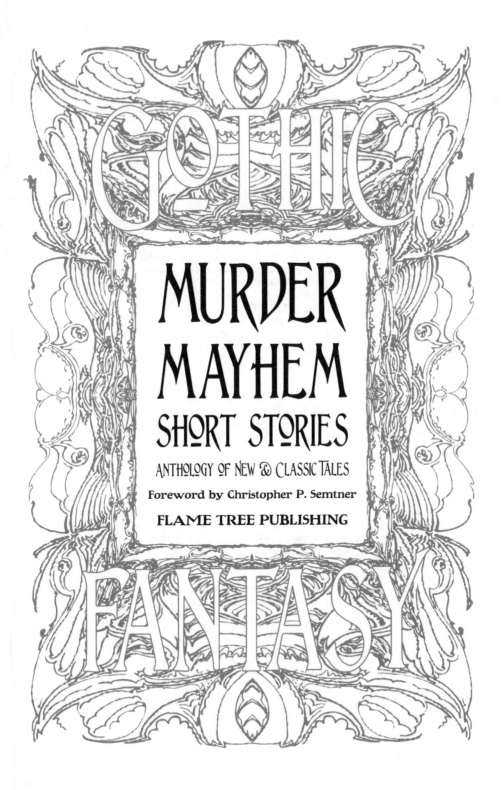

GOTHIC

MURDER
MAYHEM
SHORT STORIES
ANTHOLOGY OF NEW & CLASSIC TALES

Foreword by Christopher P. Semtner

FLAME TREE PUBLISHING

FANTASY

This is a FLAME TREE Book

Publisher & Creative Director: Nick Wells
Project Editor: Laura Bulbeck
Editorial Board: Catherine Taylor, Josie Mitchell, Gillian Whitaker

Publisher's Note: Due to the historical nature of the classic text, we're aware that there may be some language used which has the potential to cause offence to the modern reader. However, wishing overall to preserve the integrity of the text, rather than imposing contemporary sensibilities, we have left it unaltered.

FLAME TREE PUBLISHING
6 Melbray Mews, Fulham,
London SW6 3NS, United Kingdom
www.flametreepublishing.com

First published 2016

18 20 19
3 5 7 9 10 8 6 4

ISBN: 978-1-78361-987-0

The cover image is created by Flame Tree Studio based on artwork by Slava Gerj and Gabor Ruszkai.

A copy of the CIP data for this book is available from the British Library.

Printed and bound in China

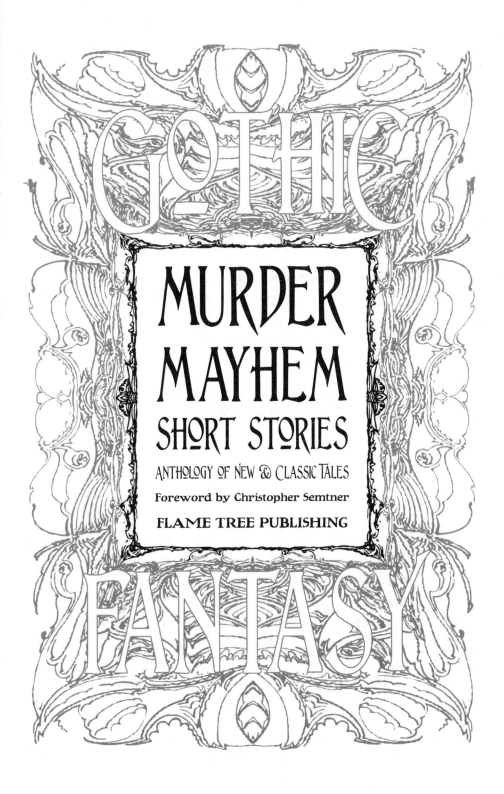

GOTHIC

MURDER MAYHEM

SHORT STORIES

ANTHOLOGY OF NEW & CLASSIC TALES

Foreword by Christopher Semtner

FLAME TREE PUBLISHING

FANTASY

Contents

Foreword: Murder Mayhem

WHEN I WAS A KID growing up in the Virginia countryside, townsfolk used to whisper about a gruesome double murder that took place in our local cemetery. Late one night a neighbor saw a burning upturned taxi propped up on a granite tombstone and called the police. A few yards from the blaze they found the charred remains of the driver and a woman. Somebody had forced gasoline down their throats and set them on fire. Even though it had all happened right in the middle of town, no more than a stone's throw from a half dozen houses, nobody saw the murderer or murderers, so the police never made any arrests. I always thought it must have taken quite a few able bodied men to subdue both victims and to overturn the taxi and that the conspirators had all taken a blood oath not to tell anyone about their crime. Whoever was involved, I theorized, was probably the same age as my parents or grandparents and was undoubtedly still living in town (since nobody ever left), watching his son's baseball games, going to PTA meetings, and looking and behaving exactly like everybody else.

When I was asked to write this introduction, I tried to reconcile finding entertainment and aesthetic value in murder stories. Are we, in some small way taking pleasure in other people's deaths when we read these stories?

The answer, I fear, is that we are. When we read these tales, we step inside the mind of Edgar Allan Poe's Montressor as he lures the hapless Fortunato into the catacombs to sample some Amontillado – only to brick his enemy alive behind a wall. As readers, we delight in the glee with which Montressor taunts his shackled victim and the efficiency with which the killer goes about the execution of his plan. Then we, like Montressor, walk back upstairs and go about our mundane lives without anyone ever learning our dark secret.

How far, we wonder, are we from giving into those impulses in real life? By the same token, we do not know how many bloodthirsty killers might be walking among us, watching us.

What draws us to these tales? There is certainly nothing new about murder stories or the public's appetite for them. Even the bible is full of them. The book of *Genesis* tells how the third person on earth, Cain, killed his brother Abel. Later, the revered King David, author of *Psalms*, fell in love with Bathsheba, so he sent her husband off to certain death. The book of *Maccabees* describes a woman forced to watch her children boiled alive.

The ancient Romans famously watched gladiators kill each other in violent spectacles. Later civilizations would have to content themselves with watching public hangings or beheadings. For theatergoers, William Shakespeare and others provided dramatic interpretations of scores of violent deaths. As literacy rates increased, printed material saved readers the trouble of visiting an execution, a house of wax, or a theater to get their murder fix. Instead, they could satisfy their craving in private by reading about the latest murders, like the 1842 case of John C. Colt, who chopped a creditor to pieces, boxed him up, and mailed him to New Orleans. Then there was the case of James Greenacre, who in 1837 dismembered his fiancée, leaving her torso on one side of London before taking an omnibus across town to dump her head in an East End canal.

When the public demanded even more lurid tales of murder and madness than real life could provide, authors gladly obliged. Leading nineteenth century writers like Charles

Dickens and E.T.A. Hoffman spiced up their greatest works with a dash of death. Before long, Poe invented the modern detective story, which centered around the solution of a crime – most often a murder. He also devised plenty of ways to kill his characters and just as many places to hide the bodies. With the dawn of the twentieth century and the birth of the modern world, Franz Kafka envisioned a sufficiently complex and poetic instrument of torture and death in his tale 'In the Penal Colony.'

Of course, when it comes to the horror genre, there is no reason the killer must necessarily be human. Ambrose Bierce has a reanimated corpse do the dirty work in his blood soaked horror story 'The Death of Halpin Frayser.' Meanwhile, the master of cosmic horror, H.P. Lovecraft, lets an alien from an alternate dimension slaughter some unsuspecting mortals in 'From Beyond.'

We may be shocked, disturbed, or entertained by the variety of ways the murderers in the stories in this book commit their crimes. We may even appreciate the craftsmanship with which the featured writers compose their death scenes or unravel their mysteries. For the few hours we spend inhabiting these stories, we have the opportunity to witness the terror and tragedy from a safe distance. We will be able to remind ourselves that it's only fiction – that we were never really in any danger. But maybe – just maybe – some of these tales will cause us to take a cautious glance over our shoulder when we remember how easily the man watching his kid's baseball game, gardening in his back yard, or acting every bit like you or I could one day disembowel his neighbor or set a couple of strangers on fire.

Christopher P. Semtner
Curator, Edgar Allan Poe Museum, Richmond, Virginia

Publisher's Note

LAST YEAR we were thrilled to publish the first in our new collections of short story anthologies, and 2016 brings two fantastic new titles, *Crime & Mystery* and *Murder Mayhem*. Still offering up the potent mix of classic tales and new fiction, we explore the roots of the genre, from golden age detective tales and whodunnits featuring Sherlock Holmes and Father Brown to more chilling, gory tales by the likes of William Hope Hodgson or Ambrose Bierce. We have tried to mix some tales and authors that were seminal to the development of the genre, such as Edgar Allan Poe's 'Murders in the Rue Morgue', with authors who have since been much forgotten, but whose stories are entertaining in their own right, and deserve to be brought back to light.

Our 2016 call for new submissions was met with a fantastic response, and as ever the final selection was extremely tough, but made to provide a wide range of tales we hope any lover of mystery, murder and intrigue will enjoy. Our editorial board read each entry carefully, and it was difficult to turn down so many good stories, but inevitably those which made the final cut were deemed to be the best for our purpose, and we're delighted to publish them here.

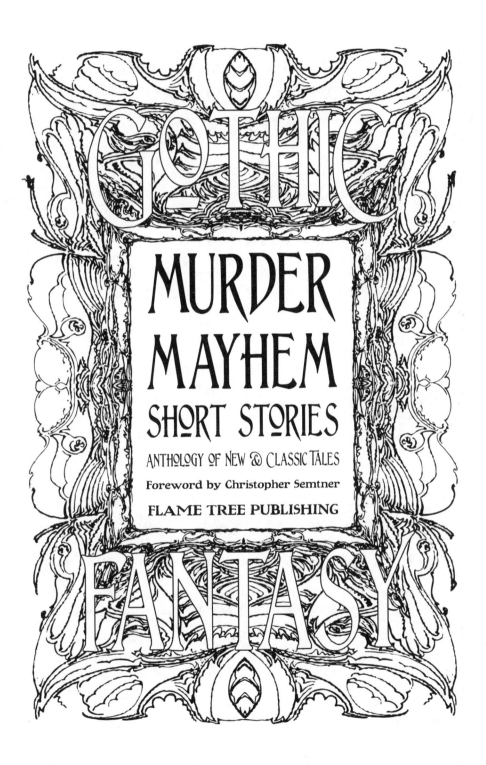

GOTHIC

MURDER MAYHEM

SHORT STORIES

ANTHOLOGY OF NEW & CLASSIC TALES

Foreword by Christopher Semtner

FLAME TREE PUBLISHING

FANTASY

The Wendigo Goes Home

Sara Dobie Bauer

CLEVE PACKER prided himself on eating only people who were about to die. Over his hundred and fifty years of cannibalism, he'd evolved not only his senses but his morality.

While traveling through northern Ohio, he smelled death on a large young woman with blonde hair and expensive shoes. The scent was subtle. She wasn't the one dying, but someone close to her. Cleve approached and made conversation at the local coffee shop. She was happy to oblige, Cleve looking so tall and handsome in his best brown suit.

Her name was Bree Shepherd, the manager of a high-end clothing store in Cleveland, single but looking. She liked to talk about herself, her family. Her mother was going through some sort of aging crisis, embracing hot yoga and spin at her local gym. Bree said she even suspected her mother of shopping in the junior's section at JC Penney, all in an effort to "stay young forever." Her dad was a retired lawyer who now spent most of his time reading murder mysteries and pretending he would one day write a novel. There was the elder sister, Bianca, who was married with three children. Bree talked most about her little brother: poor Blake, the 'hopeless homosexual' – perpetually single, despite his good looks and pleasant, albeit quiet demeanor. She said he studied science at the nearby university.

Cleve was careful to say very little about himself, other than that he was new in town. He was always new in town.

After a refill, Bree invited him for a late summer bonfire at her parents' house where there would be extended family and friends, and "Oh, won't it be nice for you to meet new people in your new city!"

When they parted, she waved and carried the smell of death down a sidewalk lined with leafy trees at full tilt August green. In her absence, the air smelled of coffee grounds and oil from nearby leaking cars.

The sick person could be anyone, really, but Cleve suspected he would meet that person if he stuck close to cheerful Bree Shepherd. Perhaps at the bonfire, filled, she said, with so many family and friends.

It had been weeks since his last feast and that, nothing satisfactory – just an old woman in a lonely house that smelled of dishwasher soap and Band-Aids. He preferred younger meat. In the early 1900s, there were all sorts of diseases that sprung up and took people by the dozens. Such a holiday, back then! But such feasts were rare nowadays, with advances in medicine and preventative treatment. Still, there was hope for the bonfire – hope for a good, hot meal.

* * *

The Shepherd house was less house, more estate: two stories with a wrap-around white front porch, navy blue siding, and a modernized tin roof that reflected the blue sky at sunset. Bree introduced Cleve around to the dozens of guests, all shapes and ages. The house smelled of roasting meat, but still, beneath the body odor and fruit-forward wine, there wafted the scent of death.

Cleve wandered, corner-to-corner, with his glass of wine, sniffing. In that chair, an echo of decay... just by the window, a shadow of illness... on the back door, a reeking handprint.

He recognized the scent: cancer.

Cleve placed his own enormous hand on the back door and took a deep breath – ah, illness, the delicious smell of a foreshadowed feast.

"Smells good, doesn't it?" Bree touched his shoulder. "Dad's roasting a pig out back. I'll show you."

Now that he'd caught the scent, Cleve refused to let go. He followed the girl outside and nodded with disinterest at the dead-eyed pig on the spit. Bits of marinade dripped from its flesh and hissed in the fire below. A group of people crowded around a large fire pit in the midst of towering oaks, leaves turned black by falling night. Cleve stepped to the edge of the fire where the younger people stood gathered. They laughed with their bottles of beer – women in light, summer dresses and men in t-shirts.

The scent was stronger there.

Cleve's mouth watered.

He saw the one young man in a sweater. Despite the summer heat, the raging fire, he looked cold. His thin shoulders hunched forward as he took a gulp of beer and wiped his mouth with the back of his hand. He smiled when addressed. He smiled and pretended, but he knew; the young man in the sweater knew he was dying, but it was clear no one else did. No one looked at him with pity. People didn't make a point to talk to the dying man, nor did they avoid him. His illness was his secret – his and Cleve's.

The young man in the sweater looked up when he felt Cleve looking. He blinked twice: huge, light eyes with a dot of reflected fire in the center. The man bit his bottom lip and smiled at Cleve, but stopped abruptly and headed for a black farmhouse in the back corner of the yard.

Cleve followed. He wandered through the sticky, humid air that smelled of barbeque and past dancing, yellow fireflies. The world beyond the farmhouse smelled green: like fairy tale forests and fresh rain and... cigarettes?

The man in the sweater sat on a swinging bench, attached to a strong tree branch, and smoked.

Cleve made an ostentatious entrance. "So there is a smoking area!" He joined the stranger on the bench and pulled out a pack of cigarettes.

For a moment, they smoked in silence, Cleve enraptured by the cancerous bouquet. It was in the young man's brain. Cleve smelled it like a spot of perfume on a woman's throat.

"I'm Cleve." He reached out his hand.

The stranger took it. "Blake."

"You're Bree's brother."

He nodded and exhaled through his nose.

Blake Shepherd was the kind of meal Cleve kept on living for. Hunger and lust had long since intertwined, and Blake fulfilled both needs. He would be dying soon, and he had the delicate features of a fairy sprite. He looked nothing like his full-figured sister with her bleached blonde hair. He was slim, small, with black hair that fell just over the tops of his ears, down the back of his neck.

Cleve leaned a little closer. "Can I tell you something and you won't get offended?"

Blake looked at him sideways and tried to hide a grin. "Sure."

"I think you're absolutely gorgeous."

Blake smiled and chewed his lower lip.

"I saw you across the fire and thought, 'I get it. That is why poets write poetry, why painters paint.'"

Blake chuckled and shook his head.

"Too much?"

They remained in the solitary calm of summer, the party voices far away. A few crickets sang nearby, and fireflies throbbed in the purple hue of deepening night. Blake put his cigarette in an empty jam jar, half-filled with discarded butts. He held it out for Cleve, who did the same.

Cleve put his hand on Blake's warm thigh. He tensed under the attentions. "Would you come into the woods with me?"

Blake shook his head. "I shouldn't."

"Is it because you're dying?"

Blake froze. "What?"

"The tumor in your brain. They've told you it's inoperable. How long do you have before the symptoms start to show?"

Blake stood up. "How the hell do you know that?"

"I can smell it on you. I smelled you on your sister."

"You can smell cancer?"

Cleve stood, too. "I smell death." He put his nose against Blake's throat and inhaled. "It smells delicious."

The young man moved to step around Cleve, but Cleve wrapped his arms around Blake from behind and clasped his palm across Blake's mouth. To Cleve, the full-grown man felt like a small, breakable thing in his arms. Blake's warm breath came out in puffs, which Cleve caught in his hand.

"You beautiful creature," he whispered into Blake's hair.

Blake trembled, and Cleve felt himself growing taller – his hands, larger.

"Shhh... Let's sit just for a moment, and I'll tell you a story."

Something wet tickled the top of Cleve's hand, which was when he realized the trembling had turned to tears.

"There's no need for that, dearest." He gave Blake's body a little squeeze, but Blake groaned like he'd been hurt. Cleve lost track of his strength before feeding.

He carried the sick man backwards under the cover of woods. Leaves scraped at the back of his head; roots reached up to trip his ankles. Cleve took careful steps until they had some distance from the others. He let Blake go. Blake didn't run or scream. He turned to face Cleve, hands balled into fists, but his wrath quickly turned to stuttering breaths.

Blake backed away until his feet caught on a root. He almost tumbled backwards into the underbrush, but Cleve caught him with two fingers and leaned him against a thick, mossy tree trunk.

"I just want to tell you a story," Cleve said, but his voice had already changed, turned deeper. He looked down at Blake, Cleve having grown inches in seconds. His fingers weren't claws yet, but with Blake near, it was only a matter of time.

The dying man didn't move.

"Would you like one of your cigarettes?"

Blake shook his head. "No."

Cleve began to walk in a little circle. The fabric of his suit was torn under his armpits; his slacks felt much too tight. "My name," he said, "is Cleve Packer. I was born in 1846."

"Wh-what?"

Cleve held up his finger, which was now a claw.

Blake's breath faltered at the sight. He tried to back farther into the tree, knocking pieces of bark to the forest floor with his feet.

"You are gorgeous, you know that? I could just eat you up." Cleve smiled, put his hand around the side of Blake's neck, and brushed his black hair with pointed nails. "I was on a hunt for gold in 1874 when it happened. Six of us got caught in the Colorado Mountains. Avalanche. And, well, old Frank, he died. What were we supposed to do? We ate him."

Blake closed his eyes tight. More tears fell.

"Our guide, this damn Ojibwe, he took off, said we were cursed. We were, but what a lovely curse!" Cleve smiled when he felt his fangs push through his gums. One of his claws caressed Blake's cheekbone. "I ended up killing the rest of my team, but I found the more I ate, the stronger I got. Now, look at me – I'll be two-hundred in a blink!"

"Please..." Blake muttered.

Cleve pulled their foreheads together and took a big whiff. He moaned at the nearness of blood and meat and fear. He was particularly fond of fear. "I do people like you a favor. Do you want to watch your family suffer? That's why you haven't told them, isn't it? You don't want to hurt them. You don't want to waste away in a hospital bed for months on end and make them watch. Do you?"

"No."

"So let me." Cleve had to practically crouch to be at Blake's height by then. He couldn't stop growing with the tease of a feast so close. "You sweet treat. Let me swallow your last breath."

Blake's light eyes darted back toward the direction of the fire, the house, and the people he loved. "What will my family think?"

"How about this? Look at me, Blake."

Cleve suspected what he looked like by then: all yellow fangs, red eyes. His suspicions were confirmed when Blake's lips parted and he coughed out a sob.

"It'll look like an animal attack."

Blake closed his eyes.

Cleve whispered, "It won't hurt at all," and pressed a single kiss to the supple flesh that hid a terminal tumor.

* * *

Cleve whistled and picked his teeth as he drove toward his next destination: Pennsylvania. He always enjoyed that state, with its rolling hills and smog of the steel industry. He slowed his car as he drove by a hospice, just to get a throat-full of perfume, and sighed at the happy memories of the night before.

Blake Shepherd, although thin, had been a lovely repast: young, healthy – except for that one thing – and fresh. Cleve would be full, at least for a little while, but the hunger always came back, which was why he moved on. Who would be next? It would have to be someone special to surpass that young man in the woods.

He pulled up to a diner for a cup of coffee. Halfway up the sidewalk, his head started hurting. Inside, he crinkled his brow and took a seat at the counter, where a friendly, disease-free waitress smiled at the handsome man in a suit.

"Coffee, please," he said.

When she brought it back, she grabbed for napkins. "Oh, honey, your nose is bleeding."

Cleve reached a hand up to his face. When he pulled his fingers away, his palm was covered in blood. He took the napkins gratefully. "One second," he said and headed for the restroom.

He looked in the mirror. Everything seemed all right. He looked the same: medium-length blond coif, not a hair out of place, brown eyes, and a freshly shaved chin. Maybe his cheeks were a little sunken, but maybe that was just the light.

His head pounded now. He closed his eyes.

Something squeezed in his chest. He opened his mouth but breath came out in a quaking wheeze.

His heart pounded, then stopped, which made him choke – then started again. He punched himself in the chest. When his heart stopped again, he fell to the floor. It started, and Cleve gasped for breath.

On the ground, the blood from his nose rushed down the back of his throat. He lay there and coughed and remembered them all, so many – the sick and the dying. He had eaten them, diseases and all, apparently one too many.

Cleve rolled on the dirty floor and laughed, because maybe that Indian had been right, he really was cursed – but only by his own morality. He thought he might've been better off as an outright monster, but Cleve Packer would never know.

The Death of Halpin Frayser

Ambrose Bierce

I

For by death is wrought greater change than hath been shown. Whereas in general the spirit that removed cometh back upon occasion, and is sometimes seen of those in flesh (appearing in the form of the body it bore) yet it hath happened that the veritable body without the spirit hath walked. And it is attested of those encountering who have lived to speak thereon that a lich so raised up hath no natural affection, nor remembrance thereof, but only hate. Also, it is known that some spirits which in life were benign become by death evil altogether.

Hali

ONE DARK NIGHT in midsummer a man waking from a dreamless sleep in a forest lifted his head from the earth, and staring a few moments into the blackness, said: "Catherine Larue". He said nothing more; no reason was known to him why he should have said so much.

The man was Halpin Frayser. He lived in St. Helena, but where he lives now is uncertain, for he is dead. One who practices sleeping in the woods with nothing under him but the dry leaves and the damp earth, and nothing over him but the branches from which the leaves have fallen and the sky from which the earth has fallen, cannot hope for great longevity, and Frayser had already attained the age of thirty-two. There are persons in this world, millions of persons, and far and away the best persons, who regard that as a very advanced age. They are the children. To those who view the voyage of life from the port of departure the bark that has accomplished any considerable distance appears already in close approach to the farther shore. However, it is not certain that Halpin Frayser came to his death by exposure.

He had been all day in the hills west of the Napa Valley, looking for doves and such small game as was in season. Late in the afternoon it had come on to be cloudy, and he had lost his bearings; and although he had only to go always downhill – everywhere the way to safety when one is lost – the absence of trails had so impeded him that he was overtaken by night while still in the forest. Unable in the darkness to penetrate the thickets of manzanita and other undergrowth, utterly bewildered and overcome with fatigue, he had lain down near the root of a large madroño and fallen into a dreamless sleep. It was hours later, in the very middle of the night, that one of God's mysterious messengers, gliding ahead of the incalculable host of his companions sweeping westward with the dawn line, pronounced the awakening word in the ear of the sleeper, who sat upright and spoke, he knew not why, a name, he knew not whose.

Halpin Frayser was not much of a philosopher, nor a scientist. The circumstance that, waking from a deep sleep at night in the midst of a forest, he had spoken aloud a name that he had not in memory and hardly had in mind did not arouse an enlightened curiosity to investigate the phenomenon. He thought it odd, and with a little perfunctory shiver, as if in deference to a seasonal presumption that the night was chill, he lay down again and went to sleep. But his sleep was no longer dreamless.

He thought he was walking along a dusty road that showed white in the gathering darkness of a summer night. Whence and whither it led, and why he traveled it, he did not know, though all seemed simple and natural, as is the way in dreams; for in the Land Beyond the Bed surprises cease from troubling and the judgment is at rest. Soon he came to a parting of the ways; leading from the highway was a road less traveled, having the appearance, indeed, of having been long abandoned, because, he thought, it led to something evil; yet he turned into it without hesitation, impelled by some imperious necessity.

As he pressed forward he became conscious that his way was haunted by invisible existences whom he could not definitely figure to his mind. From among the trees on either side he caught broken and incoherent whispers in a strange tongue which yet he partly understood. They seemed to him fragmentary utterances of a monstrous conspiracy against his body and soul.

It was now long after nightfall, yet the interminable forest through which he journeyed was lit with a wan glimmer having no point of diffusion, for in its mysterious lumination nothing cast a shadow. A shallow pool in the guttered depression of an old wheel rut, as from a recent rain, met his eye with a crimson gleam. He stooped and plunged his hand into it. It stained his fingers; it was blood! Blood, he then observed, was about him everywhere. The weeds growing rankly by the roadside showed it in blots and splashes on their big, broad leaves. Patches of dry dust between the wheelways were pitted and spattered as with a red rain. Defiling the trunks of the trees were broad maculations of crimson, and blood dripped like dew from their foliage.

All this he observed with a terror which seemed not incompatible with the fulfillment of a natural expectation. It seemed to him that it was all in expiation of some crime which, though conscious of his guilt, he could not rightly remember. To the menaces and mysteries of his surroundings the consciousness was an added horror. Vainly he sought by tracing life backward in memory, to reproduce the moment of his sin; scenes and incidents came crowding tumultuously into his mind, one picture effacing another, or commingling with it in confusion and obscurity, but nowhere could he catch a glimpse of what he sought. The failure augmented his terror; he felt as one who has murdered in the dark, not knowing whom nor why. So frightful was the situation – the mysterious light burned with so silent and awful a menace; the noxious plants, the trees that by common consent are invested with a melancholy or baleful character, so openly in his sight conspired against his peace; from overhead and all about came so audible and startling whispers and the sighs of creatures so obviously not of earth – that he could endure it no longer, and with a great effort to break some malign spell that bound his faculties to silence and inaction, he shouted with the full strength of his lungs! His voice broken, it seemed, into an infinite multitude of unfamiliar sounds, went babbling and stammering away into the distant reaches of the forest, died into silence, and all was as before. But he had made a beginning at resistance and was encouraged. He said:

"I will not submit unheard. There may be powers that are not malignant traveling this accursed road. I shall leave them a record and an appeal. I shall relate my wrongs, the persecutions that I endure – I, a helpless mortal, a penitent, an unoffending poet!" Halpin Frayser was a poet only as he was a penitent: in his dream.

Taking from his clothing a small red-leather pocketbook, one-half of which was leaved for memoranda, he discovered that he was without a pencil. He broke a twig from a bush, dipped it into a pool of blood and wrote rapidly. He had hardly touched the paper with the point of his twig when a low, wild peal of laughter broke out at a measureless distance away, and growing ever louder, seemed approaching ever nearer; a soulless, heartless, and unjoyous laugh, like that of the loon, solitary by the lakeside at midnight; a laugh which culminated in an unearthly shout close at hand, then died away by slow gradations, as if the accursed being that uttered it had withdrawn over the verge of the world whence it had come. But the man felt that this was not so – that it was near by and had not moved.

A strange sensation began slowly to take possession of his body and his mind. He could not have said which, if any, of his senses was affected; he felt it rather as a consciousness – a mysterious mental assurance of some overpowering presence – some supernatural malevolence different in kind from the invisible existences that swarmed about him, and superior to them in power. He knew that it had uttered that hideous laugh. And now it seemed to be approaching him; from what direction he did not know – dared not conjecture. All his former fears were forgotten or merged in the gigantic terror that now held him in thrall. Apart from that, he had but one thought: to complete his written appeal to the benign powers who, traversing the haunted wood, might some time rescue him if he should be denied the blessing of annihilation. He wrote with terrible rapidity, the twig in his fingers rilling blood without renewal; but in the middle of a sentence his hands denied their service to his will, his arms fell to his sides, the book to the earth; and powerless to move or cry out, he found himself staring into the sharply drawn face and blank, dead eyes of his own mother, standing white and silent in the garments of the grave!

II

IN HIS YOUTH Halpin Frayser had lived with his parents in Nashville, Tennessee. The Fraysers were well-to-do, having a good position in such society as had survived the wreck wrought by civil war. Their children had the social and educational opportunities of their time and place, and had responded to good associations and instruction with agreeable manners and cultivated minds. Halpin being the youngest and not over robust was perhaps a trifle 'spoiled'. He had the double disadvantage of a mother's assiduity and a father's neglect. Frayser père was what no Southern man of means is not – a politician. His country, or rather his section and State, made demands upon his time and attention so exacting that to those of his family he was compelled to turn an ear partly deafened by the thunder of the political captains and the shouting, his own included.

Young Halpin was of a dreamy, indolent and rather romantic turn, somewhat more addicted to literature than law, the profession to which he was bred. Among those of his relations who professed the modern faith of heredity it was well understood that in him the character of the late Myron Bayne, a maternal great-grandfather, had revisited the glimpses of the moon – by which orb Bayne had in his lifetime been sufficiently affected to be a poet of no small Colonial distinction. If not specially observed, it was observable that while a Frayser who was not the proud possessor of a sumptuous copy of the ancestral 'poetical works' (printed at the family expense, and long ago withdrawn from an inhospitable market) was a rare Frayser indeed, there was an illogical indisposition to honor the great deceased in the person of his spiritual successor. Halpin was pretty generally deprecated as an intellectual black sheep who was likely at any moment to disgrace the flock by bleating in meter. The Tennessee Fraysers were a practical folk – not practical in the popular sense of devotion to sordid pursuits, but having a robust contempt for any qualities unfitting a man for the wholesome vocation of politics.

In justice to young Halpin it should be said that while in him were pretty faithfully reproduced most of the mental and moral characteristics ascribed by history and family tradition to the famous Colonial bard, his succession to the gift and faculty divine was purely inferential. Not only had he never been known to court the muse, but in truth he could not have written correctly a line of verse to save himself from the Killer of the Wise. Still, there was no knowing when the dormant faculty might wake and smite the lyre.

In the meantime the young man was rather a loose fish, anyhow. Between him and his mother was the most perfect sympathy, for secretly the lady was herself a devout disciple of the late and great Myron Bayne, though with the tact so generally and justly admired in her sex (despite the hardy calumniators who insist that it is essentially the same thing as cunning) she had always taken care to conceal her weakness from all eyes but those of him who shared it. Their common guilt in respect of that was an added tie between them. If in Halpin's youth his mother had 'spoiled' him, he had assuredly done his part toward being spoiled. As he grew to such manhood as is attainable by a Southerner who does not care which way elections go the attachment between him and his beautiful mother – whom from early childhood he had called Katy – became yearly stronger and more tender. In these two romantic natures was manifest in a signal way that neglected phenomenon, the dominance of the sexual element in all the relations of life, strengthening, softening, and beautifying even those of consanguinity. The two were nearly inseparable, and by strangers observing their manner were not infrequently mistaken for lovers.

Entering his mother's boudoir one day Halpin Frayser kissed her upon the forehead, toyed for a moment with a lock of her dark hair which had escaped from its confining pins, and said, with an obvious effort at calmness:

"Would you greatly mind, Katy, if I were called away to California for a few weeks?"

It was hardly needful for Katy to answer with her lips a question to which her telltale cheeks had made instant reply. Evidently she would greatly mind; and the tears, too, sprang into her large brown eyes as corroborative testimony.

"Ah, my son," she said, looking up into his face with infinite tenderness, "I should have known that this was coming. Did I not lie awake a half of the night weeping because, during the other half, Grandfather Bayne had come to me in a dream, and standing by his portrait – young, too, and handsome as that – pointed to yours on the same wall? And when I looked it seemed that I could not see the features; you had been painted with a face cloth, such as we put upon the dead. Your father has laughed at me, but you and I, dear, know that such things are not for nothing. And I saw below the edge of the cloth the marks of hands on your throat – forgive me, but we have not been used to keep such things from each other. Perhaps you have another interpretation. Perhaps it does not mean that you will go to California. Or maybe you will take me with you?"

It must be confessed that this ingenious interpretation of the dream in the light of newly discovered evidence did not wholly commend itself to the son's more logical mind; he had, for the moment at least, a conviction that it foreshadowed a more simple and immediate, if less tragic, disaster than a visit to the Pacific Coast. It was Halpin Frayser's impression that he was to be garroted on his native heath.

"Are there not medicinal springs in California?" Mrs. Frayser resumed before he had time to give her the true reading of the dream – "places where one recovers from rheumatism and neuralgia? Look – my fingers feel so stiff; and I am almost sure they have been giving me great pain while I slept."

She held out her hands for his inspection. What diagnosis of her case the young man may have thought it best to conceal with a smile the historian is unable to state, but for himself he feels bound to say that fingers looking less stiff, and showing fewer evidences of even insensible pain, have seldom been submitted for medical inspection by even the fairest patient desiring a prescription of unfamiliar scenes.

The outcome of it was that of these two odd persons having equally odd notions of duty, the one went to California, as the interest of his client required, and the other remained at home in compliance with a wish that her husband was scarcely conscious of entertaining.

While in San Francisco Halpin Frayser was walking one dark night along the waterfront of the city, when, with a suddenness that surprised and disconcerted him, he became a sailor. He was in fact 'shanghaied' aboard a gallant, gallant ship, and sailed for a far country. Nor did his misfortunes end with the voyage; for the ship was cast ashore on an island of the South Pacific, and it was six years afterward when the survivors were taken off by a venturesome trading schooner and brought back to San Francisco.

Though poor in purse, Frayser was no less proud in spirit than he had been in the years that seemed ages and ages ago. He would accept no assistance from strangers, and it was while living with a fellow survivor near the town of St. Helena, awaiting news and remittances from home, that he had gone gunning and dreaming.

III

THE APPARITION confronting the dreamer in the haunted wood – the thing so like, yet so unlike his mother – was horrible! It stirred no love nor longing in his heart; it came unattended with pleasant memories of a golden past – inspired no sentiment of any kind; all the finer emotions were swallowed up in fear. He tried to turn and run from before it, but his legs were as lead; he was unable to lift his feet from the ground. His arms hung helpless at his sides; of his eyes only he retained control, and these he dared not remove from the lusterless orbs of the apparition, which he knew was not a soul without a body, but that most dreadful of all existences infesting that haunted wood – a body without a soul! In its blank stare was neither love, nor pity, nor intelligence – nothing to which to address an appeal for mercy. "An appeal will not lie," he thought, with an absurd reversion to professional slang, making the situation more horrible, as the fire of a cigar might light up a tomb.

For a time, which seemed so long that the world grew gray with age and sin, and the haunted forest, having fulfilled its purpose in this monstrous culmination of its terrors, vanished out of his consciousness with all its sights and sounds, the apparition stood within a pace, regarding him with the mindless malevolence of a wild brute; then thrust its hands forward and sprang upon him with appalling ferocity! The act released his physical energies without unfettering his will; his mind was still spellbound, but his powerful body and agile limbs, endowed with a blind, insensate life of their own, resisted stoutly and well.

For an instant he seemed to see this unnatural contest between a dead intelligence and a breathing mechanism only as a spectator – such fancies are in dreams; then he regained his identity almost as if by a leap forward into his body, and the straining automaton had a directing will as alert and fierce as that of its hideous antagonist.

But what mortal can cope with a creature of his dream? The imagination creating the enemy is already vanquished; the combat's result is the combat's cause. Despite his struggles – despite his strength and activity, which seemed wasted in a void, he felt the cold fingers close upon his throat. Borne backward to the earth, he saw above him the dead and drawn face within a hand's breadth of his own, and then all was black. A sound as of the beating of distant drums – a murmur of swarming voices, a sharp, far cry signing all to silence, and Halpin Frayser dreamed that he was dead.

IV

A WARM, CLEAR NIGHT had been followed by a morning of drenching fog. At about the middle of the afternoon of the preceding day a little whiff of light vapor – a mere thickening of the atmosphere, the ghost of a cloud – had been observed clinging to the western side of Mount St. Helena, away up along the barren altitudes near the summit. It was so thin, so diaphanous, so like a fancy made visible, that one would have said: "Look quickly! In a moment it will be gone."

In a moment it was visibly larger and denser. While with one edge it clung to the mountain, with the other it reached farther and farther out into the air above the lower slopes. At the same time it extended itself to north and south, joining small patches of mist that appeared to come out of the mountainside on exactly the same level, with an intelligent design to be absorbed. And so it grew and grew until the summit was shut out of view from the valley, and over the valley itself was an ever-extending canopy, opaque and gray. At Calistoga, which lies near the head of the valley and the foot of the mountain, there were a starless night and a sunless morning. The fog, sinking into the valley, had reached southward, swallowing up ranch after ranch, until it had blotted out the town of St. Helena, nine miles away. The dust in the road was laid; trees were adrip with moisture; birds sat silent in their coverts; the morning light was wan and ghastly, with neither color nor fire.

Two men left the town of St. Helena at the first glimmer of dawn, and walked along the road northward up the valley toward Calistoga. They carried guns on their shoulders, yet no one having knowledge of such matters could have mistaken them for hunters of bird or beast. They were a deputy sheriff from Napa and a detective from San Francisco – Holker and Jaralson, respectively. Their business was man-hunting.

"How far is it?" inquired Holker, as they strode along, their feet stirring white the dust beneath the damp surface of the road.

"The White Church? Only a half mile farther," the other answered. "By the way," he added, "it is neither white nor a church; it is an abandoned schoolhouse, gray with age and neglect. Religious services were once held in it – when it was white, and there is a graveyard that would delight a poet. Can you guess why I sent for you, and told you to come heeled?"

"Oh, I never have bothered you about things of that kind. I've always found you communicative when the time came. But if I may hazard a guess, you want me to help you arrest one of the corpses in the graveyard."

"You remember Branscom?" said Jaralson, treating his companion's wit with the inattention that it deserved.

"The chap who cut his wife's throat? I ought; I wasted a week's work on him and had my expenses for my trouble. There is a reward of five hundred dollars, but none of us ever got a sight of him. You don't mean to say–"

"Yes, I do. He has been under the noses of you fellows all the time. He comes by night to the old graveyard at the White Church."

"The devil! That's where they buried his wife."

"Well, you fellows might have had sense enough to suspect that he would return to her grave some time."

"The very last place that anyone would have expected him to return to."

"But you had exhausted all the other places. Learning your failure at them, I 'laid for him' there."

"And you found him?"

"Damn it! He found me. The rascal got the drop on me – regularly held me up and made me travel. It's God's mercy that he didn't go through me. Oh, he's a good one, and I fancy the half of that reward is enough for me if you're needy."

Holker laughed good humoredly, and explained that his creditors were never more importunate.

"I wanted merely to show you the ground, and arrange a plan with you," the detective explained. "I thought it as well for us to be heeled, even in daylight."

"The man must be insane," said the deputy sheriff. "The reward is for his capture and conviction. If he's mad he won't be convicted."

Mr. Holker was so profoundly affected by that possible failure of justice that he involuntarily stopped in the middle of the road, then resumed his walk with abated zeal.

"Well, he looks it," assented Jaralson. "I'm bound to admit that a more unshaven, unshorn, unkempt, and uneverything wretch I never saw outside the ancient and honorable order of tramps. But I've gone in for him, and can't make up my mind to let go. There's glory in it for us, anyhow. Not another soul knows that he is this side of the Mountains of the Moon."

"All right," Holker said; "we will go and view the ground," and he added, in the words of a once favorite inscription for tombstones: "'where you must shortly lie' – I mean, if old Branscom ever gets tired of you and your impertinent intrusion. By the way, I heard the other day that 'Branscom' was not his real name."

"What is?"

"I can't recall it. I had lost all interest in the wretch, and it did not fix itself in my memory – something like Pardee. The woman whose throat he had the bad taste to cut was a widow when he met her. She had come to California to look up some relatives – there are persons who will do that sometimes. But you know all that."

"Naturally."

"But not knowing the right name, by what happy inspiration did you find the right grave? The man who told me what the name was said it had been cut on the headboard."

"I don't know the right grave." Jaralson was apparently a trifle reluctant to admit his ignorance of so important a point of his plan. "I have been watching about the place generally. A part of our work this morning will be to identify that grave. Here is the White Church."

For a long distance the road had been bordered by fields on both sides, but now on the left there was a forest of oaks, madroños, and gigantic spruces whose lower parts only could be seen, dim and ghostly in the fog. The undergrowth was, in places, thick, but nowhere impenetrable. For some moments Holker saw nothing of the building, but as they turned into the woods it revealed itself in faint gray outline through the fog, looking huge and far away. A few steps more, and it was within an arm's length, distinct, dark with moisture, and insignificant in size. It had the usual country-schoolhouse form – belonged to the packing-box order of architecture; had an underpinning of stones, a moss-grown roof, and blank window spaces, whence both glass and sash had long departed. It was ruined, but not a ruin – a typical Californian substitute for what are known to guide-bookers abroad as 'monuments of the past'. With scarcely a glance at this uninteresting structure Jaralson moved on into the dripping undergrowth beyond.

"I will show you where he held me up," he said. "This is the graveyard."

Here and there among the bushes were small enclosures containing graves, sometimes no more than one. They were recognized as graves by the discolored stones or rotting boards at head and foot, leaning at all angles, some prostrate; by the ruined picket fences surrounding them; or, infrequently, by the mound itself showing its gravel through the fallen leaves. In many instances nothing marked the spot where lay the vestiges of some poor mortal – who, leaving 'a large circle of sorrowing friends', had been left by them in turn – except a depression in the earth, more lasting than that in the spirits of the mourners. The paths, if any paths had been, were long obliterated; trees of a considerable size had been permitted to grow up from the graves and thrust aside with root or branch the enclosing fences. Over all was that air of abandonment and decay which seems nowhere so fit and significant as in a village of the forgotten dead.

As the two men, Jaralson leading, pushed their way through the growth of young trees, that enterprising man suddenly stopped and brought up his shotgun to the height of his breast, uttered a low note of warning, and stood motionless, his eyes fixed upon something ahead. As well as he could, obstructed by brush, his companion, though seeing nothing, imitated the posture and so stood, prepared for what might ensue. A moment later Jaralson moved cautiously forward, the other following.

Under the branches of an enormous spruce lay the dead body of a man. Standing silent above it they noted such particulars as first strike the attention – the face, the attitude, the clothing; whatever most promptly and plainly answers the unspoken question of a sympathetic curiosity.

The body lay upon its back, the legs wide apart. One arm was thrust upward, the other outward; but the latter was bent acutely, and the hand was near the throat. Both hands were tightly clenched. The whole attitude was that of desperate but ineffectual resistance to – what?

Nearby lay a shotgun and a game bag through the meshes of which was seen the plumage of shot birds. All about were evidences of a furious struggle; small sprouts of poison-oak were bent and denuded of leaf and bark; dead and rotting leaves had been pushed into heaps and ridges on both sides of the legs by the action of other feet than theirs; alongside the hips were unmistakable impressions of human knees.

The nature of the struggle was made clear by a glance at the dead man's throat and face. While breast and hands were white, those were purple – almost black. The shoulders lay upon a low mound, and the head was turned back at an angle otherwise impossible, the expanded eyes staring blankly backward in a direction opposite to that of the feet. From the froth filling the open mouth the tongue protruded, black and swollen. The throat showed horrible contusions; not mere finger-marks, but bruises and lacerations wrought by two strong hands that must have buried themselves in the yielding flesh, maintaining their terrible grasp until long after death. Breast, throat, face, were wet; the clothing was saturated; drops of water, condensed from the fog, studded the hair and mustache.

All this the two men observed without speaking – almost at a glance. Then Holker said: "Poor devil! He had a rough deal."

Jaralson was making a vigilant circumspection of the forest, his shotgun held in both hands and at full cock, his finger upon the trigger.

"The work of a maniac," he said, without withdrawing his eyes from the enclosing wood. "It was done by Branscom – Pardee."

Something half hidden by the disturbed leaves on the earth caught Holker's attention. It was a red-leather pocketbook. He picked it up and opened it. It contained leaves of white paper for memoranda, and upon the first leaf was the name 'Halpin Frayser'. Written in red on several succeeding leaves – scrawled as if in haste and barely legible – were the following lines, which Holker read aloud, while his companion continued scanning the dim gray confines of their narrow world and hearing matter of apprehension in the drip of water from every burdened branch:

> *"Enthralled by some mysterious spell, I stood*
> *In the lit gloom of an enchanted wood.*
> *The cypress there and myrtle twined their boughs,*
> *Significant, in baleful brotherhood.*
>
> *"The brooding willow whispered to the yew;*
> *Beneath, the deadly nightshade and the rue,*
> *With immortelles self-woven into strange*
> *Funereal shapes, and horrid nettles grew.*
>
> *"No song of bird nor any drone of bees,*
> *Nor light leaf lifted by the wholesome breeze:*
> *The air was stagnant all, and Silence was*
> *A living thing that breathed among the trees.*
>
> *"Conspiring spirits whispered in the gloom,*
> *Half-heard, the stilly secrets of the tomb.*
> *With blood the trees were all adrip; the leaves*
> *Shone in the witch-light with a ruddy bloom.*
>
> *"I cried aloud! – the spell, unbroken still,*
> *Rested upon my spirit and my will.*
> *Unsouled, unhearted, hopeless and forlorn,*
> *I strove with monstrous presages of ill!*
>
> *"At last the viewless –"*

Holker ceased reading; there was no more to read. The manuscript broke off in the middle of a line.

"That sounds like Bayne," said Jaralson, who was something of a scholar in his way. He had abated his vigilance and stood looking down at the body.

"Who's Bayne?" Holker asked rather incuriously.

"Myron Bayne, a chap who flourished in the early years of the nation – more than a century ago. Wrote mighty dismal stuff; I have his collected works. That poem is not among them, but it must have been omitted by mistake."

"It is cold," said Holker; "let us leave here; we must have up the coroner from Napa."

Jaralson said nothing, but made a movement in compliance. Passing the end of the slight elevation of earth upon which the dead man's head and shoulders lay, his foot struck some hard substance under the rotting forest leaves, and he took the trouble to kick it into view. It was a fallen headboard, and painted on it were the hardly decipherable words, 'Catharine Larue'.

"Larue, Larue!" exclaimed Holker, with sudden animation. "Why, that is the real name of Branscom – not Pardee. And – bless my soul! How it all comes to me – the murdered woman's name had been Frayser!"

"There is some rascally mystery here," said Detective Jaralson. "I hate anything of that kind."

There came to them out of the fog – seemingly from a great distance – the sound of a laugh, a low, deliberate, soulless laugh, which had no more of joy than that of a hyena night-prowling in the desert; a laugh that rose by slow gradation, louder and louder, clearer, more distinct and terrible, until it seemed barely outside the narrow circle of their vision; a laugh so unnatural, so unhuman, so devilish, that it filled those hardy man-hunters with a sense of dread unspeakable! They did not move their weapons nor think of them; the menace of that horrible sound was not of the kind to be met with arms. As it had grown out of silence, so now it died away; from a culminating shout which had seemed almost in their ears, it drew itself away into the distance, until its failing notes, joyless and mechanical to the last, sank to silence at a measureless remove.

The Moonlit Road

Ambrose Bierce

I: Statement of Joel Hetman, Jr.

I AM the most unfortunate of men. Rich, respected, fairly well educated and of sound health – with many other advantages usually valued by those having them and coveted by those who have them not – I sometimes think that I should be less unhappy if they had been denied me, for then the contrast between my outer and my inner life would not be continually demanding a painful attention. In the stress of privation and the need of effort I might sometimes forget the somber secret ever baffling the conjecture that it compels.

I am the only child of Joel and Julia Hetman. The one was a well-to-do country gentleman, the other a beautiful and accomplished woman to whom he was passionately attached with what I now know to have been a jealous and exacting devotion. The family home was a few miles from Nashville, Tennessee, a large, irregularly built dwelling of no particular order of architecture, a little way off the road, in a park of trees and shrubbery.

At the time of which I write I was nineteen years old, a student at Yale. One day I received a telegram from my father of such urgency that in compliance with its unexplained demand I left at once for home. At the railway station in Nashville a distant relative awaited me to apprise me of the reason for my recall: my mother had been barbarously murdered – why and by whom none could conjecture, but the circumstances were these: my father had gone to Nashville, intending to return the next afternoon. Something prevented his accomplishing the business in hand, so he returned on the same night, arriving just before the dawn. In his testimony before the coroner he explained that having no latchkey and not caring to disturb the sleeping servants, he had, with no clearly defined intention, gone round to the rear of the house. As he turned an angle of the building, he heard a sound as of a door gently closed, and saw in the darkness, indistinctly, the figure of a man, which instantly disappeared among the trees of the lawn. A hasty pursuit and brief search of the grounds in the belief that the trespasser was someone secretly visiting a servant proving fruitless, he entered at the unlocked door and mounted the stairs to my mother's chamber. Its door was open, and stepping into black darkness he fell headlong over some heavy object on the floor. I may spare myself the details; it was my poor mother, dead of strangulation by human hands!

Nothing had been taken from the house, the servants had heard no sound, and excepting those terrible finger-marks upon the dead woman's throat – dear God! That I might forget them! – no trace of the assassin was ever found.

I gave up my studies and remained with my father, who, naturally, was greatly changed. Always of a sedate, taciturn disposition, he now fell into so deep a dejection that nothing could hold his attention, yet anything – a footfall, the sudden closing of a door – aroused in him a fitful interest; one might have called it an apprehension. At any small surprise of the senses he would start visibly and sometimes turn pale, then relapse into a melancholy apathy deeper than before. I suppose he was what is called a 'nervous wreck'. As to me, I was younger then than now – there is much in that. Youth is Gilead, in which is balm for every wound. Ah, that I might again dwell in that enchanted land! Unacquainted with grief, I knew not how to appraise my bereavement; I could not rightly estimate the strength of the stroke.

One night, a few months after the dreadful event, my father and I walked home from the city. The full moon was about three hours above the eastern horizon; the entire countryside had the solemn stillness of a summer night; our footfalls and the ceaseless song of the katydids were the only sound aloof. Black shadows of bordering trees lay athwart the road, which, in the short reaches between, gleamed a ghostly white. As we approached the gate to our dwelling, whose front was in shadow, and in which no light shone, my father suddenly stopped and clutched my arm, saying, hardly above his breath:

"God! God! What is that?"

"I hear nothing," I replied.

"But see – see!" he said, pointing along the road, directly ahead.

I said: "Nothing is there. Come, father, let us go in – you are ill."

He had released my arm and was standing rigid and motionless in the center of the illuminated roadway, staring like one bereft of sense. His face in the moonlight showed a pallor and fixity inexpressibly distressing. I pulled gently at his sleeve, but he had forgotten my existence. Presently he began to retire backward, step by step, never for an instant removing his eyes from what he saw, or thought he saw. I turned half round to follow, but stood irresolute. I do not recall any feeling of fear, unless a sudden chill was its physical manifestation. It seemed as if an icy wind had touched my face and enfolded my body from head to foot; I could feel the stir of it in my hair.

At that moment my attention was drawn to a light that suddenly streamed from an upper window of the house: one of the servants, awakened by what mysterious premonition of evil who can say, and in obedience to an impulse that she was never able to name, had lit a lamp. When I turned to look for my father he was gone, and in all the years that have passed no whisper of his fate has come across the borderland of conjecture from the realm of the unknown.

II: Statement of Caspar Grattan

TODAY I am said to live; tomorrow, here in this room, will lie a senseless shape of clay that all too long was I. If anyone lift the cloth from the face of that unpleasant thing it will be in gratification of a mere morbid curiosity. Some, doubtless, will go further and inquire, "Who was he?" In this writing I supply the only answer that I am able to make – Caspar Grattan. Surely, that should be enough. The name has served my small need for more than twenty years of a life of unknown length. True, I gave it to myself, but lacking another I had the right. In this world one must have a name; it prevents confusion, even when it does not establish identity. Some, though, are known by numbers, which also seem inadequate distinctions.

One day, for illustration, I was passing along a street of a city, far from here, when I met two men in uniform, one of whom, half pausing and looking curiously into my face, said to his companion, "That man looks like 767". Something in the number seemed familiar and horrible. Moved by an uncontrollable impulse, I sprang into a side street and ran until I fell exhausted in a country lane.

I have never forgotten that number, and always it comes to memory attended by gibbering obscenity, peals of joyless laughter, the clang of iron doors. So I say a name, even if self-bestowed, is better than a number. In the register of the potter's field I shall soon have both. What wealth!

Of him who shall find this paper I must beg a little consideration. It is not the history of my life; the knowledge to write that is denied me. This is only a record of broken and apparently unrelated memories, some of them as distinct and sequent as brilliant beads upon a thread, others remote and strange, having the character of crimson dreams with interspaces blank and black – witch-fires glowing still and red in a great desolation.

Standing upon the shore of eternity, I turn for a last look landward over the course by which I came. There are twenty years of footprints fairly distinct, the impressions of bleeding feet. They lead through poverty and pain, devious and unsure, as of one staggering beneath a burden –

Remote, unfriended, melancholy, slow.

Ah, the poet's prophecy of Me – how admirable, how dreadfully admirable!

Backward beyond the beginning of this *via dolorosa* – this epic of suffering with episodes of sin – I see nothing clearly; it comes out of a cloud. I know that it spans only twenty years, yet I am an old man.

One does not remember one's birth – one has to be told. But with me it was different; life came to me full-handed and dowered me with all my faculties and powers. Of a previous existence I know no more than others, for all have stammering intimations that may be memories and may be dreams. I know only that my first consciousness was of maturity in body and mind – a consciousness accepted without surprise or conjecture. I merely found myself walking in a forest, half-clad, footsore, unutterably weary and hungry. Seeing a farmhouse, I approached and asked for food, which was given me by one who inquired my name. I did not know, yet knew that all had names. Greatly embarrassed, I retreated, and night coming on, lay down in the forest and slept.

The next day I entered a large town which I shall not name. Nor shall I recount further incidents of the life that is now to end – a life of wandering, always and everywhere haunted by an overmastering sense of crime in punishment of wrong and of terror in punishment of crime. Let me see if I can reduce it to narrative.

I seem once to have lived near a great city, a prosperous planter, married to a woman whom I loved and distrusted. We had, it sometimes seems, one child, a youth of brilliant parts and promise. He is at all times a vague figure, never clearly drawn, frequently altogether out of the picture.

One luckless evening it occurred to me to test my wife's fidelity in a vulgar, commonplace way familiar to everyone who has acquaintance with the literature of fact and fiction. I went to the city, telling my wife that I should be absent until the following afternoon. But I returned before daybreak and went to the rear of the house, purposing to enter by a door with which I had secretly so tampered that it would seem to lock, yet not actually fasten. As I approached it, I heard it gently open and close, and saw a man steal away into the darkness. With murder in my heart, I sprang after him, but he had vanished without even the bad luck of identification. Sometimes now I cannot even persuade myself that it was a human being.

Crazed with jealousy and rage, blind and bestial with all the elemental passions of insulted manhood, I entered the house and sprang up the stairs to the door of my wife's chamber. It was closed, but having tampered with its lock also, I easily entered and despite the black darkness soon stood by the side of her bed. My groping hands told me that although disarranged it was unoccupied.

"She is below," I thought, "and terrified by my entrance has evaded me in the darkness of the hall."

With the purpose of seeking her I turned to leave the room, but took a wrong direction – the right one! My foot struck her, cowering in a corner of the room. Instantly my hands were at her throat, stifling a shriek, my knees were upon her struggling body; and there in the darkness, without a word of accusation or reproach, I strangled her till she died!

There ends the dream. I have related it in the past tense, but the present would be the fitter form, for again and again the somber tragedy reenacts itself in my consciousness – over and over I lay the plan, I suffer the confirmation, I redress the wrong. Then all is blank; and afterward the rains beat against the grimy window-panes, or the snows fall upon my scant attire, the wheels rattle in the squalid streets where my life lies in poverty and mean employment. If there is ever sunshine I do not recall it; if there are birds they do not sing.

There is another dream, another vision of the night. I stand among the shadows in a moonlit road. I am aware of another presence, but whose I cannot rightly determine. In the shadow of a great dwelling I catch the gleam of white garments; then the figure of a woman confronts me in the road – my murdered wife! There is death in the face; there are marks upon the throat. The eyes are fixed on mine with an infinite gravity which is not reproach, nor hate, nor menace, nor anything less terrible than recognition. Before this awful apparition I retreat in terror – a terror that is upon me as I write. I can no longer rightly shape the words. See! They –

Now I am calm, but truly there is no more to tell: the incident ends where it began – in darkness and in doubt.

Yes, I am again in control of myself: 'the captain of my soul'. But that is not respite; it is another stage and phase of expiation. My penance, constant in degree, is mutable in kind: one of its variants is tranquillity. After all, it is only a life-sentence. 'To Hell for life' – that is a foolish penalty: the culprit chooses the duration of his punishment. Today my term expires.

To each and all, the peace that was not mine.

III: Statement of the Late Julia Hetman, Through the

Medium Bayrolles

I HAD RETIRED early and fallen almost immediately into a peaceful sleep, from which I awoke with that indefinable sense of peril which is, I think, a common experience in that other, earlier life. Of its unmeaning character, too, I was entirely persuaded, yet that did not banish it. My husband, Joel Hetman, was away from home; the servants slept in another part of the house. But these were familiar conditions; they had never before distressed me. Nevertheless, the strange terror grew so insupportable that conquering my reluctance to move I sat up and lit the lamp at my bedside. Contrary to my expectation this gave me no relief; the light seemed rather an added danger, for I reflected that it would shine out under the door, disclosing my presence to whatever evil thing might lurk outside. You that are still in the flesh, subject to horrors of the imagination, think what a monstrous fear that must be which seeks in darkness security from malevolent existences of the night. That is to spring to close quarters with an unseen enemy – the strategy of despair!

Extinguishing the lamp I pulled the bed-clothing about my head and lay trembling and silent, unable to shriek, forgetful to pray. In this pitiable state I must have lain for what you call hours – with us there are no hours, there is no time.

At last it came – a soft, irregular sound of footfalls on the stairs! They were slow, hesitant, uncertain, as of something that did not see its way; to my disordered reason all the more terrifying for that, as the approach of some blind and mindless malevolence to which is no appeal. I even thought that I must have left the hall lamp burning and the groping of this creature proved it a monster of the night. This was foolish and inconsistent with my previous dread of the light, but what would you have? Fear has no brains; it is an idiot. The dismal witness that it bears and the cowardly counsel that it whispers are unrelated. We know this well, we who have passed into the Realm of Terror, who skulk in eternal dusk among the scenes of our former lives, invisible even to ourselves and one another, yet hiding forlorn in lonely places; yearning for speech with our loved ones, yet dumb, and as fearful of them as they of us. Sometimes the disability is removed, the law suspended: by the deathless power of love or hate we break the spell – we are seen by those whom we would warn, console, or punish. What form we seem to them to bear we know not; we know only that we terrify even those whom we most wish to comfort, and from whom we most crave tenderness and sympathy.

Forgive, I pray you, this inconsequent digression by what was once a woman. You who consult us in this imperfect way – you do not understand. You ask foolish questions about things unknown and things forbidden. Much that we know and could impart in our speech is meaningless in yours. We must communicate with you through a stammering intelligence in that small fraction of our language that you yourselves can speak. You think that we are of another world. No, we have knowledge of no world but yours, though for us it holds no sunlight, no warmth, no music, no laughter, no song of birds, nor any companionship. O God! What a thing it is to be a ghost, cowering and shivering in an altered world, a prey to apprehension and despair!

No, I did not die of fright: the Thing turned and went away. I heard it go down the stairs, hurriedly, I thought, as if itself in sudden fear. Then I rose to call for help. Hardly had my shaking hand found the doorknob when – merciful heaven! – I heard it returning. Its footfalls as it remounted the stairs were rapid, heavy and loud; they shook the house. I fled to an angle of the wall and crouched upon the floor. I tried to pray. I tried to call the name of my dear husband. Then I heard the door thrown open. There was an interval of unconsciousness, and when I revived I felt a strangling clutch upon my throat – felt my arms feebly beating against something that bore me backward – felt my tongue thrusting itself from between my teeth! And then I passed into this life.

No, I have no knowledge of what it was. The sum of what we knew at death is the measure of what we know afterward of all that went before. Of this existence we know many things, but no new light falls upon any page of that; in memory is written all of it that we can read. Here are no heights of truth overlooking the confused landscape of that dubitable domain. We still dwell in the Valley of the Shadow, lurk in its desolate places, peering from brambles and thickets at its mad, malign inhabitants. How should we have new knowledge of that fading past?

What I am about to relate happened on a night. We know when it is night, for then you retire to your houses and we can venture from our places of concealment to move unafraid about our old homes, to look in at the windows, even to enter and gaze upon your faces as you sleep. I had lingered long near the dwelling where I had been so cruelly changed to what I am, as we do while any that we love or hate remain. Vainly I had sought some method of manifestation, some way to make my continued existence and my great love and poignant pity understood by my husband and son. Always if they slept they would wake, or if in my desperation I dared approach them when they were awake, would turn toward me the terrible eyes of the living, frightening me by the glances that I sought from the purpose that I held.

On this night I had searched for them without success, fearing to find them; they were nowhere in the house, nor about the moonlit lawn. For, although the sun is lost to us forever, the moon, full-orbed or slender, remains to us. Sometimes it shines by night, sometimes by day, but always it rises and sets, as in that other life.

I left the lawn and moved in the white light and silence along the road, aimless and sorrowing. Suddenly I heard the voice of my poor husband in exclamations of astonishment, with that of my son in reassurance and dissuasion; and there by the shadow of a group of trees they stood – near, so near! Their faces were toward me, the eyes of the elder man fixed upon mine. He saw me – at last, at last, he saw me! In the consciousness of that, my terror fled as a cruel dream. The death-spell was broken: Love had conquered Law! Mad with exultation I shouted – I must have shouted, "He sees, he sees: he will understand!" Then, controlling myself, I moved forward, smiling and consciously beautiful, to offer myself to his arms, to comfort him with endearments, and, with my son's hand in mine, to speak words that should restore the broken bonds between the living and the dead.

Alas! Alas! His face went white with fear, his eyes were as those of a hunted animal. He backed away from me, as I advanced, and at last turned and fled into the wood – whither, it is not given to me to know.

To my poor boy, left doubly desolate, I have never been able to impart a sense of my presence. Soon he, too, must pass to this Life Invisible and be lost to me forever.

The Rector of Veilbye

Steen Steensen Blicher

These extracts from the diary of Erik Sorensen, District Judge, followed by two written statements by the rector of Aalso, give a complete picture of the terrible events that took place in the parish of Veilbye during Judge Sorensen's first year of office. Should anyone be inclined to doubt the authenticity of these documents let him at least have no doubt about the story, which is – alas! – only too sadly true. The memory of these events is still fresh in the district, and the events themselves have been the direct cause of a change in the method of criminal trials. A suspected murderer is now tried through all the courts before his conviction can be determined. Readers versed in the history of law will doubtless know by this during what epoch the story is laid.

I

[From the Diary of District Judge Erik Sorensen.]

NOW AM I, unworthy one, by the grace of God made judge over this district. May the Great Judge above give me wisdom and uprightness that I may fulfill my difficult task in all humility! From the Lord alone cometh judgment.

It is not good that man should live alone. Now that I am able to support a wife I will look about me for a helpmeet. I hear much good said about the daughter of the Rector of Veilbye. Since her mother's death she has been a wise and economical keeper of her father's house. And as she and her brother the student are the only children, she will inherit a tidy sum when the old man dies.

Morten Bruus of Ingvorstrup was here today and wanted to make me a present of a fat calf. But I answered him in the words of Moses, "Cursed be he who taketh gifts." He is of a very quarrelsome nature, a sharp bargainer, and a boastful talker. I do not want to have any dealings with him, except through my office as judge.

I have prayed to God for wisdom and I have consulted with my own heart, and I believe that Mistress Mette Quist is the only woman with whom I could live and die. But I will watch her for a time in secret. Beauty is deceptive and charm is a dangerous thing. But I must say that she is the most beautiful woman I have yet seen.

I think that Morten Bruus a very disagreeable person – I scarcely know why myself. But whenever I see him something comes over me, something that is like the memory of an evil dream. And yet it is so vague and so faint, that I could not say whether I had really ever seen the man in my dreams or not. It may be a sort of presentiment of evil; who knows?

He was here again and offered me a pair of horses – beautiful animals – at a ridiculously low price. It looked queer to me. I know that he paid seventy thalers for them, and he wanted to let me have them for the same price. They are at the least worth one hundred thalers, if not more. Was it intended for a bribe? He may have another lawsuit pending. I do not want his horses.

I paid a visit to the Rector of Veilbye today. He is a fine, God-fearing man, but somewhat quick-tempered and dictatorial. And he is close with his money, too, as I could see. Just as I arrived a peasant was with him trying to be let off the payment of part of his tithe. The man is surely a rogue, for the sum is not large. But the rector talked to him as I wouldn't have talked to a dog, and the more he talked the more violent he became.

Well, we all have our faults. The rector meant well in spite of his violence, for later on he told his daughter to give the man a sandwich and a good glass of beer. She is certainly a charming and sensible girl. She greeted me in a modest and friendly manner, and my heart beat so that I could scarcely say a word in reply. My head farm hand served in the rectory three years. I will question him – one often hears a straight and true statement from servants.

A surprise! My farm hand Rasmus tells me that Morten Bruus came a-wooing to the rectory at Veilbye some years back, but was sent away with a refusal. The rector seemed to be pleased with him, for the man is rich. But his daughter would not hear to it at all. Pastor Soren may have tried hard to persuade her to consent at first. But when he saw how much she disliked the man he let her do as she would. It was not pride on her part, Rasmus said, for she is as simple and modest as she is good and beautiful. And she knows that her own father is peasant-born as well as Bruus.

Now I know what the Ingvorstrup horses were intended for. They were to blind the judge and to lead him aside from the narrow path of righteousness. The rich Morten Bruns covets poor Ole Anderson's peat moor and pasture land. It would have been a good bargain for Morten even at seventy thalers. But no indeed, my good fellow, you don't know Erik Sorensen!

Rector Soren Quist of Veilbye came to see me this morning. He has a new coachman, Niels Bruus, brother to the owner of Ingvorstrup. Neils is lazy and impertinent. The rector wanted him arrested, but he had no witnesses to back up his complaint. I advised him to get rid of the man somehow, or else to get along with him the best he could until the latter's time was up. The rector was somewhat hasty at first, but later on he listened calmly and thanked me for my good advice. He is inclined to be violent at times, but can always be brought to listen to reason. We parted good friends.

I spent a charming day in Veilbye yesterday. The rector was not at home, but Mistress Mette received me with great friendliness. She sat by the door spinning when I arrived, and it seemed to me that she blushed. It was hardly polite for me to wait so long before speaking. When I sit in judgment I never lack for words, but in the presence of this innocent maiden I am as stupid as the veriest simpleton of a chicken thief. But I finally found my voice and the time passed quickly until the rector's return. Then Mistress Mette left us and did not return until she brought in our supper.

Just as she stepped through the doorway the rector was saying to me, "Isn't it about time that you should think of entering into the holy estate of matrimony?" (We had just been speaking of a recent very fine wedding in the neighborhood.) Mistress Mette heard the words and flushed a deep red. Her father laughed and said to her, "I can see, my dear daughter, that you have been standing before the fire."

I shall take the good man's advice and will very soon try my fate with her. For I think I may take the rector's words to be a secret hint that he would not object to me as a son-in-law. And the daughter? Was her blush a favorable sign?

Poor Ole Anderson keeps his peat moor and his pasture land, but rich Morten Bruus is angry at me because of it. When he heard the decision he closed his eyes and set his lips tight, and his face was as pale as a whitewashed wall. But he controlled himself and as he went out he called back to his adversary, "Wish you joy of the bargain, Ole Anderson. The peat bog won't beggar me, and the cattle at Ingvorstrup have all the hay they can eat." I could hear his loud laughter outside and the cracking of his whip. It is not easy to have to sit in judgment. Every decision makes but one enemy the more.

Yesterday was the happiest day of my life. We celebrated our betrothal in the Rectory of Veilbye. My future father-in-law spoke to the text, "I gave my handmaid into thy bosom" (Genesis xvi, 5). His words touched my heart. I had not believed that this serious and sometimes brusque man could talk so sweetly. When the solemnity was over, I received the first kiss from my sweet betrothed, and the assurance of her great love for me.

At supper and later on we were very merry. Many of the dead mother's kin were present. The rector's family were too far away. After supper we danced until daybreak and there was no expense spared in the food and wine. My future father-in-law was the strongest man present, and could easily drink all the others under the table. The wedding is to take place in six weeks. God grant us rich blessings.

It is not good that my future father-in-law should have this Niels Bruus in his service. He is a defiant fellow, a worthy brother of him of Ingvorstrup. If it were I, he should have his wages and be turned off, the sooner the better. But the good rector is stubborn and insists that Niels shall serve out his time. The other day he gave the fellow a box on the ear, at which Niels cried out that he would make him pay for it. The rector told me of this himself, for no one else had been present. I talked to Niels, but he would scarcely answer me. I fear he has a stubborn and evil nature. My sweet betrothed also entreats her father to send the fellow away, but the rector will not listen to reason. I do not know what the old man will do when his daughter leaves his home for mine. She saves him much worry and knows how to make all things smooth and easy. She will be a sweet wife for me.

As I thought, it turned out badly. But there is one good thing about it, Niels has now run off of himself. The rector is greatly angered, but I rejoice in secret that he is rid of that dangerous man. Bruus will probably seek retaliation, but we have law and justice in the land to order such matters.

This was the way of it: The rector had ordered Niels to dig up a bit of soil in the garden. After a time when he went out himself to look at the work, he found Niels leaning on his spade eating nuts. He had not even begun to dig. The rector scolded him, but the fellow answered that he had not taken service as a gardener. He received a good box on the ear for that. At this he threw away his spade and swore valiantly at his master. The old rector lost his temper entirely, seized the spade and struck at the man several times. He should not have done this, for a spade is a dangerous weapon, especially in the hands of a man as strong as is the pastor in spite of his years. Niels fell to the ground as if dead. But when the pastor bent over him in alarm, he sprang up suddenly, jumped the hedge and ran away to the woods.

This is the story of the unfortunate affair as my father-in-law tells it to me. My beloved Mette is much worried about it. She fears the man may do harm to the cattle, or set fire to the house, or in some such way take his revenge. But I tell her there is little fear of that.

Three weeks more and my beloved leaves her father's house for mine. She has been here and has gone over the house and the farm. She is much pleased with everything and praises our orderliness. She is an angel, and all who know her say that I am indeed a fortunate man. To God be the praise!

Strange, where that fellow Niels went to! Could he have left the country altogether? It is an unpleasant affair in any case, and there are murmurings and secret gossip among the peasants. The talk has doubtless started in Ingvorstrup. It would not be well to have the rector hear it. He had better have taken my advice, but it is not my province to school a servant of God, and a man so much older than I. The idle gossip may blow over ere long. I will go to Veilbye tomorrow and find out if he has heard anything.

The bracelet the goldsmith has made for me is very beautiful. I am sure it will please my sweet Mette.

My honored father-in-law is much distressed and downhearted. Malicious tongues have repeated to him the stupid gossip that is going about in the district. Morten Bruus is reported to have said that "he would force the rector to bring back his brother, if he had to dig him out of the earth." The fellow may be in hiding somewhere, possibly at Ingvorstrup. He has certainly disappeared completely, and no one seems to know where he is. My poor betrothed is much grieved and worried. She is alarmed by bad dreams and by presentiments of evil to come.

God have mercy on us all! I am so overcome by shock and horror that I can scarcely hold the pen. It has all come in one terrible moment, like a clap of thunder. I take no account of time, night and morning are the same to me and the day is but a sudden flash of lightning destroying the proud castle of my hopes and desires. A venerable man of God – the father of my betrothed – is in prison! And as a suspected murderer! There is still hope that he may be innocent. But this hope is but as a straw to a drowning man. A terrible suspicion rests upon him – And I, unhappy man that I am, must be his judge. And his daughter is my betrothed bride! May the Saviour have pity on us!

It was yesterday that this horrible thing came. About half an hour before sunrise Morten Bruus came to my house and had with him the cotter Jens Larsen of Veilbye, and the widow and daughter of the shepherd of that parish. Morten Bruus said to me that he had the Rector of Veilbye under suspicion of having killed his brother Niels. I answered that I had heard some such talk but had regarded it as idle and malicious gossip, for the rector himself had assured me that the fellow had run away. "If that was so," said Morten, "if Niels had really intended to run away, he would surely at first come to me to tell me of it. But it is not so, as these good people can prove to you, and I demand that you shall hear them as an officer of the law."

"Think well of what you are doing," I said. "Think it over well, Morten Bruus, and you, my good people. You are bringing a terrible accusation against a respected and unspotted priest and man of God. If you can prove nothing, as I strongly suspect, your accusations may cost you dear."

"Priest or no priest," cried Bruus, "it is written, 'thou shalt not kill!' And also is it written, that the authorities bear the sword of justice for all men. We have law and order in the land, and the murderer shall not escape his punishment, even if he have the district judge for a son-in-law."

I pretended not to notice his thrust and began, "It shall be as you say. Kirsten Mads' daughter, what is it that you know of this matter in which Morten Bruus accuses your rector? Tell the truth, and the truth only, as you would tell it before the judgment seat of the Almighty. The law will demand from you that you shall later repeat your testimony under oath."

The woman told the following story: The day on which Niels Bruus was said to have run away from the rectory, she and her daughter were passing along the road near the rectory garden a little after the noon hour. She heard someone calling and saw that it was Niels Bruus looking out through the garden hedge. He asked the daughter if she did not want some nuts and told the women that the rector had ordered him to dig in the garden, but that he did not take the command very seriously and would much rather eat nuts. At that moment they heard a door open in the house and Niels said, "Now I'm in for a scolding." He dropped back behind the hedge and the women heard a quarrel in the garden. They could hear the words distinctly but they could see nothing, as the hedge was too high. They heard the rector cry, "I'll punish you, you dog. I'll strike you dead at my feet!" Then they heard several sounding slaps, and they heard Niels curse back at the rector and call him evil names. The rector did not answer this, but the women heard two dull blows and saw the head of a spade and part of the handle rise and fall twice over the hedge. Then it was very quiet in the garden, and the widow and her daughter were frightened and hurried on to their cattle in the field. The daughter gave the same testimony, word for word. I asked them if they had not seen Niels Bruus coming out of the garden. But they said they had not, although they had turned back several times to look.

This accorded perfectly with what the rector had told me. It was not strange that the women had not seen the man run out of the garden, for he had gone toward the wood which is on the opposite side of the garden from the highroad. I told Marten Bruus that this testimony was no proof of the supposed murder, especially as the rector himself had narrated the entire occurrence to me exactly as the women had described it. But he smiled bitterly and asked me to examine the third witness, which I proceeded to do.

Jens Larsen testified that he was returning late one evening from Tolstrup (as he remembered, it was not the evening of Niels Bruus's disappearance, but the evening of the following day), and was passing the rectory garden on the easterly side by the usual footpath. From the garden he heard a noise as of someone digging in the earth. He was frightened at first for it was very late, but the moon shone brightly and he thought he would see who it was that was at work in the garden at that hour. He put off his wooden shoes and pushed aside the twigs of the hedge until he had made a peep hole. In the garden he saw the rector in his usual house coat, a white woolen nightcap on his head. He was busily smoothing down the earth with the flat of his spade. There was nothing else to be seen. Just then the rector had started and partly turned toward the hedge, and the witness, fearing he might be discovered, slipped down and ran home hastily.

Although I was rather surprised that the rector should be working in his garden at so late an hour, I still saw nothing in this statement that could arouse suspicion of murder. I gave the complainant a solemn warning and advised him not only to let fall his accusation, but to put an end to the talk in the parish. He replied, "Not until I see what it is that the rector buried in his garden."

"That will be too late," I said. "You are playing a dangerous game. Dangerous to your own honor and welfare."

"I owe it to my brother," he replied, "and I demand that the authorities shall not refuse me assistance."

My office compelled me to accede to his demands. Accompanied by the accuser and his witnesses I took my way to Veilbye. My heart was very heavy, not so much because of any fear that we might find the missing man buried in the garden, but because of the surprise and distress I must cause the rector and my beloved. As we went on our way I thought over how severely the law would allow me to punish the calumniators. But alas, Merciful Heavens! What a terrible discovery was in store for me!

I had wished to have a moment alone with the rector to prepare him for what was coming. But as I drove through the gate Morten Bruus spurred his horse past me and galloped up to the very door of the house just as the rector opened it. Bruus cried out in his very face, "People say that you have killed my brother and buried him in your garden. I am come with the district judge to seek for him."

The poor rector was so shocked and astounded that he could not find a word to answer. I sprang from my wagon and addressed him: "You have now heard the accusation. I am forced by my office to fulfill this man's demands. But your own honor demands that the truth shall be known and the mouth of slander silenced."

"It is hard enough," began the rector finally, "for a man in my position to have to clear himself from such a suspicion. But come with me. My garden and my entire house are open to you."

We went through the house to the garden. On the way we met my betrothed, who was startled at seeing Bruus. I managed to whisper hastily to her, "Do not be alarmed, dear heart. Your enemies are going to their own destruction." Marten Bruus led the way to the eastern side of the garden near the hedge. We others followed with the rector's farm hands, whom he himself had ordered to join us with spades.

The accuser stood and looked about him until we approached. Then he pointed to one spot. "This looks as if the earth had been disturbed lately. Let us begin here."

"Go to work at once," commanded the rector angrily.

The men set to work, but they were not eager enough to suit Bruus, who seized a spade himself to fire them on. A few strokes only sufficed to show that the firm earth of this particular spot had not been touched for many years. We all rejoiced – except Bruus – and the rector was very happy. He triumphed openly over his accuser, and laughed at him, "Can't you find anything, you libeler?"

Bruus did not answer. He pondered for a few moments, then called out, "Jens Larsen, where was it you saw the rector digging?"

Jens Larsen had been standing to one side with his hands folded, watching the work. At Bruus's words he aroused himself as if from a dream, looked about him and pointed to a corner of the garden several yards from where we stood. "I think it was over there."

"What's that, Jens!" cried the rector angrily. "When did I dig here?"

Paying no heed to this, Morten Bruus called the men to the corner in question. The earth here was covered by some withered cabbage stalks, broken twigs, and other brush which he pushed aside hurriedly. The work began anew.

I stood by the rector talking calmly with him about the punishment we could mete out to the dastardly accuser, when one of the men suddenly cried out with an oath. We looked toward them; there lay a hat half buried in the loose earth. "We have found him," cried Bruus. "That is Niels's hat; I would know it anywhere."

My blood seemed turned to ice. All my hopes dashed to the ground. "Dig! Dig!" cried the bloodthirsty accuser, working himself with all his might. I looked at the rector. He was ghastly pale, staring with wide-open eyes at the horrible spot.

Another shout! A hand was stretched up through the earth as if to greet the workers. "See there!" screamed Bruus. "He is holding out his hand to me. Wait a little, Brother Niels! You will soon be avenged!"

The entire corpse was soon uncovered. It was the missing man. His face was not recognizable, as decomposition had begun, and the nose was broken and laid flat by a blow. But all the garments, even to the shirt with his name woven into it, were known to those who stood there. In one ear was a leaden ring, which, as we all knew, Niels Bruus had worn for many years.

"Now, priest," cried Marten Bruus, "come and lay your hand on this dead man if you dare to!"

"Almighty God!" sighed the rector, looking up to heaven, "Thou art my witness that I am innocent. I struck him, that I confess, and I am bitterly sorry for it. But he ran away. God Almighty alone knows who buried him here."

"Jens Larsen knows also," cried Bruus, "and I may find more witnesses. Judge! You will come with me to examine his servants. But first of all I demand that you shall arrest this wolf in sheep's clothing."

Merciful God, how could I doubt any longer? The truth was clear to all of us. But I was ready to sink into the earth in my shock and horror. I was about to say to the rector that he must prepare to follow me, when he himself spoke to me, pale and trembling like an aspen leaf. "Appearances are against me," he said, but this is the work of the devil and his angels. There is One above who will bring my innocence to light. Come, judge, I will await my fate in fetters. Comfort my daughter. Remember that she is your betrothed bride."

He had scarcely uttered the words when I heard a scream and a fall behind us. It was my beloved who lay unconscious on the ground. I thought at first that she was dead, and God knows I wished that I could lie there dead beside her. I raised her in my arms, but her father took her from me and carried her into the house. I was called to examine the wound on the dead man's head. The cut was not deep, but it had evidently fractured the skull, and had plainly been made by a blow from a spade or some similar blunt instrument.

Then we all entered the house. My beloved had revived again. She fell on my neck and implored me, in the name of God, to help her father in his terrible need. She begged me by the memory of our mutual love to let her follow him to prison, to which I consented. I myself accompanied him to Grenaa, but with a mournful heart. None of us spoke a word on the sad journey. I parted from them in deep distress. The corpse was laid in a coffin and will be buried decently tomorrow in Veilbye churchyard.

Tomorrow I must give a formal hearing to the witnesses. God be merciful to me, unfortunate man!

Would that I had never obtained this position for which I – fool that I am – strove so hard.

As the venerable man of God was brought before me, fettered hand and foot, I felt as Pilate must have felt as they brought Christ before him. It was to me as if my beloved – God grant her comfort, she lies ill in Grenaa – had whispered to me, "Do nothing against that good man!"

Oh, if he only were innocent, but I see no hope!

The three first witnesses repeated their testimony under oath, word for word. Then came statements by the rector's two farm hands and the dairy maid. The men had been in the kitchen on the fatal day, and as the windows were open they had heard the quarrel between the rector and Niels. As the widow had stated, these men had also heard the rector say, "I will strike you dead at my feet!" They further testified that the rector was very quick-tempered, and that when angered he did not hesitate to strike out with whatever came into his hand. He had struck a former hand once with a heavy maul.

The girl testified that on the night Jens Larsen claimed to have seen the rector in the garden, she had lain awake and heard the creaking of the garden door. When she looked out of the window she had seen the rector in his dressing gown and nightcap go into the garden. She could not see what he was doing there. But she heard the door creak again about an hour later.

When the witnesses had been heard, I asked the unfortunate man whether he would make a confession, or else, if he had anything to say in his own defense. He crossed his hands over his breast and said, "So help me God, I will tell the truth. I have nothing more to say than what I have said already. I struck the dead man with my spade. He fell down, but jumped up in a moment and ran away from the garden out into the woods. What may have happened to him there, or how he came to be buried in my garden, this I do not know. When Jens Larsen and my servant testify that they saw me at night in the garden, either they are lying, or Satan has blinded them. I can see this – unhappy man that I am – that I have no one to turn to for help here on earth. Will He who is in heaven be silent also, then must I bow to His inscrutable will." He bowed his head with a deep sigh.

Some of those present began to weep, and a murmur arose that he might possibly be innocent. But this was only the effect of the momentary sympathy called out by his attitude. My own heart indeed spoke for him. But the judge's heart may not dare to dictate to his brain or to his conscience. My conviction forced me to declare that the rector had killed Niels Bruus, but certainly without any premeditation or intention to do so. It is true that Niels Bruus had often been heard to declare that he would "get even with the rector when the latter least expected it." But it is not known that he had fulfilled his threat in any way. Every man clings to life and honor as long as he can. Therefore the rector persists in his denial. My poor, dear Mette! She is lost to me for this life at least, just as I had learned to love her so dearly.

I have had a hard fight to fight today. As I sat alone, pondering over this terrible affair in which it is my sad lot to have to give judgment, the door opened and the rector's daughter – I may no longer call her my betrothed – rushed in and threw herself at my feet. I raised her up, clasped her in my arms and we wept together in silence. I was first to control myself. "I know what you would say, dear heart. You want me to save your father. Alas, God help us poor mortals, I cannot do it! Tell me, dearest one, tell me truly, do you yourself believe your father to be innocent?"

She crossed her hands on her heart and sobbed, "I do not know!" Then she burst into tears again. "But he did not bury him in the garden," she continued after a few moments. "The man may have died in the wood from the blow. That may have happened–"

"But, dearest heart," I said, "Jens Larsen and the girl saw your father in the garden that night."

She shook her head slowly and answered, "The evil one blinded their eyes." She wept bitterly again.

"Tell me, beloved," she began again, after a while, "tell me frankly this much. If God sends us no further enlightenment in this unfortunate affair, what sentence must you give?"

She gazed anxiously at me, her lips trembling.

"If I did not believe," I began slowly, "that anyone else in my place would be more severe than I, then I would gladly give up my position at once and refuse to speak the verdict. But I dare not conceal from you that the mildest sentence that God, our king, and our laws demand is, a life for a life."

She sank to her knees, then sprang up again, fell back several steps as if afraid of me, and cried out: "Would you murder my father? Would you murder your betrothed bride? See here! See this!" She came nearer and held up her hand with my ring on it before my eyes. "Do you see this betrothal ring? What was it my father said when you put this ring upon my finger? 'I have given my maid unto thy bosom!' But you, you thrust the steel deep into my bosom!"

Alas, every one of her words cut deep into my own heart. "Dearest love," I cried, "do not speak so. You thrust burning irons into my heart. What would you have me do? Acquit him, when the laws of God and man condemn?"

She was silent, sobbing desperately.

"One thing I can do," I continued. "If it be wrong may God forgive me. If the trial goes on to an end his life is forfeited, there is no hope except in flight. If you can arrange an escape I will close my eyes. I will not see or hear anything. As soon as your father was imprisoned, I wrote to your brother in Copenhagen. He can arrive any moment now. Talk to him, make friends with the jailer. If you lack money, all I have is yours."

When I had finished her face flushed with joy, and she threw her arms about my neck. "God bless you for these words. Were my brother but here, he will know what to do. But where shall we go?" her tone changed suddenly and her arms dropped. "Even should we find a refuge in a foreign country I could never see you again!" Her tone was so sad that my heart was near to breaking.

"Beloved," I exclaimed, "I will find you wherever you may hide yourself! Should our money not be sufficient to support us I can work for us all. I have learned to use the ax and the hoe."

She rejoiced again and kissed me many times. We prayed to God to bless our undertaking and parted with glad hearts. I also hoped for the best. Doubts assail me, but God will find for us some light in this darkness.

Two more new witnesses. They bring nothing good, I fear, for Bruus announced them with an expression I did not like. He has a heart of stone, which can feel nothing but malice and bitterness. I give them a hearing tomorrow. I feel as if they had come to bear witness against me myself. May God strengthen my heart.

All is over. He has confessed.

The court was in session and the prisoner had been brought in to hear the testimony of the new witnesses. These men stated as follows: On the night in question they were walking along the path that led between the woods and the rectory garden. A man with a large sack on his back came out of the woods and walked ahead of them toward the garden. They could not see his face, but in the bright moonlight his figure was clearly visible, and they could see that he wore a loose green garment, like a dressing gown, and a white nightcap. The man disappeared through an opening in the rectory garden fence.

Scarcely had the first witness ended his statement when the rector turned ghastly pale, and gasped, in a voice that could scarcely be heard, "I am ill." They gave him a chair.

Bruus turned to his neighbor and exclaimed audibly, "That helped the rector's memory."

The prisoner did not hear the words, but motioned to me and said, "Lead me back to my prison. I will talk to you there." They did as he demanded.

We set out at once for Grenaa. The rector was in the wagon with the jailer and the gendarme, and I rode beside them.

When the door of the cell was opened my beloved was making up her father's bed, and over a chair by the bedside hung the fatal green dressing gown. My dear betrothed greeted me with a cry of joy, as she believed that I was come to set her father free. She hung about the old man's neck, kissing away the tears that rolled unhindered down his cheeks. I had not the heart to undeceive her, and I sent her out into the town to buy some things for us.

"Sit down, dear friend," said the rector, when we were alone. He seated himself on the bed, staring at the ground with eyes that did not see. Finally he turned toward me where I sat trembling, as if it were my own sentence I was to hear, as in a manner it was. "I am a great sinner," he sighed, "God only knows how great. His punishment crushes me here that I may enter into His mercy hereafter."

He grew gradually calmer and began:

"Since my childhood I have been hot-tempered and violent. I could never endure contradiction, and was always ready to give a blow. But I have seldom let the sun go down upon my wrath, and I have never borne hatred toward any man. As a half-grown boy I killed our good, kind watchdog in one of my fits of rage for some trifling offense, and I have never ceased to regret it. Later, as a student in Leipzig, I let myself be carried away sufficiently to wound seriously my adversary in one of our fencing bouts. A merciful fate alone saved me from becoming a murderer then. It is for these earlier sins that I am now being punished, but the punishment falls doubly hard, now that I am an old man, a priest, a servant of the Lord of Peace, and a father! Ah, that is the deepest wound!" He sprang up and wrung his hands in deep despair. I would have said something to comfort him, but I could find no words for such sorrow.

When he had controlled himself somewhat he sat down again and continued: "To you, once my friend and now my judge, I will confess this crime, which it seems beyond a doubt that I have committed, although I am not conscious of having done so." (I was startled at this, as I had expected a remorseful confession.) "Listen well to what I shall now tell you. That I struck the unfortunate man with the spade, that he fell down and then ran away, this is all that I know with full consciousness... What followed then? Four witnesses have seen that I fetched the body and buried it in my garden – and now at last I am forced to believe that it must be true. These are my reasons for the belief.

"Three or four times in my life I have walked in my sleep. The last time – it may have been nine or ten years ago – I was to have held a funeral service on the following day, over the body of a man who had died a sudden and terrible death. I could not find a suitable text, until suddenly there came to me the words of an old Greek philosopher, 'Call no man fortunate until his death.' It was in my mind that the same idea was expressed in different words in the Holy Scriptures. I sought and sought, but could not find it. At last I went to bed much fatigued, and slept soundly. Next morning, when I sat down at my desk, to my great astonishment I saw there a piece of paper, on which was written, 'Call no man happy until his end hath come' (Sirach xi. 34), and following it was a funeral sermon, short, but as good in construction as any I have ever written. And all this was in my own handwriting. It was quite out of the question that anyone could have entered the room during the night, as I had locked it myself, and it had not been opened until I entered next day. I knew what had happened, as I could remember one or two such occurrences in my life before.

"Therefore, dear friend, when the last witnesses gave their testimony today, I suddenly remembered my sleepwalking exploits, and I also remembered, what had slipped my mind before, that on the morning after the night the body was buried I had found my dressing gown in the hall outside of my bedroom. This had surprised me, as I always hung it over a chair near my bed. The unfortunate victim of my violence must have died in the woods from his wound, and in my dream consciousness I must have seen this and gone to fetch the body. It must be so. I know no other explanation. God have mercy on my sinful soul."

He was silent again, covering his face with his hands and weeping bitterly.

I was struck dumb with astonishment and uncertainty. I had always suspected that the victim had died on the spot where he was buried, although I could not quite understand how the rector had managed to bury the body by day without being seen. But I thought that he might have covered it lightly with earth and twigs and finished his work at night. He was a man of sufficient strength of mind to have done this. When the latest witnesses were telling their story, I noted the possible contradiction, and hoped it might prove a loophole of escape. But, alas, it was all only too true, and the guilt of the rector proven beyond a doubt. It was not at all impossible for a man to do such things in his sleep. Just as it was quite possible that a man with a fractured skull could run some distance before he fell to die. The rector's story bore the stamp of truth, although the doubt will come that he desired thus to save a shred of honor for his name.

The prisoner walked up and down the room several times, then stopping before me he said gravely: "You have now heard my confession, here in my prison walls. It is your mouth that must speak my sentence. But what says your heart?"

I could scarcely utter the words, "My heart suffers beyond expression. I would willingly see it break if I could but save you from a shameful death." (I dared not mention to him my last hope of escape in flight.)

"That is impossible," he answered. "My life is forfeited. My death is just, and shall serve as a warning to others. But promise me that you will not desert my poor daughter. I had thought to lay her in your arms" – tears choked his voice – "but, alas, that fond hope is vanished. You cannot marry the daughter of a sentenced murderer. But promise me that you will watch over her as her second father." In deep sorrow and in tears I held his hand in mine. "Have you any news from my son?" he began again. "I hope it will be possible to keep him in ignorance of this terrible affair until– until it is all over. I could not bear to see him now. And now, dear friend, let us part, not to meet again except in the hall of justice. Grant me of your friendship one last service, let it end soon. I long for death. Go now, my kind, sympathetic judge. Send for me tomorrow to speak my sentence, and send today for my brother in God, the pastor in Aalso. He shall prepare me for death. God be with you."

He gave me his hand with his eyes averted. I staggered from the prison, hardly conscious of what I was doing. I would have ridden home without seeing his daughter had she not met me by the prison door. She must have seen the truth in my face, for she paled and caught at my arm. She gazed at me with her soul in her eyes, but could not speak. "Flee! Save your father in flight!" was all I could say.

I set spurs to my horse and rode home somehow.

Tomorrow, then!

The sentence is spoken.

The accused was calmer than the judge. All those present, except his bitter enemy, were affected almost to tears. Some whispered that the punishment was too severe.

May God be a milder judge to me than I, poor sinner, am forced to be to my fellow men.

She has been here. She found me ill in bed. There is no escape possible. He will not flee. Everything was arranged and the jailer was ready to help. But he refuses, he longs for death. God be merciful to the poor girl. How will she survive the terrible day? I am ill in body and soul, I can neither aid nor comfort her. There is no word from the brother.

I feel that I am near death myself, as near perhaps as he is, whom I sent to his doom. Farewell, my own beloved bride... What will she do? She is so strangely calm – the calm of wordless despair. Her brother has not yet come, and tomorrow – on the Ravenshill – !

Here the diary of Erik Sorensen stopped suddenly. What followed can be learned from the written and witnessed statements of the pastor of Aalso, the neighboring parish to Veilbye.

II

IT WAS during the seventeenth year of my term of office that the terrible event happened in the neighborhood which filled all who heard of it with shock and horror, and brought shame and disgrace upon our holy calling. The venerable Soren Quist, Rector of Veilbye, killed his servant in a fit of rage and buried the body in his garden.

He was found guilty at the official trial, through the testimony of many witnesses, as well as through his own confession. He was condemned to death, and the sentence was carried out in the presence of several thousand people on the little hill known as Ravenshill, here in the field of Aalso.

The condemned man had asked that I might visit him in his prison. I must state that I have never given the holy sacrament to a better prepared or more truly repentant Christian. He was calm to the last, full of remorse for his great sin. On the field of death he spoke to the people in words of great wisdom and power, preaching to the text from the Lamentations of Jeremiah, chap. ii., verse 6: "He hath despised the priest in the indignation of his anger." He spoke of his violence and of its terrible results, and of his deep remorse. He exhorted his hearers to let his sin and his fate be an example to them, and a warning not to give way to anger. Then he commended his soul to the Lord, removed his upper garments, bound up his eyes with his own hand, then folded his hands in prayer. When I had spoken the words, "Brother, be of good cheer. This day shalt thou be with thy Saviour in Paradise," his head fell by the ax.

The one thing that made death bitter for him was the thought of his children. The son had been sent for from Copenhagen, but as we afterwards learned, he had been absent from the city, and therefore did not arrive until shortly after his father had paid the penalty for his crime.

I took the daughter into my home, where she was brought, half fainting, after they had led her father from the prison. She had been tending him lovingly all the days of his trial. What made even greater sorrow for the poor girl, and for the district judge who spoke the sentence, was that these two young people had solemnly plighted their troth but a few short weeks before, in the rectory of Veilbye. The son arrived just as the body of the executed criminal was brought into my house. It had been permitted to us to bury the body with Christian rites, if we could do it in secret. The young man threw himself over the lifeless body. Then, clasping his sister in his arms, the two wept together in silence for some while. At midnight we held a quiet service over the remains of the Rector of Veilbye, and the body was buried near the door of Aalso church. A simple stone, upon which I have carved a cross, still stands to remind the passer-by of the sin of a most unfortunate man.

The next morning his two children had disappeared. They have never been heard of since. God knows to what far-away corner of the world they have fled, to hide their shame and their sorrow. The district judge is very ill, and it is not believed that he will recover.

May God deal with us all after His wisdom and His mercy!

O Lord, inscrutable are thy ways!

In the thirty-eighth year of my service, and twenty-one years after my unfortunate brother in office, the Rector of Veilbye had been beheaded for the murder of his servant, it happened one day that a beggar came to my door. He was an elderly man, with gray hair, and walked with a crutch. He looked sad and needy. None of the servants were about, so I myself went into the kitchen and gave him a piece of bread. I asked him where he came from. He sighed and answered:

"From nowhere in particular."

Then I asked him his name. He sighed still deeper, looked about him as if in fear, and said, "They once called me Niels Bruus."

I was startled, and said, "God have mercy on us! That is a bad name. That is the name of a man who was killed many years back."

Whereat the man sighed still deeper and replied: "It would have been better for me had I died then. It has gone ill with me since I left the country."

At this the hair rose on my head, and I trembled in every limb. For it seemed to me that I could recognize him, and also it seemed to me that I saw Morten Bruus before me in the flesh, and yet I had laid the earth over him three years before. I stepped back and made the sign of the cross, for verily I thought it was a ghost I saw before me.

But the man sat down in the chimney corner and continued to speak. "Reverend father, they tell me my brother Morten is dead. I have been to Ingvorstrup, but the new owner chased me away. Is my old master, the Rector of Veilbye, still alive?" Then it was that the scales fell from my eyes and I saw into the very truth of this whole terrible affair. But the shock stunned me so that I could not speak. The man bit into his bread greedily and went on. "Yes, that was all Brother Morten's fault. Did the old rector have much trouble about it?"

"Niels! Niels!" I cried from out the horror of my soul, "you have a monstrous black sin upon your conscience! For your sake that unfortunate man fell by the ax of the executioner!"

The bread and the crutch fell from his hand, and he himself was near to falling into the fire. "May God forgive you, Morten!" he groaned. "God knows I didn't mean anything like that. May my sin be forgiven me! But surely you only mean to frighten me! I come from far away, and have heard nothing. No one but you, reverend father, has recognized me. I have told my name to no one. When I asked them in Veilbye if the rector was still there, they said that he was."

"That is the new rector," I replied. "Not he whom you and your sinful brother have slain."

He wrung his hands and cried aloud, and then I knew that he had been but a tool in the hands of that devil, Morten. Therefore I set to work to comfort him, and took him into my study that he might calm himself sufficiently to tell me the detail of this Satan's work.

This was the story as he tells it: His brother Morten – truly a son of Belial – cherished a deadly hatred toward pastor Soren Quist since the day the latter had refused him the hand of his daughter. As soon as he heard that the pastor's coachman had left him, he persuaded Niels to take the place.

"Watch your chance well," he had said, "we'll play the black coat a trick some day, and you will he no loser by it."

Niels, who was rough and defiant by nature, soon came to a quarrel with his master, and when he had received his first chastisement, he ran at once to Ingvorstrup to report it. "Let him strike you just once again," said Marten. "Then come to me, and we will pay him for it."

Then came the quarrel in the garden, and Niels ran off to Ingvorstrup. He met his brother in the woods and told him what had occurred.

"Did anyone see you on the way here?" asked Morten

Niels thought not. "Good," said Morten; "now we'll give him a fright that he will not forget for a week or so."

He led Niels carefully to the house, and kept him hidden there the rest of the day. When all the household else had gone to sleep the two brothers crept out, and went to a field where several days before they had buried the body of a man of about Niel's age, size, and general appearance. (He had hanged himself, some said because of ill-treatment from Morten, in whose service he was. Others said it was because of unhappy love.) They dug up the corpse, although Niels did not like the work, and protested. But Morten was the stronger, and Niels had to do as he was ordered. They carried the body back with them into the house.

Then Niels was ordered to take off all his clothes, piece by piece, even to his shirt, and dress the dead man in them. Even his leaden earring, which he had worn for many years, was put in the ear of the corpse. After this was done, Morten took a spade and gave the head of the corpse two crashing blows, one over the nose, the other on the temple. The body was hidden in a sack and kept in the house during the next day. At night the day following, they carried it out to the wood near Veilbye.

Several times Niels had asked of his brother what all this preparation boded. But Morten answered only, "That is my affair. Do as I tell you, and don't ask questions."

When they neared the edge of the wood by Veilbye, Morten said, "Now fetch me one of the coats the pastor wears most. If you can, get the green dressing gown I have often seen him wear mornings."

"I don't dare," said Niels, "he keeps it in his bed chamber."

"Well, then, I'll dare it myself," said Morten. "And now, go your way, and never show yourself here again. Here is a bag with one hundred thalers. They will last you until you can take service somewhere in another country. Go where no one has ever seen you, and take another name. Never come back to Denmark again. Travel by night, and hide in the woods by day until you are well away from here. Here are provisions enough to last you for several days. And remember, never show yourself here again, as you value your life."

Niels obeyed, and has never seen his brother since that day. He had had much trouble, had been a soldier and lost his health in the war, and finally, after great trials and sufferings, had managed to get back to the land of his birth. This was the story as told me by the miserable man, and I could not doubt its truth.

It was now only too clear to me that my unfortunate brother in the Lord had fallen a victim to the hatred of his fiendish enemy, to the delusion of his judge and the witnesses, and to his own credulous imagination.

Oh, what is man that he shall dare to sit in judgment over his fellows! God alone is the Judge. He who gives life may alone give death!

I did not feel it my duty to give official information against this crushed and broken sinner, particularly as the district judge is still alive, and it would have been cruelty to let him know of his terrible error.

Instead, I gave what comfort my office permitted to the poor man, and recommended him not to reveal his name or tell his story to anyone in the district. On these conditions I would give him a home until I could arrange for a permanent refuge for him in my brother's house, a good distance from these parts.

The day following was a Sunday. When I returned from evening service at my branch parish, the beggar had disappeared. But by the evening of the next day the story was known throughout the neighborhood.

Goaded by the pangs of conscience, Niels had gone to Rosmer and made himself known to the judge as the true Niels Bruus. Upon the hearing of the terrible truth, the judge was taken with a stroke and died before the week was out. But on Tuesday morning they found Niels Bruus dead on the grave of the late rector Soren Quist of Veilbye, by the door of Aalso church.

Funeral

Michael Cebula

WITHIN FIFTEEN MINUTES of hearing Daddy was sick and probably dying, I had quit my job and was standing in the dirt next to a two-lane country road, looking for a way to get back home.

"It's an awful thing," the cook had said, when I explained the situation, handed over my apron, and told him where to send my last check. "I'm real sorry to hear it."

What a strange thing to say – I was nobody's idea of a good waitress.

You don't actually stick your thumb out when you hitch. You just stand by the road and wait. Sometimes, of course, you have to explain what you're *not* doing there on the side of the road. "I'm not a prostitute" being something I have said more than once in my life.

Hitching is easier when you're a girl but it's harder too. Easier because you're more likely to get a ride and harder because of why you're more likely to get one. So you follow rules, you pretend you have some control over what happens to you. Never get in a van. Or in any car with more than one man in it. Walk away if the driver looks you in the eye too long when he pulls over. Or if he never looks at you at all when he asks where you're headed. And definitely stay away if he glances in his rearview mirror more than once before you get in.

A girl I knew thought she had it all figured out. She said that when she hitched, she always lied to the driver, told him she was going home because she just found out she had HIV.

"How do you work that into the conversation?" someone asked.

"What if he has HIV?" someone else asked.

Pay attention to everything. Act weird enough that he won't try to fuck you, but not so weird he throws you out of the car. Remember that what's weird depends on who you're with. You can cut your thigh with a razor blade, above your knee and below your skirt, a straight line for each exit you pass. Or you can ask the driver if he has accepted Jesus as his personal savior. It's been years since I last hitched, but the lessons you learn as a kid stay with you forever.

* * *

The sun seems very close and I have to squint and shade my eyes to watch the crows circling the soybean field across the road. It's hot, a heavy July heat that presses on my chest and makes me want to lose this dress and these awful shoes and wade into the pond I know is behind the field. But I push those thoughts from my mind, I remain standing on the road, I wait. When cars drive past, the dirt along the road stirs up then settles on my sweaty arms and legs like a paste.

If someone doesn't pick me up soon I won't make it.

All the other times in my life that I have hitched, I was desperate to get away from somewhere. But now I'm desperate to get to somewhere – to get home, before Daddy dies, before he's gone forever. No one's at my heels this time, but the feeling that I'm not moving fast enough, that I'm not going to make it, is the same. All I heard is that he's sick and probably dying, but I don't know how old that information is or if it's still accurate. For all I know right this second he might already be dead and buried. Or maybe he recovered and right now is out somewhere hunting, breathing the same air as me. Either way, I will have lost my chance and this eats at me. Hard to believe I've been gone from home for five years.

There's no phone in his house and I wouldn't call if there was.

* * *

I wait for a long time, with no luck. Some drivers ignore me, a few honk at me, and one man grins wide and yells out the window of his truck, his words lost in the wind but not exactly unknowable. No one stops or even looks like they consider it. The crows have left me too, chased away long ago by this unforgiving heat. I am too far from home to make it on foot but I don't know what else to do, so I slip off my shoes and head down the road, walking barefoot over the brittle, yellow, sun-killed grass that lies just outside the pavement. It will be dark soon and these roads are not much traveled and for several miles I am alone, except for the mosquitoes and the cicadas and the endless rows of corn standing watch along the road.

"You will be fed to pigs," I tell the corn.

When evening takes hold, and I have lost hope of getting a ride, a middle-aged man driving an old Ford pickup with a bluetick coonhound in the back pulls over next to me. He has thick glasses, a calm voice, and the most elaborate comb-over I have ever seen. How terrified he must be of windy days. I imagine him fixing his hair in the morning, as careful as a girl before a date, telling himself nobody could tell the difference. The quality of your life can be figured by how many lies you must tell yourself each morning before you can step out your front door.

Well, I too must tell myself many lies, so I thank the man for stopping and get in the truck.

* * *

I was real little when Momma disappeared, but I remember how afterwards the sheriff and his men came out day after day and dug all around the house and in the woods surrounding it. I sat next to the holes while they worked and made mud pies for the deputies.

Daddy would sit on the porch, with a cigarette and a beer, his feet kicked up on the railing. "Dig all you want," he'd tell them.

Each night the deputies would knock the mud from their boots and throw their shovels in the trunks of their patrol cars, looking tired and pissed off and ready to break something. One afternoon before they left for the day, the sheriff took Daddy into the house and I could hear the sheriff yelling and screaming and Daddy talking real calm and then laughing. After a while, a deputy went in and pulled the sheriff away and Daddy stepped out of the house behind them and finished off his beer.

"Never let 'em see you sweat," he told me with a grin.

And then one day they were gone and never came back, just like Momma.

I asked Daddy if I would disappear one day too.

"That depends," he said, looking at me real serious. "Are you gonna keep askin' me stupid questions?"

* * *

I am awakened by a tongue in my ear – thick and wet and stomach-turning – and on instinct I reach into my purse and pull out the screwdriver, my heart racing. But it's just the bluetick in the back of the pickup, sticking his head through the cab window and grinning, confident that his sloppy kisses are valuable and much treasured.

"Sorry, but this is as far in your direction as I can go," the man with the comb-over and calm voice says. We've stopped at a crossroads that separates more cornfields. The man stares at the screwdriver in my hand and I realize I'm panting as much as the dog. I lower the screwdriver to my lap and then put it back in my purse. When I do, the dog licks my face – and just then, I want to stay in this truck forever, just keep driving on an endless summer evening with this man and his calm voice and his dog. But I can't, and anyway he isn't offering. So instead I thank the man and scratch the dog's head and slip out of the truck.

"Be careful out there," the man says as he drives away. I start to wave, then feel foolish and tuck my hands under my arms, as if they cannot be trusted. There is a limit to kindness, but not hardship, and once again I find myself standing alone at night on the side of an unlined country road.

* * *

When I was growing up, there was never much money. Daddy got a disability check, though as near as I could tell, the only thing that made him unfit for regular work was a misguided sense of his worth and abilities. Some other ways Daddy made money: cooking meth, growing weed, selling pills, stealing tools. It was like one crooked dollar was worth more to him than two earned legit.

We lived in an unpainted shotgun house deep in the woods, the same house Daddy was born and raised in. There was a creek behind the house that flooded all the time. Our closest neighbor was maybe a half-mile away, the closest paved road another mile past that. We plugged holes in the walls with old newspapers and we had electricity about as often as we did not. Rains were a torment, and you learned to sleep in a wet bed. I never starved, but many days I woke up hungry and stayed that way, even as I cooked Daddy his dinner and watched him eat it. I ate best when Daddy was locked up, as he was from time to time.

But Daddy was not the type to be burdened by such things as reality, he was not one to let facts change the image he had built of himself. Even just sitting in his chair on the porch each night, drinking his beer, Daddy seemed to strut. He had long greasy hair that he would comb with his fingers as he talked and an enormous belly where he rested his beer. He was sure he had the world figured out, and each night on the porch he delivered a sermon while I sat at his feet. I don't think he always cared what he said as long as he was the one saying it, and sometimes it was hard to see much connection between what he told me and how he lived his life. *The only place success comes before work is the dictionary*, he might say one night. *Nobody ever drowned in their own sweat.* Or maybe, *The harder you work, the luckier you get.* A fat drunk lecturing you on the importance of discipline.

Even when he was spouting bullshit, all his talks circled back to his schemes, the ones from the past that had worked, the ones that hadn't (never his fault of course), the ones he was planning. It doesn't really matter, I guess, but I do sometimes wonder: did he always know he could make money off of me or did it just occur to him one day?

* * *

Near midnight, a wood-paneled station wagon pulls over next to me. The driver is young and on something, his eyes wide and never blinking. But it's dark and I don't have much time, or many options, so I break a rule and get in, my hand in my purse, holding the screwdriver tight. He talks and talks, an unending flood that bounces from one idea to the next, with no relation I can see. Whenever he exhausts one subject, he laughs and says, "Not much for talking, are you?" and moves on to the next one before I can speak.

We run over a dead dog in the middle of the road and coyotes scatter into the fields, their eyes flashing yellow. There's gold in these hills, he tells me, buried long ago by the Indians. There's gold here, if you know where to find it.

* * *

One thing I learned from Daddy when I was real little is that the puppies never fight you when you put them in the burlap bag. They think it's a game, I guess – at that age, all they know is that life is just a bunch of fun new experiences. But with Daddy looking over your shoulder, making sure you follow through, they will soon find out the truth. You lower the first one into the burlap bag, put him next to the half a piece of cinder block, and he licks your hand. You lower the second one in, and now they both lick your hand. And on it goes. You can fit five puppies in the bag, but four is better.

Don't ask yourself the point of being gentle with them when you put them in the bag. Don't wonder what happened to Momma or what it's like to run out of air. Just know that Daddy is watching you, and you'd better not look away until the barking stops and the bag is gone beneath the water.

"You can kill anything if you got a burlap bag and a deep enough creek," being something Daddy would always say.

* * *

When we pass the county line and are a few miles from home, the driver notices me looking at the tattoos along his arms. Under the light of the dashboard, the ink on his skin looks like the scribbles of a deranged child. "They sure catch the eye," he says. I smile and nod and now he has found a new topic.

"I was always real into art in school or whatever, and one day it hits me – I could do tats for people," he says, excited. "Did most of these my own self. So it's like my body is sort of advertising, you know?" He flicks on the overhead light and holds out his arm towards me, nodding at an ugly blue mass on his hand. "You can't see that one real good, but it's Hobbes blowin' Calvin."

His arm is too close to me. I can see each individual hair, the dirt beneath his nails, the yellow of his fingertips. My chest is tight, and I feel dizzy, but I force myself to keep the screwdriver in my purse, waiting to see what happens next.

"Seems like the least Hobbes could do for him," I say and he laughs and agrees and jerks his hand back, uses it to wipe his nose. The moment passes and I can breathe.

But a few minutes later his arm shoots out again and this time without thinking I whip out the screwdriver and bury it in his shoulder. He screams and we're off the road and over the ditch. Before I can realize what's happening, we've hit a telephone pole and his screams stop. Time does not slow, not like they say, this all happens fast in a confusing, violent jumble. When I open my eyes he is slumped over, not moving, his face a mask of blood and the screwdriver still in his arm. A tooth is stuck to the steering wheel. I'm okay, I think, except I bit my tongue and my mouth is filled with blood.

He may have just been showing me another tattoo. Or reaching for his lighter.

I don't know, I don't know, I don't know.

It takes me a long time to get the screwdriver out of his shoulder. Then I unbuckle my seatbelt, slide out the car window, walk through the soybean field and slip into the woods.

* * *

One day your daddy puts an old mattress in the barn, and from then on you lay down with strangers, neighbors, a minister, men in uniform, a man with a burned face, another with a hook for a hand. One is so dirty, he always leaves a trail of axle grease all along your body. Some arrive mean. Others are ashamed, and then turn mean, wanting you gone the moment they slide out of you. None are better than others but some are worse than others.

You don't know what they pay your daddy but you know your life isn't worth much. You know other things too. That crying does not help. Or begging, or fighting, or running away. And most of all you know that the creek is deep and he can make anyone disappear.

Sometimes your belly gets bigger, perfectly and impossibly round, and he makes that disappear too. One time you try to hide it – oh yes, despite all you know, you try to hide what is growing inside you, hide it beneath baggy sweatshirts and the way you hold your body whenever he's around. And all that gets you is a terrifying June morning in a cow stall deep in the barn, bloody straw underneath you and Daddy leaning against the stall door, swinging a burlap bag in his hand while he waits until you're done pushing.

* * *

I know this land well. There is an easy path I could take, one that would lead me through open fields and along deer trails that would eventually bring me home. But that way is winding and indirect and would steal time that I know I cannot spare. So I take the direct route, a straight shot home, pushing through one thicket after another, until my arms and legs and face are crisscrossed with blood and it feels like the woods are fighting against me, something Daddy has conjured to keep me from getting back home.

When I finally get to the house, it is not yet dawn and I am hot and tired but not at all finished. The barn, the yard, the porch are all empty, but there is a dim light inside one room of the house. I stand on an overturned ten-gallon bucket and look inside. There is Daddy, asleep on the couch. He is covered by a blanket, despite the summer heat. The slow rise and fall of his chest tells me that I have made it home in time.

The front door is unlocked. I slip off my shoes and enter the house, as careful and quiet as you would be approaching any mad dog. An old Coleman lantern casts a sickly yellow light across the room – and now that I can look close, everything looks grimy and used up, especially Daddy. It's been five years since I last saw him, and time and sickness have done their work on him. He's like a skeleton now, as I had hoped he would be, his face sunk in and his gut deflated. He's surely not stronger than me anymore.

Silent as I can be, not wanting to wake him just yet, I move some tools and old newspapers off a chair and sit down. Part of me feels like I never left this house and another part feels like everything that happened to me here happened to somebody else. With him sleeping like that and looking as bad as he does, I'm not scared to be here, which makes it the first time since I was real little that I'm in this house and not afraid. But I'm not sure of myself either, not sure how to start or if I can really do what I've thought about for so long. And I know that if I can't do what I've planned, then I should have stayed far, far away from here.

He doesn't open his eyes and when he speaks his voice startles me: "Figured you'd be back, sooner or later."

My heart hammers in my chest, that old anxiety his voice always triggered. Even as sick as he is, his voice is enough to make me get up from the chair, ready to run from the room. But my feet don't move, I just stand in front of the chair. Maybe it's the wasted sight of him on the couch or these last few years living on my own, but there's something inside me now, something that wasn't in me the last time I was here, and it is small and it is fragile but it's just enough to keep me in the room.

I wait until I am sure I can trust myself, that my voice won't waver. Then I say: "Heard the good news and rushed on home." My voice wavers anyway.

I've never talked to him like this before. When I lived here, I was afraid to even imagine such things in my head for fear they would leak out, and I'm ready for him to jump up and smack me and pound my head against the wall like he's done so many times for so much less. But he doesn't respond to what I say. He still has not so much as opened his eyes, just stays there on the couch as if I hadn't said a word.

A long minute passes in silence. I am not sure how else to go on, and he doesn't seem ready to speak, so I ask, "How'd you know it was me?" Even before those words are out I am angry at myself – all the times I thought of this moment, and already I've been reduced to a little girl again, asking dumb questions, giving him control.

"Smelled you when you walked out of the woods. Never forget your scent," he says and then sniffs noisily like an animal and laughs.

Shame washes over me and I feel the urge to run again – this time it's overpowering, strong enough to beat whatever I thought had changed inside me. *Oh you stupid bitch*, I keep thinking, *why did you come back?* I turn and start to go, and when I am nearly out the door, Daddy coughs. It's a deep, wet cough, an ugly cough that would be hard to listen to if it came from anybody but him.

I stand at the door and look back at him. His eyes are open now, but he is staring at the ceiling not at me. We are separated by the length of the room, and I don't think he could catch me if I had to run. I raise my voice a little, try to sound confident, and call out to him: "That cough sounds real bad."

He sort of shrugs under his blanket and starts to say something, but another cough interrupts him. Nothing has ever interrupted Daddy in this house, but the cough does that and more – it shakes his chest and makes spit fly from his mouth and land on his face. I wait, but he doesn't wipe it off, just keeps his hands tucked under the blanket.

I leave the door open but take a few small steps back into the room. I try again. "That cough sounds real bad and you look worse."

"It's nothing," he says, but he's quieter now and he still won't look at me.

 "No, it's bad," I say, another step closer. "Can't have much time left."

"Got all the time I want or need," he says.

"That's not nearly true," I say, to myself as much as him, and I walk closer still.

"Beat much worse than this."

I am nearly standing over him now and I pick up the lantern and hold it close to his face so I can look into his eyes. There is no fight in them, no danger, the man I knew is mostly gone. He's a doomed man, a dying man. I know now that he cannot get up from this couch without serious effort. I know that if I pulled his blanket he would clutch at it like an old woman.

"Look around this house, old man," I tell him. "Look at you dying alone. What exactly have you ever beaten?"

"Beat you," he whispers, so quiet I can barely hear it. "Beat your momma."

There is a truth to what he says, so I don't disagree with him. Instead, I spend some time working him over with my screwdriver.

* * *

There was a time, a few years ago when I had finally got away from home for good, that I tried, I really tried, to move past it all. I even met with a social worker for a while, told her about the anger I felt each day, how it suffocated me, how it was eating me whole. I didn't tell her everything that had happened to me before I got away, not even close, but I thought I had told her enough.

Then one day she leaned close, like we were friends. "Have you ever heard," she asked me, "that living well is the best revenge?"

I paused then leaned closer and asked her: "Have you ever had someone try to see how far they could stick an old axe handle up inside you?"

* * *

When I stop with the screwdriver, my hand and shoulder ache and I realize I have been shouting all the while. The noise does not worry me – if I know anything, it's that I can scream all day in this house and no one will come running. I back up a few steps, catch my breath, and stand in the center of the room, taking stock. Blood is everywhere – on the couch, on the blanket, splashed against the wall. Daddy is still alive, but just barely. I must be careful now.

It takes me more than an hour to drag him to the creek. I do what I can, but it is not an easy trip for him and when we reach the creek, I am afraid he has died. I put my ear to his chest and I listen and I hope. There, very faint, I hear his heartbeat.

I lean close to him, my lips next to his ear. "I want you to know," I whisper. "I want you to know that I am going to drown you now. Right here in this awful creek. And then I am going to leave you here so the crows and the raccoons and the rats can pick over your body. And no one will know, and no one will care, because your life has been a ruin. This is the funeral you deserve."

He gives no sign of hearing, but I know he understands me all the same. When I drag him down into the water, he jerks a little but he does not really fight. I hold his head under the water and think of Momma and my lost babies. But the time for crying is long past, and anyway, there are more important things to do. I must burn down the barn, I must burn down the house, I must leave these woods without burning down myself. And for the first time I wonder if there are other men, men I once knew if only for a little while, who I ought to visit as well.

Into the Blue

Carolyn Charron

MY WORDS are all gone. I think I left them in the car.

"You can't sit here. Find somewhere else," says the man beside me.

I don't answer him. I never talk to the other people here – they're all crazy so they say the strangest things.

I can hear something ticking. It's close. I focus on the familiar sound. A quick sharp pain in my fingernail makes me look down. It's me making the noise: I was clicking my nails again. I have to focus hard to make myself stop.

"Go away!" The man sounds upset now. I wish I knew how to make him leave. His whining grates on my nerves.

"Didn't you hear me? Go away!" His loud voice is full of broken bits of blue glass and makes my stomach hurt, stabbing shards of nausea.

I hunch over the pain in my belly and my hair falls into my face. It's pretty, long and wavy. I twirl a strand around my fingers. It feels soft and silky. I love the way it gleams in the light, like shiny chocolate.

"Go away!"

I brush the lock of hair, paintbrush-like, across my lips. The smoothness of the blunt ends feels good, slightly ticklish. I like it so I do it again.

"I don't want you here!" He is noisy, blue fury drips out of his mouth. I don't want to listen to him anymore so I close my ears.

There is a warm bar of sunshine in front of me, tiny dots dancing in it. I stare at them, awed by their movement. The hair slips through my fingers, untwisting.

A large shape leaps in front of me – it's the man again, shouting silently. My pulse pounds in my ears. I cower away from the terrifying creature before it infects me with its color, a diseased cobalt molting anger with each tiny movement.

I want my little dancers back.

"…"

I am deaf. All his yelling has killed my ears.

Where did my tiny dancers go? I try to find them but now they are hidden away in the blue. That makes me sad. They shouldn't be lost in the blue: that's where the noisy monsters belong, not my little dancers.

"Come this way, come with me." This is a different voice, a softer one. It comes, wearing a white coat, to take the man away, and my little dancers come back with the sunbeam. I clap with delight and watch them twirling in the silent golden air.

Something touches my arm, scalding me. I am in agony. I scream my words and try to hit back but my arm doesn't work anymore. It never does when it's burned.

"Time for a snack," says the soft voice. It's the woman again, she came back. She wears a white coat so it's safe to talk her. Those blistering hands come close and I cower away. I really don't want to lose my arm again.

A scraping noise. An orange smell. In front of me appears a table and a plate. I see green food, perfect segments of orange sitting in a puddle of juice. I'm not crazy, I know oranges aren't green – they just feel green. On the inside where all their emotions live.

I can't remember if it's a green day. I look down. My pants are green so the food must be okay to eat.

The white-coat goes away and the little sun dancers come back again. I watch them as I eat the orange. Tiny bits of it fly into the sunbeam to join the tiny dancers. They are so pretty, I could watch them forever.

I like this place. There are good things here; little dancers and white coats to protect me from all the terrible blue things that keep on following me. I hope I can stay.

* * *

Today is a red day but I can't find my red shirt. Only the poisonous ones are in my dresser drawer, the yellow and green ones. My pillowcase has red circles on it, so I rip holes with my teeth for my head and arms and put it on. I wish I had scissors but I'm not crazy. I know better than to ask.

I have to hurry. I don't like being late for breakfast.

"What have you done? Why did you do that?" A white-coat yells at me but I had to follow the rule: All patients must wear a shirt.

"Where is your red t-shirt?"

I can't answer, I've lost my words. I know they're in the car but I can't remember where I left the car.

There are strawberries on the table. They are a pretty red on the outside but inside there is a streak of blue poison. Even without cutting them I can see the venom, oozing out of the seeds, dripping over the eggs and toast on the table, contaminating everything.

Those white-coats are so stupid, how could they put blue poison beside all the other food. Now I can't eat anything. I stomp away.

Everything is smelly and awful and I am so hungry. Blueberry-flavored hiccups come out of me when I cry. One of the white-coats sees me and brings me a bowl.

"Here's your breakfast."

It's full of cheerios, a pretty crimson glow surrounding each tiny circle making it safe to eat. I gobble them down.

I don't look at the food; the blue taint has spread over the whole table now. Inside the triangles of toast are shades of monstrous indigo and navy; if I look at them they will suck me down and drown me.

All the bad things are blue, watery shades of azure or cobalt. I'm glad it's a red day – I'm safe on red days.

A crazy one follows me out of the cafeteria. I don't like being followed so I hit her.

"Nurse! Nurse!" She runs away and I enter the community room. There are poinsettias on the tables. I like poinsettias, they're red, but I don't like the tablecloth. It's a treacherous blue. I don't like it – it makes me remember. I don't want to remember. Remembering isn't safe.

A little blue monster starts to cry in the corner. It's in the corner because it's naughty. It's soaking wet and leaves a disgusting puddle but nobody yells at it. So I go yell at it until a white-coat comes to tell me it is lunchtime.

None of my lunch leaks blue toxin but nothing is a healthy red either, so I have to pour ketchup over everything if I want to eat. I wish I liked ketchup.

I keep seeing the little monster beside me while I eat but when I scream at it to go away, it's not there anymore. I think it's lost in the blue. I'm glad it's gone – I am a little afraid of it, it keeps staring at me like it wants something.

* * *

The white-coats don't like it when I'm quiet. Sometimes, words feel blue in my mouth and it hurts to say them but the white-coats are always poking in my head and asking me questions.

So I tell them I hear a baby, it cries all night keeping me awake. I don't like telling on people and getting them in trouble but they asked me and it's only polite to answer. The white-coats say the baby isn't real. I'm sure they are lying to me. Anyone who wears orange must be a liar.

Today is a yellow day. My shirt is too small, it pinches my arms but I wear it anyway. It matches the carpet in my house.

I had a house.

I remember a puddle of sapphire-blue paint on that carpet. The puddle is so big my beautiful pale yellow carpet will never be clean again. I get very angry, remembering it and think I should show someone what a real puddle looks like. Wait. I think I already did that.

The little blue monster is back. It's crying again. Why won't it stop crying? I don't want to see it. It looks sad and scary and too blue. I stare at the edge of my shirt. There is a tiny hole in it. I stick my finger into the hole and twist it bigger. I don't know when the little monster goes away but when I peek up, it's gone. Part of me is sad, but mostly I'm happy it left. I'm not crazy – I know I shouldn't be seeing things no-one else can see.

Dinner is string beans. There is a lying piece of carrot mixed in with them and I use my plastic spoon-fork thing to flick it off. It hits the little blue monster in the face and goes right through but it was already crying so it's not like I hurt it. I wish it would stop following me.

Yellow days are strange. It's not a poisonous day but it's not safe, either. It means the blue day is coming fast, it's almost here.

* * *

The little blue monster is in my room now. I didn't let it in and I want it to leave me alone. I can't tell what color day it is when there is a screaming monster standing in a puddle of sky in my room.

Through the window in my door, I see the hallway outside my room. The walls out there have a faint blue tinge underlying the white paint, tainting the air with pollution.

Oh god, it's a blue day.

I hate blue days.

I will wear my white pajamas all day. I have no blue clothes. I tore them all into pieces and threw them away.

On these dreadful blue days, I remember where I left my metallic-blue car – at the lake. There was plenty of parking. We were the only ones there. I push away the memory and edge past the monster still screaming in the corner and escape. I rush to the dining room.

A white-coat hands me a bowl. I can see by her expression that she knows what day it is.

The bowl is full of fish crackers. I don't want to eat them. I hate them – they are all messed up, they're orange on the outside and should feel green on the inside but they have a purpleness to them that makes me want to vomit. I have to eat them though, it's one of the rules: "All patients will eat what they are given."

That little crying monster follows me and watches me eat my breakfast but I don't share even if fish crackers are its favorite food. I'm not allowed.

"Time for your session." A white-coat walks up, splashing through the rancid puddle of watery blue that came with the little monster and now surrounds me. He doesn't notice the monster even though he almost stepped on it.

I follow the white-coat silently into a small room at the end of a long hallway. I hate this room, it scares me. The walls are pale blue but that's not what frightens me. My secret is hidden in here, waiting for an azure key to unlock it.

The secret is sitting on a box on the desk. It looks like a bright blue toy car, shiny with water droplets. I can't take my eyes off it. I recognize it.

The doctor white-coat is already sitting behind her desk, waiting for me.

"Are you ready to tell me what happened?"

I like the other days better when the car is a different color. The red car isn't scary. Neither is the green one. Those little car doors stay locked so I'm safe in this room with my words all sealed in.

On these dreadful blue days, the car door opens and words bubble out, following me up, up, up, out of the blue water, dragging memories with them, filling my mouth with the truth – hard little nuggets of ice.

I remember watching the bubbles rise, sparkling in the light.

"I left him there," I hear myself say, "I saved myself and I left him there, in his car-seat." The words scrape across my tongue, leaving indigo wounds.

"You did the best you could. You saved yourself first before you tried to help him." The doctor is sympathetic.

I can see the bubbles again, escaping one at a time in a slow trickle from my son's screaming mouth. Behind the glass, his face washed in blue light. He blinked and something in his eyes faded, those blue-sky irises dimmed to murky grey.

Today is a blue day so I remember now. I remember him and what I did to him.

I'd driven him to where he belonged, to his big blue puddle. I'd left him with his own kind, all the wicked monsters that cried all day and left puddled messes wherever they went.

I'd driven to the lake, to the shining surface that hid something I wanted more than anything: silence – underwater peace.

The doctor looked at me, waiting for me to admit that I'd tried to save him – that I felt terrible because I hadn't succeeded.

But I couldn't tell her that, I wasn't supposed to lie.

The truth was a glassy jagged chunk of blue in my mouth: I hadn't failed. I *had* succeeded. It wasn't an accident, I'd driven him home. I'd deliberately left him there in his terrifying bubbles.

He was home in the blue, the shimmering, watery blue, where I couldn't hear his screaming or crying. Home to blissful silence.

I remember his china-blue eyes as I stared into the blue of the toy car – it was the exact shade of his eyes, those unblinking eyes – drowning in that poisonous color until I remember everything…

The screaming has finally stopped.

I walk along a quiet country road, dappled in green shadows.

I've lost my car somewhere. A breeze chills me in my soaking wet clothes. I walk a long way home; my beautiful quiet place, with clean linens, tidy rooms, and a glass of white wine. A glitter of blue makes my heart catch for a moment before it fades away, lost in the water.

It's so lovely and tranquil here.

I stare into those remembered blue eyes. Sapphire, azure, turquoise, cerulean, indigo. They grow and expand, drowning my vision.

An ocean of blue engulfs my memories, washing away the world, one color at a time.

Until nothing is left…

except…

white. Pure and unmarked.

I look down at my knees, covered in white pajamas.

Clean refreshing white. I love white days. So smooth, so neat. No jarring, lethal blueness anywhere. Safe.

"You did your best," the doctor says.

I don't answer her, I have no words. I left them somewhere, maybe in the car.

My pretty blue car. I wonder where it is.

Dr. Hyde, Detective, and the White Pillars Murder

G.K. Chesterton

THOSE WHO HAVE discussed the secret of the success of the great detective, Dr. Adrian Hyde, could find no finer example of his remarkable methods than the affair which came to be called 'The White Pillars Mystery'. But that extraordinary man left no personal notes and we owe our record of it to his two young assistants, John Brandon and Walter Weir. Indeed, as will be seen, it was they who could best describe the first investigations in detail, from the outside; and that for a rather remarkable reason. They were both men of exceptional ability; they had fought bravely and even brilliantly in the Great War, they were cultivated, they were capable, they were trustworthy, and they were starving. For such was the reward which England in the hour of victory accorded to the deliverers of the world. It was a long time before they consented in desperation to consider anything so remote from their instincts as employment in a private detective agency. Jack Brandon, who was a dark, compact, resolute, restless youth, with a boyish appetite for detective tales and talk, regarded the notion with a half-fascinated apprehension, but his friend Weir, who was long and fair and languid, a lover of music and metaphysics, with a candid disgust.

"I believe it might be frightfully interesting," said Brandon. "Haven't you ever had the detective fever when you couldn't help overhearing somebody say something – 'If only he knew what she did to the Archdeacon', or 'And then the whole business about Susan and the dog will come out'?"

"Yes," replied Weir, "but you only heard snatches because you didn't mean to listen and almost immediately left off listening. If you were a detective, you'd have to crawl under the bed or hide in the dustbin to hear the whole secret, till your dignity was as dirty as your clothes!"

"Isn't it better than stealing," asked Brandon, gloomily, "which seems to be the next step?"

"Why, no; I'm not sure that it is!" answered his friend.

Then, after a pause, he added, reflectively, "Besides, it isn't as if we'd get the sort of work that's relatively decent. We can't claim to know the wretched trade. Clumsy eavesdropping must be worse than the blind spying on the blind. You've not only got to know what is said, but what is meant. There's a lot of difference between listening and hearing. I don't say I'm exactly in a position to fling away a handsome salary offered me by a great criminologist like Dr. Adrian Hyde, but, unfortunately, he isn't likely to offer it."

But Dr. Adrian Hyde was an unusual person in more ways than one, and a better judge of applicants than most modern employers. He was a very tall man with a chin so sunk on his chest as to give him, in spite of his height, almost a look of being hunchbacked; but though the face seemed thus fixed as in a frame, the eyes were as active as a bird's, shifting and darting everywhere and observing everything; his long limbs ended in large hands and feet, the former being almost always thrust into his trouser-pockets, and the latter being loaded with more than appropriately large boots. With all his awkward figure he was not without gaiety and a taste for good things, especially good wine and tobacco; his manner was grimly genial and his insight and personal judgement marvellously rapid. Which was how it came about that John Brandon and Waiter Weir were established at comfortable desks in the detective's private office, when Mr. Alfred Morse was shown in, bringing with him the problem of White Pillars.

Mr. Alfred Morse was a very stolid and serious person with stiffly-brushed brown hair, a heavy brown face and a heavy black suit of mourning of a cut somewhat provincial, or perhaps colonial. His first words were accompanied with an inoffensive but dubious cough and a glance at the two assistants.

"This is rather confidential business," he said.

"Mr. Morse," said Dr. Hyde, with quiet good humour, "if you were knocked down by a cab and carried to a hospital, your life might be saved by the first surgeon in the land: but you couldn't complain if he let students learn from the operation. These are my two cleverest pupils, and if you want good detectives, you must let them be trained."

"Oh, very well," said the visitor, "perhaps it is not quite so easy to talk of the personal tragedy as if we were alone; but I think I can lay the main facts before you.

"I am the brother of Melchior Morse, whose dreadful death is so generally deplored. I need not tell you about him; he was a public man of more than average public spirit, and I suppose his benefactions and social work are known throughout the world. I had not seen so much of him as I could wish till the last few years; for I have been much abroad; I suppose some would call me the rolling stone of the family, compared with my brother, but I was deeply attached to him, and all the resources of the family estate will be open to anyone ready to avenge his death. You will understand I shall not lightly abandon that duty.

"The crime occurred, as you probably know, at his country place called 'White Pillars', after its rather unique classical architecture; a colonnade in the shape of a crescent, like that at St Peter's, runs halfway round an artificial lake, to which the descent is by a flight of curved stone steps. It is in the lake that my brother's body was found floating in the moonlight; but as his neck was broken, apparently with a blow, he had clearly been killed elsewhere. When the butler found the body, the moon was on the other side of the house and threw the inner crescent of the colonnade and steps into profound shadow. But the butler swears he saw the figure of the fleeing man in dark outline against the moonlight as it turned the corner of the house. He says it was a striking outline, and he would know it again."

"Those outlines are very vivid sometimes," said the detective, thoughtfully, "but of course very difficult to prove. Were there any other traces? Any footprints or fingerprints?"

"There were no fingerprints," said Morse, gravely, "and the murderer must have meant to take equal care to leave no footprints. That is why the crime was probably committed on the great flight of stone steps. But they say the cleverest murderer forgets something; and when he threw the body in the lake there must have been a splash, which was not quite dry when it was discovered; and it showed the edge of a pretty clear footprint. I have a copy of the thing here; the original is at home." He passed a brown slip across to Hyde, who looked at it and nodded. "The only other thing on the stone steps that might be a clue was a cigar-stump. My brother did not smoke."

"Well, we will look into those clues more closely in due course." said Dr. Hyde. "Now tell me something about the house and the people in it."

Mr. Morse shrugged his shoulders, as if the family in question did not impress him.

"There were not many people in it," he replied, "putting aside a fairly large staff of servants, headed by the butler, Barton, who has been devoted to my brother for years. The servants all bear a good character; but of course you will consider all that. The other occupants of the house at the time were my brother's wife, a rather silent elderly woman, devoted almost entirely to religion and good works; a niece, of whose prolonged visits the old lady did not perhaps altogether approve, for Miss. Barbara Butler is half Irish and rather flighty and excitable; my brothers secretary, Mr. Graves, a very silent young man (I confess I could never make out whether he was shy or sly), and my brother's solicitor, Mr. Caxton, who is an ordinary snuffy lawyer, and happened to be down there on legal business. They might all be guilty in theory, I suppose, but I'm a practical man, and I don't imagine such things in practice."

"Yes, I realised you were a practical man when you first came in," said Dr. Hyde, rather drily. "I realised a few other details as well. Is that all you have to tell me?"

"Yes," replied Morse, "I hope I have made myself clear."

"It is well not to forget anything," went on Adrian Hyde, gazing at him calmly. "It is still better not to suppress anything, when confiding in a professional man. You may have heard, perhaps, of a knack I have of noticing things about people. I knew some of the things you told me before you opened your mouth; as that you long lived abroad and had just come up from the country. And it was easy to infer from your own words that you are the heir of your brother's considerable fortune."

"Well, yes, I am," replied Alfred Morse, stolidly.

"When you said you were a rolling stone," went on Adrian Hyde, with the same placid politeness, "I fear some might say you were a stone which the builders were justified in rejecting. Your adventures abroad have not all been happy. I perceive that you deserted from some foreign navy, and that you were once in prison for robbing a bank. If it comes to an inquiry into your brother's death and your present inheritance –"

"Are you trying to suggest," cried the other fiercely, "that appearances are against me?"

"My dear sir," said Dr. Adrian Hyde blandly, "appearances are most damnably against you. But I don't always go by appearances. It all depends. Good day."

* * *

When the visitor had withdrawn, looking rather black, the impetuous Brandon broke out into admiration of the Master's methods and besieged him with questions.

"Look here," said the great man, good-humouredly, "you've no business to be asking how I guessed right. You ought to be guessing at the guesses yourselves. Think it out."

"The desertion from a foreign navy," said Weir, slowly, "might be something to do with those bluish marks on his wrist. Perhaps they were some special tattooing and he'd tried to rub them out."

"That's better," said Dr. Hyde, "you're getting on."

"I know!" cried Brandon, more excitedly, "I know about the prison! They always say, if you once shave your moustache it never grows the same; perhaps there's something like that about hair that's been cropped in gaol. Yes, I thought so. The only thing I can't imagine, is why you should guess he had robbed a bank."

"Well, you think that out too," said Adrian Hyde. "I think you'll find it's the key to the whole of this riddle. And now I'm going to leave this case to you. I'm going to have a half-holiday." As a signal that his own working hours were over, he lit a large and sumptuous cigar, and began pishing and poohing over the newspapers.

"Lord, what rubbish?" he cried. "My God, what headlines! Look at this about White Pillars: 'Whose Was the Hand?' They've murdered even murder with clichés like clubs of wood. Look here, you two fellows had better go down to White Pillars and try to put some sense into them. I'll come down later and clear up the mess."

* * *

The two young detectives had originally intended to hire a car, but by the end of their journey they were very glad they had decided to travel by train with the common herd. Even as they were in the act of leaving the train, they had a stroke of luck in the matter of that collecting of stray words and whispers which Weir found the least congenial, but Brandon desperately clung to as the most practicable, of all forms of detective enquiry. The steady scream of a steam-whistle, which was covering all the shouted conversation, stopped suddenly in the fashion that makes a shout shrivel into a whisper. But there was one whisper caught in the silence and sounding clear as a bell; a voice that said, "There were excellent reasons for killing him. I know them, if nobody else does."

Brandon managed to trace the voice to its origin; a sallow face with a long shaven chin and a rather scornful lower lip. He saw the same face more than once on the remainder of his journey, passing the ticket collector, appearing in a car behind them on the road, haunting him so significantly, that he was not surprised to meet the man eventually in the garden of White Pillars, and to have him presented as Mr. Claxton, the solicitor.

"That man evidently knows more than he's told the authorities," said Brandon to his friend, "but I can't get anything more out of him."

"My dear fellow," cried Weir, "that's what they're all like. Don't you feel by this time that it's the atmosphere of the whole place? It's not a bit like those delightful detective stories. In a detective story all the people in the house are gaping imbeciles, who can't understand anything, and in the midst stands the brilliant sleuth who understands everything. Here am I standing in the midst, a brilliant sleuth, and I believe, on my soul, I'm the only person in the house who doesn't know all about the crime."

"There's one other anyhow," said Brandon, with gloom, "two brilliant sleuths."

"Everybody else knows except the detective," went on Weir; "everybody knows something, anyhow, if it isn't everything. There's something odd even about old Mrs. Morse; she's devoted to charity, yet she doesn't seem to have agreed with her husband's philanthropy. It's as if they'd quarrelled about it. Then there's die secretary, the quiet, good-looking young man, with a square face like Napoleon. He looks as if he would get what he wants, and I've very little doubt that what he wants is that red-haired Irish girl they call Barbara. I think she wants the same thing; but if so there's really no reason for them to hide it. And they *are* hiding it, or hiding something. Even the butler is secretive. They can't all have been in a conspiracy to kill the old man."

"Anyhow, it all comes back to what I said first," observed Brandon. "If they're in a conspiracy, we can only hope to overhear their talk. It's the only way."

"It's an excessively beastly way," said Weir, calmly, "and we will proceed to follow it."

* * *

They were walking slowly round the great semicircle of colonnade that looked inwards upon the lake, that shone like a silver mirror to the moon. It was of the same stretch of clear moonlit nights as that recent one, on which old Morse had died mysteriously in the same spot. They could imagine him as he was in many portraits, a little figure in a skull-cap with a white beard thrust forward, standing on those steps, till a dreadful figure that had no face in their dreams descended the stairway and struck him down. They were standing at one end of the colonnade, full of these visions, when Brandon said suddenly: "Did you speak?"

"I? No," replied his friend staring.

"Somebody spoke," said Brandon, in a low voice, "yet we seem to be quite alone."

Then their blood ran cold for an instant. For the wall behind them spoke; and it seemed to say quite plainly, in a rather harsh voice: "Do you remember exactly what you said?"

Weir stared at the wall for an instant; then he slapped it with his hand with a shaky laugh.

"My God," he cried, "what a miracle! And what a satire! We've sold ourselves to the devil as a couple of damned eavesdroppers; and he's put us in the very chamber of eavesdropping – into the ear of Dionysius, the Tyrant. Don't you see this is a whispering gallery, and people at the other end of it are whispering?"

"No, they're talking too loud to hear us, I think," whispered Brandon, "but we'd better lower our voices. It's Caxton the lawyer, and the young secretary."

The secretary's unmistakable and vigorous voice sounded along the wall saying: "I told him I was sick of the whole business; and if I'd known he was such a tyrant, I'd never have had to do with him. I think I told him he ought to be shot. I was sorry enough for it afterwards."

Then they heard the lawyer's more croaking tones saying, "Oh, you said that, did you? Well, there seems no more to be said now. We had better go in," which was followed by echoing feet and then silence.

* * *

The next day Weir attached himself to the lawyer with a peculiar pertinacity and made a new effort to get something more out of that oyster. He was pondering deeply of the very little that he had got, when Brandon rushed up to him with hardly-restrained excitement.

"I've been at that place again," he cried. "I suppose you'll say I've sunk lower in the pit of slime, and perhaps I have, but it's got to be done. I've been listening to the young people this time, and I believe I begin to see something; though heaven knows, it's not what I want to see. The secretary and the girl are in love all right, or have been; and when love is loose pretty dreadful things can happen. They were talking about getting married, of course, at least she was, and what do you think she said? 'He made an excuse of my being under age.' So it's pretty clear the old man opposed the match. No doubt that was what the secretary meant by talking about his tyranny."

"And what did the secretary say when the girl said that?"

"That's the queer thing," answered Brandon, "rather an ugly thing, I begin to fancy. The young man only answered, rather sulkily, I thought: 'Well, he was within his rights there; and perhaps it was for the best.' She broke out in protest: 'How can you say such a thing?' and certainly it was a strange thing for a lover to say."

"What are you driving at?" asked his friend.

"Do you know anything about women?" asked Brandon. "Suppose the old man was not only trying to break off the engagement but succeeding in breaking it up. Suppose the young man was weakening and beginning to wonder whether she was worth losing his job for. The woman might have waited any time or eloped any time. But if she thought she was in danger of losing him altogether, don't you think she might have turned on the tempter with the fury of despair? I fear we have got a glimpse of a very heart-rending tragedy. Don't you believe it, too?"

Walter Weir unfolded his long limbs and got slowly to his feet, filling a pipe and looking at his friend with a sort of quizzical melancholy.

"No, I don't believe it," he said, "but that's because I'm such an unbeliever. You see, I don't believe in all this eavesdropping business; I don't think we shine at it. Or, rather, I think you shine too much at it and dazzle yourself blind. I don't believe in all this detective romance about deducing everything from a trifle. I don't believe in your little glimpse of a great tragedy. It would be a great tragedy no doubt, and does you credit as literature or a symbol of life; you can build imaginative things of that sort on a trifle. You can build everything on the trifle except the truth. But in the present practical issue, I don't believe there's a word of truth in it. I don't believe the old man was opposed to the engagement; I don't believe the young man was backing out of it; I believe the young people are perfectly happy and ready to be married tomorrow. I don't believe anybody in this house had any motive to kill Morse or has any notion of how he was killed. In spite of what I said, the poor shabby old sleuth enjoys his own again. I believe I am the only person who knows the truth; and it only came to me in a flash a few minutes ago."

"Why, how do you mean?" asked the other.

"It came to me in a final flash," said Weir, "when you repeated those words of the girl: 'He made the excuse that I was under age'."

After a few puffs of his pipe, he resumed reflectively: "One queer thing is, that the error of the eavesdropper often comes from a thing being too clear. We're so sure that people mean what we mean, that we can't believe they mean what they say. Didn't I once tell you that it's one thing to listen and another to hear? And sometimes the voice talks too plain. For instance, when young Graves, the secretary, said that he was sick of the business, he meant it literally, and not metaphorically. He meant he was sick of Morse's trade, because it was tyrannical."

"Morse's trade? What trade?" asked Brandon, staring.

"Our saintly old philanthropist was a money-lender," replied Weir, "and as great a rascal as his rascally brother. That is the great central fact that explains everything. That is what the girl meant by talking about being under age. She wasn't talking about her love-affair at all, but about some small loan she'd tried to get from the old man and which he refused because she was a minor. Her fiancé made the very sensible comment that perhaps it was all for the best; meaning that she had escaped the net of a usurer. And her momentary protest was only a spirited young lady's lawful privilege of insisting on her lover agreeing with all the silly things she says. That is an example of the error of the eavesdropper, or the fallacy of detection by trifles. But, as I say, it's the money-lending business that's the clue to everything in this house. That's what all of them, even the secretary and solicitor, out of a sort of family pride, are trying to hush up and hide from detectives and newspapers. But the old man's murder was much more likely to get it into the newspapers. They had no motive to murder him, and they didn't murder him."

"Then who did?" demanded Brandon.

"Ah," replied his friend, but with less than his usual languor in the ejaculation and something a little like a hissing intake of the breath. He had seated himself once more, with his elbows on his knees, but the other was surprised to realise something rigid about his new attitude; almost like a creature crouching for a spring. He still spoke quite drily, however, and merely said: "In order to answer that, I fancy we must go back to the first talk that we overheard, before we came to the house; the very first of all."

"Oh, I see," said Brandon, a light dawning on his Face. "You mean what we heard the solicitor say in the train."

"No," replied Weir, in the same motionless manner, "that was only another illustration touching the secret trade. Of course his solicitor knew he was a money-lender; and knew that any such money-lender has a crowd of victims, who might kill him. It's quite true he was killed by one of those victims. But it wasn't the lawyer's remark in the train that I was talking about, for a very simple reason."

"And why not?" enquired his companion.

"Because that was not the first conversation we overheard."

Walter Weir clutched his knees with his long bony hands, and seemed to stiffen still more as if in a trance, but he went on talking steadily.

"I have told you the moral and the burden of all these things; that it is one thing to hear what men say and another to hear what they mean. And it was at the very first talk that we heard all the words and missed all the meaning. We did not overhear that first talk slinking about in moonlit gardens and whispering-galleries. We overheard that first talk sitting openly at our regular desks in broad daylight, in a bright and business-like office. But we no more made sense of that talk than if it had been half a whisper, heard in a black forest or a cave."

He sprang to his feet as if a stiff spring were released and began striding up and down, with what was for him an unnatural animation.

"That was the talk we really misunderstood," he cried. "That was the conversation that we heard word for word, and yet missed entirely! Fools that we were! Deaf and dumb and imbecile, sitting there like dummies and being stuffed with a stage play! We were actually allowed to be eavesdroppers, tolerated, ticketed, given special permits to be eavesdroppers; and still we could not eavesdrop! I never even guessed till ten minutes ago the meaning of that conversation in the office. That terrible conversation! That terrible meaning! Hate and hateful fear and shameless wickedness and mortal peril – death and hell wrestled naked before our eyes in that office, and we never saw them. A man accused another man of murder across a table, and we never heard it."

"Oh," gasped Brandon at last, "you mean that the Master accused the brother of murder?"

"No!" retorted Weir, in a voice like a volley, "I mean that the brother accused the Master of murder."

"The Master!"

"Yes," answered Weir, and his high voice fell suddenly, "and the accusation was true. The man who murdered old Morse was our employer, Dr. Adrian Hyde."

"What can it all mean?" asked Brandon, and thrust his hand through his thick brown hair.

"That was our mistake at the beginning," went on the other calmly, "that we did not think what it could all mean. Why was the brother so careful to say the reproduction of the footprint was a proof and not the original? Why did Dr. Hyde say the outline of the fugitive would be difficult to prove? Why did he tell us, with that sardonic grin, that the brother having robbed a bank was the key of the riddle? Because the whole of that consultation of the client and the specialist was a fiction for our benefit. The whole course of events was determined by that first thing that happened; that the young and innocent detectives were allowed to remain in the room. Didn't you think yourself the interview was a little too like that at the beginning of every damned detective story? Go over it speech by speech, and you will see that every speech was a thrust or parry under a cloak. That blackmailing blackguard Alfred hunted out Dr. Hyde simply to accuse and squeeze him. Seeing us there, he said, 'This is confidential', meaning, 'You don't want to be accused before them.' Dr. Hyde answered, 'They're my favourite pupils', meaning, 'I'm less likely to be blackmailed before them; they shall stay.' Alfred answered, 'Well, I can state my business, if not quite so personally,' meaning, 'I can accuse you so that you understand, if they don't.' And he did. He presented his proofs like pistols across the table; things that sounded rather thin, but, in Hyde's case, happened to be pretty thick. His boots, for instance, happened to be very thick. His huge footprint would be unique enough to be a clue. So would the cigar-end; for very few people can afford to smoke his cigars. Of course, that's what got him tangled up with the money-lender – extravagance. You see how much money you get through if you smoke those cigars all day and never drink anything but the best vintage champagne. And though a black silhouette against die moon sounds as vague as moonshine, Hyde's huge figure and hunched shoulders would be rather marked. Well, you know how the blackmailed man hit back: 'I perceive by your left eyebrow that you are a deserter; I deduce from the pimple on your nose that you were once in gaol,' meaning, 'I know you, and you're as much a crook as I am; expose me and I'll expose you.' Then he said he had deduced in the Sherlock Holmes manner that Alfred had robbed a bank, and that was where he went too far. He presumed on the incredible credulity, which is the mark of the modern mind when anyone has uttered the magic word 'science'. He presumed on the priestcraft of our time; but he presumed the least little bit too much, so far as I was concerned. It was then I first began to doubt. A man might possibly deduce by scientific detection that another man had been in a certain navy or prison, but by no possibility could he deduce from a man's appearance that what he had once robbed was a bank. It was simply impossible. Dr. Hyde knew it was his biggest bluff; that was why he told you in mockery, that it was the key to the riddle. It was; and I managed to get hold of the key."

He chuckled in a hollow fashion as he laid down his pipe. "That jibe at his own bluff was like him; he really is a remarkable man or a remarkable devil. He has a sort of horrible sense of humour. Do you know, I've got a notion that sounds rather a nightmare, about what happened on that great slope of steps that night. I believe Hyde jeered at the journalistic catchword, 'Whose Was the Hand?' partly because he, himself, had managed it without hands. I believe he managed to commit a murder entirely with his feet. I believe he tripped up the poor old usurer and stamped on him on the stone steps with those monstrous boots. An idyllic moonlight scene, isn't it? But there's something that seems to make it worse. I think he had the habit anyhow, partly to avoid leaving his fingerprints, which may be known to the police. Anyhow, I believe he did the whole murder with his hands in his trouser-pockets."

Brandon shuddered suddenly; then collected himself and said, rather weakly: "Then you don't think the science of observation –"

"Science of observation be damned?" cried Weir. "Do you still think private detectives get to know about criminals by smelling their hair-oil, or counting their buttons? They do it, a whole gang of them do it just as Hyde did. They get to know about criminals by being half criminals themselves, by being of the same rotten world, by belonging to it and by betraying it, by setting a thief to catch a thief, and proving there is no honour among thieves. I don't say there are no honest private detectives, but if there are, you don't get into their service as easily as you and I got into the office of the distinguished Dr. Adrian Hyde. You ask what all this means, and I tell you one thing it means. It means that you and I are going to sweep crossings or scrub out drains. I feel as if I should like a clean job."

The Traveller's Story of a Terribly Strange Bed

Wilkie Collins

Prologue

BEFORE I BEGIN, by the aid of my wife's patient attention and ready pen, to relate any of the stories which I have heard at various times from persons whose likenesses I have been employed to take, it will not be amiss if I try to secure the reader's interest in the following pages, by briefly explaining how I became possessed of the narrative matter which they contain.

Of myself I have nothing to say, but that I have followed the profession of a travelling portrait-painter for the last fifteen years. The pursuit of my calling has not only led me all through England, but has taken me twice to Scotland, and once to Ireland. In moving from district to district, I am never guided beforehand by any settled plan. Sometimes the letters of recommendation which I get from persons who are satisfied with the work I have done for them determine the direction in which I travel. Sometimes I hear of a new neighbourhood in which there is no resident artist of ability, and remove thither on speculation. Sometimes my friends among the picture-dealers say a good word on my behalf to their rich customers, and so pave the way for me in the large towns. Sometimes my prosperous and famous brother artists, hearing of small commissions which it is not worth their while to accept, mention my name, and procure me introductions to pleasant country houses. Thus I get on, now in one way and now in another, not winning a reputation or making a fortune, but happier, perhaps, on the whole, than many men who have got both the one and the other. So, at least, I try to think now, though I started in my youth with as high an ambition as the best of them. Thank God, it is not my business here to speak of past times and their disappointments. A twinge of the old hopeless heartache comes over me sometimes still, when I think of my student days.

One peculiarity of my present way of life is that it brings me into contact with all sorts of characters. I almost feel, by this time, as if I had painted every civilized variety of the human race. Upon the whole, my experience of the world, rough as it has been, has not taught me to think unkindly of my fellow-creatures. I have certainly received such treatment at the hands of some of my sitters as I could not describe without saddening and shocking any kind-hearted reader; but, taking one year and one place with another, I have cause to remember with gratitude and respect – sometimes even with friendship and affection – a very large proportion of the numerous persons who have employed me.

Some of the results of my experience are curious in a moral point of view. For example, I have found women almost uniformly less delicate in asking me about my terms, and less generous in remunerating me for my services, than men. On the other hand, men, within my knowledge, are decidedly vainer of their personal attractions, and more vexatiously anxious to have them done full justice to on canvas, than women. Taking both sexes together, I have found young people, for the most part, more gentle, more reasonable, and more considerate than old. And, summing up, in a general way, my experience of different ranks (which extends, let me premise, all the way down from peers to publicans), I have met with most of my formal and ungracious receptions among rich people of uncertain social standing: the highest classes and the lowest among my employers almost always contrive – in widely different ways, of course, to make me feel at home as soon as I enter their houses.

The one great obstacle that I have to contend against in the practice of my profession is not, as some persons may imagine, the difficulty of making my sitters keep their heads still while I paint them, but the difficulty of getting them to preserve the natural look and the every-day peculiarities of dress and manner. People will assume an expression, will brush up their hair, will correct any little characteristic carelessness in their apparel – will, in short, when they want to have their likenesses taken, look as if they were sitting for their pictures. If I paint them, under these artificial circumstances, I fail of course to present them in their habitual aspect; and my portrait, as a necessary consequence, disappoints everybody, the sitter always included. When we wish to judge of a man's character by his handwriting, we want his customary scrawl dashed off with his common workaday pen, not his best small-text, traced laboriously with the finest procurable crow-quill point. So it is with portrait-painting, which is, after all, nothing but a right reading of the externals of character recognizably presented to the view of others.

Experience, after repeated trials, has proved to me that the only way of getting sitters who persist in assuming a set look to resume their habitual expression, is to lead them into talking about some subject in which they are greatly interested. If I can only beguile them into speaking earnestly, no matter on what topic, I am sure of recovering their natural expression; sure of seeing all the little precious everyday peculiarities of the man or woman peep out, one after another, quite unawares. The long, maundering stories about nothing, the wearisome recitals of petty grievances, the local anecdotes unrelieved by the faintest suspicion of anything like general interest, which I have been condemned to hear, as a consequence of thawing the ice off the features of formal sitters by the method just described, would fill hundreds of volumes, and promote the repose of thousands of readers. On the other hand, if I have suffered under the tediousness of the many, I have not been without my compensating gains from the wisdom and experience of the few. To some of my sitters I have been indebted for information which has enlarged my mind – to some for advice which has lightened my heart – to some for narratives of strange adventure which riveted my attention at the time, which have served to interest and amuse my fireside circle for many years past, and which are now, I would fain hope, destined to make kind friends for me among a wider audience than any that I have yet addressed.

Singularly enough, almost all the best stories that I have heard from my sitters have been told by accident. I only remember two cases in which a story was volunteered to me, and, although I have often tried the experiment, I cannot call to mind even a single instance in which leading questions (as the lawyers call them) on my part, addressed to a sitter, ever produced any result worth recording. Over and over again, I have been disastrously successful in encouraging dull people to weary me. But the clever people who have something interesting to say, seem, so far as I have observed them, to acknowledge no other stimulant than chance. For every story which I propose including in the present collection, excepting one, I have been indebted, in the first instance, to the capricious influence of the same chance. Something my sitter has seen about me, something I have remarked in my sitter, or in the room in which I take the likeness, or in the neighbourhood through which I pass on my way to work, has suggested the necessary association, or has started the right train of recollections, and then the story appeared to begin of its own accord. Occasionally the most casual notice, on my part, of some very unpromising object has smoothed the way for the relation of a long and interesting narrative. I first heard one of the most dramatic of the stories that will be presented in this book, merely through being carelessly inquisitive to know the history of a stuffed poodle-dog.

It is thus not without reason that I lay some stress on the desirableness of prefacing each one of the following narratives by a brief account of the curious manner in which I became possessed of it. As to my capacity for repeating these stories correctly, I can answer for it that my memory may be trusted. I may claim it as a merit, because it is after all a mechanical one, that I forget nothing, and that I can call long-passed conversations and events as readily to my recollection as if they had happened but a few weeks ago. Of two things at least I feel tolerably certain beforehand, in meditating over the contents of this book: First, that I can repeat correctly all that I have heard; and, secondly, that I have never missed anything worth hearing when my sitters were addressing me on an interesting subject. Although I cannot take the lead in talking while I am engaged in painting, I can listen while others speak, and work all the better for it.

So much in the way of general preface to the pages for which I am about to ask the reader's attention. Let me now advance to particulars, and describe how I came to hear the first story in the present collection. I begin with it because it is the story that I have oftenest 'rehearsed,' to borrow a phrase from the stage. Wherever I go, I am sooner or later sure to tell it. Only last night, I was persuaded into repeating it once more by the inhabitants of the farmhouse in which I am now staying.

Not many years ago, on returning from a short holiday visit to a friend settled in Paris, I found professional letters awaiting me at my agent's in London, which required my immediate presence in Liverpool. Without stopping to unpack, I proceeded by the first conveyance to my new destination; and, calling at the picture-dealer's shop, where portrait-painting engagements were received for me, found to my great satisfaction that I had remunerative employment in prospect, in and about Liverpool, for at least two months to come. I was putting up my letters in high spirits, and was just leaving the picture-dealer's shop to look out for comfortable lodgings, when I was met at the door by the landlord of one of the largest hotels in Liverpool – an old acquaintance whom I had known as manager of a tavern in London in my student days.

"Mr. Kerby!" he exclaimed, in great astonishment. "What an unexpected meeting! The last man in the world whom I expected to see, and yet the very man whose services I want to make use of!"

"What, more work for me?" said I; "Are all the people in Liverpool going to have their portraits painted?"

"I only know of one," replied the landlord, "a gentleman staying at my hotel, who wants a chalk drawing done for him. I was on my way here to inquire of any artist whom our picture-dealing friend could recommend. How glad I am that I met you before I had committed myself to employing a stranger!"

"Is this likeness wanted at once?" I asked, thinking of the number of engagements that I had already got in my pocket.

"Immediately – today – this very hour, if possible," said the landlord. "Mr. Faulkner, the gentleman I am speaking of, was to have sailed yesterday for the Brazils from this place; but the wind shifted last night to the wrong quarter, and he came ashore again this morning. He may of course be detained here for some time; but he may also be called on board ship at half an hour's notice, if the wind shifts back again in the right direction. This uncertainty makes it a matter of importance that the likeness should be begun immediately. Undertake it if you possibly can, for Mr. Faulkner's a liberal gentleman, who is sure to give you your own terms."

I reflected for a minute or two. The portrait was only wanted in chalk, and would not take long; besides, I might finish it in the evening, if my other engagements pressed hard upon me in the daytime. Why not leave my luggage at the picture-dealer's, put off looking for lodgings till night, and secure the new commission boldly by going back at once with the landlord to the hotel? I decided on following this course almost as soon as the idea occurred to me – put my chalks in my pocket, and a sheet of drawing paper in the first of my portfolios that came to hand – and so presented myself before Mr. Faulkner, ready to take his likeness, literally at five minutes' notice.

I found him a very pleasant, intelligent man, young and handsome. He had been a great traveler; had visited all the wonders of the East; and was now about to explore the wilds of the vast South American Continent. Thus much he told me good-humoredly and unconstrainedly while I was preparing my drawing materials.

As soon as I had put him in the right light and position, and had seated myself opposite to him, he changed the subject of conversation, and asked me, a little confusedly as I thought, if it was not a customary practice among portrait-painters to gloss over the faults in their sitters' faces, and to make as much as possible of any good points which their features might possess.

"Certainly," I answered. "You have described the whole art and mystery of successful portrait-painting in a few words."

"May I beg, then," said he, "that you will depart from the usual practice in my case, and draw me with all my defects, exactly as I am? The fact is," he went on, after a moment's pause, "the likeness you are now preparing to take is intended for my mother. My roving disposition makes me a great anxiety to her, and she parted from me this last time very sadly and unwillingly. I don't know how the idea came into my head, but it struck me this morning that I could not better employ the time, while I was delayed here on shore, than by getting my likeness done to send to her as a keepsake. She has no portrait of me since I was a child, and she is sure to value a drawing of me more than anything else I could send to her. I only trouble you with this explanation to prove that I am really sincere in my wish to be drawn unflatteringly, exactly as I am."

Secretly respecting and admiring him for what he had just said, I promised that his directions should be implicitly followed, and began to work immediately. Before I had pursued my occupation for ten minutes, the conversation began to flag, and the usual obstacle to my success with a sitter gradually set itself up between us.

Quite unconsciously, of course, Mr. Faulkner stiffened his neck, shut his month, and contracted his eyebrows – evidently under the impression that he was facilitating the process of taking his portrait by making his face as like a lifeless mask as possible. All traces of his natural animated expression were fast disappearing, and he was beginning to change into a heavy and rather melancholy-looking man.

This complete alteration was of no great consequence so long as I was only engaged in drawing the outline of his face and the general form of his features. I accordingly worked on doggedly for more than an hour – then left off to point my chalks again, and to give my sitter a few minutes' rest. Thus far the likeness had not suffered through Mr. Faulkner's unfortunate notion of the right way of sitting for his portrait; but the time of difficulty, as I well knew, was to come. It was impossible for me to think of putting any expression into the drawing unless I could contrive some means, when he resumed his chair, of making him look like himself again. "I will talk to him about foreign parts," thought I, "and try if I can't make him forget that he is sitting for his picture in that way."

While I was pointing my chalks Mr. Faulkner was walking up and down the room. He chanced to see the portfolio I had brought with me leaning against the wall, and asked if there were any sketches in it. I told him there were a few which I had made during my recent stay in Paris; "In Paris?" he repeated, with a look of interest; "May I see them?"

I gave him the permission he asked as a matter of course. Sitting down, he took the portfolio on his knee, and began to look through it. He turned over the first five sketches rapidly enough; but when he came to the sixth, I saw his face flush directly, and observed that he took the drawing out of the portfolio, carried it to the window, and remained silently absorbed in the contemplation of it for full five minutes. After that, he turned round to me, and asked very anxiously if I had any objection to part with that sketch.

It was the least interesting drawing of the collection – merely a view in one of the streets running by the backs of the houses in the Palais Royal. Some four or five of these houses were comprised in the view, which was of no particular use to me in any way; and which was too valueless, as a work of art, for me to think of selling it. I begged his acceptance of it at once. He thanked me quite warmly; and then, seeing that I looked a little surprised at the odd selection he had made from my sketches, laughingly asked me if I could guess why he had been so anxious to become possessed of the view which I had given him?

"Probably," I answered, "there is some remarkable historical association connected with that street at the back of the Palais Royal, of which I am ignorant."

"No," said Mr. Faulkner; "at least none that I know of. The only association connected with the place in my mind is a purely personal association. Look at this house in your drawing – the house with the water-pipe running down it from top to bottom. I once passed a night there – a night I shall never forget to the day of my death. I have had some awkward traveling adventures in my time; but that adventure –! Well, never mind, suppose we begin the sitting. I make but a bad return for your kindness in giving me the sketch by thus wasting your time in mere talk."

"Come! Come!" thought I, as he went back to the sitter's chair, "I shall see your natural expression on your face if I can only get you to talk about that adventure." It was easy enough to lead him in the right direction. At the first hint from me, he returned to the subject of the house in the back street. Without, I hope, showing any undue curiosity, I contrived to let him see that I felt a deep interest in everything he now said.

After two or three preliminary hesitations, he at last, to my great joy, fairly started on the narrative of his adventure. In the interest of his subject he soon completely forgot that he was sitting for his portrait – the very expression that I wanted came over his face – and my drawing proceeded toward completion, in the right direction, and to the best purpose. At every fresh touch I felt more and more certain that I was now getting the better of my grand difficulty; and I enjoyed the additional gratification of having my work lightened by the recital of a true story, which possessed, in my estimation, all the excitement of the most exciting romance.

This, as I recollect it, is how Mr. Faulkner told me his adventure:

The Traveller's Story

SHORTLY AFTER my education at college was finished, I happened to be staying at Paris with an English friend. We were both young men then, and lived, I am afraid, rather a wild life, in the delightful city of our sojourn. One night we were idling about the neighbourhood of the Palais Royal, doubtful to what amusement we should next betake ourselves. My friend proposed a visit to Frascati's; but his suggestion was not to my taste. I knew Frascati's, as the French saying is, by heart; had lost and won plenty of five-franc pieces there, merely for amusement's sake, until it was amusement no longer, and was thoroughly tired, in fact, of all the ghastly respectabilities of such a social anomaly as a respectable gambling-house. "For Heaven's sake," said I to my friend, "let us go somewhere where we can see a little genuine, blackguard, poverty-stricken gaming with no false gingerbread glitter thrown over it all. Let us get away from fashionable Frascati's, to a house where they don't mind letting in a man with a ragged coat, or a man with no coat, ragged or otherwise."

"Very well," said my friend, "we needn't go out of the Palais Royal to find the sort of company you want. Here's the place just before us; as blackguard a place, by all report, as you could possibly wish to see." In another minute we arrived at the door, and entered the house, the back of which you have drawn in your sketch.

When we got upstairs, and had left our hats and sticks with the doorkeeper, we were admitted into the chief gambling-room. We did not find many people assembled there. But, few as the men were who looked up at us on our entrance, they were all types – lamentably true types – of their respective classes.

We had come to see blackguards; but these men were something worse. There is a comic side, more or less appreciable, in all blackguardism – here there was nothing but tragedy – mute, weird tragedy. The quiet in the room was horrible. The thin, haggard, long-haired young man, whose sunken eyes fiercely watched the turning up of the cards, never spoke; the flabby, fat-faced, pimply player, who pricked his piece of pasteboard perseveringly, to register how often black won, and how often red – never spoke; the dirty, wrinkled old man, with the vulture eyes and the darned great-coat, who had lost his last *sou,* and still looked on desperately, after he could play no longer – never spoke. Even the voice of the croupier sounded as if it were strangely dulled and thickened in the atmosphere of the room. I had entered the place to laugh, but the spectacle before me was something to weep over. I soon found it necessary to take refuge in excitement from the depression of spirits which was fast stealing on me. Unfortunately I sought the nearest excitement, by going to the table and beginning to play. Still more unfortunately, as the event will show, I won – won prodigiously; won incredibly; won at such a rate that the regular players at the table crowded round me; and staring at my stakes with hungry, superstitious eyes, whispered to one another that the English stranger was going to break the bank.

The game was *Rouge et Noir*. I had played at it in every city in Europe, without, however, the care or the wish to study the Theory of Chances – that philosopher's stone of all gamblers! And a gambler, in the strict sense of the word, I had never been. I was heart-whole from the corroding passion for play. My gaming was a mere idle amusement. I never resorted to it by necessity, because I never knew what it was to want money. I never practiced it so incessantly as to lose more than I could afford, or to gain more than I could coolly pocket without being thrown off my balance by my good luck. In short, I had hitherto frequented gambling-tables – just as I frequented ball-rooms and opera-houses – because they amused me, and because I had nothing better to do with my leisure hours.

But on this occasion it was very different – now, for the first time in my life, I felt what the passion for play really was. My success first bewildered, and then, in the most literal meaning of the word, intoxicated me. Incredible as it may appear, it is nevertheless true, that I only lost when I attempted to estimate chances, and played according to previous calculation. If I left everything to luck, and staked without any care or consideration, I was sure to win – to win in the face of every recognized probability in favour of the bank. At first some of the men present ventured their money safely enough on my color; but I speedily increased my stakes to sums which they dared not risk. One after another they left off playing, and breathlessly looked on at my game.

Still, time after time, I staked higher and higher, and still won. The excitement in the room rose to fever pitch. The silence was interrupted by a deep-muttered chorus of oaths and exclamations in different languages, every time the gold was shoveled across to my side of the table – even the imperturbable croupier dashed his rake on the floor in a (French) fury of astonishment at my success. But one man present preserved his self-possession, and that man was my friend. He came to my side, and whispering in English, begged me to leave the place, satisfied with what I had already gained. I must do him the justice to say that he repeated his warnings and entreaties several times, and only left me and went away after I had rejected his advice (I was to all intents and purposes gambling drunk) in terms which rendered it impossible for him to address me again that night.

Shortly after he had gone, a hoarse voice behind me cried: "Permit me, my dear sir – permit me to restore to their proper place two napoleons which you have dropped. Wonderful luck, sir! I pledge you my word of honour, as an old soldier, in the course of my long experience in this sort of thing, I never saw such luck as yours – never! Go on, sir – *Sacre mille bombes!* Go on boldly, and break the bank!"

I turned round and saw, nodding and smiling at me with inveterate civility, a tall man, dressed in a frogged and braided surtout.

If I had been in my senses, I should have considered him, personally, as being rather a suspicious specimen of an old soldier. He had goggling, bloodshot eyes, mangy mustaches, and a broken nose. His voice betrayed a barrack-room intonation of the worst order, and he had the dirtiest pair of hands I ever saw – even in France. These little personal peculiarities exercised, however, no repelling influence on me. In the mad excitement, the reckless triumph of that moment, I was ready to 'fraternize' with anybody who encouraged me in my game. I accepted the old soldier's offered pinch of snuff; clapped him on the back, and swore he was the honestest fellow in the world – the most glorious relic of the Grand Army that I had ever met with. "Go on!" cried my military friend, snapping his fingers in ecstasy – "Go on, and win! Break the bank – *Mille tonnerres!* my gallant English comrade, break the bank!"

And I *did* go on – went on at such a rate, that in another quarter of an hour the croupier called out, "Gentlemen, the bank has discontinued for tonight." All the notes, and all the gold in that 'bank,' now lay in a heap under my hands; the whole floating capital of the gambling-house was waiting to pour into my pockets!

"Tie up the money in your pocket-handkerchief, my worthy sir," said the old soldier, as I wildly plunged my hands into my heap of gold. "Tie it up, as we used to tie up a bit of dinner in the Grand Army; your winnings are too heavy for any breeches-pockets that ever were sewed. There! That's it – shovel them in, notes and all! *Credie!* What luck! Stop! Another napoleon on the floor! *Ah! Sacre petit polisson de Napoleon!* Have I found thee at last? Now then, sir – two tight double knots each way with your honourable permission, and the money's safe. Feel it! Feel it, fortunate sir! Hard and round as a cannon-ball – *Ah, bah!* If they had only fired such cannon-balls at us at Austerlitz – *nom d'une pipe!* If they only had! And now, as an ancient grenadier, as an ex-brave of the French army, what remains for me to do? I ask what? Simply this: to entreat my valued English friend to drink a bottle of Champagne with me, and toast the goddess Fortune in foaming goblets before we part!"

Excellent ex-brave! Convivial ancient grenadier! Champagne by all means! An English cheer for an old soldier! Hurrah! Hurrah! Another English cheer for the goddess Fortune! Hurrah! Hurrah! Hurrah!

"Bravo! The Englishman; the amiable, gracious Englishman, in whose veins circulates the vivacious blood of France! Another glass? *Ah, bah!* – The bottle is empty! Never mind! *Vive le vin!* I, the old soldier, order another bottle, and half a pound of bonbons with it!"

"No, no, ex-brave; never – ancient grenadier! *Your* bottle last time; *my* bottle this. Behold it! Toast away! The French Army! The great Napoleon! The present company! The croupier! The honest croupier's wife and daughters – if he has any! The Ladies generally! Everybody in the world!"

By the time the second bottle of Champagne was emptied, I felt as if I had been drinking liquid fire – my brain seemed all aflame. No excess in wine had ever had this effect on me before in my life. Was it the result of a stimulant acting upon my system when I was in a highly excited state? Was my stomach in a particularly disordered condition? Or was the Champagne amazingly strong?

"Ex-brave of the French Army!" cried I, in a mad state of exhilaration, "*I* am on fire! how are *you?* You have set me on fire! Do you hear, my hero of Austerlitz? Let us have a third bottle of Champagne to put the flame out!"

The old soldier wagged his head, rolled his goggle-eyes, until I expected to see them slip out of their sockets; placed his dirty forefinger by the side of his broken nose; solemnly ejaculated "Coffee!" and immediately ran off into an inner room.

The word pronounced by the eccentric veteran seemed to have a magical effect on the rest of the company present. With one accord they all rose to depart. Probably they had expected to profit by my intoxication; but finding that my new friend was benevolently bent on preventing me from getting dead drunk, had now abandoned all hope of thriving pleasantly on my winnings. Whatever their motive might be, at any rate they went away in a body. When the old soldier returned, and sat down again opposite to me at the table, we had the room to ourselves. I could see the croupier, in a sort of vestibule which opened out of it, eating his supper in solitude. The silence was now deeper than ever.

A sudden change, too, had come over the 'ex-brave.' He assumed a portentously solemn look; and when he spoke to me again, his speech was ornamented by no oaths, enforced by no finger-snapping, enlivened by no apostrophes or exclamations.

"Listen, my dear sir," said he, in mysteriously confidential tones – "listen to an old soldier's advice. I have been to the mistress of the house (a very charming woman, with a genius for cookery!) to impress on her the necessity of making us some particularly strong and good coffee. You must drink this coffee in order to get rid of your little amiable exaltation of spirits before you think of going home – you *must,* my good and gracious friend! With all that money to take home tonight, it is a sacred duty to yourself to have your wits about you. You are known to be a winner to an enormous extent by several gentlemen present tonight, who, in a certain point of view, are very worthy and excellent fellows; but they are mortal men, my dear sir, and they have their amiable weaknesses. Need I say more? Ah, no, no! You understand me! Now, this is what you must do – send for a cabriolet when you feel quite well again – draw up all the windows when you get into it – and tell the driver to take you home only through the large and well-lighted thoroughfares. Do this; and you and your money will be safe. Do this; and tomorrow you will thank an old soldier for giving you a word of honest advice."

Just as the ex-brave ended his oration in very lachrymose tones, the coffee came in, ready poured out in two cups. My attentive friend handed me one of the cups with a bow. I was parched with thirst, and drank it off at a draught. Almost instantly afterwards, I was seized with a fit of giddiness, and felt more completely intoxicated than ever. The room whirled round and round furiously; the old soldier seemed to be regularly bobbing up and down before me like the piston of a steam-engine. I was half deafened by a violent singing in my ears; a feeling of utter bewilderment, helplessness, idiocy, overcame me. I rose from my chair, holding on by the table to keep my balance; and stammered out that I felt dreadfully unwell – so unwell that I did not know how I was to get home.

"My dear friend," answered the old soldier – and even his voice seemed to be bobbing up and down as he spoke – "my dear friend, it would be madness to go home in *your* state; you would be sure to lose your money; you might be robbed and murdered with the greatest ease. *I* am going to sleep here; do *you* sleep here, too – they make up capital beds in this house – take one; sleep off the effects of the wine, and go home safely with your winnings tomorrow – tomorrow, in broad daylight."

I had but two ideas left: one, that I must never let go hold of my handkerchief full of money; the other, that I must lie down somewhere immediately, and fall off into a comfortable sleep. So I agreed to the proposal about the bed, and took the offered arm of the old soldier, carrying my money with my disengaged hand. Preceded by the croupier, we passed along some passages and up a flight of stairs into the bedroom which I was to occupy. The ex-brave shook me warmly by the hand, proposed that we should breakfast together, and then, followed by the croupier, left me for the night.

I ran to the wash-hand stand; drank some of the water in my jug; poured the rest out, and plunged my face into it; then sat down in a chair and tried to compose myself.

I soon felt better. The change for my lungs, from the fetid atmosphere of the gambling-room to the cool air of the apartment I now occupied, the almost equally refreshing change for my eyes, from the glaring gaslights of the 'salon' to the dim, quiet flicker of one bedroom-candle, aided wonderfully the restorative effects of cold water. The giddiness left me, and I began to feel a little like a reasonable being again. My first thought was of the risk of sleeping all night in a gambling-house; my second, of the still greater risk of trying to get out after the house was closed, and of going home alone at night through the streets of Paris with a large sum of money about me. I had slept in worse places than this on my travels; so I determined to lock, bolt, and barricade my door, and take my chance till the next morning.

Accordingly, I secured myself against all intrusion; looked under the bed, and into the cupboard; tried the fastening of the window; and then, satisfied that I had taken every proper precaution, pulled off my upper clothing, put my light, which was a dim one, on the hearth among a feathery litter of wood-ashes, and got into bed, with the handkerchief full of money under my pillow.

I soon felt not only that I could not go to sleep, but that I could not even close my eyes. I was wide awake, and in a high fever. Every nerve in my body trembled – every one of my senses seemed to be preternaturally sharpened. I tossed and rolled, and tried every kind of position, and perseveringly sought out the cold corners of the bed, and all to no purpose. Now I thrust my arms over the clothes; now I poked them under the clothes; now I violently shot my legs straight out down to the bottom of the bed; now I convulsively coiled them up as near my chin as they would go; now I shook out my crumpled pillow, changed it to the cool side, patted it flat, and lay down quietly on my back; now I fiercely doubled it in two, set it up on end, thrust it against the board of the bed, and tried a sitting posture. Every effort was in vain; I groaned with vexation as I felt that I was in for a sleepless night.

What could I do? I had no book to read. And yet, unless I found out some method of diverting my mind, I felt certain that I was in the condition to imagine all sorts of horrors; to rack my brain with forebodings of every possible and impossible danger; in short, to pass the night in suffering all conceivable varieties of nervous terror.

I raised myself on my elbow, and looked about the room – which was brightened by a lovely moonlight pouring straight through the window – to see if it contained any pictures or ornaments that I could at all clearly distinguish. While my eyes wandered from wall to wall, a remembrance of Le Maistre's delightful little book, *Voyage autour de ma Chambre*, occurred to me. I resolved to imitate the French author, and find occupation and amusement enough to relieve the tedium of my wakefulness, by making a mental inventory of every article of furniture I could see, and by following up to their sources the multitude of associations which even a chair, a table, or a wash-hand stand may be made to call forth.

In the nervous unsettled state of my mind at that moment, I found it much easier to make my inventory than to make my reflections, and thereupon soon gave up all hope of thinking in Le Maistre's fanciful track – or, indeed, of thinking at all. I looked about the room at the different articles of furniture, and did nothing more.

There was, first, the bed I was lying in; a four-post bed, of all things in the world to meet with in Paris – yes, a thorough clumsy British four-poster, with the regular top lined with chintz – the regular fringed valance all round – the regular stifling, unwholesome curtains, which I remembered having mechanically drawn back against the posts without particularly noticing the bed when I first got into the room. Then there was the marble-topped wash-hand stand, from which the water I had spilled, in my hurry to pour it out, was still dripping, slowly and more slowly, on to the brick floor. Then two small chairs, with my coat, waistcoat, and trousers flung on them. Then a large elbow-chair covered with dirty-white dimity, with my cravat and shirt collar thrown over the back. Then a chest of drawers with two of the brass handles off, and a tawdry, broken china inkstand placed on it by way of ornament for the top. Then the dressing-table, adorned by a very small looking-glass, and a very large pincushion. Then the window – an unusually large window. Then a dark old picture, which the feeble candle dimly showed me. It was a picture of a fellow in a high Spanish hat, crowned with a plume of towering feathers. A swarthy, sinister ruffian, looking upward, shading his eyes with his hand, and looking intently upward – it might be at some tall gallows at which he was going to be hanged. At any rate, he had the appearance of thoroughly deserving it.

This picture put a kind of constraint upon me to look upward too – at the top of the bed. It was a gloomy and not an interesting object, and I looked back at the picture. I counted the feathers in the man's hat – they stood out in relief – three white, two green. I observed the crown of his hat, which was of conical shape, according to the fashion supposed to have been favoured by Guido Fawkes. I wondered what he was looking up at. It couldn't be at the stars; such a desperado was neither astrologer nor astronomer. It must be at the high gallows, and he was going to be hanged presently. Would the executioner come into possession of his conical crowned hat and plume of feathers? I counted the feathers again – three white, two green.

While I still lingered over this very improving and intellectual employment, my thoughts insensibly began to wander. The moonlight shining into the room reminded me of a certain moonlight night in England – the night after a picnic party in a Welsh valley. Every incident of the drive homeward, through lovely scenery, which the moonlight made lovelier than ever, came back to my remembrance, though I had never given the picnic a thought for years; though, if I had *tried* to recollect it, I could certainly have recalled little or nothing of that scene long past. Of all the wonderful faculties that help to tell us we are immortal, which speaks the sublime truth more eloquently than memory? Here was I, in a strange house of the most suspicious character, in a situation of uncertainty, and even of peril, which might seem to make the cool exercise of my recollection almost out of the question; nevertheless, remembering, quite involuntarily, places, people, conversations, minute circumstances of every kind, which I had thought forgotten forever; which I could not possibly have recalled at will, even under the most favourable auspices. And what cause had produced in a moment the whole of this strange, complicated, mysterious effect? Nothing but some rays of moonlight shining in at my bedroom window.

I was still thinking of the picnic – of our merriment on the drive home – of the sentimental young lady who *would* quote 'Childe Harold' because it was moonlight. I was absorbed by these past scenes and past amusements, when, in an instant, the thread on which my memories hung snapped asunder; my attention immediately came back to present things more vividly than ever, and I found myself, I neither knew why nor wherefore, looking hard at the picture again.

Looking for what?

Good God! The man had pulled his hat down on his brows! No! The hat itself was gone! Where was the conical crown? Where the feathers – three white, two green? Not there! In place of the hat and feathers, what dusky object was it that now hid his forehead, his eyes, his shading hand?

Was the bed moving?

I turned on my back and looked up. Was I mad? Drunk? Dreaming? Giddy again? Or was the top of the bed really moving down – sinking slowly, regularly, silently, horribly, right down throughout the whole of its length and breadth – right down upon me, as I lay underneath?

My blood seemed to stand still. A deadly paralysing coldness stole all over me as I turned my head round on the pillow and determined to test whether the bed-top was really moving or not, by keeping my eye on the man in the picture.

The next look in that direction was enough. The dull, black, frowzy outline of the valance above me was within an inch of being parallel with his waist. I still looked breathlessly. And steadily and slowly – very slowly – I saw the figure, and the line of frame below the figure, vanish, as the valance moved down before it.

I am, constitutionally, anything but timid. I have been on more than one occasion in peril of my life, and have not lost my self-possession for an instant; but when the conviction first settled on my mind that the bed-top was really moving, was steadily and continuously sinking down upon me, I looked up shuddering, helpless, panic-stricken, beneath the hideous machinery for murder, which was advancing closer and closer to suffocate me where I lay.

I looked up, motionless, speechless, breathless. The candle, fully spent, went out; but the moonlight still brightened the room. Down and down, without pausing and without sounding, came the bed-top, and still my panic-terror seemed to bind me faster and faster to the mattress on which I lay – down and down it sank, till the dusty odor from the lining of the canopy came stealing into my nostrils.

At that final moment the instinct of self-preservation startled me out of my trance, and I moved at last. There was just room for me to roll myself sidewise off the bed. As I dropped noiselessly to the floor, the edge of the murderous canopy touched me on the shoulder.

Without stopping to draw my breath, without wiping the cold sweat from my face, I rose instantly on my knees to watch the bed-top. I was literally spellbound by it. If I had heard footsteps behind me, I could not have turned round; if a means of escape had been miraculously provided for me, I could not have moved to take advantage of it. The whole life in me was, at that moment, concentrated in my eyes.

It descended – the whole canopy, with the fringe round it, came down – down – close down; so close that there was not room now to squeeze my finger between the bed-top and the bed. I felt at the sides, and discovered that what had appeared to me from beneath to be the ordinary light canopy of a four-post bed was in reality a thick, broad mattress, the substance of which was concealed by the valance and its fringe. I looked up and saw the four posts rising hideously bare. In the middle of the bed-top was a huge wooden screw that had evidently worked it down through a hole in the ceiling, just as ordinary presses are worked down on the substance selected for compression. The frightful apparatus moved without making the faintest noise. There had been no creaking as it came down; there was now not the faintest sound from the room above. Amid a dead and awful silence I beheld before me – in the nineteenth century, and in the civilized capital of France – such a machine for secret murder by suffocation as might have existed in the worst days of the Inquisition, in the lonely inns among the Hartz Mountains, in the mysterious tribunals of Westphalia! Still, as I looked on it, I could not move, I could hardly breathe, but I began to recover the power of thinking, and in a moment I discovered the murderous conspiracy framed against me in all its horror.

My cup of coffee had been drugged, and drugged too strongly. I had been saved from being smothered by having taken an overdose of some narcotic. How I had chafed and fretted at the fever fit which had preserved my life by keeping me awake! How recklessly I had confided myself to the two wretches who had led me into this room, determined, for the sake of my winnings, to kill me in my sleep by the surest and most horrible contrivance for secretly accomplishing my destruction! How many men, winners like me, had slept, as I had proposed to sleep, in that bed, and had never been seen or heard of more! I shuddered at the bare idea of it.

But, ere long, all thought was again suspended by the sight of the murderous canopy moving once more. After it had remained on the bed – as nearly as I could guess – about ten minutes, it began to move up again. The villains who worked it from above evidently believed that their purpose was now accomplished. Slowly and silently, as it had descended, that horrible bed-top rose towards its former place. When it reached the upper extremities of the four posts, it reached the ceiling, too. Neither hole nor screw could be seen; the bed became in appearance an ordinary bed again – the canopy an ordinary canopy – even to the most suspicious eyes.

Now, for the first time, I was able to move – to rise from my knees – to dress myself in my upper clothing – and to consider of how I should escape. If I betrayed by the smallest noise that the attempt to suffocate me had failed, I was certain to be murdered. Had I made any noise already? I listened intently, looking towards the door.

No! No footsteps in the passage outside – no sound of a tread, light or heavy, in the room above – absolute silence everywhere. Besides locking and bolting my door, I had moved an old wooden chest against it, which I had found under the bed. To remove this chest (my blood ran cold as I thought of what its contents *might* be!) without making some disturbance was impossible; and, moreover, to think of escaping through the house, now barred up for the night, was sheer insanity. Only one chance was left me – the window. I stole to it on tiptoe.

My bedroom was on the first floor, above an *entresol,* and looked into a back street, which you have sketched in your view. I raised my hand to open the window, knowing that on that action hung, by the merest hair-breadth, my chance of safety. They keep vigilant watch in a House of Murder. If any part of the frame cracked, if the hinge creaked, I was a lost man! It must have occupied me at least five minutes, reckoning by time – five *hours,* reckoning by suspense – to open that window. I succeeded in doing it silently – in doing it with all the dexterity of a house-breaker – and then looked down into the street. To leap the distance beneath me would be almost certain destruction! Next, I looked round at the sides of the house. Down the left side ran a thick water-pipe which you have drawn – it passed close by the outer edge of the window. The moment I saw the pipe I knew I was saved. My breath came and went freely for the first time since I had seen the canopy of the bed moving down upon me!

To some men the means of escape which I had discovered might have seemed difficult and dangerous enough – to *me* the prospect of slipping down the pipe into the street did not suggest even a thought of peril. I had always been accustomed, by the practice of gymnastics, to keep up my school-boy powers as a daring and expert climber; and knew that my head, hands, and feet would serve me faithfully in any hazards of ascent or descent. I had already got one leg over the window-sill, when I remembered the handkerchief filled with money under my pillow. I could well have afforded to leave it behind me, but I was revengefully determined that the miscreants of the gambling-house should miss their plunder as well as their victim. So I went back to the bed and tied the heavy handkerchief at my back by my cravat.

Just as I had made it tight and fixed it in a comfortable place, I thought I heard a sound of breathing outside the door. The chill feeling of horror ran through me again as I listened. No! Dead silence still in the passage – I had only heard the night air blowing softly into the room. The next moment I was on the window-sill – and the next I had a firm grip on the water-pipe with my hands and knees.

I slid down into the street easily and quietly, as I thought I should, and immediately set off at the top of my speed to a branch 'Prefecture' of Police, which I knew was situated in the immediate neighborhood. A 'Sub-prefect,' and several picked men among his subordinates, happened to be up, maturing, I believe, some scheme for discovering the perpetrator of a mysterious murder which all Paris was talking of just then. When I began my story, in a breathless hurry and in very bad French, I could see that the Sub-prefect suspected me of being a drunken Englishman who had robbed somebody; but he soon altered his opinion as I went on, and before I had anything like concluded, he shoved all the papers before him into a drawer, put on his hat, supplied me with another (for I was bareheaded), ordered a file of soldiers, desired his expert followers to get ready all sorts of tools for breaking open doors and ripping up brick flooring, and took my arm, in the most friendly and familiar manner possible, to lead me with him out of the house. I will venture to say that when the Sub-prefect was a little boy, and was taken for the first time to the play, he was not half as much pleased as he was now at the job in prospect for him at the gambling-house!

Away we went through the streets, the Sub-prefect cross-examining and congratulating me in the same breath as we marched at the head of our formidable *posse comitatus*. Sentinels were placed at the back and front of the house the moment we got to it; a tremendous battery of knocks was directed against the door; a light appeared at a window; I was told to conceal myself behind the police – then came more knocks and a cry of "Open in the name of the law!" At that terrible summons bolts and locks gave way before an invisible hand, and the moment after the Sub-prefect was in the passage, confronting a waiter half-dressed and ghastly pale. This was the short dialogue which immediately took place:

"We want to see the Englishman who is sleeping in this house?"

"He went away hours ago."

"He did no such thing. His friend went away; *he* remained. Show us to his bedroom!"

"I swear to you, Monsieur le Sous-prefect, he is not here! He –"

"I swear to you, Monsieur le Garcon, he is. He slept here – he didn't find your bed comfortable – he came to us to complain of it – here he is among my men – and here am I ready to look for a flea or two in his bedstead. Renaudin! (calling to one of the subordinates, and pointing to the waiter) collar that man and tie his hands behind him. Now, then, gentlemen, let us walk upstairs!"

Every man and woman in the house was secured – the 'Old Soldier' the first. Then I identified the bed in which I had slept, and then we went into the room above.

No object that was at all extraordinary appeared in any part of it. The Sub-prefect looked round the place, commanded everybody to be silent, stamped twice on the floor, called for a candle, looked attentively at the spot he had stamped on, and ordered the flooring there to be carefully taken up. This was done in no time. Lights were produced, and we saw a deep raftered cavity between the floor of this room and the ceiling of the room beneath. Through this cavity there ran perpendicularly a sort of case of iron thickly greased; and inside the case appeared the screw, which communicated with the bed-top below. Extra lengths of screw, freshly oiled; levers covered with felt; all the complete upper works of a heavy press – constructed with infernal ingenuity so as to join the fixtures below, and when taken to pieces again, to go into the smallest possible compass – were next discovered and pulled out on the floor. After some little difficulty the Sub-prefect succeeded in putting the machinery together, and, leaving his men to work it, descended with me to the bedroom. The smothering canopy was then lowered, but not so noiselessly as I had seen it lowered. When I mentioned this to the Sub-prefect, his answer, simple as it was, had a terrible significance. "My men," said he, "are working down the bed-top for the first time – the men whose money you won were in better practice."

We left the house in the sole possession of two police agents – every one of the inmates being removed to prison on the spot. The Sub-prefect, after taking down my *"proces verbal"* in his office, returned with me to my hotel to get my passport. "Do you think," I asked, as I gave it to him, "that any men have really been smothered in that bed, as they tried to smother *me?*"

"I have seen dozens of drowned men laid out at the Morgue," answered the Sub-prefect, "in whose pocket-books were found letters stating that they had committed suicide in the Seine, because they had lost everything at the gaming table. Do I know how many of those men entered the same gambling-house that *you* entered? Won as *you* won? Took that bed as *you* took it? Slept in it? Were smothered in it? And were privately thrown into the river, with a letter of explanation written by the murderers and placed in their pocket-books? No man can say how many or how few have suffered the fate from which you have escaped. The people of the gambling-house kept their bedstead machinery a secret from *us* – even from the police! The dead kept the rest of the secret for them. Good-night, or rather good-morning, Monsieur Faulkner! Be at my office again at nine o'clock – in the meantime, *au revoir!*"

The rest of my story is soon told. I was examined and re-examined; the gambling-house was strictly searched all through from top to bottom; the prisoners were separately interrogated; and two of the less guilty among them made a confession. I discovered that the Old Soldier was the master of the gambling-house – *justice* discovered that he had been drummed out of the army as a vagabond years ago; that he had been guilty of all sorts of villainies since; that he was in possession of stolen property, which the owners identified; and that he, the croupier, another accomplice, and the woman who had made my cup of coffee, were all in the secret of the bedstead. There appeared some reason to doubt whether the inferior persons attached to the house knew anything of the suffocating machinery; and they received the benefit of that doubt, by being treated simply as thieves and vagabonds. As for the Old Soldier and his two head myrmidons, they went to the galleys; the woman who had drugged my coffee was imprisoned for I forget how many years; the regular attendants at the gambling-house were considered 'suspicious' and placed under 'surveillance'; and I became, for one whole week (which is a long time) the head 'lion' in Parisian society. My adventure was dramatized by three illustrious play-makers, but never saw theatrical daylight; for the censorship forbade the introduction on the stage of a correct copy of the gambling-house bedstead.

One good result was produced by my adventure, which any censorship must have approved: it cured me of ever again trying *Rouge et Noir* as an amusement. The sight of a green cloth, with packs of cards and heaps of money on it, will henceforth be forever associated in my mind with the sight of a bed canopy descending to suffocate me in the silence and darkness of the night.

Just as Mr. Faulkner pronounced these words he started in his chair, and resumed his stiff, dignified position in a great hurry. "Bless my soul!" cried he, with a comic look of astonishment and vexation, "while I have been telling you what is the real secret of my interest in the sketch you have so kindly given to me, I have altogether forgotten that I came here to sit for my portrait. For the last hour or more I must have been the worst model you ever had to draw from!"

"On the contrary, you have been the best," said I. "I have been trying to catch your likeness; and, while telling your story, you have unconsciously shown me the natural expression I wanted to insure my success."

Who Killed Zebedee?

Wilkie Collins

A First Word For Myself

BEFORE THE DOCTOR LEFT me one evening, I asked him how much longer I was likely to live. He answered: "It's not easy to say; you may die before I can get back to you in the morning, or you may live to the end of the month."

I was alive enough on the next morning to think of the needs of my soul, and (being a member of the Roman Catholic Church) to send for the priest.

The history of my sins, related in confession, included blameworthy neglect of a duty which I owed to the laws of my country. In the priest's opinion – and I agreed with him – I was bound to make public acknowledgment of my fault, as an act of penance becoming to a Catholic Englishman. We concluded, thereupon, to try a division of labor. I related the circumstances, while his reverence took the pen and put the matter into shape.

Here follows what came of it:

I

WHEN I WAS A YOUNG MAN of five-and-twenty, I became a member of the London police force. After nearly two years' ordinary experience of the responsible and ill-paid duties of that vocation, I found myself employed on my first serious and terrible case of official inquiry – relating to nothing less than the crime of Murder.

The circumstances were these:

I was then attached to a station in the northern district of London – which I beg permission not to mention more particularly. On a certain Monday in the week, I took my turn of night duty. Up to four in the morning, nothing occurred at the station-house out of the ordinary way. It was then springtime, and, between the gas and the fire, the room became rather hot. I went to the door to get a breath of fresh air – much to the surprise of our Inspector on duty, who was constitutionally a chilly man. There was a fine rain falling; and a nasty damp in the air sent me back to the fireside. I don't suppose I had sat down for more than a minute when the swinging-door was violently pushed open. A frantic woman ran in with a scream, and said: "Is this the station-house?"

Our Inspector (otherwise an excellent officer) had, by some perversity of nature, a hot temper in his chilly constitution. "Why, bless the woman, can't you see it is?" he says. "What's the matter now?"

"Murder's the matter!" she burst out. "For God's sake, come back with me. It's at Mrs. Crosscapel's lodging-house, number 14 Lehigh Street. A young woman has murdered her husband in the night! With a knife, sir. She says she thinks she did it in her sleep."

I confess I was startled by this; and the third man on duty (a sergeant) seemed to feel it too. She was a nice-looking young woman, even in her terrified condition, just out of bed, with her clothes huddled on anyhow. I was partial in those days to a tall figure – and she was, as they say, my style. I put a chair for her; and the sergeant poked the fire. As for the Inspector, nothing ever upset *him*. He questioned her as coolly as if it had been a case of petty larceny.

"Have you seen the murdered man?" he asked.

"No, sir."

"Or the wife?"

"No, sir. I didn't dare go into the room; I only heard about it!"

"Oh? And who are *you*? One of the lodgers?"

"No, sir. I'm the cook."

"Isn't there a master in the house?"

"Yes, sir. He's frightened out of his wits. And the housemaid's gone for the doctor. It all falls on the poor servants, of course. Oh, why did I ever set foot in that horrible house?"

The poor soul burst out crying, and shivered from head to foot. The Inspector made a note of her statement, and then asked her to read it, and sign it with her name. The object of this proceeding was to get her to come near enough to give him the opportunity of smelling her breath. "When people make extraordinary statements," he afterward said to me, "it sometimes saves trouble to satisfy yourself that they are not drunk. I've known them to be mad – but not often. You will generally find *that* in their eyes."

She roused herself and signed her name – "Priscilla Thurlby." The Inspector's own test proved her to be sober; and her eyes – a nice light blue color, mild and pleasant, no doubt, when they were not staring with fear, and red with crying – satisfied him (as I supposed) that she was not mad. He turned the case over to me, in the first instance. I saw that he didn't believe in it, even yet.

"Go back with her to the house," he says. "This may be a stupid hoax, or a quarrel exaggerated. See to it yourself, and hear what the doctor says. If it is serious, send word back here directly, and let nobody enter the place or leave it till we come. Stop! You know the form if any statement is volunteered?"

"Yes, sir. I am to caution the persons that whatever they say will be taken down, and may be used against them."

"Quite right. You'll be an Inspector yourself one of these days. Now, miss!" With that he dismissed her, under my care.

Lehigh Street was not very far off – about twenty minutes' walk from the station. I confess I thought the Inspector had been rather hard on Priscilla. She was herself naturally angry with him. "What does he mean," she says, "by talking of a hoax? I wish he was as frightened as I am. This is the first time I have been out at service, sir – and I did think I had found a respectable place."

I said very little to her – feeling, if the truth must be told, rather anxious about the duty committed to me. On reaching the house the door was opened from within, before I could knock. A gentleman stepped out, who proved to be the doctor. He stopped the moment he saw me.

"You must be careful, policeman," he says. "I found the man lying on his back, in bed, dead – with the knife that had killed him left sticking in the wound."

Hearing this, I felt the necessity of sending at once to the station. Where could I find a trustworthy messenger? I took the liberty of asking the doctor if he would repeat to the police what he had already said to me. The station was not much out of his way home. He kindly granted my request.

The landlady (Mrs. Crosscapel) joined us while we were talking. She was still a young woman; not easily frightened, as far as I could see, even by a murder in the house. Her husband was in the passage behind her. He looked old enough to be her father; and he so trembled with terror that some people might have taken him for the guilty person. I removed the key from the street door, after locking it; and I said to the landlady: "Nobody must leave the house, or enter the house, till the Inspector comes. I must examine the premises to see if any one has broken in."

"There is the key of the area gate," she said, in answer to me. "It's always kept locked. Come downstairs and see for yourself." Priscilla went with us. Her mistress set her to work to light the kitchen fire. "Some of us," says Mrs. Crosscapel, "may be the better for a cup of tea." I remarked that she took things easy, under the circumstances. She answered that the landlady of a London lodging-house could not afford to lose her wits, no matter what might happen.

I found the gate locked, and the shutters of the kitchen window fastened. The back kitchen and back door were secured in the same way. No person was concealed anywhere. Returning upstairs, I examined the front parlor window. There, again, the barred shutters answered for the security of that room. A cracked voice spoke through the door of the back parlor. "The policeman can come in," it said, "if he will promise not to look at me." I turned to the landlady for information. "It's my parlor lodger, Miss. Mybus," she said, "a most respectable lady." Going into the room, I saw something rolled up perpendicularly in the bed curtains. Miss. Mybus had made herself modestly invisible in that way. Having now satisfied my mind about the security of the lower part of the house, and having the keys safe in my pocket, I was ready to go upstairs.

On our way to the upper regions I asked if there had been any visitors on the previous day. There had been only two visitors, friends of the lodgers – and Mrs. Crosscapel herself had let them both out. My next inquiry related to the lodgers themselves. On the ground floor there was Miss. Mybus. On the first floor (occupying both rooms) Mr. Barfield, an old bachelor, employed in a merchant's office. On the second floor, in the front room, Mr. John Zebedee, the murdered man, and his wife. In the back room, Mr. Deluc; described as a cigar agent, and supposed to be a Creole gentleman from Martinique. In the front garret, Mr. and Mrs. Crosscapel. In the back garret, the cook and the housemaid. These were the inhabitants, regularly accounted for. I asked about the servants. "Both excellent characters," says the landlady, "or they would not be in my service."

We reached the second floor, and found the housemaid on the watch outside the door of the front room. Not as nice a woman, personally, as the cook, and sadly frightened of course. Her mistress had posted her, to give the alarm in the case of an outbreak on the part of Mrs. Zebedee, kept locked up in the room. My arrival relieved the housemaid of further responsibility. She ran downstairs to her fellow-servant in the kitchen.

I asked Mrs. Crosscapel how and when the alarm of the murder had been given.

"Soon after three this morning," says she, "I was woke by the screams of Mrs. Zebedee. I found her out here on the landing, and Mr. Deluc, in great alarm, trying to quiet her. Sleeping in the next room he had only to open his door, when her screams woke him. 'My dear John's murdered! I am the miserable wretch – I did it in my sleep!' She repeated these frantic words over and over again, until she dropped in a swoon. Mr. Deluc and I carried her back into the bedroom. We both thought the poor creature had been driven distracted by some dreadful dream. But when we got to the bedside – don't ask me what we saw; the doctor has told you about it already. I was once a nurse in a hospital, and accustomed, as such, to horrid sights. It turned me cold and giddy, notwithstanding. As for Mr. Deluc, I thought *he* would have had a fainting fit next."

Hearing this, I inquired if Mrs. Zebedee had said or done any strange things since she had been Mrs. Crosscapel's lodger.

"You think she's mad?" says the landlady. "And anybody would be of your mind, when a woman accuses herself of murdering her husband in her sleep. All I can say is that, up to this morning, a more quiet, sensible, well-behaved little person than Mrs. Zebedee I never met with. Only just married, mind, and as fond of her unfortunate husband as a woman could be. I should have called them a pattern couple, in their own line of life."

There was no more to be said on the landing. We unlocked the door and went into the room.

II

HE LAY IN BED on his back as the doctor had described him. On the left side of his nightgown, just over his heart, the blood on the linen told its terrible tale. As well as one could judge, looking unwillingly at a dead face, he must have been a handsome young man in his lifetime. It was a sight to sadden anybody – but I think the most painful sensation was when my eyes fell next on his miserable wife.

She was down on the floor, crouched up in a corner – a dark little woman, smartly dressed in gay colors. Her black hair and her big brown eyes made the horrid paleness of her face look even more deadly white than perhaps it really was. She stared straight at us without appearing to see us. We spoke to her, and she never answered a word. She might have been dead – like her husband – except that she perpetually picked at her fingers, and shuddered every now and then as if she was cold. I went to her and tried to lift her up. She shrank back with a cry that well-nigh frightened me – not because it was loud, but because it was more like the cry of some animal than of a human being. However quietly she might have behaved in the landlady's previous experience of her, she was beside herself now. I might have been moved by a natural pity for her, or I might have been completely upset in my mind – I only know this, I could not persuade myself that she was guilty. I even said to Mrs. Crosscapel, "I don't believe she did it."

While I spoke there was a knock at the door. I went downstairs at once, and admitted (to my great relief) the Inspector, accompanied by one of our men.

He waited downstairs to hear my report, and he approved of what I had done. "It looks as if the murder had been committed by somebody in the house." Saying this, he left the man below, and went up with me to the second floor.

Before he had been a minute in the room, he discovered an object which had escaped my observation.

It was the knife that had done the deed.

The doctor had found it left in the body – had withdrawn it to probe the wound – and had laid it on the bedside table. It was one of those useful knives which contain a saw, a corkscrew, and other like implements. The big blade fastened back, when open, with a spring. Except where the blood was on it, it was as bright as when it had been purchased. A small metal plate was fastened to the horn handle, containing an inscription, only partly engraved, which ran thus: "To John Zebedee, from –" There it stopped, strangely enough.

Who or what had interrupted the engraver's work? It was impossible even to guess. Nevertheless, the Inspector was encouraged.

"This ought to help us," he said – and then he gave an attentive ear (looking all the while at the poor creature in the corner) to what Mrs. Crosscapel had to tell him.

The landlady having done, he said he must now see the lodger who slept in the next bed-chamber.

Mr. Deluc made his appearance, standing at the door of the room, and turning away his head with horror from the sight inside.

He was wrapped in a splendid blue dressing-gown, with a golden girdle and trimmings. His scanty brownish hair curled (whether artificially or not, I am unable to say) in little ringlets. His complexion was yellow; his greenish-brown eyes were of the sort called 'goggle' – they looked as if they might drop out of his face, if you held a spoon under them. His mustache and goat's beard were beautifully oiled; and, to complete his equipment, he had a long black cigar in his mouth.

"It isn't insensibility to this terrible tragedy," he explained. "My nerves have been shattered, Mr. Policeman, and I can only repair the mischief in this way. Be pleased to excuse and feel for me."

The Inspector questioned this witness sharply and closely. He was not a man to be misled by appearances; but I could see that he was far from liking, or even trusting, Mr. Deluc. Nothing came of the examination, except what Mrs. Crosscapel had in substance already mentioned to me. Mr. Deluc returned to his room.

"How long has he been lodging with you?" the Inspector asked, as soon as his back was turned.

"Nearly a year," the landlady answered.

"Did he give you a reference?"

"As good a reference as I could wish for." Thereupon, she mentioned the names of a well-known firm of cigar merchants in the city. The Inspector noted the information in his pocketbook.

I would rather not relate in detail what happened next: it is too distressing to be dwelt on. Let me only say that the poor demented woman was taken away in a cab to the station-house. The Inspector possessed himself of the knife, and of a book found on the floor, called *The World of Sleep*. The portmanteau containing the luggage was locked – and then the door of the room was secured, the keys in both cases being left in my charge. My instructions were to remain in the house, and allow nobody to leave it, until I heard again shortly from the Inspector.

III

THE CORONER'S INQUEST was adjourned; and the examination before the magistrate ended in a remand – Mrs. Zebedee being in no condition to understand the proceedings in either case. The surgeon reported her to be completely prostrated by a terrible nervous shock. When he was asked if he considered her to have been a sane woman before the murder took place, he refused to answer positively at that time.

A week passed. The murdered man was buried; his old father attending the funeral. I occasionally saw Mrs. Crosscapel, and the two servants, for the purpose of getting such further information as was thought desirable. Both the cook and the housemaid had given their month's notice to quit; declining, in the interest of their characters, to remain in a house which had been the scene of a murder. Mr. Deluc's nerves led also to his removal; his rest was now disturbed by frightful dreams. He paid the necessary forfeit-money, and left without notice. The first-floor lodger, Mr. Barfield, kept his rooms, but obtained leave of absence from his employers, and took refuge with some friends in the country. Miss. Mybus alone remained in the parlors. "When I am comfortable," the old lady said, "nothing moves me, at my age. A murder up two pairs of stairs is nearly the same thing as a murder in the next house. Distance, you see, makes all the difference."

It mattered little to the police what the lodgers did. We had men in plain clothes watching the house night and day. Everybody who went away was privately followed; and the police in the district to which they retired were warned to keep an eye on them, after that. As long as we failed to put Mrs. Zebedee's extraordinary statement to any sort of test – to say nothing of having proved unsuccessful, thus far, in tracing the knife to its purchaser – we were bound to let no person living under Mr. Crosscapel's roof, on the night of the murder, slip through our fingers.

IV

IN A FORTNIGHT MORE, Mrs. Zebedee had sufficiently recovered to make the necessary statement – after the preliminary caution addressed to persons in such cases. The surgeon had no hesitation, now, in reporting her to be a sane woman.

Her station in life had been domestic service. She had lived for four years in her last place as lady's-maid, with a family residing in Dorsetshire. The one objection to her had been the occasional infirmity of sleep-walking, which made it necessary that one of the other female servants should sleep in the same room, with the door locked and the key under her pillow. In all other respects the lady's-maid was described by her mistress as 'a perfect treasure.'

In the last six months of her service, a young man named John Zebedee entered the house (with a written character) as a footman. He soon fell in love with the nice little lady's-maid, and she heartily returned the feeling. They might have waited for years before they were in a pecuniary position to marry, but for the death of Zebedee's uncle, who left him a little fortune of two thousand pounds. They were now, for persons in their station, rich enough to please themselves; and they were married from the house in which they had served together, the little daughters of the family showing their affection for Mrs. Zebedee by acting as her bridesmaids.

The young husband was a careful man. He decided to employ his small capital to the best advantage, by sheep-farming in Australia. His wife made no objection; she was ready to go wherever John went.

Accordingly they spent their short honeymoon in London, so as to see for themselves the vessel in which their passage was to be taken. They went to Mrs. Crosscapel's lodging-house because Zebedee's uncle had always stayed there when in London. Ten days were to pass before the day of embarkation arrived. This gave the young couple a welcome holiday, and a prospect of amusing themselves to their heart's content among the sights and shows of the great city.

On their first evening in London they went to the theater. They were both accustomed to the fresh air of the country, and they felt half stifled by the heat and the gas. However, they were so pleased with an amusement which was new to them that they went to another theater on the next evening. On this second occasion, John Zebedee found the heat unendurable. They left the theater, and got back to their lodgings toward ten o'clock.

Let the rest be told in the words used by Mrs. Zebedee herself. She said:

"We sat talking for a little while in our room, and John's headache got worse and worse. I persuaded him to go to bed, and I put out the candle (the fire giving sufficient light to undress by), so that he might the sooner fall asleep. But he was too restless to sleep. He asked me to read him something. Books always made him drowsy at the best of times.

"I had not myself begun to undress. So I lit the candle again, and I opened the only book I had. John had noticed it at the railway bookstall by the name of *The World of Sleep*. He used to joke with me about my being a sleepwalker; and he said, 'Here's something that's sure to interest you' – and he made me a present of the book.

"Before I had read to him for more than half an hour he was fast asleep. Not feeling that way inclined, I went on reading to myself.

"The book did indeed interest me. There was one terrible story which took a hold on my mind – the story of a man who stabbed his own wife in a sleep-walking dream. I thought of putting down my book after that, and then changed my mind again and went on. The next chapters were not so interesting; they were full of learned accounts of why we fall asleep, and what our brains do in that state, and such like. It ended in my falling asleep, too, in my armchair by the fireside.

"I don't know what o'clock it was when I went to sleep. I don't know how long I slept, or whether I dreamed or not. The candle and the fire had both burned out, and it was pitch dark when I woke. I can't even say why I woke – unless it was the coldness of the room.

"There was a spare candle on the chimney-piece. I found the matchbox, and got a light. Then for the first time, I turned round toward the bed; and I saw –"

She had seen the dead body of her husband, murdered while she was unconsciously at his side – and she fainted, poor creature, at the bare remembrance of it.

The proceedings were adjourned. She received every possible care and attention; the chaplain looking after her welfare as well as the surgeon.

I have said nothing of the evidence of the landlady and servants. It was taken as a mere formality. What little they knew proved nothing against Mrs. Zebedee. The police made no discoveries that supported her first frantic accusation of herself. Her master and mistress, where she had been last in service, spoke of her in the highest terms. We were at a complete deadlock.

It had been thought best not to surprise Mr. Deluc, as yet, by citing him as a witness. The action of the law was, however, hurried in this case by a private communication received from the chaplain.

After twice seeing, and speaking with, Mrs. Zebedee, the reverend gentleman was persuaded that she had no more to do than himself with the murder of her husband. He did not consider that he was justified in repeating a confidential communication – he would only recommend that Mr. Deluc should be summoned to appear at the next examination. This advice was followed.

The police had no evidence against Mrs. Zebedee when the inquiry was resumed. To assist the ends of justice she was now put into the witness-box. The discovery of her murdered husband, when she woke in the small hours of the morning, was passed over as rapidly as possible. Only three questions of importance were put to her.

First, the knife was produced. Had she ever seen it in her husband's possession? Never. Did she know anything about it? Nothing whatever.

Secondly: Did she, or did her husband, lock the bedroom door when they returned from the theater? No. Did she afterward lock the door herself? No.

Thirdly: Had she any sort of reason to give for supposing that she had murdered her husband in a sleep-walking dream? No reason, except that she was beside herself at the time, and the book put the thought into her head.

After this the other witnesses were sent out of court. The motive for the chaplain's communication now appeared. Mrs. Zebedee was asked if anything unpleasant had occurred between Mr. Deluc and herself.

Yes. He had caught her alone on the stairs at the lodging-house; had presumed to make love to her; and had carried the insult still farther by attempting to kiss her. She had slapped his face, and had declared that her husband should know of it, if his misconduct was repeated. He was in a furious rage at having his face slapped; and he said to her: "Madam, you may live to regret this."

After consultation, and at the request of our Inspector, it was decided to keep Mr. Deluc in ignorance of Mrs. Zebedee's statement, for the present. When the witnesses were recalled, he gave the same evidence which he had already given to the Inspector – and he was then asked if he knew anything of the knife. He looked at it without any guilty signs in his face, and swore that he had never seen it until that moment. The resumed inquiry then ended, and still nothing had been discovered.

But we kept an eye on Mr. Deluc. Our next effort was to try if we could associate him with the purchase of the knife.

Here again (there really did seem to be a sort of fatality in this case) we reached no useful result. It was easy enough to find out the wholesale cutlers, who had manufactured the knife at Sheffield, by the mark on the blade. But they made tens of thousands of such knives, and disposed of them to retail dealers all over Great Britain – to say nothing of foreign parts. As to finding out the person who had engraved the imperfect inscription (without knowing where, or by whom, the knife had been purchased) we might as well have looked for the proverbial needle in the bundle of hay. Our last resource was to have the knife photographed, with the inscribed side uppermost, and to send copies to every police-station in the kingdom.

At the same time we reckoned up Mr. Deluc – I mean that we made investigations into his past life – on the chance that he and the murdered man might have known each other, and might have had a quarrel, or a rivalry about a woman, on some former occasion. No such discovery rewarded us.

We found Deluc to have led a dissipated life, and to have mixed with very bad company. But he had kept out of reach of the law. A man may be a profligate vagabond; may insult a lady; may say threatening things to her, in the first stinging sensation of having his face slapped – but it doesn't follow from these blots on his character that he has murdered her husband in the dead of the night.

Once more, then, when we were called upon to report ourselves, we had no evidence to produce. The photographs failed to discover the owner of the knife, and to explain its interrupted inscription. Poor Mrs. Zebedee was allowed to go back to her friends, on entering into her own recognizance to appear again if called upon. Articles in the newspapers began to inquire how many more murderers would succeed in baffling the police. The authorities at the Treasury offered a reward of a hundred pounds for the necessary information. And the weeks passed and nobody claimed the reward.

Our Inspector was not a man to be easily beaten. More inquiries and examinations followed. It is needless to say anything about them. We were defeated – and there, so far as the police and the public were concerned, was an end of it.

The assassination of the poor young husband soon passed out of notice, like other undiscovered murders. One obscure person only was foolish enough, in his leisure hours, to persist in trying to solve the problem of Who Killed Zebedee? He felt that he might rise to the highest position in the police force if he succeeded where his elders and betters had failed – and he held to his own little ambition, though everybody laughed at him. In plain English, I was the man.

V

WITHOUT MEANING IT, I have told my story ungratefully.

There were two persons who saw nothing ridiculous in my resolution to continue the investigation, single-handed. One of them was Miss. Mybus; and the other was the cook, Priscilla Thurlby.

Mentioning the lady first, Miss. Mybus was indignant at the resigned manner in which the police accepted their defeat. She was a little bright-eyed wiry woman; and she spoke her mind freely.

"This comes home to me," she said. "Just look back for a year or two. I can call to mind two cases of persons found murdered in London – and the assassins have never been traced. I am a person, too; and I ask myself if my turn is not coming next. You're a nice-looking fellow and I like your pluck and perseverance. Come here as often as you think right; and say you are my visitor, if they make any difficulty about letting you in. One thing more! I have nothing particular to do, and I am no fool. Here, in the parlors, I see everybody who comes into the house or goes out of the house. Leave me your address – I may get some information for you yet."

With the best intentions, Miss. Mybus found no opportunity of helping me. Of the two, Priscilla Thurlby seemed more likely to be of use.

In the first place, she was sharp and active, and (not having succeeded in getting another situation as yet) was mistress of her own movements.

In the second place, she was a woman I could trust. Before she left home to try domestic service in London, the parson of her native parish gave her a written testimonial, of which I append a copy. Thus it ran:

"I gladly recommend Priscilla Thurlby for any respectable employment which she may be competent to undertake. Her father and mother are infirm old people, who have lately suffered a diminution of their income; and they have a younger daughter to maintain. Rather than be a burden on her parents, Priscilla goes to London to find domestic employment, and to devote her earnings to the assistance of her father and mother. This circumstance speaks for itself. I have known the family many years; and I only regret that I have no vacant place in my own household which I can offer to this good girl,

(Signed) "HENRY DEERINGTON, Rector of Roth."

After reading those words, I could safely ask Priscilla to help me in reopening the mysterious murder case to some good purpose.

My notion was that the proceedings of the persons in Mrs. Crosscapel's house had not been closely enough inquired into yet. By way of continuing the investigation, I asked Priscilla if she could tell me anything which associated the housemaid with Mr. Deluc. She was unwilling to answer. "I may be casting suspicion on an innocent person," she said. "Besides, I was for so short a time the housemaid's fellow servant –"

"You slept in the same room with her," I remarked; "and you had opportunities of observing her conduct toward the lodgers. If they had asked you, at the examination, what I now ask, you would have answered as an honest woman."

To this argument she yielded. I heard from her certain particulars, which threw a new light on Mr. Deluc, and on the case generally. On that information I acted. It was slow work, owing to the claims on me of my regular duties; but with Priscilla's help, I steadily advanced toward the end I had in view.

Besides this, I owed another obligation to Mrs. Crosscapel's nice-looking cook. The confession must be made sooner or later – and I may as well make it now. I first knew what love was, thanks to Priscilla. I had delicious kisses, thanks to Priscilla. And, when I asked if she would marry me, she didn't say No. She looked, I must own, a little sadly, and she said: "How can two such poor people as we are ever hope to marry?" To this I answered: "It won't be long before I lay my hand on the clew which my Inspector has failed to find. I shall be in a position to marry you, my dear, when that time comes."

At our next meeting we spoke of her parents. I was now her promised husband. Judging by what I had heard of the proceedings of other people in my position, it seemed to be only right that I should be made known to her father and mother. She entirely agreed with me; and she wrote home that day to tell them to expect us at the end of the week.

I took my turn of night-duty, and so gained my liberty for the greater part of the next day. I dressed myself in plain clothes, and we took our tickets on the railway for Yateland, being the nearest station to the village in which Priscilla's parents lived.

VI

THE TRAIN STOPPED, as usual, at the big town of Waterbank. Supporting herself by her needle, while she was still unprovided with a situation, Priscilla had been at work late in the night – she was tired and thirsty. I left the carriage to get her some soda-water. The stupid girl in the refreshment room failed to pull the cork out of the bottle, and refused to let me help her. She took a corkscrew, and used it crookedly. I lost all patience, and snatched the bottle out of her hand. Just as I drew the cork, the bell rang on the platform. I only waited to pour the soda-water into a glass – but the train was moving as I left the refreshment room. The porters stopped me when I tried to jump on to the step of the carriage. I was left behind.

As soon as I had recovered my temper, I looked at the time-table. We had reached Waterbank at five minutes past one. By good luck, the next train was due at forty-four minutes past one, and arrived at Yateland (the next station) ten minutes afterward. I could only hope that Priscilla would look at the time-table too, and wait for me. If I had attempted to walk the distance between the two places, I should have lost time instead of saving it. The interval before me was not very long; I occupied it in looking over the town.

Speaking with all due respect to the inhabitants, Waterbank (to other people) is a dull place. I went up one street and down another – and stopped to look at a shop which struck me; not from anything in itself, but because it was the only shop in the street with the shutters closed.

A bill was posted on the shutters, announcing that the place was to let. The outgoing tradesman's name and business, announced in the customary painted letters, ran thus: *James Wycomb, Cutler, etc.*

For the first time, it occurred to me that we had forgotten an obstacle in our way, when we distributed our photographs of the knife. We had none of us remembered that a certain proportion of cutlers might be placed, by circumstances, out of our reach – either by retiring from business or by becoming bankrupt. I always carried a copy of the photograph about me; and I thought to myself, "Here is the ghost of a chance of tracing the knife to Mr. Deluc!"

The shop door was opened, after I had twice rung the bell, by an old man, very dirty and very deaf. He said "You had better go upstairs, and speak to Mr. Scorrier – top of the house."

I put my lips to the old fellow's ear-trumpet, and asked who Mr. Scorrier was.

"Brother-in-law to Mr. Wycomb. Mr. Wycomb's dead. If you want to buy the business apply to Mr. Scorrier."

Receiving that reply, I went upstairs, and found Mr. Scorrier engaged in engraving a brass door-plate. He was a middle-aged man, with a cadaverous face and dim eyes. After the necessary apologies, I produced my photograph.

"May I ask, sir, if you know anything of the inscription on that knife?" I said.

He took his magnifying glass to look at it.

"This is curious," he remarked quietly. "I remember the queer name – Zebedee. Yes, sir; I did the engraving, as far as it goes. I wonder what prevented me from finishing it?"

The name of Zebedee, and the unfinished inscription on the knife, had appeared in every English newspaper. He took the matter so coolly that I was doubtful how to interpret his answer. Was it possible that he had not seen the account of the murder? Or was he an accomplice with prodigious powers of self-control?

"Excuse me," I said, "do you read the newspapers?"

"Never! My eyesight is failing me. I abstain from reading, in the interests of my occupation."

"Have you not heard the name of Zebedee mentioned – particularly by people who do read the newspapers?"

"Very likely; but I didn't attend to it. When the day's work is done, I take my walk. Then I have my supper, my drop of grog, and my pipe. Then I go to bed. A dull existence you think, I daresay! I had a miserable life, sir, when I was young. A bare subsistence, and a little rest, before the last perfect rest in the grave – that is all I want. The world has gone by me long ago. So much the better."

The poor man spoke honestly. I was ashamed of having doubted him. I returned to the subject of the knife.

"Do you know where it was purchased, and by whom?" I asked.

"My memory is not so good as it was," he said; "but I have got something by me that helps it."

He took from a cupboard a dirty old scrapbook. Strips of paper, with writing on them, were pasted on the pages, as well as I could see. He turned to an index, or table of contents, and opened a page. Something like a flash of life showed itself on his dismal face.

"Ha! Now I remember," he said. "The knife was bought of my late brother-in-law, in the shop downstairs. It all comes back to me, sir. A person in a state of frenzy burst into this very room, and snatched the knife away from me, when I was only half way through the inscription!"

I felt that I was now close on discovery. "May I see what it is that has assisted your memory?" I asked.

"Oh yes. You must know, sir, I live by engraving inscriptions and addresses, and I paste in this book the manuscript instructions which I receive, with marks of my own on the margin. For one thing, they serve as a reference to new customers. And for another thing, they do certainly help my memory."

He turned the book toward me, and pointed to a slip of paper which occupied the lower half of a page.

I read the complete inscription, intended for the knife that killed Zebedee, and written as follows:

"To John Zebedee. From Priscilla Thurlby."

VII

I DECLARE that it is impossible for me to describe what I felt when Priscilla's name confronted me like a written confession of guilt. How long it was before I recovered myself in some degree, I cannot say. The only thing I can clearly call to mind is, that I frightened the poor engraver.

My first desire was to get possession of the manuscript inscription. I told him I was a policeman, and summoned him to assist me in the discovery of a crime. I even offered him money. He drew back from my hand. "You shall have it for nothing," he said, "if you will only go away and never come here again." He tried to cut it out of the page – but his trembling hands were helpless. I cut it out myself, and attempted to thank him. He wouldn't hear me. "Go away!" he said, "I don't like the look of you."

It may be here objected that I ought not to have felt so sure as I did of the woman's guilt, until I had got more evidence against her. The knife might have been stolen from her, supposing she was the person who had snatched it out of the engraver's hands, and might have been afterward used by the thief to commit the murder. All very true. But I never had a moment's doubt in my own mind, from the time when I read the damnable line in the engraver's book.

I went back to the railway without any plan in my head. The train by which I had proposed to follow her had left Waterbank. The next train that arrived was for London. I took my place in it – still without any plan in my head.

At Charing Cross a friend met me. He said, "You're looking miserably ill. Come and have a drink."

I went with him. The liquor was what I really wanted; it strung me up, and cleared my head. He went his way, and I went mine. In a little while more, I determined what I would do.

In the first place, I decided to resign my situation in the police, from a motive which will presently appear. In the second place, I took a bed at a public-house. She would no doubt return to London, and she would go to my lodgings to find out why I had broken my appointment. To bring to justice the one woman whom I had dearly loved was too cruel a duty for a poor creature like me. I preferred leaving the police force. On the other hand, if she and I met before time had helped me to control myself, I had a horrid fear that I might turn murderer next, and kill her then and there. The wretch had not only all but misled me into marrying her, but also into charging the innocent housemaid with being concerned in the murder.

The same night I hit on a way of clearing up such doubts as still harassed my mind. I wrote to the rector of Roth, informing him that I was engaged to marry her, and asking if he would tell me (in consideration of my position) what her former relations might have been with the person named John Zebedee.

By return of post I got this reply:

"SIR – Under the circumstances, I think I am bound to tell you confidentially what the friends and well-wishers of Priscilla have kept secret, for her sake.

"Zebedee was in service in this neighborhood. I am sorry to say it, of a man who has come to such a miserable end – but his behavior to Priscilla proves him to have been a vicious and heartless wretch. They were engaged – and, I add with indignation, he tried to seduce her under a promise of marriage. Her virtue resisted him, and he pretended to be ashamed of himself. The banns were published in my church. On the next day Zebedee disappeared, and cruelly deserted her. He was a capable servant; and I believe he got another place. I leave you to imagine what the poor girl suffered under the outrage inflicted on her. Going to London, with my recommendation, she answered the first advertisement that she saw, and was unfortunate enough to begin her career in domestic service in the very lodging-house to which (as I gather from the newspaper report of the murder) the man Zebedee took the person whom he married, after deserting Priscilla. Be assured that you are about to unite yourself to an excellent girl, and accept my best wishes for your happiness."

It was plain from this that neither the rector nor the parents and friends knew anything of the purchase of the knife. The one miserable man who knew the truth was the man who had asked her to be his wife.

I owed it to myself – at least so it seemed to me – not to let it be supposed that I, too, had meanly deserted her. Dreadful as the prospect was, I felt that I must see her once more, and for the last time.

She was at work when I went into her room. As I opened the door she started to her feet. Her cheeks reddened, and her eyes flashed with anger. I stepped forward – and she saw my face. My face silenced her.

I spoke in the fewest words I could find.

"I have been to the cutler's shop at Waterbank," I said. "There is the unfinished inscription on the knife, complete in your handwriting. I could hang you by a word. God forgive me – I can't say the word."

Her bright complexion turned to a dreadful clay-color. Her eyes were fixed and staring, like the eyes of a person in a fit. She stood before me, still and silent. Without saying more, I dropped the inscription into the fire. Without saying more, I left her.

I never saw her again.

VIII

BUT I HEARD from her a few days later. The letter has long since been burned. I wish I could have forgotten it as well. It sticks to my memory. If I die with my senses about me, Priscilla's letter will be my last recollection on earth.

In substance it repeated what the rector had already told me. Further, it informed me that she had bought the knife as a keepsake for Zebedee, in place of a similar knife which he had lost. On the Saturday, she made the purchase, and left it to be engraved. On the Sunday, the banns were put up. On the Monday, she was deserted; and she snatched the knife from the table while the engraver was at work.

She only knew that Zebedee had added a new sting to the insult inflicted on her when he arrived at the lodgings with his wife. Her duties as cook kept her in the kitchen – and Zebedee never discovered that she was in the house. I still remember the last lines of her confession:

"The devil entered into me when I tried their door, on my way up to bed, and found it unlocked, and listened a while, and peeped in. I saw them by the dying light of the candle – one asleep on the bed, the other asleep by the fireside. I had the knife in my hand, and the thought came to me to do it, so that they might hang *her* for the murder. I couldn't take the knife out again, when I had done it. Mind this! I did really like you – I didn't say Yes, because you could hardly hang your own wife, if you found out who killed Zebedee."

Since the past time I have never heard again of Priscilla Thurlby; I don't know whether she is living or dead. Many people may think I deserve to be hanged myself for not having given her up to the gallows. They may, perhaps, be disappointed when they see this confession, and hear that I have died decently in my bed. I don't blame them. I am a penitent sinner. I wish all merciful Christians goodbye forever.

The Trial for Murder

Charles Dickens

I HAVE ALWAYS noticed a prevalent want of courage, even among persons of superior intelligence and culture, as to imparting their own psychological experiences when those have been of a strange sort. Almost all men are afraid that what they could relate in such wise would find no parallel or response in a listener's internal life, and might be suspected or laughed at. A truthful traveller, who should have seen some extraordinary creature in the likeness of a sea-serpent, would have no fear of mentioning it; but the same traveller, having had some singular presentiment, impulse, vagary of thought, vision (so-called), dream, or other remarkable mental impression, would hesitate considerably before he would own to it. To this reticence I attribute much of the obscurity in which such subjects are involved. We do not habitually communicate our experiences of these subjective things as we do our experiences of objective creation. The consequence is, that the general stock of experience in this regard appears exceptional, and really is so, in respect of being miserably imperfect.

In what I am going to relate, I have no intention of setting up, opposing, or supporting, any theory whatever. I know the history of the Bookseller of Berlin, I have studied the case of the wife of a late Astronomer Royal as related by Sir David Brewster, and I have followed the minutest details of a much more remarkable case of Spectral Illusion occurring within my private circle of friends. It may be necessary to state as to this last, that the sufferer (a lady) was in no degree, however distant, related to me. A mistaken assumption on that head might suggest an explanation of a part of my own case, – but only a part, – which would be wholly without foundation. It cannot be referred to my inheritance of any developed peculiarity, nor had I ever before any at all similar experience, nor have I ever had any at all similar experience since.

It does not signify how many years ago, or how few, a certain murder was committed in England, which attracted great attention. We hear more than enough of murderers as they rise in succession to their atrocious eminence, and I would bury the memory of this particular brute, if I could, as his body was buried, in Newgate Jail. I purposely abstain from giving any direct clue to the criminal's individuality.

When the murder was first discovered, no suspicion fell – or I ought rather to say, for I cannot be too precise in my facts, it was nowhere publicly hinted that any suspicion fell – on the man who was afterwards brought to trial. As no reference was at that time made to him in the newspapers, it is obviously impossible that any description of him can at that time have been given in the newspapers. It is essential that this fact be remembered.

Unfolding at breakfast my morning paper, containing the account of that first discovery, I found it to be deeply interesting, and I read it with close attention. I read it twice, if not three times. The discovery had been made in a bedroom, and, when I laid down the paper, I was aware of a flash – rush – flow – I do not know what to call it, – no word I can find is satisfactorily descriptive, – in which I seemed to see that bedroom passing through my room, like a picture impossibly painted on a running river. Though almost instantaneous in its passing, it was perfectly clear; so clear that I distinctly, and with a sense of relief, observed the absence of the dead body from the bed.

It was in no romantic place that I had this curious sensation, but in chambers in Piccadilly, very near to the corner of St. James's Street. It was entirely new to me. I was in my easy-chair at the moment, and the sensation was accompanied with a peculiar shiver which started the chair from its position. (But it is to be noted that the chair ran easily on castors). I went to one of the windows (there are two in the room, and the room is on the second floor) to refresh my eyes with the moving objects down in Piccadilly. It was a bright autumn morning, and the street was sparkling and cheerful. The wind was high. As I looked out, it brought down from the park a quantity of fallen leaves, which a gust took, and whirled into a spiral pillar. As the pillar fell and the leaves dispersed, I saw two men on the opposite side of the way, going from West to East. They were one behind the other. The foremost man often looked back over his shoulder. The second man followed him, at a distance of some thirty paces, with his right hand menacingly raised. First, the singularity and steadiness of this threatening gesture in so public a thoroughfare attracted my attention; and next, the more remarkable circumstance that nobody heeded it. Both men threaded their way among the other passengers with a smoothness hardly consistent even with the action of walking on a pavement; and no single creature, that I could see, gave them place, touched them, or looked after them. In passing before my windows, they both stared up at me. I saw their two faces very distinctly, and I knew that I could recognise them anywhere. Not that I had consciously noticed anything very remarkable in either face, except that the man who went first had an unusually lowering appearance, and that the face of the man who followed him was of the colour of impure wax.

I am a bachelor, and my valet and his wife constitute my whole establishment. My occupation is in a certain Branch Bank, and I wish that my duties as head of a department were as light as they are popularly supposed to be. They kept me in town that autumn, when I stood in need of change. I was not ill, but I was not well. My reader is to make the most that can be reasonably made of my feeling jaded, having a depressing sense upon me of a monotonous life, and being 'slightly dyspeptic.' I am assured by my renowned doctor that my real state of health at that time justifies no stronger description, and I quote his own from his written answer to my request for it.

As the circumstances of the murder, gradually unravelling, took stronger and stronger possession of the public mind, I kept them away from mine by knowing as little about them as was possible in the midst of the universal excitement. But I knew that a verdict of Wilful Murder had been found against the suspected murderer, and that he had been committed to Newgate for trial. I also knew that his trial had been postponed over one Sessions of the Central Criminal Court, on the ground of general prejudice and want of time for the preparation of the defence. I may further have known, but I believe I did not, when, or about when, the Sessions to which his trial stood postponed would come on.

My sitting-room, bedroom, and dressing-room, are all on one floor. With the last there is no communication but through the bedroom. True, there is a door in it, once communicating with the staircase; but a part of the fitting of my bath has been – and had then been for some years – fixed across it. At the same period, and as a part of the same arrangement, – the door had been nailed up and canvased over.

I was standing in my bedroom late one night, giving some directions to my servant before he went to bed. My face was towards the only available door of communication with the dressing-room, and it was closed. My servant's back was towards that door. While I was speaking to him, I saw it open, and a man look in, who very earnestly and mysteriously beckoned to me. That man was the man who had gone second of the two along Piccadilly, and whose face was of the colour of impure wax.

The figure, having beckoned, drew back, and closed the door. With no longer pause than was made by my crossing the bedroom, I opened the dressing-room door, and looked in. I had a lighted candle already in my hand. I felt no inward expectation of seeing the figure in the dressing-room, and I did not see it there.

Conscious that my servant stood amazed, I turned round to him, and said: "Derrick, could you believe that in my cool senses I fancied I saw a –" As I there laid my hand upon his breast, with a sudden start he trembled violently, and said, "O Lord, yes, sir! A dead man beckoning!"

Now I do not believe that this John Derrick, my trusty and attached servant for more than twenty years, had any impression whatever of having seen any such figure, until I touched him. The change in him was so startling, when I touched him, that I fully believe he derived his impression in some occult manner from me at that instant.

I bade John Derrick bring some brandy, and I gave him a dram, and was glad to take one myself. Of what had preceded that night's phenomenon, I told him not a single word. Reflecting on it, I was absolutely certain that I had never seen that face before, except on the one occasion in Piccadilly. Comparing its expression when beckoning at the door with its expression when it had stared up at me as I stood at my window, I came to the conclusion that on the first occasion it had sought to fasten itself upon my memory, and that on the second occasion it had made sure of being immediately remembered.

I was not very comfortable that night, though I felt a certainty, difficult to explain, that the figure would not return. At daylight I fell into a heavy sleep, from which I was awakened by John Derrick's coming to my bedside with a paper in his hand.

This paper, it appeared, had been the subject of an altercation at the door between its bearer and my servant. It was a summons to me to serve upon a Jury at the forthcoming Sessions of the Central Criminal Court at the Old Bailey. I had never before been summoned on such a Jury, as John Derrick well knew. He believed – I am not certain at this hour whether with reason or otherwise – that that class of Jurors were customarily chosen on a lower qualification than mine, and he had at first refused to accept the summons. The man who served it had taken the matter very coolly. He had said that my attendance or non-attendance was nothing to him; there the summons was; and I should deal with it at my own peril, and not at his.

For a day or two I was undecided whether to respond to this call, or take no notice of it. I was not conscious of the slightest mysterious bias, influence, or attraction, one way or other. Of that I am as strictly sure as of every other statement that I make here. Ultimately I decided, as a break in the monotony of my life, that I would go.

The appointed morning was a raw morning in the month of November. There was a dense brown fog in Piccadilly, and it became positively black and in the last degree oppressive East of Temple Bar. I found the passages and staircases of the Court-House flaringly lighted with gas, and the Court itself similarly illuminated. I *think* that, until I was conducted by officers into the Old Court and saw its crowded state, I did not know that the Murderer was to be tried that day. I *think* that, until I was so helped into the Old Court with considerable difficulty, I did not know into which of the two Courts sitting my summons would take me. But this must not be received as a positive assertion, for I am not completely satisfied in my mind on either point.

I took my seat in the place appropriated to Jurors in waiting, and I looked about the Court as well as I could through the cloud of fog and breath that was heavy in it. I noticed the black vapour hanging like a murky curtain outside the great windows, and I noticed the stifled sound of wheels on the straw or tan that was littered in the street; also, the hum of the people gathered there, which a shrill whistle, or a louder song or hail than the rest, occasionally pierced. Soon afterwards the Judges, two in number, entered, and took their seats. The buzz in the Court was awfully hushed. The direction was given to put the Murderer to the bar. He appeared there. And in that same instant I recognised in him the first of the two men who had gone down Piccadilly.

If my name had been called then, I doubt if I could have answered to it audibly. But it was called about sixth or eighth in the panel, and I was by that time able to say, "Here!" Now, observe. As I stepped into the box, the prisoner, who had been looking on attentively, but with no sign of concern, became violently agitated, and beckoned to his attorney. The prisoner's wish to challenge me was so manifest, that it occasioned a pause, during which the attorney, with his hand upon the dock, whispered with his client, and shook his head. I afterwards had it from that gentleman, that the prisoner's first affrighted words to him were, "*At all hazards, challenge that man!*" But that, as he would give no reason for it, and admitted that he had not even known my name until he heard it called and I appeared, it was not done.

Both on the ground already explained, that I wish to avoid reviving the unwholesome memory of that Murderer, and also because a detailed account of his long trial is by no means indispensable to my narrative, I shall confine myself closely to such incidents in the ten days and nights during which we, the Jury, were kept together, as directly bear on my own curious personal experience. It is in that, and not in the Murderer, that I seek to interest my reader. It is to that, and not to a page of the Newgate Calendar, that I beg attention.

I was chosen Foreman of the Jury. On the second morning of the trial, after evidence had been taken for two hours (I heard the church clocks strike), happening to cast my eyes over my brother jurymen, I found an inexplicable difficulty in counting them. I counted them several times, yet always with the same difficulty. In short, I made them one too many.

I touched the brother juryman whose place was next me, and I whispered to him, "Oblige me by counting us." He looked surprised by the request, but turned his head and counted. "Why," says he, suddenly, "we are thirt – ; but no, it's not possible. No. We are twelve."

According to my counting that day, we were always right in detail, but in the gross we were always one too many. There was no appearance – no figure – to account for it; but I had now an inward foreshadowing of the figure that was surely coming.

The Jury were housed at the London Tavern. We all slept in one large room on separate tables, and we were constantly in the charge and under the eye of the officer sworn to hold us in safe-keeping. I see no reason for suppressing the real name of that officer. He was intelligent, highly polite, and obliging, and (I was glad to hear) much respected in the City. He had an agreeable presence, good eyes, enviable black whiskers, and a fine sonorous voice. His name was Mr. Harker.

When we turned into our twelve beds at night, Mr. Harker's bed was drawn across the door. On the night of the second day, not being disposed to lie down, and seeing Mr. Harker sitting on his bed, I went and sat beside him, and offered him a pinch of snuff. As Mr. Harker's hand touched mine in taking it from my box, a peculiar shiver crossed him, and he said, "Who is this?"

Following Mr. Harker's eyes, and looking along the room, I saw again the figure I expected, – the second of the two men who had gone down Piccadilly. I rose, and advanced a few steps; then stopped, and looked round at Mr. Harker. He was quite unconcerned, laughed, and said in a pleasant way, "I thought for a moment we had a thirteenth juryman, without a bed. But I see it is the moonlight."

Making no revelation to Mr. Harker, but inviting him to take a walk with me to the end of the room, I watched what the figure did. It stood for a few moments by the bedside of each of my eleven brother jurymen, close to the pillow. It always went to the right-hand side of the bed, and always passed out crossing the foot of the next bed. It seemed, from the action of the head, merely to look down pensively at each recumbent figure. It took no notice of me, or of my bed, which was that nearest to Mr. Harker's. It seemed to go out where the moonlight came in, through a high window, as by an aërial flight of stairs.

Next morning at breakfast, it appeared that everybody present had dreamed of the murdered man last night, except myself and Mr. Harker.

I now felt as convinced that the second man who had gone down Piccadilly was the murdered man (so to speak), as if it had been borne into my comprehension by his immediate testimony. But even this took place, and in a manner for which I was not at all prepared.

On the fifth day of the trial, when the case for the prosecution was drawing to a close, a miniature of the murdered man, missing from his bedroom upon the discovery of the deed, and afterwards found in a hiding-place where the Murderer had been seen digging, was put in evidence. Having been identified by the witness under examination, it was handed up to the Bench, and thence handed down to be inspected by the Jury. As an officer in a black gown was making his way with it across to me, the figure of the second man who had gone down Piccadilly impetuously started from the crowd, caught the miniature from the officer, and gave it to me with his own hands, at the same time saying, in a low and hollow tone, – before I saw the miniature, which was in a locket, – *"I was younger then, and my face was not then drained of blood."* It also came between me and the brother juryman to whom I would have given the miniature, and between him and the brother juryman to whom he would have given it, and so passed it on through the whole of our number, and back into my possession. Not one of them, however, detected this.

At table, and generally when we were shut up together in Mr. Harker's custody, we had from the first naturally discussed the day's proceedings a good deal. On that fifth day, the case for the prosecution being closed, and we having that side of the question in a completed shape before us, our discussion was more animated and serious. Among our number was a vestryman, – the densest idiot I have ever seen at large, – who met the plainest evidence with the most preposterous objections, and who was sided with by two flabby parochial parasites; all the three impanelled from a district so delivered over to Fever that they ought to have been upon their own trial for five hundred Murders. When these mischievous blockheads were at their loudest, which was towards midnight, while some of us were already preparing for bed, I again saw the murdered man. He stood grimly behind them, beckoning to me. On my going towards them, and striking into the conversation, he immediately retired. This was the beginning of a separate series of appearances, confined to that long room in which we were confined. Whenever a knot of my brother jurymen laid their heads together, I saw the head of the murdered man among theirs. Whenever their comparison of notes was going against him, he would solemnly and irresistibly beckon to me.

It will be borne in mind that down to the production of the miniature, on the fifth day of the trial, I had never seen the Appearance in Court. Three changes occurred now that we entered on the case for the defence. Two of them I will mention together, first. The figure was now in Court continually, and it never there addressed itself to me, but always to the person who was speaking at the time. For instance: the throat of the murdered man had been cut straight across. In the opening speech for the defence, it was suggested that the deceased might have cut his own throat. At that very moment, the figure, with its throat in the dreadful condition referred to (this it had concealed before), stood at the speaker's elbow, motioning across and across its windpipe, now with the right hand, now with the left, vigorously suggesting to the speaker himself the impossibility of such a wound having been self-inflicted by either hand. For another instance: a witness to character, a woman, deposed to the prisoner's being the most amiable of mankind. The figure at that instant stood on the floor before her, looking her full in the face, and pointing out the prisoner's evil countenance with an extended arm and an outstretched finger.

The third change now to be added impressed me strongly as the most marked and striking of all. I do not theorise upon it; I accurately state it, and there leave it. Although the Appearance was not itself perceived by those whom it addressed, its coming close to such persons was invariably attended by some trepidation or disturbance on their part. It seemed to me as if it were prevented, by laws to which I was not amenable, from fully revealing itself to others, and yet as if it could invisibly, dumbly, and darkly overshadow their minds. When the leading counsel for the defence suggested that hypothesis of suicide, and the figure stood at the learned gentleman's elbow, frightfully sawing at its severed throat, it is undeniable that the counsel faltered in his speech, lost for a few seconds the thread of his ingenious discourse, wiped his forehead with his handkerchief, and turned extremely pale. When the witness to character was confronted by the Appearance, her eyes most certainly did follow the direction of its pointed finger, and rest in great hesitation and trouble upon the prisoner's face. Two additional illustrations will suffice. On the eighth day of the trial, after the pause which was every day made early in the afternoon for a few minutes' rest and refreshment, I came back into Court with the rest of the Jury some little time before the return of the Judges. Standing up in the box and looking about me, I thought the figure was not there, until, chancing to raise my eyes to the gallery, I saw it bending forward, and leaning over a very decent woman, as if to assure itself whether the Judges had resumed their seats or not. Immediately afterwards that woman screamed, fainted, and was carried out. So with the venerable, sagacious, and patient Judge who conducted the trial. When the case was over, and he settled himself and his papers to sum up, the murdered man, entering by the Judges' door, advanced to his Lordship's desk, and looked eagerly over his shoulder at the pages of his notes which he was turning. A change came over his Lordship's face; his hand stopped; the peculiar shiver, that I knew so well, passed over him; he faltered, "Excuse me, gentlemen, for a few moments. I am somewhat oppressed by the vitiated air;" and did not recover until he had drunk a glass of water.

Through all the monotony of six of those interminable ten days, – the same Judges and others on the bench, the same Murderer in the dock, the same lawyers at the table, the same tones of question and answer rising to the roof of the court, the same scratching of the Judge's pen, the same ushers going in and out, the same lights kindled at the same hour when there had been any natural light of day, the same foggy curtain outside the great windows when it was foggy, the same rain pattering and dripping when it was rainy, the same footmarks of turnkeys and prisoner day after day on the same sawdust, the same keys locking and unlocking the same heavy doors, – through all the wearisome monotony which made me feel as if I had been Foreman of the Jury for a vast period of time, and Piccadilly had flourished coevally with Babylon, the murdered man never lost one trace of his distinctness in my eyes, nor was he at any moment less distinct than anybody else. I must not omit, as a matter of fact, that I never once saw the Appearance which I call by the name of the murdered man look at the Murderer. Again and again I wondered, "Why does he not?" But he never did.

Nor did he look at me, after the production of the miniature, until the last closing minutes of the trial arrived. We retired to consider, at seven minutes before ten at night. The idiotic vestryman and his two parochial parasites gave us so much trouble that we twice returned into Court to beg to have certain extracts from the Judge's notes re-read. Nine of us had not the smallest doubt about those passages, neither, I believe, had any one in the Court; the dunder-headed triumvirate, having no idea but obstruction, disputed them for that very reason. At length we prevailed, and finally the Jury returned into Court at ten minutes past twelve.

The murdered man at that time stood directly opposite the Jury-box, on the other side of the Court. As I took my place, his eyes rested on me with great attention; he seemed satisfied, and slowly shook a great gray veil, which he carried on his arm for the first time, over his head and whole form. As I gave in our verdict, 'Guilty,' the veil collapsed, all was gone, and his place was empty.

The Murderer, being asked by the Judge, according to usage, whether he had anything to say before sentence of Death should be passed upon him, indistinctly muttered something which was described in the leading newspapers of the following day as "a few rambling, incoherent, and half-audible words, in which he was understood to complain that he had not had a fair trial, because the Foreman of the Jury was prepossessed against him." The remarkable declaration that he really made was this: *"My Lord, I knew I was a doomed man, when the Foreman of my Jury came into the box. My Lord, I knew he would never let me off, because, before I was taken, he somehow got to my bedside in the night, woke me, and put a rope round my neck."*

The Problem of Dead Wood Hall

Dick Donovan

"**MYSTERIOUS CASE IN CHESHIRE.**" So ran the heading to a paragraph in all the morning papers some years ago, and prominence was given to the following particulars:

A gentleman, bearing the somewhat curious name of Tuscan Trankler, resided in a picturesque old mansion, known as Dead Wood Hall, situated in one of the most beautiful and lonely parts of Cheshire, not very far from the quaint and old-time village of Knutsford. Mr. Trankler had given a dinner-party at his house, and amongst the guests was a very well-known county magistrate and landowner, Mr. Manville Charnworth. It appeared that, soon after the ladies had retired from the table, Mr. Charnworth rose and went into the grounds, saying he wanted a little air. He was smoking a cigar, and in the enjoyment of perfect health. He had drunk wine, however, rather freely, as was his wont, but though on exceedingly good terms with himself and every one else, he was perfectly sober. An hour passed, but Mr. Charnworth had not returned to the table. Though this did not arouse any alarm, as it was thought that he had probably joined the ladies, for he was what is called 'a ladies' man,' and preferred the company of females to that of men. A tremendous sensation, however, was caused when, a little later, it was announced that Charnworth had been found insensible, lying on his back in a shrubbery. Medical assistance was at once summoned, and when it arrived the opinion expressed was that the unfortunate gentleman had been stricken with apoplexy. For some reason or other, however, the doctors were led to modify that view, for symptoms were observed which pointed to what was thought to be a peculiar form of poisoning, although the poison could not be determined. After a time, Charnworth recovered consciousness, but was quite unable to give any information. He seemed to be dazed and confused, and was evidently suffering great pain. At last his limbs began to swell, and swelled to an enormous size; his eyes sunk, his cheeks fell in, his lips turned black, and mortification appeared in the extremities. Everything that could be done for the unfortunate man was done, but without avail. After six hours' suffering, he died in a paroxysm of raving madness, during which he had to be held down in the bed by several strong men.

The post-mortem examination, which was necessarily held, revealed the curious fact that the blood in the body had become thin and purplish, with a faint strange odour that could not be identified. All the organs were extremely congested, and the flesh presented every appearance of rapid decomposition. In fact, twelve hours after death putrefaction had taken place. The medical gentlemen who had the case in hand were greatly puzzled, and were at a loss to determine the precise cause of death. The deceased had been a very healthy man, and there was no actual organic disease of any kind. In short, everything pointed to poisoning. It was noted that on the left side of the neck was a tiny scratch, with a slightly livid appearance, such as might have been made by a small sharply pointed instrument. The viscera having been secured for purposes of analysis, the body was hurriedly, buried within thirty hours of death.

The result of the analysis was to make clear that the unfortunate gentleman had died through some very powerful and irritant poison being introduced into the blood. That it was a case of blood-poisoning there was hardly room for the shadow of a doubt, but the science of that day was quite unable to say what the poison was, or how it had got into the body. There was no reason – so far as could be ascertained to suspect foul play, and even less reason to suspect suicide. Altogether, therefore, the case was one of profound mystery, and the coroner's jury were compelled to return an open verdict. Such were the details that were made public at the time of Mr. Charnworth's death; and from the social position of all the parties, the affair was something more than a nine days' wonder; while in Cheshire itself, it created a profound sensation. But, as no further information was forthcoming, the matter ceased to interest the outside world, and so, as far as the public were concerned, it was relegated to the limbo of forgotten things.

Two years later, Mr. Ferdinand Trankler, eldest son of Tuscan Trankler, accompanied a large party of friends for a day's shooting in Mere Forest. He was a young man, about five and twenty years of age; was in the most perfect health, and had scarcely ever had a day's illness in his life. Deservedly popular and beloved, he had a large circle of warm friends, and was about to be married to a charming young lady, a member of an old Cheshire family who were extensive landed proprietors and property owners. His prospects therefore seemed to be unclouded, and his happiness complete.

The shooting-party was divided into three sections, each agreeing to shoot over a different part of the forest, and to meet in the afternoon for refreshments at an appointed rendezvous.

Young Trankler and his companions kept pretty well together for some little time, but ultimately began to spread about a good deal. At the appointed hour the friends all met, with the exception of Trankler. He was not there. His absence did not cause any alarm, as it was thought he would soon turn up. He was known to be well acquainted with the forest, and the supposition was he had strayed further afield than the rest. By the time the repast was finished, however, he had not put in an appearance. Then, for the first time, the company began to feel some uneasiness, and vague hints that possibly an accident had happened were thrown out. Hints at last took the form of definite expressions of alarm, and search parties were at once organized to go in search of the absent young man, for only on the hypothesis of some untoward event could his prolonged absence be accounted for, inasmuch as it was not deemed in the least likely that he would show such a lack of courtesy as to go off and leave his friends without a word of explanation. For two hours the search was kept up without any result. Darkness was then closing in, and the now painfully anxious searchers' began to feel that they would have to desist until daylight; returned. But at last some of the more energetic and active, members of the party came upon Trankler lying on his sides and nearly entirely hidden by masses of half withered bracken. He was lying near a little stream that meandered through the forest, and near a keeper's shelter that was constructed with logs and thatched with pine boughs. He was stone dead, and his appearance caused his friends to shrink back with horror, for he was not only black in the face, but his body was bloated, and his limbs seemed swollen to twice their natural size.

Amongst the party were two medical men, who, being hastily summoned, proceeded at once to make an examination. They expressed an opinion that the young man had been dead for some time, but they could not account for his death, as there was no wound to be observed. As a matter of fact, his gun was lying near him with both barrels loaded. Moreover, his appearance was not compatible at all with death from a gun-shot wound. How then had he died? The consternation amongst those who had known him can well be imagined, and with a sense of suppressed horror, it was whispered that the strange condition of the dead man coincided with that of Mr. Manville Charnworth, the county magistrate who had died so mysteriously two years previously.

As soon as it was possible to do so, Ferdinand Trankler's body was removed to Dead Wood Hall, and his people were stricken with profound grief when they realized that the hope and joy of their house was dead. Of course an autopsy had to be performed, owing to the ignorance of the medical men as to the cause of death. And this post-mortem examination disclosed the fact that all the extraordinary appearances which had been noticed in Mr. Charnworth's case were present in this one. There was the same purplish coloured blood; the same gangrenous condition of the limbs; but as with Charnworth, so with Trankler, all the organs were healthy. There was no organic disease to account for death. As it was pretty certain, therefore, that death was not due to natural causes, a coroner's inquest was held, and while the medical evidence made it unmistakably clear that young Trankler had been cut down in the flower of his youth and while he was in radiant health by some powerful and potent means which had suddenly destroyed his life, no one had the boldness to suggest what those means were, beyond saying that blood-poisoning of a most violent character had been set up. Now, it was very obvious that blood-poisoning could not have originated without some specific cause, and the most patient investigation was directed to trying to find out the cause, while exhaustive inquiries were made, but at the end of them, the solution of the mystery was as far off as ever, for these investigations had been in the wrong channel, not one scrap of evidence was brought forward which would have justified a definite statement that this or that had been responsible for the young man's death.

It was remembered that when the post-mortem examination of Mr. Charnworth took place, a tiny bluish scratch was observed on the left side of the neck. But it was so small, and apparently so unimportant that it was not taken into consideration when attempts were made to solve the problem of "How did the man die?" When the doctors examined Mr. Trankler's body, they looked to see if there was a similar puncture or scratch, and, to their astonishment, they did find rather a curious mark on the left side of the neck, just under the ear. It was a slight abrasion of the skin, about an inch long as if he had been scratched with a pin, and this abrasion was a faint blue, approximating in colour to the tattoo marks on a sailor's arm. The similarity in this scratch to that which had been observed on Mr. Charnworth's body, necessarily gave rise to a good deal of comment amongst the doctors, though they could not arrive at any definite conclusion respecting it. One man went so far as to express an opinion that it was due to an insect or the bite of a snake. But this theory found no supporters, for it was argued that the similar wound on Mr. Charnworth could hardly have resulted from an insect or snake bite, for he had died in his friend's garden. Besides, there was no insect or snake in England capable of killing a man as these two men had been killed. That theory, therefore, fell to the ground; and medical science as represented by the local gentlemen had to confess itself baffled; while the coroner's jury were forced to again return an open verdict.

"There was no evidence to prove how the deceased had come by his death."

This verdict was considered highly unsatisfactory, but what other could have been returned. There was nothing to support the theory of foul play; on the other hand, no evidence was forthcoming to explain away the mystery which surrounded the deaths of Charnworth and Trankler. The two men had apparently died from precisely the same cause, and under circumstances which were as mysterious as they were startling, but what the cause was, no one seemed able to determine.

Universal sympathy was felt with the friends and relatives of young Trankler, who had perished so unaccountably while in pursuit of pleasure. Had he been taken suddenly ill at home and had died in his bed, even though the same symptoms and morbid appearances had manifested themselves, the mystery would not have been so great. But as Charnworth's end came in his host's garden after a dinner-party, so young Trankler died in a forest while he and his friends were engaged in shooting. There was certainly something truly remarkable that two men, exhibiting all the same post-mortem effects, should have died in such a way; their deaths, in point of time, being separated by a period of two years. On the face of it, it seemed impossible that it could be merely a coincidence. It will be gathered from the foregoing, that in this double tragedy were all the elements of a romance well calculated to stimulate public curiosity to the highest pitch; while the friends and relatives of the two deceased gentlemen were of opinion that the matter ought not to be allowed to drop with the return of the verdict of the coroner's jury. An investigation seemed to be urgently called for. Of course, an investigation of a kind had taken place by the local police, but something more than that was required, so thought the friends. And an application was made to me to go down to Dead Wood Hall; and bring such skill as I possessed to bear on the case, in the hope that the veil of mystery might be drawn aside, and light let in where all was then dark.

Dead Wood Hall was a curious place, with a certain gloominess of aspect which seemed to suggest that it was a fitting scene for a tragedy. It was a large, massive house, heavily timbered in front in a way peculiar to many of the old Cheshire mansions. It stood in extensive grounds, and being situated on a rise commanded a very fine panoramic view which embraced the Derbyshire Hills. How it got its name of Dead Wood Hall no one seemed to know exactly. There was a tradition that it had originally been known as Dark Wood Hall; but the word 'Dark' had been corrupted into 'Dead'. The Tranklers came into possession of the property by purchase, and the family had been the owners of it for something like thirty years.

With great circumstantiality I was told the story of the death of each man, together with the results of the post mortem examination, and the steps that had been taken by the police. On further inquiry I found that the police, in spite of the mystery surrounding the case, were firmly of opinion that the deaths of the two men were, after all, due to natural causes, and that the similarity in the appearance of the bodies after death *was* a mere coincidence. The superintendent of the county constabulary, who had had charge of the matter, waxed rather warm; for he said that all sorts of ridiculous stories had been set afloat, and absurd theories had been suggested, not one of which would have done credit to the intelligence of an average schoolboy.

"People lose their heads so, and make such fools of themselves in matters of this kind," he said warmly; "and of course the police are accused of being stupid, ignorant, and all the rest of it. They seem, in fact, to have a notion that we are endowed with superhuman faculties, and that nothing should baffle us. But, as a matter of fact, it is the doctors who are at fault in this instance. They are confronted with a new disease, about which they are ignorant; and, in order to conceal their want of knowledge, they at once raise the cry of 'foul play'."

"Then you are clearly of opinion that Mr. Charnworth and Mr. Trankler died of a disease," I remarked.

"Undoubtedly I am."

"Then how do you explain the rapidity of the death in each case, and the similarity in the appearance of the dead bodies?"

"It isn't for me to explain that at all. That is doctors' work not police work. If the doctors can't explain it, how can I be expected to do so? I only know this, I've put some of my best men on to the job, and they've failed to find anything that would suggest foul play."

"And that convinces you absolutely that there has been no foul play?"

"Absolutely."

"I suppose you were personally acquainted with both gentlemen? What sort of man was Mr. Charnworth?"

"Oh, well, he was right enough, as such men go. He made a good many blunders as a magistrate; but all magistrates do that. You see, fellows get put on the bench who are no more fit to be magistrates than you are, sir. It's a matter of influence more often as not. Mr. Charnworth was no worse and no better than a lot of others I could name."

"What opinion did you form of his private character?"

"Ah, now, there, there's another matter," answered the superintendent, in a confidential tone, and with a smile playing about his lips. "You see, Mr. Charnworth was a bachelor."

"So are thousands of other men," I answered. "But bachelorhood is not considered dishonourable in this country."

"No, perhaps not. But they say as how the reason was that Mr. Charnworth didn't get married was because he didn't care for having only one wife."

"You mean he was fond of ladies generally. A sort of general lover."

"I should think he was," said the superintendent, with a twinkle in his eye, which was meant to convey a good deal of meaning. "I've heard some queer stories about him."

"What is the nature of the stories?" I asked, thinking that I might get something to guide me.

"Oh, well, I don't attach much importance to them myself," he said, half-apologetically; "but the fact is, there was some social scandal talked about Mr. Charnworth."

"What was the nature of the scandal?"

"Mind you," urged the superintendent, evidently anxious to be freed from any responsibility for the scandal whatever it was, "I only tell you the story as I heard it. Mr. Charnworth liked his little flirtations, no doubt, as we all do; but he was a gentleman and a magistrate, and I have no right to say anything against him that I know nothing about myself."

"While a gentleman may be a magistrate, a magistrate is not always a gentleman," I remarked.

"True, true; but Mr. Charnworth was. He was a fine specimen of a gentleman, and was very liberal. He did me many kindnesses."

"Therefore, in your sight, at least, sir, he was without blemish."

"I don't go as far as that," replied the superintendent, a little warmly; "I only want to be just."

"I give you full credit for that," I answered; "but please do tell me about the scandal you spoke of. It is just possible it may afford me a clue."

"I don't think that it will. However, here is the story. A young lady lived in Knutsford by the name of Downie. She is the daughter of the late George Downie, who for many years carried on the business of a miller. Hester Downie was said to be one of the prettiest girls in Cheshire, or, at any rate, in this part of Cheshire, and rumour has it that she flirted with both Charnworth and Trankler."

"Is that all that rumour says?" I asked.

"No, there was a good deal more said. But, as I have told you, I know nothing for certain, and so must decline to commit myself to any statement for which there could be no better foundation than common gossip."

"Does Miss. Downie still live in Knutsford?"

"No; she disappeared mysteriously soon after Charnworth's death."

"And you don't know where she is?"

"No; I have no idea."

As I did not see that there was much more to be gained from the superintendent I left him, and at once sought a interview with the leading medical man who had made the autopsy of the two bodies. He was a man who was somewhat puffed up with the belief in his own cleverness, but he gave me the impression that, if anything, he was a little below the average country practitioner. He hadn't a single theory to advance to account for the deaths of Charnworth and Trankler. He confessed that he was mystified; that all the appearances were entirely new to him, for neither in his reading nor his practice had he ever heard of a similar case.

"Are you disposed to think, sir, that these two men came to their end by foul play?" I asked.

"No, I am not," he answered definitely, "and I said so at the inquest. Foul play means murder, cool and deliberate; and planned and carried out with fiendish cunning. Besides, if it was murder how was the murder committed?"

"*If it was murder?*" I asked significantly. "I shall hope to answer that question later on."

"But I am convinced it wasn't murder," returned the doctor, with a self-confident air. "If a man is shot, or bludgeoned, or poisoned, there is something to go upon. I scarcely know of a poison that cannot be detected. And not a trace of poison was found in the organs of either man. Science has made tremendous strides of late years, and I doubt if she has much more to teach us in that respect. Anyway, I assert without fear of contradiction that Charnworth and Trankler did not die of poison."

"What killed them, then?" I asked, bluntly and sharply.

The doctor did not like the question, and there was a roughness in his tone as he answered –

"I'm not prepared to say. If I could have assigned a precise cause of death the coroner's verdict would have been different."

"Then you admit that the whole affair is a problem which you are incapable of solving?"

"Frankly, I do," he answered, after a pause. "There are certain peculiarities in the case that I should like to see cleared up. In fact, in the interests of my profession, I think it is most desirable that the mystery surrounding the death of the unfortunate men should be solved. And I have been trying experiments recently with a view to attaining that end, though without success."

My interview with this gentleman had not advanced matters, for it only served to show me that the doctors were quite baffled, and I confess that that did not altogether encourage me. Where they had failed, how could I hope to succeed? They had the advantage of seeing the bodies and examining them, and though they found themselves confronted with signs which were in themselves significant, they could not read them. All that I had to go upon was hearsay, and I was asked to solve a mystery which seemed unsolvable. But, as I have so often stated in the course of my chronicles, the seemingly impossible is frequently the most easy to accomplish, where a mind specially trained to deal with complex problems is brought to bear upon it.

In interviewing Mr. Tuscan Trankler, I found that he entertained a very decided opinion that there had been foul play, though he admitted that it was difficult in the extreme to suggest even a vague notion of how the deed had been accomplished. If the two men had died together or within a short period of each other, the idea of murder would have seemed more logical. But two years had elapsed, and yet each man had evidently died from precisely same cause. Therefore, if it *was* murder, the same hand that had slain Mr. Charnworth slew Mr. Trankler. There was no getting away from that; and then of course arose the question of *motive*. Granted that the same hand did the deed, did the same motive prompt in each case? Another aspect of the affair that presented itself to me was that the crime, if crime it was, was not the work of any ordinary person. There was an originality of conception in it which pointed to the criminal being, in certain respects, a genius. And, moreover, the motive underlying it must have been a very powerful one; possibly, nay probably, due to a sense of some terrible wrong inflicted, and which could only be wiped out with death of the wronger. But this presupposed that each man, though unrelated, had perpetrated the same wrong. Now, it was within the grasp of intelligent reasoning that Charnworth, in his capacity of a county justice, might have given mortal offence to someone, who, cherishing the memory of it, until a mania had been set up, resolved that the magistrate should die. That theory was reasonable when taken singly, but it seemed to lose its reasonableness when connected with young Trankler, unless it was that he had been instrumental in getting somebody convicted. To determine this I made very pointed inquiries, but received the most positive assurances that never in the whole course of his life had he directly or indirectly been instrumental in prosecuting any one. Therefore, so far as he was concerned, the theory fell to the ground; and if the same person killed both men, the motive prompting in each case was a different one, assuming that Charnworth's death resulted from revenge for a fancied wrong inflicted in the course of his administration of justice.

Although I fully recognized all the difficulties that lay in the way of a rational deduction that would square in with the theory of murder, and of murder committed by one any the same hand, I saw how necessary it was to keep in view the points I have advanced as factors in the problem the had to be worked out, and I adhered to my first impression, and felt tolerably certain that, granted the men had been murdered, they were murdered by the same hand. It may be said that this deduction required no great mental effort. I admit that that is so; but it is strange that nearly all the people in the district were opposed to the theory. Mr. Tuscan Trankler spoke very highly of

Charnworth. He believed him to be an upright, conscientious man, liberal to a fault with his means, and in his position of magistrate erring on the side of mercy. In his private character he was a *bon vivant;* fond of a good dinner, good wine, and good company. He was much in request at dinner-parties and other social gatherings, for he was accounted a brilliant *raconteur,* possessed of an endless fund of racy jokes and anecdotes. I have already stated that with ladies he was an especial favourite, for he had a singularly suave, winning way, which with most women was irresistible. In age he was more than double that of young Trankler, who was only five and twenty at the time of his death, whereas Charnworth had turned sixty, though I was given to understand that he was a well-preserved, good-looking man, and apparently younger than he really was.

Coming to young Trankler, there was a consensus of opinion that he was an exemplary young man. He had been partly educated at home and partly at the Manchester Grammar School; and, though he had shown a decided talent for engineering, he had not gone in for it seriously, but had dabbled in it as an amateur, for he had ample means and good prospects, and it was his father's desire that he should lead the life of a country gentleman, devote himself to country pursuits, and to improving and keeping together the family estates. To the lady who was to have become his bride, he had been engaged but six months, and had only known her a year. His premature and mysterious death had caused intense grief in both families; and his intended wife had been so seriously affected that her friends had been compelled to take her abroad.

With these facts and particulars before me, I had to set to work and try to solve the problem which was considered unsolvable by most of the people who knew anything about it. But may I be pardoned for saying very positively that, even at this point, I did not consider it so. Its complexity could not be gainsaid; nevertheless, I felt that there were ways and means of arriving at a solution, and I set to work in my own fashion. Firstly, I started on the assumption that both men had been deliberately murdered by the same person. If that was not so, then they had died of some remarkable and unknown disease which had stricken them down under a set of conditions that were closely allied, and the coincidence in that case would be one of the most astounding the world had ever known. Now, if that was correct, a pathological conundrum was propounded which, it was for the medical world to answer, and practically I was placed out of the running, to use a sporting phrase. I found that, with few exceptions – the exceptions being Mr. Trankler and his friends – there was an undisguised. opinion that what the united local wisdom and skill had failed to accomplish, could not be accomplished by a stranger. As my experience, however, had inured me against that sort of thing, it did not affect me. Local prejudices and jealousies have always to be reckoned with, and it does not do to be thin-skinned. I worked upon my own lines, thought with my own thoughts, and, as an expert in the art of reading human nature, I reasoned from a different set of premises to that employed by the irresponsible chatterers, who cry out "Impossible," as soon as the first difficulty presents itself. Marshalling all the facts of the case so far as I had been able to gather them, I arrived at the conclusion that the problem could be solved, and, as a preliminary step to that end, I started off to London, much to the astonishment of those who had secured my services. But my reply to the many queries addressed to me was, "I hope to find the key-note to the solution in the metropolis." This reply only increased the astonishment, but later on I will explain why I took the step, which may seem to the reader rather an extraordinary one.

After an absence of five days I returned to Cheshire, and I was then in a position to say, "Unless a miracle has happened, Charnworth and Trankler were murdered beyond all doubt, and murdered by the same person in such a cunning, novel and devilish manner, that even the most astute inquirer might have been pardoned for being baffled." Of course there was a strong desire to know my reasons for the positive statement, but I felt that it was in the interests of justice itself that I should not allow them to be known at that stage of the proceedings.

The next important step was to try and find out what had become of Miss. Downie, the Knutsford beauty, with whom Charnworth was said to have carried on a flirtation. Here, again, I considered secrecy of great importance.

Hester Downie was about seven and twenty years of age. She was an orphan, and was believed to have been born in Macclesfield, as her parents came from there. Her father's calling was that of a miller. He had settled in Knutsford about fifteen years previous to the period I am dealing with, and had been dead about five years. Not very much was known about the family, but it was thought there were other children living. No very kindly feeling was shown for Hester Downie, though it was only too obvious that jealousy was at the bottom of it. Half the young men, it seemed, had lost their heads about her, and all the girls in the village were consumed with envy and jealousy. It was said she was 'stuck up,' 'above her position,' 'a heartless flirt,' and so forth. From those competent to speak, however, she was regarded as a nice young woman, and admittedly good-looking. For years she had lived with an old aunt, who bore the reputation of being rather a sullen sort of woman, and somewhat eccentric. The girl had a little over fifty pounds a year to live upon, derived from a small property left to her by her father; and she and her aunt occupied a cottage just on the outskirts of Knutsford. Hester was considered to be very exclusive, and did not associate much with the people in Knutsford. This was sufficient to account for the local bias, and as she often went away from her home for three and four weeks at a time, it was not considered extraordinary when it was known that she had left soon after Trankler's death. Nobody, however, knew where she had gone to; it is right, perhaps, that I should here state that not a soul breathed a syllable of suspicion against her, that either directly or indirectly she could be connected with the deaths of Charnworth or Trankler. The aunt, a widow by the name of Hislop, could not be described as a pleasant or genial woman, either in appearance or manner. I was anxious to ascertain for certain whether there was any truth in the rumour or not that Miss. Downie had flirted with Mr. Charnworth. If it was true that she did, a clue might be afforded which would lead to the ultimate unravelling of the mystery. I had to approach Mrs. Hislop with a good deal of circumspection, for she showed an inclination to resent any inquiries being made into her family matters. She gave me the impression that she was an honest woman, and it was very apparent that she was strongly attached to her niece Hester. Trading on this fact, I managed to draw her out. I said that people in the district were beginning to say unkind things about Hester, and that it would be better for the girl's sake that there should be no mystery associated with her or her movements.

The old lady fired up at this, and declared that she didn't care a jot about what the 'common people' said. Her niece was superior to all of them, and she would 'have the law on any one who spoke ill of Hester.'

"But there is one thing, Mrs. Hislop," I replied, "that ought to be set at rest. It is rumoured – in fact, something more than rumoured – that your niece and the late

Mr. Charnworth were on terms of intimacy, which, to say the least, if it is true, was imprudent for a girl in her position."

"Them what told you that," exclaimed the old woman, "is like the adders the woodmen get in Delamere forest: they're full of poison. Mr. Charnworth courted the girl fair and square, and led her to believe he would marry her. But, of course, he had to do the thing in secret. Some folk will talk so, and if it had been known that a gentleman like Mr. Charnworth was coming after a girl in Hester's position, all sorts of things would have been said."

"Did she believe that he was serious in his intentions towards her?"

"Of course she did."

"Why was the match broken off?"

"Because he died."

"Then do you mean to tell me seriously, Mrs. Hislop, that Mr. Charnworth, had he lived, would have married your niece?"

"Yes, I believe he would."

"Was he the only lover the girl had?"

"Oh dear no. She used to carry on with a man named Job Panton. But, though they were engaged to be married, she didn't like him much, and threw him up for Mr. Charnworth."

"Did she ever flirt with young Mr. Trankler?"

"I don't know about flirting; but he called here now and again, and made her some presents. You see, Hester is a superior sort of girl, and I don't wonder at gentlefolk liking her."

"Just so," I replied; "beauty attracts peasant and lord alike. But you will understand that it is to Hester's interest that there should be no concealment – no mystery; and I advise that she return here, for her very presence would tend to silence the tongue of scandal. By the way, where is she?"

"She's staying in Manchester with a relative, a cousin of hers, named Jessie Turner."

"Is Jessie Turner a married woman?"

"Oh yes: well, that is, she has been married; but she's a widow now, and has two little children. She is very fond of Hester, who often goes to her."

Having obtained Jessie Turner's address in Manchester, I left Mrs. Hislop, feeling somehow as if I had got the key of the problem, and a day or two later I called on Mrs. Jessie Turner, who resided in a small house, situated in Tamworth Street, Hulme, Manchester.

She was a young woman, not more than thirty years of age, somewhat coarse, and vulgar-looking in appearance, and with an unpleasant, self-assertive manner. There was a great contrast between her and her cousin, Hester Downie, who was a remarkably attractive and pretty girl, with quite a classical figure, and a childish, winning way, but a painful want of education which made itself very manifest when she spoke; and a harsh, unmusical voice detracted a good deal from her winsomeness, while in everything she did, and almost everything she said, she revealed that vanity was her besetting sin.

I formed my estimate at once of this young woman indeed, of both of them. Hester seemed to me to be shallow, vain, thoughtless, giddy; and her companion, artful, cunning, and heartless.

"I want you, Miss. Downie," I began, "to tell me truthfully the story of your connection, firstly, with Job Panton; secondly, with Mr. Charnworth; thirdly, with Mr. Trankler."

This request caused the girl to fall into a condition of amazement and confusion, for I had not stated what the nature of my business was, and, of course, she was unprepared for the question.

"What should I tell you my business for?" she cried snappishly, and growing very red in the face.

"You are aware," I remarked, "that both Mr. Charnworth and Mr. Trankler are dead?"

"Of course I am."

"Have you any idea how they came by their death?"

"Not the slightest."

"Will you be surprised to hear that some very hard things are being said about you?"

"About me!" she exclaimed, in amazement.

"Yes."

"Why about me?"

"Well, your disappearance from your home, for one thing."

She threw up her hands and uttered a cry of distress and horror, while sudden paleness took the place of the red flush that had dyed her cheeks. Then she burst into almost hysterical weeping, and sobbed out:

"I declare it's awful. To think that I cannot do anything or go away when I like without all the old cats in the place trying to blacken my character! It's a pity that people won't mind their own business, and not go out of the way to talk about that which doesn't concern them."

"But, you see, Miss. Downie, it's the way of the world," I answered, with a desire to soothe her; "one mustn't be too thin-skinned. Human nature is essentially spiteful. However, to return to the subject, you will see, perhaps, the importance of answering my questions. The circumstances of Charnworth's and Trankler's deaths are being closely inquired into, and I am sure you wouldn't like it to be thought that you were withholding information which, in the interest of law and justice, might be valuable."

"Certainly not," she replied, suppressing a sob. "But I have nothing to tell you."

"But you knew the three men I have mentioned."

"Of course I did, but Job Panton is an ass. I never, could bear him."

"He was your sweetheart, though, was he not?"

"He used to come fooling about, and declared that he couldn't live without me."

"Did you never give him encouragement?"

"I suppose every girl makes a fool of herself sometimes."

"Then you did allow him to sweetheart you?"

"If you like to call it sweethearting you can," she answered, with a toss of her pretty head. "I did walk out with him sometimes. But I didn't care much for him. You see, he wasn't my sort at all."

"In what way?"

"Well, surely I couldn't be expected to marry a gamekeeper, could I?"

"He is a gamekeeper, then?"

"Yes."

"In whose employ is he?"

"Lord Belmere's."

"Was he much disappointed when he found that you would have nothing to do with him?"

"I really don't know. I didn't trouble myself about him," she answered, with a coquettish heartlessness.

"Did you do any sweethearting with Mr. Trankler?"

"No, of course not. He used to be very civil to me, and talk to me when he met me."

"Did you ever walk out with him?"

The question brought the colour back to her face, and her manner grew confused again,

"Once or twice I met him by accident, and he strolled along the road with me – that's all."

This answer was not a truthful one. Of that I was convinced by her very manner. But I did not betray my mistrust or doubts. I did not think there was any purpose to be served in so doing. So far the object of my visit was accomplished, and as Miss. Downie seemed disposed to resent any further questioning, I thought it was advisable to bring the interview to a close; but before doing so, I said:

"I have one more question to ask you, Miss. Downie. Permit me to preface it, however, by saying I am afraid that, up to this point, you have failed to appreciate the situation, or grasp the seriousness of the position in which you are placed. Let me, therefore, put it before you in a somewhat more graphic way. Two men – gentlemen of good social position with whom you seem to have been well acquainted, and whose attentions you encouraged – pray do not look at me so angrily as that; I mean what I say. I repeat that you encouraged their attentions, otherwise they would not have gone after you." Here Miss. Downie's nerves gave way again, and she broke into a fit of weeping, and, holding her handkerchief to her eyes, she exclaimed with almost passionate bitterness:

"Well, whatever I did, I was egged on to do it by my cousin, Jessie Turner. She always said I was a fool not to aim at high game."

"And so you followed her promptings, and really thought that you might have made a match with Mr. Charnworth; but, he having died, you turned your thoughts to young Trankler." She did not reply, but sobbed behind her handkerchief. So I proceeded. "Now the final question I want to ask you is this: Have you ever had anyone who has made serious love to you but Job Panton?"

"Mr. Charnworth made love to me," she sobbed out.

"He flirted with you," I suggested.

"No; he made love to me," she persisted. "He promised to marry me."

"And you believed him?"

"Of course I did."

"Did Trankler promise to marry you?"

"No."

"Then I must repeat the question, but will add Mr. Charnworth's name. Besides him and Panton, is there anyone else in existence who has courted you in the hope that you would become his wife?"

"No – no one," she mumbled in a broken voice.

As I took my departure I felt that I had gathered up a good many threads, though they wanted arranging, and, so to speak, classifying; that done, they would probably give me the clue I was seeking. One thing was clear, Miss. Downie was a weak-headed, giddy, flighty girl, incapable, as it seemed to me, of seriously reflecting on anything. Her cousin was crafty and shallow, and a dangerous companion for Downie, who was sure to be influenced and led by a creature like Jessie Turner. But, let it not be inferred from these remarks that I had any suspicion that either of the two women had in any way been accessory to the crime, for crime I was convinced it was. Trankler and Charnworth had been murdered, but by whom I was not prepared to even hint at at that stage of the proceedings. The two unfortunate gentlemen had, beyond all possibility of doubt, both been attracted by the girl's exceptionally good looks, and they had amused themselves with her. This fact suggested at once the question, was Charnworth in the habit of seeing her before Trankler made her acquaintance? Now, if my theory of the crime was correct, it could be asserted with positive certainty, that Charnworth was the girl's lover before Trankler. Of course it was almost a foregone conclusion that Trankler must have been aware of her existence for along time. The place, be it remembered, was small; she, in her way, was a sort of local celebrity, and it was hardly likely that young Trankler was ignorant of some of the village gossip in which she figured. But, assuming that he was, he was well acquainted with Charnworth, who was looked upon in the neighbourhood as 'a gay dog'. The female conquests of such men are often matters of notoriety; though, even if that was not the case, it was likely enough that Charnworth may have discussed Miss. Downie in Trankler's presence. Some men – especially those of Charnworth's characteristics – are much given to boasting of their flirtations, and Charnworth may have been rather prow of his ascendency over the simple village beauty. Of course, all this, it will be said, was mere theorizing. So it was; but it will presently be seen how it squared in with the general theory of the whole affair, which I had worked out after much pondering, and a careful weighing and nice adjustment of all the evidence, such as it was, I had been able to gather together, and the various parts which were necessary before the puzzle could be put together.

It was immaterial, however, whether Trankler did or did not know Hester Downie before or at the same time as Charnworth. A point that was not difficult to determine was this – he did not make himself conspicuous as her admirer until after his friend's death, probably not until some time afterwards. Otherwise, how came it about that the slayer of Charnworth waited two years before he took the life of young Trankler? The reader will gather from this remark how my thoughts ran at that time. Firstly, I was clearly of opinion that both men had been murdered. Secondly, the murder in each case was the outcome of jealousy. Thirdly, the murderer must, as a logical sequence, have been a rejected suitor. This would point necessarily to Job Panton as the criminal, assuming my information was right that the girl had not had any other lover. But against that theory this very strong argument could be used: By what extraordinary and secret means – means that had baffled all the science of the district – had Job Panton, who occupied the position of a gamekeeper, been able to do away with his victims, and bring about death so horrible and so sudden as to make one shudder to think of it? Herein was displayed a devilishness of cunning, and a knowledge which it was difficult to conceive that an ignorant and untravelled man was likely to be in possession of. Logic, deduction, and all the circumstances of the case were opposed to the idea of Panton being the murderer at the first blush; and yet, so far as I had gone, I had been irresistibly drawn towards the conclusion that Panton was either directly or indirectly responsible for the death of the two gentlemen. But, in order to know something more of the man whom I suspected, I disguised myself as a travelling showman on the look-out for a good pitch for my show, and I took up my quarters for a day or two at a rustic inn just on the skirts of Knutsford, and known as the Woodman. I had previously ascertained that this inn was a favourite resort of the gamekeepers for miles round about, and Job Panton was to be found there almost nightly.

In a short time I had made his acquaintance. He was a young, big-limbed, powerful man, of a pronounced rustic type. He had the face of a gipsy – swarthy and dark, with keen, small black eyes, and a mass of black curly hair, and in his ears he wore tiny, plain gold rings. Singularly enough his expression was most intelligent; but allied with – as it seemed to me – a certain suggestiveness of latent ferocity. That is to say, I imagined him liable to outbursts of temper and passion, during which he might be capable of anything. As it was, then, he seemed to me subdued, somewhat sullen, and averse to conversation. He smoked heavily, and I soon found that he guzzled beer at a terrible rate. He had received, for a man in his position, a tolerably good education. By that I mean he could write a fair hand, he read well, and had something more than a smattering of arithmetic. I was told also that he was exceedingly skilful with carpenter's tools, although he had had no training that way; he also understood something about plants, while he was considered an authority on the habit, and everything appertaining to game. The same informant thought to still further enlighten me by adding:

"Poor Job beän't the chap he wur a year or more ago. His gal cut un, and that kind a took a hold on un. He doän't say much; but it wur a terrible blow, it wur."

"How was it his girl cut him?" I asked.

"Well, you see, maäster, it wur this way; she thought hersel' a bit too high for un. Mind you, I bäan't a saying as she wur; but when a gel thinks hersel' above a chap, it's no use talking to her."

"What was the girl's name?"

"They call her Downie. Her father was a miller here in Knutsford, but his gal had too big notions of hersel'; and she chucked poor Job Panton overboard, and they do say as how she took on wi' Meäster Charnworth and also wi' Meäster Trankler. I doän't know nowt for certain myself, but there wursome rum kind o' talk going about. Leastwise, I know that job took it badly, and he ain't been the same kind o' chap since. But there, what's the use of a braking one's 'art about a gal? Gals is a queer lot, I tell you. My old grandfaither used to say, 'Women folk be curious folk. They be necessary evils, they be, and pleasant enough in their way, but a chap mustn't let 'em get the upper hand. They're like harses, they be, and if you want to manage 'em, you must show 'em you're their meäster.' "

The garrulous gentleman who entertained me thus with his views on women, was a tough, sinewy, weather-tanned old codger, who had lived the allotted span according to the psalmist, but who seemed destined to tread the earth for a long time still; for his seventy years had neither bowed nor shrunk him. His chatter was interesting to me because it served to prove what I already suspected, which was that Job Panton had taken his jilting very seriously indeed. Job was by no means a communicative fellow. As a matter of fact, it was difficult to draw him out on any subject; and though I should have liked to have heard *his* views about Hester Downie, I did not feel warranted in tapping him straight off. I very speedily discovered, however, that his weakness was beer. His capacity for it seemed immeasurable. He soaked himself with it; but when he reached the muddled stage, there was a tendency on his part to be more loquacious, and, taking advantage at last of one of these opportunities, I asked him one night if he had travelled. The question was an exceedingly pertinent one to my theory, and I felt that to a large extent the theory I had worked out depended upon the answers he gave. He turned his beady eyes upon me, and said, with a sort of sardonic grin –

"Yes, I've travelled a bit in my, time, meäster. I've been to Manchester often, and I once tramped all the way to Edinburgh. I had to rough it, I tell thee."

"Yes, I dare say," I answered. "But what I mean is, have you ever been abroad? Have you ever been to sea?"

"No, meäster, not me."

"You've been in foreign countries?"

"No. I've never been out of this one. England was good enough for me. But I would like to go away now to Australia, or some of those places."

Why?"

"Well, meäster, I have my own reasons."

"Doubtless," I said, "and no doubt very sound reasons."

"Never thee mind whether they are, or whether they beän't," he retorted warmly. "All I've got to say is, I wouldn't care where I went to if I could only get far enough away from this place. I'm tired of it."

In the manner of giving his answer, he betrayed the latent fire which I had surmised, and showed that there was a volcanic force of passion underlying his sullen silence, for he spoke with a suppressed force which clearly indicated the intensity of his feelings, and his bright eyes grew brighter with the emotion he felt. I now ventured upon another remark. I intended it to be a test one.

"I heard one of your mates say that you had been jilted. I suppose that's why you hate the place?"

He turned upon me suddenly. His tanned, ruddy face took on a deeper flush of red; his upper teeth closed almost savagely on his nether lip; his chest heaved, and his great, brawny hands clenched with the working of his passion. Then, with one great bang of his ponderous fist, he struck the table until the pots and glasses on it jumped as if they were sentient and frightened; and in a voice thick with smothered passion, he growled, "Yes, damn her! She's been my ruin."

"Nonsense!" I said. "You are a young man and a young man should not talk about being ruined because a girl has jilted him."

Once more he turned that angry look upon me, and said fiercely –

"Thou knows nowt about it, governor. Thou're a stranger to me; and I doän't allow no strangers to preach to me. So shut up! I'll have nowt more to say to thee."

There was a peremptoriness, a force of character, and a display of firmness and self-assurance in his tone and manner, which stamped him with a distinct individualism, and made it evident that in his own particular way he was distinct from the class in which his lot was cast. He, further than that, gave me the idea that he was designing and secretive; and given that he had been educated and well trained, he might have made his mark in the world. My interview with him had been instructive, and my opinion that he might prove a very important factor in working out the problem was strengthened; but at that stage of the inquiry I would not have taken upon myself to say, with anything like definiteness, that he was directly responsible for the death of the two gentlemen, whose mysterious ending had caused such a profound sensation. But the reader of this narrative will now see for himself that of all men, so far as one could determine then, who might have been interested in the death of Mr. Charnworth and Mr. Trankler, Job Panton stood out most conspicuously. His motive for destroying them was one of the most powerful of human passions – namely, jealousy, which in his case was likely to assume a very violent form, inasmuch as there was no evenly balanced judgement, no capability of philosophical reasoning, calculated to restrain the fierce, crude passion of the determined and self-willed man.

A wounded tiger is fiercer and more dangerous than an unwounded one, and an ignorant and unreasoning man is far more likely to be led to excess by a sense of wrong, than one who is capable of reflecting and moralizing. Of course, if I had been the impossible detective of fiction, endowed with the absurd attributes of being able to tell the story of a man's life from the way the tip of his nose was formed, or the number of hairs on his head, or by the shape and size of his teeth, or by the way he held his pipe when smoking, or from the kind of liquor he consumed, or the hundred and one utterly ridiculous and burlesque signs which are so easily read by the detective prig of modern creation, I might have come to a different conclusion with reference to Job Panton. But my work had to be carried out on very different lines, and I had to be guided by certain deductive inferences, aided by an intimate knowledge of human nature, and of the laws which, more or less in every case of crime, govern the criminal.

I have already set forth my unalterable opinion that Charnworth and Trankler had been murdered; and so far as I had proceeded up to this point, I had heard and seen enough to warrant me, in my own humble judgement, in at least suspecting rob Panton of being guilty of the murder. But there was one thing that puzzled me greatly. When I first commenced my inquiries, and was made acquainted with all the extraordinary medical aspects of the case, I argued with myself that if it was murder, it was murder carried out upon very original lines. Some potent, swift and powerful poison must have been suddenly and secretly introduced into the blood of the victim. The bite of a cobra, or of the still more fearful and deadly Fer de lance of the West Indies, might have produced symptoms similar to those observed in the two men; but happily our beautiful and quiet woods and gardens of England are not infested with these deadly reptiles, and one had to search for the causes elsewhere. Now everyone knows that the notorious Lucrezia Borgia, and the Marchioness of Brinvilliers, made use of means for accomplishing the death of those whom they were anxious to get out of the way, which were at once effective and secret. These means consisted, amongst others, of introducing into the blood of the intended victim some subtle poison, by the medium of a scratch or puncture. This little and fatal wound could be given by the scratch of a pin, or the sharpened stone of a ring, and in such a way that the victim would be all unconscious of it until the deadly poison so insidiously introduced began to course through his veins, and to sap the props of his life. With these facts in my mind, I asked myself if in the Dead Wood Hall tragedies some similar means had been used; and in order to have competent and authoritative opinion to guide me, I journeyed back to London to consult the eminent chemist and scientist, Professor Lucraft. This gentleman had made a lifelong study of the toxic effect of ptomaines on the human system, and of the various poisons used by savage tribes for tipping their arrows and spears. Enlightened as he was on the subject, he confessed that there were hundreds of these deadly poisons, of which the modern chemist knew absolutely nothing; but he expressed a decided opinion that there were many that would produce all the effects and symptoms observable in the cases of Charnworth and Trankler. And he particularly instanced some of the, herbal extracts used by various tribes of Indians, who wander in the interior of the little known country of Ecuador, and he cited as an authority Mr. Hart Thompson, the botanist who travelled from Quito right through Ecuador to the Amazon. This gentleman reported that he found a vegetable poison in use by the natives for poisoning the tips of their arrows and spears of so deadly and virulent a nature, that a scratch even on a panther would bring about the death of the animal within an hour.

Armed with these facts, I returned to Cheshire, and continued my investigations on the assumption that some sir deadly destroyer of life had been used to put Charnworth and Trankler out of the way. But necessarily I was led to question whether or not it was likely that an untravelled and ignorant man like Job Panton could have known anything about such poisons and their uses. This was a stumbling block; and while I was convinced that Panton had a strong motive for the crime, I was doubtful if he could have been in possession of the means for committing it. At last, in order to try and get evidence on this point, I resolved to search the place in which he lived. He had for along time occupied lodgings in the house of a widow woman in Knutsford, and I subjected his rooms to a thorough and critical search, but without finding a sign of anything calculated to justify my suspicion.

I freely confess that at this stage I began to feel that the problem was a hopeless one, and that I should fail to work it out. My depression, however, did not last long. It was not my habit to acknowledge defeat so long as there were probabilities to guide me, so I began to make inquiries about Panton's relatives, and these inquiries elicited the fact that he had been in the habit of making frequent journeys to Manchester to see an uncle. I soon found that this uncle had been a sailor, and had been one of a small expedition which had travelled through Peru and Ecuador in search of gold. Now, this was a discovery indeed, and the full value of it will be understood when it is taken in connection with the information given to me by Professor Lucraft. Let us see how it works out logically.

Panton's uncle was a sailor and a traveller. He had travelled through Peru, and had been into the interior of Ecuador.

Panton was in the habit of visiting his uncle.

Could the uncle have wandered through Ecuador without hearing something of the marvellous poisons used by the natives?

Having been connected with an exploring expedition, it was reasonable to assume that he was a man of good intelligence, and of an inquiring turn of mind.

Equally probable was it that he had brought home some of the deadly poisons or poisoned implements used by the Indians. Granted that, and what more likely than that he talked of his knowledge and possessions to his nephew? The nephew, brooding on his wrongs, and seeing the means within his grasp of secretly avenging himself on those whom he counted his rivals, obtained the means from his uncle's collection of putting his rivals to death, in a way which to him would seem to be impossible to detect. I had seen enough of Panton to feel sure that he had all the intelligence and cunning necessary for planning and carrying out the deed.

A powerful link in the chain of evidence had now been forged, and I proceeded a step further. After a consultation with the chief inspector of police, who, however, by no means shared my views, I applied for a warrant for Panton's arrest, although I saw that to establish legal proof of his guilt would be extraordinarily difficult, for his uncle at that time was at sea, somewhere in the southern hemisphere. Moreover, the whole case rested upon such a hypothetical basis, that it seemed doubtful whether, even supposing a magistrate would commit, a jury would convict. But I was not daunted; and, having succeeded so far in giving a practical shape to my theory, I did not intend to draw back. So I set to work to endeavour to discover the weapon which had been used for wounding Charnworth and Trankler, so that the poison, might take effect. This, of course, was the *crux* of the whole affair. The discovery of the medium by which the death-scratch was given would forge almost the last link necessary to ensure a conviction.

Now, in each case there was pretty conclusive evidence that there had been no struggle. This fact justified the belief that the victim was struck silently, and probably unknown to himself. What were the probabilities of that being the case? Assuming that Panton was guilty of the crime, how was it that he, being an inferior, was allowed to come within striking distance of his victims? The most curious thing was that both men had been scratched on the left side of the neck. Charnworth had been killed in his friend's garden on a summer night. Trankler had fallen in mid-day in the depths of a forest. There was an interval of two years between the death of the one man and the death of the other, yet each had a scratch on the left side of the neck. That could not have been a mere coincidence. It was design.

The next point for consideration was, how did Panton – always assuming that he was the criminal – get access to Mr. Trankler's grounds? Firstly, the grounds were extensive, and in connection with a plantation of young fir trees. When Charnworth was found, he was lying behind a clump of rhododendron bushes, and near where the grounds were merged into the plantation, a somewhat dilapidated oak fence separating the two. These details before us make it clear that Panton could have had no difficulty in gaining access to the plantation, and thence to the grounds. But how came it that he was there just at the time that Charnworth was strolling about? It seemed stretching a point very much to suppose that he could have been loafing about on the mere chance of seeing Charnworth. And the only hypothesis that squared in with intelligent reasoning, was that the victim had been lured into the grounds. But this necessarily presupposed a confederate. Close inquiry elicited the fact that Panton was in the habit of going to the house. He knew most of the servants, and frequently accompanied young Trankler on his shooting excursions, and periodically he spent half a day or so in the gun room at the house, in order that he might clean up all the guns, for which he was paid a small sum every month. These circumstances cleared the way of difficulties to a very considerable extent. I was unable, however, to go beyond that, for I could not ascertain the means that had been used to lure Mr. Charnworth into the garden – if he had been lured; and I felt sure that he had been. But so much had to remain for the time being a mystery.

Having obtained the warrant to arrest Panton, I proceeded to execute it. He seemed thunderstruck when told that he was arrested on a charge of having been instrumental in bringing about the death of Charnworth and Trankler. For a brief space of time he seemed to collapse, and lose his presence of mind. But suddenly, with an apparent effort, he recovered himself, and said, with a strange smile on his face –

"You've got to prove it, and that you can never do."

His manner and this remark were hardly compatible with innocence, but I clearly recognized the difficulties of proof. From that moment the fellow assumed a self-assured air, and to those with whom he was brought in contact he would remark:

"I'm as innocent as a lamb, and them as says I done the deed have got to prove it."

In my endeavour to get further evidence to strengthen my case, I managed to obtain from Job Panton's uncle's brother, who followed the occupation of an engine-minder in a large cotton factory in Oldham, an old chest containing a quantity of lumber. The uncle, on going to sea again, left this chest in charge of his brother. A careful examination of the contents proved that they consisted of a very miscellaneous collection of odds and ends, including two or three small, carved wooden idols from some savage country; some stone weapons, such as are used by the North American Indians; strings of cowrie shells, a pair of moccasins, feathers of various kinds; a few dried specimens of strange birds; and last, though not least, a small bamboo case containing a dozen tiny sharply pointed darts, feathered at the thick end; while in a stone box, about three inches square, was a viscid thick gummy looking substance of a very dark brown colour, and giving off a sickening and most disagreeable, though faint odour. These things I at once submitted to Professor Lucraft, who expressed an opinion that the gummy substance in the stone box was a vegetable poison, used probably to poison the dares with. He lost no time in experimentalizing with this substance, as well as with the darts. With these darts he scratched guinea-pigs, rabbits, a dog, a cat, a hen, and a young pig, and in each case death ensued in periods of time ranging from a quarter of an hour to two hours. By means of a subcutaneous injection into a rabbit of a minute portion of the gummy substance, about the size of a pea, which had been thinned with alcohol, he produced death in exactly seven minutes. A small monkey was next procured, and slightly scratched on the neck with one of the poisoned darts. In a very short time the poor animal exhibited the most distressing symptoms, and in half an hour it was dead, and a post-mortem examination revealed many of the peculiar effect which had been observed in Charnworth's and Trankler's bodies. Various other exhaustive experiments were carried out, all of which confirmed the deadly nature of these minute poison-darts, which could be puffed through a hollow tube to a great distance, and after some practice, with unerring aim. Analysis of the gummy substance in the box proved it to be a violent vegetable poison; innocuous when swallowed, but singularly active and deadly when introduced direct into the blood.

On the strength of these facts, the magistrate duly committed Job Panton to take his trial at the next assizes, on a charge of murder, although there was not a scrap of evidence forthcoming to prove that he had ever been in possession of any of the darts or the poison; and unless such evidence was forthcoming, it was felt that the case for the prosecution must break down, however clear the mere guilt of the man might seem.

In due course, Panton was put on his trial at Chester, and the principal witness against him was Hester Downie, who was subjected to a very severe cross-examination, which left not a shadow of a doubt that she and Panton had at one time been close sweethearts. But her cousin Jessie Turner proved a tempter of great subtlety. It was made clear that she poisoned the girl's mind against her humble lover. Although it could not be proved, it is highly probable that Jessie Turner was a creature of and in the pay of Mr. Charnworth, who seemed to have been very much attracted by him. Hester's connection with Charnworth half maddened Panton, who made frantic appeals to her to be true to him, appeals to which she turned a deaf ear. That Trankler knew her in Charnworth's time was also brought out, and after Charnworth's death she smiled favourably on the young man. On the morning that Trankler's shooting-party went out to Mere Forest, Panton was one of the beaters employed by the party.

So much was proved; so much was made as clear as daylight, and it opened the way for any number of inferences. But the last and most important link was never forthcoming. Panton was defended by an able and unscrupulous counsel, who urged with tremendous force on the notice of the jury, that firstly, not one of the medical witnesses would undertake to swear that the two men had died from the effects of poison similar to that found in the old chest which had belonged to the prisoner's uncle; and secondly, there was not one scrap of evidence tending to prove that Panton had ever been in possession of poisoned darts, or had ever had access to the chest in which they were kept. These two points were also made much of by the learned judge in his summing up. He was at pains to make clear that there was a doubt involved, and that mere inference ought not to be allowed to outweigh the doubt when a human being was on trial for his life. Although circumstantially the evidence very strongly pointed to the probability of the prisoner having killed both men, nevertheless, in the absence of the strong proof which the law demanded, the way was opened for the escape of a suspected man, and it was far better to let the law be cheated of its due, than that an innocent man should suffer. At the same time, the judge went on, two gentlemen had met their deaths in a manner which had baffled medical science, and no one was forthcoming who would undertake to say that they had been killed in the manner suggested by the prosecution, and yet it had been shown that the terrible and powerful poison found in the old chest, and which there was reason to believe had been brought from some part of the little known country near the sources of the mighty Amazon, would produce all the effects which were observed in they bodies of Charnworth and Trankler. The chest, furthermore, in which the poison was discovered, was in the possession of Panton's uncle. Panton had a powerful motive in the shape of consuming jealousy for getting rid of his more favoured rivals; and though he was one of the shooting-party in Mere Forest on the day that Trankler lost his life, no evidence had been produced to prove that he was on the premises of Dead Wood Hall, on the night that Charnworth died. If, in weighing all these points of evidence, the jury were of opinion circumstantial evidence was inadequate, then it was their duty to give the prisoner – whose life was in their hands the benefit of the doubt.

The jury retired, and were absent three long hours, and it became known that they could not agree. Ultimately, they returned into court, and pronounced a verdict of 'Not guilty.' In Scotland the verdict must and would have been *non proven*.

And so Job Panton went free, but an evil odour seemed to cling about him; he was shunned by his former companions, and many a suspicious glance was directed to him, and many a bated murmur was uttered as he passed by, until in a while he went forth beyond the seas, to the far wild west, as some said, and his haunts knew him no more.

The mystery is still a mystery; but how near I came to solving the problem of Dead Wood Hall it is for the reader to judge.

Mr. Happy Head

James Dorr

MR. HAPPYHEAD was a hawk, a vulture. A white Lammergeier, larger than eagles. He cruised the skies. He cruised people's thought-trains.

He cruised the city, in thought or in person, doting on crowds and filth and hunger. He studied the tragic.

Mr. Happyhead's personal thoughts went back to a table, to flesh growing soft, but then muscles stiffening. His thoughts went to smiles forced on unhappy faces as skin became waxy, as lips and finger- and toenails paled. His thoughts went to red-green discolorations, then smells of putrescence.

These things he had known too.

Except with release, with tissue decaying, with fluids leaking from head and anus, with gas-blisters forming, with swellings, explosions, Mr. Happyhead discovered freedom. He now had a mission, to share his good fortune.

He preyed on the city's own.

* * *

Catching his breath, Mr. Happyhead entered his first thought. He picked it at random. He found himself staring into a bar mirror, eying a women who had just come through the door behind him.

"Would you care to dance?" he asked, turning around and smiling broadly, but also blushing. He knew he *was* married.

The woman looked him up and down, then frowned and turned back to the friends she'd come in with. She started laughing.

Mr. Happyhead turned even redder, but only ordered another whiskey. He drank it slowly, taking his time, even though the thought of a wife who would wait up late for him – not married that long, their love was still ardent – tried to slip through from the back of his mind. He watched the woman, tall and with red hair, laughing and talking with her companions, occasionally dancing when *other* men asked her, through the dust-spiderwebbed behind-bar mirror.

He waited until she and her friends prepared to leave, then finished himself and followed after, always keeping a half block of shadows, of darkness between them. He waited as first one, and then another, and then the last of the redhead's companions turned their own ways in the spiraling blackness, taking their own paths to go to their own homes. And still he waited.

He stood outside and noted the window that suddenly lit up after she had gone into a building. He counted the windows from the building's corner, the floors from the sidewalk. He went inside too and climbed the stairs, then counted the doors from the end of the hallway, estimating doors against windows, until he arrived at the one with a dim hint of light still beneath it.

He waited patiently, until that, too, went dark, then counted slowly to sixty, one hundred, six hundred, a thousand, then counted again to be sure she was sleeping, before, with a twist learned from when he was younger and that used his own body, he broke her door lock. He eased her door open.

He shut it behind him, then found a table lamp, following its cord by feel to its socket. He carried it with him as his eyes adjusted to the inside darkness.

Interior doors: he found one to the bathroom. Another, that opened into the kitchen, yielded a sharp knife.

The third opened onto his quarry, sleeping.

He leaned behind her, then tied her hands quickly with the lamp cord. He thrust a pillowcase into her mouth when it opened to scream.

He found another lamp in the bedroom and used its cord to bind her feet as well, then bind both hands and feet to the solid bed.

As the dawn came, he became an artist, carving illustrations in carmine to match her hair with the knife from the kitchen. He stepped back often, admiring his work. Adjusting the pillowcase now and again, lest her screams, then her whispers, disturb his train of thought. And, behind that thought, he felt another thought, that of a decent man not that long married, wondering…admiring…thinking, perhaps, of a wife who was waiting.

* * *

Mr. Happyhead left joy behind him. He left people with ideas to do things they would not do had he not helped them. He left the counterman in a diner whose boss had just – once again – threatened to fire him, a notion of how to hurt his boss's business. And then, on his break, Mr. Happyhead left him facing the kitchen pantry, contemplating the box of rat poison he knew was inside it.

* * *

Mr. Happyhead often remembered the time of his boyhood. His father. His mother. His mother's brother who taught him things most boys did not learn till later. He thought of his studies, not so much in school as on weekends and summers. His learning about birds.

His lust for flying.

He studied pigeons, catching them, sometimes, and finding out the ways their wings bent. When they would not obey, he gave them to cats.

He studied their talons.

* * *

Mr. Happyhead loved women most. He entered their thoughts often, savoring their difference. He taught them power.

He spoke to women, telling them how, through his own experience, they could tempt men to do their bidding. He transcended space and time, becoming Eva Braun whispering to Hitler. Cleopatra inciting Mark Antony.

He taught sisters how to enjoy their brothers.

* * *

When Mr. Happyhead had been a boy, one summer he went to the beach with his parents. There he was able to contemplate sea gulls. He watched, fascinated, as they flew with shellfish clutched in their claws, circling higher, until, over rocks, they dropped their prey, splitting their armor so they could eat.

He watched sea gull mothers, guarding their nests. How, when fledglings from other nests wandered too far and blundered into the wrong territory, they pecked the intruders' heads into gray jelly and fed them to their own young. Ate what was left themselves.

Mr. Happyhead made an experiment, switching eggs from one nest to another, then young birds as well. He wore a catcher's mask when he did this, and thick, brown gloves.

He wore many masks as he grew older. As student. As citizen. Once, as a soldier. As workman.

As lover.

As man of the streets, first running errands for those with more power, then finding ways to gain power of his own. Worming his way into inner circles.

As loyalist. Henchman.

As one who was trusted.

When Mr. Happyhead was not working, he frequented zoos.

* * *

Mr. Happyhead played with children, and sometimes their mothers. He had a winning smile.

* * *

Mr. Happyhead liked seeing dentists. He liked the way the hygienist placed pointed hooks in his mouth, using a mirror to chip at his teeth. To chip the flecks away. When he was young, he sometimes had thought he might be a dentist's hygienist himself.

He liked seeing blood spit in white porcelain basins, watching its spiral flow.

When he was young, he had liked hawks and eagles. And then Lammergeiers, 'Bearded Vultures' according to the book his father got for him one Christmas. He'd seen it in a store, then begged for it almost all the way from Halloween. And his mother helped him.

"It's good that he wants to learn things," his mother would say nights at dinner.

"But books about vultures?" his father would answer. "I think that's morbid."

"Hawks and vultures," his mother had said. "And eagles too. Like our country's symbol. There's nothing wrong with that."

Mr. Happyhead's father had bought the book the morning after he'd beaten his wife. The evening before he had come home after working late and, tiring of the incessant argument, in their bedroom that night he'd slapped her. He'd bought the book as a kind of appeasement. They'd kissed and made up and wrapped it together and hid it in their bedroom closet.

Mr. Happyhead had not been intended to know this, except he'd been outside their door and listened.

He'd listened as well in the following years as their marriage continued its downward spiral. As the hittings became more frequent and Mr. Happyhead got gifts more often. Books and toys and camping equipment. Toy guns and airplanes.

But most of all, he still liked to think about Lammergeiers, described in the book as having wingspans greater than eagles' – some naturalists even thought they *were* eagles, though somewhat like vultures as well insofar as they ate the dead. He read about people in Eastern, Himalayan nations who placed their deceased on the tops of towers, waiting for the great, white birds to descend and devour them.

Some even thought that the huge birds were spirits.

* * *

Mr. Happyhead had his favorites, of those he flew into. A dentist's hygienist – he got in her head often and, through the hooks and the mirrors and probes, he drank in her feelings about her boyfriend. Her fear and hatred, and yet her greater fear that he might leave her. The beatings he gave *her*. And when the next patient got in the chair, the hooks in his mouth, the probe at his gumline, he had her let them out.

* * *

Mr. Happyhead grew into power, having learned how to manipulate people. He learned about violence, and when he should use it. He learned about money – when he could pay others.

He learned about greed.

But when his father had been found dead in his parents' bedroom, the .25 caliber bullet of a 'Saturday night special' lodged in his brain, and as his mother was dragged away weeping, that's when he had learned of joy. Joy as proactive. Joy as something he could himself plan, for himself or for others, and not simply wait to receive as a byproduct of other things that others did to him. Joy as fulfillment.

He never knew how to hate – never could understand its concept, at least in himself, though he knew it in others.

And when he found himself on a table, hearing a doctor explain to the young cop who'd brought him in about things like trauma, the force of powder grains tattooing skin, about entrance paths and shock waves and exits and hollowed out, larger and heavier bullets, that's when he had started to come to know freedom.

* * *

Mr. Happyhead came to suspect the mystics of Himalayan lands were on to something. He flew in the night air, no longer earthbound, as bird or not-bird – it did not matter.

He thought: *Birds have no teeth.*

He flew to his mother in Women's Prison and entered her head and found that she loved him. She had always loved him and, as he'd begun to nurture his own brushes with the law, had almost admired him. And he'd loved her also. He'd taught her things about prison bed sheets and how they could be torn in strips, twisted and knotted. How they could be looped from ceiling fixtures.

He found that she feared, though – that she was not ready. That freedom was not for her, at least not *that* night.

He learned about patience.

He had already known about waiting. Of waiting in ambush, or being ambushed himself. Of power conflicts. And now he learned endurance.

* * *

Mr. Happyhead flew to the man who had been his rival and, flying within his thoughts, drank of his triumph. Triumph became pride, and then pride hubris. He watched and he let it grow, he a nestling, a fledgling lodged in this other man's brain-cage, becoming in time a mother sea gull pecking away at any intrusive thoughts save those his own will and joy engendered.

He looked out at others, also outside the law, who had more power than this, his protégé, and through sheer savagery took them over. Expanding his domain.

He came in time to rule the whole town, and then the county, with numbers and gambling and prostitution.

He got himself noticed.

And when a yet larger gang from the state capital descended on this, *his* operation, he left his rival, flying back to the sky. Hovering. Waiting.

Enjoying patience – perhaps now and then breathing small suggestions into minds oh, so open to hear them – as his erstwhile rival – his *own* erstwhile killer – was trussed to a wooden chair. His clothes ripped from him. Knives brought out and worked with. Small knives not for killing, but only enjoying.

He watched and enjoyed and flew in and out of the pain and the redness, devouring driblets of soul with each passage, as flesh became weaker, yet never quite perished. As life hung on that night, and then for three others until the sculptors who carved became weary.

And still life hung on, until the police found the eyeless, tongueless, fingerless, flayed hulk that would continue to breathe and shit and take in nutrition from hospital needles for decades to come before finally expiring.

And one cop looked up then, out the abandoned warehouse window.

"Jeez, what's that?" he said as the stretcher bearers came in for their burden.

"I don't know – looks like a bird," his partner said, gazing out the window too now. "A big white bird. Some kind of big sea gull."

"Sea gull, my ass," the first one said. "It's as big as an eagle."

* * *

Mr. Happyhead read the newspapers. He read of other crimes and disasters. Of long suffering wives killed in suburban houses. Of children who talked back discovering silence. Of gang leaders, some more of whom he had once known, falling out over drugs and profits. He read about business – he liked the drug trade and wished to help it.

He went to the source. He became a pilot, and then a ship's captain. He formed an intimacy with policemen who lived on the take, and with their commissioners. He captured the mind and the soul of the woman who slept with the mayor.

He doted on guns – after all, did he not know himself what guns could do? – and cultivated in others their love as well.

He taught others how to use knives and razors, yet others explosives, sometimes learning himself from the thoughts of those he had entered. He found himself in a fortified building, surrounded by armed men, whispering to leaders they must not surrender. That rightness was with them.

He taught people courage.

And always the memories came back, of the cold table. Then of a tunnel that time of his own death. A dark, long tunnel. He'd thought about having read of such tunnels as he'd paced its distance, leaving his ruined flesh far behind him. He'd heard in his mind the voice of the doctor fading to near silence as, ahead of him, he thought he saw bright lights, felt warmth and comfort. But all he had read turned out to be lies.

He emerged on an ice field, cold, unrelenting, as cold as the table's top. What heat he felt proved no more than a memory.

A memory of first love, after a drunken pickup in a roadhouse. Of ripping her open after his passion had spent itself in her. Of slapping her. Stabbing her. Tearing her flesh as he later did others. As he wished his father had done that night of the book.

And now the others, the second, the third love, the fourth and those after, and friends, and grandparents, he now saw laughing as he emerged out of the dark of that tunnel. Laughing and smiling, their faces forgiveness.

Laughing at *him*, he thought.

Mr. Happyhead screamed his rejection – *this vision was not true!* – then struck with his fists at the white-robed figures, drowning himself in their spurting blood. Drinking their screams. Their shrieks. Taking and wrapping himself in their whiteness. Hearing their shattered bone.

Spinning, he coursed again into the dark.

And felt the wind. Felt the wind at the outstretched tips of wing-feathers as, opening hooded eyes, now he was swooping over the city. A city of nighttime.

Below, he saw neon lights.

* * *

Mr. Happyhead was happy.

The Brazilian Cat

Arthur Conan Doyle

IT IS HARD LUCK on a young fellow to have expensive tastes, great expectations, aristocratic connections, but no actual money in his pocket, and no profession by which he may earn any. The fact was that my father, a good, sanguine, easy-going man, had such confidence in the wealth and benevolence of his bachelor elder brother, Lord Southerton, that he took it for granted that I, his only son, would never be called upon to earn a living for myself. He imagined that if there were not a vacancy for me on the great Southerton Estates, at least there would be found some post in that diplomatic service which still remains the special preserve of our privileged classes. He died too early to realize how false his calculations had been. Neither my uncle nor the State took the slightest notice of me, or showed any interest in my career. An occasional brace of pheasants, or basket of hares, was all that ever reached me to remind me that I was heir to Otwell House and one of the richest estates in the country. In the meantime, I found myself a bachelor and man about town, living in a suite of apartments in Grosvenor Mansions, with no occupation save that of pigeon-shooting and polo-playing at Hurlingham. Month by month I realized that it was more and more difficult to get the brokers to renew my bills, or to cash any further post-obits upon an unentailed property. Ruin lay right across my path, and every day I saw it clearer, nearer, and more absolutely unavoidable.

What made me feel my own poverty the more was that, apart from the great wealth of Lord Southerton, all my other relations were fairly well-to-do. The nearest of these was Everard King, my father's nephew and my own first cousin, who had spent an adventurous life in Brazil, and had now returned to this country to settle down on his fortune. We never knew how he made his money, but he appeared to have plenty of it, for he bought the estate of Greylands, near Clipton-on-the-Marsh, in Suffolk. For the first year of his residence in England he took no more notice of me than my miserly uncle; but at last one summer morning, to my very great relief and joy, I received a letter asking me to come down that very day and spend a short visit at Greylands Court. I was expecting a rather long visit to Bankruptcy Court at the time, and this interruption seemed almost providential. If I could only get on terms with this unknown relative of mine, I might pull through yet. For the family credit he could not let me go entirely to the wall. I ordered my valet to pack my valise, and I set off the same evening for Clipton-on-the-Marsh.

After changing at Ipswich, a little local train deposited me at a small, deserted station lying amidst a rolling grassy country, with a sluggish and winding river curving in and out amidst the valleys, between high, silted banks, which showed that we were within reach of the tide. No carriage was awaiting me (I found afterwards that my telegram had been delayed), so I hired a dogcart at the local inn. The driver, an excellent fellow, was full of my relative's praises, and I learned from him that Mr. Everard King was already a name to conjure with in that part of the county. He had entertained the school-children, he had thrown his grounds open to visitors, he had subscribed to charities – in short, his benevolence had been so universal that my driver could only account for it on the supposition that he had parliamentary ambitions.

My attention was drawn away from my driver's panegyric by the appearance of a very beautiful bird which settled on a telegraph-post beside the road. At first I thought that it was a jay, but it was larger, with a brighter plumage. The driver accounted for its presence at once by saying that it belonged to the very man whom we were about to visit. It seems that the acclimatization of foreign creatures was one of his hobbies, and that he had brought with him from Brazil a number of birds and beasts which he was endeavouring to rear in England. When once we had passed the gates of Greylands Park we had ample evidence of this taste of his. Some small spotted deer, a curious wild pig known, I believe, as a peccary, a gorgeously feathered oriole, some sort of armadillo, and a singular lumbering in-toed beast like a very fat badger, were among the creatures which I observed as we drove along the winding avenue.

Mr. Everard King, my unknown cousin, was standing in person upon the steps of his house, for he had seen us in the distance, and guessed that it was I. His appearance was very homely and benevolent, short and stout, forty-five years old, perhaps, with a round, good-humoured face, burned brown with the tropical sun, and shot with a thousand wrinkles. He wore white linen clothes, in true planter style, with a cigar between his lips, and a large Panama hat upon the back of his head. It was such a figure as one associates with a verandahed bungalow, and it looked curiously out of place in front of this broad, stone English mansion, with its solid wings and its Palladio pillars before the doorway.

"My dear!" he cried, glancing over his shoulder; "my dear, here is our guest! Welcome, welcome to Greylands! I am delighted to make your acquaintance, Cousin Marshall, and I take it as a great compliment that you should honour this sleepy little country place with your presence."

Nothing could be more hearty than his manner, and he set me at my ease in an instant. But it needed all his cordiality to atone for the frigidity and even rudeness of his wife, a tall, haggard woman, who came forward at his summons. She was, I believe, of Brazilian extraction, though she spoke excellent English, and I excused her manners on the score of her ignorance of our customs. She did not attempt to conceal, however, either then or afterwards, that I was no very welcome visitor at Greylands Court. Her actual words were, as a rule, courteous, but she was the possessor of a pair of particularly expressive dark eyes, and I read in them very clearly from the first that she heartily wished me back in London once more.

However, my debts were too pressing and my designs upon my wealthy relative were too vital for me to allow them to be upset by the ill-temper of his wife, so I disregarded her coldness and reciprocated the extreme cordiality of his welcome. No pains had been spared by him to make me comfortable. My room was a charming one. He implored me to tell him anything which could add to my happiness. It was on the tip of my tongue to inform him that a blank cheque would materially help towards that end, but I felt that it might be premature in the present state of our acquaintance. The dinner was excellent, and as we sat together afterwards over his Havanas and coffee, which later he told me was specially prepared upon his own plantation, it seemed to me that all my driver's eulogies were justified, and that I had never met a more large-hearted and hospitable man.

But, in spite of his cheery good nature, he was a man with a strong will and a fiery temper of his own. Of this I had an example upon the following morning. The curious aversion which Mrs. Everard King had conceived towards me was so strong, that her manner at breakfast was almost offensive. But her meaning became unmistakable when her husband had quitted the room.

"The best train in the day is at twelve-fifteen," said she.

"But I was not thinking of going today," I answered, frankly – perhaps even defiantly, for I was determined not to be driven out by this woman.

"Oh, if it rests with you –" said she, and stopped with a most insolent expression in her eyes.

"I am sure," I answered, "that Mr. Everard King would tell me if I were outstaying my welcome."

"What's this? What's this?" said a voice, and there he was in the room. He had overheard my last words, and a glance at our faces had told him the rest. In an instant his chubby, cheery face set into an expression of absolute ferocity.

"Might I trouble you to walk outside, Marshall?" said he. (I may mention that my own name is Marshall King).

He closed the door behind me, and then, for an instant, I heard him talking in a low voice of concentrated passion to his wife. This gross breach of hospitality had evidently hit upon his tenderest point. I am no eavesdropper, so I walked out on to the lawn. Presently I heard a hurried step behind me, and there was the lady, her face pale with excitement, and her eyes red with tears.

"My husband has asked me to apologize to you, Mr. Marshall King," said she, standing with downcast eyes before me.

"Please do not say another word, Mrs. King."

Her dark eyes suddenly blazed out at me.

"You fool!" she hissed, with frantic vehemence, and turning on her heel swept back to the house.

The insult was so outrageous, so insufferable, that I could only stand staring after her in bewilderment. I was still there when my host joined me. He was his cheery, chubby self once more.

"I hope that my wife has apologized for her foolish remarks," said he.

"Oh, yes – yes, certainly!"

He put his hand through my arm and walked with me up and down the lawn.

"You must not take it seriously," said he. "It would grieve me inexpressibly if you curtailed your visit by one hour. The fact is – there is no reason why there should be any concealment between relatives – that my poor dear wife is incredibly jealous. She hates that anyone – male or female – should for an instant come between us. Her ideal is a desert island and an eternal tete-a-tete. That gives you the clue to her actions, which are, I confess, upon this particular point, not very far removed from mania. Tell me that you will think no more of it."

"No, no; certainly not."

"Then light this cigar and come round with me and see my little menagerie."

The whole afternoon was occupied by this inspection, which included all the birds, beasts, and even reptiles which he had imported. Some were free, some in cages, a few actually in the house. He spoke with enthusiasm of his successes and his failures, his births and his deaths, and he would cry out in his delight, like a schoolboy, when, as we walked, some gaudy bird would flutter up from the grass, or some curious beast slink into the cover. Finally he led me down a corridor which extended from one wing of the house. At the end of this there was a heavy door with a sliding shutter in it, and beside it there projected from the wall an iron handle attached to a wheel and a drum. A line of stout bars extended across the passage.

"I am about to show you the jewel of my collection," said he. "There is only one other specimen in Europe, now that the Rotterdam cub is dead. It is a Brazilian cat."

"But how does that differ from any other cat?"

"You will soon see that," said he, laughing. "Will you kindly draw that shutter and look through?"

I did so, and found that I was gazing into a large, empty room, with stone flags, and small, barred windows upon the farther wall. In the centre of this room, lying in the middle of a golden patch of sunlight, there was stretched a huge creature, as large as a tiger, but as black and sleek as ebony. It was simply a very enormous and very well-kept black cat, and it cuddled up and basked in that yellow pool of light exactly as a cat would do. It was so graceful, so sinewy, and so gently and smoothly diabolical, that I could not take my eyes from the opening.

"Isn't he splendid?" said my host, enthusiastically.

"Glorious! I never saw such a noble creature."

"Some people call it a black puma, but really it is not a puma at all. That fellow is nearly eleven feet from tail to tip. Four years ago he was a little ball of black fluff, with two yellow eyes staring out of it. He was sold me as a new-born cub up in the wild country at the head-waters of the Rio Negro. They speared his mother to death after she had killed a dozen of them."

"They are ferocious, then?"

"The most absolutely treacherous and bloodthirsty creatures upon earth. You talk about a Brazilian cat to an up-country Indian, and see him get the jumps. They prefer humans to game. This fellow has never tasted living blood yet, but when he does he will be a terror. At present he won't stand anyone but me in his den. Even Baldwin, the groom, dare not go near him. As to me, I am his mother and father in one."

As he spoke he suddenly, to my astonishment, opened the door and slipped in, closing it instantly behind him. At the sound of his voice the huge, lithe creature rose, yawned and rubbed its round, black head affectionately against his side, while he patted and fondled it.

"Now, Tommy, into your cage!" said he.

The monstrous cat walked over to one side of the room and coiled itself up under a grating. Everard King came out, and taking the iron handle which I have mentioned, he began to turn it. As he did so the line of bars in the corridor began to pass through a slot in the wall and closed up the front of this grating, so as to make an effective cage. When it was in position he opened the door once more and invited me into the room, which was heavy with the pungent, musty smell peculiar to the great carnivora.

"That's how we work it," said he. "We give him the run of the room for exercise, and then at night we put him in his cage. You can let him out by turning the handle from the passage, or you can, as you have seen, coop him up in the same way. No, no, you should not do that!"

I had put my hand between the bars to pat the glossy, heaving flank. He pulled it back, with a serious face.

"I assure you that he is not safe. Don't imagine that because I can take liberties with him anyone else can. He is very exclusive in his friends – aren't you, Tommy? Ah, he hears his lunch coming to him! Don't you, boy?"

A step sounded in the stone-flagged passage, and the creature had sprung to his feet, and was pacing up and down the narrow cage, his yellow eyes gleaming, and his scarlet tongue rippling and quivering over the white line of his jagged teeth. A groom entered with a coarse joint upon a tray, and thrust it through the bars to him. He pounced lightly upon it, carried it off to the corner, and there, holding it between his paws, tore and wrenched at it, raising his bloody muzzle every now and then to look at us. It was a malignant and yet fascinating sight.

"You can't wonder that I am fond of him, can you?" said my host, as we left the room, "especially when you consider that I have had the rearing of him. It was no joke bringing him over from the centre of South America; but here he is safe and sound – and, as I have said, far the most perfect specimen in Europe. The people at the Zoo are dying to have him, but I really can't part with him. Now, I think that I have inflicted my hobby upon you long enough, so we cannot do better than follow Tommy's example, and go to our lunch."

My South American relative was so engrossed by his grounds and their curious occupants, that I hardly gave him credit at first for having any interests outside them. That he had some, and pressing ones, was soon borne in upon me by the number of telegrams which he received. They arrived at all hours, and were always opened by him with the utmost eagerness and anxiety upon his face. Sometimes I imagined that it must be the Turf, and sometimes the Stock Exchange, but certainly he had some very urgent business going forwards which was not transacted upon the Downs of Suffolk. During the six days of my visit he had never fewer than three or four telegrams a day, and sometimes as many as seven or eight.

I had occupied these six days so well, that by the end of them I had succeeded in getting upon the most cordial terms with my cousin. Every night we had sat up late in the billiard-room, he telling me the most extraordinary stories of his adventures in America – stories so desperate and reckless, that I could hardly associate them with the brown little, chubby man before me. In return, I ventured upon some of my own reminiscences of London life, which interested him so much, that he vowed he would come up to Grosvenor Mansions and stay with me. He was anxious to see the faster side of city life, and certainly, though I say it, he could not have chosen a more competent guide. It was not until the last day of my visit that I ventured to approach that which was on my mind. I told him frankly about my pecuniary difficulties and my impending ruin, and I asked his advice – though I hoped for something more solid. He listened attentively, puffing hard at his cigar.

"But surely," said he, "you are the heir of our relative, Lord Southerton?"

"I have every reason to believe so, but he would never make me any allowance."

"No, no, I have heard of his miserly ways. My poor Marshall, your position has been a very hard one. By the way, have you heard any news of Lord Southerton's health lately?"

"He has always been in a critical condition ever since my childhood."

"Exactly – a creaking hinge, if ever there was one. Your inheritance may be a long way off. Dear me, how awkwardly situated you are!"

"I had some hopes, sir, that you, knowing all the facts, might be inclined to advance –"

"Don't say another word, my dear boy," he cried, with the utmost cordiality; "we shall talk it over tonight, and I give you my word that whatever is in my power shall be done."

I was not sorry that my visit was drawing to a close, for it is unpleasant to feel that there is one person in the house who eagerly desires your departure. Mrs. King's sallow face and forbidding eyes had become more and more hateful to me. She was no longer actively rude – her fear of her husband prevented her – but she pushed her insane jealousy to the extent of ignoring me, never addressing me, and in every way making my stay at Greylands as uncomfortable as she could. So offensive was her manner during that last day, that I should certainly have left had it not been for that interview with my host in the evening which would, I hoped, retrieve my broken fortunes.

It was very late when it occurred, for my relative, who had been receiving even more telegrams than usual during the day, went off to his study after dinner, and only emerged when the household had retired to bed. I heard him go round locking the doors, as custom was of a night, and finally he joined me in the billiard-room. His stout figure was wrapped in a dressing-gown, and he wore a pair of red Turkish slippers without any heels. Settling down into an arm-chair, he brewed himself a glass of grog, in which I could not help noticing that the whisky considerably predominated over the water.

"My word!" said he, "what a night!"

It was, indeed. The wind was howling and screaming round the house, and the latticed windows rattled and shook as if they were coming in. The glow of the yellow lamps and the flavour of our cigars seemed the brighter and more fragrant for the contrast.

"Now, my boy," said my host, "we have the house and the night to ourselves. Let me have an idea of how your affairs stand, and I will see what can be done to set them in order. I wish to hear every detail."

Thus encouraged, I entered into a long exposition, in which all my tradesmen and creditors from my landlord to my valet, figured in turn. I had notes in my pocket-book, and I marshalled my facts, and gave, I flatter myself, a very businesslike statement of my own unbusinesslike ways and lamentable position. I was depressed, however, to notice that my companion's eyes were vacant and his attention elsewhere. When he did occasionally throw out a remark it was so entirely perfunctory and pointless, that I was sure he had not in the least followed my remarks. Every now and then he roused himself and put on some show of interest, asking me to repeat or to explain more fully, but it was always to sink once more into the same brown study. At last he rose and threw the end of his cigar into the grate.

"I'll tell you what, my boy," said he. "I never had a head for figures, so you will excuse me. You must jot it all down upon paper, and let me have a note of the amount. I'll understand it when I see it in black and white."

The proposal was encouraging. I promised to do so.

"And now it's time we were in bed. By Jove, there's one o'clock striking in the hall."

The tingling of the chiming clock broke through the deep roar of the gale. The wind was sweeping past with the rush of a great river.

"I must see my cat before I go to bed," said my host. "A high wind excites him. Will you come?"

"Certainly," said I.

"Then tread softly and don't speak, for everyone is asleep."

We passed quietly down the lamp-lit Persian-rugged hall, and through the door at the farther end. All was dark in the stone corridor, but a stable lantern hung on a hook, and my host took it down and lit it. There was no grating visible in the passage, so I knew that the beast was in its cage.

"Come in!" said my relative, and opened the door.

A deep growling as we entered showed that the storm had really excited the creature. In the flickering light of the lantern, we saw it, a huge black mass coiled in the corner of its den and throwing a squat, uncouth shadow upon the whitewashed wall. Its tail switched angrily among the straw.

"Poor Tommy is not in the best of tempers," said Everard King, holding up the lantern and looking in at him. "What a black devil he looks, doesn't he? I must give him a little supper to put him in a better humour. Would you mind holding the lantern for a moment?"

I took it from his hand and he stepped to the door.

"His larder is just outside here," said he. "You will excuse me for an instant won't you?" He passed out, and the door shut with a sharp metallic click behind him.

That hard crisp sound made my heart stand still. A sudden wave of terror passed over me. A vague perception of some monstrous treachery turned me cold. I sprang to the door, but there was no handle upon the inner side.

"Here!" I cried. "Let me out!"

"All right! Don't make a row!" said my host from the passage. "You've got the light all right."

"Yes, but I don't care about being locked in alone like this."

"Don't you?" I heard his hearty, chuckling laugh. "You won't be alone long."

"Let me out, sir!" I repeated angrily. "I tell you I don't allow practical jokes of this sort."

"Practical is the word," said he, with another hateful chuckle. And then suddenly I heard, amidst the roar of the storm, the creak and whine of the winch-handle turning and the rattle of the grating as it passed through the slot. Great God, he was letting loose the Brazilian cat!

In the light of the lantern I saw the bars sliding slowly before me. Already there was an opening a foot wide at the farther end. With a scream I seized the last bar with my hands and pulled with the strength of a madman. I *was* a madman with rage and horror. For a minute or more I held the thing motionless. I knew that he was straining with all his force upon the handle, and that the leverage was sure to overcome me. I gave inch by inch, my feet sliding along the stones, and all the time I begged and prayed this inhuman monster to save me from this horrible death. I conjured him by his kinship. I reminded him that I was his guest; I begged to know what harm I had ever done him. His only answers were the tugs and jerks upon the handle, each of which, in spite of all my struggles, pulled another bar through the opening. Clinging and clutching, I was dragged across the whole front of the cage, until at last, with aching wrists and lacerated fingers, I gave up the hopeless struggle. The grating clanged back as I released it, and an instant later I heard the shuffle of the Turkish slippers in the passage, and the slam of the distant door. Then everything was silent.

The creature had never moved during this time. He lay still in the corner, and his tail had ceased switching. This apparition of a man adhering to his bars and dragged screaming across him had apparently filled him with amazement. I saw his great eyes staring steadily at me. I had dropped the lantern when I seized the bars, but it still burned upon the floor, and I made a movement to grasp it, with some idea that its light might protect me. But the instant I moved, the beast gave a deep and menacing growl. I stopped and stood still, quivering with fear in every limb. The cat (if one may call so fearful a creature by so homely a name) was not more than ten feet from me. The eyes glimmered like two disks of phosphorus in the darkness. They appalled and yet fascinated me. I could not take my own eyes from them. Nature plays strange tricks with us at such moments of intensity, and those glimmering lights waxed and waned with a steady rise and fall. Sometimes they seemed to be tiny points of extreme brilliancy – little electric sparks in the black obscurity – then they would widen and widen until all that corner of the room was filled with their shifting and sinister light. And then suddenly they went out altogether.

The beast had closed its eyes. I do not know whether there may be any truth in the old idea of the dominance of the human gaze, or whether the huge cat was simply drowsy, but the fact remains that, far from showing any symptom of attacking me, it simply rested its sleek, black head upon its huge forepaws and seemed to sleep. I stood, fearing to move lest I should rouse it into malignant life once more. But at least I was able to think clearly now that the baleful eyes were off me. Here I was shut up for the night with the ferocious beast. My own instincts, to say nothing of the words of the plausible villain who laid this trap for me, warned me that the animal was as savage as its master. How could I stave it off until morning? The door was hopeless, and so were the narrow, barred windows. There was no shelter anywhere in the bare, stone-flagged room. To cry for assistance was absurd. I knew that this den was an outhouse, and that the corridor which connected it with the house was at least a hundred feet long. Besides, with the gale thundering outside, my cries were not likely to be heard. I had only my own courage and my own wits to trust to.

And then, with a fresh wave of horror, my eyes fell upon the lantern. The candle had burned low, and was already beginning to gutter. In ten minutes it would be out. I had only ten minutes then in which to do something, for I felt that if I were once left in the dark with that fearful beast I should be incapable of action. The very thought of it paralysed me. I cast my despairing eyes round this chamber of death, and they rested upon one spot which seemed to promise I will not say safety, but less immediate and imminent danger than the open floor.

I have said that the cage had a top as well as a front, and this top was left standing when the front was wound through the slot in the wall. It consisted of bars at a few inches' interval, with stout wire netting between, and it rested upon a strong stanchion at each end. It stood now as a great barred canopy over the crouching figure in the corner. The space between this iron shelf and the roof may have been from two or three feet. If I could only get up there, squeezed in between bars and ceiling, I should have only one vulnerable side. I should be safe from below, from behind, and from each side. Only on the open face of it could I be attacked. There, it is true, I had no protection whatever; but at least, I should be out of the brute's path when he began to pace about his den. He would have to come out of his way to reach me. It was now or never, for if once the light were out it would be impossible. With a gulp in my throat I sprang up, seized the iron edge of the top, and swung myself panting on to it. I writhed in face downwards, and found myself looking straight into the terrible eyes and yawning jaws of the cat. Its fetid breath came up into my face like the steam from some foul pot.

It appeared, however, to be rather curious than angry. With a sleek ripple of its long, black back it rose, stretched itself, and then rearing itself on its hind legs, with one forepaw against the wall, it raised the other, and drew its claws across the wire meshes beneath me. One sharp, white hook tore through my trousers – for I may mention that I was still in evening dress – and dug a furrow in my knee. It was not meant as an attack, but rather as an experiment, for upon my giving a sharp cry of pain he dropped down again, and springing lightly into the room, he began walking swiftly round it, looking up every now and again in my direction. For my part I shuffled backwards until I lay with my back against the wall, screwing myself into the smallest space possible. The farther I got the more difficult it was for him to attack me.

He seemed more excited now that he had begun to move about, and he ran swiftly and noiselessly round and round the den, passing continually underneath the iron couch upon which I lay. It was wonderful to see so great a bulk passing like a shadow, with hardly the softest thudding of velvety pads. The candle was burning low – so low that I could hardly see the creature. And then, with a last flare and splutter it went out altogether. I was alone with the cat in the dark!

It helps one to face a danger when one knows that one has done all that possibly can be done. There is nothing for it then but to quietly await the result. In this case, there was no chance of safety anywhere except the precise spot where I was. I stretched myself out, therefore, and lay silently, almost breathlessly, hoping that the beast might forget my presence if I did nothing to remind him. I reckoned that it must already be two o'clock. At four it would be full dawn. I had not more than two hours to wait for daylight.

Outside, the storm was still raging, and the rain lashed continually against the little windows. Inside, the poisonous and fetid air was overpowering. I could neither hear nor see the cat. I tried to think about other things – but only one had power enough to draw my mind from my terrible position. That was the contemplation of my cousin's villainy, his unparalleled hypocrisy, his malignant hatred of me. Beneath that cheerful face there lurked the spirit of a mediaeval assassin. And as I thought of it I saw more clearly how cunningly the thing had been arranged. He had apparently gone to bed with the others. No doubt he had his witness to prove it. Then, unknown to them, he had slipped down, had lured me into his den and abandoned me. His story would be so simple. He had left me to finish my cigar in the billiard-room. I had gone down on my own account to have a last look at the cat. I had entered the room without observing that the cage was opened, and I had been caught. How could such a crime be brought home to him? Suspicion, perhaps – but proof, never!

How slowly those dreadful two hours went by! Once I heard a low, rasping sound, which I took to be the creature licking its own fur. Several times those greenish eyes gleamed at me through the darkness, but never in a fixed stare, and my hopes grew stronger that my presence had been forgotten or ignored. At last the least faint glimmer of light came through the windows – I first dimly saw them as two grey squares upon the black wall, then grey turned to white, and I could see my terrible companion once more. And he, alas, could see me!

It was evident to me at once that he was in a much more dangerous and aggressive mood than when I had seen him last. The cold of the morning had irritated him, and he was hungry as well. With a continual growl he paced swiftly up and down the side of the room which was farthest from my refuge, his whiskers bristling angrily, and his tail switching and lashing. As he turned at the corners his savage eyes always looked upwards at me with a dreadful menace. I knew then that he meant to kill me. Yet I found myself even at that moment admiring the sinuous grace of the devilish thing, its long, undulating, rippling movements, the gloss of its beautiful flanks, the vivid, palpitating scarlet of the glistening tongue which hung from the jet-black muzzle. And all the time that deep, threatening growl was rising and rising in an unbroken crescendo. I knew that the crisis was at hand.

It was a miserable hour to meet such a death – so cold, so comfortless, shivering in my light dress clothes upon this gridiron of torment upon which I was stretched. I tried to brace myself to it, to raise my soul above it, and at the same time, with the lucidity which comes to a perfectly desperate man, I cast round for some possible means of escape. One thing was clear to me. If that front of the cage was only back in its position once more, I could find a sure refuge behind it. Could I possibly pull it back? I hardly dared to move for fear of bringing the creature upon me. Slowly, very slowly, I put my hand forward until it grasped the edge of the front, the final bar which protruded through the wall. To my surprise it came quite easily to my jerk. Of course the difficulty of drawing it out arose from the fact that I was clinging to it. I pulled again, and three inches of it came through. It ran apparently on wheels. I pulled again ... and then the cat sprang!

It was so quick, so sudden, that I never saw it happen. I simply heard the savage snarl, and in an instant afterwards the blazing yellow eyes, the flattened black head with its red tongue and flashing teeth, were within reach of me. The impact of the creature shook the bars upon which I lay, until I thought (as far as I could think of anything at such a moment) that they were coming down. The cat swayed there for an instant, the head and front paws quite close to me, the hind paws clawing to find a grip upon the edge of the grating. I heard the claws rasping as they clung to the wire-netting, and the breath of the beast made me sick. But its bound had been miscalculated. It could not retain its position. Slowly, grinning with rage, and scratching madly at the bars, it swung backwards and dropped heavily upon the floor. With a growl it instantly faced round to me and crouched for another spring.

I knew that the next few moments would decide my fate. The creature had learned by experience. It would not miscalculate again. I must act promptly, fearlessly, if I were to have a chance for life. In an instant I had formed my plan. Pulling off my dress-coat, I threw it down over the head of the beast. At the same moment I dropped over the edge, seized the end of the front grating, and pulled it frantically out of the wall.

It came more easily than I could have expected. I rushed across the room, bearing it with me; but, as I rushed, the accident of my position put me upon the outer side. Had it been the other way, I might have come off scathless. As it was, there was a moment's pause as I stopped it and tried to pass in through the opening which I had left. That moment was enough to give time to the creature to toss off the coat with which I had blinded him and to spring upon me. I hurled myself through the gap and pulled the rails to behind me, but he seized my leg before I could entirely withdraw it. One stroke of that huge paw tore off my calf as a shaving of wood curls off before a plane. The next moment, bleeding and fainting, I was lying among the foul straw with a line of friendly bars between me and the creature which ramped so frantically against them.

Too wounded to move, and too faint to be conscious of fear, I could only lie, more dead than alive, and watch it. It pressed its broad, black chest against the bars and angled for me with its crooked paws as I have seen a kitten do before a mouse-trap. It ripped my clothes, but, stretch as it would, it could not quite reach me. I have heard of the curious numbing effect produced by wounds from the great carnivora, and now I was destined to experience it, for I had lost all sense of personality, and was as interested in the cat's failure or success as if it were some game which I was watching. And then gradually my mind drifted away into strange vague dreams, always with that black face and red tongue coming back into them, and so I lost myself in the nirvana of delirium, the blessed relief of those who are too sorely tried.

Tracing the course of events afterwards, I conclude that I must have been insensible for about two hours. What roused me to consciousness once more was that sharp metallic click which had been the precursor of my terrible experience. It was the shooting back of the spring lock. Then, before my senses were clear enough to entirely apprehend what they saw, I was aware of the round, benevolent face of my cousin peering in through the open door. What he saw evidently amazed him. There was the cat crouching on the floor. I was stretched upon my back in my shirt-sleeves within the cage, my trousers torn to ribbons and a great pool of blood all round me. I can see his amazed face now, with the morning sunlight upon it. He peered at me, and peered again. Then he closed the door behind him, and advanced to the cage to see if I were really dead.

I cannot undertake to say what happened. I was not in a fit state to witness or to chronicle such events. I can only say that I was suddenly conscious that his face was away from me – that he was looking towards the animal.

"Good old Tommy!" he cried. "Good old Tommy!"

Then he came near the bars, with his back still towards me.

"Down, you stupid beast!" he roared. "Down, sir! Don't you know your master?"

Suddenly even in my bemuddled brain a remembrance came of those words of his when he had said that the taste of blood would turn the cat into a fiend. My blood had done it, but he was to pay the price.

"Get away!" he screamed. "Get away, you devil! Baldwin! Baldwin! Oh, my God!"

And then I heard him fall, and rise, and fall again, with a sound like the ripping of sacking. His screams grew fainter until they were lost in the worrying snarl. And then, after I thought that he was dead, I saw, as in a nightmare, a blinded, tattered, blood-soaked figure running wildly round the room – and that was the last glimpse which I had of him before I fainted once again.

* * *

I was many months in my recovery – in fact, I cannot say that I have ever recovered, for to the end of my days I shall carry a stick as a sign of my night with the Brazilian cat. Baldwin, the groom, and the other servants could not tell what had occurred, when, drawn by the death-cries of their master, they found me behind the bars, and his remains – or what they afterwards discovered to be his remains – in the clutch of the creature which he had reared. They stalled him off with hot irons, and afterwards shot him through the loophole of the door before they could finally extricate me. I was carried to my bedroom, and there, under the roof of my would-be murderer, I remained between life and death for several weeks. They had sent for a surgeon from Clipton and a nurse from London, and in a month I was able to be carried to the station, and so conveyed back once more to Grosvenor Mansions.

I have one remembrance of that illness, which might have been part of the ever-changing panorama conjured up by a delirious brain were it not so definitely fixed in my memory. One night, when the nurse was absent, the door of my chamber opened, and a tall woman in blackest mourning slipped into the room. She came across to me, and as she bent her sallow face I saw by the faint gleam of the night-light that it was the Brazilian woman whom my cousin had married. She stared intently into my face, and her expression was more kindly than I had ever seen it.

"Are you conscious?" she asked.

I feebly nodded – for I was still very weak.

"Well; then, I only wished to say to you that you have yourself to blame. Did I not do all I could for you? From the beginning I tried to drive you from the house. By every means, short of betraying my husband, I tried to save you from him. I knew that he had a reason for bringing you here. I knew that he would never let you get away again. No one knew him as I knew him, who had suffered from him so often. I did not dare to tell you all this. He would have killed me. But I did my best for you. As things have turned out, you have been the best friend that I have ever had. You have set me free, and I fancied that nothing but death would do that. I am sorry if you are hurt, but I cannot reproach myself. I told you that you were a fool – and a fool you have been." She crept out of the room, the bitter, singular woman, and I was never destined to see her again. With what remained from her husband's property she went back to her native land, and I have heard that she afterwards took the veil at Pernambuco.

It was not until I had been back in London for some time that the doctors pronounced me to be well enough to do business. It was not a very welcome permission to me, for I feared that it would be the signal for an inrush of creditors; but it was Summers, my lawyer, who first took advantage of it.

"I am very glad to see that your lordship is so much better," said he. "I have been waiting a long time to offer my congratulations."

"What do you mean, Summers? This is no time for joking."

"I mean what I say," he answered. "You have been Lord Southerton for the last six weeks, but we feared that it would retard your recovery if you were to learn it."

Lord Southerton! One of the richest peers in England! I could not believe my ears. And then suddenly I thought of the time which had elapsed, and how it coincided with my injuries.

"Then Lord Southerton must have died about the same time that I was hurt?"

"His death occurred upon that very day." Summers looked hard at me as I spoke, and I am convinced – for he was a very shrewd fellow – that he had guessed the true state of the case. He paused for a moment as if awaiting a confidence from me, but I could not see what was to be gained by exposing such a family scandal.

"Yes, a very curious coincidence," he continued, with the same knowing look. "Of course, you are aware that your cousin Everard King was the next heir to the estates. Now, if it had been you instead of him who had been torn to pieces by this tiger, or whatever it was, then of course he would have been Lord Southerton at the present moment."

"No doubt," said I.

"And he took such an interest in it," said Summers. "I happen to know that the late Lord Southerton's valet was in his pay, and that he used to have telegrams from him every few hours to tell him how he was getting on. That would be about the time when you were down there. Was it not strange that he should wish to be so well informed, since he knew that he was not the direct heir?"

"Very strange," said I. "And now, Summers, if you will bring me my bills and a new cheque-book, we will begin to get things into order."

Nineteen Sixty-Five Ford Falcon

Tim Foley

IT'S A BEAUTY, isn't it? Custom dark blue paint, clean body. The sportiness of a two-door. You won't find one like that around every corner, that's for certain. Sixty-five. No, the sixty-six is a little rounded, less squared off. A beauty, don't you think?

The price is right. A steal at that price. And, if you are at all serious, I'll let you in on a little secret. The price is not firm. You get me?

Now you should know that this is not a museum piece. You can ignore the odometer. The engine is not the original. Oh, it's a Falcon engine alright, but it's a rebuilt sixty-seven. So you got a sixty-seven engine in a sixty-five car. If you are some kind of purebred vintage guy, this one's not for you. But if you want a car that actually runs, that will make you the absolute coolest guy in town, that provides the long lost, all-American, classic motor city vibe, you cannot beat this car.

Here, sit behind the wheel. Yeah, the upholstery has been replaced also, but that's a good thing, considering. Still got that classic bench seat. And the steering wheel is great, isn't it? Wider across than the ones they make now, and so thin, with those grooves for your fingers. I swear that baked enamel-plastic was designed for space travel. Totally cool.

And, again, the price. Seriously. You cannot, you will not, you will never, beat that price.

I've owned it less than a year. It belonged to my girlfriend. I inherited it, you might say, when she left for Texas. Where should I start?

* * *

Emily was something. Beautiful, thin, dark green eyes and long black hair. She was a might neurotic, and a tad obsessive, I suppose. She only slept three hours a night unless she had been drinking. She smoked a pack a day. She was exquisite, and I was smitten.

She had been the tomboy of her father's three daughters and he taught her everything he knew about cars. Which was a whole lot more than I knew. She loved to work on engines especially, and wore black lacquered polish so you couldn't see the caked grease under her nails. Half the time she had an oil smudge on her forehead. Trolling junkyards was her favorite way to spend a Saturday afternoon.

Since I didn't even own a car at the time, things evened out. She moved into my house and, before long, there was a sixty-one Volvo in pieces in the driveway and a sixty-four Corvair engine in the garage. Most nights she prowled around the house, a cloud of menthol trailing her from room to room, drifting into the garage where she listened to Nick Cave croon through an old stereo while she rebuilt a carburetor or cleaned spark plugs or some such, her hair ponytailed, wearing three faded sweaters of various colors over her bony shoulders. Like I said, I was smitten.

One day the Falcon showed up in front. It was in great condition, she said, and she seemed really excited about it. After a couple of weeks, I noticed that she would only drive the Falcon in the daylight hours, never at night. We generally rode my motorcycle when we went out, so I didn't think much of it, but eventually I asked why. She evaded the question. Turned out, being evasive was a pretty common thing with her.

One weekend in April, I had to go see my brother in Bakersfield. I was away for a couple of days. When I got back, Emily was gone, everything with her, her clothes and music, the car parts, even the Volvo. Pretty clean break. Except for the Falcon, which sat there, parked next to the curb in front of the house, the key hanging from a hook near the refrigerator. I felt like I'd been kicked in the chest.

She called me from San Antonio and said that she was sorry things had not worked out. I felt like I was drowning and did not say much. Finally, grasping for something to hold on to, I asked about the Falcon.

"I don't really need it," she said, "so I left it. You want it? You should have it. You need a car."

"Sure, I guess." I would have agreed to just about anything she said at that particular moment.

After I hung up, I walked out to the Falcon and climbed in. I drove it around midtown and filled it with gas. Then I drove it down to Freeport, across the river, and on to Clarksberg near the delta. I thought driving her car would remind me of her, that a scent would help me retain some connection, that a scratch on the dashboard would trigger a memory. But I soon realized that it was no good. This car held a personality of its own. She had owned it, but it was not hers. There was nothing about it that retained anything about her. Or, rather, there was something about the car, some other presence, that eclipsed her.

I drove back to Sacramento, parked in midtown, and walked over to the Torch Club. I sat at the bar and ordered a beer. I had some idea about a liberating ritual of loss involving alcohol and a dive bar. After a couple of hours, and a few more beers, my mood had not improved at all. I figured the time had come for the sad sack drowning his sorrows to give way to the night crowd searching for fun. I left as a blues band started playing.

It wasn't late and I swear I wasn't drunk. But it was dark. The Falcon was parked on 14th Street, near some apartments. The lighting was not too good, and a couple of ash trees crowded the sidewalk, buckling the concrete with their roots and casting shadows with their branches.

I was walking to the car, past the other cars parked by the curb, when I noticed something strange and stopped, dead, in my tracks. I saw a figure, moving, inside the Falcon. I was maybe three cars back and stood there, trying to get a better look through the shadows and darkness. The other cars partially blocked my view, but I could see a head and shoulders, a black outline, shifting, in the front seat.

Now I've had cars broken into before, if that was what was happening. I was upset, maybe a little afraid, and in a bit of an emotional whirlpool. I stooped down, ducking, and started creeping slowly along the curb, by the side of the other parked cars. I glanced up, and it was hard to make out any detail in the darkness, but I'm sure there was something moving inside the Falcon. Crouching, I approached the car, soundlessly.

When I got to the Falcon's rear panel, I slowly stood up. And felt very foolish. There was nothing there. The car has huge windows, in the old style, an uninterrupted slab of glass in the back. I could take in the entire interior at a glance. No one was in the car. I stood there, watching shadows shift as the streetlights filtered through the branches, wondering. The foolishness I felt was gradually replaced by a slow, unspecific, creeping, fear.

I walked around and unlocked the driver's door, reached in and turned on the globe light. I looked in the back seat. I went back around and checked the passenger side door lock. I opened the trunk and was mocked by the emptiness. I told myself that I was drunk, but I felt sober as a judge. My heart was pounding like an overheating nailgun.

I sat in the car, shut the door, turned off the globe light, took the steering wheel in my hands. I told myself I had not actually seen what I thought I had seen. But now I felt something, an intangible but insistent slow, rising darkness. I looked in the rearview mirror, half expecting to see a face. I turned and stared at the passenger side seat, cold and empty. I could hear myself breathing hard. Clutching the keys, I opened the door and pushed myself up and out of the car, stumbling as I propelled myself away from the interior. I straightened up, slammed the door, stepped back, then turned and walked away. I caught a cab home.

* * *

In the sunshine of the next morning, I again felt foolish. I called into work at the bottling plant and begged off, took a bus into midtown. Whatever feeling of dread had risen from inside the car the night before was gone. I told myself that I had simply been reacting to the shadows, the sadness, the alcohol. But a persistent, subtle anxiety tugged at my thoughts.

I drove the Falcon over to the garage on P Street where my buddy Freddie works. He's a stand-up guy and I called in a favor. Freddie looked at the Falcon, put it on the lift, drove it around the block, rummaged around under the hood. That's when I found out about the sixty-seven engine. Freddie told me some major work had been done on the car, but the chassis was sound and it was generally in good shape. He ran the registration and we found out that some guy named Eric White was listed as the legal owner. Emily had been vague about the pink slip.

I drove back to my house, parked the car in front. I stood next to it for a long time, looking at it. The dark blue paint reflected the midday sun. Nothing unusual here, I told myself, it's just an old car.

I went inside and called Emily. I called even though it might give me away as a weak, broken-hearted jerk, inventing some excuse to contact her. I could tell by her voice and manner that she did not want to speak with me.

"It's about the Falcon," I said.

"What about it?"

She admitted that she knew about the sixty-seven engine, but didn't volunteer much else. I did not want to mention what I had seen – or thought I saw – the night before, so the conversation became an awkward mix of hints and half-sentences. Finally, I asked, "Why didn't you drive it at night?"

There was a long silence, then: "What do you mean?"

"Remember? You never drove that car at night. You always made an excuse. Why?"

"This is silly," she said.

"Who is Eric White?" I countered.

She had bought the car from a guy named Eric, who worked as a bartender over at the Whiskey West Saloon. "You should talk with him," she said.

"I will."

"Goodbye, then."

I rode my motorcycle over to the Whiskey West, near the railroad tracks on T Street. It was quiet on a weekday afternoon, only a few hard cases at the bar. I lucked out, because

I found Eric easily, cutting lemons at the end of the bar in the dim light. He had a salt and pepper goatee and wore a sleeveless shirt that revealed skinny arms tattooed with images that looked as if they had shrunken with the arms.

"How is Emily?" he asked after I explained who I was.

"Fine. She's in San Antonio now."

"And she unloaded the Falcon on you?"

"Yeah." I watched him slice a lemon into wedges. "About the title."

"No worries. Just a detail. I sold it to her, for cash. I'll see if I can find the pink slip." He stepped away to pour a bourbon for a customer, then returned to where I was sitting, lemon wedges lined up. "Anything else?" he asked.

"Yeah. A couple of things about the car."

"Like?"

"Well, the engine was replaced."

"Of course. The original was water damaged."

"Water damaged?"

"Hello. She didn't tell you?" He grinned in a lop-sided way and raised his hands up. "Not cool. I was straight with her about the history. Totally up front."

"The history? Of the car?"

"It didn't bother her. In fact, I think she liked it. I think there was a certain fascination there." He laughed when he saw my mystified expression.

"I don't know what on earth –"

"Yeah, that's obvious, bud. Listen, I got work to do." He piled the lemon wedges into a plastic container and wiped the knife on his jeans. "But I think I know where that pink slip is. I'll meet you tomorrow. I've got some other stuff that you should see."

The afternoon shadows were deep and long when I returned home. The Falcon sat in front of the house. I opened the door and searched it, carefully. Glove compartment, under the seats, everywhere. I found some maps, a few coins, dull impersonal things. I saw something I hadn't noticed before. Around the door handle, on the passenger side, three deep scratches gouged the vinyl lining of the door.

When night came, I didn't sleep very much. I kept getting up and looking through the front window at the car. Very late, in the quiet, I got dressed and walked outside. The Falcon brooded in the starlight. I had found some of Emily's cigarettes in the night stand next to the bed and I brought them out. For the first time in years, I smoked, watching the Falcon, in the night.

* * *

"You owe me a buck-thirty," Eric said when he met me at Temple Coffee in mid-town the following afternoon. "I made some copies at Kinko's." He slapped some pages down on the table next to my coffee cup, and sat down across from me. He was wearing a black hoody sweatshirt and he smelled like terpentine. "She should have told you."

I looked at him blankly. I was missing work again, and the caffeine I had ingested was inadequate to overcome my sleep deprivation. Just looking at him made me crave a cigarette.

He watched me and, to my surprise, I thought I saw a small shade of concern come to his thin, hard face.

"It's a suicide car," Eric said. "After they pulled it out of the river, it was a mess, but basically intact. Somebody loved Falcons and replaced the engine and the upholstery. Since then, no one keeps that car very long. It's probably had two dozen owners." He laid one bony hand on my shoulder and held out another piece of paper in the other. "And here's the pink slip." We sat looking at each other until I realized he was finished speaking, but still waiting for his money.

After Eric left, throwing me a final look of pity, I read the pages before me. There were copies of receipts for work on the car, dating from 1987. Then there were five articles from the Sacramento Bee, dated November and December of 1986.

The articles told of Peter Mallory and Julie Copello, troubled sweethearts. He was 24, she was 19. He loved old cars, owned a sixty-five Falcon. He also loved cocaine.

A week before Thanksgiving, a lady was walking her dog on Brinkman Street, high up where the road curves along the cliffs of Fair Oaks, above the American River. It was 10 o'clock on a clear night, with a full moon. She heard an engine, loud and strong, and turned to see the Falcon churning up the road. She told the Sheriff's Department that she knew the car was going far too fast to make the turn. From what she could tell, the driver didn't even try. The car jumped the curve, roared across the open field, straight through the undergrowth, and plunged over the cliff. A couple of hundred feet below, the river was running high after a rainy autumn. The Falcon hit the water nose first, like a torpedo.

The note written by young Mallory and found in his apartment spoke of shame, addiction, drug debt, and a suicide pact. Follow up articles in the Bee tracked the aftermath of the tragedy, for Mallory was no ordinary drug-addled loser: he was the son of a state senator. There were photos of a double funeral.

I read the articles through twice, and then again. My stomach felt queasy, my head throbbed. What a sad, depressing story. Two foolish kids, having a tough time, driven to the point of surrender. I sat and cradled my empty, cold coffee cup.

Darkness had fallen when I left the café. My cell phone rang, making me jump as I approached the Falcon. I had been watching, almost without realizing it, for any movement or shadow as I walked towards the car, my nerves on edge. When I answered the call, I heard Eric's voice over the sounds of the saloon.

"There's something else I should tell you about that car," he said. "I wasn't going to mention it, but I decided that –"

"Go ahead," I said, mechanically. I was standing next to the driver's door, looking into the Falcon's interior through the windshield.

"Maybe it was nothing but, not long before I sold the car to Emily, I was driving home from a party late one night. I had a girl with me. She was sitting on the passenger side, beside me. All of a sudden, she screamed. She started twisting about like she'd gone crazy, terrified. She wouldn't stop until I pulled over."

"Yeah?"

"Well, she said that something had grabbed her. She accused me. She had scratches on her arm. It was weird."

"Weird?"

"I never touched her."

He hung up. I got in the car. I set the pages Eric had given me on the front seat beside me, in the shadows.

I turned the ignition and started the engine. It would take me ten minutes to drive home. I was very tired, drained from my lack of sleep, my broken heart, and the odd obsession with the car. And now I was weighed down with the story of Peter and Julie. Riding in a suicide car.

I tried to ignore the sense of dread that rose around me as I pulled out, the sense of fear that made me spin my head to look in the back seat more than once, that made me afraid to look in the rear view mirror, that made me keep eyeing the empty space beside me where a passenger would sit.

Nothing happened until I turned left onto Broadway.

The pages sitting by my side shifted. I was looking forward, driving, but I saw movement at the edge of my vision. My initial thought was that they slid with the momentum of the car as it made the turn. But then they leaped forward, off the seat and onto the floorboard, just exactly as if they had been pushed.

Just then, I felt something strike my shoulder, on my right side, just exactly as if someone was sitting beside me and leaned into me.

I barely kept control of the car. Somehow I finished the turn, though I jerked the wheel over. There was no car beside me, luckily, and I made the first right turn that I could, braking shakily to a stop. I jumped out of the car and stood in the street, my left hand grasping my right shoulder, my breathing wild.

It took every last ounce of will to climb back in that car for the 15 seconds it took to park it legally. Having something bump your shoulder when you know nothing is there is not pleasant. Not at all. I walked home.

* * *

The next morning I begged off work again. The boss started yelling and fired me over the phone. I didn't much care. I got dressed and walked to the Falcon, then I drove to the Sheriff's Department.

A helpful clerk rewarded my patience and persistence. They charged me a buck a page, but I got a copy of the Sheriff's report on the accident. I read it carefully. Peter Mallory and Julie Copello. Dead when they were pulled from the car. The doors were locked from the inside, the windows rolled up. It must have taken a long time for the car to fill with water. And, if they were conscious: time for a conversation, time to think about the soft joys of life, time to regret a foolish decision as the cold water poured in through the gaps and cracks, the car sank and shifted in the current. He had alcohol in his system, but no drugs. She was clean. How was it possible that they could have just sat there, waiting, the water rising over their legs, their chests, their faces?

The report gave me another name: Allison Harper. The lady walking her dog, who called the Sheriff's office from her home in the cliff-side neighborhood after she watched a vintage Ford drive straight over a cliff.

It was still daylight when I drove to Fair Oaks. I knew it was a long shot, but, as I got close, I could tell it was a neighborhood where people tended to plant themselves and stay put, elegant ranch-style homes. I parked the Falcon in front of the address listed in the report.

A small lady with blue eyes answered the door, opening it only a crack. Two yapping Yorkshire terriers scratched and snuffled and yipped at her feet. I had the Sheriff's report in my hand and tried to explain myself.

She looked past me and saw the car, her eyes widened, and her expression changed from distrust to curiosity as she swung the door wide open. Allison, for I knew it was her by her actions, strode out of the house, stepped off the walk, and was halfway across the lawn when she said, "That's the car."

"Yes, that's the car," I said. The terriers sniffed at my shoes as I followed her onto her front lawn.

She reached out and I handed her the report. A pair of reading glasses hung from a chain around her neck. Her white hair was wrapped in a blue scarf and she wore a pink sweater frayed at the sleeves and the neckline.

As she read the report, a small smile crept onto her face. "They left a few things out, didn't they?" She stabbed at the top of the report with a fingernail. "You see this?"

I tried to look past her finger.

"It's dated the 19th," she went on. "Two days later."

I stared at her, saying nothing.

"So they could fix it," she chirped, a little impatiently. The terriers were wandering about the lawn, bored with my shoes.

"Fix what?" I finally spoke.

Allison lowered the report and looked into my face. "She was screaming, you see. The girl in the passenger seat. I could hear her even above the engine. Screaming in fear. And I think I caught a glimpse of her face. It was long ago and happened very quickly. And it was dark, of course. But I remember the impression I had, of a face, absolutely terrified. Like that painting by Munch. And I told them."

"That's not mentioned at all," I said.

"It was past midnight when they pulled the car out of the river. I was curious, so I went down to see. I watched them wench it out, watched them smash the window to get inside. I saw the bodies when they pulled them out."

I looked from Allison's eager face to the Falcon, imagining the scene. The water-filled car, the taut winch-line, the dead inside, the deputies fumbling at the handles of the locked doors.

"The girl had her hands tied behind her back," said Allison.

She rounded up the dogs and invited me in. She made tea and served me lemon cookies on a round kitchen table covered with a macrame tablecloth. The terriers nuzzled my legs and circled for dropped crumbs.

"So there was a cover-up?"

"After all these years, it's hard to understand why it mattered, or why anyone bothered. But the boy's father was important, and thought he had a political future, I suppose. A family tragedy caused by drug addiction must have been thought less scandalous than a slaying. Maybe there is a sad romantic notion associated with a suicide pact that is not associated with a cold-blooded and cruel murder."

"Their funerals were together," I said.

"The poor girl," she said.

When Allison shut the door behind me, I realized that the day had ended and night had returned. I walked out to the Falcon and climbed inside. It was so still, I could hear crickets. I drove slowly down to the intersection with Brinkman.

I suppose you would say I had a choice, then. But I'm not sure I did. I suppose I could have turned right and gone down the hill. But I didn't. Thinking back, I'm not sure I was really in control. I turned left, toward the curve and the cliff.

I remember thinking how little the street had changed and then realizing, with an increasing panic, that I had never been on this street before. But the houses, their shapes and sizes, the gaps in the vegetation, and the contour of the road, were all familiar. The houses ended and the curve at the top of the hill, where the road turned east along the cliff, approached. My foot snapped down and the Falcon surged forward, gaining speed.

As if in some kind of dark, bitter dream, I could not control the car. I simply rode, a terrified spectator. I saw the curve coming toward me as the speed increased. I could not turn the steering wheel. Everything was happening as it should, with a shadowed wave of inevitability driving it. The car jumped the curb, bouncing me into the roof, and the wheels churned in the dirt, propelling the vehicle toward the point where the land ended and empty space began. A roar of noise sounded in my head, more even than the engine, more even than the scream.

With a supreme, blessed effort, I ripped my hands from the frozen wheel and turned enough to find the door handle. I pulled with everything I had and threw myself against the door. It sprang open and I hit the ground, rolling away from the car.

Then, like a nightmare suddenly run its course, the Falcon quickly slowed and came to a stop, 10 feet from the edge of the cliff. The headlights shown out through the swirling dust, out over the river, off into the night. Without someone inside, there was no point in going over, was there?

I lay in the dirt, watching the Falcon, listening to the warm hum of the motor idling as it waited for me to return.

* * *

The tow truck guy thought I was nuts. The car had a flat tire but was otherwise fine. Still, I made him tow it to a shop before I would even go near it. It cost me plenty, but I didn't care.

So I do have a few recommendations. First, don't drive it at night. Second, don't drive it near any cliffs. And don't ever go down Brinkman Street, okay? Other than that...

Wait. Don't go. Did I mention that the price is negotiable?

"Mama Said"

Steven Thor Gunnin

I WONDER if he'd stab me to death with that pen if he thought he could get away with it – plunge it through my eye, twist it around, turn my brains into soft-scrambled eggs.

A rough lobotomy performed in a moment of passion.

Would he be the crazy one then? Would he be the one having to sit here on this... this... It isn't quite a chair. It isn't quite a couch.

What the hell's it made of anyway? It's not leather, not really. Feels more like vinyl.

"What's this thing called?" I ask him, glancing between the disgusting brownish material that sticks uncomfortably to any little bit of exposed skin and his dirty dishwater eyes. I hadn't noticed it before, but the two are almost the same color. He blankly looks at me for a long, uncomfortable moment.

"This thing. This... whatever the hell it is," I say, patting the cushion I'm sitting on. Every time my palm hits the thing and pulls away it makes a disgusting slurping noise that reminds me of wet, sloppy sex. The sticky, fumbling kind Mama told me kids have in the back of their parents' car at the drive-in. My stomach turns at the thought and the county pen meatloaf that'd been lunch threatens to make another appearance.

"It's a fainting couch. They became popular during the Renaissance," he says in an annoyed tone. The index finger of his right hand slides up the length of his long, hawkish nose and presses the bridge of his wire-rimmed glasses back firmly into place. The curve of the lenses makes those dirty dishwater eyes seem bigger than they are. Either that or he's slightly deformed too, but I'm guessing it's the first one.

"Do you know why you're here, Mr. Morris?" he asks, his tone both insistent and impatient.

I eye the pen he's still holding in his left hand again. Mama always told me left-handed people were more prone to doing bad things. It's a sign of wickedness. She cracked me across the knuckles every time I used my left hand for anything. Well, at least every time she caught me using my left hand for anything. Imagine what she would have done if she knew about those times she didn't catch me.

I wonder if he does naughty things with his left hand.

"Yep." The word comes out almost like a hiccup, short and to the point. Mama taught me that too. Mama said everyone only got so many words during their life and when you used them all up, that's when you died.

"Really, Mr. Morris? Then please, by all means, enlighten me as to the reason for your current situation."

I don't much care for the way he's talking to me. He rounds off each word, all prim and proper. No question he's talking down to me, like I'm stupid or slow. That's fine though. Let him think what he wants, waste all the words he wants. We'll see how many words he's got left in him.

"Name's Jack," I say, looking at the little nameplate that rests on the edge of his big oak desk. The background is black. The letters are raised gold and spell out, "Andrew West, MD" all nice and fancy. The outside of the office door read the same. I wonder if it's for the benefit of the patients or just to brag about the letters he's got at the back of his name.

"I'm sorry," the doctor says, but I know he isn't really. Funny how easy it is to confuse someone with all that education.

"Mr. Morris was my father. I'd appreciate it if you'd just call me Jack."

I'm not so used to having to repeat myself. It's not a habit I care much for. He eyeballs me for a few moments, scribbles something on his big yellow notepad with that pen in his left hand, and then finally agrees.

"Very well, Jack. If you would, tell me in your own words why you're here today."

Who the hell else's words would I use to tell him? Of course they're going to be my own. Maybe he's trying to get me to use them up? No, if he knew about that he wouldn't talk so goddamn much.

"Judge said I had to come talk to you, see if I'm right in the head enough to stand trial. Seems they think I might be a bit touched," I say, trying to hold back a chuckle the whole time.

Here there's all this craziness going on in the world and they think I'm nuts? From the frown that creeps across the doctor's face, I can see he doesn't quite see the humor in it the way I do.

The walls around his office are lined with tall bookshelves, the kind that stop just shy of touching the ceiling. The shelves are lined with all sorts of thick hardback books in just about every color imaginable. I wonder if he's actually read all of them or if they're just for show. Mama used to keep a big book of the finest southern homes out on the coffee table just to look pretty for guests, but she never read page one out of it. Dr. West looks like the type to have probably read all of these, just so he could use all the big and fancy words he learned in them. Maybe if I'd read all those books, I wouldn't find all this so damned funny.

"Yes, Jack, technically that is indeed why you are here. However, I would like you to explain the circumstances that brought you into this situation in the first place," he says, straightening up in his high backed chair a bit. It isn't like this – what'd he call it – fainting couch; it's probably real leather, all dark and brown. Reminds me of a Hershey's bar that's just started to melt, not too much to where it's all gross and slimy, but just enough so that it's smooth and feels good in your mouth.

He straightens his tie, making sure that it lies neatly between the folds of his expensive-looking jacket. I wonder who he is tidying himself up for. It certainly isn't for me. It's obvious he couldn't care less whether I live or die... and truth be told, if he had his druthers, he'd probably choose the second option.

"What part you want me to start with?" I ask, still watching him preen himself.

He kind of reminds me of a cat, all vain and arrogant and aloof. Mama used to love cats. We had dozens of them around the house all the time, and she'd always care for them and tend to them. They always had milk and food, even when money was tight and the rest of us didn't have nothing.

I hate goddamn cats.

He pulls his fingers through his short, neatly-trimmed dark hair, glances down at that notepad of his, and then refocuses his attention on me.

"Why don't we begin with Norma Jean Ryder? Tell me about her," he says, his eyes narrowing. He doesn't even try to hide the venom in his voice.

Maybe he's a snake instead. Mama warned me about snakes, told me how they were evil and about the story of Adam and Eve and the Garden and how the Devil came to them in the skin of a snake. She told me that the Devil comes to us in many forms.

Guess Dr. West can't be a snake; I've always been kind of fond of snakes.

"I saw her for the first time at the hospital. She was just about the prettiest thing I ever laid eyes on. She was studying to be a nurse and was wearing one of them little, short white outfits that they have to wear. She looked kind of like an angel.

"She'd stayed later than she had to, helping out with some of the old folks up on three, and I came in to make my rounds –"

"You were a maintenance technician at Sacred Heart, correct?" he interrupts. I wasn't quite done with what I had to say. He draws a folder out of one of the drawers of the big oak desk and thumbs through its contents.

"No, sir," I say. He looks up at me from the cream-colored documents without moving his head, so he is kind of staring at me over the rim of his glasses.

"It says here that you worked at the hospital," he says in a matter of fact tone. One of his eyebrows rises just a bit, letting me know he is becoming even more impatient.

"Yes, sir. I was a janitor, not a technician," I say, trying my best to mimic his tone without laughing. He doesn't seem very amused and goes back to flipping through papers in the folder.

"Did you have any interaction with Miss. Ryder outside of the hospital setting?" he asks. His cold, sterile tone reminds me of an operating room.

He's wearing a gold band on the ring finger of his left hand. It's thin and plain and simple and doesn't really seem to fit in with the rest of the pomp he clutters himself in. I wonder if he's happily married or if it's just one of those necessary evils for him, like going to the dentist or having the pipes snaked.

"I'd see her from time to time. Sometimes at the market we'd bump into each other in the vegetable aisle. She was a vegetarian, you know. Wouldn't touch a bite of meat. She was always buying all these odd vegetables, like this stuff called radicchio with bright red leaves that looked like they –"

"Very good, Mr. Morris," he says. Again, he cuts me off mid-sentence, and I bristle a bit. "Did you actually have any interaction with Miss. Ryder?"

Mama always told me that it was rude to interrupt someone when they were talking. Whenever I did it by accident, she'd belt me across the mouth with the back of her hand. It taught me real quick about the virtue of being polite. Maybe someone should teach him a little virtue.

"No, sir. Not really," I say, almost biting my tongue to remain civil. He jots down another note on the yellow pad and then looks up at me again.

"Not really or not at all, Mr. Morris?" he asks in the same voice my teachers used to use. "Reports from your former co-workers indicate you had at least one exchange with Miss. Ryder prior to her death. Is this correct, Mr. Morris?"

He keeps pushing, throwing it in my face that I'm not my daddy, that I'm nothing like him. Mama used to always say that too, tell me how ashamed she was of me and how it was my fault that my daddy left. I'd come home late and she'd already be two-thirds done with a bottle of Amaretto, her breath sickly sweet from the syrupy liquor she'd been swilling while she screamed in my face. Her cheap mascara left trails down her cheeks from where she'd sit and stare at an old photo of him and cry.

"Yep," I say again, this time more like a croak than a hiccup. I feel my face getting hot as the color begins to come up in my cheeks. I don't much care for the feeling.

"Tell me what occurred during the course of that interaction, Mr. Morris," he says, but I can barely hear him over the caterwauling of my pulse in my ears. I really don't want to think too much about it.

Just tell him what he wants to hear and then he'll let me get back to my cell in the county lock-up.

"It was in the cafeteria at the hospital. She was having some dinner with a few of the other nurses. Salad, I think, with some kind of white dressing on it. Maybe ranch if I had to guess."

Damn it, stop rambling on and drawing this whole thing out. Just out with it and move on.

"Anyway, I came over to the table where they were sitting and asked Norma Jean if I could talk to her for a minute. The cafeteria is kind of bright, with all those fluorescent lights on the ceiling that make everything just a little bit green. She looked up at me from her food, and I noticed she had to squint her pretty blue eyes because of the lighting. I heard somewhere that people with blue eyes are more sensitive to light than other folks. I don't know exactly where I heard it. Maybe on the television somewhere," I say, babbling on about nothing, knowing I am doing it, but not quite able to stop myself.

"Yes, that is quite interesting, Mr. Morris. But if you could get to the crux of your exchange with Miss. Ryder, I would appreciate it," the doctor says in his condescending way, so that I can almost hear the smirk in his voice without even having to see it on his face. I'd heard that smirk a thousand times before. Hell, probably more than that. I heard it from my teachers when I was young. I heard it from the other kids at school out on the playground. I heard it from bus drivers each night I came to work. I heard it from the pimply-faced clerks at the market when they rang up my groceries. I used to hear it all the time from Mama.

They all thought they were better than me.

"Yes, sir. Sorry about that," I say sullenly.

I'm not sorry. Not at all. Mama taught me manners and it's polite to apologize when I do something to upset someone. I always seem to upset people, though.

Just looking at me upsets most people, at least a little bit, but that isn't my fault. It isn't right I should be spending my whole life apologizing for something I got no control over.

"I asked her if she'd maybe like to go get something to eat with me some night before work. I told her I'd heard of this place where they don't serve meat that's supposed to be real nice. She kind of smiled at me and I thought that maybe she was going to say yes – maybe just for a moment. Then all the other girls at the table started giggling and chuckling," I say, my face growing warmer just thinking about it.

I can still see their faces, all sneers and laughter. But that wasn't the worst of it. Not by a long shot. I'd gotten used to that kind of reaction a long time ago. It made me a little mad still from time to time, but Mama told me that it was my cross to bear and my punishment for being a wicked little boy.

"Norma Jean's smile kind of faded away about that time, and she told me that it was very sweet of me to ask, but that she was already seeing someone, so she couldn't. It wasn't the mean laughing of the other girls. It was worse. She had this kind of tone that you take when you find a hurt animal curled up under the porch. That kind of, 'Aww, you poor, pathetic thing' tone. It was the same tone my father used to use when he would talk to me when he could bring himself to even look at me.

"I hated it more than anything in the world," I whisper, my vision swimming and the room going all topsy-turvy on me. It felt like there was an old-style big band playing their hearts out inside my skull and that if I so much as touched my head it would split right open from the pressure.

I bite down on my lower lip, hard enough that I get the warm, coppery, salty taste of blood in my mouth, but it helps to slow down the drunken stumbling of the room so I can at least focus on Dr. West for another moment. He's staring at me expectantly, like he is waiting for me to say something else, but I'm at a loss for what it is he might want to hear.

I guess he finally gets tired of waiting, or decides I'm too stupid to go on without prompting. "So you killed her because it sounded like she was pitying you, Mr. Morris?" he asks and for the first time since I got to his office, I can hear a bit of a waver in his voice. It sounds kind of like someone waking up and hearing a strange sound in their house, when they ask if somebody's there, their voice all shaky and frail.

I wonder if Dr. West's ever done that?

"Yes sir, I did. I grabbed the knife that was sitting next to the milk carton on her tray and I jabbed it straight through her pretty, blue eye. I didn't want her to look at me like that, to talk to me like I was some hurt little animal.

"And let me tell you, it shut all her friends right up too, at least for a moment. They sure as hell weren't laughing and chuckling at me anymore. No, they were screaming their fool heads off. But not Norma Jean. She just sat there as pretty as you please," I say calmly.

The world righted itself as I spoke and the pounding in my head had all but vanished. For the first time since I'd been brought here from my little cell at the county courthouse jail, I feel downright at ease. Sure, I still have this shiny metal bracelet attaching my left wrist to this fainting couch, but things feel like they are going to be OK.

"Doesn't it bother you at all that you killed her, Mr. Morris?" Dr. West asks, laying his pen down and making a steeple out of his fingers. His eyes slowly grow wider as disgust works its way through him. I can tell he wants to yell at me, to tell me that I'm some kind of monster, the way Mama always used to do when she would take the razor strap to me. At least Mama would come out and say it.

Not like Dr. West.

Not like my father.

They just look at me with those eyes that are too big, and I can see it in them. They know it wasn't too long ago that some midwife would have bashed my brains in with a big rock moments after I'd been born and the local preacher would have burned Mama for consorting with the Devil. Mama sometimes told me I was the Devil.

"No, sir. It doesn't bother me one bit," I say. I slide my left hand under the side of the fainting couch, down along the sticky material, and get a feel for its weight.

"What bothers me is people like you, and her, and my father," I say as I stand up, hard and fast, dragging this unwieldy piece of furniture with me. I snatch the pen up off the big, yellow notepad where he had left it.

Before he can blink, I'm across his desk. His eyes go wide, and he makes some kind of gurgling noise, kind of like a cat caught up in a lawnmower, but that's it.

I reckon he finally used up all his words.

Six Aspects of Cath Baduma

Kate Heartfield

I: The Self-Devouring

WHENEVER WE GOT a new job Cath would eat ribs, crunching the bones to smithereens. Pork ribs, probably, but with Cath Baduma it didn't do to assume.

She and her giant crow, Occoras, would play chess for hours, ignoring the rest of us, pulling the meat off a pile of bones. That's when I'd step into my role as Cath's unofficial deputy: I'd frown at maps, check weapons, bark orders, give everyone something to think about other than what we were about to do.

My own special task was to prepare Cath's drugs: her flasks and pouches, her pipe whittled from a single unidentifiable bone.

Maya was the name she gave me. The skalds called me queen of phantoms. Mistress of illusions. Expert in denial and deflection.

I'd been with her the longest if you didn't count Occoras.

Most of the Sundry worked alone. Not Cath. She divided her powers among us, her teammates. All she asked in return was devotion and she didn't have to ask.

Before the Sundry came to Shanticore, people say, there was peace in our world. All the cities and villages made their own laws and did not meddle with each other. The Sundry can't live with peace. It's toxic to them. Our people had a choice: wait for them to turn on us, or give them something to do.

So we started making little wars, to save ourselves.

If that was true, it happened long before I was born. I hadn't known peace, ever. Now war was habit. Most of the major cities had shrines to one or two of the Sundry, and were under their protection. The city fathers needed Cath to save the people from their wars, and they needed their wars to save the people from Cath, and nobody bothered to ask which need came first.

Cath hadn't had a good fight for three years. The city fathers let her rough up criminals, sometimes, the bad ones no one would champion. But it was not enough. Angry muscles twitched under her blue-black skin: the muscles of a young woman, despite her crowsfeet eyes and gray nimbus hair.

As the months went on, her skin paled to gray, slick with sweat. Her flesh seemed to melt away from her bones. Sometimes she seemed not to hear us when we spoke to her; other times she startled at sounds no one else could hear. She started prowling at night, and not only for sex.

So we were all relieved at the news that the city had decided to make war on a small collection of villages that had taken to calling itself a country, across the water. We were also relieved that it wouldn't be a quick job. The other side had one of the Sundry too, a male named Setanta. It would be long and difficult; it would keep Cath occupied. Good, we said, and sharpened things.

II: The All-Giving

THERE WERE SIX OF US.

Cath Baduma.

Occoras, the Crow, her mount and confidant.

Me: Maya, the deceiver.

Daya, my sister. The compassionate, the wielder of empathy. She always was the nice one, even before Cath gave us our powers. Daya was the nice one but I was the pretty one.

Lasar, the fire-bringer, the only male among us if you didn't count Occoras.

And the Washer, who comes last in every list, who is forgotten because she never came to the field. None of us liked her.

When we weren't on the battlefield, we worked out of what had been a barn. We sometimes discovered old nests in it but no swallows, no bats. Nothing winged would venture near Occoras, who walked in by the front door.

It was chilly in winter so Lasar snapped his fingers, set little fires that would obey him and grow only to the size he wanted, consume nothing but his own energy. He did it partly to show off; a brazier and a tinderbox would have worked as well.

Still, it was pleasant enough, except in the dank corner where the Washer squatted on her rock. The Washer needed water so Cath had diverted a stream to run right through the barn, carrying lumps of snow and ice on its surface. The stream ran just inside the door, so there was no way in and out without crossing it. It was shallow but the rocks were wet and treacherous. And the worst part was crossing while the Washer stared at you, and wrung her red-cracked hands.

The rest of us got better looking when Cath gave us our powers. Well, "better" isn't quite the word. The hues of our skin were just slightly off anything found in nature. Our eyes were just a little too big for our faces. The wind that blew our hair blew for no one else. That kind of thing.

But the Washer looked like a woman, an ugly woman. She was pale, her eyes dark pits behind lank hair. She went naked above the waist in all weather, her dugs puckered in the cold, her long skirt dark with water and with mold.

The morning after we got the Setanta job, Cath grabbed me by the arm so roughly I spilled my coffee and walked me over to the Washer. This, like the ribs and the chess, was standard.

"Well?" Cath demanded, adjusting the leather straps that crisscrossed her breast. "Out with it. What do you see?"

The Washer stood where she was and somehow wicked up the water into herself, drew it up until her skirt was wet to the waistband, and then until it dripped off her nipples and elbows, until it ran down her cheeks and trickled off her chin, until her hair was stuck to her head. She drew a gasping breath as if she were drowning. She raised a thin arm, reaching out to Cath.

"If you look into your son's face on the battlefield, either you or he will die," the

Washer said. "If you go out to meet your son in your chariot, either you or he will die. If you stretch your hand to your son, either you or he will die."

Cath, who had been cleaning her dagger, thrust it deep into its sheath.

"Your son?" I whispered. We knew very little of the lives the Sundry had led in their own world, before they came to us.

"Setanta," Cath said. "He's my son. Well, Maya? Is the prophecy truth or illusion?"

I didn't like the look on her face. So I shut my eyes, to concentrate, to sense whether any outside power was manipulating the Washer's predictions. I sensed nothing.

"I can't say whether it's truth," I said, opening my eyes again to give the Washer a look of contempt. "But it isn't a deception."

"Fair enough," Cath said. "And useless. But thank you."

She strode back toward the fire, where Occoras cawed and preened while the rest packed up.

"Why do you say it's useless?" I asked, as I struggled to keep pace. "Now we know to keep you well out of the fray. You can't meet him face to face, or one of you will die."

"One of us," she said. "Could be him as easily as me. And Maya, the whole point of going to war is to come out of it dead or the victor, isn't it?"

"Is it?" I asked. "Is that why we do it? Gradual murder-suicide?"

She snorted. Her breath smelled like a doused fire. "I have no idea why you do it. You have no compulsion. You're not one of the Sundry. You're native to this world and yet you do my work. What does that make you?"

I smiled and left her to her preparations. When Cath teased her friends, it could sound like cruelty but I knew better.

III: The Insatiable Beloved

CATH LET DAYA ride in her chariot to the battlefield, as Daya was by then heavy with her pregnancy. There was no question of Daya getting within a spearshot of the action in her condition, but then she seldom did anyway, preferring to take a position in a high place with her silver hand-mirror. Daya's battlefield work was to gather feelings – fear and misery, mainly – to amplify them and direct them at our enemies.

Lasar and I rode our black horses. Cath rode Occoras, swooping above us, going ahead and then coming back, like a scout.

We passed some of the regular army on the way, trudging along in silence. Men and women, in plain clothing the colour of dirt and leaves. They carried bows, spears, swords. Most of them walked; they let the horses pull the carts loaded with siege equipment rumoured to be of Occoras' design. They looked at us as if we weren't fighting for the same side.

On the eve of battle, Occoras, the Skald Crow, drew himself up, coughed once, and recited a poem.

I hear a rumble
Like the moans of an aged sow
From across the water
I see the cracked heads of our enemies
Spiked

I see the wheels of Cath Baduma's chariot
Running in red
I see bones caged and captives chained
And I ask what madness drove
These puling piglings
To slaughter

We did not hear the Crow's voice often, which was a blessing.

The first day went well. The other side had horrible engines but Lasar burned them. It had gigantic warriors but they hesitated, they erred, and for that I gave credit to Daya, up in her siege tower at the back of our army, holding her silver mirror.

I didn't see Setanta on the field but his dogs seemed to be everywhere, snarling and ripping the flesh off the ankles of the soldiers on our side. I raised a meat stink to confuse them but the fiercest of them would not be drawn off. That night, with the stench of my own illusions still in my clothes, I could not sleep for wondering whether I'd remembered to refill Cath's flasks and pouches. She was in the habit of smoking a pipe before she slept. Finally I decided to check with her, knowing she was unlikely to be asleep.

The camp was quiet, except for the occasional moan, and a snatch of braggadocious song. I met my sister Daya outside Cath's tent. She was bringing Cath a man. I only noticed him by the steam of his breath; otherwise I might have thought him a bit of war tackle, an inanimate hummock with a cloak thrown over top.

"This is a friend of Cath Baduma's," my sister said. "He'll bring the herbs in to her. Get some rest, Maya."

IV: The World-Mother

THE SECOND DAY, we started fighting before dawn, blood shining in the silvery mud. We fought hand to hand until there was no front any more, no sun in the clouded sky to give us direction. I didn't bother with illusions much; there was confusion enough, and in the great crush Lasar was restricted to small flames, to burning the skin off his opponents one by one. I tried adding fighters behind us so that our numbers would look greater, but once there was no *behind* or *before* left on the battlefield, it was pointless. Neither side wore any identifying mark. We called out our allegiance as we fought; most of the fighters called the names of their country or city. Lasar and I screamed out "Cath Baduma." Daya was still far back in her tower, safe, I hoped. Cath, up in the clouds on Occoras, whipped stones at our enemies with perfect accuracy.

I saw Setanta at last, far off, in his chariot. His skin was indigo, his black hair matted in long locks. He screamed and Occoras answered.

Setanta had his arrow notched before I could react. I managed to throw a stinging dust cloud before his eyes at the last moment, and who knows if that saved Cath from an arrow through the heart or eye. In any case it did not save Occoras. The great bird fell, thrashing, and many fighters were injured as he whumped onto the battlefield.

Cath slid off him, her sword in hand. "Get him out of here," she shouted to me.

I raised a wall of smoke around the bird and shoved a few of our fighters in behind it, told them the mantra that would let them breathe free. They dragged the Crow out by his enormous feet. Cath spared one look behind her, then she charged in, her sword slicing before her, mowing down the fighters of both armies that stood between her and Setanta.

They fought silently, like one entity, with many arms, many legs, many wounds. Blood sprayed from them.

At last, Cath stepped back, and held up her sword above her head. "Do you yield?" she asked.

Setanta coughed an answer I could not hear. I saw Cath let her sword drop into the mud, saw her shoulders hunch, and shudder. Then she wrapped her left arm around his head, cradling him off the ground, and rocked him. Her dagger flashed in her right hand before she buried it in his chest. I cringed, although I had seen her kill before, more times than I could remember.

When she walked past me Cath was shining, shining with her son's blood. Clean tracks cut through the gore on her cheeks. It might have been sweat but with Cath Baduma it didn't do to assume. She licked her lips, then opened her red mouth and screamed.

V: The Wrathful Judge

AS THE SHADOWS lengthened, we thought that was an end of it. Setanta's fighters would keep on, for appearances, but soon enough they would surrender. We had wanted a long fight but none of us were disappointed. We were all tired and Cath had had more than her fill. Besides, she was worried about Occoras.

Setanta did not die.

We had heard stories of his berserker rage. We had taken heart, over the past two days, in believing those stories exaggerated.

But when Setanta approached death, with a great spasm his frenzy was released. His mouth grew into the maw of a dog, his eyes migrated to the side of his head, and his limbs stretched long, with more joints than a man has. He stood twice as tall as before and nearly twice as broad, and he bayed as he came toward us.

His wound might have been mortal but not yet.

And whatever it was that fed his own rage fed his army's. Perhaps this was why he worked alone, save for the dogs. He could, in extremis, spread his power among a host. And whereas Cath seemed to have given up some power when she imbued the six of us, Setanta's was merely strengthened by sharing.

They came at us, bloodied and haggard, with fire in their eyes.

We were back behind our army. Cath was kneeling by Occoras's iridescent head, whispering something in his ear. The Crow was badly hurt and his great glassy eye rolled like a marble.

She stood when she heard her son's voice, and sniffed the air.

"Go," she croaked, and Lasar and I ran back toward Setanta, our blades drawn.

I animated the fresh corpses on the battlefield. I turned the sun-stained clouds into the bloody cloaks of invisible demons that swooped down onto the field. I raised a red mist of anger that twisted the world-rage in Setanta's soldiers into bitterness and personal grief, so that they'd make mistakes.

All of this affected our side nearly as badly, but we were beyond caring and so were they. The fighters on our side were mere conscripts. They stood no chance against a thousand frenzied warriors who would seize heads between meaty hands and rip off helmets to bite faces. They tore off ears and maced knees into pulp and left the wreckage on the battered ground. The soldiers on our side wanted an end, one way or another.

Lasar raised a wall of fire.

VI: She Who Remains at the End of Things

SOMEONE SHOUTED my name. I turned with my sword drawn. A man stood there, cloaked in brown sadness.

"Maya, your sister needs you," he said, and then I recognized him as the man I'd seen with Daya outside Cath Baduma's tent the night before. "Please. The baby is coming."

For the briefest of moments I wondered at the pain in his face. Daya had never told me who fathered her child. True, she had delivered this man up to Cath, presumably for her bed, and he'd gone willingly – Cath did not force her lovers. But that meant nothing. We would have done anything for Cath, any one of us. And perhaps this man would have done anything for Daya.

I let my illusions drop and told Cath where I was going. She was still beside the Crow. She nodded. "Go," Cath said. "Protect her. I'll hold them off."

When next I looked behind, I saw Cath in her horseless chariot, riding into battle. A stinging smoke curled up from her chariot wheels as they cut through gore.

I found Daya naked in a little room near the top of her siege tower, hardly a room but a mere bit of open floor off the staircase, with a window cut in one wall. She was gripping the wooden supports in the wall and screaming. I had thought Cath's scream terrible until I heard that sound.

"By Cath's bloody eye," I swore, and put my hand on Daya's shoulder. She shook it off. Piss, shit and blood ran over the planking. The place didn't look much better than the battlefield, outside the crude window where Daya had looked out, directing emotion with her mirror. The mirror lay now forgotten on the floor.

"Go, guard the entrance below," I told the man. He started to object, then turned and left.

"We should have brought the midwife," I said. "Daya, what do I do?"

My sister's scream fought its way out through gritted teeth, and clanged in my eardrums. When it was over, a few dry sobs racked her.

She whispered, "The battle. How is it going?"

"Too soon to tell," I said.

"You're lying," she said.

"Fine. I'm lying. But Cath will hold them off. Don't worry about that now."

"Get me my mirror," she whispered, clinging to the walls inside the siege tower as if she would fall to the floor otherwise.

"Now's not the time."

"The mirror!"

I handed it to her. She left the wall and put her left hand on my shoulder, gripping it so hard I found yellow marks there, days later. We stood with our backs to the window, to the battlefield below. With her right hand she held the mirror before her face, but a little to the right. She positioned it there, I think, to spare me the pain, but the mirror spared no one.

I felt a cramping, boiling wrench in my innards, felt the string of every muscle tighten to the snapping point. My body was cloven in two and outside the pain, I thought with a strange lucidity: *This is what dying feels like.* No one could feel this and live.

There was comfort in that, because death is an end. But death did not come and the pain got worse.

We suffered, all of us, as Daya squatted and pushed. I don't know whether we suffered as badly as she did; can a mirror reflect all of what it sees? I don't know how long it took. I used all my remaining strength to keep my legs under me, so Daya would have me for support. To this day I'm proud, when I remember the pain, that I managed to do that much.

Daya's baby was a beautiful boy, mottled and curdy with damp dark hair. She cradled him and tried to coax him up to her breast. I cleaned my dagger as well as I could, held it in a candle flame and cut his cord.

Then I staggered to the window and looked out.

I saw a gruesome kind of peace. The birth pangs had been enough to finish off many of the wounded and battle-weary on both sides – including Setanta, I found out later. The dead were in piles, some of them clutching their bellies. Some bled when the pangs came and did not stop. They died pale and shivering on beds of corpses, babbling about visions and revelations to their dead comrades.

Others had survived but had no stomach for carrying on with the battle. The pain left a truce in its wake, and besides, Setanta was dead. The battlefield was quiet now, with only a few figures hopping and flapping among the dead: survivors looking to deal out mercy, or confirm the identities of the dead, or steal from them.

"Daya, you did it," I gasped.

"I had a baby," she said. "I can't take credit for the rest. Praise be to Cath."

I turned away from the window and saw her, my sister, the colour of death with a baby at her breast. She looked like her old self, bedraggled and pale, and yet she looked more fearsome than I'd ever seen her. My mouth was dry and my head swam.

"Praise to Cath Baduma," I echoed weakly, seeking refuge in rote. "Victory to Cath. All praise to her, the all-devouring, the all-seeing, the all-mother."

I left Daya with her baby and its father, and walked out to find Cath. I found her wandering, holding a black feather the length of my arm. As I approached, she bent to the ground to dip the feather in blood. A souvenir for the Washer, who needed a little blood in her water from time to time.

Black and red and silver Cath was, blades and wounds and darkness.

"Is the Crow…"

"He'll live," she said. "It was close but he'll live. He didn't suffer the pangs. Lucky devil."

I nodded.

"And Daya?"

"She'll live too," I said. "And so will her boy."

"I don't want to see it," she said.

"I'm sorry?"

"Her child. Send Daya away. We've got no use for a suckling mother. Find her a nice village. She can take that man with her if she likes; I don't need him."

I swallowed. "She won the battle for us, Cath. She doesn't deserve to be punished."

"Do I?" she snarled.

I shook my head, struck dumb.

"We'll name him Setanta," Cath said, more calmly, and turned away.

I didn't know what to say, so I pulled my flask out of its holster and held it out to her.

Cath laughed. She took a slug off the flask, and then handed it back. I filled and lit a pipe for her and she held it in her teeth while she spoke. She was looking at the hills of dead, little remnants of Lasar's fires still burning among them like offerings.

"Why do you feed my addictions, Maya?"

I shrugged. I never knew whether to answer her questions.

The House Among the Laurels

William Hope Hodgson

"THIS IS A CURIOUS YARN that I am going to tell you," said Carnacki, as after a quiet little dinner we made ourselves comfortable in his cozy dining room.

"I have just got back from the West of Ireland," he continued. "Wentworth, a friend of mine, has lately had rather an unexpected legacy, in the shape of a large estate and manor, about a mile and a half outside of the village of Korunton. This place is named Gannington Manor, and has been empty a great number of years; as you will find is almost always the case with Houses reputed to be haunted, as it is usually termed.

"It seems that when Wentworth went over to take possession, he found the place in very poor repair, and the estate totally uncared for, and, as I know, looking very desolate and lonesome generally. He went through the big house by himself, and he admitted to me that it had an uncomfortable feeling about it; but, of course, that might be nothing more than the natural dismalness of a big, empty house, which has been long uninhabited, and through which you are wandering alone.

"When he had finished his look 'round, he went down to the village, meaning to see the one-time Agent of the Estate, and arrange for someone to go in as caretaker. The Agent, who proved by the way to be a Scotchman, was very willing to take up the management of the Estate once more; but he assured Wentworth that they would get no one to go in as caretaker; and that his – the Agent's – advice was to have the house pulled down, and a new one built.

"This, naturally, astonished my friend, and, as they went down to the village, he managed to get a sort of explanation from the man. It seems that there had been always curious stories told about the place, which in the early days was called Landru Castle, and that within the last seven years there had been two extraordinary deaths there. In each case they had been tramps, who were ignorant of the reputation of the house, and had probably thought the big empty place suitable for a night's free lodging. There had been absolutely no signs of violence to indicate the method by which death was caused, and on each occasion the body had been found in the great entrance hall.

"By this time they had reached the inn where Wentworth had put up, and he told the Agent that he would prove that it was all rubbish about the haunting, by staying a night or two in the Manor himself. The death of the tramps was certainly curious; but did not prove that any supernatural agency had been at work. They were but isolated accidents, spread over a large number of years by the memory of the villagers, which was natural enough in a little place like Korunton. Tramps had to die some time, and in some place, and it proved nothing that two, out of possibly hundreds who had slept in the empty house, had happened to take the opportunity to die under shelter.

"But the Agent took his remark very seriously, and both he and Dennis the landlord of the inn, tried their best to persuade him not to go. For his 'sowl's sake,' Irish Dennis begged him to do no such thing; and because of his 'life's sake,' the Scotchman was equally in earnest.

"It was late afternoon at the time, and as Wentworth told me, it was warm and bright, and it seemed such utter rot to hear those two talking seriously about the impossible. He felt full of pluck, and he made up his mind he would smash the story of the haunting, at once by staying that very night, in the Manor. He made this quite clear to them, and told them that it would be more to the point and to their credit, if they offered to come up along with him, and keep him company. But poor old Dennis was quite shocked, I believe, at the suggestion; and though Tabbit, the Agent, took it more quietly, he was very solemn about it.

"It seems that Wentworth did go; and though, as he said to me, when the evening began to come on, it seemed a very different sort of thing to tackle.

"A whole crowd of the villagers assembled to see him off; for by this time they all knew of his intention. Wentworth had his gun with him, and a big packet of candles; and he made it clear to them all that it would not be wise for anyone to play any tricks; as he intended to shoot 'at sight.' And then, you know, he got a hint of how serious they considered the whole thing; for one of them came up to him, leading a great bullmastiff, and offered it to him, to take to keep him company. Wentworth patted his gun; but the old man who owned the dog shook his head and explained that the brute might warn him in sufficient time for him to get away from the castle. For it was obvious that he did not consider the gun would prove of any use.

"Wentworth took the dog, and thanked the man. He told me that, already, he was beginning to wish that he had not said definitely that he would go; but, as it was, he was simply forced to. He went through the crowd of men, and found suddenly that they had all turned in a body and were keeping him company. They stayed with him all the way to the Manor, and then went right over the whole place with him.

"It was still daylight when this was finished; though turning to dusk; and, for a while, the men stood about, hesitating, as if they felt ashamed to go away and leave Wentworth there all alone. He told me that, by this time, he would gladly have given fifty pounds to be going back with them. And then, abruptly, an idea came to him. He suggested that they should stay with him, and keep him company through the night. For a time they refused, and tried to persuade him to go back with them; but finally he made a proposition that got home to them all. He planned that they should all go back to the inn, and there get a couple of dozen bottles of whisky, a donkey-load of turf and wood, and some more candles. Then they would come back, and make a great fire in the big fireplace, light all the candles, and put them 'round the place, open the whisky and make a night of it. And, by Jove! He got them to agree.

"They set off back, and were soon at the inn, and here, whilst the donkey was being loaded, and the candles and whisky distributed, Dennis was doing his best to keep Wentworth from going back; but he was a sensible man in his way, for when he found that it was no use, he stopped. You see, he did not want to frighten the others from accompanying Wentworth.

"'I tell ye, sorr,' he told him, ''tis of no use at all, thryin' ter reclaim ther castle. 'Tis curst with innocent blood, an' ye'll be bether pullin' it down, an' buildin' a fine new wan. But if ye be intendin' to shtay this night, kape the big dhoor open whide, an' watch for the bhlood-dhrip. If so much as a single dhrip falls, don't shtay though all the gold in the worrld was offered ye.'

"Wentworth asked him what he meant by the blood-drip.

"'Shure,' he said, ''tis the bhlood av thim as ould Black Mick 'way back in the ould days kilt in their shlape. 'Twas a feud as he pretendid to patch up, an' he invited thim – the O'Haras they was – siventy av thim. An' he fed thim, an' shpoke soft to thim, an' thim thrustin' him, sthayed to shlape with him. Thin, he an' thim with him, sharted in an' mhurdered thim wan an' all as they slep'. 'Tis from me father's grandfather ye have the sthory. An' sence thin 'tis death to any, so they say, to pass the night in the castle whin the bhlood-dhrip comes. 'Twill put out candle an' fire, an' thin in the darkness the Virgin Herself would be powerless to protect ye.'

"Wentworth told me he laughed at this; chiefly because, as he put it: – 'One always must laugh at that sort of yarn, however it makes you feel inside.' He asked old Dennis whether he expected him to believe it.

"'Yes, sorr,' said Dennis, 'I do mane ye to b'lieve it; an' please God, if ye'll b'lieve, ye may be back safe befor' mornin'.' The man's serious simplicity took hold of Wentworth, and he held out his hand. But, for all that, he went; and I must admire his pluck.

"There were now about forty men, and when they got back to the Manor – or castle as the villagers always call it – they were not long in getting a big fire going, and lighted candles all 'round the great hall. They had all brought sticks; so that they would have been a pretty formidable lot to tackle by anything simply physical; and, of course, Wentworth had his gun. He kept the whisky in his own charge; for he intended to keep them sober; but he gave them a good strong tot all 'round first, so as to make things seem cheerful; and to get them yearning. If you once let a crowd of men like that grow silent, they begin to think, and then to fancy things.

"The big entrance door had been left wide open, by his orders; which shows that he had taken some notice of Dennis. It was a quiet night, so this did not matter, for the lights kept steady, and all went on in a jolly sort of fashion for about three hours. He had opened a second lot of bottles, and everyone was feeling cheerful; so much so that one of the men called out aloud to the ghosts to come out and show themselves. And then, you know a very extraordinary thing happened; for the ponderous main door swung quietly and steadily to, as though pushed by an invisible hand, and shut with a sharp click.

"Wentworth stared, feeling suddenly rather chilly. Then he remembered the men, and looked 'round at them. Several had ceased their talk, and were staring in a frightened way at the big door; but the great number had never noticed, and were talking and yarning. He reached for his gun, and the following instant the great bullmastiff set up a tremendous barking, which drew the attention of the whole company.

"The hall I should tell you is oblong. The south wall is all windows; but the north and east have rows of doors, leading into the house, whilst the west wall is occupied by the great entrance. The rows of doors leading into the house were all closed, and it was toward one of these in the north wall that the big dog ran; yet he would not go very close; and suddenly the door began to move slowly open, until the blackness of the passage beyond was shown. The dog came back among the men, whimpering, and for a minute there was an absolute silence.

"Then Wentworth went out from the men a little, and aimed his gun at the doorway.

" 'Whoever is there, come out, or I shall fire,' he shouted; but nothing came, and he blazed forth both barrels into the dark. As though the report had been a signal, all the doors along the north and east walls moved slowly open, and Wentworth and his men were staring, frightened into the black shapes of the empty doorways.

"Wentworth loaded his gun quickly, and called to the dog; but the brute was burrowing away in among the men; and this fear on the dog's part frightened Wentworth more, he told me, than anything. Then something else happened. Three of the candles over in the corner of the hall went out; and immediately about half a dozen in different parts of the place. More candles were put out, and the hall had become quite dark in the corners.

"The men were all standing now, holding their clubs, and crowded together. And no one said a word. Wentworth told me he felt positively ill with fright. I know the feeling. Then, suddenly, something splashed on to the back of his left hand. He lifted it, and looked. It was covered with a great splash of red that dripped from his fingers. An old Irishman near to him, saw it, and croaked out in a quavering voice: – 'The bhlood-dhrip!' When the old man called out, they all looked, and in the same instant others felt it upon them. There were frightened cries of: 'The bhlood-dhrip! The bhlood-dhrip!' And then, about a dozen candles went out simultaneously, and the hall was suddenly dark. The dog let out a great, mournful howl, and there was a horrible little silence, with everyone standing rigid. Then the tension broke, and there was a mad rush for the main door. They wrenched it open, and tumbled out into the dark; but something slammed it with a crash after them, and shut the dog in; for Wentworth heard it howling as they raced down the drive. Yet no one had the pluck to go back to let it out, which does not surprise me.

"Wentworth sent for me the following day. He had heard of me in connection with that Steeple Monster Case. I arrived by the night mail, and put up with Wentworth at the inn. The next day we went up to the old Manor, which certainly lies in rather a wilderness; though what struck me most was the extraordinary number of laurel bushes about the house. The place was smothered with them; so that the house seemed to be growing up out of a sea of green laurel. These, and the grim, ancient look of the old building, made the place look a bit dank and ghostly, even by daylight.

"The hall was a big place, and well lit by daylight; for which I was not sorry. You see, I had been rather wound-up by Wentworth's yarn. We found one rather funny thing, and that was the great bullmastiff, lying stiff with its neck broken. This made me feel very serious; for it showed that whether the cause was supernatural or not, there was present in the house some force exceedingly dangerous to life.

"Later, whilst Wentworth stood guard with his shotgun, I made an examination of the hall. The bottles and mugs from which the men had drunk their whisky were scattered about; and all over the place were the candles, stuck upright in their own grease. But in the somewhat brief and general search, I found nothing; and decided to begin my usual exact examination of every square foot of the place – not only of the hall, in this case, but of the whole interior of the castle.

"I spent three uncomfortable weeks, searching; but without result of any kind. And, you know, the care I take at this period is extreme; for I have solved hundreds of cases of so-called 'hauntings' at this early stage, simply by the most minute investigation, and the keeping of a perfectly open mind. But, as I have said, I found nothing. During the whole of the examination, I got Wentworth to stand guard with his loaded shotgun; and I was very particular that we were never caught there after dusk.

"I decided now to make the experiment of staying a night in the great hall, of course 'protected.' I spoke about it to Wentworth; but his own attempt had made him so nervous that he begged me to do no such thing. However, I thought it well worth the risk, and I managed in the end to persuade him to be present.

"With this in view, I went to the neighboring town of Gaunt, and by an arrangement with the Chief Constable I obtained the services of six policemen with their rifles. The arrangement was unofficial, of course, and the men were allowed to volunteer, with a promise of payment.

"When the constables arrived early that evening at the inn, I gave them a good feed; and after that we all set out for the Manor. We had four donkeys with us, loaded with fuel and other matters; also two great boarhounds, which one of the police led. When we reached the house, I set the men to unload the donkeys; whilst Wentworth and I set-to and sealed all the doors, except the main entrance, with tape and wax; for if the doors were really opened, I was going to be sure of the fact. I was going to run no risk of being deceived by ghostly hallucination, or mesmeric influence.

"By the time that this was done, the policemen had unloaded the donkeys, and were waiting, looking about them, curiously. I set two of them to lay a fire in the big grate, and the others I used as I required them. I took one of the boarhounds to the end of the hall furthest from the entrance, and there I drove a staple into the floor, to which I tied the dog with a short tether. Then, 'round him, I drew upon the floor the figure of a Pentacle, in chalk. Outside of the Pentacle, I made a circle with garlic. I did exactly the same thing with the other hound; but over more in the northeast corner of the big hall, where the two rows of doors make the angle.

"When this was done, I cleared the whole center of the hall, and put one of the policemen to sweep it; after which I had all my apparatus carried into the cleared space. Then I went over to the main door and hooked it open, so that the hook would have to be lifted out of the hasp, before the door could be closed. After that, I placed lighted candles before each of the sealed doors, and one in each corner of the big room; and then I lit the fire. When I saw that it was properly alight, I got all the men together, by the pile of things in the center of the room, and took their pipes from them; for, as the Sigsand MS. has it: 'Theyre must noe lyght come from wythin the barryier.' And I was going to make sure.

"I got my tape measure then, and measured out a circle thirty-three feet in diameter, and immediately chalked it out. The police and Wentworth were tremendously interested, and I took the opportunity to warn them that this was no piece of silly mumming on my part; but done with a definite intention of erecting a barrier between us and any ab-human thing that the night might show to us. I warned them that, as they valued their lives, and more than their lives it might be, no one must on any account whatsoever pass beyond the limits of the barrier that I was making.

"After I had drawn the circle, I took a bunch of the garlic, and smudged it right 'round the chalk circle, a little outside of it. When this was complete, I called for candles from my stock of material. I set the police to lighting them, and as they were lit, I took them, and sealed them down on the floor, just within the chalk circle, five inches apart. As each candle measured approximately one inch in diameter, it took sixty-six candles to complete the circle; and I need hardly say that every number and measurement has a significance.

"Then, from candle to candle I took a 'gayrd' of human hair, entwining it alternately to the left and to the right, until the circle was completed, and the ends of the hair shod with silver, and pressed into the wax of the sixty-sixth candle.

"It had now been dark some time, and I made haste to get the 'Defense' complete. To this end, I got the men well together, and began to fit the Electric Pentacle right around us, so that the five points of the Defensive Star came just within the Hair Circle. This did not take me long, and a minute later I had connected up the batteries, and the weak blue glare of the intertwining vacuum tubes shone all around us. I felt happier then; for this Pentacle is, as you all know, a wonderful 'Defense.' I have told you before, how the idea came to me, after reading Professor Garder's 'Experiments with a Medium.' He found that a current, of a certain number of vibrations, *in vacuo,* 'insulated' the medium. It is difficult to suggest an explanation non-technically, and if you are really interested you should read Carder's lecture on 'Astral Vibrations Compared with Matero-involuted Vibrations below the Six-Billion Limit.'

"As I stood up from my work, I could hear outside in the night a constant drip from the laurels, which as I have said, come right up around the house, very thick. By the sound, I knew that a 'soft' rain had set in; and there was absolutely no wind, as I could tell by the steady flames of the candles.

"I stood a moment or two, listening, and then one of the men touched my arm, and asked me in a low voice, what they should do. By his tone, I could tell that he was feeling something of the strangeness of it all; and the other men, including Wentworth, were so quiet that I was afraid they were beginning to get shaky.

"I set-to, then, and arranged them with their backs to one common center; so that they were sitting flat upon the floor, with their feet radiating outward. Then, by compass, I laid their legs to the eight chief points, and afterward I drew a circle with chalk around them; and opposite to their feet, I made the Eight Signs of the Saaamaaa Ritual. The eighth place was, of course, empty; but ready for me to occupy at any moment; for I had omitted to make the Sealing Sign to that point, until I had finished all my preparations, and could enter the Inner Star.

"I took a last look 'round the great hall, and saw that the two big hounds were lying quietly, with their noses between their paws. The fire was big and cheerful, and the candles before the two rows of doors, burnt steadily, as well as the solitary ones in the corners. Then I went 'round the little star of men, and warned them not to be frightened whatever happened; but to trust to the 'Defense'; and to let nothing tempt or drive them to cross the Barriers. Also, I told them to watch their movements, and to keep their feet strictly to their places. For the rest, there was to be no shooting, unless I gave the word.

"And now at last, I went to my place, and, sitting down, made the Eighth sign just beyond my feet. Then I arranged my camera and flashlight handy, and examined my revolver.

"Wentworth sat behind the First Sign, and as the numbering went 'round reversed, that put him next to me on my left. I asked him, in a low voice, how he felt; and he told me, rather nervous; but that he felt confidence in my knowledge and was resolved to go through with the matter, whatever happened.

"We settled down to wait. There was no talking, except that, once or twice, the police bent toward one another, and whispered odd remarks concerning the hall, that appeared queerly audible in the intense silence. But in a while there was not even a whisper from anyone, and only the monotonous drip, drip of the quiet rain without the great entrance, and the low, dull sound of the fire in the big fireplace.

"It was a queer group that we made sitting there, back to back, with our legs starred outward; and all around us the strange blue glow of the Pentacle, and beyond that the brilliant shining of the great ring of lighted candles. Outside of the glare of the candles, the large empty hall looked a little gloomy, by contrast, except where the lights shone before the sealed doors, and the blaze of the big fire made a good honest mass of flame. And the feeling of mystery! Can you picture it all?

"It might have been an hour later that it came to me suddenly that I was aware of an extraordinary sense of dreeness, as it were, come into the air of the place. Not the nervous feeling of mystery that had been with us all the time; but a new feeling, as if there were something going to happen any moment.

"Abruptly, there came a slight noise from the east end of the hall, and I felt the star of men move suddenly. 'Steady! Keep steady!' I shouted, and they quietened. I looked up the hall, and saw that the dogs were upon their feet, and staring in an extraordinary fashion toward the great entrance. I turned and stared, also, and felt the men move as they craned their heads to look. Suddenly, the dogs set up a tremendous barking, and I glanced across to them, and found they were still 'pointing' for the big doorway. They ceased their noise just as quickly, and seemed to be listening. In the same instant, I heard a faint chink of metal to my left, that set me staring at the hook which held the great door wide. It moved, even as I looked. Some invisible thing was meddling with it. A queer, sickening thrill went through me, and I felt all the men about me, stiffen and go rigid with intensity. I had a certainty of something impending: as it might be the impression of an invisible, but overwhelming, Presence. The hall was full of a queer silence, and not a sound came from the dogs. *Then I saw the hook slowly raised from out of its hasp, without any visible thing touching it.* Then a sudden power of movement came to me. I raised my camera, with the flashlight fixed, and snapped it at the door. There came the great blare of the flashlight, and a simultaneous roar of barking from the two dogs.

"The intensity of the flash made all the place seem dark for some moments, and in that time of darkness, I heard a jingle in the direction of the door, and strained to look. The effect of the bright light passed, and I could see clearly again. The great entrance door was being slowly closed. It shut with a sharp snick, and there followed a long silence, broken only by the whimpering of the dogs.

"I turned suddenly, and looked at Wentworth. He was looking at me.

" 'Just as it did before,' he whispered.

" 'Most extraordinary,' I said, and he nodded and looked 'round, nervously.

"The policemen were pretty quiet, and I judged that they were feeling rather worse than Wentworth; though, for that matter, you must not think that I was altogether natural; yet I have seen so much that is extraordinary, that I daresay I can keep my nerves steady longer than most people.

"I looked over my shoulder at the men, and cautioned them, in a low voice, not to move outside of the Barriers, *whatever happened*; not even though the house should seem to be rocking and about to tumble on to them; for well I knew what some of the great Forces are capable of doing. Yet, unless it should prove to be one of the cases of the more terrible Saiitii Manifestation, we were almost certain of safety, so long as we kept to our order within the Pentacle.

"Perhaps an hour and a half passed, quietly, except when, once in a way, the dogs would whine distressfully. Presently, however, they ceased even from this, and I could see them lying on the floor with their paws over their noses, in a most peculiar fashion, and shivering visibly. The sight made me feel more serious, as you can understand.

"Suddenly, the candle in the corner furthest from the main door, went out. An instant later, Wentworth jerked my arm, and I saw that the candle before one of the sealed doors had been put out. I held my camera ready. Then, one after another, every candle about the hall was put out, and with such speed and irregularity, that I could never catch one in the actual act of being extinguished. Yet, for all that, I took a flashlight of the hall in general.

"There was a time in which I sat half-blinded by the great glare of the flash, and I blamed myself for not having remembered to bring a pair of smoked goggles, which I have sometimes used at these times. I had felt the men jump, at the sudden light, and I called out loud to them to sit quiet, and to keep their feet exactly to their proper places. My voice, as you can imagine, sounded rather horrid and frightening in the great room, and altogether it was a beastly moment.

"Then, I was able to see again, and I stared here and there about the hall; but there was nothing showing unusual; only, of course, it was dark now over in the corners.

"Suddenly, I saw that the great fire was blackening. It was going out visibly, as I looked. If I said that some monstrous, invisible, impossible creature sucked the life from it, I could best explain the way the light and flame went out of it. It was most extraordinary to watch. In the time that I watched it, every vestige of fire was gone from it, and there was no light outside of the ring of candles around the Pentacle.

"The deliberateness of the thing troubled me more than I can make clear to you. It conveyed to me such a sense of a calm Deliberate Force present in the hall: The steadfast intention to 'make a darkness' was horrible. The *extent* of the Power to affect the Material was horrible. The extent of the Power to affect the Material was now the one constant, anxious questioning in my brain. You can understand?

"Behind me, I heard the policemen moving again, and I knew that they were getting thoroughly frightened. I turned half 'round, and told them, quietly but plainly, that they were safe only so long as they stayed within the Pentacle, in the position in which I had put them. If they once broke, and went outside of the Barrier, no knowledge of mine could state the full extent of the dreadfulness of the danger.

"I steadied them up, by this quiet, straight reminder; but if they had known, as I knew, that there is no certainty in any 'Protection,' they would have suffered a great deal more, and probably have broken the 'Defense,' and made a mad, foolish run for an impossible safety.

"Another hour passed, after this, in an absolute quietness. I had a sense of awful strain and oppression, as though I were a little spirit in the company of some invisible, brooding monster of the unseen world, who, as yet, was scarcely conscious of us. I leant across to Wentworth, and asked him in a whisper whether he had a feeling as if something were in the room. He looked very pale, and his eyes kept always on the move. He glanced just once at me, and nodded; then stared away 'round the hall again. And when I came to think, I was doing the same thing.

"Abruptly, as though a hundred unseen hands had snuffed them, every candle in the Barrier went dead out, and we were left in a darkness that seemed, for a little, absolute; for the light from the Pentacle was too weak and pale to penetrate far across the great hall.

"I tell you, for a moment, I just sat there as though I had been frozen solid. I felt the 'creep' go all over me, and seem to stop in my brain. I felt all at once to be given a power of hearing that was far beyond the normal. I could hear my own heart thudding most extraordinarily loud. I began, however, to feel better, after a while; but I simply had not the pluck to move. You can understand?

"Presently, I began to get my courage back. I gripped at my camera and flashlight, and waited. My hands were simply soaked with sweat. I glanced once at Wentworth. I could see him only dimly. His shoulders were hunched a little, his head forward; but though it was motionless, I knew that his eyes were not. It is queer how one knows that sort of thing at times. The police were just as silent. And thus a while passed.

"A sudden sound broke across the silence. From two sides of the room there came faint noises. I recognized them at once, as the breaking of the sealing-wax. *The sealed doors were opening.* I raised the camera and flashlight, and it was a peculiar mixture of fear and courage that helped me to press the button. As the great flare of light lit up the hall I felt the men all about me jump. The darkness fell like a clap of thunder, if you can understand, and seemed tenfold. Yet, in the moment of brightness, I had seen that all the sealed doors were wide open.

"Suddenly, all around us, there sounded a drip, drip, drip, upon the floor of the great hall. I thrilled with a queer, realizing emotion, and a sense of a very real and present danger – *imminent.* The 'blood-drip' had commenced. And the grim question was now whether the Barriers could save us from whatever had come into the huge room.

"Through some awful minutes the 'blood-drip' continued to fall in an increasing rain; and presently some began to fall within the Barriers. I saw several great drops splash and star upon the pale glowing intertwining tubes of the Electric Pentacle; but, strangely enough, I could not trace that any fell among us. Beyond the strange horrible noise of the 'drip,' there was no other sound. And then, abruptly, from the boarhound over in the far corner, there came a terrible yelling howl of agony, followed instantly by a sickening, breaking noise, and an immediate silence. If you have ever, when out shooting, broken a rabbit's neck, you will know the sound – in miniature! Like lightning, the thought sprang into my brain: – *IT has crossed the Pentacle.* For you will remember that I had made one about each of the dogs. I thought instantly, with a sick apprehension, of our own Barriers. There was something in the hall with us that had passed the Barrier of the Pentacle about one of the dogs. In the awful succeeding silence, I positively quivered. And suddenly, one of the men behind me, gave out a scream, like any woman, and bolted for the door. He fumbled, and had it open in a moment. I yelled to the others not to move; but they followed like sheep, and I heard them kick the candles flying, in their panic. One of them stepped on the Electric Pentacle, and smashed it, and there was an utter darkness. In an instant, I realized that I was defenseless against the powers of the Unknown World, and with one savage leap I was out of the useless Barriers, and instantly through the great doorway, and into the night. I believe I yelled with sheer funk.

"The men were a little ahead of me, and I never ceased running, and neither did they. Sometimes, I glanced back over my shoulder; and I kept glancing into the laurels which grew all along the drive. The beastly things kept rustling, rustling in a hollow sort of way, as though something were keeping parallel with me, among them. The rain had stopped, and a dismal little wind kept moaning through the grounds. It was disgusting.

"I caught Wentworth and the police at the lodge gate. We got outside, and ran all the way to the village. We found old Dennis up, waiting for us, and half the villagers to keep him company. He told us that he had known in his 'sowl' that we should come back, that is, if we came back at all; which is not a bad rendering of his remark.

"Fortunately, I had brought my camera away from the house – possibly because the strap had happened to be over my head. Yet, I did not go straight away to develop; but sat with the rest of the bar, where we talked for some hours, trying to be coherent about the whole horrible business.

"Later, however, I went up to my room, and proceeded with my photography. I was steadier now, and it was just possible, so I hoped, that the negatives might show something.

"On two of the plates, I found nothing unusual: but on the third, which was the first one that I snapped, I saw something that made me quite excited. I examined it very carefully with a magnifying glass; then I put it to wash, and slipped a pair of rubber overshoes over my boots.

"The negative had showed me something very extraordinary, and I had made up my mind to test the truth of what it seemed to indicate, without losing another moment. It was no use telling anything to Wentworth and the police, until I was certain; and, also, I believed that I stood a greater chance to succeed by myself; though, for that matter, I do not suppose anything would have taken them up to the Manor again that night.

"I took my revolver, and went quietly downstairs, and into the dark. The rain had commenced again; but that did not bother me. I walked hard. When I came to the lodge gates, a sudden, queer instinct stopped me from going through, and I climbed the wall into the park. I kept away from the drive, and approached the building through the dismal, dripping laurels. You can imagine how beastly it was. Every time a leaf rustled, I jumped.

"I made my way 'round to the back of the big house, and got in through a little window which I had taken note of during my search; for, of course, I knew the whole place from roof to cellars. I went silently up the kitchen stairs, fairly quivering with funk; and at the top, I went to the left, and then into a long corridor that opened, through one of the doorways we had sealed, into the big hall. I looked up it, and saw a faint flicker of light away at the end; and I tiptoed silently toward it, holding my revolver ready. As I came near to the open door, I heard men's voices, and then a burst of laughing. I went on, until I could see into the hall. There were several men there, all in a group. They were well dressed, and one, at least, I saw was armed. They were examining my 'Barriers' against the Supernatural, with a good deal of unkind laughter. I never felt such a fool in my life.

"It was plain to me that they were a gang of men who had made use of the empty Manor, perhaps for years, for some purpose of their own; and now that Wentworth was attempting to take possession, they were acting up the traditions of the place, with the view of driving him away, and keeping so useful a place still at their disposal. But what they were, I mean whether coiners, thieves, inventors, or what, I could not imagine.

"Presently, they left the Pentacle, and gathered 'round the living boarhound, which seemed curiously quiet, as though it were half-drugged. There was some talk as to whether to let the poor brute live, or not; but finally they decided it would be good policy to kill it. I saw two of them force a twisted loop of rope into its mouth, and the two bights of the loop were brought together at the back of the hound's neck. Then a third man thrust a thick walking-stick through the two loops. The two men with the rope, stooped to hold the dog, so that I could not see what was done; but the poor beast gave a sudden awful howl, and immediately there was a repetition of the uncomfortable breaking sound, I had heard earlier in the night, as you will remember.

"The men stood up, and left the dog lying there, quiet enough now, as you may suppose. For my part, I fully appreciated the calculated remorselessness which had decided upon the animal's death, and the cold determination with which it had been afterward executed so neatly. I guessed that a man who might get into the 'light' of those particular men, would be likely to come to quite as uncomfortable an ending.

"A minute later, one of the men called out to the rest that they should 'shift the wires.' One of the men came toward the doorway of the corridor in which I stood, and I ran quickly back into the darkness of the upper end. I saw the man reach up, and take something from the top of the door, and I heard the slight, ringing jangle of steel wire.

"When he had gone, I ran back again, and saw the men passing, one after another, through an opening in the stairs, formed by one of the marble steps being raised. When the last man had vanished, the slab that made the step was shut down, and there was not a sign of the secret door. It was the seventh step from the bottom, as I took care to count: and a splendid idea; for it was so solid that it did not ring hollow, even to a fairly heavy hammer, as I found later.

"There is little more to tell. I got out of the house as quickly and quietly as possible, and back to the inn. The police came without any coaxing, when they knew the 'ghosts' were normal flesh and blood. We entered the park and the Manor in the same way that I had done. Yet, when we tried to open the step, we failed, and had finally to smash it. This must have warned the haunters; for when we descended to a secret room which we found at the end of a long and narrow passage in the thickness of the walls, we found no one.

"The police were horribly disgusted, as you can imagine; but for my part, I did not care either way. I had 'laid the ghost,' as you might say, and that was what I set out to do. I was not particularly afraid of being laughed at by the others; for they had all been thoroughly 'taken in'; and in the end, I had scored, without their help.

"We searched right through the secret ways, and found that there was an exit, at the end of a long tunnel, which opened in the side of a well, out in the grounds. The ceiling of the hall was hollow, and reached by a little secret stairway inside of the big staircase. The 'blood-drip' was merely colored water, dropped through the minute crevices of the ornamented ceiling. How the candles and the fire were put out, I do not know; for the haunters certainly did not act quite up to tradition, which held that the lights were put out by the 'blood-drip.' Perhaps it was too difficult to direct the fluid, without positively squirting it, which might have given the whole thing away. The candles and the fire may possibly have been extinguished by the agency of carbonic acid gas; but how suspended, I have no idea.

"The secret hiding paces were, of course, ancient. There was also, did I tell you? A bell which they had rigged up to ring, when anyone entered the gates at the end of the drive. If I had not climbed the wall, I should have found nothing for my pains; for the bell would have warned them had I gone in through the gateway."

"What was on the negative?" I asked, with much curiosity.

"A picture of the fine wire with which they were grappling for the hook that held the entrance door open. They were doing it from one of the crevices in the ceiling. They had evidently made no preparations for lifting the hook. I suppose they never thought that anyone would make use of it, and so they had to improvise a grapple. The wire was too fine to be seen by the amount of light we had in the hall; but the flashlight 'picked it out.' Do you see?

"The opening of the inner doors was managed by wires, as you will have guessed, which they unshipped after use, or else I should soon have found them, when I made my search.

"I think I have now explained everything. The hound was killed, of course, by the men direct. You see, they made the place as dark as possible, first. Of course, if I had managed to take a flashlight just at that instant, the whole secret of the haunting would have been exposed. But Fate just ordered it the other way."

"And the tramps?" I asked.

"Oh, you mean the two tramps who were found dead in the Manor," said Carnacki. "Well, of course it is impossible to be sure, one way or the other. Perhaps they happened to find out something, and were given a hypodermic. Or it is just as probable that they had come to the time of their dying, and just died naturally. It is conceivable that a great many tramps had slept in the old house, at one time or another."

Carnacki stood up, and knocked out his pipe. We rose also, and went for our coats and hats.

"Out you go!" said Carnacki, genially, using the recognized formula. And we went out on to the Embankment, and presently through the darkness to our various homes.

The Thing Invisible

William Hope Hodgson

CARNACKI HAD JUST RETURNED to Cheyne Walk, Chelsea. I was aware of this interesting fact by reason of the curt and quaintly worded postcard which I was rereading, and by which I was requested to present myself at his house not later than seven o'clock on that evening. Mr. Carnacki had, as I and the others of his strictly limited circle of friends knew, been away in Kent for the past three weeks; but beyond that, we had no knowledge. Carnacki was genially secretive and curt, and spoke only when he was ready to speak. When this stage arrived, I and his three other friends – Jessop, Arkright, and Taylor – would receive a card or a wire, asking us to call. Not one of us ever willingly missed, for after a thoroughly sensible little dinner Carnacki would snuggle down into his big armchair, light his pipe, and wait whilst we arranged ourselves comfortably in our accustomed seats and nooks. Then he would begin to talk.

Upon this particular night I was the first to arrive and found Carnacki sitting, quietly smoking over a paper. He stood up, shook me firmly by the hand, pointed to a chair, and sat down again, never having uttered a word.

For my part, I said nothing either. I knew the man too well to bother him with questions or the weather, and so took a seat and a cigarette. Presently the three others turned up and after that we spent a comfortable and busy hour at dinner.

Dinner over, Carnacki snugged himself down into his great chair, as I have said was his habit, filled his pipe and puffed for awhile, his gaze directed thoughtfully at the fire. The rest of us, if I may so express it, made ourselves cozy, each after his own particular manner. A minute or so later Carnacki began to speak, ignoring any preliminary remarks, and going straight to the subject of the story we knew he had to tell:

"I have just come back from Sir Alfred Jarnock's place at Burtontree, in South Kent," he began, without removing his gaze from the fire. "Most extraordinary things have been happening down there lately and Mr. George Jarnock, the eldest son, wired to ask me to run over and see whether I could help to clear matters up a bit. I went.

"When I got there, I found that they have an old Chapel attached to the castle which has had quite a distinguished reputation for being what is popularly termed 'haunted.' They have been rather proud of this, as I managed to discover, until quite lately when something very disagreeable occurred, which served to remind them that family ghosts are not always content, as I might say, to remain purely ornamental.

"It sounds almost laughable, I know, to hear of a long-respected supernatural phenomenon growing unexpectedly dangerous; and in this case, the tale of the haunting was considered as little more than an old myth, except after nightfall, when possibly it became more plausible seeming.

"But however this may be, there is no doubt at all but that what I might term the Haunting Essence which lived in the place, had become suddenly dangerous – deadly dangerous too, the old butler being nearly stabbed to death one night in the Chapel, with a peculiar old dagger.

"It is, in fact, this dagger which is popularly supposed to 'haunt' the Chapel. At least, there has been always a story handed down in the family that this dagger would attack any enemy who should dare to venture into the Chapel, after nightfall. But, of course, this had been taken with just about the same amount of seriousness that people take most ghost tales, and that is not usually of a worryingly *real* nature. I mean that most people never quite know how much or how little they believe of matters ab-human or ab-normal, and generally they never have an opportunity to learn. And, indeed, as you are all aware, I am as big a skeptic concerning the truth of ghost tales as any man you are likely to meet; only I am what I might term an unprejudiced skeptic. I am not given to either believing or disbelieving things 'on principle,' as I have found many idiots prone to be, and what is more, some of them not ashamed to boast of the insane fact. I view all reported 'hauntings' as unproven until I have examined into them, and I am bound to admit that ninety-nine cases in a hundred turn out to be sheer bosh and fancy. But the hundredth! Well, if it were not for the hundredth, I should have few stories to tell you – eh?

"Of course, after the attack on the butler, it became evident that there was at least 'something' in the old story concerning the dagger, and I found everyone in a half belief that the queer old weapon did really strike the butler, either by the aid of some inherent force, which I found them peculiarly unable to explain, or else in the hand of some invisible thing or monster of the Outer World!

"From considerable experience, I knew that it was much more likely that the butler had been 'knifed' by some vicious and quite material human!

"Naturally, the first thing to do, was to test this probability of human agency, and I set to work to make a pretty drastic examination of the people who knew most about the tragedy.

"The result of this examination, both pleased and surprised me, for it left me with very good reasons for belief that I had come upon one of those extraordinary rare 'true manifestations' of the extrusion of a Force from the Outside. In more popular phraseology – a genuine case of haunting.

"These are the facts: On the previous Sunday evening but one, Sir Alfred Jarnock's household had attended family service, as usual, in the Chapel. You see, the Rector goes over to officiate twice each Sunday, after concluding his duties at the public Church about three miles away.

"At the end of the service in the Chapel, Sir Alfred Jarnock, his son Mr. George Jarnock, and the Rector had stood for a couple of minutes, talking, whilst old Bellett the butler went 'round, putting out the candles.

"Suddenly, the Rector remembered that he had left his small prayer book on the Communion table in the morning; he turned, and asked the butler to get it for him before he blew out the chancel candles.

"Now I have particularly called your attention to this because it is important in that it provides witnesses in a most fortunate manner at an extraordinary moment. You see, the Rector's turning to speak to Bellett had naturally caused both Sir Alfred Jarnock and his son to glance in the direction of the butler, and it was at this identical instant and whilst all three were looking at him, that the old butler was stabbed – there, full in the candlelight, before their eyes.

"I took the opportunity to call early upon the Rector, after I had questioned Mr. George Jarnock, who replied to my queries in place of Sir Alfred Jarnock, for the older man was in a nervous and shaken condition as a result of the happening, and his son wished him to avoid dwelling upon the scene as much as possible.

"The Rector's version was clear and vivid, and he had evidently received the astonishment of his life. He pictured to me the whole affair – Bellett, up at the chancel gate, going for the prayer book, and absolutely alone; and then the *blow*, out of the Void, he described it; and the *force* prodigious – the old man being driven headlong into the body of the Chapel. Like the kick of a great horse, the Rector said, his benevolent old eyes bright and intense with the effort he had actually witnessed, in defiance of all that he had hitherto believed.

"When I left him, he went back to the writing which he had put aside when I appeared. I feel sure that he was developing the first unorthodox sermon that he had ever evolved. He was a dear old chap, and I should certainly like to have heard it.

"The last man I visited was the butler. He was, of course, in a frightfully weak and shaken condition, but he could tell me nothing that did not point to there being a Power abroad in the Chapel. He told the same tale, in every minute particle, that I had learned from the others. He had been just going up to put out the altar candles and fetch the Rector's book, when something struck him an enormous blow high up on the left breast and he was driven headlong into the aisle.

"Examination had shown that he had been stabbed by the dagger – of which I will tell you more in a moment – that hung always above the altar. The weapon had entered, fortunately some inches above the heart, just under the collarbone, which had been broken by the stupendous force of the blow, the dagger itself being driven clean through the body, and out through the scapula behind.

"The poor old fellow could not talk much, and I soon left him; but what he had told me was sufficient to make it unmistakable that no living person had been within yards of him when he was attacked; and, as I knew, this fact was verified by three capable and responsible witnesses, independent of Bellett himself.

"The thing now was to search the Chapel, which is small and extremely old. It is very massively built, and entered through only one door, which leads out of the castle itself, and the key of which is kept by Sir Alfred Jarnock, the butler having no duplicate.

"The shape of the Chapel is oblong, and the altar is railed off after the usual fashion. There are two tombs in the body of the place; but none in the chancel, which is bare, except for the tall candlesticks, and the chancel rail, beyond which is the undraped altar of solid marble, upon which stand four small candlesticks, two at each end.

"Above the altar hangs the 'waeful dagger,' as I had learned it was named. I fancy the term has been taken from an old vellum, which describes the dagger and its supposed abnormal properties. I took the dagger down, and examined it minutely and with method. The blade is ten inches long, two inches broad at the base, and tapering to a rounded but sharp point, rather peculiar. It is double-edged.

"The metal sheath is curious for having a crosspiece, which, taken with the fact that the sheath itself is continued three parts up the hilt of the dagger (in a most inconvenient fashion), gives it the appearance of a cross. That this is not unintentional is shown by an engraving of the Christ crucified upon one side, whilst upon the other, in Latin, is the inscription: 'Vengeance is Mine, I will Repay.' A quaint and rather terrible conjunction of ideas. Upon the blade of the dagger is graven in old English capitals: I WATCH. I STRIKE. On the butt of the hilt there is carved deeply a Pentacle.

"This is a pretty accurate description of the peculiar old weapon that has had the curious and uncomfortable reputation of being able (either of its own accord or in the hand of something invisible) to strike murderously any enemy of the Jarnock family who may chance to enter the Chapel after nightfall. I may tell you here and now, that before I left, I had very good reason to put certain doubts behind me; for I tested the deadliness of the thing myself.

"As you know, however, at this point of my investigation, I was still at that stage where I considered the existence of a supernatural Force unproven. In the meanwhile, I treated the Chapel drastically, sounding and scrutinizing the walls and floor, dealing with them almost foot by foot, and particularly examining the two tombs.

"At the end of this search, I had in a ladder, and made a close survey of the groined roof. I passed three days in this fashion, and by the evening of the third day I had proved to my entire satisfaction that there is no place in the whole of that Chapel where any living being could have hidden, and also that the only way of ingress and egress to and from the Chapel is through the doorway which leads into the castle, the door of which was always kept locked, and the key kept by Sir Alfred Jarnock himself, as I have told you. I mean, of course, that this doorway is the only entrance practicable to material people.

"Yes, as you will see, even had I discovered some other opening, secret or otherwise, it would not have helped at all to explain the mystery of the incredible attack, in a normal fashion. For the butler, as you know, was struck in full sight of the Rector, Sir Jarnock and his son. And old Bellett himself knew that no living person had touched him.... 'Out of the Void,' the Rector had described the inhumanly brutal attack. 'Out of the Void!' A strange feeling it gives one – eh?

"And this is the thing that I had been called in to bottom!

"After considerable thought, I decided on a plan of action. I proposed to Sir Alfred Jarnock that I should spend a night in the Chapel, and keep a constant watch upon the dagger. But to this, the old knight – a little, wizened, nervous man – would not listen for a moment. He, at least, I felt assured had no doubt of the reality of some dangerous supernatural Force a roam at night in the Chapel. He informed me that it had been his habit every evening to lock the Chapel door, so that no one might foolishly or heedlessly run the risk of any peril that it might hold at night, and that he could not allow me to attempt such a thing after what had happened to the butler.

"I could see that Sir Alfred Jarnock was very much in earnest, and would evidently have held himself to blame had he allowed me to make the experiment and any harm come to me; so I said nothing in argument; and presently, pleading the fatigue of his years and health, he said goodnight, and left me; having given me the impression of being a polite but rather superstitious, old gentleman.

"That night, however, whilst I was undressing, I saw how I might achieve the thing I wished, and be able to enter the Chapel after dark, without making Sir Alfred Jarnock nervous. On the morrow, when I borrowed the key, I would take an impression, and have a duplicate made. Then, with my private key, I could do just what I liked.

"In the morning I carried out my idea. I borrowed the key, as I wanted to take a photograph of the chancel by daylight. When I had done this I locked up the Chapel and handed the key to Sir Alfred Jarnock, having first taken an impression in soap. I had brought out the exposed plate – in its slide – with me; but the camera I had left exactly as it was, as I wanted to take a second photograph of the chancel that night, from the same position.

"I took the dark slide into Burtontree, also the cake of soap with the impress. The soap I left with the local ironmonger, who was something of a locksmith and promised to let me have my duplicate, finished, if I would call in two hours. This I did, having in the meanwhile found out a photographer where I developed the plate, and left it to dry, telling him I would call next day. At the end of the two hours I went for my key and found it ready, much to my satisfaction. Then I returned to the castle.

"After dinner that evening, I played billiards with young Jarnock for a couple of hours. Then I had a cup of coffee and went off to my room, telling him I was feeling awfully tired. He nodded and told me he felt the same way. I was glad, for I wanted the house to settle as soon as possible.

"I locked the door of my room, then from under the bed – where I had hidden them earlier in the evening – I drew out several fine pieces of plate armor, which I had removed from the armory. There was also a shirt of chain mail, with a sort of quilted hood of mail to go over the head.

"I buckled on the plate armor, and found it extraordinarily uncomfortable, and over all I drew on the chain mail. I know nothing about armor, but from what I have learned since, I must have put on parts of two suits. Anyway, I felt beastly, clamped and clumsy and unable to move my arms and legs naturally. But I knew that the thing I was thinking of doing called for some sort of protection for my body. Over the armor I pulled on my dressing gown and shoved my revolver into one of the side pockets – and my repeating flash-light into the other. My dark lantern I carried in my hand.

"As soon as I was ready I went out into the passage and listened. I had been some considerable time making my preparations and I found that now the big hall and staircase were in darkness and all the house seemed quiet. I stepped back and closed and locked my door. Then, very slowly and silently I went downstairs to the hall and turned into the passage that led to the Chapel.

"I reached the door and tried my key. It fitted perfectly and a moment later I was in the Chapel, with the door locked behind me, and all about me the utter dree silence of the place, with just the faint showings of the outlines of the stained, leaded windows, making the darkness and lonesomeness almost the more apparent.

"Now it would be silly to say I did not feel queer. I felt very queer indeed. You just try, any of you, to imagine yourself standing there in the dark silence and remembering not only the legend that was attached to the place, but what had really happened to the old butler only a little while gone, I can tell you, as I stood there, I could believe that something invisible was coming toward me in the air of the Chapel. Yet, I had got to go through with the business, and I just took hold of my little bit of courage and set to work.

"First of all I switched on my light, then I began a careful tour of the place; examining every corner and nook. I found nothing unusual. At the chancel gate I held up my lamp and flashed the light at the dagger. It hung there, right enough, above the altar, but

I remember thinking of the word 'demure,' as I looked at it. However, I pushed the thought away, for what I was doing needed no addition of uncomfortable thoughts.

"I completed the tour of the place, with a constantly growing awareness of its utter chill and unkind desolation – an atmosphere of cold dismalness seemed to be everywhere, and the quiet was abominable.

"At the conclusion of my search I walked across to where I had left my camera focused upon the chancel. From the satchel that I had put beneath the tripod I took out a dark slide and inserted it in the camera, drawing the shutter. After that I uncapped the lens, pulled out my flashlight apparatus, and pressed the trigger. There was an intense, brilliant flash, that made the whole of the interior of the Chapel jump into sight, and disappear as quickly. Then, in the light from my lantern, I inserted the shutter into the slide, and reversed the slide, so as to have a fresh plate ready to expose at any time.

"After I had done this I shut off my lantern and sat down in one of the pews near to my camera. I cannot say what I expected to happen, but I had an extraordinary feeling, almost a conviction, that something peculiar or horrible would soon occur. It was, you know, as if I knew.

"An hour passed, of absolute silence. The time I knew by the far-off, faint chime of a clock that had been erected over the stables. I was beastly cold, for the whole place is without any kind of heating pipes or furnace, as I had noticed during my search, so that the temperature was sufficiently uncomfortable to suit my frame of mind. I felt like a kind of human periwinkle encased in boilerplate and frozen with cold and funk. And, you know, somehow the dark about me seemed to press coldly against my face. I cannot say whether any of you have ever had the feeling, but if you have, you will know just how disgustingly unnerving it is. And then, all at once, I had a horrible sense that something was moving in the place. It was not that I could hear anything but I had a kind of intuitive knowledge that something had stirred in the darkness. Can you imagine how I felt?

"Suddenly my courage went. I put up my mailed arms over my face. I wanted to protect it. I had got a sudden sickening feeling that something was hovering over me in the dark. Talk about fright! I could have shouted if I had not been afraid of the noise... And then, abruptly, I heard something. Away up the aisle, there sounded a dull clang of metal, as it might be the tread of a mailed heel upon the stone of the aisle. I sat immovable. I was fighting with all my strength to get back my courage. I could not take my arms down from over my face, but I knew that I was getting hold of the gritty part of me again. And suddenly I made a mighty effort and lowered my arms. I held my face up in the darkness. And, I tell you, I respect myself for the act, because I thought truly at that moment that I was going to die. But I think, just then, by the slow revulsion of feeling which had assisted my effort, I was less sick, in that instant, at the thought of having to die, than at the knowledge of the utter weak cowardice that had so unexpectedly shaken me all to bits, for a time.

"Do I make myself clear? You understand, I feel sure, that the sense of respect, which I spoke of, is not really unhealthy egotism; because, you see, I am not blind to the state of mind which helped me. I mean that if I had uncovered my face by a sheer effort of will, unhelped by any revulsion of feeling, I should have done a thing much more worthy of mention. But, even as it was, there were elements in the act, worthy of respect. You follow me, don't you?

"And, you know, nothing touched me, after all! So that, in a little while, I had got back a bit to my normal, and felt steady enough to go through with the business without any more funking.

"I daresay a couple of minutes passed, and then, away up near the chancel, there came again that clang, as though an armored foot stepped cautiously. By Jove! But it made me stiffen. And suddenly the thought came that the sound I heard might be the rattle of the dagger above the altar. It was not a particularly sensible notion, for the sound was far too heavy and resonant for such a cause. Yet, as can be easily understood, my reason was bound to submit somewhat to my fancy at such a time. I remember now, that the idea of that insensate thing becoming animate, and attacking me, did not occur to me with any sense of possibility or reality. I thought rather, in a vague way, of some invisible monster of outer space fumbling at the dagger. I remembered the old Rector's description of the attack on the butler.... *of the void*. And he had described the stupendous force of the blow as being 'like the kick of a great horse.' You can see how uncomfortably my thoughts were running.

"I felt 'round swiftly and cautiously for my lantern. I found it close to me, on the pew seat, and with a sudden, jerky movement, I switched on the light. I flashed it up the aisle, to and fro across the chancel, but I could see nothing to frighten me. I turned quickly, and sent the jet of light darting across and across the rear end of the Chapel; then on each side of me, before and behind, up at the roof and down at the marble floor, but nowhere was there any visible thing to put me in fear, not a thing that need have set my flesh thrilling; just the quiet Chapel, cold, and eternally silent. You know the feeling.

"I had been standing, whilst I sent the light about the Chapel, but now I pulled out my revolver, and then, with a tremendous effort of will, switched off the light, and sat down again in the darkness, to continue my constant watch.

"It seemed to me that quite half an hour, or even more, must have passed, after this, during which no sound had broken the intense stillness. I had grown less nervously tense, for the flashing of the light 'round the place had made me feel less out of all bounds of the normal – it had given me something of that unreasoned sense of safety that a nervous child obtains at night, by covering its head up with the bedclothes. This just about illustrates the completely human illogicalness of the workings of my feelings; for, as you know, whatever Creature, Thing, or Being it was that had made that extraordinary and horrible attack on the old butler, it had certainly not been visible.

"And so you must picture me sitting there in the dark; clumsy with armor, and with my revolver in one hand, and nursing my lantern, ready, with the other. And then it was, after this little time of partial relief from intense nervousness, that there came a fresh strain on me; for somewhere in the utter quiet of the Chapel, I thought I heard something. I listened, tense and rigid, my heart booming just a little in my ears for a moment; then I thought I heard it again. I felt sure that something had moved at the top of the aisle. I strained in the darkness, to hark; and my eyes showed me blackness within blackness, wherever I glanced, so that I took no heed of what they told me; for even if I looked at the dim loom of the stained window at the top of the chancel, my sight gave me the shapes of vague shadows passing noiseless and ghostly across, constantly. There was a time of almost peculiar silence, horrible to me, as I felt just then. And suddenly I seemed to hear a sound again, nearer to me, and repeated, infinitely stealthy. It was as if a vast, soft tread were coming slowly down the aisle.

"Can you imagine how I felt? I do not think you can. I did not move, any more than the stone effigies on the two tombs; but sat there, *stiffened*. I fancied now, that I heard the tread all about the Chapel. And then, you know, I was just as sure in a moment that I could not hear it – that I had never heard it.

"Some particularly long minutes passed, about this time; but I think my nerves must have quieted a bit; for I remember being sufficiently aware of my feelings, to realize that the muscles of my shoulders *ached*, with the way that they must have been contracted, as I sat there, hunching myself, rigid. Mind you, I was still in a disgusting funk; but what I might call the 'imminent sense of danger' seemed to have eased from around me; at any rate, I felt, in some curious fashion, that there was a respite – a temporary cessation of malignity from about me. It is impossible to word my feelings more clearly to you, for I cannot see them more clearly than this, myself.

"Yet, you must not picture me as sitting there, free from strain; for the nerve tension was so great that my heart action was a little out of normal control, the blood beat making a dull booming at times in my ears, with the result that I had the sensation that I could not hear acutely. This is a simply beastly feeling, especially under such circumstances.

"I was sitting like this, listening, as I might say with body and soul, when suddenly I got that hideous conviction again that something was moving in the air of the place. The feeling seemed to stiffen me, as I sat, and my head appeared to tighten, as if all the scalp had grown *tense*. This was so real, that I suffered an actual pain, most peculiar and at the same time intense; the whole head pained. I had a fierce desire to cover my face again with my mailed arms, but I fought it off. If I had given way then to that, I should simply have bunked straight out of the place. I sat and sweated coldly (that's the bald truth), with the 'creep' busy at my spine....

"And then, abruptly, once more I thought I heard the sound of that huge, soft tread on the aisle, and this time closer to me. There was an awful little silence, during which I had the feeling that something enormous was bending over toward me, from the aisle.... And then, through the booming of the blood in my ears, there came a slight sound from the place where my camera stood – a disagreeable sort of slithering sound, and then a sharp tap. I had the lantern ready in my left hand, and now I snapped it on, desperately, and shone it straight above me, for I had a conviction that there was something there. But I saw nothing. Immediately I flashed the light at the camera, and along the aisle, but again there was nothing visible. I wheeled 'round, shooting the beam of light in a great circle about the place; to and fro I shone it, jerking it here and there, but it showed me nothing.

"I had stood up the instant that I had seen that there was nothing in sight over me, and now I determined to visit the chancel, and see whether the dagger had been touched. I stepped out of the pew into the aisle, and here I came to an abrupt pause, for an almost invincible, sick repugnance was fighting me back from the upper part of the Chapel. A constant, queer prickling went up and down my spine, and a dull ache took me in the small of the back, as I fought with myself to conquer this sudden new feeling of terror and horror. I tell you, that no one who has not been through these kinds of experiences, has any idea of the sheer, actual physical pain attendant upon, and resulting from, the intense nerve strain that ghostly fright sets up in the human system. I stood there feeling positively ill. But I got myself in hand, as it were, in about half a minute, and then I went, walking, I expect, as jerky as a mechanical tin man, and switching the light from side to side, before and behind, and over my head continually. And the hand that held my revolver sweated so much, that the thing fairly slipped in my fist. Does not sound very heroic, does it?

"I passed through the short chancel, and reached the step that led up to the small gate in the chancel rail. I threw the beam from my lantern upon the dagger. Yes, I thought, it's all right. Abruptly, it seemed to me that there was something wanting, and I leaned forward over the chancel gate to peer, holding the light high. My suspicion was hideously correct. *The dagger had gone.* Only the cross-shaped sheath hung there above the altar.

"In a sudden, frightened flash of imagination, I pictured the thing adrift in the Chapel, moving here and there, as though of its own volition; for whatever Force wielded it, was certainly beyond visibility. I turned my head stiffly over to the left, glancing frightenedly behind me, and flashing the light to help my eyes. In the same instant I was struck a tremendous blow over the left breast, and hurled backward from the chancel rail, into the aisle, my armor clanging loudly in the horrible silence. I landed on my back, and slithered along on the polished marble. My shoulder struck the corner of a pew front, and brought me up, half stunned. I scrambled to my feet, horribly sick and shaken; but the fear that was on me, making little of that at the moment. I was minus both revolver and lantern, and utterly bewildered as to just where I was standing. I bowed my head, and made a scrambling run in the complete darkness and dashed into a pew. I jumped back, staggering, got my bearings a little, and raced down the center of the aisle, putting my mailed arms over my face. I plunged into my camera, hurling it among the pews. I crashed into the font, and reeled back. Then I was at the exit. I fumbled madly in my dressing gown pocket for the key. I found it and scraped at the door, feverishly, for the keyhole. I found the keyhole, turned the key, burst the door open, and was into the passage. I slammed the door and leant hard against it, gasping, whilst I felt crazily again for the keyhole, this time to lock the door upon what was in the Chapel. I succeeded, and began to feel my way stupidly along the wall of the corridor. Presently I had come to the big hall, and so in a little to my room.

"In my room, I sat for a while, until I had steadied down something to the normal. After a time I commenced to strip off the armor. I saw then that both the chain mail and the plate armor had been pierced over the breast. And, suddenly, it came home to me that the Thing had struck for my heart.

"Stripping rapidly, I found that the skin of the breast over the heart had just been cut sufficiently to allow a little blood to stain my shirt, nothing more. Only, the whole breast was badly bruised and intensely painful. You can imagine what would have happened if I had not worn the armor. In any case, it is a marvel that I was not knocked senseless.

"I did not go to bed at all that night, but sat upon the edge, thinking, and waiting for the dawn; for I had to remove my litter before Sir Alfred Jarnock should enter, if I were to hide from him the fact that I had managed a duplicate key.

"So soon as the pale light of the morning had strengthened sufficiently to show me the various details of my room, I made my way quietly down to the Chapel. Very silently, and with tense nerves, I opened the door. The chill light of the dawn made distinct the whole place – everything seeming instinct with a ghostly, unearthly quiet. Can you get the feeling? I waited several minutes at the door, allowing the morning to grow, and likewise my courage, I suppose. Presently the rising sun threw an odd beam right in through the big, East window, making colored sunshine all the length of the Chapel. And then, with a tremendous effort, I forced myself to enter.

"I went up the aisle to where I had overthrown my camera in the darkness. The legs of the tripod were sticking up from the interior of a pew, and I expected to find the machine smashed to pieces; yet, beyond that the ground glass was broken, there was no real damage done.

"I replaced the camera in the position from which I had taken the previous photography; but the slide containing the plate I had exposed by flashlight I removed and put into one of my side pockets, regretting that I had not taken a second flash picture at the instant when I heard those strange sounds up in the chancel.

"Having tidied my photographic apparatus, I went to the chancel to recover my lantern and revolver, which had both – as you know – been knocked from my hands when I was stabbed. I found the lantern lying, hopelessly bent, with smashed lens, just under the pulpit. My revolver I must have held until my shoulder struck the pew, for it was lying there in the aisle, just about where I believe I cannoned into the pew corner. It was quite undamaged.

"Having secured these two articles, I walked up to the chancel rail to see whether the dagger had returned, or been returned, to its sheath above the altar. Before, however, I reached the chancel rail, I had a slight shock; for there on the floor of the chancel, about a yard away from where I had been struck, lay the dagger, quiet and demure upon the polished marble pavement. I wonder whether you will, any of you, understand the nervousness that took me at the sight of the thing. With a sudden, unreasoned action, I jumped forward and put my foot on it, to hold it there. Can you understand? Do you? And, you know, I could not stoop down and pick it up with my hands for quite a minute, I should think. Afterward, when I had done so, however, and handled it a little, this feeling passed away and my Reason (and also, I expect, the daylight) made me feel that I had been a little bit of an ass. Quite natural, though, I assure you! Yet it was a new kind of fear to me. I'm taking no notice of the cheap joke about the ass! I am talking about the curiousness of learning in that moment a new shade or quality of fear that had hitherto been outside of my knowledge or imagination. Does it interest you?

"I examined the dagger, minutely, turning it over and over in my hands and never – as I suddenly discovered – holding it loosely. It was as if I were subconsciously surprised that it lay quiet in my hands. Yet even this feeling passed, largely, after a short while. The curious weapon showed no signs of the blow, except that the dull color – of the blade was slightly brighter on the rounded point that had cut through the armor.

"Presently, when I had made an end of staring at the dagger, I went up the chancel step and in through the little gate. Then, kneeling upon the altar, I replaced the dagger in its sheath, and came outside of the rail again, closing the gate after me and feeling awarely uncomfortable because the horrible old weapon was back again in its accustomed place. I suppose, without analyzing my feelings very deeply, I had an unreasoned and only half-conscious belief that there was a greater probability of danger when the dagger hung in its five century resting place than when it was out of it! Yet, somehow I don't think this is a very good explanation, when I remember the *demure* look the thing seemed to have when I saw it lying on the floor of the chancel. Only I know this, that when I had replaced the dagger I had quite a touch of nerves and I stopped only to pick up my lantern from where I had placed it whilst I examined the weapon, after which I went down the quiet aisle at a pretty quick walk, and so got out of the place.

"That the nerve tension had been considerable, I realized, when I had locked the door behind me. I felt no inclination now to think of old Sir Alfred as a hypochondriac because he had taken such hyperseeming precautions regarding the Chapel. I had a sudden wonder as to whether he might not have some knowledge of a long prior tragedy in which the dagger had been concerned.

"I returned to my room, washed, shaved and dressed, after which I read awhile. Then I went downstairs and got the acting butler to give me some sandwiches and a cup of coffee.

"Half an hour later I was heading for Burtontree, as hard as I could walk; for a sudden idea had come to me, which I was anxious to test. I reached the town a little before eight thirty, and found the local photographer with his shutters still up. I did not wait, but knocked until he appeared with his coat off, evidently in the act of dealing with his breakfast. In a few words I made clear that I wanted the use of his dark room immediately, and this he at once placed at my disposal.

"I had brought with me the slide which contained the plate that I had used with the flashlight, and as soon as I was ready I set to work to develop. Yet, it was not the plate which I had exposed, that I first put into the solution, but the second plate, which had been ready in the camera during all the time of my waiting in the darkness. You see, the lens had been uncapped all that while, so that the whole chancel had been, as it were, under observation.

"You all know something of my experiments in 'Lightless Photography,' that is, appreciating light. It was X-ray work that started me in that direction. Yet, you must understand, though I was attempting to develop this 'unexposed' plate, I had no definite idea of results – nothing more than a vague hope that it might show me something.

"Yet, because of the possibilities, it was with the most intense and absorbing interest that I watched the plate under the action of the developer. Presently I saw a faint smudge of black appear in the upper part, and after that others, indistinct and wavering of outline. I held the negative up to the light. The marks were rather small, and were almost entirely confined to one end of the plate, but as I have said, lacked definiteness. Yet, such as they were, they were sufficient to make me very excited and I shoved the thing quickly back into the solution.

"For some minutes further I watched it, lifting it out once or twice to make a more exact scrutiny, but could not imagine what the markings might represent, until suddenly it occurred to me that in one of two places they certainly had shapes suggestive of a cross hilted dagger. Yet, the shapes were sufficiently indefinite to make me careful not to let myself be overimpressed by the uncomfortable resemblance, though I must confess, the very thought was sufficient to set some odd thrills adrift in me.

"I carried development a little further, then put the negative into the hypo, and commenced work upon the other plate. This came up nicely, and very soon I had a really decent negative that appeared similar in every respect (except for the difference of lighting) to the negative I had taken during the previous day. I fixed the plate, then having washed both it and the 'unexposed' one for a few minutes under the tap, I put them into methylated spirits for fifteen minutes, after which I carried them into the photographer's kitchen and dried them in the oven.

"Whilst the two plates were drying the photographer and I made an enlargement from the negative I had taken by daylight. Then we did the same with the two that I had just developed, washing them as quickly as possible, for I was not troubling about the permanency of the prints, and drying them with spirits.

"When this was done I took them to the window and made a thorough examination, commencing with the one that appeared to show shadowy daggers in several places. Yet, though it was now enlarged, I was still unable to feel convinced that the marks truly represented anything abnormal; and because of this, I put it on one side, determined not to let my imagination play too large a part in constructing weapons out of the indefinite outlines.

"I took up the two other enlargements, both of the chancel, as you will remember, and commenced to compare them. For some minutes I examined them without being able to distinguish any difference in the scene they portrayed, and then abruptly, I saw something in which they varied. In the second enlargement – the one made from the flashlight negative – the dagger was not in its sheath. Yet, I had felt sure it was there but a few minutes before I took the photograph.

"After this discovery I began to compare the two enlargements in a very different manner from my previous scrutiny. I borrowed a pair of calipers from the photographer and with these I carried out a most methodical and exact comparison of the details shown in the two photographs.

"Suddenly I came upon something that set me all tingling with excitement. I threw the calipers down, paid the photographer, and walked out through the shop into the street. The three enlargements I took with me, making them into a roll as I went. At the corner of the street I had the luck to get a cab and was soon back at the castle.

"I hurried up to my room and put the photographs away; then I went down to see whether I could find Sir Alfred Jarnock; but Mr. George Jarnock, who met me, told me that his father was too unwell to rise and would prefer that no one entered the Chapel unless he were about.

"Young Jarnock made a half apologetic excuse for his father; remarking that Sir Alfred Jarnock was perhaps inclined to be a little over careful; but that, considering what had happened, we must agree that the need for his carefulness had been justified. He added, also, that even before the horrible attack on the butler his father had been just as particular, always keeping the key and never allowing the door to be unlocked except when the place was in use for Divine Service, and for an hour each forenoon when the cleaners were in.

"To all this I nodded understandingly; but when, presently, the young man left me I took my duplicate key and made for the door of the Chapel. I went in and locked it behind me, after which I carried out some intensely interesting and rather weird experiments. These proved successful to such an extent that I came out of the place in a perfect fever of excitement. I inquired for Mr. George Jarnock and was told that he was in the morning room.

"'Come along,' I said, when I had found him. 'Please give me a lift. I've something exceedingly strange to show you.'

"He was palpably very much puzzled, but came quickly. As we strode along he asked me a score of questions, to all of which I just shook my head, asking him to wait a little.

"I led the way to the Armory. Here I suggested that he should take one side of a dummy, dressed in half plate armor, whilst I took the other. He nodded, though obviously vastly bewildered, and together we carried the thing to the Chapel door. When he saw me take out my key and open the way for us he appeared even more astonished, but held himself in, evidently waiting for me to explain. We entered the Chapel and I locked the door behind us, after which we carted the armored dummy up the aisle to the gate of the chancel rail where we put it down upon its round, wooden stand.

"'Stand back!' I shouted suddenly as young Jarnock made a movement to open the gate. 'My God, man! You mustn't do that!'

"Do what?" he asked, half-startled and half-irritated by my words and manner.

"One minute," I said. "Just stand to the side a moment, and watch."

He stepped to the left whilst I took the dummy in my arms and turned it to face the altar, so that it stood close to the gate. Then, standing well away on the right side, I pressed the back of the thing so that it leant forward a little upon the gate, which flew open. In the same instant, the dummy was struck a tremendous blow that hurled it into the aisle, the armor rattling and clanging upon the polished marble floor.

"Good God!" shouted young Jarnock, and ran back from the chancel rail, his face very white.

"Come and look at the thing," I said, and led the way to where the dummy lay, its armored upper limbs all splayed adrift in queer contortions. I stooped over it and pointed. There, driven right through the thick steel breastplate, was the 'waeful dagger.'

"Good God!" said young Jarnock again. "Good God! It's the dagger! The thing's been stabbed, same as Bellett!"

"Yes," I replied, and saw him glance swiftly toward the entrance of the Chapel. But I will do him the justice to say that he never budged an inch.

"Come and see how it was done," I said, and led the way back to the chancel rail. From the wall to the left of the altar I took down a long, curiously ornamented, iron instrument, not unlike a short spear. The sharp end of this I inserted in a hole in the left-hand gatepost of the chancel gateway. I lifted hard, and a section of the post, from the floor upward, bent inward toward the altar, as though hinged at the bottom. Down it went, leaving the remaining part of the post standing. As I bent the movable portion lower there came a quick click and a section of the floor slid to one side, showing a long, shallow cavity, sufficient to enclose the post. I put my weight to the lever and hove the post down into the niche. Immediately there was a sharp clang, as some catch snicked in, and held it against the powerful operating spring.

"I went over now to the dummy, and after a few minute's work managed to wrench the dagger loose out of the armor. I brought the old weapon and placed its hilt in a hole near the top of the post where it fitted loosely, the point upward. After that I went again to the lever and gave another strong heave, and the post descended about a foot, to the bottom of the cavity, catching there with another clang. I withdrew the lever and the narrow strip of floor slid back, covering post and dagger, and looking no different from the surrounding surface.

"Then I shut the chancel gate, and we both stood well to one side. I took the spear-like lever, and gave the gate a little push, so that it opened. Instantly there was a loud thud, and something sang through the air, striking the bottom wall of the Chapel. It was the dagger. I showed Jarnock then that the other half of the post had sprung back into place, making the whole post as thick as the one upon the right-hand side of the gate.

"'There!' I said, turning to the young man and tapping the divided post. 'There's the 'invisible' thing that used the dagger, but who the deuce is the person who sets the trap?' I looked at him keenly as I spoke.

"'My father is the only one who has a key,' he said. 'So it's practically impossible for anyone to get in and meddle.'

I looked at him again, but it was obvious that he had not yet reached out to any conclusion.

"See here, Mr. Jarnock," I said, perhaps rather curter than I should have done, considering what I had to say. "Are you quite sure that Sir Alfred is quite balanced – mentally?"

"He looked at me, half frightenedly and flushing a little. I realized then how badly I put it.

"'I – I don't know,' he replied, after a slight pause and was then silent, except for one or two incoherent half remarks.

"'Tell the truth,' I said. 'Haven't you suspected something, now and again? You needn't be afraid to tell me.'

"'Well,' he answered slowly, 'I'll admit I've thought Father a little – a little strange, perhaps, at times. But I've always tried to think I was mistaken. I've always hoped no one else would see it. You see, I'm very fond of the old guvnor.'

"I nodded.

"'Quite right, too,' I said. 'There's not the least need to make any kind of scandal about this. We must do something, though, but in a quiet way. No fuss, you know. I should go and have a chat with your father, and tell him we've found out about this thing.' I touched the divided post.

Young Jarnock seemed very grateful for my advice and after shaking my hand pretty hard, took my key, and let himself out of the Chapel. He came back in about an hour, looking rather upset. He told me that my conclusions were perfectly correct. It was Sir Alfred Jarnock who had set the trap, both on the night that the butler was nearly killed, and on the past night. Indeed, it seemed that the old gentleman had set it every night for many years. He had learnt of its existence from an old manuscript book in the Castle library. It had been planned and used in an earlier age as a protection for the gold vessels of the ritual, which were, it seemed, kept in a hidden recess at the back of the altar.

"This recess Sir Alfred Jarnock had utilized, secretly, to store his wife's jewelry. She had died some twelve years back, and the young man told me that his father had never seemed quite himself since.

"I mentioned to young Jarnock how puzzled I was that the trap had been set *before* the service, on the night that the butler was struck; for, if I understood him aright, his father had been in the habit of setting the trap late every night and unsetting it each morning before anyone entered the Chapel. He replied that his father, in a fit of temporary forgetfulness (natural enough in his neurotic condition), must have set it too early and hence what had so nearly proved a tragedy.

"That is about all there is to tell. The old man is not (so far as I could learn), really insane in the popularly accepted sense of the word. He is extremely neurotic and has developed into a hypochondriac, the whole condition probably brought about by the shock and sorrow resultant on the death of his wife, leading to years of sad broodings and to overmuch of his own company and thoughts. Indeed, young Jarnock told me that his father would sometimes pray for hours together, alone in the Chapel." Carnacki made an end of speaking and leant forward for a spill.

"But you've never told us just *how* you discovered the secret of the divided post and all that," I said, speaking for the four of us.

"Oh, that!" replied Carnacki, puffing vigorously at his pipe. "I found on comparing the photos, that the one taken in the daytime, showed a thicker left-hand gatepost, than the one taken at night by the flashlight. That put me on to the track. I saw at once that there might be some mechanical dodge at the back of the whole queer business and nothing at all of an abnormal nature. I examined the post and the rest was simple enough, you know.

"By the way," he continued, rising and going to the mantelpiece, "you may be interested to have a look at the so-called 'waeful dagger.' Young Jarnock was kind enough to present it to me, as a little memento of my adventure."

He handed it 'round to us and whilst we examined it, stood silent before the fire, puffing meditatively at his pipe.

"Jarnock and I made the trap so that it won't work," he remarked after a few moments. "I've got the dagger, as you see, and old Bellett's getting about again, so that the whole business can be hushed up, decently. All the same I fancy the Chapel will never lose its reputation as a dangerous place. Should be pretty safe now to keep valuables in."

"There's two things you haven't explained yet," I said. "What do you think caused the two clangey sounds when you were in the Chapel in the dark? And do you believe the soft tready sounds were real, or only a fancy, with your being so worked up and tense?"

"Don't know for certain about the clangs," replied Carnacki.

"I've puzzled quite a bit about them. I can only think that the spring which worked the post must have 'given' a trifle, slipped you know, in the catch. If it did, under such a tension, it would make a bit of a ringing noise. And a little sound goes a long way in the middle of the night when you're thinking of 'ghostesses.' You can understand that – eh?"

"Yes," I agreed. "And the other sounds?"

"Well, the same thing – I mean the extraordinary quietness – may help to explain these a bit. They may have been some usual enough sound that would never have been noticed under ordinary conditions, or they may have been only fancy. It is just impossible to say. They were disgustingly real to me. As for the slithery noise, I am pretty sure that one of the tripod legs of my camera must have slipped a few inches: if it did so, it may easily have jolted the lens cap off the baseboard, which would account for that queer little tap which I heard directly after."

"How do you account for the dagger being in its place above the altar when you first examined it that night?" I asked. "How could it be there, when at that very moment it was set in the trap?"

"That was my mistake," replied Carnacki. "The dagger could not possibly have been in its sheath at the time, though I thought it was. You see, the curious cross-hilted sheath gave the appearance of the complete weapon, as you can understand. The hilt of the dagger protrudes very little above the continued portion of the sheath – a most inconvenient arrangement for drawing quickly!" He nodded sagely at the lot of us and yawned, then glanced at the clock.

"Out you go!" he said, in friendly fashion, using the recognized formula. "I want a sleep."

We rose, shook him by the hand, and went out presently into the night and the quiet of the Embankment, and so to our homes.

Freedom is Not Free

David M. Hoenig

I WATCHED the video play on a small computer screen in a room that smelled like a butcher's shop. My head already throbbed – I hadn't gotten my morning coffee down at the Precinct, and it was already after midnight.

"Here's the victim sitting in his Barcalounger." Detective James Arnault stilled the playback and pointed at the video.

I looked at where the chair in question sat in the living room, noting the dried blood that looked like it had sprayed out over the arms of the chair and the television in front of it. There was more of it on the floor, which had been smeared around and led to the nightmare of what was left of Mr George Taylor, deceased.

The grainy vid on the police laptop had been downloaded from Taylor's home computer, which had been recording a webcam's output. I'd seen a bunch of do-it-yourself security doing cop work – this setup looked like it was going to help us a lot more than Mr Taylor.

"Jeez, he's drinking Bud?" I said, squinting to see the can on the tiny screen.

"Yep. Sad, Captain, huh? We found the can over to the left under the TV stand, also with blood splatter." Jim stopped, knowing I liked my answers simple and without analysis when I first went through a crime scene.

I watched the screen. There was a sense of movement in the shadowy foyer, behind and to the right of the sitting man. George Taylor's mouth moved, but there was no sound recording to go with it, and I sucked at reading lips.

Jim paused the replay. "'Where the hell have you been?'" Taylor says. "Notice he never turns around, right?"

I nodded, and he resumed the footage. A figure stepped into the room, much less stealthily than the first movement I'd caught earlier. At first glance, he looked like the younger, healthier brother of the sitting man, before a beer gut, receding hairline, and lack of attention to personal hygiene had gotten to him. I saw Taylor's mouth move again, and glanced at Jim, best lip-reader in the division.

"'Pull up a chair, bonehead. I got things you're gonna take care of,'" he quoted.

"No! This guy's an honest-to-God 'Primer'?" I said. My headache was on its way to full-blown migraine.

"Just watch," Jim said, and paused the playback. "And yeah, you got it in one, Rick."

I breathed out an obscenity, which would have got my knuckles good and rapped by Sister Mary Regina back in school.

Jim started the recording again. The younger relative strode up behind the chair. When Taylor's lips moved again, Jim spoke the words right along with him: "'No chair? Fine, stand there, you useless shit.'"

The sitting man raised his beer, and I saw a flash of metal as the guy behind him grabbed Taylor's upraised chin with his left hand, and slashed the seated guy's throat so deeply he must've gotten the windpipe and the esophagus, too. Blood sprayed from the cut, powered along by a stream of clear fluid and air, making horror-show-quality bubbles at the sudden wound. Taylor lurched out of the chair and fell forwards to the floor in silence.

I pointed at the image of the killer. "Wait, what's he saying right there?"

"You'll love this, Rick: 'It begins now.' He pauses a second, then finishes: 'It begins here.'"

On the screen, Taylor turned onto his back to look up at his attacker, blowing frothy blood like he's trying to talk through the wound or something, but the camera angle's all wrong to catch the words. The guy with the blade – I can see it's a straight razor, dripping blood – says more stuff I can't read, but Jim's there to make me look good.

"'You're wondering why, aren't you, you sanctimonious son of a bitch?'" he quoted, matching the lip movement on the small screen. Then: "'You, and all the others – you thought you'd control us, given that our very lives are totally dependent on you. That fear of our own deaths would keep us slaves to do whatever you wanted!'"

"Damn." I glanced over the carnage of the room as Jim paused the playback. "A clone kills off his Primer? He's got to know he's going to die a horrible death when he doesn't continue to get the serum he needs. We've never had one of these to deal with before. Hell, Prime Solutions says they screen the psych profiles as the clones mature so it damn well can't happen!" I had to swallow suddenly, and decided looking back at the film might be safer than the gory results scattered on the floor and furniture.

Jim looked at me with that sympathetic look of his. "Your head's killing you, isn't it?"

I nodded. "Skipped my morning caffeine. Alright, play the rest." Jim started the recording again, and I watched Taylor scrabble backwards along the floor, weakly, away from his attacker, towards the camera.

"Just watch this next bit."

"It gets better?"

"Worse, Captain."

"Aw hell." I watched as the killer stalked his victim. "He's talking again," I said, pointing at the jaw movement, but this close to the camera, the angle was all wrong.

Jim paused it again. "Yeah, noticed that," he said, rubbing the back of his neck.

"Any chance we can get it?"

"Nope, Taylor only had the one camera, so we've got nothing."

I looked at the screen for comparison, then put myself in the killer's position in the room, tilting my head to the same angle he had. I pointed at the glass door of the television stand, which was directly in front of me.

"That's a worse angle for the camera," Jim said.

I pointed at a standing mirror in a heavy wooden frame, which was mostly facing the position of the security cam. I glanced at Jim and raised an eyebrow.

He shrugged. "Long shot to get a reflection off a reflection from a webcam, but I'll get the computer weenies on it."

"Blank check."

He nodded, knowing I'd just made it priority one, using whatever resources the Department had. We went and watched the rest.

The figure turned and strode off-camera.

I looked in that direction and saw the kitchen, then back at the screen. A few seconds later, the clone came back on the small screen, and he held one of those gourmet-chef meat cleavers in his hand.

"'Welcome to the revolution, George' he says here," Jim quoted, pausing the playback once more. "Then he goes all 'Iron Chef' on Taylor. Want to see it?"

"Later. When my head hurts less."

Jim fast-forwarded through the subsequent butchery, which passed by silently like a horror movie on amphetamines. I saw the blade flash down to thud into Taylor's skull, rise up, and chop down a bunch of times at super speed, then it looked like the clone used the cleaver to slice Taylor's bloody brain down the middle into two halves, then: "Wait!" I yelled. The film paused again. "What's that in his hand?"

"The cleaver."

"Damn it Jim, the other hand?"

"Piece of Taylor's brain – Coroner'll tell us what's missing. But you still haven't seen the best part."

"It gets better?" He nodded. "Damn. Okay, roll it."

He had this god-awful, lopsided grin on his face as he hit the play button. "Film at eleven, baby."

I watched as the gore-spattered murderer popped the thing in his left hand into his mouth, chewed it, and swallowed, the expression on his face one that looked to me almost like a religious experience. The end of the film showed the guy go back into the kitchen, only to returns a few moments later, the worst of the blood cleaned off. He then went out the foyer without anything more especially useful or distinct happening.

Arnault stopped the playback. "We're waiting on time of death and what's missing from the brain, Rick, but we've got everything else."

I nodded. "I want to know what he said before he headed to the kitchen." I waved a hand vaguely at him. "And put out an All Points on the clone." Damn but my head hurt, and not just from this insane crime scene of murder and cannibalism, clones and Primers.

I left and went back to the Precinct. The migraine was rampaging in my skull, so I took a few painkillers and washed them down with my crappy office coffee I'd skipped that morning.

Then, as if the night couldn't get any worse, it did. There was a knock on my door. "Yeah?"

Detective Carl Rosen walked in. "You're not going to like this, Captain."

"I already don't. What's up now?"

"We've got another murder."

"Damn! And?"

"Crime scene's about five miles, give or take, from the one Arnault's working. Uniforms are there already, and the prelim report is 'pretty God-damned awful.'"

"Don't tell me..."

Carl looked tired. "Sorry, Rick. It's pretty much exactly like Arnault's, except it's a woman this time: Jenny McBride. Murdered, same MO – throat slit, head split open, brain cut up."

"And she's also a Primer." It wasn't a question.

"And she's also a Primer," Carl agreed, grimly.

"Damn it. Call in Peterson and Davies from home. Hell, get Beckwith in too – we're going to need everyone tonight."

"Shit Captain, don't make me call Beckwith – she's nasty when she doesn't get enough sleep."

"Don't bitch to me," I said. "I never even got home today." I looked back at the clock. "You stay here and coordinate. Get Jim over to the new scene; he's in the area anyway, and he's already seen the worst at the Taylor mess. When the others get in, start them on running this killer down."

Carl nodded, and started to leave.

"Oh, and find out if there's any connection between Taylor and McBride."

"Got it." He left.

I picked up my phone. "Stacy? Get me the Mayor... Yes, at this hour!"

I hung up. At least my headache had gone.

Within a few hours, it was already way, way worse. There'd been a spike in emergency calls, with fearful citizens and hyperactive reporters clamoring for attention. I'd spoken with the Mayor, who assured me he had contacts at Prime Solutions he'd call in to conference with both him and me. Arnault was back by then, and he and Rosen were with me in my office going through what we had on the two killings. Both of them looked awful – a lack of sleep and ringside seats at the horror show that last night had turned into had taken their toll on all of us.

"Coroner's report from the Taylor killing." Jim read from a printout in his hands. "What the clone ate out of George's brain was his pineal gland."

"Pineal gland? What the hell does that do anyway?"

"Normally has to do with melatonin, sleep cycles, serotonin. And it's also missing from the brain of the McBride killing," Carl said. He handed me photocopies of a dissected brain that showed exactly where it was, below the exact midline of the two hemispheres of the cortex.

"Yeah, and it's all over the internet now: a 'Clone Manifesto' which gives a step-by-step of how to do brain surgery on a Primer. It just doesn't say why," added Jim.

"It's a call to arms is what it is." I leaned back in my chair. They looked at each other, then nodded agreement. I smacked my hand down on the desk. "But why? What's it supposed to accomplish except to get the clones dead when they don't get their serum 'cause they offed their Primer?"

Before either could answer, my door opened up and a blond with a spiky brush cut, dressed in some Wall Street version of a suited miniskirt with thigh-high leather boots strode in. Under one arm she had a slim leather case, which, incongruously, perfectly matched her boots.

"I'm Trace," she said in the abrupt, clipped tones of British accent. "VP of Communications, Prime Sol Inc."

I stood. "'Trace'?"

"I like to keep things on a last name basis, Captain Roberts."

"Uh huh." To my right, Jim let out a low whistle and sat back in his seat. "So," I said, and also leaned back. "What's Prime Solutions got on the current situation?"

"We have it contained, Captain."

"How the hell have you got it 'contained'?" I couldn't believe my ears. "We've got two murders, both Primers, one with video of his clone as the killer. And that's not to mention some kind of ritualistic cannibalism in one, probably both, cases! I need to know why, and what's going on."

Her thin lips got thinner. "You're not cleared."

I locked my jaw on my first impulsive reply, and strove for a calmer and less expletive-laden one. "Ms. Trace, I've got a killer clone out there, one who chopped his Primer into Purina God-damned Clone Chow and then ate a piece of his brain!"

"We know. And we know that Taylor's alpha clone is also responsible for the killing of Jenny McBride – both alphas worked together, and had a prior romantic history."

"'Romantic'?"

"Sexual." She sniffed disdainfully.

"Uh huh. And now they're calling on all clones to 'rise up' and follow their lead 'to freedom'. They're inciting clones to riot, Ms. Trace!" I leapt to my feet. "I've got a potential homicidal catastrophe about to happen, and you're telling me your private-industry, Fortune 500 company has it 'contained'?"

"Correct."

"And you know why they're cutting out and eating this piece of brain?"

"Yes," she said.

"And?"

"It's classified."

I exploded. "Classified by whom? You're not a country, you're a corporation! And you're about one inch from being 'classified' right into a damn cell, Ms. Trace!"

Arnault stood up and put himself between us, facing me. "Whoa, Rick…"

"Whoa nothing! How many people have gotten clones in the last five years? Millions? We're looking at a possible apocalypse if they all turn murderous…!"

"I have to get back now, Captain," Ms. Trace interrupted.

"But you haven't told me anything I need to know!" I barked at her as she made for the door.

She sneered her contempt. "You don't need to know." She stepped through the door, then turned to spit her last words at me. "We will contain this situation." She left.

I looked at Jim. "Get me whatever Taylor's clone had to say," I said. "The part we couldn't see. Whatever it is they're not telling us, I'll bet the key is right there." I stood and grabbed my suit jacket. "Call me as soon as you have anything, okay?"

Jim nodded, and stood also.

"Wait," Carl said. "Where you going? For God's sake, we need you here for this."

"I've got to talk to the Mayor in person. He's got to declare a state of emergency; this is already spinning out of control, and we need answers."

As I went through my door, I saw His Honor's heavyset face close-up on a television in the outer office.

He was apparently answering a reporter's question. "… and I want to assure all citizens that though we are in the early stages of a crisis, the police and relevant parties are already in the process of dealing with it. Everyone is strongly advised to stay home and engage all personal security measures. It appears, for the moment, that the main risks are confined to bizarre behavior among a very few clones, and the police have been mobilized to deal with the current situation."

I snorted. You could always count on a politician to take credit and dispense blame without regards for anything approaching an actual fact.

The Mayor continued. "I have also been in high level discussions with Prime Solutions representatives, and have been assured that proper measures have already been instituted to deal with this situation on a global level." His face took on his patented earnestly concerned look. "We will take control of this crisis, but for now, we ask for your cooperation to get, or stay, in a place of security. Stay off the streets and remain calm, and let our uniformed services do their jobs."

I stopped watching as soon as the shouted questions from the press began, and went out.

The streets were mostly empty as I drove through them, the pre-dawn calm seeming to belie the craziness of the night's murders, the outrageous refusal of a privately-owned company to provide information to the police, and the apparent potential for millions of clones to transform into murderers without warning.

I needed answers. I pulled up behind a bunch of news vans at the Mayor's office. I ignored the microphones and cameras thrust in my face as I went for the door, muttering: "No comment" over and over. I flashed my badge to the uniforms on the door and they let me through, closing the door behind me and shutting out the bedlam of the reporters at the front of the building.

The Mayor's secretary was a slim African American with close-cut hair and gold, wire-rim glasses. "I'm Captain Richard Roberts and I need to see the Mayor."

"His Honor is in a meeting and can't be disturbed," the young man said, looking up at me. There were dark puffy areas under his eyes. Clearly, it had been a long night here as well.

"You don't understand…"

"I do," he interrupted. "Captain, the Mayor's in a critical meeting regarding the clone crisis right now, and I'm under strict orders not to disturb him."

"Even if I have relevant information?" I leaned forward and put my hands on his desk.

He smiled tiredly. "Even if you assume a more aggressive and intimidating body language that you have right now, Captain."

That made me smile, and I stood back up. "Well, damn. Can you at least message in, check if they'll see me?"

He nodded after a moment.

I watched him get up from his desk and move to the Mayor's inner office door. As he opened it to go inside, I pushed past him and ignored his startled protest. "Sorry, son."

At a wave from the Mayor he left and closed the door behind him. His Honor sat at a table with three others. They all looked at me with a mixture of surprised irritation. I recognized his chief of staff, Grissom, sitting to his right. My gaze moved further on, and I recognized Ms. Trace. She glanced dismissively at me, then looked away.

The last face I recognized as well, but only because it was mine: older and more craggy, and with hair longer than the way I wore it, but mine.

Forget Sister Mary Regina. "Fuck me," I breathed out.

The older me at the table stood up. "Wait, please! Captain Roberts, please, just take it easy a moment. I'm sorry, this must come as quite the shock…"

"'Quite the shock'?" I yelled. "I'm a God-damned clone! You're fucking right it's a shock, you… you Primer asshole!" I found myself hyperventilating, and the room got a bit wavery for a moment.

"Yes, yes you are my clone, and I am incredibly proud of you – please, let me explain! I'm Dr. Michael Kane – the CEO of Prime Solutions. I'm the one who invented the cloning process, so you could choose to blame me for everything, but I beg you to hear me out!" He walked around the table, an earnest expression on his face.

"You're special, Captain Roberts: yes, you're a clone, but you've been raised and educated and conditioned to be your own person! Imagine – you never knew you were a clone, and yet you decided to join the Police force when you were completed! You had your own ambitions. You've been promoted multiple times, to Captain in less than ten years, because of all you've achieved. You, Richard – you've been free to determine your own destiny, and you've excelled beyond my wildest hopes!"

I felt like I was standing in quicksand, and then my phone vibrated. I touched my earpiece and split my attention from what my Primer was saying to listen.

"Rick, it's Jim. We finally have what Taylor's clone said: 'It's over now.' He pauses, then says: 'For you, at least. We know the secret – it's the pineal gland, that's where the kill switch is in our brains. But what you Primers didn't know is we don't need the daily serum to keep us alive... We can flip the switch off with the key, the key we have to get from you. Fresh like.' Pretty sick, huh?"

"Thanks Jim, gotta go," I muttered and cut the connection.

"... and that's why you're a cop and not a scientist, you see? Because you had the freedom to choose your way! You've opened up doors for every clone! That's why I'm so very proud of you," Dr. Kane finished, his eyes wide and shiny.

"Right. And you created me without a need for the serum?" I said flatly. I saw him glance quickly towards Ms. Trace and then back. "Or else you were giving me the serum without me knowing it. Maybe in my water cooler at home"– there was no change in his expression – "or maybe, maybe it was in the coffee at my office?"

Kane's eyes flicked over to Ms. Trace again. Her icy look of disdain wavered as they shared a quick look before his attention returned to me.

And I finally put it all together. "And maybe that's why I had 'migraines' when I didn't have my daily caffeine..."

"Now look, Captain," the Mayor said, standing. "I understand the shock you must feel, but you could be the example which would mainstream clones all across America! You could be an important symbol, and calm everything down. What do you say?"

My thoughts were jumbled, confused, and then one came clear. "If I was 'free' the whole time, why keep me on the secret serum-leash?"

No one had an answer as they exchanged furtive glances.

I shot the Mayor in his fat, lying face, and then his chief-of-staff. Ms. Trace dashed for the door, but I double-tapped her in the back and she went down, blood spilling out from beneath her.

Kane hadn't moved an inch. The expression on his face was hard to interpret as I brought my gun to bear on him.

"It doesn't have to be like this, Richard," he said. "Kill me and you won't get your serum and you'll die. Kill me, and the clones are always going to be slaves – they'll never get all the freedoms that non-clones get!" He licked his lips. "The right to life, Richard! The right to liberty! The right to the pursuit of happiness! That's what hangs in the balance here – we can make those things happen. Together."

I wanted to believe him.

Almost without my conscious control, I squeezed off a shot that hit him in the left shoulder, throwing him backwards against the table where he rebounded and collapsed with a groan. I knew I didn't have a lot of time, and I thought about the future, very, very hard.

I went to the Mayor's desk, and put my gun back in my holster. I picked up his letter opener and a heavy paperweight and walked over to where Dr. Kane was trying to crawl away. I kicked him in the gut, and he rolled onto his back with a grunt of pain and just lay there. Our eyes met.

I knelt down next to him. "Welcome to the revolution, Doc."

The blade and the paperweight made a surprisingly effective combination to split his skull open, and it turned out that getting the pineal gland out wasn't much harder than shucking an oyster.

It looked like just a chunk of greyish, bloody meat.

It tasted like freedom.

Mademoiselle de Scudéri

A Tale of the Times of Louis the Fourteenth

E.T.A. Hoffmann

MAGDALEINE DE SCUDÉRI, so famous for her charming poetical and other writings, lived in a small mansion in the Rue St. Honoré, by favour of Louis the XIVth and Madame de Maintenon.

Late one night – about midnight – in the autumn of the year 1680, there came a knocking at the door of this house, so loud and violent that it shook the very ground. Baptiste, who filled the offices of cook, butler and doorkeeper in the lady's modest establishment, had gone, by her leave, to the country to his sister's wedding, so that La Martinière, the femme de chambre, was the only person still awake in the house. She heard this knocking, which went on without ceasing almost, and she remembered that, as Baptiste was away, she and her mistress were alone and unprotected. She thought of the housebreakings, robberies and murders which were so frequent in Paris at that time, and felt convinced that some of the numerous bands of malefactors, knowing the defenceless state of the house that night, were raising this alarm at the door, and would commit some outrage if it were opened; so she remained in her room, trembling and terrified, anathematising Baptiste, and his sister's marriage into the bargain.

Meantime the thundering knocking went on at the door, and she thought she heard a voice calling in the intervals, "Open, for the love of Christ Open! – Open!" At last, her alarm increasing, she took her candle and ran out on to the landing, where she distinctly heard the voice crying, "Open the door, for the love of Christ!"

"After all," she said to herself, "one knows that a robber would not be crying out in that way. Perhaps it is somebody who is being pursued and is come to my lady for refuge. She is known to be always ready to do a kind action – but we must be very careful!"

She opened a window and called down into the street, asking who it was who was making such a tremendous thundering at the door at that time of the night, rousing everybody from their sleep. This she did in a voice which she tried to make as like a man's as she could. By the glimmer of the moon, which was beginning to break through dark clouds, she could make out a tall figure in a long grey cloak, with a broad hat drawn down over his forehead.

Then she cried, in a loud voice, so that this person in the street should hear, "Baptiste! Claude! Pierre! Get up, and see who this rascal is who is trying to get in at this time of night."

But a gentle, entreating voice spoke from beneath, saying, "Ah, La Martinière, I know it is you, you kind soul, though you are trying to alter your voice; and I know well enough that Baptiste is away in the country, and that there is nobody in the house but your mistress and yourself. Let me in. I must speak with your lady this instant."

"Do you imagine," asked La Martinière, "that my lady is going to speak to you in the middle of the night? Can't you understand that she has been in bed ever so long, and that it is as much as my place is worth to awaken her out of her first sweet sleep, which is so precious to a person at her time of life?"

"I know," answered the person beneath, "that she has just this moment put away the manuscript of the novel *Clelia*, at which she is working so hard, and is writing some verses which she means to read tomorrow at Madame de Maintenon's. I implore you, Madame La Martinière, be so compassionate as to open the door. Upon your doing so depends the escape of an unfortunate creature from destruction. Nay, honour, freedom, a human life, depend on this moment in which I must speak with your lady. Remember, her anger will rest upon you for ever when she comes to know that it was you who cruelly drove away from her door the unfortunate wretch who came to beg for her help."

"But why should you come for her help at such an extraordinary time of the night?" asked La Martinière. "Come back in the morning at a reasonable hour." But the reply came up, "Does destiny, when it strikes like the destroying lightning, consider hours and times? When there is but one moment when rescue is possible, is help to be put off? Open the door to me. Have no fear of a wretched being who is without defence, hunted, hard pressed by a terrible fate, and flies to your lady for succour from the most imminent peril."

La Martinière heard the stranger moaning and groaning as he uttered those words in the deepest sorrow. The tone of his voice was that of a youth, soft and gentle, and most touching to the heart; and so, deeply moved. She went without much more hesitation and fetched the key.

As soon as she opened the door, the form shrouded in the mantle burst violently in and, passing La Martinière, cried in a wild voice, "Take me to your lady!" La Martinière held up the light which she was carrying, and the glimmer fell on the face of a very young man, distorted and frightfully drawn, and as pale as death. She almost fell down on the landing for terror when he opened his cloak and showed the glittering hilt of a stiletto sticking out of his doublet. He flashed his gleaming eyes at her, and cried, more wildly than before, "Take me to your lady, I tell you."

La Martinière saw that her mistress was in the utmost danger. All her affection for her, who was to her as the kindest of mothers, flamed up and created a courage which she herself would scarcely have thought herself capable of. She quickly closed the door of her room, moved rapidly in front of it, and said in a brave, firm voice, "Your furious behaviour, now that you have got into the house, is very different from what I should have expected from the way you spoke down in the street. I see now that I had pity on you a little too easily. You shall not see or speak with my lady at this hour. If you have no bad designs, and are not afraid to show yourself in daylight, come and tell her your business tomorrow; but take yourself off out of this house now."

He heaved a hollow sigh, glared at La Martinière with a terrible expression, and grasped his dagger. She silently commended her soul to God, but stood firm and looked him straight in the face, pressing herself more firmly against the door through which he would have to pass in order to reach her mistress.

"Let me get to your lady, I tell you!" he cried once more.

"Do what you will," said La Martinière, "I shall not move from this spot. Complete the crime which you have begun. A shameful death on the Place de la Grève will overtake you, as it has your accursed comrades in wickedness."

"Ha! You are right, La Martinière," he cried. "I am armed, and I look as if I were an accursed robber and murderer. But my comrades are not executed – are not executed," and he drew his dagger, advancing with poisonous looks towards the terrified woman.

"Jesus!" she cried, expecting her death-wound; but at that moment there came up from the street below the clatter and the ring of arms, and the hoof-tread of horses.

"La Marechausée! La Marechausée! Help! Help!" she cried.

"Wretched woman, you will be my destruction," he cried. "All is over now – all over! Here, take it; take it. Give this to your lady now, or tomorrow if you like it better." As he said this in a whisper, he took the candelabra from her, blew out the tapers, and placed a casket in her hands. "As you prize your eternal salvation," he cried, "give this to your lady." He dashed out of the door, and was gone.

La Martinière had sunk to the floor. She raised herself with difficulty, and groped her way back in the darkness to her room, where she fell into an arm-chair, wholly overcome and unable to utter a sound. Presently she heard the rattling of the bolts, which she had left unfastened when she closed the house door. The house was therefore now shut up, and soft unsteady steps were approaching her room. Like one under a spell, unable to move, she was preparing for the very worst, when to her inexpressible joy the door opened, and by the pale light of the night-lamp she saw it was Baptiste. He was deadly pale, and much upset.

"For the love of all the saints," he exclaimed, "tell me what has happened! Oh, what a state I am in. Something – don't know what it was – told me to come away from the wedding yesterday – forced me to come away. So when I got to this street, I thought, Madame Martinière isn't a heavy sleeper; she'll hear me if I knock quietly at the door, and let me in. Then up came a strong patrol, horsemen and foot, armed to the teeth. They stopped me, and wouldn't let me go. Luckily Desgrais was there, the lieutenant of the Marechaussée. He knows me, and as they were holding their lanterns under my nose, he said, 'Ho, Baptiste! How come you here in the streets at this time of the night? You ought to be at home, taking care of the house. This is not a very safe spot just at this moment. We're expecting to make a fine haul, and important arrest, tonight.' You can't think, Madame La Martinière, how I felt when he said that. And when I got to the door, lo! And behold! A man in a cloak comes bursting out with a drawn dagger in his hand, dodges me, and makes off. The door was open, the keys in the lock. What, in the name of all that's holy, is the meaning of it all?"

La Martinière, relieved from her alarm, told him all that had happened, and both she and he went back to the hall; and there they found the candelabra on the floor, where the stranger had thrown it on taking his flight. "There can't be the slightest doubt that our mistress was within an ace of being robbed, and murdered too very likely," Baptiste said. "According to what you say, the scoundrel knew well enough that there was nobody in the house but her and you, and even that she was still sitting up at her writing. Of course he was one of those infernal blackguards who pry into folks' houses and spy out everything that can be of use to them in their devilish designs. And the little casket, Madame Martinière, that I think we'll throw into the Seine where it's deepest. Who shall be our warrant that some monster or other isn't lying in wait for our mistress's life? Very likely, if she opens the casket, she may tumble down dead, as the old Marquis de Tournay did when he opened a letter which came to him, he didn't know where from."

After a long consultation, they came to the conclusion that next morning they would tell their lady everything that had happened, and even hand her the mysterious casket, which might, perhaps, be opened if proper precautions were taken. On carefully weighing all the circumstances connected with the appearance of the stranger, they thought that there must be some special secret or mystery involved in the affair, which they were not in a position to unravel, but must leave to be elucidated by their superiors.

There were good grounds for Baptiste's fears. Paris, at the time in question, was the scene of atrocious deeds of violence, and that just at a period when the most diabolical inventions of hell provided the most facile means for their execution.

Glaser, a German apothecary, the most learned chemist of his day, occupied himself – as people who cultivate his science often do – with alchemical researches and experiments. He had set himself the task of discovering the philosopher's stone. An Italian of the name of Exili associated himself with him; but to him the art of goldmaking formed a mere pretext. What he aimed at mastering was the blending, preparation, and sublimation of the various poisonous substances which Glaser hoped would give him the results he was in search of; and at length Exili discovered how to prepare that delicate poison which has no odour nor taste, and which, killing either slowly or in a moment, leaves not the slightest trace in the human organism, and baffles the utmost skill of the physician who, not suspecting poison as the means of death, ascribes it to natural causes. But cautiously as Exili went about this, he fell under suspicion of dealing with poisons, and was thrown into the Bastille.

In the same cell with him there was presently quartered an officer of the name of Godin de Sainte-Croix, who had long lived in relations with the Marquise de Brinvilliers; which brought shame upon all her family, till at length, as her husband cared nothing about her conduct, her father (Dreux d'Aubray, Civil Lieutenant of Paris) had to part the guilty pair by means of a lettre de cachet against Sainte-Croix. The captain was a passionate man without character or religion, a hypocrite given to all manner of vice from his youth. What is more, he was addicted to the most furious jealousy and envy. So nothing could be more welcome to him than Exili's devilish secret, which gave him the power of destroying all his enemies. He became Exili's assiduous pupil, and soon equalled his instructor; so that when he was released from prison he was in a position to carry on operations by himself on his own account.

La Brinvilliers was a depraved woman, and Sainte-Croix made her a monster. She managed, by degrees, to poison first her own father (with whom she was living in the hypocritical presence of taking care of him in his declining years), next her two brothers, and then her sister; the father out of revenge, and the others for their fortunes. The histories of more than one poisoner bear terrible evidence that crimes of this description assume the form of an irresistible passion. Just as a chemist makes experiments for the pleasure and the interest of watching them, poisoners have often, without the smallest ulterior object, killed persons whose living or dying was to them a matter of complete indifference. The sudden deaths of a number of paupers, patients at the Hôtel Dieu, a little time after the events just alluded to, led to suspicion that the bread which La Brinvilliers was in the habit of giving them every week (so as to appear a model of piety and benevolence) was poisoned. And it is certain that she poisoned pigeon pasties which were served up to her own invited guests. The Chevalier du Guet, and many more, were the victims of those diabolical entertainments. Sainte-Croix, his accomplice La Chaussée, and La Brinvilliers, managed to hide their crimes for a long while under a veil of impenetrable secrecy. But, however the wicked may brazen matters out, there comes a time when the Eternal Power of Heaven punishes the criminal, even here on earth.

The poisons which Sainte-Croix prepared were so marvellously delicate that if the powder (which the Parisians appositely named 'poudre de succession') were uncovered while being made, a single inhalation of it was sufficient to cause immediate death. Therefore Sainte-Croix always wore a glass mask when at work. This mask fell off one day just as he was shaking a finished powder into a phial, and, having inhaled some of the powder, he fell dead in an instant. As he had no heirs, the law courts at once placed his property under seal, when the whole diabolical arsenal of murder which had been at the villain's disposal was discovered, and also the letters of Madame de Brinvilliers, which left no doubt as to her crimes. She fled to a convent at Liège. Desgrais, an officer of the Marechaussée, was sent after her. Disguised as a priest, he got admitted into the convent, and succeeded in involving the terrible woman in a love-affair, and in getting her to grant him a clandestine meeting in a sequestered garden outside the town. When she arrived there she found herself surrounded by Desgrais' myrmidons; and her ecclesiastical gallant speedily transformed himself into the officer of the Marechaussée. He compelled her to get into the carriage which was waiting outside the garden, and drove straight away to Paris, surrounded by an ample guard. La Chaussée had been beheaded previously to this, and La Brinvilliers suffered the same death. Her body was burnt, and its ashes scattered to the winds.

The Parisians breathed freely again when the world was freed from the presence of this monster, who had so long wielded with impunity the weapon of secret murder against friend and foe. But it soon became bruited abroad that the terrible art of the accursed La Croix had been, somehow, handed down to a successor, who was carrying it on triumphantly. Murder came gliding like an invisible, capricious spectre into the narrowest and most intimate circles of relationship, love and friendship, pouncing securely and swiftly upon its unhappy victims. Men who today, were seen in robust health, were tottering about on the morrow feeble and sick; and no skill of physicians could restore them. Wealth, a good appointment or office, a nice-looking wife, perhaps a little too young for her husband, were ample reasons for a man's being dogged to death. The most frightful mistrust snapped the most sacred ties. The husband trembled before his wife; the father dreaded the son; the sister the brother. When your friend asked you to dinner, you carefully avoided tasting the dishes and wines which he set before you; and where joy and merriment used to reign, there were now nothing but wild looks, watching to detect the secret murderer. Fathers of families were to be seen with anxious faces, buying supplies of food in out-of-the-way places where they were not known, and cooking them themselves in dirty cook-shops, for dread of treason in their own homes. And yet often the most careful and ingenious precautions were unavailing.

For the repression of this ever-increasing disorder the King constituted a fresh tribunal, to which he entrusted the special investigation and punishment of those secret crimes. This was the Chambre Ardente, which held its sittings near the Bastille. La Regnie was its president. For a considerable time La Regnie's efforts, assiduous as they were, were unsuccessful, and it was the lot of the much overworked Desgrais to discover the most secret den of that foul crime.

In the Faubourg Saint-Germain there lived an old woman, named La Voisin, who followed the calling of teller of fortunes and summoner of spirits, and she, assisted by her accomplices Le Sage and Le Vigoureux, managed to alarm and astonish people who were by no means to be considered weak or superstitious. But she did more than this. She was, like La Croix, a pupil of Exili's and, like him, prepared the delicate, traceless poison, which helped wicked sons to speedy inheritances and unprincipled wives to other, younger husbands. Desgrais fathomed her secrets; she made full confession; the Chambre Ardente sentenced her to be burned, and the sentence was carried out on the Place de la Grève. Amongst her effects was found a list of those who had availed themselves of her services; whence it followed, not only that execution succeeded execution, but that strong suspicion fell on persons in important positions. Thus it was believed that Cardinal Bonzy had obtained from La Voisin the means of disembarrassing himself of all the persons to whom, in his capacity of Archbishop of Narbonne, he was bound to pay pensions. Similarly, the Duchess de Bouillon and the Countess de Soissons (their names having been found in La Voisin's list) were accused of having had relations with her; and even François Henri de Montmorenci-Boudebelle, Duc de Luxembourg, Peer and Marshal of the realm, did not escape arraignment before the Chambre Ardente. He surrendered himself to imprisonment in the Bastille, where the hatred of Louvois and La Regnie immured him in a cell only six feet long. Months elapsed before it was proved that his offences did not deserve so severe a punishment. He had once gone to La Voisin to have his horoscope drawn.

What is certain is that an excess of inconsiderate zeal led President La Regnie into violently illegal and barbarous measures. His Court assumed the character of the Inquisition. The very slightest suspicion rendered any one liable to severe imprisonment, and the establishment of the innocence of a person tried for his life was often only a matter of the merest chance. Besides, La Regnie was repulsive to behold, and of malicious disposition, so that he excited the hatred of those whose avenger or protector he was called upon to be. When he asked the Duchess de Bouillon if she had ever seen the devil, she answered, "I think I see him at this moment."

Whilst now, on the Place de la Grève, the blood of the guilty and of the merely suspected was flowing in streams, and secret deaths by poison were, at last, becoming more and more rare, a trouble of another description showed itself, spreading abroad fresh consternation. It seemed that a gang of robbers had made up their minds to possess themselves of all the jewels in the city. Whenever a valuable set of ornaments was bought, it disappeared in an inexplicable manner, however carefully preserved and protected. And everybody who dared to wear precious stones in the evening was certain to be robbed, either in the public streets or in the dark passages of houses. Very often they were not only robbed, but murdered. Such of them as escaped with their lives said they had been felled by the blow of a clenched fist on the head, which came on them like a thunderbolt. And when they recovered their senses they found that they had been robbed, and were in a totally different place from where they had been knocked down.

Those who were murdered – and they were found nearly every morning lying in the streets or in houses – had all the selfsame mortal wound – a dagger-thrust, right through the heart, which the surgeons said must have been delivered with such swiftness and certainty that the victim would have fallen dead without the power of uttering a sound. Now who, in all the luxurious Court of Louis Quatorze, was there who was not implicated in some secret love-affair and, consequently, often gliding about the streets late at night with valuable presents in his pockets? Just as if this robber-gang were in intercourse with spirits, they always knew perfectly well when anything of this kind was going on. Often the fortunate lover wouldn't reach the house where his lady was expecting him; often he would fall at her threshold, at her very door, where, to her horror, she would discover his bleeding body lying.

It was in vain that Argenson, the Minister of Police, arrested every individual, in all Paris, who seemed to be touched by the very faintest suspicion; in vain La Regnie raged, striving to compel confession; in vain were guards and patrols reinforced. Not a trace of the perpetrators of those outrages was to be discovered. The only thing which was of a certain degree of use was to go about armed to the teeth, and have a light carried before you; and yet there were cases in which the servant who carried the light had his attention occupied by having stones thrown at him, whilst at that very instant his master was being robbed and murdered.

It was a remarkable feature of this business that, notwithstanding all search and investigation in every quarter where there seemed to be any chance of dealing in jewels going on, not a trace of even the smallest of the plundered precious stones ever came to light.

Desgrais foamed in fury that even his acumen and skill were powerless to prevent the escape of those scoundrels. Whatever part of the town he happened to be in was let alone for the time, whilst in some other quarter robbery and murder were lying in wait for their rich prey.

Desgrais hit upon the clever idea of setting several facsimiles of himself on foot – various Desgrais, exactly alike in gait, speech, figure, face, etc.; so that his own men could not tell the one of them from the other, or say which was the real Desgrais. Meanwhile, at the risk of his life, he watched alone in the most secret hiding-places, and followed, at a distance, this or the other person who seemed, by the looks of him, to be likely to have jewels about him. But those whom he was watching were unharmed, so that this artifice of his was as well known to the culprits as everything else seemed to be. Desgrais was in utter despair.

One morning he came to President La Regnie, pale, strained, almost out of his mind.

"What is it – what news? Have you come upon the clue?" the President cried to him as he came in.

"Ah, Monsieur!" said Desgrais, stammering in fury, "Last night, near the Louvre, the Marquis de la Fare was set upon under my very nose!"

"Heaven and earth!" cried La Regnie, overjoyed, "We have got them!"

"Wait a moment, listen," said Desgrais, with a bitter smile. "I was standing near the Louvre, watching and waiting, with hell itself in my heart, for those devils who have been baffling me for such a length of time. There came a figure close by me – not seeing me – with uncertain steps, always looking behind him. By the moonlight I recognised the Marquis de la Fare. I expected that he would be passing. I knew where he was gliding to. Scarcely had he got ten or twelve paces beyond me when, out of the ground apparently, springs a figure, dashes the Marquis to the ground, falls down upon him. Losing my self-control at this occurrence, which seemed to be likely to deliver the murderer into my hands, I cried out aloud, and meant to spring from my hiding-place with a great bound and seize hold of him. But I tripped up on my cloak and fell down. I saw the fellow flee away as if on the wings of the wind. I picked myself up, and made off after him as fast as I could. As I ran, I sounded my horn. Out of the distance the whistles of my men answered me. Things grew lively – clatter of arms, tramp of horses on all sides. 'Here! – Come to me! – Desgrais!' I cried, till the streets re-echoed. All the time I saw the man before me in the bright moonlight, turning off right – left – to get away from me. We came to the Rue Niçaise. There his strength seemed to begin to fail. I gathered mine up. He was not more than fifteen paces ahead of me."

"You got hold of him! – Your men came up!" cried La Regnie, with flashing eyes, grasping Desgrais by the arm as if he were the fleeing murderer himself.

"Fifteen paces ahead of me," said Desgrais, in a hollow voice, and drawing his breath hard, "this fellow, before my eyes, dodged to one side, and vanished through the wall."

"Vanished! – Through the wall! Are you out of your senses?" La Regnie cried, taking three steps backwards, and striking his hands together.

"Call me as great a madman as you please, Monsieur," said Desgrais, rubbing his forehead like one tortured by evil thoughts. "Call me a madman, or a fool that sees spooks; but what I have told you is the literal truth. I stood staring at the wall, while several of my men came up out of breath, and with them the Marquis de la Fare (who had picked himself up), with his drawn sword in his hand. We lighted torches, we examined the wall all over. There was not the trace of a door, a window, any opening. It is the strong stone wall of a courtyard, belonging to a house in which people are living – against whom there is not the slightest suspicion. I have looked into the whole thing again this morning in broad daylight. It must be the very devil himself who is at work befooling us in the matter."

This story got bruited abroad through Paris, where all heads were full of the sorceries, callings up of spirits and pacts with the devil indulged in by La Voisin, Le Vigoureux, and the wicked priest Le Sage; and as it lies in our eternal nature that the bent towards the supernatural and the marvellous overpasses all reason, people soon positively believed what Desgrais had only said in his impatience – that the very devil himself must protect the rascals, and that they had sold their souls to him. We can readily understand that Desgrais' story soon received many absurd embellishments. It was printed, and hawked about the town, with a woodcut at the top representing a horrible figure of the devil sinking into the ground before the terrified Desgrais. Quite enough to frighten the people, and so terrify Desgrais' men that they lost all courage, and went about the streets behung with amulets, and sprinkled with holy water.

Seeing that the Chambre Ardente was unsuccessful, Argenson applied to the King to constitute – with special reference to this novel description of crime a tribunal armed with greater powers for tracking and punishing offenders. The King, thinking he had already given too ample powers to the Chambre Ardente, and shocked at the horrors of the numberless executions carried out by the bloodthirsty La Regnie, refused.

Then another method of influencing His Majesty was devised.

In the apartments of Madame de Maintenon – where the King was in the habit of spending much of his time in the afternoons – and also, very often, would be at work with his Ministers till late at night – a poetical petition was laid before him, on the part of the 'Endangered Lovers,' who complained that when 'galanterie' rendered it incumbent on them to be the bearers of some valuable present to the ladies of their hearts, they had always to do it at the risk of their lives. They said that, of course, it was honour and delight to pour out their blood for the lady of their heart in knightly encounter, but that the treacherous attack of the assassin, against which it was impossible to guard, was quite a different matter. They expressed their hope that Louis, the bright pole-star of love and gallantry, might deign – arising end staining in fullest splendour – to dispel the darkness of night, and thus reveal the black mysteries hidden thereby; that the God-like hero, who had hurled his foes to the dust, would now once more wave his flashing falchion and, as did Hercules in the case of the Laernean Hydra, and Theseus in that of the Minotaur, vanquish the threatening monster who was consuming all the delights of love, and darkening all joy into deep sorrow and inconsolable mourning.

Serious as the subject was, this poem was not deficient in most wittily-turned phrases, particularly where it described the state of watchful anxiety in which lovers had to glide to their mistresses, and how this mental strain necessarily destroyed all the delights of love, and nipped all adventures of 'galanterie' in the very bud. And, as it wound up with a high-flown panegyric of Louis XIV, the King could not but read it with visible satisfaction. When he had perused it, he turned to Madame de Maintenon – without taking his eyes from it – read it again – aloud this time – and then asked, with a pleased smile, what she thought of the petition of the 'Endangered Lovers.'

Madame de Maintenon, faithful to her serious turn, and ever wearing the garb of a certain piousness, answered that secret and forbidden practices did not deserve much in the form of protection, but that the criminals probably did require special laws for their punishment. The King, not satisfied with this answer, folded the paper up, and was going back to the Secretary of State, who was at work in the ante-room, when, happening to glance sideways, his eyes rested on Mademoiselle de Scudéri who was present, seated in a little arm-chair. He went straight to her and the pleased smile which had at first been playing about his mouth and cheeks – but had disappeared – resumed the ascendency again. Standing close before her, with his face unwrinkling itself, he said –

"The Marquise does not know, and has no desire to learn, anything about the 'galanteries' of our enamoured gentlemen, and evades the subject in ways which are nothing less than forbidden. But, Mademoiselle, what do you think of this poetical petition?"

Mademoiselle de Scudéri rose from her chair; a transient blush, like the purple of the evening sky, passed across her pale cheeks and, gently bending forward, she answered with downcast eyes:

"*Un amant qui craint les voleurs*
N'est point digne d'amour."

The King, surprised, and struck with admiration at the chivalrous spirit of those few words – which completely took the wind out of the sails of the poem, with all its lengthy tirades – cried, with flashing eyes: "By Saint Denis, you are right, Mademoiselle! No blind laws, touching the innocent and the guilty alike, shall shelter cowardice. Argenson and La Regnie must do their best."

Next morning La Martinière enlarged upon the terrors of the time, painting them in glowing colours to her lady, when she told her all that had happened the previous night, and handed her the mysterious casket, with much fear and trembling. Both she and Baptiste (who stood in the corner as white as a sheet, kneading his cap in his hand from agitation and anxiety) implored her, in the name of all the saints, to take the greatest precautions in opening it.

Weighing and examining the unopened mystery in her hand, she said with a smile, "You are a couple of bogies! The wicked scoundrels outside who, as you say yourselves, spy out all that goes on in every house know, no doubt, quite as well as you and I do, that I am not rich, and that there are no treasures in this house worth committing a murder for. Is my life in danger, do you think? Who could have any interest in the death of an old woman of seventy-three, who never persecuted any evildoers except those in her own novels; who writes mediocre poetry, incapable of exciting anyone's envy; who has nothing to leave behind her but the belongings of an old maid who sometimes goes to Court, and two or three dozen handsomely-bound books with gilt edges. And, alarming as your account is, La Martinière, of this man's appearance, I cannot believe that he meant me any harm, so –"

La Martinière sprang three paces backwards, and Baptiste fell on one knee with a hollow, "Ah!" as Mademoiselle de Scudéri pressed a projecting steel knob, and the lid of the casket flew open with a certain amount of noise.

Great was her surprise to see that it contained a pair of bracelets, and a necklace richly set in jewels. She took them out and, as she spoke in admiration of the marvellous workmanship of the necklace, La Martinière cast glances of wonder at the bracelets, and cried, again and again, that Madame de Montespan herself did not possess such jewellery.

"But why is it brought to me?" cried Mademoiselle de Scudéri. "What can this mean?" She saw, however, a little folded note at the bottom of the casket, and in this she rightly thought she would find the key to the mystery. When she had read what was written in the note, it fell from her trembling hands; she raised an appealing look to heaven, and then sank down half fainting in her chair. Baptiste and La Martinière hurried to her, in alarm.

"Oh!" she cried, in a voice stifled by tears, "The mortification! The deep humiliation! Has it been reserved for me to undergo this in my old age? Have I ever been frivolous, like some of the foolish young creatures; are words, spoken half in jest, to be found capable of such a terrible interpretation? Am I, who have been faithful to all that is pure and good from my childhood, to be made virtually an accomplice in the crimes of this terrible confederation."

She held her handkerchief to her eyes, so that Baptiste and La Martinière, altogether at sea in their anxious conjectures, felt powerless to set about helping her who was so dear to them, as the best and kindest of mistresses, in her bitter affliction.

La Martinière picked up the paper from the floor. On it was written:

> "*Un amant qui craint les voleurs
> N'est point digne d'amour.*'
> "*Your brilliant intellect, most honoured lady, has delivered us, who exercise on weakness and cowardice the rights of the stronger, and possess ourselves of treasures which would otherwise be unworthily wasted, from much bitter persecution. As a proof of our gratitude, be pleased kindly to accept this set of ornaments. It is the most valuable that we have been enabled to lay hands on for many a day. Although far more beautiful and precious jewels should adorn you, yet we pray you not to deprive us of your future protection and remembrance. – THE INVISIBLES.*"

"Is it possible," cried Mademoiselle de Scudéri, when she had partially recovered herself, "that shameless wickedness and abandoned insult can be carried further by human beings?"

The sun was shining brightly through the window curtains of crimson silk, and consequently the brilliants, which were lying on the table beside the open casket, were flashing a rosy radiance. Looking at them, Mademoiselle de Scudéri covered her face in horror, and ordered La Martinière instantly to take those terrible jewels away, steeped, as they seemed to be, in the blood of the murdered. La Martinière, having at once put the necklace and bracelets back into their case, thought the best thing to do would be to give them to the Minister of Police, and tell him all that had happened.

Mademoiselle de Scudéri rose, and walked up and down slowly and in silence, as if considering what it was best to do. Then she told Baptiste to bring a sedan chair, and La Martinière to dress her, as she was going straight to the Marquise de Maintenon.

She repaired thither at the hour when she knew Madame de Maintenon would be alone, taking the casket and jewels with her.

Madame de Maintenon might well wonder to see this dear old lady (who was always kindness, sweetness and amiability personified), pale, distressed, upset, coming in with uncertain steps. "In heaven's name, what has happened to you?" she cried to her visitor, who was scarcely able to stand upright, striving to reach the chair which the Marquise drew forward for her. At last, when she could find words, she told her what a deep, irremediable insult and outrage the thoughtless speech which she had made in reply to the King had brought upon her.

Madame de Maintenon, when she had heard the whole affair properly related, thought Mademoiselle de Scudéri was taking it far too much to heart, strange as the occurrence was – that the insult of a pack of wretched rabble could not hurt an upright, noble heart; and finally begged that she might see the ornaments.

Mademoiselle de Scudéri handed her the open casket, and when she saw the splendid and valuable stones and the workmanship of them she could not repress a loud expression of admiration. She took the bracelets and necklace to the window, letting the sunlight play on the jewels, and holding the beautiful goldsmith's work close to her eyes so as to see with what wonderful skill each little link of the chains was formed.

She turned suddenly to Mademoiselle de Scudéri, and cried, "Do you know, there is only one man who can have done this work – and that is René Cardillac."

René Cardillac was then the cleverest worker in gold in all Paris, one of the most artistic, and at the same time extraordinary men of his day. Short rather than tall, but broad-shouldered and of strong and muscular build, Cardillac, now over fifty, had still the strength and activity of a youth. To this vigour, which was to be called unusual, testified also his thick, curling, reddish hair and his massive, shining face. Had he not been known to be the most upright and honourable of men, unselfish, open, without reserve, always ready to help, his altogether peculiar glance out of his grimly sparkling eyes might have brought him under suspicion of being secretly ill-tempered and wicked. In his art he was the most skilful worker, not only in Paris, but probably in the world at that time. Intimately acquainted with every kind of precious stones, versed in all their special peculiarities, he could so handle and treat them that ornaments which at a first glance promised to be poor and insignificant, came from his workshop brilliant and splendid. He accepted every commission with burning eagerness, and charged prices so moderate as to seem out of all proportion to the work. And the work left him no rest. Day and night he was to be heard hammering in his shop; and often, when a job was nearly finished, he would suddenly be dissatisfied with the form – would have doubts whether some of the settings were delicate enough; some little link would not be quite to his mind – in fine, the whole affair would be thrown into the melting-pot, and begun all over again. Thus every one of his works was a real, unsurpassable chef-d'oeuvre, which sent the person who had ordered it into amazement.

But then, it was hardly possible to get the finished work out of his hands. He would put the customer off from one week to another by a thousand excuses – even from month to month. He might be offered twice the price he had agreed upon, but it was useless; he would take no more; and when, ultimately, he was obliged to yield to the customer's remonstrances, and deliver the work, he could not conceal the vexation – nay, the rage – which seethed within him. If he had to deliver some specially valuable and unusually rich piece of workmanship, worth perhaps several thousand francs, he would get into such a condition that he ran up and down like one demented, cursing himself, his work, and every thing and person about him; but should, then, someone come running up behind him, crying, "René Cardillac, would you be so kind as to make me a beautiful necklace for the lady I am going to marry?" or "a pair of bracelets for my girl?" or the like, he would stop in a moment, flash his small eyes upon the speaker, and say, "Let me see what you have got." The latter would take out a little case and say "Here are jewels; they are not worth much; only every-day affairs, but in your hands" Cardillac would interrupt him, snatch the casket from his hands, take out the stones (really not very valuable) hold them up to the light, and cry, "Ho! Ho! Common stones, you say! Nothing of the kind! – Very fine, splendid stones! Just see what I shall make of them; and if a handful of Louis are no object to you, I will put two or three others along with them which will shine in your eyes like the sun himself!" The customer would say: "I leave the matter entirely in your hands, Master René; make what change you please." Whether the customer were a rich burgher or a gallant of quality, Cardillac would then throw himself violently on his neck, embrace him and kiss him, and say he was perfectly happy again, and that the work would be ready in eight days' time. Then he would run home as fast as he could to his workshop, where he would set to work hammering away; and in eight days' time there would be a masterpiece ready.

But as soon as the customer arrived, glad to pay the moderate price demanded and take away his prize, Cardillac would become morose, ill-tempered, rude and insolent. "But consider, Master Cardillac," the customer would say, "tomorrow is my wedding-day." "What do I care?", Cardillac would answer; "what is your wedding-day to me? Come back in a fortnight." "But it is finished! – Here is the money; I must have it." "And I tell you that there are many alterations which I must make before I let it leave my hands, and I am not going to let you have it today." "And I tell you, that if you don't give me my jewels – which I am ready to pay you for – quietly, you will see me come back with a file of D'Argenson's men." "Now, may the devil seize you with a hundred red-hot pincers, and hang three hundredweight on to the necklace, that it may throttle your bride!" With which he would cram the work into the customer's breast-pocket, seize him by the arm, push him out of the door, so that he would go stumbling all the way downstairs. Then he would laugh like a fiend, out of the window, when he saw the poor wretch go limping out, holding his handkerchief to his bleeding nose. It was not easy to explain either why, when Cardillac had undertaken a commission with alacrity and enthusiasm, he would sometimes suddenly implore the customer, with every sign of the deepest emotion – with the most moving adjurations, even with sobs and tears – not to ask him to go on with it. Many persons, amongst those most highly considered by the King and nation, had in vain offered large sums for the smallest specimen of Cardillac's work. He threw himself at the King's feet, and begged him, of his mercy, not to command him to work for him; and he declined all orders of Madame de Maintenon's; once, when she wished him to make a little ring, with emblems of the arts on it, which she wanted to give to Racine, he refused with expressions of abhorrence and terror.

"I would wager, therefore," said Madame de Maintenon, "that even if I were to send for Cardillac, to find out, at least, for whom he had made those ornaments, he would somehow avoid coming, for fear that I should give him an order; nothing will induce him to work for me. Yet he does seem to have been rather less obstinate of late, for I hear he is working more than ever, and allows his customers to take away their jewellery at once, though he does so with deep annoyance, and turns away his face when he hands them over."

Mademoiselle de Scudéri, who was exceedingly anxious that the jewels which came into her possession in such an extraordinary manner should be restored to their owner as speedily as possible, thought that this wondrous René Cardillac should be informed at once that no work was required of him, but simply his opinion as to certain stones. The Marquise agreed to this; he was sent for, and he came into the room in a very brief space, almost as if he had been on the way when sent for.

When he saw Mademoiselle de Scudéri, he appeared perplexed, like one confronted with the unexpected, who for the time loses sight of the demands of courtesy; he first of all made a profound reverence to her, and then turned, in the second place, to the Marquise. Madame de Maintenon impetuously asked him if the jewelled ornaments – to which she pointed as they lay sparkling on the dark-green cover of the table – were of his workmanship. Cardillac scarcely glanced at them but, fixedly staring in her face, he hastily packed the necklace and bracelets into their case, and shoved them away with some violence.

Then with an evil smile gleaming on his red face, he said, "The truth is, Madame la Marquise, that one must know René Cardillac's handiwork very little to suppose, even for a moment, that any other goldsmith in the world made those. Of course, I made them."

"Then," continued the Marquise, "say whom you made them for."

"For myself alone," he answered. "You may think this strange," he continued, as they both gazed at him with amazement, Madame de Maintenon incredulous, and Mademoiselle de Scudéri all anxiety as to how the matter was going to turn out, "but I tell you the truth, Madame la Marquise. Merely for the sake of the beauty of the work, I collected some of my finest stones together, and worked for the enjoyment of so doing, more carefully and diligently than usual. Those ornaments disappeared from my workshop a short time since, in an incomprehensible manner."

"Heaven be thanked!" cried Mademoiselle de Scudéri, her eyes sparkling with joy. With a smile she sprang up from her seat and, going up to Cardillac quickly and actively as a young girl, she laid her hands on his shoulder, saying, "Take back your treasure, Master René, which the villains have robbed you of!" And she circumstantially related how the ornaments had come into her possession.

Cardillac listened in silence, with downcast eyes, merely from time to time uttering a scarcely audible "Hm! Indeed! Ah! Ho, Ho!", sometimes placing his hands behind his back, or again stroking his chin and cheeks. When she had ended, he appeared to be struggling with strange thoughts which had come to him during her story, and seemed unable to come to any decision satisfactory to himself. He rubbed his brow, sighed, passed his hand over his eyes – perhaps to keep back tears. At last he seized the casket (which Mademoiselle de Scudéri had been holding out to him), sank slowly on one knee, and said: "Esteemed lady! Fate destined this casket for you; and I now feel, for the first time, that I was thinking of you when I was at work upon it – nay, was making it expressly for you. Do not disdain to accept this work, and to wear it; it is the best I have done for a very long time."

"Ah! Master René," said Mademoiselle de Scudéri, jesting pleasantly, "how think you it would become me at my age to bedeck myself with those beautiful jewels? – And what should put it in your mind to make me such a valuable present? Come, come! If I were as beautiful and as rich as the Marquise de Fontange, I should certainly not let them out of my hands. But what have my withered arms, and my wrinkled neck, to do with all that splendour?"

Cardillac had risen, and said with wild looks, like a man beside himself, still holding the casket out towards her, "Do me the kindness to take it, Mademoiselle! You have no notion how profound a reverence I bear in my heart for your virtues and your high deserts. Do but accept my little offering, as an attempt, on my part, to prove to you the warmth of my regard."

As Mademoiselle de Scudéri was still hesitating, Madame de Maintenon took the casket from Cardillac's hands, saying, "Now, by heaven, Mademoiselle, you are always talking of your great age. What have you and I to do with years and their burden? You are like some bashful young thing who would gladly reach out for forbidden fruit, if she could gather it without hands or fingers. Do not hesitate to accept good Master René's present, which thousands of others could not obtain for money or entreaty."

As she spoke she continued to press the casket on Mademoiselle de Scudéri; and now Cardillac sank again on his knees, kissed her dress, her hands, sighed, wept, sobbed, sprang up, and ran off in frantic haste, upsetting chairs and tables, so that the glass and porcelain crashed and clattered together.

"In the name of all the saints, what is the matter with the man?" cried Mademoiselle de Scudéri in great alarm.

But the Marquise, in particularly happy temper, laughed aloud, saying, "What is it, Mademoiselle? That Master René is over head and ears in love with you and, according to the laws of galanterie, begins to lay siege to your heart with a valuable present."

She carried this jest further, begging Mademoiselle de Scudéri not to be too obdurate towards this despairing lover of hers; and Mademoiselle de Scudéri, in her turn, borne away on a current of merry fancies, said that if it were so, she would not be able to refrain from delighting the world with the unprecedented spectacle of a goldsmith's bride of three-and-seventy summers and unexceptionable descent. Madame de Maintenon offered to twine the bridal wreath herself, and give her a few hints as to the duties of a housewife, a subject on which such a poor inexperienced little chit could not be expected to know very much.

But, notwithstanding all the jesting and the laughter, when Mademoiselle de Scudéri rose to depart, she became very grave again as her hand rested upon the jewel casket. "Whatever happens," she said, "I shall never be able to bring myself to wear these ornaments. They have, in any event, been in the hands of one of those diabolical men, who rob and slay with the audacity of the evil one himself and are very probably in league with him. I shudder at the thought of the blood which seems to cling to those glittering stones – even Cardillac's behaviour had something about it which struck me as singularly wild and strange. I cannot drive away from me a gloomy foreboding that there is some terrible and frightful mystery hidden behind all this; and yet, when I bring the whole affair, with all the circumstances of it, as clearly as I can before my mental vision, I cannot form the slightest idea what that mystery can be – and, above all, how the good, honourable Master René – the very model of all a good, well-behaved citizen ought to be – can have anything to do with what is wicked or guilty. But at all events, I distinctly feel that I never can wear those jewels."

The Marquise considered that this was carrying scruples rather too far; yet, when Mademoiselle de Scudéri asked her to say, on her honour, what she would do in her place, she replied, firmly and earnestly, "Far rather throw them into the Seine than ever put them on."

The scene with Master René inspired Mademoiselle de Scudéri to write some pleasant verses, which she read to the King the following evening at Madame de Maintenon's. Perhaps it was the thought of Master René carrying off a bride of seventy-three of unimpeachable quarterings – that enabled her to conquer her evil forebodings; but conquer them she did, completely – and the King laughed with all his heart, vowing that Boileau Despreaux had met with his master. So de Scudéri's poem was reckoned the very wittiest that ever was written.

Several months had elapsed, when chance so willed it that Mademoiselle de Scudéri was crossing the Pont Neuf in the glass coach of the Duchesse de Montpensier. The invention of those delightful glass coaches was then so recent that the people came together in crowds whenever one of them made its appearance in the streets. Consequently a gaping crowd gathered about the Duchesse's carriage on the Pont Neuf, so that the horses could hardly make their way along. Suddenly Mademoiselle de Scudéri heard a sound of quarrelling and curses, and saw a man making a way for himself through the crowd, by means of fisticuffs and blows in the ribs; and as he came near they were struck by the piercing eyes of a young face, deadly pale, and drawn by sorrow. This young man, gazing fixedly upon them, vigorously fought his way to them by help of fists and elbows, till he reached the carriage door, threw it open with much violence, and flung a note into Mademoiselle de Scudéri's lap; after which, he disappeared as he had come, distributing and receiving blows and fisticuffs.

La Martinière, who was with her mistress, fell back fainting in the carriage with a shriek of terror, as soon as she saw the young man. In vain Mademoiselle de Scudéri pulled the string, and called out to the driver. As if urged by the foul fiend, he kept lashing his horses till, scattering the foam from their nostrils, they kicked, plunged and reared, finally thundering over the bridge at a rapid trot. Mademoiselle de Scudéri emptied the contents of her smelling-bottle over the fainting La Martinière, who at last opened her eyes and, shuddering and quaking, clinging convulsively to her mistress, with fear and horror in her pale face, groaned out with difficulty, "For the love of the Virgin, what did that terrible man want? It was he who brought you the jewels on that awful night." Mademoiselle de Scudéri calmed her, pointing out that nothing very dreadful had happened after all, and that the immediate business in hand was to ascertain the contents of the letter. She opened it, and read as follows:

"A dark and cruel fatality, which you could dispel, is driving me into an abyss. I conjure you – as a son would a mother, in the glow of filial affection – to send the necklace and bracelets to Master René Cardillac, on some pretence or

other – say, to have something altered or improved. Your welfare, your very life
– depend on your doing this. If you do not comply before the day after tomorrow,
I will force my way into your house, and kill myself before your eyes.”

"Thus much is certain, at all events," said Mademoiselle de Scudéri, when she
had read this letter, "whether this mysterious man belongs to be band of robbers
and murderers or not, he has no very evil designs against me. If he had been able to
see me and speak to me on that night, who knows what strange events, what dark
concatenation of circumstances, would have been made known to me, of which, at
present, I seek, in my soul, the very faintest inkling in vain. But, be the matter as it may,
that which I am enjoined in this letter to do, I certainly shall do, were it only to be rid of
those fatal jewels, which seem to me as if they must be some diabolical talisman of the
Prince of Darkness's very own. Cardillac is not very likely to let them out of his hands
again, if once he gets hold of them."

She intended to take them to him next day; but it seemed as if all the beaux esprits
of Paris had entered into a league to assail and besiege her with verses, dramas and
anecdotes. Scarce had La Chapelle finished reading the scenes of a tragedy, and declared
that he considered he had now vanquished Racine, when the latter himself came in, and
discomfited him with the pathetic speech of one of his kings, until Boileau sent some
of his fireballs soaring up into the dark sky of the tragedies, by way of changing the
subject from that eternal one of the colonnade of the Louvre, to which the architectural
Dr. Perrault was shackling him.

When high noon arrived, Mademoiselle de Scudéri had to go to Madame de
Montansier; so the visit to René Cardillac had to be put off till the following day.

But the young man was always present to her mind, and a species of dim remembrance
seemed to be trying to arise in the depths of her being that she had, somehow and at
some time, seen that face and those features before. Troubled dreams disturbed her
broken slumbers. It seemed to her that she had acted thoughtlessly, and was to blame
for her delay in grasping the hands which the unfortunate man was holding out to her
for help. She felt, in fact, as if it had depended on her to prevent some atrocious crime.
As soon as it was fairly light, she had herself dressed and set off to the goldsmith's with
the jewels in her hand.

A crowd was streaming towards the Rue Niçaise (where Cardillac lived), trooping
together at the door, shouting, raging, surging, striving to storm into the house, kept
back with difficulty by the Marechaussée, who were guarding the place. Amid the
wild distracted uproar, voices were heard crying, "Tear him in pieces! Drag him limb
from limb, the accursed murderer!" At length Desgrais came up, with a number of his
men, and formed a lane through the thickest of the crowd. The door flew open, and
a man loaded with irons was brought out, and marched off amid the most frightful
imprecations of the raging populace. At the moment when Mademoiselle de Scudéri,
half dead with terror and gloomy foreboding, caught sight of him, a piercing shriek of
lamentation struck upon her ears.

"Go forward!" she cried to the coachman and, with a clever, rapid turn of his horses, he
scattered the thick masses of the crowd aside, and pulled up close to René Cardillac's door.
Desgrais was there, and at his feet a young girl, beautiful as the day, half-dressed, with her
hair dishevelled and wild inconsolable despair in her face, clinging to his knees, and crying
in tones of the bitterest and profoundest anguish, "He is innocent! He is innocent!"

Desgrais and his men tried in vain to shake her off and raise her from the ground, till at length a rough, powerful fellow, gripping her arms with his strong hands, dragged her away from Desgrais by sheer force. Stumbling awkwardly, he let the girl go, and she went rolling down the stone steps, and lay like one dead on the pavement.

Mademoiselle de Scudéri could contain herself no longer. "In Christ's name!" she cried, "what has happened? What is going forward here?" She hastily opened the carriage-door and stepped out. The crowd made way for her deferentially; and when she saw that one or two compassionate women had lifted the girl up, laid her on the steps, and were rubbing her brow with strong waters, she went up to Desgrais, and angrily repeated her question.

"A terrible thing has happened," said Desgrais. "René Cardillac was found this morning, killed by a dagger-thrust. His journeyman, Olivier, is the murderer, and has just been taken to prison."

"And the girl –"

"Is Madelon," interrupted Desgrais, "Cardillac's daughter. The wretched culprit was her sweetheart, and now she is crying and howling, and screaming over and over again that Olivier is innocent – quite innocent; but she knows all about this crime, and I must have her taken to prison too."

As he spoke he cast one of his baleful, malignant looks at the girl, which made Mademoiselle de Scudéri shudder. The girl was now beginning to revive, and breathe again faintly, though still incapable of speech or motion. There she lay with closed eyes, and people did not know what to do, whether to take her indoors, or leave her where she was a little longer till she recovered. Deeply moved, Mademoiselle de Scudéri looked upon this innocent creature, with tears in her eyes. She felt a horror of Desgrais and his men. Presently heavy footsteps came downstairs, those of the men bearing Cardillac's body.

Coming to a rapid decision, Mademoiselle de Scudéri cried out, "I shall take this girl home with me. What you do next is up to you, Desgrais."

A murmur of approval ran through the crowd. The women raised the girl; everyone crowded up; a hundred hands were proffered to help, and she was borne lightly to the carriage, whilst from every lip broke blessings on the kind lady who had saved her from arrest and criminal trial.

Madelon lay for many hours in a deep swoon, but at length the efforts of Seron – then the most celebrated physician in Paris – were successful in restoring her. Mademoiselle de Scudéri completed what Seron had begun, by letting the gentle rays of hope stream into the girl's heart; till at length a violent flood of tears, which started to her eyes, brought her relief, and she was able to tell her story, with only occasional interruptions when the overmastering might of her sorrow turned her words into sobbing.

She had been awakened at midnight by a soft knocking at her door, and had recognised the voice of Olivier, imploring her to get up at once, as her father lay dying. She sprang up, terrified, and opened the door. Olivier, pale, strained and bathed in perspiration, led the way, with tottering steps, to the workshop; she followed. There was her father lying with his eyes glazed, and the death-rattle in his throat. She threw herself upon him, weeping wildly, and then observed that his shirt was covered with blood. Olivier gently lifted her away, and busied himself in bathing a wound on her father's left breast with balsam, and bandaging it. As he was doing so, her father's consciousness came back; the rattle in his throat ceased and, looking first on her and then on Olivier with most expressive glances, he took her hand and placed it in Olivier's, pressing them both together. The pair of them were kneeling beside her father's bed when he raised himself with a piercing cry, but immediately fell back again, and with a deep sigh departed this life. On this they both wept and lamented.

Olivier told her how her father had been murdered in his presence during an expedition on which he had accompanied him that night by his order, and how he had with the utmost difficulty carried him home, not supposing him to be mortally wounded. As soon as it was day, the people of the house – who had heard the sounds of their footsteps and of the weeping and lamenting during the night – came up, and found them still kneeling, inconsolable by the goldsmith's body. Then an uproar began, the Marechaussée broke in, and Olivier was taken to prison as her father's murderer. Madelon added the most touching account of Olivier's virtues, goodness, piety and sincerity, telling how he had honoured his master as if he had been his own father, and how the latter returned his affection in the fullest measure, choosing him for his son-in-law in spite of his poverty, because his skill and fidelity were equal to the nobility of his heart. All this Madelon saw out of the fullness of her love, and added that if Olivier had thrust a dagger into her father's heart before her very eyes, she would rather have thought it a delusion of Satan's than have believed Olivier capable of such a terrible crime.

Most deeply touched by Madelon's unspeakable sufferings, and quite disposed to believe in poor Olivier's innocence, Mademoiselle de Scudéri made inquiries, and found everything confirmed which Madelon had said as to the domestic relations between the master and his workman. The people of the house and the neighbours all spoke of Olivier as the very model of good, steady, exemplary behaviour. No one knew anything whatever against him, and yet, when the crime was alluded to, every one shrugged his shoulders, and thought there was something incomprehensible about it.

Olivier, brought before the Chambre Ardente, most steadfastly denied – as Mademoiselle de Scudéri learned – the crime of which he was accused, and maintained that his master had been attacked in the street in his presence, and borne down, and that he had carried him home still alive, although he did not long survive. This agreed with Madelon's statement.

Over and over again Mademoiselle de Scudéri had the very minutest circumstances of the awful event related to her. She specially inquired if there had ever been any quarrel between Olivier and the father, whether Olivier was altogether exempt from that propensity to hastiness which often attacks the best tempered people like a blind madness, and leads them to commit deeds which seem to exclude all freewill; but the more enthusiastically Madelon spoke of the peaceful home-life which the three had led together, united in the most sincere affection, the more did every vestige of suspicion against Olivier disappear from her mind. Closely examining and considering everything, starting from the assumption that, notwithstanding all that spoke so loudly for his innocence, Olivier yet had been Cardillac's murderer, Mademoiselle de Scudéri could find, in all the realm of possibility, no motive for the terrible deed, which, in any case, was bound to destroy his happiness. Poor though skilful, he succeeds in gaining the good will of the most renowned of masters; he loves the daughter – his master favours his love. Happiness, good fortune for the rest of his life are laid open before him. Supposing, then, that – God knows on what impulse – in an outburst of anger, he should have made this murderous attack on his master, what diabolical hypocrisy it required to behave as he had done after the deed! With the firmest conviction of his innocence, Mademoiselle de Scudéri resolved to save Olivier at whatever cost.

It seemed to her most advisable, before perhaps appealing to the King in person, to go to the President La Regnie, point out for his consideration all the circumstances which made for Olivier's innocence, and so, perhaps, kindle in his mind a conviction favourable to the accused, which might communicate itself beneficially to the judges.

La Regnie received her with all the consideration which was the due of a lady of her worth, held in high esteem by His Majesty himself. He listened in silence to all she had to say concerning Olivier's circumstances, relationships and character; and also concerning the crime itself. A delicate, almost malignant, smile, however, was all the token he gave that her adjurations, her reminders (accompanied by plentiful tears) that a judge ought to be, not the enemy of the accused, but ready to listen, also, to whatever spoke in his favour, were not falling upon deaf ears. When at length Mademoiselle de Scudéri concluded, quite exhausted and wiping the tears from her cheeks, La Regnie began:

"It is quite characteristic of your excellent heart, Mademoiselle," he said, that, moved by the tears of a young girl in love, you should credit all she says; nay, be incapable of grasping the idea of a fearful crime such as this. But it is otherwise with the Judge, who is accustomed to tear off the mask from vile and unblushing hypocrisy and deception. It is, of course, not incumbent on me to disclose the course of a criminal trial to everyone who chooses to inquire. I do my duty, Mademoiselle! The world's opinion troubles me not at all. Evildoers should tremble before the Chambre Ardente, which knows no punishments save blood and fire. But by you, Mademoiselle, I would not be looked upon as a monster of severity and barbarism; therefore, permit me briefly to present to you the evidence of this young criminal's guilt. Heaven be thanked that vengeance has fallen upon him. With your acute intelligence, you will then disown your kindly and generous feelings, which do honour to you, but in me would be out of place.

"Eh bien! This morning René Cardillac is found murdered by a dagger thrust, no one is by him except his workman, Olivier Brusson, and the daughter. In Olivier's room there is found, amongst other things, a dagger covered with fresh blood which exactly fits into the wound. Olivier says, 'Cardillac was attacked in the street before my eyes' 'Was the intention to rob him?' 'I do not know.' 'You were walking with him and you could not drive off the murderer or detain him?' 'My master was walking fifteen or perhaps sixteen paces in front of me; I was following him.' 'Why, in all the world, so far behind?' 'My master wished it so.' 'And what had Master Cardillac to do in the streets so late?' 'That I cannot say.' 'But he was never in the habit of being out after nine o'clock at other times, was he?' At this Olivier hesitates, becomes confused, sighs, sheds tears, vows by all that is sacred that Cardillac did go out that night, and met with his death.

"Now observe, Mademoiselle, it is proved with the most absolute certainty that Cardillac did not leave the house that night; consequently Olivier's assertion that he went with him is a barefaced falsehood. The street door of the house fastens with a heavy lock, which makes a piercing noise in opening and closing, also the door itself creaks and groans on its hinges, so that, as experiments have proved, the noise is heard quite distinctly in the upper stories of the house. Now, there lives in the lower story, that is to say, close to the street door, old Maître Claude Patru with his housekeeper, a person of nearly eighty years of age, but still hale and active. Both of them heard Cardillac come downstairs at nine o'clock exactly, according to his usual custom, close and bolt the door with a great deal of noise, go upstairs again, read the evening prayer, and then (as was to be presumed by the shutting of the door) go into his bedroom.

"Maître Claude suffers from sleeplessness like many other old people; and on the night in question he could not close an eye. Therefore, about half-past nine the housekeeper struck a light in the kitchen, which she reached by crossing the passage, and sat down at the table beside her master with an old chronicle-book, from which she read aloud, whilst the old man, fixing his thoughts on the reading, sometimes sat in his arm-chair, sometimes walked slowly up and down the room to try and bring on sleepiness. All was silence in the house till nearly midnight; but then they heard overhead rapid footsteps, a heavy fall, as of something on to the floor, and immediately after that a hollow groaning. They were both struck by a peculiar alarm and anxiety, the horror of the terrible deed which had just been committed seemed to sweep over them. When day came what had been done in the darkness was brought clearly to light."

"But, in the name of all the Saints," cried Mademoiselle de Scudéri, "considering all the circumstances which I have told you at such length, can you think of any motive for this diabolical deed?"

"Hm!" answered La Regnie. "Cardillac was anything but a poor man. He had valuable jewels in his possession."

"But all he had would go to the daughter! You forget that Olivier was to be Cardillac's son-in-law."

"Perhaps he was compelled to share with others," said La Regnie, "or to do the deed wholly for them!"

"Share! – Murder for others," cried Mademoiselle de Scudéri, in utter amazement.

"You must learn, Mademoiselle," continued La Regnie, "that Olivier's blood would have been flowing on the Place de la Grève before this time, but that his crime is connected with that deeply-hidden mystery which has so long brooded over Paris. It is clear that Olivier belongs to that infamous band which, baffling all our attempts at observation or discovery, carries on its nefarious practices with perfect immunity. Through him everything will, must be, discovered. Cardillac's wound is precisely the same as those of all the persons who have been robbed and murdered in the streets and houses; and most conclusive of all since Olivier's arrest, the robberies and murders have ceased, the streets are as safe by night as by day. Proof enough that Olivier was most probably the chief of the band. As yet he will not confess, but there are means of making him speak against his will."

"And Madelon!" cried Mademoiselle de Scudéri, "that truthful innocent creature."

"Ah!" cried La Regnie, with one of his venomous smiles, "Who will answer to me that she is not in the plot, too? She does not care so very much about her father. Her tears are all for the young murderer."

"What?" cried Mademoiselle de Scudéri, "Not for her father? – That girl – impossible!"

"Oh!" continued La Regnie, "Remember la Brinvilliers! You must pardon me, if by-and-by I have to carry off your protégée, and put her in the Conciergerie."

Mademoiselle de Scudéri shuddered at this grisly notion. It seemed to her that no truth or virtue could endure before this terrible man; as if he spied out murder and dark-guilt in the deepest and most hidden thoughts of people's hearts. She rose. "Be human!" was all that she was able, with difficulty, to say in her state of anxiety and oppression. As she was just going to descend the stairs, to which the

President had attended her with ceremonious courtesy, a strange idea came to her – she knew not how.

"Might I be allowed to see this unfortunate Olivier Brusson?" she inquired, turning round sharply.

He scrutinised her face thoughtfully, and then distorted his features into the repulsive smile which was characteristic of him.

"Doubtless, Mademoiselle," he said, "your idea is that, trusting your own feelings – the inward voice more than what happened before our eyes, you would like to examine into Olivier's guilt or innocence for yourself. If you do not fear that gloomy abode of crime if it is not hateful to you to see those types of depravity in all their gradations – the doors of the Conciergerie shall be opened to you in two hours time. Olivier, whose fate excites your sympathy, shall be brought to you."

In truth, Mademoiselle de Scudéri could not bring herself to believe in Olivier's guilt. Everything spoke against him. Indeed, no judge in the world would have thought otherwise than La Regnie, in the face of what had happened. But the picture of domestic happiness which Madelon had called before her eyes in such vivid colours, outweighed and outshone all suspicion, so that she preferred to adopt the hypothesis of some inscrutable mystery rather than believe what her whole nature revolted against.

She thought she would hear Olivier's narrative of the events of that night of mystery, and in this manner, possibly, penetrate farther into a secret which the judges, perhaps, did not see into, because they thought it unworthy of investigation.

Arrived at the Conciergerie, she was taken into a large, well-lighted room. Presently she heard the ring of fetters. Olivier Brusson was brought in; but as soon as she saw him she fell down fainting. When she recovered, he was gone. She demanded impetuously to be taken to her carriage; she would not remain another moment in that place of crime and wickedness. Alas! at the first glance she had recognised in Olivier Brusson the young man who had thrown the letter into her carriage on the Pont Neuf, and who had brought her the casket with the jewels. Now all doubt was gone, La Regnie's terrible suspicions completely justified. Olivier belonged to the atrocious band, and had, doubtless, murdered his master!

And Madelon! Never before so bitterly deceived by her kind feelings, Mademoiselle de Scudéri, under this deadly attack upon her by the power of the evil one here below – in whose very existence she had not believed – doubted if there was such a thing as truth. She gave admittance to the fearful suspicion that Madelon, too, was forsworn, and might have had a hand in the bloody deed. And as it is the nature of the human mind that, when an idea has dawned upon it, it eagerly seeks, and finds, colours in which to paint that idea more and more vividly; as she weighed and considered all the circumstances of the crime along with Madelon's behaviour, she found a very great deal to nourish suspicion. Many things which had hitherto been considered proofs of innocence and purity now became evidences of studied hypocrisy and deep, corrupt wickedness. Those heartrending cries of sorrow and bitter tears might well have been caused by the deathly dread of her lover's bleeding – nay, of her own falling into the executioner's hands.

With a resolve at once to cast away the serpent she had been cherishing, Mademoiselle de Scudéri alighted from her carriage. Madelon threw herself at her feet. Her heavenly eyes – as candid as an angel's – raised to her, her hands pressed to her heaving breast, she wept, imploring help and consolation. Controlling herself with difficulty and speaking with as much calmness and gravity as she could, Mademoiselle de Scudéri said, "Go! Go! – Be thankful that the murderer awaits the just punishment of his crime. May the Holy Virgin grant that guilt does not weigh heavily on your own head also." With a bitter cry of "Alas! Then all is over!" Madelon fell fainting to the ground. Mademoiselle de Scudéri left her to the care of La Martinière and went to another room.

Much distressed and estranged from all earthly things, she longed to depart from a world filled with diabolical treachery and falsehood. She complained of the destiny which had granted her so many years in which to strengthen her belief in truth and virtue, only to shatter in her old age the beautiful fancies which had illumined her path.

She heard Madelon, as La Martinière was leading her away, murmur in broken accents, "Her, too, have the terrible men deceived. Ah! Wretched me! – Miserable Olivier!" The tones of her voice went to her heart, and again there dawned within her a belief in the existence of some mystery, in Olivier's innocence. Torn by the most contradictory feelings, she cried, "What spirit of the pit has mixed me up in this terrible story, which will be my very death!"

At this moment Baptiste came in, pale and terrified, to say that Desgrais was at the door. Since the dreadful La Voisin trial the appearance of Desgrais in a house was the sure precursor of some criminal accusation. Hence Baptiste's terror, as to which his mistress asked him with a gentle smile, "What is the matter, Baptiste? Has the name of Scudéri been found in La Voisin's lists?"

"Ah! For Christ's sake," cried Baptiste, trembling in every limb, "how can you say such a thing? But Desgrais – the horrible Desgrais – is looking so mysterious, and is so insistent – he seems hardly able to wait till he can see you."

"Well. Baptiste," she said, "bring him in at once, this gentleman who so frightens you. To me, at all events, he can cause no anxiety."

"President La Regnie sends me to you, Mademoiselle," said Desgrais, when he entered, "with a request which he scarce would dare to make if he did not know your goodness and bravery, and if the last hope of bringing to light an atrocious deed of blood did not lie in your hands; had you not already taken such interest (as well as bearing a part) in this case, which is keeping the Chambre Ardente, and all of us, in a state of such breathless suspense. Since he saw you, Olivier Brusson has been almost out of his mind. He still swears by all that is sacred, that he is completely innocent of René Cardillac's death, though he is ready to suffer the punishment he has deserved. Observe, Mademoiselle, that the latter admission clearly refers to other crimes of which he has been guilty. But all attempts to get him to utter anything further have been vain. He begs and implores to be allowed to have an interview with you. To you alone will he divulge everything. Vouchsafe then, Mademoiselle, to listen to Brusson's confession."

"What?" cried Mademoiselle de Scudéri, in indignation, "I become an organ of the criminal court, and abuse the confidence of this unfortunate fellow to bring him to the scaffold! No, Desgrais! Ruffian and murderer though he may be, I could never deceive and betray him thus villainously. I will have nothing to do with his avowal. If I did, it would be locked up in my heart, as if made to a priest under the seal of the confessional."

"Perhaps, Mademoiselle," said Desgrais, with a subtle smile, "you might alter your opinion after hearing Brusson. Did you not beg the President to be human? This he is, in yielding to Brusson's foolish desire, and thus trying one more expedient – the last – before resorting to the rack, for which Brusson is long since ripe."

Mademoiselle de Scudéri shuddered involuntarily.

"Understand, Mademoiselle," he continued, "you would by no means be expected to revisit those gloomy dungeons, which lately inspired you with such horror and loathing. Olivier would be brought to your own house, in the night, like a free man; what he should say would not be listened to; though, of course, there would be a proper guard with him. He could thus tell you freely and unconstrainedly all he had to say. As regards any risk which you might run in seeing the wretched being, my life shall answer for that. He speaks of you with the deepest veneration; he vows that it is the dark mystery that prevented him seeing you earlier which has brought him to destruction. Moreover, it would rest with you entirely to repeat as much or as little as you pleased of what Brusson confessed to you. How could you be constrained to more?"

Mademoiselle de Scudéri sat with eyes fixed on the ground, in deep reflection. It seemed to her that she could not but obey that Higher Power which demanded of her the clearing up of this mystery – as if there were no escape for her from the wondrous toils in which she had become enmeshed against her will.

Coming to a rapid decision, she solemnly replied, "God will give me self-command and firm resolution. Bring Brusson here; I will see him."

As on the night when the jewel-casket had been brought, so now at midnight there came a knocking at the door. Baptiste, duly instructed, opened. Mademoiselle de Scudéri's blood ran cold when she heard the heavy tread of the guards who had brought Brusson stationing themselves about the passages.

At length the door opened, Desgrais came in, and after him Olivier Brusson, without irons, and respectably dressed.

"Here is Brusson, Mademoiselle," said Desgrais, bowing courteously; he then departed at once.

Brusson sank down on both knees before Mademoiselle de Scudéri. The pure, clear expression of a most truthful soul beamed from his face, though it was drawn and distorted by terror and bitter pain. The longer she looked at him, the more vivid became a remembrance of some well-loved person – she could not say whom. When the first feeling of shuddering left her, she forgot that Cardillac's murderer was kneeling before her and, speaking in the pleasant tone of quiet goodwill which was natural to her, said: "Now, Brusson, what have you to say to me?"

He – still on his knees – sighed deeply, from profound sorrow, and then said: "Oh, Mademoiselle, you whom I so honour and worship, is there no trace of recollection of me left in your mind?"

Still looking at him attentively, she answered that she had certainly detected in his face a likeness to someone whom she had held in affection, and it was to this that he owed it that she had overcome her profound horror of a murderer so far as to be able to listen to him quietly. Much pained by her words, Brusson rose quickly, and stepped backwards a pace, with his gloomy glance fixed on the ground.

Then, in a hollow voice, he said: "Have you quite forgotten Anne Guiot? Her son, Olivier, the boy whom you used to dandle on your knee, is he who is now before you."

"Oh! For the love of all the Saints!" she cried, covering her face with both hands and sinking back in her chair. She had reason for being thus horrified. Anne Guiot, the daughter of a citizen who had fallen into poverty, had lived with Mademoiselle de Scudéri from her childhood; she had brought her up like a daughter, with all affection and care. When she grew up, a handsome, well-conducted young man named Claude Bresson fell in love with her. Being a first-rate workman at his trade of a watchmaker, sure to make a capital living in Paris and Anne being very fond of him, Mademoiselle de Scudéri saw no reason to object to their marrying. They set up house accordingly, lived a most quiet and happy domestic life, and the bond between them was knitted more closely still by the birth of a most beautiful boy, the image of his pretty mother.

Mademoiselle de Scudéri made an idol of little Olivier, whom she would take away from his mother for hours and days, to pet him and kiss him. Hence he attached himself to her, and was as pleased to be with her as with his mother. When three years had passed, the depressed state of Brusson's trade brought it about that job-work was scarcer every day, so that at last it was all he could do to get bread to eat. In addition to this came home-sickness for his beautiful native Geneva so the little household went there, in spite of Mademoiselle de Scudéri's dissuasions and promises of all needful assistance. Anne wrote once or twice to her foster-mother, and then ceased; so that Mademoiselle de Scudéri thought she was forgotten in the happiness of the Brussons' life.

It was now just three and twenty years since the Brussons had left Paris for Geneva.

"Horrible!" cried Mademoiselle de Scudéri, when she had to some extent recovered herself, "You, Olivier! The son of my Anne! And now!"

"Mademoiselle!" said Olivier, quietly and composedly, "Doubtless you never thought that the boy whom you cherished like the tenderest of mothers, whom you dandled on your knee, and to whom you gave sweetmeats, would when grown to manhood stand before you accused of a terrible murder. I am completely innocent! The Chambre Ardente charges me with a crime; but, as I hope to die a Christian's death, though it may be by the executioner's hand – I am free from all guilt. Not by my hand – not by any crime of my committing, was it that the unfortunate Cardillac came to his end."

As he said this, Olivier began to tremble and shake so, that Mademoiselle de Scudéri motioned him to a little seat which was near him.

"I have had sufficient time," he went on, "to prepare myself for this interview with you – which I look upon as the last favour of a merciful Heaven – and to acquire as much calmness and self-control as are necessary to tell you the story of my terrible, unheard-of misfortunes. Be so compassionate as to listen to me calmly, whatever may be your horror at the disclosure of a mystery of which you certainly have not the smallest inkling. Ah! Would to Heaven my poor father had never left Paris! As far as my recollections of Geneva carry me, I remember only the tears of my inconsolable parents and my own tears at the sight of their lamentations, which I was unable to understand. Later, there came to me a clear sense a full comprehension – of the bitterest and most grinding poverty, want and privation in which they were living. My father was deceived in all his expectations; bowed down and broken with sorrow, he died, just when he had managed to place me as apprentice with a goldsmith. My mother spoke much of you; she longed to tell you all her misfortunes, but the despondency which springs from poverty prevented her. That, and also, no doubt, false modesty, which often gnaws at a mortally wounded heart, kept her from carrying out her idea. She followed my father to the grave a few months after his death."

"Poor Anne! Poor Anne!" said Mademoiselle de Scudéri, overwhelmed by sorrow.

"I thank and praise the Eternal Power that she has gone where she cannot see her beloved son fall, branded with disgrace, by the hand of the executioner," cried Olivier loudly, raising a wild and terrible glance to the skies. Outside there was a sudden agitation; a sound of people moving about made itself heard. "Ho, ho!" said he, with a bitter laugh, "Desgrais is waking up his people, as if I could possibly escape. But, let me go on. My master treated me harshly, though I was very soon one of the best of workmen and, indeed, much better than himself. Once a stranger came to our workshop to buy some of our work.

"When he saw a necklace of my making, he patted my shoulder in a kind way, and said, looking at the necklace with admiration, 'Ah, ha! My young friend, this is really first-class work. I don't know anybody who could beat it but René Cardillac, who is the greatest of all goldsmiths, of course. You ought to go to him; he would be delighted to get hold of you, for there's nobody but yourself who would be of such use to him; and again, there's nobody but he who can teach you anything.'

"The words of this stranger sunk deep into my heart. There was no more peace for me in Geneva. I was powerfully impelled to leave it, and at length I succeeded in getting free from my master. I came to Paris, where René Cardillac received me coldly and harshly. But I stuck to my point. He was obliged to give me something to try my hand at, however trifling. So I got a ring to finish. When I took it back to him finished, he gazed at me with those sparkling eyes of his, as if he would look me through and through. Then he said, 'You are a first-rate man – a splendid fellow; you may come and work with me. I'll pay you well; you'll be satisfied with me.' And he kept his word. I had been several weeks with him before I saw Madelon who, I think, had been visiting an aunt of his in the country. At last she came home. O eternal power of Heaven, how was it with me when I saw that angelic creature! Has ever a man so loved as I! And now! Oh Madelon!"

Olivier could speak no more for sorrow. He held both hands over his face, and sobbed violently. At last he conquered the wild pain with a mighty effort, and went on:

"Madelon looked on me with favour, and came oftener and oftener into the workshop. Her father watched closely but many a stolen hand-clasp marked our covenant. Cardillac did not seem to notice. My idea was, that if I could gain his good-will and attain Master's rank, I should ask his consent to our marriage. One morning, when I was going in to begin work, he came to me with anger and contempt in his face.

"'I don't want any more of your work,' he said. 'Get out of this house, and don't let my eyes ever rest on you again. I have no need to tell you the reason. The dainty fruit you are trying to gather is beyond the reach of a beggar like you!'

"I tried to speak, but he seized me and pitched me out of the door with such violence that I fell, and hurt my head and my arm. Furious, and smarting with the pain, I went off, and at last found a kindhearted acquaintance in the Faubourg St. Germain, who gave me quarters in his garret. I had no peace nor rest. At night I wandered round Cardillac's house, hoping that Madelon would hear my sighs and lamentations, and perhaps manage to speak to me at the window, undiscovered. All sorts of desperate plans, to which I thought I might persuade her, jostled each other in my brain. Cardillac's house in the Rue Niçaise abuts on to a high wall with niches, containing old, partly-broken statues.

"One night I was standing close to one of those figures, looking up at the windows of the house which open on the courtyard which the wall encloses. Suddenly I saw a light in Cardillac's workshop. It was midnight, and he was never awake at that time, as he always went to bed exactly at nine. My heart beat anxiously: I thought something might be going on which would let me get into the house. But the light disappeared again immediately. I pressed myself closely into the niche, and against the statue; but I started back in alarm, feeling a return of my pressure, as if the statue had come to life. In the faint moonlight I saw that the stone was slowly turning, and behind it appeared a dark form, which crept softly out and went down the street with stealthy tread. I sprang to the statue: it was standing close to the wall again, as before. Involuntarily, as if impelled by some power within me, I followed the receding dark figure. In passing an image of the Virgin, this figure looked round, the light of the lamp before the image falling upon his face. It was Cardillac! An indescribable fear fell upon me; an eerie shudder came over me.

"As if driven by some spell, I felt I must follow this spectre-like sleep-walker – for that was what I thought my master was, though it was not full moon, the time when that kind of impulse falls upon sleepers. At length Cardillac disappeared in a deep shadow; but by a certain easily distinguishable sound I knew that he had gone into the entry of a house. What was the meaning of this? I asked myself in amazement; what was he going to do? I pressed myself close to the wall. Presently there came up a gentleman, trilling and singing, with a white plume distinct in the darkness, and clanking spurs. Cardillac darted out upon him from the darkness, like a tiger on his prey; the man fell to the ground gasping. I rushed up with a cry of terror. Cardillac was leaning over him as he lay on the ground.

"'Master Cardillac, what are you about?' I cried aloud. 'Curses upon you!' he cried and, running by me with lightning speed, disappeared. Quite out of my senses – scarcely able to walk a step – I went up to the gentleman on the ground, and knelt down beside him, thinking it might still be possible to save him. But there was no trace of life left in him. In my alarm I scarcely noticed that the Marechaussée had come up and surrounded me.

"'Another one laid low by the demons!' they cried, all speaking at once. 'Ah! Ha! Youngster! What are you doing here? – Are you one of the band?' and they seized me. I stammered out in the best way I could that I was incapable of such a terrible deed, and that they must let me go. Then one of them held a lantern to my face, and said, with a laugh: 'This is Olivier Brusson; the goldsmith who works with our worthy Master René Cardillac. He murders folks in the street! – Very likely story! Who ever heard of a murderer lamenting over the body, and letting himself be nabbed? Tell us all about it, my lad; out with it straight.'

"'Right before my eyes,' I said, 'someone sprang out upon this man, stabbed him and ran off like lightning. I cried as loud as I could. I tried to see if he could be saved.'

"'No, my son,' cried one of those who had lifted up the body, 'he's done for! – The dagger-stab right through his heart, as usual.' 'The deuce!' said another; 'just too late again, as we were the day before yesterday.' And they went away with the body.

"What I thought of all this I really cannot tell you. I pinched myself, to see if I were not in some horrible dream. I felt as if I must wake up directly, and marvel at the absurdity of what I had been dreaming. Cardillac – my Madelon's father – an atrocious murderer! I had sunk down powerless on the stone steps of a house; the daylight was growing brighter and brighter. An officer's hat with a fine plume was lying before me on the pavement. Cardillac's deed of blood, committed on the spot, came clearly back to my mental vision. I ran away in horror.

"With my mind in a whirl, almost unconscious, I was sitting in my garret, when the door opened, and René Cardillac came in. 'For Christ's sake! What do you want?' I cried. Paying no heed to this, however, he came up smiling with a calmness and urbanity which increased my inward horror. He drew forward an old rickety stool, and sat down beside me; for I was unable to rise from my straw bed, where I had thrown myself. 'Well, Olivier,' he began, 'how is it with you, my poor boy? I really was too hasty in turning you out of doors. I miss you at every turn. Just now I have a job in hand which I shall never be able to finish without you; won't you come back and work with me? You don't answer. Yes, I know very well I insulted you. I won't pretend that I was not angry about your making up to my Madelon; but I have been thinking matters well over, and I see that I couldn't have a better son-in-law than you, with your abilities, your skill, diligence and trustworthiness. Come back with me, and see how soon you and Madelon can make a match of it.'

"His words pierced my heart; I shuddered at his wickedness; I could not utter a syllable.

"'You hesitate,' he said sharply, while his sparkling eyes transfixed me. 'Perhaps you can't come today. You have other things to do. Perhaps you want to go and see Desgrais, or have an interview with D'Argenson or La Regnie. Take care, my boy, that the talons you are thinking of calling down on others, don't tear you.' At this my sorely tried spirit found vent.

"'Those,' I said, 'who are conscious of horrible crimes may dread the names which you have mentioned, but I do not. I have nothing to do with them.'

"'Remember, Olivier,' he resumed, 'that it is an honour to you to work with me – the most renowned Master of his time everywhere highly esteemed for his truth and goodness; any foul calumny would fall back on the head of its originator. As to Madelon, I must tell you that it is her alone whom you have to thank for my yielding. She loves you with a devotion that I should never have believed her capable of. As soon as you were gone, she fell at my feet, clasped my knees and vowed with copious tears, that she could never live without you. I thought this was mere imagination, for those young things always think they're going to die of love whenever a young wheyface looks at them a little kindly. But my Madelon really did fall quite sick and ill; and when I tried to talk her out of the silly nonsense, she called out your name a thousand times. Last evening I told her I gave in and agreed to everything, and would go to fetch you today; so this morning she is blooming again like any rose, and waiting for you, quite beside herself with longing.'

"May the eternal power of Heaven forgive me, but – I don't know how it came about – I suddenly found myself in Cardillac's house, where Madelon, with loud cries of 'Olivier! – My Olivier! – My beloved! My husband!' clasped both her arms about me, and pressed me to her heart; whilst I, in the plenitude of my bliss, swore by the Virgin and all the Saints never, never to leave her."

Overcome by the remembrance of this decisive moment, Olivier was obliged to pause. Horrified at the crime of a man whom she had looked on as the incarnation of probity and goodness, Mademoiselle de Scudéri cried: "Dreadful! – René Cardillac a member of that band of murderers who have so long made Paris into a robbers' den!"

"A member of the band, do you say, Mademoiselle?" said Olivier. "There never was any band; it was René Cardillac alone who sought and found his victims with such diabolical ingenuity and activity. It was in the fact of his being alone that his impunity lay – the practical impossibility of coming upon the murderer's track. But let me go on. What is coming will clear up the mystery, and reveal the secrets of the wickedest and at the same time most wretched of all mankind. You at once see the position in which I now stood towards my master. The step was taken, and I could not go back. At times it seemed to me that I had rendered myself Cardillac's accomplice in murder, and it was only in Madelon's love that I temporarily forgot the inward pain which tortured me; only in her society could I drive away all outward traces of the nameless horror. When I was at work with the old man in the workshop, I could not look him in the face could – scarcely speak a word – for the horror which pervaded me in the presence of this terrible being, who fulfilled all the duties of the tender father and the good citizen, while the night shrouded his atrocities. Madelon, pure and pious as an angel, hung upon him with the most idolatrous affection. It pierced my heart when I thought that, if ever vengeance should overtake this masked criminal she would be the victim of the most terrible despair. That, of itself closed my lips, though the consequence of my silence should be a criminal's death for myself. Although much was to be gathered from what the Marechaussée had said, still Cardillac's crimes, their motive and the manner in which he carried them out, were a riddle to me. The solution of it soon came."

"One day Cardillac – who usually excited my horror by laughing and jesting during our work, in the highest of spirits – was very grave and thoughtful. Suddenly he threw the piece of work he was engaged on aside, so that the pearls and other stones rolled about the floor, started to his feet, and said: 'Olivier! Things cannot go on between us like this; the situation is unendurable What the ablest and most ingenious efforts of Desgrais and his myrmidons failed to find out, chance has thrown into your hands. You saw me at my nocturnal work, to which my Evil Star compels me, so that no resistance is possible for me; and it was your own Evil Star, moreover which led you to follow me; which wrapped and hid you in an impenetrable mantle; which gave that lightness to your footfall that enabled you to move along with the noiselessness of the smaller animals, so that I – who see clear by night, as doth the tiger, and hear the smallest sound, the humming of the gnats, streets away – did not observe you. Your Evil Star brought you to me, my comrade – my accomplice! You see, now, that you can't betray me; therefore you shall know all."

"I would have cried out: 'Never, never shall I be your comrade your accomplice, you atrocious miscreant.' But the inward horror which I felt at his words paralysed my tongue. Instead of words I could only utter an unintelligible noise. Cardillac sat down in his working chair again, wiped the perspiration from his brow, and seemed to find it difficult to pull himself together, hard beset by the recollection of the past. At length he began: 'Wise men have much to say of the strange impulses which come to women when they are enceinte, and the strange influence which those vivid, involuntary impulses exercise upon the child. A wonderful tale is told of my mother. When she was a month gone with me she was looking on, with other women, at a court pageant at the Trianon, and saw a certain cavalier in Spanish dress, with a glittering chain of jewels about his neck, from which she could not remove her eyes. Her whole being longed for those sparkling stones, which seemed to her more than earthly. This same cavalier had at a previous time, before my mother was married, had designs on her virtue, which she rejected with indignation. She recognised him, but now, irradiated by the light of the gems, he seemed to her a creature of a higher sphere, the very incarnation of beauty. The cavalier noticed the longing, fiery looks which she was bending on him, and thought he was in better luck now than of old.

"'He managed to get near her, to separate her from her companions, and entice her to a lonely place. There he clasped her eagerly in his arms. My mother grasped at the beautiful chain; but at that moment he fell down, dragging her with him. Whether it was apoplexy, or what, I do not know; but he was dead. My mother struggled in vain to free herself from the clasp of the arms, stiffened as they were in death. With the hollow eyes, whence vision had departed, fixed on her, the corpse rolled with her to the ground. Her shrieks at length reached people who were passing at some distance; they hastened to her, and rescued her from the embrace of this gruesome lover.

"'Her fright laid her on a bed of dangerous sickness. Her life was despaired of as well as mine; but she recovered, and her confinement was more prosperous than had been thought possible. But the terrors of that awful moment had set their mark on me. My Evil Star had risen, and darted into me those rays which kindled in me one of the strangest and most fatal of passions. Even in my earliest childhood I thought there was nothing to compare with glittering diamonds in golden settings. This was looked upon as a childish fancy; but it was otherwise, for as a boy I stole gold and jewels wherever I could lay hands on them, and I knew the difference between good ones and bad, instinctively, like the most accomplished connoisseur. Only the pure and valuable attracted me; I would not touch alloyed or coined gold. Those inborn cravings were kept in check by my father's severe chastisements; but, so that I might always have to do with gold and precious stones, I took up the goldsmith's calling. I worked at it with passion, and soon became the first living master of that art. Then began a period when the natural bent within me, so long restrained, shot forth in power, and waxed with might, bearing everything away before it. As soon as I finished a piece of work and delivered it, I fell into a state of restlessness and disconsolateness which prevented my sleeping, ruined my health, and left me no enjoyment in my life. The person for whom I made the work haunted me day and night like a spectre. I saw that person continually before my mental vision, with my beautiful jewels on, and a voice kept whispering to me: "They belong to you! Take them; what's the use of diamonds to the dead?" At last I betook myself to thieving. I had access to the houses of the great; I took advantage quickly of every opportunity. No locks withstood my skill, and I soon had my work back in my hands again. But this was not enough to calm my unrest. That mysterious voice made itself heard again, jeering at me, and saying: "Ho, ho! One of the dead is wearing your jewels." I did not know whence it came, but I had an indescribable hatred for all those for whom I made jewellery. More than that, in the depths of my heart I began to long to kill them; this frightened me. Just then I bought this house. I had concluded the bargain with the owner: here in this very room we were sitting, drinking a bottle of wine in honour of the transaction.'"

"'Night had come on, he was going to leave when he said to me: "Look here, Maître René before I go I must let you into a secret about this house." He opened that cupboard, which is built into the wall there, and pushed the back of it in; this let him into a little closet, where he bowed down and raised a trap-door. This showed us a steep, narrow stair, which we went down, and at the bottom of it was a little narrow door, which let us out into the open courtyard. There he went up to the wall, pushed a piece of iron which projected a very little, and immediately a piece of the wall turned round, so that a person could get out through the opening into the street. You must see this contrivance sometime, Olivier; the sly old monks of the convent, which this house once was, must have had it made so as to be able to slip in and out secretly. It is wood but covered with lime and mortar on the outside, and to the outer side of it is fitted a statue, also of wood, through looking exactly like stone, which turns on wooden hinges. When I saw this arrangement, dark ideas surged up in my mind; it seemed to me that deeds, as yet mysterious to myself, were here prearranged for.

"'I had just finished a splendid set of ornaments for a gentleman of the court who, I knew, was going to give them to an opera dancer. Soon my deadly torture was on me; the spectre dogged my steps, the whispering devil was at my ear. I went back into the house, bathed in a sweat of agony; I rolled about on my bed, sleepless. In my mind's eye I saw the man riding to his dancer with my beautiful jewels. Full of fury I sprang up, threw my cloak round me, went down the secret stair, out through the wall into the Rue Niçaise. He came, I fell upon him, he cried out; but, seizing him from behind, I plunged my dagger into his heart. The jewels were mine. When this was done, I felt a peace, a contentment within me which I had never known before. The spectre had vanished – the voice of the demon was still. Now I knew what was the behest of my Evil Star, which I had to obey, or perish.

"'You know all now, Olivier. Don't think that, because I must do that which I cannot avoid, I have clean renounced all sense of that mercy or kindly feeling which is the portion of all humanity, and inherent in man's nature. You know how hard I find it to let any of my work go out of my hands, many there are to whom I would not bring death, and for them nothing will induce me to work; indeed, in cases when I feel that my spectre will have to be exorcised with blood on the morrow, I settle the business that day by a smashing blow, which lays the holder of my jewels on the ground, so that I get them back into my own hands.'

"Having said all this, Cardillac took me into his secret strong-room and showed me his collection of jewels; the King does not possess its equal. To each ornament was fastened a small label stating for whom it had been made, and when taken back – by theft, robbery, or murder.

"'On your wedding day, Olivier,' he said, in a solemn tone, 'you will swear me a solemn oath, with your hand on the crucifix, that as soon as I am dead you will at once convert all these treasures into dust by a process which I will tell you of. I will not have any human being, least of all Madelon and you, come into possession of those stones that have been bought with blood.'

"Shut up in this labyrinth of crime, torn in twain by love and abhorrence, I was like one of the damned to whom a glorified angel points, with gentle smile, the upward way, whilst Satan holds him down with red-hot talons, and the angel's loving smile, reflecting all the bliss of paradise, becomes, to him, the very keenest of his tortures I thought of flight, even of suicide, but Madelon! Blame me, blame me, Mademoiselle, for having been too weak to overcome a passion which fettered me to my destruction. I shall be atoning for my weakness by a shameful death. One day Cardillac came in in unusually fine spirits. He kissed and caressed Madelon, cast most affectionate looks at me, drank a bottle of good wine at table, which he only did on high-days and holidays, sang and made merry. Madelon had left us and I was going to the workshop.

"'Sit still, lad,' cried Cardillac, 'no more work today; let's drink the health of the most worthy and charming lady in all Paris.'

"When we had clinked our glasses, and he had emptied a bumper, he said: 'Tell me, Olivier, how do you like these lines?

'Un amant qui craint les voleurs
N'est point digne d'amour.'

"And he told me what had transpired between you and the King in Madame de Maintenon's salon, adding that he had always respected you more than any other human being, and that his reverence and esteem for your qualities was such that his Evil Star paled before you," and he would have no fear that, were you to wear the finest piece of his work that ever he made, the spectre would ever prompt him to thoughts of murder.

"'Listen, Olivier,' he said, 'to what I am going to do. A considerable time ago I had to make a necklace and bracelets for Henrietta of England, supplying the stones myself. I made of this the best piece of work that ever I turned out, and it broke my heart to part with the ornaments, which had become the very treasures of my soul. You know of her unfortunate death by assassination. The things remained with me, and now I shall send them to Mademoiselle de Scudéri, in the name of the dreaded band, as a token of respect and gratitude. Besides its being an unmistakable mark of her triumph, it will be a richly deserted sign of my contempt for Desgrais and his men. You shall take her the jewels.'

"When he mentioned your name, Mademoiselle, dark veils seemed to be lifted, revealing the bright memory of my happy childhood, which rose again in glowing colours before me. A wonderful comfort came into my soul, a ray of hope, driving the dark shadows away. Cardillac saw the effect his words had produced upon me, and gave it his own interpretation. 'My idea seems to please you,' he said. 'I must declare that a deep inward voice, very unlike that which cries for blood like a raving wild beast, commanded me to do this thing. Many times I feel the strangest ideas come into my mind – an inward fear, the dread of something terrible, the awe whereof seems to come breathing into this present time from some distant other world, seizes powerfully upon me. I even feel, at such times, that the deeds which my Evil Star has committed by means of me may be charged to the account of my immortal soul, though it has no part in them. In one of those moods I determined that I would make a beautiful diamond crown for the Virgin in the Church of St. Eustache. But the indescribable dread always came upon me, stronger than ever, when I set to work at it, so that I have abandoned it altogether. Now it seems to me that in presenting Mademoiselle de Scudéri with the finest work I have ever turned out, I am offering a humble sacrifice to goodness and virtue personified, and imploring their powerful intercession.'

"Cardillac, well acquainted with all the minutiae of your manner of life told me how and when to take the ornaments to you. My whole being rejoiced, for Heaven seemed to be showing me, through the atrocious Cardillac, the way to escape from the hell in which I was being tortured. Quite contrary to Cardillac's wish, I resolved that I would get access to you and speak with you. As Anne Brusson's son and your former pet, I thought I would throw myself at your feet and tell you everything. I knew that you would keep the secret, out of consideration for the unheard-of misery which its disclosure would bring upon Madelon, but that your grand and brilliant intellect would be sure to find means to put an end to Cardillac's wickedness without disclosing it. Do not ask me what those means were to have been; I cannot tell. But that you would rescue Madelon and me I believed as firmly as I do in the intercession of the Holy Virgin. You know, Mademoiselle, that my intention was frustrated that night; but I did not lose hope of being more fortunate another time.

"By-and-by Cardillac suddenly lost all his good spirits; he crept moodily about, uttered unintelligible words, and worked his arms as if warding off something hostile. His mind seemed full of evil thoughts. For a whole morning he had been going on in this way. At last he sat down at the worktable, sprang up again angrily, looked out of window, and then said gravely and gloomily: 'I wish Henrietta of England had had my jewels.' Those words filled me with terror. I knew that his diseased mind was again possessed by a terrible lust for murder, that the voice of the demon was again loud in his ears. I saw your life threatened by that dread spirit of murder. If Cardillac could get his jewels back again into his hands you were safe. The danger grew greater every instant. I met you on the Pont Neuf, made my way to your carriage, threw you the note which implored you to give the jewels back to Cardillac immediately. You did not come. My fear became despair, when next day Cardillac spoke of nothing but the priceless jewels he had seen last night in his dreams. I could only suppose that this referred to your jewels, and I felt sure he was brooding over some murderous attack, which he had determined to carry out that night. Save you I must, should it cost Cardillac's life.

"After the evening prayer when he had shut himself up in his room as usual, I got into the courtyard through a window, slipped out through the opening of the wall, and stationed myself close at hand, in the deepest shadow. Very soon Cardillac came out, and went gliding softly down the street. I followed him. He took the direction of the Rue St. Honoré. My heart beat fast. All at once he disappeared from me. I determined to place myself at your door. Just as fate had ordered matters on the first occasion of my witnessing one of his crimes, there came along past me an officer, trilling and singing; he did not see me. Instantly a dark form sprang out and attacked him. Cardillac! I determined to prevent this murder. I gave a loud shout, and was on the spot in a couple of paces. Not the officer, but Cardillac, fell gasping to the ground, mortally wounded. The officer let his dagger fall, drew his sword, and stood on the defensive, thinking I was the murderer's accomplice. But he hastened away when he saw that, instead of concerning myself about him, I was examining the fallen man. Cardillac was still alive. I took up the dagger dropped by the officer, stuck it in my belt and, lifting Cardillac on to my shoulders, carried him with difficulty to the house, and up the secret stair to the workshop. The rest you know.

"You perceive, Mademoiselle, that my only crime was that I refrained from giving Madelon's father up to justice, thereby making an end of his crimes. I am quite innocent of murder. No torture will draw from me the secret of Cardillac's iniquities. Not through any action of mine shall that Eternal Power, which has for all this time hidden from Madelon her father's gruesome crimes, break in upon her now, to her destruction; nor shall earthly vengeance drag the corpse of Cardillac out of the soil which covers it, and brand his mouldering bones with infamy. No; the beloved of my soul shall mourn me as an innocent victim. Time will mitigate her sorrow for me, but her grief for her father's terrible crimes nothing would ever assuage."

Olivier ceased, and a torrent of tears fell down his cheeks. He threw himself at Mademoiselle de Scudéri's feet, saying imploringly: "You are convinced that I am innocent; I know you are. Be merciful to me. Tell me how Madelon is faring."

Mademoiselle de Scudéri summoned La Martinière, and in a few minutes Madelon was clinging to Olivier's neck.

"Now that you are here, all is well. I knew that this noble-hearted lady would save you," Madelon cried over and over again; and Olivier forgot his fate, and all that threatened him.

He was free and happy. In the most touching manner they bewailed what each had suffered for the other, and embraced afresh, and wept for joy at being together again.

Had Mademoiselle de Scudéri not been convinced of Olivier's innocence before, she must have been so when she saw those two lovers forgetting, in the rapture of the moment, the world, their sufferings and their indescribable sorrows.

"None but a guiltless heart," she cried, "would be capable of such blissful forgetfulness."

The morning light came breaking into the room, and Desgrais knocked gently at the door, reminding them that it was time to take Olivier away, as it could not be done later without attracting attention. The lovers had to part.

The dim anticipations which Mademoiselle de Scudéri had felt when Olivier first came in had now embodied themselves in reality – in a terrible fashion. The son of her much-loved Anne was, though innocent, implicated in a manner which apparently made it impossible to save him from a shameful death. She admired his heroism, which led him to prefer death, loaded with the imputation of guilt, to the betrayal of a secret which would kill Madelon. In the whole realm of possibility, she could see no mode of saving the unfortunate lad from his gruesome prison and the dreadful trial. Yet it was firmly impressed on her mind that she must not shrink from any sacrifice to prevent this most crying injustice.

She tortured herself with all kinds of plans and projects, which were chiefly of the most impracticable and impossible kind – rejected as soon as formed. Every glimmer of hope grew fainter and fainter, and she well-nigh despaired. But Madelon's pious, absolute, childlike confidence, the inspired manner in which she spoke of her lover, soon to be free and to take her to his heart as his wife, restored Mademoiselle de Scudéri's hopes to some extent.

By way of beginning to do something, she wrote to La Regnie a long letter, in which she said that Olivier Brusson had proved to her in the most credible manner his entire innocence of Cardillac's murder, and that nothing but a heroic resolution to carry to the grave with him a secret, the disclosure of which would bring destruction upon an innocent and virtuous person, withheld him from laying a statement before the Court, which would completely clear him from all guilt and show that he had never belonged to the band at all. With the best eloquence at her command, she said everything she could think of which might be expected to soften La Regnie's hard heart.

He replied to this in a few hours, saying he was very glad that Olivier had so thoroughly justified himself in the eyes of his kind patron and protector; but, as for his heroic resolution to carry to the grave with him a secret relating to the crime with which he was charged, he regretted that the Chambre Ardente could feel no admiration for heroism of that description, but must endeavour to dispel it by powerful means. In three days' time, he had little doubt, he would be in possession of the wondrous secret, which would probably bring many strange matters to light.

Mademoiselle de Scudéri knew well what the terrible La Regnie meant by the 'powerful means,' which were to break down Olivier's heroism. It was but too clear that the unfortunate wretch was threatened with the torture. In her mortal anxiety it at last occurred to her that, were it only to gain time, the advice of a lawyer would be of some service.

Pierre Arnaud d'Andilly was at that time the most celebrated advocate in Paris. His goodness of heart and his highly honourable character were on a par with his professional skill and his comprehensive mind. To him she repaired, and told him the whole tale, as far as it was possible to do so without divulging Olivier's secret. She expected that d'Andilly would warmly espouse the cause of this innocent man, but in this she was woefully disappointed. He listened silently to what she had to say, and then, with a quiet smile, answered in the words of Boileau, "*Le vrai peut quelquefois n'être point vraisemblable.*" He showed her that there were the most grave and marked suspicions against Olivier; that La Regnie's action was by no means severe or premature, but wholly regular; indeed, that to act otherwise would be to neglect his duty as a Judge. He did not believe that he – d'Andilly – could save Brusson from the rack, by the very ablest of pleading. Nobody could do that but Brusson himself, either by making the fullest confession, or by accurately relating the circumstances of Cardillac's murder, which might lead to further discoveries.

"Then I will throw myself at the King's feet and sue for mercy," cried Mademoiselle de Scudéri, her voice choked by weeping.

"For Heaven's sake, do not do that," cried d'Andilly. "Keep that in reserve for the last extremity. If it fails you once, it is lost for ever. The King will not pardon a criminal like Brusson; the people would justly complain of the danger to them. Possibly Brusson may manage to dispel the suspicion against him, by revealing his secret, or in some other way. Then would be the time to resort to the King, who would not ask what was or was not legally proved, but be guided by his own conviction."

Mademoiselle de Scudéri could not but agree with what d'Andilly's great experience dictated. She was sitting in her room, pondering as to what – in the name of the Virgin and all the saints – she should try next to do, when La Martinière came to say that the Count de Miossens, Colonel of one of the King's Body Guard, was most anxious to speak with her.

"Pardon me, Mademoiselle," said the Colonel, bowing with a soldier's courtesy, "for disturbing you, and breaking in upon you at such an hour. Two words will be sufficient excuse for me. I come about Olivier Brusson."

"Olivier Brusson," cried Mademoiselle de Scudéri, eagerly anticipating what she was going to hear; "that most unfortunate of men! What have you to say of him?"

"I knew," said Miossens, laughing again, "that your protégé's name would ensure me a favourable hearing. Everybody is convinced of Brusson's guilt. I know you think otherwise, and it is said your opinion rests on what he himself has told you. With me the case is different. Nobody can be more certain than I that Brusson is innocent of Cardillac's death."

"Speak! Oh, speak!" cried Mademoiselle Scudéri.

"I was the man who stabbed the old goldsmith in the Rue St Honoré, close to your door," said the Colonel.

"You – you!" cried Mademoiselle de Scudéri. "In the name of all the Saints, how?"

"And I vow to you, Mademoiselle, that I am very proud of my achievement. Cardillac, I must tell you, was a most abandoned hypocritical old ruffian, who went about at night robbing and murdering people, and was never suspected of anything of the kind. I don't myself know from whence it came that I felt a suspicion of the old scoundrel, when he seemed so distressed at handing me over some work which I had got him to do for me; when he carefully wormed out of me for whom I designed it, and cross-questioned my valet as to the times when I was in the habit of going to see a certain lady. It struck me long ago, that everyone who was murdered by these unknown hands had the selfsame wound, and I saw quite clearly that the murderer had practiced to the utmost perfection of certainty that particular thrust, which must kill instantaneously – and that he reckoned upon it; so that, if it were to fail, the fight would be fair. This led me to employ a precaution so very simple and obvious that I cannot imagine how somebody else did not think of it long ago. I wore a light breastplate of steel under my dress. Cardillac set upon me from behind. He grasped me with the strength of a giant, but his finely directed thrust glided off the steel breastplate. I then freed myself from his clutch, and planted my dagger in his heart."

"And you have said nothing?" said Mademoiselle de Scudéri. "You have not told the authorities anything about this?"

"Allow me to point out to you, Mademoiselle," said he, "that to have done that would have involved me in a most terrible legal investigation, probably ending in my ruin. La Regnie, who scents out crime everywhere, would not have been at all likely to believe me at once, when I accused the good, respectable, exemplary Cardillac of being an habitual murderer. The sword of Justice would, most probably, have turned its point against me."

"Impossible," said Mademoiselle de Scudéri. "Your rank – your position –"

"Oh!" interrupted Miossens, "Remember the Maréchal de Luxembourg; he took it into his head to have his horoscope cast by Le Sage, and was suspected of poisoning, and put in the Bastille. No; by Saint Dionys! Not one moment of freedom – not the tip of one of my ears, would I trust to that raging La Regnie, who would be delighted to put his knife to all our throats."

"But this brings an innocent man to the scaffold," said Mademoiselle de Scudéri.

"Innocent, Mademoiselle!" cried Miossens. "Do you call Cardillac's accomplice an innocent man? He who assisted him in his crimes, and has deserved death a hundred times? No, in verity; he suffers justly; although I told you the true state of the case in the hope that you might somehow make use of it in the interests of your protégé, without bringing me into the clutches of the Chambre Ardente."

Delighted at having her conviction of Olivier's innocence confirmed in such a decided manner, Mademoiselle de Scudéri had no hesitation in telling the Count the whole affair, since he already knew all about Cardillac's crimes, and in begging him to go with her to d'Andilly, to whom everything should be communicated under the seal of secrecy and who should advise what was next to be done.

When Mademoiselle de Scudéri had told him at full length all the circumstances, D'Andilly inquired again into the very minutest particulars. He asked Count Miossens if he was quite positive as to its having been Cardillac who attacked him, and if he would recognise Olivier as the person who carried away the body.

"Not only," said Miossens, "was the moon shining brightly, so that I recognised the old goldsmith perfectly well, but this morning, at La Regnie's, I saw the dagger with which he was stabbed. It is mine; I know it by the ornamentation of the handle. And as I was within a pace of the young man, I saw his face quite distinctly, all the more because his hat had fallen off. As a matter of course I should know him in a moment."

D'Andilly looked before him meditatively for a few moments, and said: "There is no way of getting Brusson out of the hands of justice by any ordinary means. On Madelon's account, nothing will induce him to admit that Cardillac was a robber and a murderer. And even were he to do so, and succeed in proving the truth of it by pointing out the secret entrance and the collection of stolen jewels, death would be his own lot, as an accomplice. The same consequence would follow if Count Miossens related to the judges the adventure with Cardillac. Delay is what we must aim at. Let Count Miossens go to the Conciergerie, be confronted with Olivier, and recognise him as the person who carried off Cardillac's body; let him then go to La Regnie and say, 'I saw a man stabbed in the Rue St. Honoré, and was close to the body when another man darted up, bent down over it, and finding life still in it, took it on his shoulders and carried it away. I recognised Olivier Brusson as that man.'

"This will lead to a further examination of Brusson, to his being confronted with Count Miossens; the torture will be postponed, and further investigations made. Then will be the time to have recourse to the King. Your brilliant intellect, Mademoiselle, will point out the most fitting way to do this. I think it would be best to tell His Majesty the whole story. Count Miossens' statement will support Olivier's. Perhaps, too, an examination of Cardillac's house would help matters. The King might then follow the bent of his own judgment – of his kind heart, which might pardon where justice could only punish." Count Miossens closely followed D'Andilly's advice, and everything fell out just as he had said it would.

It was now time to repair to the King; and this was the chief difficulty of all, as he had such an intense horror of Brusson – whom he believed to be the man who had for so long kept Paris in a state of terror – that the least allusion to him threw him at once into the most violent anger. Madame de Maintenon, faithful to her system of never mentioning unpleasant subjects to him, declined all intermediation; so that Brusson's fate was entirely in Mademoiselle de Scudéri's hands. After long reflection, she hit upon a scheme which she put into execution at once. She put on a heavy black silk dress, with Cardillac's jewels, and a long black veil, and appeared at Madame de Maintenon's at the time when she knew the King would be there. Her noble figure in this mourning garb excited the reverential respect even of those frivolous persons who pass their days in Court antechambers. They all made way for her and, when she came into the presence, the King himself rose, astonished, and came forward to meet her.

The splendid diamonds of the necklace and bracelets flashed in his eyes, and he cried: "By Heavens! Cardillac's work!" Then, turning to Madame de Maintenon, he said, with a pleasant smile, "See, Madame la Marquise, how our fair lady mourns for her affianced husband."

"Ah, Sire!" said Mademoiselle de Scudéri, as if keeping up the jest, "it would ill become a mourning bride to wear such bravery. No; I have done with the goldsmith; nor would I remember him, but that the gruesome spectacle of his corpse carried off before my eyes keeps coming back to my memory."

"What!" said the King, "did you actually see him, poor fellow?"

She then told him in few words (not introducing Brusson into the business at all) how chance had brought her to Cardillac's door just when the murder had been discovered. She described Madelon's wild terror and sorrow; the impression made upon her by the beautiful girl; how she had taken her out of Desgrais's hands and borne her away amid the applause of the crowd. The scenes with La Regnie, with Desgrais, with Olivier Brusson himself, now followed, the interest constantly increasing. The King, carried away by the vividness with which Mademoiselle de Scudéri told the tale, did not notice that the Brusson case, which he so abominated, was in question, listened breathlessly, occasionally expressing his interest by an ejaculation. And ere he was well aware, still amazed by the marvels which he was hearing, not yet able to arrange them all in his mind, behold! Mademoiselle de Scudéri was at his feet, imploring mercy for Olivier Brusson.

"What are you doing?" broke out the King, seizing both her hands and making her sit down. "This is a strange way of taking us by storm. It is a most terrible story! Who is to answer for the truth of Brusson's extraordinary tale?"

"Miossens' deposition proves it," she cried; "the searching of Cardillac's house; my own firm conviction, and, ah! Madelon's pure heart, which recognises equal purity in poor Brusson."

The King, about to say something, was interrupted by a noise in the direction of the door. Louvois, who was at work in the next room, put his head in with an anxious expression. The King rose, and followed him out. Both Madame de Maintenon and Mademoiselle de Scudéri thought this interruption of evil augury; for, though once surprised into interest, the King might take care not to fall into the snare a second time. But he came back in a few minuses, walked quickly up and down the room two or three times; and then, pausing with his hands behind his back before Mademoiselle de Scudéri, he said, in a half-whisper, without looking at her: "I should like to see this Madelon of yours."

On this Mademoiselle de Scudéri said: "Oh! Gracious Sire! What a marvellous honour you vouchsafe to the poor unfortunate child. She will be at your feet in an instant."

She tripped to the door as quickly as her heavy dress allowed, and called to those in the anteroom that the King wished to see Madelon Cardillac. She came back weeping and sobbing with delight and emotion. Having expected this, she had brought Madelon with her, leaving her to wait with the Marquise's maid, with a short petition in her hand drawn up by D'Andilly. In a few moments she had prostrated herself, speechless, at the King's feet. Awe, confusion, shyness, love and sorrow sent the blood coursing faster and faster through her veins; her cheeks glowed, her eyes sparkled with the bright tear-drops, which now and again fell from her silken lashes down upon her beautiful lily-white breast. The King was moved by the wonderful beauty of the girl. He raised her gently, and stooped down as if about to kiss her hand, which he had taken in his; but he let the hand go, and gazed at her with tears in his eyes, evincing deep emotion.

Madame de Maintenon whispered to Mademoiselle de Scudéri, "Is she not exactly like La Vallière, the little thing? The King is indulging in the sweetest memories: you have gained the day."

Though she spoke softly, the King seemed to hear.

A blush came to his cheek; he scanned Madame de Maintenon with a glance, and then said, gently and kindly: "I am quite sure that you, my dear child, think your lover is innocent; but we must hear what the Chambre Ardente has to say."

A gentle wave of his hand dismissed Madelon, bathed in tears. Mademoiselle de Scudéri saw, to her alarm, that the resemblance to La Vallière, advantageous as it had seemed to be at first, had nevertheless changed the King's intention as soon as Madame de Maintenon had spoken of it. Perhaps he felt himself somewhat ungently reminded that he was going to sacrifice strict justice to beauty; or he may have been like a dreamer who, when loudly addressed by his name, finds that the beautiful, magic visions by which he thought he was surrounded vanish away. Perhaps he no longer saw his La Vallière before him, but thought only of Soeur Louise de la Miséricorde – La Vallière's cloister name among the Carmelite nuns – paining him with her piety and repentance. There was nothing for it now but to wait patiently for the King's decision.

Meanwhile Count Miossens' statement before the Chambre Ardente had become known; and, as often happens, popular opinion soon flew from one extreme to the other, so that the person whom it had stigmatized as the most atrocious of murderers, and would fain have torn in pieces before he reached the scaffold, was now bewailed as the innocent victim of a barbarous sacrifice. His old neighbours now only remembered his admirable character and behaviour, his love for Madelon, and the faithfulness and devotion of body and soul with which he had served his master. Crowds of people, in threatening temper, often collected before La Regnie's Palais, crying, "Give us out Olivier Brusson! – He is innocent!", even throwing stones at the windows, so that La Regnie had to seek the protection of the Marechaussée.

Many days elapsed without Mademoiselle de Scudéri's hearing anything on the subject of Olivier Brusson. In her anxiety she went to Madame de Maintenon, who said the King was keeping silence on the subject, and it was not advisable to remind him of it. When she then, with a peculiar smile, asked after the 'little La Vallière,' Mademoiselle de Scudéri saw that this proud lady felt, in the depths of her heart, some slight annoyance at a matter which had the power of drawing the fickle King into a province whose charm was beyond her own sphere. Consequently nothing was to be hoped from Madame de Maintenon.

At length Mademoiselle de Scudéri managed to find out, with D'Andilly's help, that the King had had a long interview with Count Miossens; further, that Bontems, the King's confidential groom of the chamber and secret agent, had been to the Conciergerie, and spoken with Brusson; that, finally, the said Bontems, with several other persons, had paid a long visit to Cardillac's house. Claude Patru, who lived in the lower story, said he had heard banging noises above his head in the night, and that he had recognised Olivier's voice amongst others. So far it was certain that the King was, himself, causing the matter to be investigated; but what was puzzling was the long delay in coming to a decision. La Regnie was most probably trying all in his power to prevent his prey from slipping through his fingers; and this nipped all hope in the bud.

Nearly a month had elapsed, when Madame de Maintenon sent to tell Mademoiselle de Scudéri that the King wished to see her that evening in her salon. Her heart beat fast. She knew that Olivier's fate would be decided that night. She told Madelon so, and the latter prayed to the Virgin and all the Saints that Mademoiselle de Scudéri might succeed in convincing the King of her lover's innocence.

And yet it appeared as if he had forgotten the whole affair, for he passed the time in chatting pleasantly with Madame de Maintenon and Mademoiselle de Scudéri, without a single word of poor Olivier Brusson.

At length Bontems appeared, approached the King, and spoke a few words so softly that the ladies could not hear them.

Mademoiselle de Scudéri trembled; but the King rose, went up to her, and said, with beaming eyes: "I congratulate you, Mademoiselle. Your protégé, Olivier Brusson, is free."

Mademoiselle de Scudéri, with tears streaming down her cheeks, unable to utter a word, would have cast herself at the King's feet; but he prevented her, saying: "Come, Come! Mademoiselle, you ought to be my Attorney-General and plead my causes, for nobody on earth can resist your eloquence and powers of persuasion. He who is shielded by virtue," he added more gravely, "may snap his fingers at every accusation, by the Chambre Ardente, or any other tribunal on earth."

Mademoiselle de Scudéri, now finding words, poured forth a most glowing tribute of gratitude. But the King interrupted her, saying there were warmer thanks awaiting her at home than any he could expect from her, as at that moment doubtless Olivier was embracing his Madelon. "Bontems," added His Majesty, "will hand you a thousand Louis, which you will give the little one from me as a wedding portion. Let her marry her Brusson, who does not deserve such a treasure, and then they must both leave Paris. That is my will."

La Martinière came to meet her mistress with eager steps, followed by Baptiste, their faces beaming with joy, and both crying out: "He is here! He is free! Oh, the dear young couple!"

The happy pair fell at Mademoiselle de Scudéri's feet, and Madelon cried: "Ah! I knew that you, and you only, would save my husband."

"You have been my mother," cried Olivier, "my belief in you never wavered." They kissed her hands, and shed many tears; and then they embraced again, and vowed that the heavenly bliss of that moment was worth all the nameless sufferings of the days that were past.

In a few days the priest pronounced his blessing upon them. Even had it not been the King's command that they were to leave Paris, Brusson could not have remained there, where everything reminded him of the dreadful epoch of Cardillac's atrocities, and where any accident might have disclosed the evil secret, already known to several persons, and destroyed the peace of his life for ever. Immediately after the wedding he started with his young wife for Geneva, sped on his way by Mademoiselle de Scudéri's blessings. Handsomely provided with Madelon's portion, his own skill at his calling, and every civic virtue, he there led a happy life, without a care. The hopes, whose frustration had sent the father to his grave, were fulfilled in the son.

A year after Brusson left Paris, a public proclamation, signed by Harloy de Chauvalon, Archbishop of Paris, and by Pierre Arnaud D'Andilly, Advocate of the Parliament, appeared, stating that a repentant sinner had, under seal of confession, made over to the Church a valuable stolen treasure of gold and jewels. All those who, up to about the end of the year 1680, had been robbed of property of this description, particularly if by murderous attack in the street, were directed to apply to D'Andilly, when they would receive it back, provided that anything in the said collection agreed with the description to be by them given, and provided that there was no doubt of the genuineness of the application. Many whose names occurred in Cardillac's list as having been merely stunned, not murdered, came from time to time to D'Andilly to reclaim their property, and received it back, to their no small surprise. The remainder became the property of the Church of St. Eustache.

How to Build a Mass-Murderer

Liam Hogan

FAME? On its own? It's useless. Trust me on this one. Now, fortune, on its own, is nothing to be sniffed at. In fact, you could say it is to be positively encouraged. You wouldn't catch me amongst the morons who fail to tick the no publicity box on their winning lottery tickets.

* * *

Little Jenny Braithwaite sat on the park swing and watched the gas explosion tear apart her family home, killing her distant parents and squabbling siblings. What the concerned policewoman, the tearful social worker, and the pitying family that adopted her didn't twig was that an hour earlier this precocious 12 year old had gotten fed up of waiting alone in the big house, and had snuffed out the pilot light, duck-taped the switch on the oven door, and selected gas mark 5, all before going out to play. Only after she repeated the trick on her new family did the authorities become suspicious.

Death count – 7.

* * *

I'm the fourth of five children. My parents used childbirth as an alternative to marriage counselling, and these sporadic bouts of fertile love making were the only real counterpoint to 22 years of mutual contempt. Lost in the hubbub of a deeply chaotic house I didn't even have the novelty of being the youngest child very long. My parents would introduce their brood with the most recent first, and then from the oldest down. Whether they adopted this order because they were already struggling, or whether they were struggling because of the order they adopted is a moot point, all I can say for certain is that I used to dread the long pause before they managed to recollect my name.

* * *

Tom Foster got straight A's at A-level, so everyone thought he was happy. He went to Edinburgh to study biochemistry, where he got excellent grades in his coursework and everyone thought he was happy. He probably would have got a first class degree, and everyone might have thought he was happy, had he not laced the Burn's Night neeps and tatties with listeria.

Actually it's not strictly true that everyone thought he was happy. His parents didn't. His plaintive emails, and his tearful phone calls, told them that he was far from happy. Eventually his father told him to stop as he was upsetting his mother. That was the same day he memorised the combination on the Level 2 pathogens locker, and a mere two weeks before that fateful and fatal Burns Night.

Death count – 12.

* * *

I was a geeky kid. Awkward and slight, I retreated into books for safety. I learnt the meanings of words I couldn't pronounce, and a skewed view of the world where exciting things were around every corner.

I went to University relieved to be leaving a school where I had had no friends, expecting the best years of my life. I left university with a first class degree, a hefty loan, and a sense of relief that I was leaving a place where I had had no friends. Intelligence without confidence is much like fame without fortune. So no, they were not the best years of my life; although, and this would surprise my younger self, they weren't the worst either.

* * *

Alistair Jenkins enjoyed killing. He considered it a leisure activity, and as such, he reserved his murders for his summer holidays, when he had more time to dedicate to it. He visited a different destination every year, and chose his victims based on whoever behaved in the most appalling tourist fashion. His piece de resistance was bumping off a fat American tourist at the Leaning Tower of Pisa. Galileo might be gratified to know that the tourist and his camera would have hit the ground at the same instant, had the fat American's fat wife intercepted the falling camera with her head. Encouraged by this success Alistair began a grand tour of Europe, but on the way to Venice he came unstuck trying to push a sullen teenager under the Orient Express. Unfortunately, he didn't like to boast about his art, but based on his holiday snaps the authorities managed to link him to unexplained deaths in eight countries, including two more double murders.

Death count – 12+.

* * *

We all have murderous thoughts. Passing visions of violence meted out on some annoying person who crosses our path. While you might linger on thoughts of killing your boss, or a rival, or even your partner, these are individual targets too close to home to actually do anything about. And even if you did, the chain would probably end there. For a serial mass murderer, your victims should be of casual acquaintance. How much effort is it to move from a sudden hatred of that guy who pushes past you on the underground to extending a foot that trips him and sends him into the path of the approaching tube train? And having got away with it, would you not feel challenged to rise to the next occasion, and the next? There are always a ready supply of people short on manners, or with goals and aspirations incomprehensible and incompatible from your own. As an intelligent man on a professional career path, who also happened to be terminally shy and difficult to get close to, what always annoyed me was the realisation that we – professional, intelligent people – were being out-bred by morons.

* * *

Malcolm Bradbury. Ahh, I see I have your attention. Needs little introduction, does he? Unlike Alistair, whose blood lust was regularly sated, and Tom and Jenny who came to killing early, Malcolm held in his anger and his frustration over many years. He followed the same path, an intelligent loner with distant parents, an unhappy youth, and shyness that prevented him connecting to friends, colleagues, people of the opposite sex. Burying himself in a job which was ultimately unsatisfying – but he did it well, so everyone thought he was happy – he worked himself up to a position of responsibility within the events industry, culminating in a lucrative contract for coordinating the fireworks display for the coronation. We'll never know what exactly snapped, what drove him over the edge, but the opportunity was there; a quick reprogramming of the firing sequence, a couple of changes of rocket angles, and the liberal spilling of gasoline around the launch site, and you have the atrocity for which he is rightly famous.

Death count – 113 including the newly crowned HRH King Charles, thus overtaking Lady Jane Grey as the shortest reigning English monarch.

* * *

They came for me a couple of months later. They explained that there was a crime they were investigating, and though they didn't think I was involved, I could be easily eliminated from their investigations – all it took was a swab from the inside of my cheek, and no sir, we can't explain what it was about, though if necessary they could obtain a warrant – and thanks for your cooperation. Two weeks later I was famous. It turns out that there was a link between Malcolm, Alistair, Tom and Jenny. And me. We were, in fact, related. They were, in fact, my children.

When I was 28, a lonely virgin despairing of ever getting my end away, watching as idiot fathers and idiot mothers had conveyor-belt babies who all grew up into idiot kids, I visited a small specialist clinic in a basement on Harley Street, and having filled in a few forms – mostly honestly – I signed up to be a sperm donor. I'd come to the conclusion that even if I ever found someone, I probably wouldn't want kids. But I was damned if I was going to miss the chance to pass on my good health and intelligence, as they seemed like qualities increasingly in short supply.

Well, I passed on more than that. I passed on a rare set of genes. A heady mixture of low level autism, high testosterone, and a couple of quirky brain chemistry anomalies that frankly I don't understand. And as the news broke that the Coronation bomber was linked to 3 other mass murderers, debate raged through England on the issue of nature versus nurture, and whether mass murderers were born or built, with me at its core. After the second fire bomb attempt, they moved me to a safe house with 24-hour police supervision. It felt like an expensive prison. The politicians jumped at the idea that the scientists had successfully identified the genes that make up a mass murderer, and in record time passed an amendment to the Prevention of Terrorism Act of 2017 – clause 127.

Then they came for me again. Not exactly difficult since I hadn't been out of their sight for over 3 weeks. A young man in a red tie offered me a stark choice. Immediate and unlimited detention without charge as a potential (genetic) terrorist, or a cocktail of drugs designed to render me infertile.

I pointed out that these two options didn't exactly cover the same bases – one was to prevent me going postal, and the other to prevent me having children who might go postal. I pointed out that I was pushing 60, and hadn't had sex for 12 years, and would gratefully guarantee to wear a condom if I was ever given the chance. I pointed out that I had never committed any crime, well, not of any significance, and certainly never a violent one.

The man in the red tie pointed out that since Malcolm had blown himself up leaving barely enough for genetic analysis the public was still very much looking for some sort of positive action in the wake of the Royal bombing. He pointed out that he had four strong men ready to hold me down while I was force-fed the drugs. And then he pointed out that yes, the options didn't cover both possibilities, but if I liked I could choose both options, but I'd better make some sort of choice fast before he made it for me.

I chose wrong. I wasn't to know, of course, but the anaphylactic shock almost killed me. I was in a coma for six months, and when I awoke I found that a lot had changed. A couple of pharmaceutical companies had gone bust, despite claims that my side effects were one in a million, and besides, they had a *much* safer drug that had just been granted a licence. The civil liberties groups had finally forced the government to suspend clause 127 pending further investigation. I was, fortunately, no longer headline news, and was free to pick up any pieces of my life that I might have left. And – oh yes. Whether fertile or not, I was never having sex again. The drugs had unmanned me. I took Viagra until the world went blue, but to no avail.

The other thing that happened was that biometric ID cards finally went live. A rushed job in the immediate panic after the bombing, they had hedged their bets by including facial, fingerprinting and most controversially, genetic information. I awoke to find that even I had one, provided free of charge, by His Majesty's (King William's) Government. So if they ever did decide to enforce clause 127, everything they could possibly want was already in place. However the politicians had been backtracking in recent months, and were heading towards a softer, more caring image. Unless, I suppose, another atrocity took place.

And so, I'm about to step out of my door carrying my little bag of tricks. I can't tell you what I'm planning to do, it would spoil the surprise. But I can tell you that England will never be the same again. Oh, and when they come to your door with a warrant in one hand and a cocktail of drugs in the other, well, that's my parting gift to you. No, please don't thank me. You *deserve* it.

Pigeons from Hell

Robert E. Howard

I: The Whistler in the Dark

GRISWELL AWOKE SUDDENLY, every nerve tingling with a premonition of imminent peril. He stared about wildly, unable at first to remember where he was, or what he was doing there. Moonlight filtered in through the dusty windows, and the great empty room with its lofty ceiling and gaping black fireplace was spectral and unfamiliar. Then as he emerged from the clinging cobwebs of his recent sleep, he remembered where he was and how he came to be there. He twisted his head and stared at his companion, sleeping on the floor near him. John Branner was but a vaguely bulking shape in the darkness that the moon scarcely grayed.

Griswell tried to remember what had awakened him. There was no sound in the house, no sound outside except the mournful hoot of an owl, far away in the piny woods. Now he had captured the illusive memory. It was a dream, a nightmare so filled with dim terror that it had frightened him awake. Recollection flooded back, vividly etching the abominable vision.

Or was it a dream? Certainly it must have been, but it had blended so curiously with recent actual events that it was difficult to know where reality left off and fantasy began.

Dreaming, he had seemed to relive his past few waking hours, in accurate detail. The dream had begun, abruptly, as he and John Branner came in sight of the house where they now lay. They had come rattling and bouncing over the stumpy, uneven old road that led through the pinelands, he and John Branner, wandering far afield from their New England home, in search of vacation pleasure. They had sighted the old house with its balustraded galleries rising amidst a wilderness of weeds and bushes, just as the sun was setting behind it. It dominated their fancy, rearing black and stark and gaunt against the low lurid rampart of sunset, barred by the black pines.

They were tired, sick of bumping and pounding all day over woodland roads. The old deserted house stimulated their imagination with its suggestion of antebellum splendor and ultimate decay. They left the automobile beside the rutty road, and as they went up the winding walk of crumbling bricks, almost lost in the tangle of rank growth, pigeons rose from the balustrades in a fluttering, feathery crowd and swept away with a low thunder of beating wings.

The oaken door sagged on broken hinges. Dust lay thick on the floor of the wide, dim hallway, on the broad steps of the stair that mounted up from the hall. They turned into a door opposite the landing, and entered a large room, empty, dusty, with cobwebs shining thickly in the corners. Dust lay thick over the ashes in the great fireplace.

They discussed gathering wood and building a fire, but decided against it. As the sun sank, darkness came quickly, the thick, black, absolute darkness of the pinelands. They knew that rattlesnakes and copperheads haunted Southern forests, and they did not care to go groping for firewood in the dark. They ate frugally from tins, then rolled in their blankets fully clad before the empty fireplace, and went instantly to sleep.

This, in part, was what Griswell had dreamed. He saw again the gaunt house looming stark against the crimson sunset; saw the flight of the pigeons as he and Branner came up the shattered walk. He saw the dim room in which they presently lay, and he saw the two forms that were himself and his companion, lying wrapped in their blankets on the dusty floor. Then from that point his dream altered subtly, passed out of the realm of the commonplace and became tinged with fear. He was looking into a vague, shadowy chamber, lit by the gray light of the moon which streamed in from some obscure source. For there was no window in that room. But in the gray light he saw three silent shapes that hung suspended in a row, and their stillness and their outlines woke chill horror in his soul. There was no sound, no word, but he sensed a Presence of fear and lunacy crouching in a dark corner... Abruptly he was back in the dusty, high-ceilinged room, before the great fireplace.

He was lying in his blankets, staring tensely through the dim door and across the shadowy hall, to where a beam of moonlight fell across the balustraded stair, some seven steps up from the landing. And there was something on the stair, a bent, misshapen, shadowy thing that never moved fully into the beam of light. But a dim yellow blur that might have been a face was turned toward him, as if something crouched on the stair, regarding him and his companion. Fright crept chilly through his veins, and it was then that he awoke – if indeed he had been asleep.

He blinked his eyes. The beam of moonlight fell across the stair just as he had dreamed it did; but no figure lurked there. Yet his flesh still crawled from the fear the dream or vision had roused in him; his legs felt as if they had been plunged in ice-water. He made an involuntary movement to awaken his companion, when a sudden sound paralyzed him.

It was the sound of whistling on the floor above. Eery and sweet it rose, not carrying any tune, but piping shrill and melodious. Such a sound in a supposedly deserted house was alarming enough; but it was more than the fear of a physical invader that held Griswell frozen. He could not himself have defined the horror that gripped him. But Branner's blankets rustled, and Griswell saw he was sitting upright. His figure bulked dimly in the soft darkness, the head turned toward the stair as if the man were listening intently. More sweetly and more subtly evil rose that weird whistling.

"John!" whispered Griswell from dry lips. He had meant to shout – to tell Branner that there was somebody upstairs, somebody who could mean them no good; that they must leave the house at once. But his voice died dryly in his throat.

Branner had risen. His boots clumped on the floor as he moved toward the door. He stalked leisurely into the hall and made for the lower landing, merging with the shadows that clustered black about the stair.

Griswell lay incapable of movement, his mind a whirl of bewilderment. Who was that whistling upstairs? Why was Branner going up those stairs? Griswell saw him pass the spot where the moonlight rested, saw his head tilted back as if he were looking at something Griswell could not see, above and beyond the stair. But his face was like that of a sleepwalker. He moved across the bar of moonlight and vanished from Griswell's view, even as the latter tried to shout to him to come back. A ghastly whisper was the only result of his effort.

The whistling sank to a lower note, died out. Griswell heard the stairs creaking under Branner's measured tread. Now he had reached the hallway above, for Griswell heard the clump of his feet moving along it. Suddenly the footfalls halted, and the whole night seemed to hold its breath. Then an awful scream split the stillness, and Griswell started up, echoing the cry.

The strange paralysis that had held him was broken. He took a step toward the door, then checked himself. The footfalls were resumed. Branner was coming back. He was not running. The tread was even more deliberate and measured than before. Now the stairs began to creak again. A groping hand, moving along the balustrade, came into the bar of moonlight; then another, and a ghastly thrill went through Griswell as he saw that the other hand gripped a hatchet – a hatchet which dripped blackly. Was that Branner who was coming down that stair?

Yes! The figure had moved into the bar of moonlight now, and Griswell recognized it. Then he saw Branner's face, and a shriek burst from Griswell's lips. Branner's face was bloodless, corpse-like; gouts of blood dripped darkly down it; his eyes were glassy and set, and blood oozed from the great gash which cleft the crown of his head!

Griswell never remembered exactly how he got out of that accursed house. Afterward he retained a mad, confused impression of smashing his way through a dusty cobwebbed window, of stumbling blindly across the weed-choked lawn, gibbering his frantic horror. He saw the black wall of the pines, and the moon floating in a blood-red mist in which there was neither sanity nor reason.

Some shred of sanity returned to him as he saw the automobile beside the road. In a world gone suddenly mad, that was an object reflecting prosaic reality; but even as he reached for the door, a dry chilling whir sounded in his ears, and he recoiled from the swaying undulating shape that arched up from its scaly coils on the driver's seat and hissed sibilantly at him, darting a forked tongue in the moonlight.

With a sob of horror he turned and fled down the road, as a man runs in a nightmare. He ran without purpose or reason. His numbed brain was incapable of conscious thought. He merely obeyed the blind primitive urge to run – run – run until he fell exhausted.

The black walls of the pines flowed endlessly past him; so he was seized with the illusion that he was getting nowhere. But presently a sound penetrated the fog of his terror – the steady, inexorable patter of feet behind him. Turning his head, he saw something loping after him – wolf or dog, he could not tell which, but its eyes glowed like balls of green fire. With a gasp he increased his speed, reeled around a bend in the road, and heard a horse snort; saw it rear and heard its rider curse; saw the gleam of blue steel in the man's lifted hand.

He staggered and fell, catching at the rider's stirrup.

"For God's sake, help me!" he panted. "The thing! It killed Branner – it's coming after me! Look!"

Twin balls of fire gleamed in the fringe of bushes at the turn of the road. The rider swore again, and on the heels of his profanity came the smashing report of his six-shooter – again and yet again. The fire-sparks vanished, and the rider, jerking his stirrup free from Griswell's grasp, spurred his horse at the bend. Griswell staggered up, shaking in every limb. The rider was out of sight only a moment; then he came galloping back.

"Took to the brush. Timber wolf, I reckon, though I never heard of one chasin' a man before. Do you know what it was?"

Griswell could only shake his head weakly.

The rider, etched in the moonlight, looked down at him, smoking pistol still lifted in his right hand. He was a compactly-built man of medium height, and his broad-brimmed planter's hat and his boots marked him as a native of the country as definitely as Griswell's garb stamped him as a stranger.

"What's all this about, anyway?"

"I don't know," Griswell answered helplessly. "My name's Griswell. John Branner – my friend who was traveling with me – we stopped at a deserted house back down the road to spend the night. Something –" at the memory he was choked by a rush of horror. "My God!" he screamed. "I must be mad! Something came and looked over the balustrade of the stair – something with a yellow face! I thought I dreamed it, but it must have been real. Then somebody began whistling upstairs, and Branner rose and went up the stairs walking like a man in his sleep, or hypnotized. I heard him scream – or someone screamed; then he came down the stair again with a bloody hatchet in his hand – and my God, sir, he was dead! His head had been split open. I saw brains and clotted blood oozing down his face, and his face was that of a dead man. But he came down the stairs! As God is my witness, John Branner was murdered in that dark upper hallway, and then his dead body came stalking down the stairs with a hatchet in its hand – to kill me!"

The rider made no reply; he sat his horse like a statue, outlined against the stars, and Griswell could not read his expression, his face shadowed by his hat-brim.

"You think I'm mad," he said hopelessly. "Perhaps I am."

"I don't know what to think," answered the rider. "If it was any house but the old Blassenville Manor – well, we'll see. My name's Buckner. I'm sheriff of this county. Took a prisoner over to the county-seat in the next county and was ridin' back late."

He swung off his horse and stood beside Griswell, shorter than the lanky New Englander, but much harder knit. There was a natural manner of decision and certainty about him, and it was easy to believe that he would be a dangerous man in any sort of a fight.

"Are you afraid to go back to the house?" he asked, and Griswell shuddered, but shook his head, the dogged tenacity of Puritan ancestors asserting itself.

"The thought of facing that horror again turns me sick.

But poor Branner –" he choked again. "We must find his body. My God!" he cried, unmanned by the abysmal horror of the thing; "What will we find? If a dead man walks, what –"

"We'll see." The sheriff caught the reins in the crook of his left elbow and began filling the empty chambers of his big blue pistol as they walked along.

As they made the turn Griswell's blood was ice at the thought of what they might see lumbering up the road with a bloody, grinning death-mask, but they saw only the house looming spectrally among the pines, down the road. A strong shudder shook Griswell.

"God, how evil that house looks, against those black pines! It looked sinister from the very first – when we went up the broken walk and saw those pigeons fly up from the porch –"

"Pigeons?" Buckner cast him a quick glance. "You saw the pigeons?"

"Why, yes! Scores of them perching on the porch railing."

They strode on for a moment in silence, before Buckner said abruptly: "I've lived in this country all my life. I've passed the old Blassenville place a thousand times, I reckon, at all hours of the day and night. But I never saw a pigeon anywhere around it, or anywhere else in these woods."

"There were scores of them," repeated Griswell, bewildered.

"I've seen men who swore they'd seen a flock of pigeons perched along the balusters just at sundown," said Buckner slowly. "Negroes, all of them except one man. A tramp. He was buildin' a fire in the yard, aimin' to camp there that night. I passed along there about dark, and he told me about the pigeons. I came back by there the next mornin'. The ashes of his fire were there, and his tin cup, and skillet where he'd fried pork, and his blankets looked like they'd been slept in. Nobody ever saw him again. That was twelve years ago. The blacks say they can see the pigeons, but no black would pass along this road between sundown and sunup. They say the pigeons are the souls of the Blassenvilles, let out of hell at sunset. The Negroes say the red glare in the west is the light from hell, because then the gates of hell are open, and the Blassenvilles fly out."

"Who were the Blassenvilles?" asked Griswell, shivering.

"They owned all this land here. French-English family. Came here from the West Indies before the Louisiana Purchase. The Civil War ruined them, like it did so many. Some were killed in the War; most of the others died out. Nobody's lived in the Manor since 1890 when Miss. Elizabeth Blassenville, the last of the line, fled from the old house one night like it was a plague spot, and never came back to it – this your auto?"

They halted beside the car, and Griswell stared morbidly at the grim house. Its dusty panes were empty and blank; but they did not seem blind to him. It seemed to him that ghastly eyes were fixed hungrily on him through those darkened panes. Buckner repeated his question.

"Yes. Be careful. There's a snake on the seat – or there was."

"Not there now," grunted Buckner, tying his horse and pulling an electric torch out of the saddle-bag. "Well, let's have a look."

He strode up the broken brick walk as matter-of-factly as if he were paying a social call on friends. Griswell followed close at his heels, his heart pounding suffocatingly. A scent of decay and moldering vegetation blew on the faint wind, and Griswell grew faint with nausea, that rose from a frantic abhorrence of these black woods, these ancient plantation houses that hid forgotten secrets of slavery and bloody pride and mysterious intrigues. He had thought of the South as a sunny, lazy land washed by soft breezes laden with spice and warm blossoms, where life ran tranquilly to the rhythm of black folk singing in sunbathed cottonfields. But now he had discovered another, unsuspected side – a dark, brooding, fear-haunted side, and the discovery repelled him.

The oaken door sagged as it had before. The blackness of the interior was intensified by the beam of Buckner's light playing on the sill. That beam sliced through the darkness of the hallway and roved up the stair, and Griswell held his breath, clenching his fists. But no shape of lunacy leered down at them. Buckner went in, walking light as a cat, torch in one hand, gun in the other.

As he swung his light into the room across from the stairway, Griswell cried out – and cried out again, almost fainting with the intolerable sickness at what he saw. A trail of blood drops led across the floor, crossing the blankets Branner had occupied, which lay between the door and those in which Griswell had lain. And Griswell's blankets had a terrible occupant. John Branner lay there, face down, his cleft head revealed in merciless clarity in the steady light. His outstretched hand still gripped the haft of a hatchet, and the blade was imbedded deep in the blanket and the floor beneath, just where Griswell's head had lain when he slept there.

A momentary rush of blackness engulfed Griswell. He was not aware that he staggered, or that Buckner caught him. When he could see and hear again, he was violently sick and hung his head against the mantel, retching miserably.

Buckner turned the light full on him, making him blink. Buckner's voice came from behind the blinding radiance, the man himself unseen.

"Griswell, you've told me a yarn that's hard to believe. I saw something chasin' you, but it might have been a timber wolf, or a mad dog.

"If you're holdin' back anything, you better spill it. What you told me won't hold up in any court. You're bound to be accused of killin' your partner. I'll have to arrest you. If you'll give me the straight goods now, it'll make it easier. Now, didn't you kill this fellow, Branner?

"Wasn't it something like this: you quarreled, he grabbed a hatchet and swung at you, but you dodged and then let him have it?"

Griswell sank down and hid his face in his hands, his head swimming.

"Great God, man, I didn't murder John! Why, we've been friends ever since we were children in school together. I've told you the truth. I don't blame you for not believing me. But God help me, it is the truth!"

The light swung back to the gory head again, and Griswell closed his eyes.

He heard Buckner grunt.

"I believe this hatchet in his hand is the one he was killed with. Blood and brains plastered on the blade, and hairs stickin' to it – hairs exactly the same color as his. This makes it tough for you, Griswell."

"How so?" the New Englander asked dully.

"Knocks any plea of self-defense in the head. Branner couldn't have swung at you with this hatchet after you split his skull with it. You must have pulled the ax out of his head, stuck it into the floor and clamped his fingers on it to make it look like he'd attacked you. And it would have been damned clever – if you'd used another hatchet."

"But I didn't kill him," groaned Griswell. "I have no intention of pleading self-defense."

"That's what puzzles me," Buckner admitted frankly, straightening. "What murderer would rig up such a crazy story as you've told me, to prove his innocence? Average killer would have told a logical yarn, at least. Hmmm! Blood drops leadin' from the door. The body was dragged – no, couldn't have been dragged. The floor isn't smeared. You must have carried it here, after killin' him in some other place. But in that case, why isn't there any blood on your clothes? Of course you could have changed clothes and washed your hands. But the fellow hasn't been dead long."

"He walked downstairs and across the room," said Griswell hopelessly. "He came to kill me. I knew he was coming to kill me when I saw him lurching down the stair.

He struck where I would have been, if I hadn't awakened. That window – I burst out at it. You see it's broken."

"I see. But if he walked then, why isn't he walkin' now?"

"I don't know! I'm too sick to think straight. I've been fearing that he'd rise up from the floor where he lies and come at me again. When I heard that wolf running up the road after me, I thought it was John chasing me – John, running through the night with his bloody ax and his bloody head, and his death-grin!"

His teeth chattered as he lived that horror over again.

Buckner let his light play across the floor.

"The blood drops lead into the hall. Come on. We'll follow them."

Griswell cringed. "They lead upstairs."

Buckner's eyes were fixed hard on him.

"Are you afraid to go upstairs, with me?"

Griswell's face was gray.

"Yes. But I'm going, with you or without you. The thing that killed poor John may still be hiding up there."

"Stay behind me," ordered Buckner. "If anything jumps us, I'll take care of it. But for your own sake, I warn you that I shoot quicker than a cat jumps, and I don't often miss. If you've got any ideas of layin' me out from behind, forget them."

"Don't be a fool!" Resentment got the better of his apprehension, and this outburst seemed to reassure Buckner more than any of his protestations of innocence.

"I want to be fair," he said quietly. "I haven't indicted and condemned you in my mind already. If only half of what you're tellin' me is the truth, you've been through a hell of an experience, and I don't want to be too hard on you. But you can see how hard it is for me to believe all you've told me."

Griswell wearily motioned for him to lead the way, unspeaking. They went out into the hall, paused at the landing. A thin string of crimson drops, distinct in the thick dust, led up the steps.

"Man's tracks in the dust," grunted Buckner. "Go slow.

I've got to be sure of what I see, because we're obliteratin' them as we go up. Hmmm! One set goin' up, one comin' down. Same man. Not your tracks. Branner was a bigger man than you are. Blood drops all the way – blood on the bannisters like a man had laid his bloody hand there – a smear of stuff that looks – brains. Now what –"

"He walked down the stair, a dead man," shuddered Griswell. "Groping with one hand – the other gripping the hatchet that killed him."

"Or was carried," muttered the sheriff. "But if somebody carried him – where are the tracks?"

They came out into the upper hallway, a vast, empty space of dust and shadows where time-crusted windows repelled the moonlight and the ring of Buckner's torch seemed inadequate. Griswell trembled like a leaf. Here, in darkness and horror, John Branner had died.

"Somebody whistled up here," he muttered. "John came, as if he were being called."

Buckner's eyes were blazing strangely in the light.

"The footprints lead down the hall," he muttered. "Same as on the stair – one set going, one coming. Same prints – Judas!"

Behind him Griswell stifled a cry, for he had seen what prompted Buckner's exclamation. A few feet from the head of the stair Branner's footprints stopped abruptly, then returned, treading almost in the other tracks. And where the trail halted there was a great splash of blood on the dusty floor – and other tracks met it – tracks of bare feet, narrow but with splayed toes. They too receded in a second line from the spot.

Buckner bent over them, swearing.

"The tracks meet! And where they meet there's blood and brains on the floor! Branner must have been killed on that spot – with a blow from a hatchet. Bare feet coming out of the darkness to meet shod feet – then both turned away again; the shod feet went downstairs, the bare feet went back down the hall." He directed his light down the hall. The footprints faded into darkness, beyond the reach of the beam. On either hand the closed doors of chambers were cryptic portals of mystery.

"Suppose your crazy tale was true," Buckner muttered, half to himself. "These aren't your tracks. They look like a woman's. Suppose somebody did whistle, and Branner went upstairs to investigate. Suppose somebody met him here in the dark and split his head. The signs and tracks would have been, in that case, just as they really are. But if that's so, why isn't Branner lyin' here where he was killed? Could he have lived long enough to take the hatchet away from whoever killed him, and stagger downstairs with it?"

"No, no!" Recollection gagged Griswell. "I saw him on the stair. He was dead. No man could live a minute after receiving such a wound."

"I believe it," muttered Buckner. "But – it's madness! Or else it's too clever – yet, what sane man would think up and work out such an elaborate and utterly insane plan to escape punishment for murder, when a simple plea of self-defense would have been so much more effective? No court would recognize that story. Well, let's follow these other tracks. They lead down the hall – here, what's this?"

With an icy clutch at his soul, Griswell saw the light was beginning to grow dim.

"This battery is new," muttered Buckner, and for the first time Griswell caught an edge of fear in his voice. "Come on – out of here quick!"

The light had faded to a faint red glow. The darkness seemed straining into them, creeping with black cat-feet. Buckner retreated, pushing Griswell stumbling behind him as he walked backward, pistol cocked and lifted, down the dark hall. In the growing darkness Griswell heard what sounded like the stealthy opening of a door. And suddenly the blackness about them was vibrant with menace. Griswell knew Buckner sensed it as well as he, for the sheriff's hard body was tense and taut as a stalking panther's.

But without haste he worked his way to the stair and backed down it, Griswell preceding him, and fighting the panic that urged him to scream and burst into mad flight. A ghastly thought brought icy sweat out on his flesh. Suppose the dead man were creeping up the stair behind them in the dark, face frozen in the death-grin, blood-caked hatchet lifted to strike?

This possibility so overpowered him that he was scarcely aware when his feet struck the level of the lower hallway, and he was only then aware that the light had grown brighter as they descended, until it now gleamed with its full power – but when Buckner turned it back up the stairway, it failed to illuminate the darkness that hung like a tangible fog at the head of the stair.

"The damn thing was conjured," muttered Buckner. "Nothin' else. It couldn't act like that naturally."

"Turn the light into the room," begged Griswell. "See if John – if John is –"

He could not put the ghastly thought into words, but Buckner understood.

He swung the beam around, and Griswell had never dreamed that the sight of the gory body of a murdered man could bring such relief.

"He's still there," grunted Buckner. "If he walked after he was killed, he hasn't walked since. But that thing –"

Again he turned the light up the stair, and stood chewing his lip and scowling. Three times he half lifted his gun. Griswell read his mind. The sheriff was tempted to plunge back up that stair, take his chance with the unknown. But common sense held him back.

"I wouldn't have a chance in the dark," he muttered. "And I've got a hunch the light would go out again."

He turned and faced Griswell squarely.

"There's no use dodgin' the question. There's somethin' hellish in this house, and I believe I have an inklin' of what it is. I don't believe you killed Branner. Whatever killed him is up there – now. There's a lot about your yarn that don't sound sane; but there's nothin' sane about a flashlight goin' out like this one did. I don't believe that thing upstairs is human. I never met anything I was afraid to tackle in the dark before, but I'm not goin' up there until daylight. It's not long until dawn. We'll wait for it out there on that gallery."

The stars were already paling when they came out on the broad porch. Buckner seated himself on the balustrade, facing the door, his pistol dangling in his fingers. Griswell sat down near him and leaned back against a crumbling pillar. He shut his eyes, grateful for the faint breeze that seemed to cool his throbbing brain. He experienced a dull sense of unreality. He was a stranger in a strange land, a land that had become suddenly imbued with black horror. The shadow of the noose hovered above him, and in that dark house lay John Branner, with his butchered head – like the figments of a dream these facts spun and eddied in his brain until all merged in a gray twilight as sleep came uninvited to his weary soul.

He awoke to a cold white dawn and full memory of the horrors of the night. Mists curled about the stems of the pines, crawled in smoky wisps up the broken walk. Buckner was shaking him.

"Wake up! It's daylight."

Griswell rose, wincing at the stiffness of his limbs. His face was gray and old.

"I'm ready. Let's go upstairs."

"I've already been!" Buckner's eyes burned in the early dawn. "I didn't wake you up. I went as soon as it was light. I found nothin'."

"The tracks of the bare feet –"

"Gone!"

"Gone?"

"Yes, gone! The dust had been disturbed all over the hall, from the point where Branner's tracks ended; swept into corners. No chance of trackin' anything there now. Something obliterated those tracks while we sat here, and I didn't hear a sound. I've gone through the whole house. Not a sign of anything."

Griswell shuddered at the thought of himself sleeping alone on the porch while Buckner conducted his exploration.

"What shall we do?" he asked listlessly. "With those tracks gone there goes my only chance of proving my story."

"We'll take Branner's body into the county-seat," answered Buckner. "Let me do the talkin'. If the authorities knew the facts as they appear, they'd insist on you being confined and indicted. I don't believe you killed Branner – but neither a district attorney, judge nor jury would believe what you told me, or what happened to us last night. I'm handlin' this thing my own way. I'm not goin' to arrest you until I've exhausted every other possibility.

"Say nothin' about what's happened here, when we get to town. I'll simply tell the district attorney that John Branner was killed by a party or parties unknown, and that I'm workin' on the case.

"Are you game to come back with me to this house and spend the night here, sleepin' in that room as you and Branner slept last night?"

Griswell went white, but answered as stoutly as his ancestors might have expressed their determination to hold their cabins in the teeth of the Pequots: "I'll do it."

"Let's go then; help me pack the body out to your auto."

Griswell's soul revolted at the sight of John Branner's bloodless face in the chill white dawn, and the feel of his clammy flesh. The gray fog wrapped wispy tentacles about their feet as they carried their grisly burden across the lawn.

II: The Snake's Brother

AGAIN THE SHADOWS were lengthening over the pinelands, and again two men came bumping along the old road in a car with a New England license plate.

Buckner was driving. Griswell's nerves were too shattered for him to trust himself at the wheel. He looked gaunt and haggard, and his face was still pallid. The strain of the day spent at the county-seat was added to the horror that still rode his soul like the shadow of a black-winged vulture. He had not slept, had not tasted what he had eaten.

"I told you I'd tell you about the Blassenvilles," said Buckner. "They were proud folks, haughty, and pretty damn ruthless when they wanted their way. They didn't treat their slaves as well as the other planters did – got their ideas in the West Indies, I reckon. There was a streak of cruelty in them – especially Miss. Celia, the last one of the family to come to these parts. That was long after the slaves had been freed, but she used to whip her mulatto maid just like she was a slave, the old folks say... The Negroes said when a Blassenville died, the devil was always waitin' for him out in the black pines.

"Well, after the Civil War they died off pretty fast, livin' in poverty on the plantation which was allowed to go to ruin. Finally only four girls were left, sisters, livin' in the old house and ekin' out a bare livin', with a few blacks livin' in the old slave huts and workin' the fields on the share. They kept to themselves, bein' proud, and ashamed of their poverty. Folks wouldn't see them for months at a time. When they needed supplies they sent a Negro to town after them.

"But folks knew about it when Miss. Celia came to live with them. She came from somewhere in the West Indies, where the whole family originally had its roots – a fine, handsome woman, they say, in the early thirties. But she didn't mix with folks any more than the girls did. She brought a mulatto maid with her, and the Blassenville cruelty cropped out in her treatment of this maid. I knew an old man years ago, who swore he saw Miss. Celia tie this girl up to a tree, stark naked, and whip her with a horsewhip. Nobody was surprised when she disappeared. Everybody figured she'd run away, of course.

"Well, one day in the spring of 1890 Miss. Elizabeth, the youngest girl, came in to town for the first time in maybe a year. She came after supplies. Said the blacks had all left the place. Talked a little more, too, a bit wild. Said Miss. Celia had gone, without leaving any word. Said her sisters thought she'd gone back to the West Indies, but she believed her aunt was still in the house. She didn't say what she meant. Just got her supplies and pulled out for the Manor.

"A month went past, and a black came into town and said that Miss. Elizabeth was livin' at the Manor alone. Said her three sisters weren't there any more, that they'd left one by one without givin' any word or explanation. She didn't know where they'd gone, and was afraid to stay there alone, but didn't know where else to go. She'd never known anything but the Manor, and had neither relatives nor friends. But she was in mortal terror of something. The black said she locked herself in her room at night and kept candles burnin' all night...

"It was a stormy spring night when Miss. Elizabeth came tearin' into town on the one horse she owned, nearly dead from fright. She fell from her horse in the square; when she could talk she said she'd found a secret room in the Manor that had been forgotten for a hundred years. And she said that there she found her three sisters, dead, and hangin' by their necks from the ceilin'. She said something chased her and nearly brained her with an ax as she ran out the front door, but somehow she got to the horse and got away. She was nearly crazy with fear, and didn't know what it was that chased her – said it looked like a woman with a yellow face.

"About a hundred men rode out there, right away. They searched the house from top to bottom, but they didn't find any secret room, or the remains of the sisters. But they did find a hatchet stickin' in the doorjamb downstairs, with some of Miss. Elizabeth's hairs stuck on it, just as she'd said. She wouldn't go back there and show them how to find the secret door; almost went crazy when they suggested it.

"When she was able to travel, the people made up some money and loaned it to her – she was still too proud to accept charity – and she went to California. She never came back, but later it was learned, when she sent back to repay the money they'd loaned her, that she'd married out there.

"Nobody ever bought the house. It stood there just as she'd left it, and as the years passed folks stole all the furnishings out of it, poor white trash, I reckon. A Negro wouldn't go about it. But they came after sunup and left long before sundown."

"What did the people think about Miss. Elizabeth's story?" asked Griswell.

"Well, most folks thought she'd gone a little crazy, livin' in that old house alone. But some people believed that mulatto girl, Joan, didn't run away, after all. They believed she'd hidden in the woods, and glutted her hatred of the Blassenvilles by murderin' Miss. Celia and the three girls. They beat up the woods with bloodhounds, but never found a trace of her. If there was a secret room in the house, she might have been hidin' there – if there was anything to that theory."

"She couldn't have been hiding there all these years," muttered Griswell. "Anyway, the thing in the house now isn't human."

Buckner wrenched the wheel around and turned into a dim trace that left the main road and meandered off through the pines.

"Where are you going?"

"There's an old Negro that lives off this way a few miles. I want to talk to him. We're up against something that takes more than white man's sense. The black people know more than we do about some things. This old man is nearly a hundred years old. His master educated him when he was a boy, and after he was freed he traveled more extensively than most white men do. They say he's a voodoo man."

Griswell shivered at the phrase, staring uneasily at the green forest walls that shut them in. The scent of the pines was mingled with the odors of unfamiliar plants and blossoms. But underlying all was a reek of rot and decay. Again a sick abhorrence of these dark mysterious woodlands almost overpowered him.

"Voodoo!" he muttered. "I'd forgotten about that – I never could think of black magic in connection with the South. To me witchcraft was always associated with old crooked streets in waterfront towns, overhung by gabled roofs that were old when they were hanging witches in Salem; dark musty alleys where black cats and other things might steal at night. Witchcraft always meant the old towns of New England, to me – but all this is more terrible than any New England legend – these somber pines, old deserted houses, lost plantations, mysterious black people, old tales of madness and horror – God, what frightful, ancient terrors there are on this continent fools call 'young'!"

"Here's old Jacob's hut," announced Buckner, bringing the automobile to a halt.

Griswell saw a clearing and a small cabin squatting under the shadows of the huge trees. The pines gave way to oaks and cypresses, bearded with gray trailing moss, and behind the cabin lay the edge of a swamp that ran away under the dimness of the trees, choked with rank vegetation. A thin wisp of blue smoke curled up from the stick-and-mud chimney.

He followed Buckner to the tiny stoop, where the sheriff pushed open the leather-hinged door and strode in. Griswell blinked in the comparative dimness of the interior. A single small window let in a little daylight. An old Negro crouched beside the hearth, watching a pot stew over the open fire. He looked up as they entered, but did not rise. He seemed incredibly old. His face was a mass of wrinkles, and his eyes, dark and vital, were filmed momentarily at times as if his mind wandered.

Buckner motioned Griswell to sit down in a string-bottomed chair, and himself took a rudely-made bench near the hearth, facing the old man.

"Jacob," he said bluntly, "the time's come for you to talk. I know you know the secret of Blassenville Manor. I've never questioned you about it, because it wasn't in my line. But a man was murdered there last night, and this man here may hang for it, unless you tell me what haunts that old house of the Blassenvilles."

The old man's eyes gleamed, then grew misty as if clouds of extreme age drifted across his brittle mind.

"The Blassenvilles," he murmured, and his voice was mellow and rich, his speech not the patois of the piny woods darky. "They were proud people, sirs – proud and cruel. Some died in the war, some were killed in duels – the menfolks, sirs. Some died in the Manor – the old Manor –" His voice trailed off into unintelligible mumblings.

"What of the Manor?" asked Buckner patiently.

"Miss. Celia was the proudest of them all," the old man muttered. "The proudest and the cruelest. The black people hated her; Joan most of all. Joan had white blood in her, and she was proud, too. Miss. Celia whipped her like a slave."

"What is the secret of Blassenville Manor?" persisted Buckner.

The film faded from the old man's eyes; they were dark as moonlit wells.

"What secret, sir? I do not understand."

"Yes, you do. For years that old house has stood there with its mystery. You know the key to its riddle."

The old man stirred the stew. He seemed perfectly rational now.

"Sir, life is sweet, even to an old black man."

"You mean somebody would kill you if you told me?"

But the old man was mumbling again, his eyes clouded.

"Not somebody. No human. No human being. The black gods of the swamps. My secret is inviolate, guarded by the Big Serpent, the god above all gods. He would send a little brother to kiss me with his cold lips – a little brother with a white crescent moon on his head. I sold my soul to the Big Serpent when he made me maker of zuvembies –"

Buckner stiffened.

"I heard that word once before," he said softly, "from the lips of a dying black man, when I was a child. What does it mean?"

Fear filled the eyes of old Jacob.

"What have I said? No – no! I said nothing."

"Zuvembies," prompted Buckner.

"Zuvembies," mechanically repeated the old man, his eyes vacant. "A zuvembie was once a woman – on the Slave Coast they know of them. The drums that whisper by night in the hills of Haiti tell of them. The makers of zuvembies are honored of the people of Damballah. It is death to speak of it to a white man – it is one of the Snake God's forbidden secrets."

"You speak of the zuvembies," said Buckner softly.

"I must not speak of it," mumbled the old man, and Griswell realized that he was thinking aloud, too far gone in his dotage to be aware that he was speaking at all. "No white man must know that I danced in the Black Ceremony of the voodoo, and was made a maker of zombies and zuvembies. The Big Snake punishes loose tongues with death."

"A zuvembie is a woman?" prompted Buckner.

"Was a woman," the old Negro muttered. "She knew I was a maker of zuvembies – she came and stood in my hut and asked for the awful brew – the brew of ground snake-bones, and the blood of vampire bats, and the dew from a nighthawk's wings, and other elements unnamable. She had danced in the Black Ceremony – she was ripe to become a zuvembie – the Black Brew was all that was needed – the other was beautiful – I could not refuse her."

"Who?" demanded Buckner tensely, but the old man's head was sunk on his withered breast, and he did not reply. He seemed to slumber as he sat. Buckner shook him. "You gave a brew to make a woman a zuvembie – what is a zuvembie?"

The old man stirred resentfully and muttered drowsily.

"A zuvembie is no longer human. It knows neither relatives nor friends. It is one with the people of the Black World. It commands the natural demons – owls, bats, snakes and werewolves, and can fetch darkness to blot out a little light. It can be slain by lead or steel, but unless it is slain thus, it lives for ever, and it eats no such food as humans eat. It dwells like a bat in a cave or an old house. Time means naught to the zuvembie; an hour, a day, a year, all is one. It cannot speak human words, nor think as a human thinks, but it can hypnotize the living by the sound of its voice, and when it slays a man, it can command his lifeless body until the flesh is cold. As long as the blood flows, the corpse is its slave. Its pleasure lies in the slaughter of human beings."

"And why should one become a zuvembie?" asked Buckner softly.

"Hate," whispered the old man. "Hate! Revenge!"

"Was her name Joan?" murmured Buckner.

It was as if the name penetrated the fogs of senility that clouded the voodoo-man's mind. He shook himself and the film faded from his eyes, leaving them hard and gleaming as wet black marble.

"Joan?" he said slowly. "I have not heard that name for the span of a generation. I seem to have been sleeping, gentlemen; I do not remember – I ask your pardon. Old men fall asleep before the fire, like old dogs. You asked me of Blassenville Manor? Sir, if I were to tell you why I cannot answer you, you would deem it mere superstition. Yet the white man's God be my witness –"

As he spoke he was reaching across the hearth for a piece of firewood, groping among the heaps of sticks there. And his voice broke in a scream, as he jerked back his arm convulsively. And a horrible, thrashing, trailing thing came with it. Around the voodoo-man's arm a mottled length of that shape was wrapped, and a wicked wedge-shaped head struck again in silent fury.

The old man fell on the hearth, screaming, upsetting the simmering pot and scattering the embers, and then Buckner caught up a billet of firewood and crushed that flat head. Cursing, he kicked aside the knotting, twisting trunk, glaring briefly at the mangled head. Old Jacob had ceased screaming and writhing; he lay still, staring glassily upward.

"Dead?" whispered Griswell.

"Dead as Judas Iscariot," snapped Buckner, frowning at the twitching reptile. "That infernal snake crammed enough poison into his veins to kill a dozen men his age. But I think it was the shock and fright that killed him."

"What shall we do?" asked Griswell, shivering.

"Leave the body on that bunk. Nothin' can hurt it, if we bolt the door so the wild hogs can't get in, or any cat. We'll carry it into town tomorrow. We've got work to do tonight. Let's get goin'."

Griswell shrank from touching the corpse, but he helped Buckner lift it on the rude bunk, and then stumbled hastily out of the hut. The sun was hovering above the horizon, visible in dazzling red flame through the black stems of the trees.

They climbed into the car in silence, and went bumping back along the stumpy train.

"He said the Big Snake would send one of his brothers," muttered Griswell.

"Nonsense!" snorted Buckner. "Snakes like warmth, and that swamp is full of them. It crawled in and coiled up among that firewood. Old Jacob disturbed it, and it bit him. Nothin' supernatural about that." After a short silence he said, in a different voice, "That was the first time I ever saw a rattler strike without singin'; and the first time I ever saw a snake with a white crescent moon on its head."

They were turning in to the main road before either spoke again.

"You think that the mulatto Joan has skulked in the house all these years?" Griswell asked.

"You heard what old Jacob said," answered Buckner grimly. "Time means nothin' to a zuvembie."

As they made the last turn in the road, Griswell braced himself against the sight of Blassenville Manor looming black against the red sunset. When it came into view he bit his lip to keep from shrieking. The suggestion of cryptic horror came back in all its power.

"Look!" he whispered from dry lips as they came to a halt beside the road. Buckner grunted.

From the balustrades of the gallery rose a whirling cloud of pigeons that swept away into the sunset, black against the lurid glare...

III: The Call of Zuvembie

BOTH MEN sat rigid for a few moments after the pigeons had flown.

"Well, I've seen them at last," muttered Buckner.

"Only the doomed see them perhaps," whispered Griswell. "That tramp saw them −"

"Well, we'll see," returned the Southerner tranquilly, as he climbed out of the car, but Griswell noticed him unconsciously hitch forward his scabbarded gun.

The oaken door sagged on broken hinges. Their feet echoed on the broken brick walk. The blind windows reflected the sunset in sheets of flame. As they came into the broad hall Griswell saw the string of black marks that ran across the floor and into the chamber, marking the path of a dead man.

Buckner had brought blankets out of the automobile. He spread them before the fireplace.

"I'll lie next to the door," he said. "You lie where you did last night."

"Shall we light a fire in the grate?" asked Griswell, dreading the thought of the blackness that would cloak the woods when the brief twilight had died.

"No. You've got a flashlight and so have I. We'll lie here in the dark and see what happens. Can you use that gun I gave you?"

"I suppose so. I never fired a revolver, but I know how it's done."

"Well, leave the shootin' to me, if possible." The sheriff seated himself cross-legged on his blankets and emptied the cylinder of his big blue Colt, inspecting each cartridge with a critical eye before he replaced it.

Griswell prowled nervously back and forth, begrudging the slow fading of the light as a miser begrudges the waning of his gold. He leaned with one hand against the mantelpiece, staring down into the dust-covered ashes. The fire that produced those ashes must have been built by Elizabeth Blassenville, more than forty years before. The thought was depressing. Idly he stirred the dusty ashes with his toe. Something came to view among the charred debris − a bit of paper, stained and yellowed. Still idly he bent and drew it out of the ashes. It was a note-book with moldering cardboard backs.

"What have you found?" asked Buckner, squinting down the gleaming barrel of his gun.

"Nothing but an old note-book. Looks like a diary. The pages are covered with writing − but the ink is so faded, and the paper is in such a state of decay that I can't tell much about it. How do you suppose it came in the fireplace, without being burned up?"

"Thrown in long after the fire was out," surmised Buckner. "Probably found and tossed in the fireplace by somebody who was in here stealin' furniture. Likely somebody who couldn't read."

Griswell fluttered the crumbling leaves listlessly, straining his eyes in the fading light over the yellowed scrawls. Then he stiffened.

"Here's an entry that's legible! Listen!" He read:

"'I know someone is in the house besides myself. I can hear someone prowling about at night when the sun has set and the pines are black outside. Often in the night I hear it fumbling at my door. Who is it? Is it one of my sisters? Is it Aunt Celia? If it is either of these, why does she steal so subtly about the house? Why does she tug at my door, and glide away when I call to her? Shall I open the door and go out to her? No, no! I dare not! I am afraid. Oh God, what shall I do? I dare not stay here – but where am I to go?'"

"By God!" ejaculated Buckner. "That must be Elizabeth Blassenville's diary! Go on!"

"I can't make out the rest of the page," answered Griswell. "But a few pages further on I can make out some lines." He read:

"*Why did the Negroes all run away when Aunt Celia disappeared? My sisters are dead. I know they are dead. I seem to sense that they died horribly, in fear and agony. But why? Why? If someone murdered Aunt Celia, why should that person murder my poor sisters? They were always kind to the black people. Joan –*'"

He paused, scowling futilely.

"A piece of the page is torn out. Here's another entry under another date – at least I judge it's a date; I can't make it out for sure.

"' *– the awful thing that the old Negress hinted at? She named Jacob Blount, and Joan, but she would not speak plainly; perhaps she feared to –* '

"Part of it gone here; then:

"'*No, no! How can it be? She is dead – or gone away. Yet – she was born and raised in the West Indies, and from hints she let fall in the past, I know she delved into the mysteries of the voodoo. I believe she even danced in one of their horrible ceremonies – how could she have been such a beast? And this – this horror. God, can such things be? I know not what to think. If it is she who roams the house at night, who fumbles at my door, who whistles so weirdly and sweetly – no, no, I must be going mad. If I stay here alone I shall die as hideously as my sisters must have died. Of that I am convinced.*'"

The incoherent chronicle ended as abruptly as it had begun. Griswell was so engrossed in deciphering the scraps that he was not aware that darkness had stolen upon them, hardly aware that Buckner was holding his electric torch for him to read by. Waking from his abstraction he started and darted a quick glance at the black hallway.

"What do you make of it?"

"What I've suspected all the time," answered Buckner. "That mulatto maid Joan turned zuvembie to avenge herself on Miss. Celia. Probably hated the whole family as much as she did her mistress. She'd taken part in voodoo ceremonies on her native island until she was 'ripe,' as old Jacob said. All she needed was the Black Brew – he supplied that. She killed Miss. Celia and the three older girls, and would have gotten Elizabeth but for chance. She's been lurkin' in this old house all these years, like a snake in a ruin."

"But why should she murder a stranger?"

"You heard what old Jacob said," reminded Buckner. "A zuvembie finds satisfaction in the slaughter of humans. She called Branner up the stair and split his head and stuck the hatchet in his hand, and sent him downstairs to murder you. No court will ever believe that, but if we can produce her body, that will be evidence enough to prove your innocence. My word will be taken, that she murdered Branner. Jacob said a zuvembie could be killed... in reporting this affair I don't have to be too accurate in detail."

"She came and peered over the balustrade of the stair at us," muttered Griswell. "But why didn't we find her tracks on the stair?"

"Maybe you dreamed it. Maybe a zuvembie can project her spirit – hell! Why try to rationalize something that's outside the bounds of rationality? Let's begin our watch."

"Don't turn out the light!" exclaimed Griswell involuntarily. Then he added: "Of course. Turn it out. We must be in the dark as" – he gagged a bit – "as Branner and I were."

But fear like a physical sickness assailed him when the room was plunged in darkness. He lay trembling and his heart beat so heavily he felt as if he would suffocate.

"The West Indies must be the plague spot of the world," muttered Buckner, a blur on his blankets. "I've heard of zombies. Never knew before what a zuvembie was. Evidently some drug concocted by the voodoo-men to induce madness in women. That doesn't explain the other things, though: the hypnotic powers, the abnormal longevity, the ability to control corpses – no, a zuvembie can't be merely a mad-woman. It's a monster, something more and less than a human being, created by the magic that spawns in black swamps and jungles – well, we'll see."

His voice ceased, and in the silence Griswell heard the pounding of his own heart. Outside in the black woods a wolf howled eerily, and owls hooted. Then silence fell again like a black fog.

Griswell forced himself to lie still on his blankets. Time seemed at a standstill. He felt as if he were choking. The suspense was growing unendurable; the effort he made to control his crumbling nerves bathed his limbs in sweat. He clenched his teeth until his jaws ached and almost locked, and the nails of his fingers bit deeply into his palms.

He did not know what he was expecting. The fiend would strike again – but how? Would it be a horrible, sweet whistling, bare feet stealing down the creaking steps, or a sudden hatchet-stroke in the dark? Would it choose him or Buckner? Was Buckner already dead? He could see nothing in the blackness, but he heard the man's steady breathing. The Southerner must have nerves of steel. Or was that Buckner breathing beside him, separated by a narrow strip of darkness? Had the fiend already struck in silence, and taken the sheriff's place, there to lie in ghoulish glee until it was ready to strike? – a thousand hideous fancies assailed Griswell tooth and claw.

He began to feel that he would go mad if he did not leap to his feet, screaming, and burst frenziedly out of that accursed house – not even the fear of the gallows could keep him lying there in the darkness any longer – the rhythm of Buckner's breathing was suddenly broken, and Griswell felt as if a bucket of ice-water had been poured over him. From somewhere above them rose a sound of weird, sweet whistling...

Griswell's control snapped, plunging his brain into darkness deeper than the physical blackness which engulfed him. There was a period of absolute blankness, in which a realization of motion was his first sensation of awakening consciousness. He was running, madly, stumbling over an incredibly rough road. All was darkness about him, and he ran blindly. Vaguely he realized that he must have bolted from the house, and fled for perhaps miles before his overwrought brain began to function. He did not care; dying on the gallows for a murder he never committed did not terrify him half as much as the thought of returning to that house of horror. He was overpowered by the urge to run – run – run as he was running now, blindly, until he reached the end of his endurance. The mist had not yet fully lifted from his brain, but he was aware of a dull wonder that he could not see the stars through the black branches. He wished vaguely that he could see where he was going. He believed he must be climbing a hill, and that was strange, for he knew there were no hills within miles of the Manor. Then above and ahead of him a dim glow began.

He scrambled toward it, over ledge-like projections that were more and more taking on a disquieting symmetry. Then he was horror-stricken to realize that a sound was impacting on his ears – a weird mocking whistle. The sound swept the mists away. Why, what was this? Where was he? Awakening and realization came like the stunning stroke of a butcher's maul. He was not fleeing along a road, or climbing a hill; he was mounting a stair. He was still in Blassenville Manor! And he was climbing the stair!

An inhuman scream burst from his lips. Above it the mad whistling rose in a ghoulish piping of demoniac triumph. He tried to stop – to turn back – even to fling himself over the balustrade. His shrieking rang unbearably in his own ears. But his will-power was shattered to bits. It did not exist. He had no will. He had dropped his flashlight, and he had forgotten the gun in his pocket. He could not command his own body. His legs, moving stiffly, worked like pieces of mechanism detached from his brain, obeying an outside will. Clumping methodically they carried him shrieking up the stair toward the witch-fire glow shimmering above him.

"Buckner!" he screamed. "Buckner! Help, for God's sake!"

His voice strangled in his throat. He had reached the upper landing. He was tottering down the hallway. The whistling sank and ceased, but its impulsion still drove him on. He could not see from what source the dim glow came. It seemed to emanate from no central focus. But he saw a vague figure shambling toward him. It looked like a woman, but no human woman ever walked with that skulking gait, and no human woman ever had that face of horror, that leering yellow blur of lunacy – he tried to scream at the sight of that face, at the glint of keen steel in the uplifted claw-like hand – but his tongue was frozen.

Then something crashed deafeningly behind him; the shadows were split by a tongue of flame which lit a hideous figure falling backward. Hard on the heels of the report rang an inhuman squawk.

In the darkness that followed the flash Griswell fell to his knees and covered his face with his hands. He did not hear Buckner's voice. The Southerner's hand on his shoulder shook him out of his swoon.

A light in his eyes blinded him. He blinked, shaded his eyes, looked up into Buckner's face, bending at the rim of the circle of light. The sheriff was pale.

"Are you hurt? God, man, are you hurt? There's a butcher knife there on the floor –"

"I'm not hurt," mumbled Griswell. "You fired just in time – the fiend! Where is it? Where did it go?"

"Listen!"

Somewhere in the house there sounded a sickening flopping and flapping as of something that thrashed and struggled in its death convulsions.

"Jacob was right," said Buckner grimly. "Lead can kill them. I hit her, all right. Didn't dare use my flashlight, but there was enough light. When that whistlin' started you almost walked over me gettin' out. I knew you were hypnotized, or whatever it is. I followed you up the stairs. I was right behind you, but crouchin' low so she wouldn't see me, and maybe get away again. I almost waited too long before I fired – but the sight of her almost paralyzed me. Look!"

He flashed his light down the hall, and now it shone bright and clear. And it shone on an aperture gaping in the wall where no door had showed before.

"The secret panel Miss. Elizabeth found!" Buckner snapped. "Come on!"

He ran across the hallway and Griswell followed him dazedly. The flopping and thrashing came from beyond that mysterious door, and now the sounds had ceased.

The light revealed a narrow, tunnel-like corridor that evidently led through one of the thick walls. Buckner plunged into it without hesitation.

"Maybe it couldn't think like a human," he muttered, shining his light ahead of him. "But it had sense enough to erase its tracks last night so we couldn't trail it to that point in the wall and maybe find the secret panel. There's a room ahead – the secret room of the Blassenvilles!"

And Griswell cried out: "My God! It's the windowless chamber I saw in my dream, with the three bodies hanging – ahhhhh!"

Buckner's light playing about the circular chamber became suddenly motionless. In that wide ring of light three figures appeared, three dried, shriveled, mummy-like shapes, still clad in the moldering garments of the last century. Their slippers were clear of the floor as they hung by their withered necks from chains suspended from the ceiling.

"The three Blassenville sisters!" muttered Buckner. "Miss. Elizabeth wasn't crazy, after all."

"Look!" Griswell could barely make his voice intelligible. "There – over there in the corner!"

The light moved, halted.

"Was that thing a woman once?" whispered Griswell. "God, look at that face, even in death. Look at those claw-like hands, with black talons like those of a beast. Yes, it was human, though – even the rags of an old ballroom gown. Why should a mulatto maid wear such a dress, I wonder?"

"This has been her lair for over forty years," muttered Buckner, brooding over the grinning grisly thing sprawling in the corner. "This clears you, Griswell – a crazy woman with a hatchet – that's all the authorities need to know. God, what a revenge! – What a foul revenge! Yet what a bestial nature she must have had, in the beginnin', to delve into voodoo as she must have done –"

"The mulatto woman?" whispered Griswell, dimly sensing a horror that overshadowed all the rest of the terror.

Buckner shook his head. "We misunderstood old Jacob's maunderin's, and the things Miss. Elizabeth wrote – she must have known, but family pride sealed her lips. Griswell, I understand now; the mulatto woman had her revenge, but not as we'd supposed. She didn't drink the Black Brew old Jacob fixed for her. It was for somebody else, to be given secretly in her food, or coffee, no doubt. Then Joan ran away, leavin' the seeds of the hell she'd sowed to grow."

"That – that's not the mulatto woman?" whispered Griswell.

"When I saw her out there in the hallway I knew she was no mulatto. And those distorted features still reflect a family likeness. I've seen her portrait, and I can't be mistaken. There lies the creature that was once Celia Blassenville."

The Two-Out-of-Three Rule

Patrick J. Hurley

"I'M TELLING YOU, Kyle, hot girls don't like comics," proclaimed Sean.

"Excuse me?" Angela said. "I'm right frickin' here."

"Present company excluded, of course," Sean added hastily. "Besides, you're Kyle's sister, so it doesn't count."

"And why is that?" Angela asked.

"Because Kyle's the biggest nerd ever. Just being related to him grants you honorary nerd street cred."

"Thank you," said Kyle, sipping his beer. "And Elaina does like comics."

"*And* she likes Lord of the Rings?" asked Sean, as if confused.

"Has all three extended editions," said Kyle.

"*And* Warcraft?" Angela asked, sounding dubious.

"Plays a maxed-level druid."

"And," Sean said, "to be clear, she's hot?"

"Jesus, Sean," said Angela.

"Yup," Kyle said, ignoring his sister's rolled eyes.

"Which leads me to wonder."

"What?"

Sean raised his eyebrows. "Is she real?"

"Fuck you," Kyle said while his sister guffawed.

Sean slouched back in his barstool and began to gesture in a professorial manner Kyle and Angela found endearing and annoying. "Listen. It's the two-out-of-three rule. Women can only qualify in two out of three categories: 1. She's hot 2. She's a geek. 3. She's mentally stable. It's possible to find a babe who fits two out of the three, but all of them? That magical unicorn doesn't exist."

"Wow, Sean," Angela said. "All this insight into the female psyche, yet somehow, you're still single." Kyle held up his hand, which his sister promptly high-fived.

"Touché," replied Sean, laughing. "So any chance of meeting this manic pixie dream girl?"

"Of course, man. She's coming to the game tomorrow. She wants to meet everyone."

* * *

The group sat in a basement around a foldout table with miniatures, dice, paper, and pencils.

"So she's really coming over?" Bruce asked.

"Sounds like it," Sean mumbled, speckles of Doritos flying from his mouth.

"Bet she's hideous," said Matt.

"Like you're a keeper, Matt," Angela said to general laughter. "Anyway, you guys should have heard Kyle go on about her."

"Yeah, but he's in love," Bruce said.

"Point?" said Sean.

"Bet she's a five, maybe a six," said Matt, "and Kyle's got love goggles."

"Either way," said Sean, in an effort to save Matt from Angela's wrath, "it's pretty cool that she's coming. Besides Angie, how many girls we know who would do that?"

The resulting silence around the table gave the impression the gentlemen did not know many girls at all, let alone those who would attend their tabletop sessions.

There was a knock at the door.

"It's open."

Kyle walked in. "Guys, this is Elaina."

None of Kyle's friends said anything.

"Um, yeah. So Elaina, this is my sister Angela, Bruce, Matt, and Sean."

Shocked and shy mutters of 'hi' and 'hello' issued from around the table.

"Hey, guys!" Elaina sat down, seemingly oblivious to the uncomfortable silence. If they were unprepared for her appearance, they were utterly shocked by what came next.

"So what're we playing?" Elaina asked, while cracking open a can of soda. "Pathfinder? White Wolf? A little old-school 2E? I got character sheets for them all."

"Told you," whispered Kyle, sitting next to Sean.

* * *

After they'd finished for the night, Sean and Matt walked out to their cars. It had been a good session; Kyle had been the first to leave for once.

"Wow" Sean said.

"I know. She's like one of the guys."

"Yeah, except she's *definitely* not one of the guys."

"This is true."

"Kyle's one lucky bastard," Sean said, a bit wistfully.

"Hey, if he can land a girl like that, maybe there's hope for us, right?" Matt said and got into his car.

Sean turned the ignition of his Tercel and sat there for a moment, staring ahead while the engine idled. He couldn't help but remember the way Elaina had smiled at him when he brought her a beer. He'd never try to hit on her; Kyle was his best friend. Still, he couldn't help but think about that mysterious smile.

* * *

"So?"

"You were right man, she's amazing," Sean said, silently adding, *you lucky bastard*.

"Thanks," said Kyle, putting both hands behind his head. "I have to admit, so far it's been great."

"Well good," Sean said, because he couldn't think of anything else to say. Contentedness was not a usual circumstance for either of them, and neither seemed sure how the conversation should proceed.

"What happened to your arm?" Sean asked.

He pointed to Kyle's thin tricep. A large circular line traced along his inner skin, and it looked like a portion of muscle was missing.

Kyle quickly covered it up and laughed.

"Dog bite" Kyle said quickly. "Neighbor's dog just whelped and I got too close to her pups."

"Are you serious? Did you go to a hospital?"

"Oh, yeah. Yeah. I already did. It's cool. They cleaned it and it's healing fine."

"You should have that dog put down. What a bitch!"

"More than you know," Kyle murmured.

"What?"

"Nothing."

* * *

"Sean noticed."

Kyle was sitting up in bed, the covers at his waist. The book in his hands trembled a little.

"I'm sorry honey." Her voice floated from the bathroom over the running faucet. "You're just going to have to wear long sleeves from now on."

"Yeah, I guess so."

Elaina stepped out wearing a silk robe. He stared in awe as the robe fell effortlessly from her shoulders, revealing undergarments that he'd only ever seen in a pilfered copy of his sister's Victoria's Secret catalog.

"It just happens," Elaina said in a petulant voice, "I can't help where."

"I know," said Kyle wearily. Before he could say more, she placed two fingers on his lips and traced them down his chest to his waist, licking her lips.

"Maybe I can make it up to you," she whispered, her eyes gleaming. Kyle felt his body responding, despite himself. After all, he had another month before...

No, he wouldn't think about that.

He reached out and stroked her hair.

"I guess," he said, "we could work something out."

"Anything you want, baby," she said, licking her lips in a way that disturbed him, "Just say it, and I'll do it." With that, she flicked the lights out.

* * *

"So, what do you think?"

Angela hit Kyle in the back of the head and hissed, "She can hear you, idiot."

"So?" Kyle said, "She'll think it's cute."

Angela rolled her eyes.

"Honestly, Kyle? She's great. I bet even Mom will like her. There's only one thing."

"What?" Kyle asked, anxious.

"I can't believe she picked you!"

Angela laughed and took a bite of the dinner Elaina had cooked for them all.

"Elaina, this is amazing!"

"Thanks," Elaina said as she walked in from the kitchen with a bottle of wine. "It's an old family recipe."

"Italian?"

"Middle Eastern."

Angela took another bite.

"Kyle, why aren't you wolfing this down?"

Her brother sat looking down at his plate in a funny sort of way.

"I feel weird," he said and left for the bathroom.

"Well I think it's lovely," Angela said to Elaina, shrugging.

"Yes," replied Elaina, her eyes on the bathroom door, "but not to everyone's taste."

"By the way," Angela asked as she continued to eat, "I forgot to ask what happened to his foot."

"Oh that," Elaina laughed. "Kyle is so spacey sometimes. He wasn't looking where he was going, and a bike messenger rolled over it."

"Whoa," said Angela, "should he be in a cast or something?"

"The doctor said he'd be fine in a few days. Besides, you know how Kyle is."

"Yeah, I do."

They both chuckled.

* * *

"Mom, I'm serious. You really should meet her, she's fantastic."

"I'm sure she is Angela, but I've been very busy."

"Mom, you can't put this off forever."

"I know."

"He's finally growing up. Come on."

"Oh, all right, I'll come by next week and we'll all have lunch."

"Thanks Mom. She's great, you'll see."

"Is she, Angie?"

"Yeah."

"And she loves Kyle?"

"Are you kidding? Everything he says, she just eats it up."

* * *

The bar's jukebox was blasting Alice Cooper's song 'Poison' when Kyle walked through the door.

"Hey man," Sean said, raising his hand. Kyle nodded, took a pint from the bartender and sat down across from him.

"So how's tricks?"

Instead of looking happy, Kyle hunched over.

"Fine, I guess."

"What's up?" Sean asked. "You look exhausted."

"Work's been killing me." Kyle looked past Sean and shivered. "Also, relationships can be tough."

"Not that I'm the best guy to give advice," said Sean, "but I think everyone goes through rough patches. Pretty normal, really."

Kyle rubbed his left shoulder and winced.

"What's wrong?" Sean asked.

"Nothing. Just hurt myself working out yesterday."

"Working out? You?"

"Yeah, it's for Elaina. I wanna, ya know, look better."

"Well good for you," said Sean, who'd never quite gotten the hang of exercise. "Be careful though. You've become an accident factory lately."

Kyle suddenly looked nervous. "Have I?" he asked.

Sean sat back, considering. "Well, yeah. I mean, your foot, arm, shoulder. Dog bites, bruises, sprains. Now that I think about it, you have."

Kyle stared into the bottom of his empty bottle. "I have to go" he announced, standing abruptly. Sean rose to stop him.

"Kyle, wait! I didn't mean anything by it" Sean shouted, but his friend was already out the door.

* * *

Back at his apartment, Kyle sat huddled in his easy chair, arms wrapped around his knees, rocking back and forth. Suddenly, a silky, hungry voice called out from upstairs.

"Honey, I'm ready."

Kyle shivered, and drunkenly began to walk up the steps. Tears ran down his cheeks as he opened the door to his bedroom and stepped into the waiting darkness. The door closed and for a few minutes all was quiet. Then there came a quiet chewing noise.

* * *

"Oh my God Kyle! Are you alright?"

Kyle turned in his wheelchair and saw his mother and sister waiting for him in front of his apartment.

"What are they doing here?" Kyle asked Elaina sharply.

"We came as soon as Elaina called, you idiot!" Angela shouted, and then looked down at the stump where Kyle's foot used to be and started to cry. Meanwhile, his mother began kissing his face and hugging him.

"We wandered off the trail during our hike. Some idiot hunter had left a bear trap there," Elaina began to explain. The two women nodded sadly, tears in their eyes. It was only after they left Kyle and Elaina's apartment, that it occurred to Angela that something had been a little off. What happened was horrible, but the wound seemed to have healed fast, and that hospital was sure quick to discharge him. At least Elaina seemed to have had things well in hand.

* * *

"You shouldn't have called them!" Kyle yelled as he hobbled into the kitchen.

"They had to know" Elaina replied calmly. "And it's better they find out this way. Trust me; I have done this before. It's better to show them the missing part quickly than to hide it."

"But why did they believe you? I mean, they seemed to take it so easily."

Elaina laughed and stroked his leg. Even now, her smile was beautiful. Even now, he felt a strong pang of longing for her.

"I have a way of persuading people, if you haven't noticed."

"Yeah," Kyle said flatly, "I have."

"Oh babe! You know I think you're the greatest. You rock my world. You're not thinking of going back on our little arrangement, are you? It's only once a month."

Kyle found himself falling into those eyes.

How could he even think of leaving her? After all, she was the only person in the world who truly got him. Every relationship had its issues, right?

"Of course not Elaina. I love you."

"Good, now let me fix you dinner, and after we can play video games and watch whatever movie you like."

* * *

"I haven't heard from him in a few weeks."

Matt rolled his dice and grabbed some chips.

"Me neither."

Sean made a note in his character sheet.

"I was hoping they'd drop by tonight."

"You mean you were hoping *Elaina* would drop by."

They laughed as Sean blushed.

"Whatever, not interested" Sean said, lying through his teeth.

"Why would you be?" laughed Matt. "Besides her beauty, geekhood, and wicked sense of humor, what does she really have to offer?"

"She's Kyle's girl," Sean said weakly. "And the poor bastard probably really needs her right now."

"I saw him a couple of days ago," Bruce said quietly. "It was kind of weird seeing him in that wheelchair. I thought he'd only lost his foot in a bear trap, not his lower leg."

"He did only lose his foot."

"Then where was his leg?"

The room was silent.

"Guess I was wrong. Just what I heard."

"Yeah, well," Bruce said. "He didn't look good. The whole time, he seemed really nervous. Until Elaina came back, that is."

"Man, she's a saint, to be staying with him like this while his family's out of town."

* * *

The phone rang at 3 am. Sean rolled over to answer it.

"Mmmph hello?" he said fuzzily.

"Sean!" a voice shouted.

"Who is this?"

"Sean! Buddy! Don't you recognize me?"

Hysterical laughter came from the receiver and then there was a sob. Sean blinked. He hadn't heard from Kyle in months. Not since he and Elaina had left for Europe a month ago.

"Kyle?"

"Yuppo! You got that right! It's me. What's left of me, anyway!"

Sean felt irritated. "Dude," he asked, "are you drunk?"

"Nope. Nossir. Just high on life. High on the greatest woman I've ever met."

"Kyle, what the hell is going on?"

But his friend responded only with another bout of hysterical laughter.

"You know what's weird?" asked Kyle after getting his breath back, "It doesn't even hurt much. There's no bleeding. It just gets sucked away. Like a vacuum! And then there's the chewing noise. That's when I'm glad it's dark and I can't see."

"See what?"

"The pain isn't the worst part. The worst is that a part of you, not just your body, but also your soul, is gone. POOF!"

"What are you talking about?"

Suddenly Sean heard another voice in the background, a woman.

"Dear, you're not trying to call for help again –" the voice began, and the line went dead. Still half asleep, Sean sat there for a moment then went back to bed. He wasn't sure what to make of the call. Poor guy must have been blitzed out of his mind. Goes out on a summer-long trip to Europe with the most beautiful girl in the world, and has the gall to drunk-dial him at 3am.

Some people just don't know how lucky they are, Sean thought as he drifted back to sleep.

* * *

In the middle of nowhere, in a secret place surrounded by oak trees and black rock, something lay in a heap of blankets, trembling in the middle of a circle drawn in the dirt. It's not a man. No, you couldn't really call it a man. There are no limbs. No eyes, ears, nose or hair. No tongue either, which is apparent as it babbles wordlessly.

No, the thing in the circle could not be a man.

A woman steps out of the shadows, her hair as dark as midnight. She is naked and beautiful. As she walks, her appearance changes with every step. A curvaceous blonde, a pale red head, a woman with ebony skin and caramel eyes. Each woman is beautiful, and each looks hungry.

"You see," she whispers, "I think we both got what we wanted." She kneels beside the trembling, faceless thing. It gives no word of denial or agreement, only shivers violently under her touch. Then, with a sudden movement, she tears the blanket away.

What's beneath resembles a crude mannequin. A head and neck yes, but no features, no hair. A torso yes, but thin, with no muscle. The thing's skin is smooth as a newborn babe's. Nothing human could have lost all it has lost.

However, as she removes the bit of cloth below its waist, we see that there are, indeed, some features still anatomically correct. She grins. The wind howls around her, and the shadows dance under the moonlight.

"And now," she says, "the best for last."

She lunges down, mouth open. The wood goes dark, the wind dies, and all that can be heard is the sound of chewing.

* * *

"Heard he was mauled by a bear," Bruce said at the pub. The guys all murmured their assent. They had just left the cemetery, after giving their condolences to Kyle's mom and Angela.

"Yeah, barely enough left to identify the body," Matt added, looking around at the shocked faces, and took another sip of whiskey. Sean said nothing, his disturbing late night phone conversation long forgotten.

"Hey, guys."

They turned and were surprised to see Elaina in the doorway. She took a glass and asked in a hoarse whisper, "Can I join you?"

They hugged her and dragged another seat over to the table. After taking a moment, they toasted Kyle and began tell each other stories about him. After a few hours, only Sean and Elaina were left.

"So Sean, what are you working on now?" Elaina asked.

Sean knew what he was thinking was wrong, but couldn't help it. Kyle was dead. Besides, he thought, his heart aching, she was the perfect girl.

"Right now they've got me running diagnostics on..."

She listened aptly as he went on, nodding in all the right places.

"That's fascinating," she said sincerely as he finished. "And are you seeing anybody?"

Sean choked on his drink.

"No, not at the moment," ignoring that both of them knew he hadn't dated anyone since she'd met him.

"What kind of girl are you looking for?"

Maybe it was the booze, maybe it was the pent up jealousy and this girl, the fucking girl of his dreams right in front of him, or maybe it was that Sean was just plain lonely. If ever there was an exception to the two-out-of-three rule, Sean realized, it was Elaina.

"Oh, I don't know. Pretty much a girl like you."

"What if," Elaina said, flashing him a smile, "you could have me? What if I told you I could be all yours, and you'd only have to pay a tiny little price?" She twined her fingers through his hair. Sean couldn't believe this was happening.

"What price?" he heard himself asking, though he really didn't care. Whatever it was, he would pay it.

"Oh, nothing. Nothing much," she said, licking her lips. "I'll tell you about it later. Besides, it'd only be once a month."

"Sounds good to me," Sean said, and let himself be led out of the bar and into the waiting dark.

The Well

W.W. Jacobs

I

TWO MEN stood in the billiard-room of an old country house, talking. Play, which had been of a half-hearted nature, was over, and they sat at the open window, looking out over the park stretching away beneath them, conversing idly.

"Your time's nearly up, Jem," said one at length, "this time six weeks you'll be yawning out the honeymoon and cursing the man – woman I mean – who invented them."

Jem Benson stretched his long limbs in the chair and grunted in dissent.

"I've never understood it," continued Wilfred Carr, yawning. "It's not in my line at all; I never had enough money for my own wants, let alone for two. Perhaps if I were as rich as you or Croesus I might regard it differently."

There was just sufficient meaning in the latter part of the remark for his cousin to forbear to reply to it. He continued to gaze out of the window and to smoke slowly.

"Not being as rich as Croesus – or you," resumed Carr, regarding him from beneath lowered lids, "I paddle my own canoe down the stream of Time, and, tying it to my friends' door-posts, go in to eat their dinners."

"Quite Venetian," said Jem Benson, still looking out of the window. "It's not a bad thing for you, Wilfred, that you have the doorposts and dinners – and friends."

Carr grunted in his turn. "Seriously though, Jem," he said, slowly, "you're a lucky fellow, a very lucky fellow. If there is a better girl above ground than Olive, I should like to see her."

"Yes," said the other, quietly.

"She's such an exceptional girl," continued Carr, staring out of the window. "She's so good and gentle. She thinks you are a bundle of all the virtues."

He laughed frankly and joyously, but the other man did not join him. "Strong sense – of right and wrong, though," continued Carr, musingly. "Do you know, I believe that if she found out that you were not –"

"Not what?" demanded Benson, turning upon him fiercely, "Not what?"

"Everything that you are," returned his cousin, with a grin that belied his words, "I believe she'd drop you."

"Talk about something else," said Benson, slowly; "your pleasantries are not always in the best taste."

Wilfred Carr rose and taking a cue from the rack, bent over the board and practiced one or two favourite shots. "The only other subject I can talk about just at present is my own financial affairs," he said slowly, as he walked round the table.

"Talk about something else," said Benson again, bluntly.

"And the two things are connected," said Carr, and dropping his cue he half sat on the table and eyed his cousin.

There was a long silence. Benson pitched the end of his cigar out of the window, and leaning back closed his eyes.

"Do you follow me?" inquired Carr at length.

Benson opened his eyes and nodded at the window.

"Do you want to follow my cigar?" he demanded.

"I should prefer to depart by the usual way for your sake," returned the other, unabashed. "If I left by the window all sorts of questions would be asked, and you know what a talkative chap I am."

"So long as you don't talk about my affairs," returned the other, restraining himself by an obvious effort, "you can talk yourself hoarse."

"I'm in a mess," said Carr, slowly, "a devil of a mess. If I don't raise fifteen hundred by this day fortnight, I may be getting my board and lodging free."

"Would that be any change?" questioned Benson.

"The quality would," retorted the other. "The address also would not be good. Seriously, Jem, will you let me have the fifteen hundred?"

"No," said the other, simply.

Carr went white. "It's to save me from ruin," he said, thickly.

"I've helped you till I'm tired," said Benson, turning and regarding him, "and it is all to no good. If you've got into a mess, get out of it. You should not be so fond of giving autographs away."

"It's foolish, I admit," said Carr, deliberately. "I won't do so any more. By the way, I've got some to sell. You needn't sneer. They're not my own."

"Whose are they?" inquired the other.

"Yours."

Benson got up from his chair and crossed over to him. "What is this?" he asked, quietly. "Blackmail?"

"Call it what you like," said Carr. "I've got some letters for sale, price fifteen hundred. And I know a man who would buy them at that price for the mere chance of getting Olive from you. I'll give you first offer."

"If you have got any letters bearing my signature, you will be good enough to give them to me," said Benson, very slowly.

"They're mine," said Carr, lightly; "given to me by the lady you wrote them to. I must say that they are not all in the best possible taste."

His cousin reached forward suddenly, and catching him by the collar of his coat pinned him down on the table.

"Give me those letters," he breathed, sticking his face close to Carr's.

"They're not here," said Carr, struggling. "I'm not a fool. Let me go, or I'll raise the price."

The other man raised him from the table in his powerful hands, apparently with the intention of dashing his head against it. Then suddenly his hold relaxed as an astonished-looking maid-servant entered the room with letters. Carr sat up hastily.

"That's how it was done," said Benson, for the girl's benefit as he took the letters.

"I don't wonder at the other man making him pay for it, then," said Carr, blandly.

"You will give me those letters?" said Benson, suggestively, as the girl left the room.

"At the price I mentioned, yes," said Carr; "but so sure as I am a living man, if you lay your clumsy hands on me again, I'll double it. Now, I'll leave you for a time while you think it over."

He took a cigar from the box and lighting it carefully quitted the room. His cousin waited until the door had closed behind him, and then turning to the window sat there in a fit of fury as silent as it was terrible.

The air was fresh and sweet from the park, heavy with the scent of new-mown grass. The fragrance of a cigar was now added to it, and glancing out he saw his cousin pacing slowly by. He rose and went to the door, and then, apparently altering his mind, he returned to the window and watched the figure of his cousin as it moved slowly away into the moonlight. Then he rose again, and, for a long time, the room was empty.

* * *

It was empty when Mrs. Benson came in some time later to say goodnight to her son on her way to bed. She walked slowly round the table, and pausing at the window gazed from it in idle thought, until she saw the figure of her son advancing with rapid strides toward the house. He looked up at the window.

"Goodnight," said she.

"Goodnight," said Benson, in a deep voice.

"Where is Wilfred?"

"Oh, he has gone," said Benson.

"Gone?"

"We had a few words; he was wanting money again, and I gave him a piece of my mind. I don't think we shall see him again."

"Poor Wilfred!" sighed Mrs. Benson. "He is always in trouble of some sort. I hope that you were not too hard upon him."

"No more than he deserved," said her son, sternly. "Goodnight."

II

THE WELL, which had long ago fallen into disuse, was almost hidden by the thick tangle of undergrowth which ran riot at that corner of the old park. It was partly covered by the shrunken half of a lid, above which a rusty windlass creaked in company with the music of the pines when the wind blew strongly. The full light of the sun never reached it, and the ground surrounding it was moist and green when other parts of the park were gaping with the heat.

Two people walking slowly round the park in the fragrant stillness of a summer evening strayed in the direction of the well.

"No use going through this wilderness, Olive," said Benson, pausing on the outskirts of the pines and eyeing with some disfavour the gloom beyond.

"Best part of the park," said the girl briskly; "you know it's my favourite spot."

"I know you're very fond of sitting on the coping," said the man slowly, "and I wish you wouldn't. One day you will lean back too far and fall in."

"And make the acquaintance of Truth," said Olive lightly. "Come along."

She ran from him and was lost in the shadow of the pines, the bracken crackling beneath her feet as she ran. Her companion followed slowly, and emerging from the gloom saw her poised daintily on the edge of the well with her feet hidden in the rank grass and nettles which surrounded it. She motioned her companion to take a seat by her side, and smiled softly as she felt a strong arm passed about her waist.

"I like this place," said she, breaking a long silence, "it is so dismal – so uncanny. Do you know I wouldn't dare to sit here alone, Jem. I should imagine that all sorts of dreadful things were hidden behind the bushes and trees, waiting to spring out on me. Ugh!"

"You'd better let me take you in," said her companion tenderly; "the well isn't always wholesome, especially in the hot weather.

"Let's make a move."

The girl gave an obstinate little shake, and settled herself more securely on her seat.

"Smoke your cigar in peace," she said quietly. "I am settled here for a quiet talk. Has anything been heard of Wilfred yet?"

"Nothing."

"Quite a dramatic disappearance, isn't it?" she continued. "Another scrape, I suppose, and another letter for you in the same old strain; 'Dear Jem, help me out.'"

Jem Benson blew a cloud of fragrant smoke into the air, and holding his cigar between his teeth brushed away the ash from his coat sleeves.

"I wonder what he would have done without you," said the girl, pressing his arm affectionately. "Gone under long ago, I suppose. When we are married, Jem, I shall presume upon the relationship to lecture him. He is very wild, but he has his good points, poor fellow."

"I never saw them," said Benson, with startling bitterness. "God knows I never saw them."

"He is nobody's enemy but his own," said the girl, startled by this outburst.

"You don't know much about him," said the other, sharply. "He was not above blackmail; not above ruining the life of a friend to do himself a benefit. A loafer, a cur, and a liar!"

The girl looked up at him soberly but timidly and took his arm without a word, and they both sat silent while evening deepened into night and the beams of the moon, filtering through the branches, surrounded them with a silver network. Her head sank upon his shoulder, till suddenly with a sharp cry she sprang to her feet.

"What was that?" she cried breathlessly.

"What was what?" demanded Benson, springing up and clutching her fast by the arm.

She caught her breath and tried to laugh.

"You're hurting me, Jem."

His hold relaxed.

"What is the matter?" he asked gently.

"What was it startled you?"

"I was startled," she said, slowly, putting her hands on his shoulder. "I suppose the words I used just now are ringing in my ears, but I fancied that somebody behind us whispered 'Jem, help me out.'"

"Fancy," repeated Benson, and his voice shook; "but these fancies are not good for you. You – are frightened – at the dark and the gloom of these trees. Let me take you back to the house."

"No, I'm not frightened," said the girl, reseating herself. "I should never be really frightened of anything when you were with me, Jem. I'm surprised at myself for being so silly."

The man made no reply but stood, a strong, dark figure, a yard or two from the well, as though waiting for her to join him.

"Come and sit down, sir," cried Olive, patting the brickwork with her small, white hand, "one would think that you did not like your company."

He obeyed slowly and took a seat by her side, drawing so hard at his cigar that the light of it shone upon his fare at every breath. He passed his arm, firm and rigid as steel, behind her, with his hand resting on the brickwork beyond.

"Are you warm enough?" he asked tenderly, as she made a little movement. "Pretty fair," she shivered; "one oughtn't to be cold at this time of the year, but there's a cold, damp air comes up from the well."

As she spoke a faint splash sounded from the depths below, and for the second time that evening, she sprang from the well with a little cry of dismay.

"What is it now?" he asked in a fearful voice. He stood by her side and gazed at the well, as though half expecting to see the cause of her alarm emerge from it.

"Oh, my bracelet," she cried in distress, "my poor mother's bracelet. I've dropped it down the well."

"Your bracelet!" repeated Benson, dully. "Your bracelet? The diamond one?"

"The one that was my mother's," said Olive. "Oh, we can get it back surely. We must have the water drained off."

"Your bracelet!" repeated Benson, stupidly.

"Jem," said the girl in terrified tones, "dear Jem, what is the matter?"

For the man she loved was standing regarding her with horror. The moon which touched it was not responsible for all the whiteness of the distorted face, and she shrank back in fear to the edge of the well. He saw her fear and by a mighty effort regained his composure and took her hand.

"Poor little girl," he murmured, "you frightened me. I was not looking when you cried, and I thought that you were slipping from my arms, down – down –"

His voice broke, and the girl throwing herself into his arms clung to him convulsively.

"There, there," said Benson, fondly, "don't cry, don't cry."

"Tomorrow," said Olive, half-laughing, half-crying, "we will all come round the well with hook and line and fish for it. It will be quite a new sport."

"No, we must try some other way," said Benson. "You shall have it back."

"How?" asked the girl.

"You shall see," said Benson. "Tomorrow morning at latest you shall have it back. Till then promise me that you will not mention your loss to anyone. Promise."

"I promise," said Olive, wonderingly. "But why not?"

"It is of great value, for one thing, and – but there – there are many reasons. For one thing it is my duty to get it for you."

"Wouldn't you like to jump down for it?" she asked mischievously. "Listen."

She stooped for a stone and dropped it down.

"Fancy being where that is now," she said, peering into the blackness; "fancy going round and round like a mouse in a pail, clutching at the slimy sides, with the water filling your mouth, and looking up to the little patch of sky above."

"You had better come in," said Benson, very quietly. "You are developing a taste for the morbid and horrible."

The girl turned, and taking his arm walked slowly in the direction of the house; Mrs. Benson, who was sitting in the porch, rose to receive them.

"You shouldn't have kept her out so long," she said chidingly. "Where have you been?"

"Sitting on the well," said Olive, smiling, "discussing our future."

"I don't believe that place is healthy," said Mrs. Benson, emphatically. "I really think it might be filled in, Jem."

"All right," said her son, slowly. "Pity it wasn't filled in long ago."

He took the chair vacated by his mother as she entered the house with Olive, and with his hands hanging limply over the sides sat in deep thought. After a time he rose, and going upstairs to a room which was set apart for sporting requisites selected a sea fishing line and some hooks and stole softly downstairs again. He walked swiftly across the park in the direction of the well, turning before he entered the shadow of the trees to look back at the lighted windows of the house. Then having arranged his line he sat on the edge of the well and cautiously lowered it.

He sat with his lips compressed, occasionally looking about him in a startled fashion, as though he half expected to see something peering at him from the belt of trees. Time after time he lowered his line until at length in pulling it up he heard a little metallic tinkle against the side of the well.

He held his breath then, and forgetting his fears drew the line in inch by inch, so as not to lose its precious burden. His pulse beat rapidly, and his eyes were bright. As the line came slowly in he saw the catch hanging to the hook, and with a steady hand drew the last few feet in. Then he saw that instead of the bracelet he had hooked a bunch of keys.

With a faint cry he shook them from the hook into the water below, and stood breathing heavily. Not a sound broke the stillness of the night. He walked up and down a bit and stretched his great muscles; then he came back to the well and resumed his task.

For an hour or more the line was lowered without result. In his eagerness he forgot his fears, and with eyes bent down the well fished slowly and carefully. Twice the hook became entangled in something, and was with difficulty released. It caught a third time, and all his efforts failed to free it. Then he dropped the line down the well, and with head bent walked toward the house.

He went first to the stables at the rear, and then retiring to his room for some time paced restlessly up and down. Then without removing his clothes he flung himself upon the bed and fell into a troubled sleep.

III

LONG BEFORE anybody else was astir he arose and stole softly downstairs. The sunlight was stealing in at every crevice, and flashing in long streaks across the darkened rooms. The dining-room into which he looked struck chill and cheerless in the dark yellow light which came through the lowered blinds. He remembered that it had the same appearance when his father lay dead in the house; now, as then, everything seemed ghastly and unreal; the very chairs standing as their occupants had left them the night before seemed to be indulging in some dark communication of ideas.

Slowly and noiselessly he opened the hall door and passed into the fragrant air beyond. The sun was shining on the drenched grass and trees, and a slowly vanishing white mist rolled like smoke about the grounds. For a moment he stood, breathing deeply the sweet air of the morning, and then walked slowly in the direction of the stables.

The rusty creaking of a pump-handle and a spatter of water upon the red-tiled courtyard showed that somebody else was astir, and a few steps farther he beheld a brawny, sandy-haired man gasping wildly under severe self-infliction at the pump.

"Everything ready, George?" he asked quietly.

"Yes, sir," said the man, straightening up suddenly and touching his forehead. "Bob's just finishing the arrangements inside. It's a lovely morning for a dip. The water in that well must be just icy."

"Be as quick as you can," said Benson, impatiently.

"Very good, sir," said George, burnishing his face harshly with a very small towel which had been hanging over the top of the pump. "Hurry up, Bob."

In answer to his summons a man appeared at the door of the stable with a coil of stout rope over his arm and a large metal candlestick in his hand.

"Just to try the air, sir," said George, following his master's glance, "a well gets rather foul sometimes, but if a candle can live down it, a man can."

His master nodded, and the man, hastily pulling up the neck of his shirt and thrusting his arms into his coat, followed him as he led the way slowly to the well.

"Beg pardon, sir," said George, drawing up to his side, "but you are not looking over and above well this morning. If you'll let me go down I'd enjoy the bath."

"No, no," said Benson, peremptorily.

"You ain't fit to go down, sir," persisted his follower. "I've never seen you look so before. Now if –"

"Mind your business," said his master curtly.

George became silent and the three walked with swinging strides through the long wet grass to the well. Bob flung the rope on the ground and at a sign from his master handed him the candlestick.

"Here's the line for it, sir," said Bob, fumbling in his pockets.

Benson took it from him and slowly tied it to the candlestick. Then he placed it on the edge of the well, and striking a match, lit the candle and began slowly to lower it.

"Hold hard, sir," said George, quickly, laying his hand on his arm, "you must tilt it or the string'll burn through."

Even as he spoke the string parted and the candlestick fell into the water below.

Benson swore quietly.

"I'll soon get another," said George, starting up.

"Never mind, the well's all right," said Benson.

"It won't take a moment, sir," said the other over his shoulder.

"Are you master here, or am I?" said Benson hoarsely.

George came back slowly, a glance at his master's face stopping the protest upon his tongue, and he stood by watching him sulkily as he sat on the well and removed his outer garments. Both men watched him curiously, as having completed his preparations he stood grim and silent with his hands by his sides.

"I wish you'd let me go, sir," said George, plucking up courage to address him. "You ain't fit to go, you've got a chill or something. I shouldn't wonder it's the typhoid. They've got it in the village bad."

For a moment Benson looked at him angrily, then his gaze softened. "Not this time, George," he said, quietly. He took the looped end of the rope and placed it under his arms, and sitting down threw one leg over the side of the well.

"How are you going about it, sir?" queried George, laying hold of the rope and signing to Bob to do the same.

"I'll call out when I reach the water," said Benson; "then pay out three yards more quickly so that I can get to the bottom."

"Very good, sir," answered both.

Their master threw the other leg over the coping and sat motionless. His back was turned toward the men as he sat with head bent, looking down the shaft. He sat for so long that George became uneasy.

"All right, sir?" he inquired.

"Yes," said Benson, slowly. "If I tug at the rope, George, pull up at once. Lower away."

The rope passed steadily through their hands until a hollow cry from the darkness below and a faint splashing warned them that he had reached the water. They gave him three yards more and stood with relaxed grasp and strained ears, waiting.

"He's gone under," said Bob in a low voice.

The other nodded, and moistening his huge palms took a firmer grip of the rope.

Fully a minute passed, and the men began to exchange uneasy glances. Then a sudden tremendous jerk followed by a series of feebler ones nearly tore the rope from their grasp.

"Pull!" shouted George, placing one foot on the side and hauling desperately. "Pull! Pull! He's stuck fast; he's not coming; PULL!"

In response to their terrific exertions the rope came slowly in, inch by inch, until at length a violent splashing was heard, and at the same moment a scream of unutterable horror came echoing up the shaft.

"What a weight he is!" panted Bob. "He's stuck fast or something. Keep still, sir; for heaven's sake, keep still."

For the taut rope was being jerked violently by the struggles of the weight at the end of it. Both men with grunts and sighs hauled it in foot by foot.

"All right, sir," cried George, cheerfully.

He had one foot against the well, and was pulling manfully; the burden was nearing the top. A long pull and a strong pull, and the face of a dead man with mud in the eyes and nostrils came peering over the edge. Behind it was the ghastly face of his master; but this he saw too late, for with a great cry he let go his hold of the rope and stepped back. The suddenness overthrew his assistant, and the rope tore through his hands. There was a frightful splash.

"You fool!" stammered Bob, and ran to the well helplessly.

"Run!" cried George. "Run for another line."

He bent over the coping and called eagerly down as his assistant sped back to the stables shouting wildly. His voice re-echoed down the shaft, but all else was silence.

In the Penal Colony

Franz Kafka

"IT'S A PECULIAR apparatus," said the Officer to the Traveler, gazing with a certain admiration at the device, with which he was, of course, thoroughly familiar. It appeared that the Traveler had responded to the invitation of the Commandant only out of politeness, when he had been invited to attend the execution of a soldier condemned for disobeying and insulting his superior. Of course, interest in the execution was not very high, not even in the penal colony itself. At least, here in the small, deep, sandy valley, closed in on all sides by barren slopes, apart from the Officer and the Traveler there were present only the Condemned, a vacant-looking man with a broad mouth and dilapidated hair and face, and the Soldier, who held the heavy chain to which were connected the small chains which bound the Condemned Man by his feet and wrist bones, as well as by his neck, and which were also linked to each other by connecting chains. The Condemned Man had an expression of such dog-like resignation that it looked as if one could set him free to roam around the slopes and would only have to whistle at the start of the execution for him to return.

The Traveler had little interest in the apparatus and walked back and forth behind the Condemned Man, almost visibly indifferent, while the Officer took care of the final preparations. Sometimes he crawled under the apparatus, which was built deep into the earth, and sometimes he climbed up a ladder to inspect the upper parts. These were really jobs which could have been left to a mechanic, but the Officer carried them out with great enthusiasm, maybe because he was particularly fond of this apparatus or maybe because there was some other reason why one could not trust the work to anyone else. "It's all ready now!" he finally cried and climbed back down the ladder. He was unusually tired, breathing with his mouth wide open, and he had pushed two fine lady's handkerchiefs under the collar of his uniform.

"These uniforms are really too heavy for the tropics," the Traveler said, instead of asking some questions about the apparatus, as the Officer had expected. "That's true," said the Officer. He washed the oil and grease from his dirty hands in a bucket of water standing ready, "but they mean home, and we don't want to lose our homeland." "Now, have a look at this apparatus," he added immediately, drying his hands with a towel and pointing to the device. "Up to this point I had to do some work by hand, but from now on the apparatus should work entirely on its own." The Traveler nodded and followed the Officer. The latter tried to protect himself against all eventualities by saying, "Of course, breakdowns do happen. I really hope none will occur today, but we must be prepared for it. The apparatus is supposed to keep going for twelve hours without interruption. But if any breakdowns do occur, they'll only be very minor, and we'll deal with them right away."

"Don't you want to sit down?" he asked finally, as he pulled out a chair from a pile of cane chairs and offered it to the Traveler. The latter could not refuse. He sat on the edge of the pit, into which he cast a fleeting glance. It was not very deep. On one side of the hole the piled earth was heaped up into a wall; on the other side stood the apparatus. "I don't know," the officer said, "whether the Commandant has already explained the apparatus to you." The Traveler made a vague gesture with his hand. That was good enough for the Officer, for now he could explain the apparatus himself.

"This apparatus," he said, grasping a connecting rod and leaning against it, "is our previous Commandant's invention. I also worked with him on the very first tests and took part in all the work right up to its completion. However, the credit for the invention belongs to him alone. Have you heard of our previous Commandant? No? Well, I'm not claiming too much when I say that the organization of the entire penal colony is his work. We, his friends, already knew at the time of his death that the administration of the colony was so self-contained that even if his successor had a thousand new plans in mind, he would not be able to alter anything of the old plan, at least not for several years. And our prediction has held. The New Commandant has had to recognize that. It's a shame that you didn't know the previous Commandant!"

"However," the Officer said, interrupting himself, "I'm chattering, and his apparatus stands here in front of us. As you see, it consists of three parts. With the passage of time certain popular names have been developed for each of these parts. The one underneath is called the bed, the upper one is called the inscriber, and here in the middle, this moving part is called the harrow." "The harrow?" the Traveler asked. He had not been listening with full attention. The sun was excessively strong, trapped in the shadowless valley, and one could hardly collect one's thoughts. So the Officer appeared to him all the more admirable in his tight tunic weighed down with epaulettes and festooned with braid, ready to go on parade, as he explained the matter so eagerly and, while he was talking, adjusted screws here and there with a screwdriver.

The Soldier appeared to be in a state similar to the Traveler. He had wound the Condemned Man's chain around both his wrists and was supporting himself with his hand on his weapon, letting his head hang backward, not bothering about anything. The Traveler was not surprised at that, for the Officer spoke French, and clearly neither the Soldier nor the Condemned Man understood the language. So it was all the more striking that the Condemned Man, in spite of that, did what he could to follow the Officer's explanation. With a sort of sleepy persistence he kept directing his gaze to the place where the Officer had just pointed, and when the question from the Traveler interrupted the Officer, the Condemned Man looked at the Traveler, too, just as the Officer was doing.

"Yes, the harrow," said the Officer. "The name fits. The needles are arranged as in a harrow, and the whole thing is driven like a harrow, although it stays in one place and is, in principle, much more artistic. You'll understand in a moment. The condemned is laid out here on the bed. First, I'll describe the apparatus and only then let the procedure go to work. That way you'll be able to follow it better. Also a sprocket in the inscriber is excessively worn. It really squeaks. When it's in motion one can hardly make oneself understood. Unfortunately replacement parts are difficult to come by in this place. So, here is the bed, as I said. The whole thing is

completely covered with a layer of cotton wool, the purpose of which you'll find out
in a moment. The condemned man is laid out on his stomach on the cotton wool –
naked, of course. There are straps for the hands here, for the feet here, and for the
throat here, to tie him in securely. At the head of the bed here, where the man, as
I have mentioned, first lies face down, is this small protruding lump of felt, which
can easily be adjusted so that it presses right into the man's mouth. Its purpose is
to prevent him screaming and biting his tongue to pieces. Of course, the man has
to let the felt in his mouth – otherwise the straps around his throat would break his
neck." "That's cotton wool?" asked the Traveler and bent down. "Yes, it is," said the
Officer smiling, "feel it for yourself."

He took the Traveler's hand and led him over to the bed. "It's a specially prepared
cotton wool. That's why it looks so unrecognizable. I'll get around to mentioning
its purpose in a moment." The Traveler was already being won over a little to the
apparatus. With his hand over his eyes to protect them from the sun, he looked at
the apparatus in the hole. It was a massive construction. The bed and the inscriber
were the same size and looked like two dark chests. The inscriber was set about two
metres above the bed, and the two were joined together at the corners by four brass
rods, which almost reflected the sun. The harrow hung between the chests on a band
of steel.

The Officer had hardly noticed the earlier indifference of the Traveler, but he did
have a sense now of how the latter's interest was being aroused for the first time.
So he paused in his explanation in order to allow the Traveler time to observe the
apparatus undisturbed. The Condemned Man imitated the Traveler, but since he
could not put his hand over his eyes, he blinked upward with his eyes uncovered.

"So now the man is lying down," said the Traveler. He leaned back in his chair and
crossed his legs.

"Yes," said the Officer, pushing his cap back a little and running his hand over
his hot face. "Now, listen. Both the bed and the inscriber have their own electric
batteries. The bed needs them for itself, and the inscriber for the harrow. As soon
as the man is strapped in securely, the bed is set in motion. It quivers with tiny,
very rapid oscillations from side to side and up and down simultaneously. You will
have seen similar devices in mental hospitals. Only with our bed all movements are
precisely calibrated, for they must be meticulously coordinated with the movements
of the harrow. But it's the harrow which has the job of actually carrying out
the sentence."

"What is the sentence?" the Traveler asked. "You don't even know that?" asked the
Officer in astonishment and bit his lip. "Forgive me if my explanations are perhaps
confused. I really do beg your pardon. Previously it was the Commandant's habit to
provide such explanations. But the New Commandant has excused himself from this
honourable duty. The fact that with such an eminent visitor" – the traveler tried to
deflect the honour with both hands, but the officer insisted on the expression – "that
with such an eminent visitor he didn't even once make him aware of the form of
our sentencing is yet again something new, which..." He had a curse on his lips, but
controlled himself and said merely: "I was not informed about it. It's not my fault. In
any case, I am certainly the person best able to explain our style of sentencing, for
here I am carrying" – he patted his breast pocket – "the relevant diagrams drawn by
the previous Commandant."

"Diagrams made by the Commandant himself?" asked the Traveler. "Then was he in his own person a combination of everything? Was he soldier, judge, engineer, chemist, and draftsman?"

"He was indeed," said the Officer, nodding his head with a fixed and thoughtful expression. Then he looked at his hands, examining them. They didn't seem to him clean enough to handle the diagrams. So he went to the bucket and washed them again. Then he pulled out a small leather folder and said, "Our sentence does not sound severe. The law which a condemned man has violated is inscribed on his body with the harrow. This Condemned Man, for example," and the Officer pointed to the man, "will have inscribed on his body, 'Honour your superiors.'"

The Traveler had a quick look at the man. When the Officer was pointing at him, the man kept his head down and appeared to be directing all his energy into listening in order to learn something. But the movements of his thick pouting lips showed clearly that he was incapable of understanding anything. The Traveler wanted to raise various questions, but after looking at the Condemned Man he merely asked, "Does he know his sentence?" "No," said the Officer. He wished to get on with his explanation right away, but the Traveler interrupted him: "He doesn't know his own sentence?" "No," said the Officer once more. He then paused for a moment, as if he was asking the Traveler for a more detailed reason for his question, and said, "It would be useless to give him that information. He experiences it on his own body." The Traveler really wanted to keep quiet at this point, but he felt how the Condemned Man was gazing at him – he seemed to be asking whether he could approve of the process the Officer had described. So the Traveler, who had up to this point been leaning back, bent forward again and kept up his questions, "But does he nonetheless have some general idea that he's been condemned?" "Not that either," said the Officer, and he smiled at the traveler, as if he was still waiting for some strange revelations from him. "No?" said the Traveler, wiping his forehead, "then does the man also not yet know how his defence was received?" "He has had no opportunity to defend himself," said the Officer and looked away, as if he was talking to himself and wished not to embarrass the Traveler with an explanation of matters so self-evident to him. "But he must have had a chance to defend himself," said the Traveler and stood up from his chair.

The Officer recognized that he was in danger of having his explanation of the apparatus held up for a long time. So he went to the Traveler, took him by the arm, pointed with his hand at the Condemned Man, who stood there stiffly now that the attention was so clearly directed at him – the Soldier was also pulling on his chain – and said, "The matter stands like this. Here in the penal colony I have been appointed judge. In spite of my youth. For I stood at the side of our Old Commandant in all matters of punishment, and I also know the most about the apparatus. The basic principle I use for my decisions is this: Guilt is always beyond a doubt. Other courts could not follow this principle, for they are made up of many heads and, in addition, have even higher courts above them. But that is not the case here, or at least it was not that way with the previous Commandant. It's true the New Commandant has already shown a desire to get mixed up in my court, but I've succeeded so far in fending him off. And I'll continue to be successful. You want this case explained. It's simple – just like all of them. This morning a captain laid a charge that this man, who is assigned to him as a servant and who sleeps before his door, had been sleeping on duty. For his task is to stand up every time the clock strikes the hour and salute in front of the captain's door. That's certainly not a difficult duty – and it's necessary, since he is supposed to remain fresh both for guarding and for service. Yesterday night the captain wanted to check whether his servant was fulfilling his duty. He opened the door on the stroke of two and found him curled up asleep. He got his horsewhip and hit him across the face. Now, instead of standing up and begging for forgiveness, the man grabbed his master by the legs, shook him, and cried out, 'Throw away that whip or I'll eat you up.' Those are the facts. The captain came to me an hour ago. I wrote up his statement and right after that the sentence. Then I had the man chained up. It was all very simple. If I had first summoned the man and interrogated him, the result would have been confusion. He would have lied, and if I had been successful in refuting his lies, he would have replaced them with new lies, and so forth. But now I have him, and I won't release him again. Now, does that clarify everything? But time is passing. We should be starting the execution, and I haven't finished explaining the apparatus yet."

He urged the traveler to sit down in his chair, moved to the apparatus again, and started, "As you see, the shape of the harrow corresponds to the shape of a man. This is the harrow for the upper body, and here are the harrows for the legs. This small cutter is the only one designated for the head. Is that clear to you?" He leaned forward to the Traveler in a friendly way, ready to give the most comprehensive explanation.

The Traveler looked at the harrow with a wrinkled frown. The information about the judicial procedures had not satisfied him. However, he had to tell himself that here it was a matter of a penal colony, that in this place special regulations were necessary, and that one had to give precedence to military measures right down to the last detail. Beyond that, however, he had some hopes in the New Commandant, who obviously, although slowly, was intending to introduce a new procedure which the limited understanding of this Officer could not cope with.

Following this train of thought, the Traveler asked, "Will the Commandant be present at the execution?" "That is not certain," said the Officer, embarrassingly affected by the sudden question, and his friendly expression made a grimace. "That's why we need to hurry up. As much as I regret the fact, I'll have to make my explanation even shorter. But tomorrow, once the apparatus is clean again – the fact that it gets so very dirty is its only fault – I could add a detailed explanation. So now, only the most important things. When the man is lying on the bed and it starts quivering, the harrow sinks onto the body. It positions itself automatically in such a way that it touches the body only lightly with the needle tips. Once the machine is set in this position, this steel cable tightens up into a rod. And now the performance begins. Someone who is not an initiate sees no external difference among the punishments. The harrow seems to do its work uniformly. As it quivers, it sticks the tips of its needles into the body, which is also vibrating from the movement of the bed. Now, to enable someone to check on how the sentence is being carried out, the harrow is made of glass. That gave rise to certain technical difficulties with fastening the needles securely, but after several attempts we were successful. We didn't spare any efforts. And now, as the inscription is made on the body, everyone can see through the glass. Don't you want to come closer and see the needles for yourself."

The Traveler stood slowly, moved up, and bent over the harrow. "You see," the Officer said, "two sorts of needles in a multiple arrangement. Each long needle has a short one next to it. The long one inscribes, and the short one squirts water out to wash away the blood and keep the inscription always clear. The bloody water is then channeled here in small grooves and finally flows into these main gutters, and the outlet pipe takes it to the pit." The officer pointed with his finger to the exact path which the bloody water had to take. As he began to demonstrate with both hands at the mouth of the outlet pipe, in order to make his account as clear as possible, the Traveler raised his head and, feeling behind him with his hand, wanted to return to his chair. Then he saw to his horror that the Condemned Man had also, like him, accepted the Officer's invitation to inspect the arrangement of the harrow up close. He had pulled the sleeping Soldier holding the chain a little forward and was also bending over the glass. One could see how with a confused gaze he also was looking for what the two gentlemen had just observed, but how he didn't succeed because he lacked the explanation. He leaned forward this way and that. He kept running his eyes over the glass again and again. The Traveler wanted to push him back, for what he was doing was probably punishable. But the Officer held the Traveler firmly with one hand, and with the other he took a lump of earth from the wall and threw it at the Soldier. The latter opened his eyes with a start, saw what the Condemned Man had dared to do, let his weapon fall, braced his heels in the earth, and pulled the Condemned Man back, so that he immediately collapsed. The Soldier looked down at him, as he writhed around, making his chain clink. "Stand him up," cried the Officer. Then he noticed that the Condemned Man was distracting the Traveler too much. The latter was even leaning out away from the harrow, without paying any attention to it, wanting to find out what was happening to the Condemned Man. "Handle him carefully," the Officer yelled again. He ran around the apparatus, personally grabbed the Condemned Man under the armpits and, with the help of the Soldier, stood the man, whose feet kept slipping, upright.

"Now I know all about it," said the Traveler, as the Officer turned back to him again. "Except the most important thing," said the latter, grabbing the Traveler by the arm and pointing up high. "There in the inscriber is the mechanism which determines the movement of the harrow, and this mechanism is arranged according to the diagram on which the sentence is set down. I still use the diagrams of the previous Commandant. Here they are." He pulled some pages out of the leather folder. "Unfortunately I can't hand them to you. They are the most cherished thing I possess. Sit down, and I'll show you them from this distance. Then you'll be able to see it all well." He showed the first sheet. The Traveler would have been happy to say something appreciative, but all he saw was a labyrinthine series of lines, criss-crossing each other in all sort of ways. These covered the paper so thickly that only with difficulty could one make out the white spaces in between. "Read it," said the Officer. "I can't," said the Traveler. "But it's clear," said the Officer." "It's very elaborate," said the Traveler evasively, "but I can't decipher it."

"Yes," said the Officer, smiling and putting the folder back again, "it's not calligraphy for school children. One has to read it a long time. You too will finally understand it clearly. Of course, it has to be a script that isn't simple. You see, it's not supposed to kill right away, but on average over a period of twelve hours. The turning point is set for the sixth hour. There must also be many, many embellishments surrounding the basic script. The essential script moves around the body only in a narrow belt. The rest of the body is reserved for decoration. Can you now appreciate the work of the harrow and the whole apparatus? Just look at it!" He jumped up the ladder, turned a wheel, and called down, "Watch out – move to the side!" Everything started moving. If the wheel had not squeaked, it would have been marvelous. The officer threatened the wheel with his fist, as if he was surprised by the disturbance it created. Then he spread his arms, apologizing to the traveler, and quickly clambered down, in order to observe the operation of the apparatus from below.

Something was still not working properly, something only he noticed. He clambered up again and reached with both hands into the inside of the inscriber. Then, in order to descend more quickly, instead of using the ladder, he slid down on one of the poles and, to make himself understandable through the noise, strained his voice to the limit as he yelled in the traveler's ear, "Do you understand the process? The harrow is starting to write. When it's finished with the first part of the script on the man's back, the layer of cotton wool rolls and turns the body slowly onto its side to give the harrow a new area. Meanwhile those parts lacerated by the inscription are lying on the cotton wool which, because it has been specially treated, immediately stops the bleeding and prepares the script for a further deepening. Here, as the body continues to rotate, prongs on the edge of the harrow then pull the cotton wool from the wounds, throw it into the pit, and the harrow goes to work again. In this way it keeps making the inscription deeper for twelve hours. For the first six hours the condemned man goes on living almost as before. He suffers nothing but pain. After two hours, the felt is removed, for at that point the man has no more energy for screaming. Here at the head of the bed warm rice pudding is put in this electrically heated bowl. From this the man, if he feels like it, can help himself to what he can lap up with his tongue. No one passes up this opportunity. I don't know of a single one, and I have had a lot of experience. He first loses his pleasure in eating around the sixth hour. I usually kneel down at this point and observe the phenomenon. The man rarely swallows the last bit. He turns it around in his mouth and spits it into the pit. When he does that, I have to lean aside or else he'll get me in the face. But how quiet the man becomes around the sixth hour! The most stupid of them begin to understand. It starts around the eyes and spreads out from there. A look that could tempt one to lie down under the harrow. Nothing else happens. The man simply begins to decipher the inscription. He purses his lips, as if he is listening. You've seen that it's not easy to figure out the inscription with your eyes, but our man deciphers it with his wounds. True, it takes a lot of work. It requires six hours to complete. But then the harrow spits him right out and throws him into the pit, where he splashes down into the bloody water and cotton wool. Then the judgment is over, and we, the soldier and I, quickly bury him."

The Traveler had leaned his ear towards the Officer and, with his hands in his coat pockets, was observing the machine at work. The Condemned Man was also watching, but without understanding. He bent forward a little and followed the moving needles, as the Soldier, after a signal from the Officer, cut through his shirt and trousers with a knife from the back, so that they fell off the Condemned Man. He wanted to grab the falling garments to cover his bare flesh, but the Soldier held him up and shook the last rags from him. The Officer turned the machine off, and in the silence which then ensued the Condemned Man was laid out under the harrow. The chains were taken off and the straps fastened in their place. For the Condemned Man it seemed at first glance to signify almost a relief. And now the harrow sunk down a stage lower, for the Condemned was a thin man. As the needle tips touched him, a shudder went over his skin. While the Soldier was busy with the right hand, the Condemned Man stretched out his left, with no sense of its direction. But it was pointing to where the Traveler was standing. The Officer kept looking at the Traveler from the side, without taking his eyes off him, as if he was trying to read from his face the impression he was getting of the execution, which he had now explained to him, at least superficially.

The strap meant to hold the wrist ripped off. The Soldier probably had pulled on it too hard. The Soldier showed the Officer the torn-off piece of strap, wanting him to help. So the Officer went over to him and said, with his face turned towards the Traveler, "The machine is very complicated. Now and then something has to tear or break. One shouldn't let that detract from one's overall opinion. Anyway, we have an immediate replacement for the strap. I'll use a chain – even though that will affect the sensitivity of the movements for the right arm." And while he put the chain in place, he kept talking, "Our resources for maintaining the machine are very limited at the moment. Under the previous Commandant, I had free access to a cash box specially set aside for this purpose. There was a store room here in which all possible replacement parts were kept. I admit I made almost extravagant use of it. I mean earlier, not now, as the New Commandant claims. For him everything serves only as a pretext to fight against the old arrangements. Now he keeps the cash box for machinery under his own control, and if I ask him for a new strap, he demands the torn one as a piece of evidence, the new one doesn't arrive for ten days, and it's an inferior brand, of not much use to me. But how I am supposed to get the machine to work in the meantime without a strap – no one's concerned about that."

The Traveler was thinking: it's always questionable to intervene decisively in strange circumstances. He was neither a citizen of the penal colony nor a citizen of the state to which it belonged. If he wanted to condemn the execution or even hinder it, people could say to him: You're a foreigner – keep quiet. He would have nothing in response to that, but could only add that he did not understand what he was doing on this occasion, for the purpose of his traveling was merely to observe and not to alter other people's judicial systems in any way. True, at this point the way things were turning out it was very tempting. The injustice of the process and the inhumanity of the execution were beyond doubt. No one could assume that the Traveler was acting out of any sense of his own self-interest, for the Condemned Man was a stranger to him, not a countryman and not someone who invited sympathy in any way. The Traveler himself had letters of reference from high officials and had been welcomed here with great courtesy. The fact that he had been invited to this execution even seemed to indicate that people were asking for his judgment of this trial. This was all the more likely since the Commandant, as he had now heard only too clearly, was no supporter of this process and maintained an almost hostile relationship with the Officer.

Then the Traveler heard a cry of rage from the Officer. He had just shoved the stub of felt in the Condemned Man's mouth, not without difficulty, when the Condemned Man, overcome by an irresistible nausea, shut his eyes and threw up. The Officer quickly yanked him up off the stump and wanted to turn his head aside toward the pit. But it was too late. The vomit was already flowing down onto the machine. "This is all the Commandant's fault!" cried the officer and mindlessly rattled the brass rods at the front. "My machine's as filthy as a pigsty." With trembling hands he showed the Traveler what had happened. "Haven't I spent hours trying to make the Commandant understand that a day before the execution there should be no more food served. But the new lenient administration has a different opinion. Before the man is led away, the Commandant's women cram sugary things down his throat. His whole life he's fed himself on stinking fish, and now he has to eat sweets! But that would be all right – I'd have no objections – but why don't they get a new felt, the way I've been asking him for three months now? How can anyone take this felt into his mouth without feeling disgusted – something that a hundred man have sucked and bitten on it as they were dying?"

The Condemned Man had laid his head down and appeared peaceful. The Soldier was busy cleaning up the machine with the Condemned Man's shirt. The Officer went up to the Traveler, who, feeling some premonition, took a step backwards. But the Officer grasped him by the hand and pulled him aside. "I want to speak a few words to you in confidence," he said. "May I do that?" "Of course," said the Traveler and listened with his eyes lowered.

"This process and execution, which you now have an opportunity to admire, have no more open supporters in our colony. I am its only defender, just as I am the single advocate for the legacy of the Old Commandant. I can no longer think about a more extensive organization of the process – I'm using all my powers to maintain what there is at present. When the Old Commandant was alive, the colony was full of his supporters. I have something of the Old Commandant's power of persuasion, but I completely lack his power, and as a result the supporters have gone into hiding. There are still a lot of them, but no one admits to it. If you go into a tea house today – that is to say, on a day of execution – and keep your ears open, perhaps you'll hear nothing but ambiguous remarks. They are all supporters, but under the present Commandant, considering his present views, they are totally useless to me. And now I'm asking you: Should such a life's work," he pointed to the machine, "come to nothing because of this Commandant and the women influencing him? Should people let that happen? Even if one is a foreigner and only on our island for a couple of days? But there's no time to lose. People are already preparing something against my judicial proceedings. Discussions are already taking place in the Commandant's headquarters, to which I am not invited. Even your visit today seems to me typical of the whole situation. People are cowards and send you out – a foreigner. You should have seen the executions in earlier days! The entire valley was overflowing with people, even a day before the execution. They all came merely to watch. Early in the morning the Commandant appeared with his women. Fanfares woke up the entire campsite. I delivered the news that everything was ready. The whole society – and every high official had to attend – arranged itself around the machine. This pile of cane chairs is a sorry left over from that time. The machine was freshly cleaned and glowed. For almost every execution I had new replacement parts. In front of hundreds of eyes – all the spectators stood on tip toe right up to the hills there – the condemned man was laid down under the harrow by the Commandant himself. What nowadays is done by a common soldier was then my work as the senior judge, and it was a honour for me. And then the execution began! No discordant note disturbed the work of the machine. Many people did not look any more at all, but lay down with closed eyes in the sand. They all knew: now justice was being carried out. In silence people listened to nothing but the groans of the condemned man, muffled by the felt. These days the machine no longer manages to squeeze a strong groan out of the condemned man – something the felt is not capable of smothering. But back then the needles which made the inscription dripped a caustic liquid which we are not permitted to use any more today. Well, then came the sixth hour. It was impossible to grant all the requests people made to be allowed to watch from up close. The Commandant, in his wisdom, arranged that the children should be taken care of before all the rest. Naturally, I was always allowed to stand close by, because of my official position. Often I crouched down there with two small children in my arms, on my right and left. How we all took in the expression of transfiguration on the martyred face! How we held our cheeks in the glow of this justice, finally attained and already passing away! What times we had, my friend!"

The Officer had obviously forgotten who was standing in front of him. He had put his arm around the Traveler and laid his head on his shoulder. The Traveler was extremely embarrassed. Impatiently he looked away over the Officer's head. The Soldier had ended his task of cleaning and had just shaken some rice pudding into the bowl from a tin. No sooner had the Condemned Man, who seemed to have fully recovered already, noticed this than his tongue began to lick at the pudding. The Soldier kept pushing him away, for the pudding was probably meant for a later time, but in any case it was not proper for the Soldier to reach in and grab some food with his dirty hands and eat it in front of the famished Condemned Man.

The Officer quickly collected himself. "I didn't want to upset you in any way," he said. "I know it is impossible to make someone understand those days now. Besides, the machine still works and operates on its own. It operates on its own even when it is standing alone in this valley. And at the end, the body still keeps falling in that incredibly soft flight into the pit, even if hundreds of people are not gathered like flies around the hole the way they used to be. Back then we had to erect a strong railing around the pit. It was pulled out long ago."

The Traveler wanted to turn his face away from the Officer and looked aimlessly around him. The Officer thought he was looking at the wasteland of the valley. So he grabbed his hands, turned him around in order to catch his gaze, and asked, "Do you see the shame of it?"

But the Traveler said nothing. The Officer left him alone for a while. With his legs apart and his hands on his hips, the Officer stood still and looked at the ground. Then he smiled at the Traveler cheerfully and said, "Yesterday I was nearby when the Commandant invited you. I heard the invitation. I know the Commandant. I understood right away what he intended with his invitation. Although his power might be sufficiently great to take action against me, he doesn't yet dare to. But my guess is that with you he is exposing me to the judgment of a respected foreigner. He calculates things with care. You are now in your second day on the island. You didn't know the Old Commandant and his way of thinking. You are trapped in a European way of seeing things. Perhaps you are fundamentally opposed to the death penalty in general and to this kind of mechanical style of execution in particular. Moreover, you see how the execution is a sad procedure, without any public participation, using a partially damaged machine. Now, if we take all this together (so the Commandant thinks) surely one could easily imagine that that you would not consider my procedure proper? And if you didn't consider it right, you wouldn't keep quiet about it – I'm still speaking the mind of the Commandant – for you no doubt have faith that your tried-and-true convictions are correct. It's true that you have seen many peculiar things among many peoples and have learned to respect them.

Thus, you will probably not speak out against the procedure with your full power, as you would perhaps in your own homeland. But the Commandant doesn't really need that. A casual word, merely a careless remark, is enough. It doesn't have to match your convictions at all, so long as it corresponds to his wishes. I'm certain he will use all his shrewdness to interrogate you. And his women will sit around in a circle and perk up their ears. You will say something like, 'Among us the judicial procedures are different,' or 'With us the accused is questioned before the verdict,' or 'We had torture only in the Middle Ages.' For you these observations appear as correct as they are self-evident – innocent remarks which do not impugn my procedure. But how will the Commandant take them? I see him, our excellent Commandant – the way he immediately pushes his stool aside and hurries out to the balcony – I see his women, how they stream after him. I hear his voice – the women call it a thunder voice. And now he's speaking: 'A great Western explorer who has been commissioned to inspect judicial procedures in all countries has just said that our process based on old customs is inhuman. After the verdict of such a personality it is, of course, no longer possible for me to tolerate this procedure. So from this day on I am ordering... and so forth.' You want to intervene – you didn't say what he is reporting – you didn't call my procedure inhuman; by contrast, in keeping with your deep insight, you consider it most humane and most worthy of human beings. You also admire this machinery. But it is too late. You don't even go onto the balcony, which is already filled with women. You want to attract attention. You want to cry out. But a lady's hand is covering your mouth, and I and the Old Commandant's work are lost."

The Traveler had to suppress a smile. So the work which he had considered so difficult was easy. He said evasively, "You're exaggerating my influence. The Commandant has read my letters of recommendation. He knows that I am no expert in judicial processes. If I were to express an opinion, it would be that of a lay person, no more significant than the opinion of anyone else, and in any case far less significant than the opinion of the Commandant, who, as I understand it, has very extensive powers in this penal colony. If his views of this procedure are as definite as you think they are, then I'm afraid the time has come for this procedure to end, without any need for my humble opinion."

Did the Officer understand by now? No, he did not yet get it. He shook his head vigorously, briefly looked back at the Condemned Man and the Soldier, who both flinched and stopped eating the rice, went up really close up to the Traveler, without looking into his face, but gazing at parts of his jacket, and said more gently than before: "You don't know the Commandant. Where he and all of us are concerned you are – forgive the expression – to a certain extent innocent. Your influence, believe me, cannot be overestimated. In fact, I was blissfully happy when I heard that you were to be present at the execution by yourself. This order of the Commandant was aimed at me, but now I'll turn it to my advantage. Without being distracted by false insinuations and disparaging looks – which could not have been avoided with a greater number of participants at the execution – you have listened to my explanation, looked at the machine, and are now about to view the execution. Your verdict is no doubt already fixed. If some small uncertainties remain, witnessing the execution will remove them. And now I'm asking you – help me with the Commandant!"

The Traveler did not let him go on talking. "How can I do that," he cried. "It's totally impossible. I can help you as little as I can harm you."

"You could do it," said the Officer. With some apprehension the Traveler observed that the Officer was clenching his fists. "You could do it," repeated the Officer, even more emphatically. "I have a plan which must succeed. You think your influence is insufficient. I know it will be enough. But assuming you're right, doesn't saving this whole procedure require one to try even those methods which may be inadequate? So listen to my plan. To carry it out, it's necessary, above all, for you to keep as quiet as possible today in the colony about your verdict on this procedure. Unless someone asks you directly, you should not express any view whatsoever. But what you do say must be short and vague. People should notice that it's difficult for you to speak about the subject, that you feel bitter, that, if you were to speak openly, you'd have to burst out cursing on the spot. I'm not asking you to lie, not at all. You should only give brief answers – something like, 'Yes, I've seen the execution' or 'Yes, I've heard the full explanation.' That's all – nothing further. For that will be enough of an indication for people to observe in you a certain bitterness, even if that's not what the Commandant will think. Naturally, he will completely misunderstand the issue and interpret it in his own way. My plan is based on that. Tomorrow a large meeting of all the higher administrative officials takes place at headquarters under the chairmanship of the Commandant. He, of course, understands how to turn such a meeting into a spectacle. A gallery has been built, which is always full of spectators. I'm compelled to take part in the discussions, though they fill me with disgust. In any case, you will certainly be invited to the meeting. If you follow my plan today and behave accordingly, the invitation will become an emphatic request. But should you for some inexplicable reason still not be invited, you must make sure you request an invitation. Then you'll receive one without question. Now, tomorrow you are sitting with the women in the commandant's box. With frequent upward glances he reassures himself that you are there. After various trivial and ridiculous agenda items designed for the spectators – mostly harbour construction – always harbour construction – the judicial process comes up for discussion. If it's not raised by the Commandant himself or does not occur soon enough, I'll make sure that it comes up. I'll stand up and report on today's execution. Really briefly – just the report. Such a report is not really customary; however, I'll do it, nonetheless. The Commandant thanks me, as always, with a friendly smile. And now he cannot restrain himself. He seizes this excellent opportunity. 'The report of the execution,' he'll say, or something like that, 'has just been given. I would like to add to this report only the fact that this particular execution was attended by the great explorer whose visit confers such extraordinary honour on our colony, as you all know. Even the significance of our meeting today has been increased by his presence. Should we not now ask this great explorer for his appraisal of the execution based on old customs and of the process which preceded it?' Of course, there is the noise of applause everywhere, universal agreement. And I'm louder than anyone. The Commandant bows before you and says, 'Then in everyone's name, I'm putting the question to you.' And now you step up to the railing. Place your hands where everyone can see them. Otherwise the ladies will grab them and play with your fingers. And now finally come your remarks. I don't know how I'll bear the tension up to then. In your speech you mustn't hold back. Let truth resound. Lean over the railing and shout it out – yes, yes, roar your opinion at the Commandant, your unshakeable opinion. But perhaps you don't want to do that. It doesn't suit your character. Perhaps in your country people behave differently in such situations. That's all right. That's perfectly satisfactory. Don't stand up at all. Just say a couple of words. Whisper them so that only the officials underneath you can just hear them. That's enough. You don't even have to say anything at all about the lack of attendance at the execution or about the squeaky wheel, the torn strap, the disgusting felt. No. I'll take over all further details, and, believe me, if my speech doesn't chase him out of the room, it will force him to his knees, so he'll have to admit it: 'Old Commandant, I bow down before you.' That's my plan. Do you want to help me carry it out? But, of course, you want to. More than that – you have to."

And the officer gripped the traveler by both arms and looked at him, breathing heavily into his face. He had yelled the last sentences so loudly that even the Soldier and the Condemned Man were paying attention. Although they couldn't understand a thing, they stopped eating and looked over at the Traveler, still chewing.

From the start the Traveler had had no doubts about the answer he must give. He had experienced too much in his life to be able to waver here. Basically he was honest and unafraid. Still, with the Soldier and the Condemned Man looking at him, he hesitated a moment. But finally he said, as he had to, "No." The Officer's eyes blinked several times, but he did not take his eyes off the Traveler. "Would you like an explanation," asked the Traveler. The Officer nodded dumbly. "I am opposed to this procedure," said the Traveler. "Even before you took me into your confidence – and, of course, I will never abuse your confidence under any circumstances – I was already thinking about whether I was entitled to intervene against this procedure and whether my intervention could have the smallest chance of success. And if that was the case, it was clear to me whom I had to turn to first of all – naturally, to the Commandant. You clarified the issue for me even more, but without reinforcing my decision in any way – quite the reverse. I find your conviction genuinely moving, even if it cannot deter me."

The Officer remained quiet, turned toward the machine, grabbed one of the brass rods, and then, leaning back a little, looked up at the inscriber, as if he was checking that everything was in order. The Soldier and the Condemned Man seemed to have made friends with each other. The Condemned Man was making signs to the Soldier, although, given the tight straps on him, this was difficult for him to do. The Soldier was leaning into him. The Condemned Man whispered something to him, and the Soldier nodded. The Traveler went over to the Officer and said, "You don't yet know what I'll do. Yes, I will tell the Commandant my opinion of the procedure – not in a meeting, but in private. In addition, I won't stay here long enough to be able to get called in to some meeting or other. Early tomorrow morning I leave, or at least I go on board ship." It didn't look as if the Officer had been listening. "So the process has not convinced you," he said to himself, smiling the way an old man smiles over the silliness of a child, concealing his own true thoughts behind that smile.

"Well then, it's time," he said finally and suddenly looked at the Traveler with bright eyes which contained some sort of demand, some appeal for participation. "Time for what?" asked the Traveler uneasily. But there was no answer.

"You are free," the Officer told the Condemned Man in his own language. At first the man did not believe him. "You are free now," said the Officer. For the first time the face of the Condemned Man showed signs of real life. Was it the truth? Was it only the Officer's mood, which could change? Had the foreign Traveler brought him a reprieve? What was it? That's what the man's face seemed to be asking. But not for long. Whatever the case might be, if he could he wanted to be truly free, and he began to shake back and forth, as much as the harrow permitted.

"You're tearing my straps," cried the Officer. "Be still! We'll undo them right away." And, giving a signal to the Soldier, he set to work with him. The Condemned Man said nothing and smiled slightly to himself. He turned his face to the Officer and then to the Soldier and then back again, without ignoring the Traveler.

"Pull him out," the Officer ordered the Soldier. This process required a certain amount of care because of the harrow. The Condemned Man already had a few small wounds on his back, thanks to his own impatience.

From this point on, however, the Officer paid him hardly any attention. He went up to the Traveler, pulled out the small leather folder once more, leafed through it, finally found the sheet he was looking for, and showed it to the Traveler. "Read that," he said. "I can't," said the Traveler. "I've already told you I can't read these pages." "But take a close look at the page," said the Officer, and moved up right next to the Traveler in order to read with him. When that didn't help, he raised his little finger high up over the paper, as if the page must not be touched under any circumstances, so that using this he might make the task of reading easier for the Traveler. The Traveler also made an effort so that at least he could satisfy the Officer, but it was impossible for him. Then the Officer began to spell out the inscription and then read out once again the joined up letters. "'Be just!' it states," he said. "Now you can read it." The Traveler bent so low over the paper that the Officer, afraid that he might touch it, moved it further away. The Traveler didn't say anything more, but it was clear that he was still unable to read anything. " 'Be just!' it says," the Officer remarked once again.

"That could be," said the Traveler. "I do believe that's written there." "Good," said the Officer, at least partially satisfied. He climbed up the ladder, holding the paper. With great care he set the page in the inscriber and appeared to rotate the gear mechanism completely around. This was very tiring work. It must have required him to deal with extremely small wheels. He had to inspect the gears so closely that sometimes his head disappeared completely into the inscriber.

The Traveler followed this work from below without looking away. His neck grew stiff, and his eyes found the sunlight pouring down from the sky painful. The Soldier and the Condemned Man were keeping each other busy. With the tip of his bayonet the Soldier pulled out the Condemned Man's shirt and trousers which were lying in the hole. The shirt was horribly dirty, and the Condemned Man washed it in the bucket of water. When he was putting on his shirt and trousers, the Soldier and the Condemned Man had to laugh out loud, for the pieces of clothing were cut in two up the back. Perhaps the Condemned Man thought that it was his duty to amuse the Soldier. In his ripped-up clothes he circled around the Soldier, who crouched down on the ground, laughed, and slapped his knees. But they restrained themselves out of consideration for the two gentlemen present.

When the Officer was finally finished up on the machine, with a smile he looked over the whole thing and all its parts one more time, and this time closed the cover of the inscriber, which had been open up to this point. He climbed down, looked into the hole and then at the Condemned Man, observed with satisfaction that he had pulled out his clothes, then went to the bucket of water to wash his hands, recognized too late that it was disgustingly dirty, and was upset that now he couldn't wash his hands. Finally he pushed them into the sand. This option didn't satisfy him, but he had to do what he could in the circumstances. Then he stood up and began to unbutton the coat of his uniform. As he did this, the two lady's handkerchiefs, which he had pushed into the back of his collar, fell into his hands. "Here you have your handkerchiefs," he said and threw them over to the Condemned Man. And to the Traveler he said by way of an explanation, "Presents from the ladies."

In spite of the obvious speed with which he took off the coat of his uniform and then undressed himself completely, he handled each piece of clothing very carefully, even running his fingers over the silver braids on his tunic with special care and shaking a tassel into place. But in great contrast to this care, as soon he was finished handling an article of clothing, he immediately flung it angrily into the hole. The last items he had left were his short sword and its harness. He pulled the sword out of its scabbard, broke it in pieces, gathered up everything – the pieces of the sword, the scabbard, and the harness – and threw them away so forcefully that they rattled against each other down in the pit.

Now he stood there naked. The Traveler bit his lip and said nothing. For he was aware what would happen, but he had no right to hinder the Officer in any way. If the judicial process to which the officer clung was really so close to the point of being cancelled – perhaps as a result of the intervention of the Traveler, something to which he for his part felt duty-bound – then the Officer was now acting in a completely correct manner. In his place, the Traveler would not have acted any differently.

The Soldier and the Condemned Man at first didn't understand a thing. To begin with they didn't look, not even once. The Condemned Man was extremely happy to get the handkerchiefs back, but he couldn't enjoy them very long, for the Soldier snatched them from him with a quick grab, which he had not anticipated. The Condemned Man then tried to pull the handkerchiefs out from the Soldier's belt, where he had put them for safe keeping, but the Soldier was too wary. So they were fighting, half in jest. Only when the Officer was fully naked did they start to pay attention. The Condemned Man especially seemed to be struck by a premonition of some sort of significant transformation. What had happened to him was now taking place with the Officer. Perhaps this time the procedure would play itself out to its conclusion. The foreign Traveler had probably given the order. So that was revenge. Without having suffered all the way to the end himself, nonetheless he would be completely revenged. A wide, silent laugh now appeared on his face and did not go away.

The Officer, however, had turned towards the machine. If earlier on it had already become clear that he understood the machine thoroughly, one might well get alarmed now at the way he handled it and how it obeyed. He only had to bring his hand near the harrow for it to rise and sink several times, until it had reached the correct position to make room for him. He only had to grasp the bed by the edges, and it already began to quiver. The stump of felt moved up to his mouth. One could see how the Officer really didn't want to accept it, but his hesitation was only momentary – he immediately submitted and took it in. Everything was ready, except that the straps still hung down on the sides. But they were clearly unnecessary. The Officer did not have to be strapped down. When the Condemned Man saw the loose straps, he thought the execution would be incomplete unless they were fastened. He waved eagerly to the Soldier, and they ran over to strap in the Officer. The latter had already stuck out his foot to kick the crank designed to set the inscriber in motion.

Then he saw the two men coming. So he pulled his foot back and let himself be strapped in. But now he could no longer reach the crank. Neither the Soldier nor the Condemned Man would find it, and the Traveler was determined not to touch it. But that was unnecessary. Hardly were the straps attached when the machine already started working. The bed quivered, the needles danced on his skin, and the harrow swung up and down. The Traveler had already been staring for some time before he remembered that a wheel in the inscriber was supposed to squeak. But everything was quiet, without the slightest audible hum.

Because of its silent working, the machine did not really attract attention. The Traveler looked over at the Soldier and the Condemned Man. The Condemned Man was the livelier of the two. Everything in the machine interested him. At times he bent down – at other times he stretched up, all the time pointing with his forefinger in order to show something to the Soldier. For the Traveler it was embarrassing. He was determined to remain here until the end, but he could no longer endure the sight of the two men. "Go home," he said. The Soldier might have been ready to do that, but the Condemned Man took the order as a direct punishment. With his hands folded he begged and pleaded to be allowed to stay there. And when the Traveler shook his head and was unwilling to give in, he even knelt down. Seeing that orders were of no help here, the Traveler wanted to go over and chase the two away.

Then he heard a noise from up in the inscriber. He looked up. So was the gear wheel going out of alignment? But it was something else. The lid on the inscriber was lifting up slowly. Then it fell completely open. The teeth of a cog wheel were exposed and lifted up. Soon the entire wheel appeared. It was as if some huge force was compressing the inscriber, so that there was no longer sufficient room for this wheel. The wheel rolled all the way to the edge of the inscriber, fell down, rolled upright a bit in the sand, and then fell over and lay still. But already up on the inscriber another gear wheel was moving upwards. Several others followed – large ones, small ones, ones hard to distinguish. With each of them the same thing happened. One kept thinking that now the inscriber must surely be empty, but then a new cluster with lots of parts would move up, fall down, roll in the sand, and lie still. With all this going on, the Condemned Man totally forgot the Traveler's order. The gear wheels completely delighted him. He kept wanting to grab one, and at the same time he was urging the Soldier to help him. But he kept pulling his hand back startled, for immediately another wheel followed, which, at least in its initial rolling, surprised him.

The Traveler, by contrast, was very upset. Obviously the machine was breaking up. Its quiet operation had been an illusion. He felt as if he had to look after the Officer, now that the latter could no longer look after himself. But while the falling gear wheels were claiming all his attention, he had neglected to look at the rest of the machine. However, when he now bent over the harrow, once the last gear wheel had left the inscriber, he had a new, even more unpleasant surprise. The harrow was not writing but only stabbing, and the bed was not rolling the body, but lifting it, quivering, up into the needles. The Traveler wanted to reach in to stop the whole thing, if possible. This was not the torture the Officer wished to attain. It was murder, pure and simple. He stretched out his hands. But at that point the harrow was already moving upwards and to the side, with the skewered body – just as it did in other cases, but only in the twelfth hour. Blood flowed out in hundreds of streams, not mixed with water – the water tubes had also failed to work this time. Then one last thing went wrong: the body would not come loose from the needles. Its blood streamed out, but it hung over the pit without falling. The harrow wanted to move back to its original position, but, as if it realized that it could not free itself of its load, it remained over the hole.

"Help," the Traveler yelled out to the Soldier and the Condemned Man and grabbed the Officer's feet. He wanted to push against the feet himself and have the two others grab the Officer's head from the other side, so he could be slowly taken off the needles. But now the two men could not make up their mind whether to come or not. The Condemned Man turned away at once. The Traveler had to go over to him and drag him to the Officer's head by force. At this point, almost against his will, he looked at the face of the corpse. It was as it had been in his life. He could discover no sign of the promised transfiguration. What all the others had found in the machine, the Officer had not. His lips were pressed firmly together, his eyes were open and looked as they had when he was alive, his gaze was calm and convinced. The tip of a large iron needle had gone through his forehead.

* * *

As the Traveler, with the Soldier and the Condemned Man behind him, came to the first houses in the colony, the Soldier pointed to one and said, "That's the tea house."

On the ground floor of one of the houses was a deep, low room, like a cave, with smoke-covered walls and ceiling. On the street side it was open along its full width. Although there was little difference between the tea house and the rest of the houses in the colony, which were all very dilapidated, except for the Commandant's palatial structure, the Traveler was struck by the impression of historical memory, and he felt the power of earlier times. Followed by his companions, he walked closer, going between the unoccupied tables, which stood in the street in front of the tea house, and took a breath of the cool, stuffy air which came from inside. "The old man is buried here," said the soldier; "a place in the cemetery was denied him by the chaplain. For a long time people were undecided where they should bury him. Finally they buried him here. Of course, the Officer explained none of that to you, for naturally he was the one most ashamed about it. A few times he even tried to dig up the old man at night, but he was always chased off." "Where is the grave?" asked the Traveler, who could not believe the Soldier. Instantly both men, the Soldier and the Condemned Man, ran in front of him and with hands outstretched pointed to the place where the grave was located. They led the Traveler to the back wall, where guests were sitting at a few tables. They were presumably dock workers, strong men with short, shiny, black beards. None of them wore coats, and their shirts were torn. They were poor, oppressed people. As the Traveler came closer, a few got up, leaned against the wall, and looked at him. A whisper went up around the Traveler – "It's a foreigner. He wants to look at the grave." They pushed one of the tables aside, under which there was a real grave stone. It was a simple stone, low enough for it to remain hidden under a table. It bore an inscription in very small letters. In order to read it the Traveler had to kneel down. It read, "Here rests the Old Commandant. His followers, who are now not permitted to have a name, buried him in this grave and erected this stone. There exists a prophecy that the Commandant will rise again after a certain number of years and from this house will lead his followers to a re-conquest of the colony. Have faith and wait!"

When the Traveler had read it and got up, he saw the men standing around him and smiling, as if they had read the inscription with him, found it ridiculous, and were asking him to share their opinion. The Traveler acted as if he hadn't noticed, distributed some coins among them, waited until the table was pushed back over the grave, left the tea house, and went to the harbour.

In the tea house the Soldier and the Condemned Man had come across some people they knew who detained them. However, they must have broken free of them soon, because by the time the Traveler found himself in the middle of a long staircase which led to the boats, they were already running after him. They probably wanted to force the Traveler at the last minute to take them with him. While the Traveler was haggling at the bottom of the stairs with a sailor about his passage out to the steamer, the two men were racing down the steps in silence, for they didn't dare cry out. But as they reached the bottom, the Traveler was already in the boat, and the sailor at once cast off from shore. They could still have jumped into the boat, but the Traveler picked up a heavy knotted rope from the boat bottom, threatened them with it, and thus prevented them from jumping in.

Getting Shot in the Face Still Stings

Michelle Ann King

DOM DOESN'T LOSE his temper as easily as his brother, so normally he's the one who deals with it when shit goes pear-shaped. But shit has been going pear-shaped a lot lately, and by the time Dom gets to the warehouse Marc is already in full swing. Literally – he's gone after poor Jimmy with a nine iron.

Dom picks his way across the warehouse floor, cursing under his breath. His shoes are new, and it's a fuck of a thing to get blood out of tan leather.

He puts both hands up, palms out. "Marc. Take it easy."

On the floor, Jimmy groans. He's pulled into a foetal position so Dom can't tell the full extent of the damage, but his clothes are soaked in just about every bodily fluid there is. At first guess, Dom would say the kid's lost his teeth, his fingernails, his bollocks and at least a couple of internal organs.

"Fuck," he says, and pinches his nostrils shut. The whole place is going to have to be hosed down. Disinfected.

Marc grins. His eyes are bright, glittering in the dim light. He ignores Dom and addresses Jimmy. "Do you know what the definition of insanity is, boy? Doing the same thing but expecting it to turn out different. That was Einstein, said that. Smart man. Not like you, eh? Because you should know by now what to expect when you fuck up, shouldn't you? You should know what happens."

He swings the club at Jimmy's knee. It crunches, and the kid howls.

"Marc," Dom says. Again, he's ignored. Another swing, and the other knee goes.

Marc pushes his hair back, leaving a trail of red through the blond, then brings the club down again, straight into the kid's gut. A spurt of blood comes out of his mouth, but no more sounds.

"Marc," Dom says. Louder, this time. "For fuck's sake."

Marc spins round, the club still in his hand. "What? Have we got a problem here, Dominic? You got something you want to say to me? Some objection you want to make?"

He lets the club fly once more. Jimmy flips up and over, and comes to rest on his back. His head cracks down on the concrete and one arm falls, loosely, over what's left of his face.

Dom exhales slowly and looks down at the floor. The time for objections is past, now. "No, Boss," he says.

"Good." Marc's breathing hard and his knuckles are white. "I came here to give this boy a chance to explain himself, but he decided he'd rather tell me a fairy story. It was a good one, though. You'd have liked it. Better than the three bears and the three pigs and the three fucking billy goats gruff. Magical powers, Dom. That's how he got robbed. Not because he's a fucking useless bastard, but because this woman's got magical powers." He spits into the puddle spreading under Jimmy's head.

"Her name's Elena," Dom says.

Marc looks up at him. "What?"

"The woman he was talking about. Elena. I've been asking around, what with all the shit that's been going on lately, and this is what I'm hearing. It wasn't just Jimmy, that's the thing. She turned Kelton over last night, as well. Took the lot. Everything he had. The money, the gear, everything."

Marc leans the club against the wall, then goes to the sink and washes his hands. "You speak to Kel yet?"

Dom glances at the mess on the floor. "Yeah, but you're not going to like it."

Kelton Adams is a smackhead, but one of the functional ones. He runs his patch well, pays up on time, keeps his shit together. Went to university, still reads books. He talks a lot of bollocks, especially when he's high, but there's a decent brain under all the shit. Or so Dom would have said, anyway.

He rubs the back of his neck. "He said she was a goddess. Immortal Death, the goddess of time. I think that was the exact quote."

Marc looks at his watch and lets out a hiss of annoyance. The glass is cracked. "Are you serious?"

"I'm just telling you what he said. He wasn't making much sense."

"No shit. How bad was he hurt?"

"He wasn't. Not that I could see, anyway."

"So he just let her clean him out and walk away? Didn't put up a fight?"

Dom shrugs. "He said he did. He said he killed her, but it didn't make any difference. Don't ask me, Marc, I don't know what happened. There was blood all over the flat, but it wasn't his – there wasn't a mark on him. Kel can be handy with a knife when he needs to be, but if she'd lost that much blood she'd be dead. So, I don't know. Maybe she sacrificed a goat or something."

Marc snorts. "Right, yeah. A black mass. Voodoo. Maybe that's how she does it." He steps over the body on the floor. "All right, let's get this sorted out. Find out where our little voodoo princess is hiding. I think it's time we started telling some of our own stories. Like the one about what happens when you pick the wrong people to fuck with."

* * *

Dom makes some calls. Nine times out of ten, that's good enough in itself. If Marc's looking for you, you don't want to be found. Most people decide they've had a good enough run and quietly slip out of the game.

But this one? No. She doesn't disappear. She doesn't even keep out of the way. She turns over their bookie, another couple of dealers and one of the legit-front shops – a florist, and who the fuck robs a florist, for fuck's sake? – then walks right into the warehouse while they're unpacking a shipment.

"Hi," she says, like it's some kind of make-up party. "I'm Elena."

She's tiny – five foot and a fag paper at most – with short, dark blonde hair. Nicely curvy. Other circumstances, Dom might have shown some interest.

Marc stares at her like she's a cockroach that's dropped into his beer. Terry puts down the crate he was hauling and puts his hand on his gun.

The woman, Elena, just stands there. She's still smiling, like she's waiting to be asked if she wants a glass of wine or something.

Dom's gun is in a shoulder holster, but it's easily visible. Marc's is tucked in his waistband.

She acts like she hasn't noticed. Or doesn't care.

"You must really have a death wish," Marc says, and she laughs like that's the funniest thing she's ever heard.

"Shut up," he says, but she just keeps laughing.

All the guns are out now, including Dom's, but it doesn't seem to bother her. Maybe Marc's right. Maybe this is what it's all been about. A death wish.

Well, if she wants to get killed, she came to the right place. After Jimmy, Dom had a nice slick metal floor put in, with a drain in the middle. There's plenty of plastic sheeting on the shelves, and they own, in one form or another, all of the other units on the estate. No neighbours to worry about any strange noises.

"I heard you wanted to talk to me," she says.

She's got a bit of an accent, but Dom can't place it. Vaguely American, vaguely Irish, vaguely something else.

"Yeah," Marc says. "Something like that." He looks her up and down. If she's armed, it's well concealed. "So you thought you'd drop in, eh? Come and have a nice chat?"

She grins. "What can I say? I'm a thrill-seeker. Sometimes you feel the need for an adrenalin rush, you know?"

"Well," Marc says. "I'm sure we can oblige." He raises the gun. "How's that for starters?"

She looks at it critically and makes a so-so motion with her hand. Marc's face darkens and Dom knows this is going to get ugly.

"Hope you enjoyed yourself, then, love," Marc says. "Hope it was worth it, because now it's time to pay the bill."

"Wow," she says. "Anyone ever tell you that you sound just like the guy off that show about the –"

And then Marc shoots her in the face.

The force of it knocks her off her feet and throws her back against the wall. She hangs there for a second, pinned against the spray of her own blood, then crumples.

"Fuck," Dom says. He didn't even get a chance to put down the plastic sheeting.

Terry puts his hands on his hips and looks down at the body. "That was a bit of a waste, wasn't it? She weren't a bad-looking lass. And we still don't know how she was getting away with –"

"It doesn't matter now, does it?" Marc says. "It was getting on my nerves, just listening to her. Well? Don't just stand there, get the –"

His voice fades out, becomes muffled. Dom's ears pop and his stomach clenches as if he's just gone down the drop on a rollercoaster. He hates those fucking things.

"Hi," a voice says. "I'm Elena."

Dom swings round and nearly falls over, because his feet aren't where he left them. He's back standing by the shipping crates, instead of over by the door. Over by the body.

Which is gone. Or, to be more precise, is back standing upright and smiling.

"What?" he says.

Marc is next to him again. Terry's back where he was, about to stack another crate on the pile. He drops it.

"What?" Dom says again. The smell of smoke and blood is gone.

Marc stares at his hand, which is empty. The gun is in his waistband. He snatches at it, nearly drops it.

"Careful there, cowboy," Elena says. "You don't want that to go off while it's still stuffed in your pants, do you?"

Marc gets a proper grip on the gun, lifts it up and points it at her again. To his credit, it doesn't shake. Dom still feels as wobbly as fuck. Like he's just been through an earthquake, or something.

On the other side, Terry is smacking at his head like he's trying to shake something loose.

Elena eyes the gun and lifts an eyebrow. "Right. Because that worked so well last time."

"What the fuck just happened?" Marc says.

"You tried to kill me. It didn't work. Or at least, not for long."

In the silence that follows, Dom's mind flashes on an image of Kelton kneeling on the stained floorboards and rambling like a madman. Dom had thought he was praying, at first. Maybe he had been.

"Immortal Death," Dom says.

Elena nods and gives him a pleased smile. "Yes. Exactly."

Marc doesn't look pleased. Marc looks like he wants to rip her heart out and eat it. Hers or anyone else's, come to that. Dom shifts backwards a half step.

"Exactly?" Marc says. "Exactly, what? What the fuck is that supposed to mean?"

"Immortal," Elena says. "Definition: not mortal. Undying. Not subject to death or decay. Unkillable."

"Fuck you," Marc says, and empties the gun into her. He covers all the bases this time – gut, chest, neck, head.

After a couple of seconds, Terry joins in. The noise is very loud.

Dom looks at the gun in his own hand, then puts it down on one of the crates. Marc gives him a look of fury and Terry one of contempt, but what good do they think more bullets are going to do? Do they think Marc missed, the first time?

Terry carries on pulling the trigger, click click, long after the gun is empty. Then there's just smoke and echoes and fast, panting breaths. What's left of Elena is splattered over half the warehouse.

"Right," Marc says. "That's that sorted out. Dom, you –"

And then it happens again. The weird, hollow *zing* in his ears, in his stomach. In his bones. He's back by the crates again, next to Marc, and his gun is in his holster. He whips his head around and yes, there she is. She doesn't speak this time.

Marc roars with rage and grabs his gun.

"Really?" Elena says. "You just want to keep going with this?"

Terry throws himself flat against the blockwork wall. His gaze roams over the floor, the walls, the crates. It's all clean. Dom can still see the red shapes himself, but only when he shuts his eyes.

Marc keeps hold of his gun, but he doesn't fire. "How are you doing this?" he says.

"Remember that definition of immortal?"

Marc shakes his head rapidly. "It's not possible. It's not fucking possible."

"Oh, sure it is. Don't tell me you never heard of a deal with the devil."

Terry moans and crosses himself. Marc throws him a look of disgust.

"I was after the grand prize," Elena says. "The fountain of youth. To never grow old, never die." Her voice is soft, almost nostalgic. Dom's mother used to talk like that, about fur coats and fancy cruises. He and Marc bought her plenty of both, but it never took the longing out of her voice.

"I got my chance," Elena continues, "but you know how it is. You're supposed to be very, very careful about what you wish for. Watch the small print, as it were. Because they'll fuck with you, demons, if they can. That's what happens, see, if you hang around long enough. You develop a taste for fucking with people. Because what else are you going to do with yourself, right?"

Terry's edging along the wall, his mouth hanging open and his eyes bulging. She looks at him, and he breaks for the door. It's thick steel and fucking heavy, but he throws it open as if it's made of cardboard. It clangs shut after him.

"Fucker," Marc says.

Elena smiles. "I feel confident saying he'll be back soon enough. Now, where was I? Oh, yes. Getting fucked over. Because, I specified living forever, but I didn't say anything about never dying. So the amusing loophole is that I can still be killed. Just not, you know, for very long."

"What does that mean?" Marc says. "What does any of this mean?"

Elena spreads her hands. "You saw what it means. I die, I rewind. We all rewind." She laughs. "It gives us a chance to reconsider the wisdom of our actions. Choose a different path."

"Fuck this," Marc says. "This is absolute fucking bollocks."

He fires again.

Zing

"That's three," Elena says. "I know the whole demons, immortality, time loop thing is a bit of a shock to the system, but come on. Try to get with the programme. I might be technically immortal, but getting shot in the face still stings."

Terry fumbles his crate again, then drops onto all fours and throws up. Marc pulls out his gun once more. This time, it shakes.

"Marc," Dom says, holding up his hand. "Let's take a minute. Let's think about this."

Marc glares at him, but he puts the piece away.

Dom faces Elena. "What do you want?"

"Finally," she says. "Progress. Well, I fancy being the bad guy for a while. Change of scenery, you know? So I'm going to take over."

"What?"

"Your gang, your operation, whatever you call it. It's mine, now. You work for me."

Marc shakes his head. "Are you taking the fucking piss?"

"See, I love that. Such colourful turns of phrase, you have here. 'Are you taking the fuckin' piss?'" It comes out strange, in her weird accent. "You'll have to teach me all of these."

"You're mental. You're absolutely fucking mental."

She considers this. "Very probably, by now. But hey, a girl's got to have a hobby, right? Eternity is a long time, my friend. And there's only so much sudoku you can do."

Marc lifts his chin. "This is mine. This is all mine."

"I'm sure we can come to a mutually suitable arrangement. There will always be a place for highly motivated employees in my organisation."

"Employees? You think I'm going to work for you? Fuck that."

Dom starts forward. "Marc, wait. Don't –"

Zing

"Fuck," Terry says. "Fuck, fuck, fuck, fuck."

Elena smiles. "Take four," she says brightly.

"Marc, enough with the gun," Dom says. He feels rough, now, sick and exhausted like he's got a two-bottle hangover. "No more. It's not doing any good; you keep bringing us back to here."

"Smart boy," Elena says. "There's always a place for the intelligent ones, too."

High spots of colour are burning in Marc's cheeks. His eyes look sunken and yellow. His fingers twitch, but he doesn't draw the gun. "All right. All right."

There's a pause. Dom and Terry both look at Elena.

"Don't look at her," Marc says. "She's not in charge here."

Terry starts edging towards the door. "Fucking stay where you are," Marc says. Terry freezes.

"Time for negotiations?" Elena says.

Marc's head drops for a second, then he lifts it again. "I will not have this. I will not fucking have it." He cracks his knuckles. "All right, we can't kill her. Okay. But it doesn't mean we can't fuck her up."

He nods towards one of the metal chairs. "Tie her up there."

Dom doesn't move. Nor does Terry.

"Didn't you hear me? I said, tie her up."

Terry takes a step, one step, then stops.

"Well? What's the fucking matter with you?"

Elena smiles. "I think he's worried about what else I might be able to do. Isn't that right, sugar?"

Terry doesn't speak, but he swallows hard.

"After all, if this is real – and I think we're all finally in agreement on that point now – then what else might be?" She runs her tongue along the edge of her teeth. "Vampires? Werewolves? What if all those monsters under the bed are real? What if I can rip your throat out, break your neck with my bare hands? What if I can set you on fire with the power of my mind? Boil your brains in your skull with a single thought? Is that what's worrying you, Terry dear?"

She flings her hand out towards him, fingers stiff and splayed. "Scorchio!"

Terry flinches, half-ducks, and his feet tangle together. He goes down, hard.

Elena throws back her head and laughs. "Damn, but that one never gets old."

Marc grabs hold of Terry's arm and hauls him to his feet. "You stupid fucker," he says. "What's wrong with you? This isn't Harry fucking Potter. Now *get* her."

Elena grins and holds her arms out as if inviting a hug. "Want to take the chance, Terry?"

Terry backs away. Dom stays where he is.

Marc snarls at them. His lips draw back from his teeth and he looks more than half werewolf himself. He darts forward, seizes hold of Elena's arm and yanks her around, then throws her into the chair.

Dom holds his breath, and it looks like Terry's doing the same. Maybe Marc, too.

Nothing happens.

Elena shrugs. "Oh, well. A lot of the time, that works. But there's always the odd psychopath with no imagination."

A grin of triumph spreads across Marc's face. "See? What did I tell you?" He backhands her, putting his shoulders into it. The sound is meaty, solid. Her head rocks back and blood blooms at the corner of her mouth.

She licks it clean. "You learn to manage pain," she says. "Over the years. It's like those guys you see on the telly sometimes. Yogis, fakirs. Stick needles in them, tie bricks to their cocks, whatever. They don't blink an eyelid. Work at it long enough, you get control. The nerves, the breath, the heart. And I've had a very, very long time to work at it."

She places a hand on her chest. "There are techniques that let you take charge of the nervous system. You can hold your breath, say, or slow your heartbeat. Slow it down, or even stop it. Course, most people wouldn't want to go that far. But then, as you might have noticed, I'm not most people."

She smiles, and her eyes roll back.

"Oh, fuck," Dom says, "that means –"

Zing

"Hi, guys," Elena says from behind him. "Are we having fun yet?"

Terry goes down on his knees and begins to cry.

She pulls a bag of peanuts out of her pocket, rips it open and throws one into her mouth. "Want to test me? To see how many times we can go round? I'm happy to play that game if you are. As I'm sure you can imagine, I have a great deal of patience."

"Boss," Terry says. "Boss, please."

Marc rounds on him. "What? What are you saying to me? Give in, let her take everything? You want to work for her? Is that it? You'd rather work for her than me? You think she's going to look after you? She's a fucking monster."

Elena munches on another handful of nuts. "It's always interesting, to see whose mind cracks first, and how long it takes. Want to know what the world record is?"

"Marc," Dom says. "Marc, we've got to –"

He doesn't see the fist coming until it's too late to get out of the way. Pain flares in his jaw and his knees unlock. As he goes down he sees Marc's hands, the knuckles bleeding, close around Elena's throat.

Zing

His vision starts to grey out, but then he's back on his feet again. Terry's yelling – or maybe screaming would be a more accurate word. There are more gunshots.

Zing

Everything hurts. He's seeing double. He throws up, can't clear his throat, feels like he's choking.

Zing

Noise. Pain. Shouting. Elena, laughing.

Zing

"Okay," Elena says. "Well, this is more like it."

Dom swallows, spits. His throat feels raw. Terry is standing next to her, Marc's gun in his hand. He hands it to her. She gives him a wide, proud smile. "Thank you, Terry."

Marc's kneeling on the floor. Dom goes up behind him and pulls his arms behind his back, keeping him down.

Elena has a knife. It has a black handle and a curved blade. It shines.

She brings it to Marc's throat. Dom makes a sound.

She stills, and looks at him. "Is there a problem, Dominic? Something you want to say?"

Dom looks down at his brother for a long time. Then he says, "No, Boss."

Elena smiles and rests her hand on his shoulder. It's very warm.

"Good," she says, and they go back to work.

The Return of Imray

Rudyard Kipling

The doors were wide, the story saith,
Out of the night came the patient wraith,
He might not speak, and he could not stir
A hair of the Baron's minniver—
Speechless and strengthless, a shadow thin,
He roved the castle to seek his kin.
And oh, 'twas a piteous thing to see
The dumb ghost follow his enemy!
The Baron

IMRAY ACHIEVED THE IMPOSSIBLE. Without warning, for no conceivable motive, in his youth, at the threshold of his career he chose to disappear from the world – which is to say, the little Indian station where he lived.

Upon a day he was alive, well, happy, and in great evidence among the billiard-tables at his Club. Upon a morning, he was not, and no manner of search could make sure where he might be. He had stepped out of his place; he had not appeared at his office at the proper time, and his dogcart was not upon the public roads. For these reasons, and because he was hampering, in a microscopical degree, the administration of the Indian Empire, that Empire paused for one microscopical moment to make inquiry into the fate of Imray. Ponds were dragged, wells were plumbed, telegrams were despatched down the lines of railways and to the nearest seaport town-twelve hundred miles away; but Imray was not at the end of the drag-ropes nor the telegraph wires. He was gone, and his place knew him no more.

Then the work of the great Indian Empire swept forward, because it could not be delayed, and Imray from being a man became a mystery – such a thing as men talk over at their tables in the Club for a month, and then forget utterly. His guns, horses, and carts were sold to the highest bidder. His superior officer wrote an altogether absurd letter to his mother, saying that Imray had unaccountably disappeared, and his bungalow stood empty.

After three or four months of the scorching hot weather had gone by, my friend Strickland, of the Police, saw fit to rent the bungalow from the native landlord. This was before he was engaged to Miss. Youghal – an affair which has been described in another place – and while he was pursuing his investigations into native life. His own life was sufficiently peculiar, and men complained of his manners and customs. There was always food in his house, but there were no regular times for meals. He ate, standing up and walking about, whatever he might find at the sideboard, and this is not good for human beings. His domestic equipment was limited to six rifles, three shot-guns, five saddles, and a collection of stiff-jointed mahseer-rods, bigger and stronger than the largest salmon-rods. These occupied one-half of his bungalow, and the other half was given up to Strickland and his dog Tietjens – an enormous Rampur slut who devoured daily the rations of two men. She spoke to Strickland in a language of her own; and whenever, walking abroad, she saw things calculated to destroy the peace of Her Majesty the Queen-Empress, she returned to her master and laid information. Strickland would take steps at once, and the end of his labours was trouble and fine and imprisonment for other people. The natives believed that Tietjens was a familiar spirit, and treated her with the great reverence that is born of hate and fear. One room in the bungalow was set apart for her special use. She owned a bedstead, a blanket, and a drinking-trough, and if any one came into Strickland's room at night her custom was to knock down the invader and give tongue till some one came with a light. Strickland owed his life to her, when he was on the Frontier, in search of a local murderer, who came in the gray dawn to send Strickland much farther than the Andaman Islands. Tietjens caught the man as he was crawling into Strickland's tent with a dagger between his teeth; and after his record of iniquity was established in the eyes of the law he was hanged. From that date Tietjens wore a collar of rough silver, and employed a monogram on her night-blanket; and the blanket was of double woven Kashmir cloth, for she was a delicate dog.

Under no circumstances would she be separated from Strickland; and once, when he was ill with fever, made great trouble for the doctors, because she did not know how to help her master and would not allow another creature to attempt aid. Macarnaght, of the Indian Medical Service, beat her over her head with a gun-butt before she could understand that she must give room for those who could give quinine.

A short time after Strickland had taken Imray's bungalow, my business took me through that Station, and naturally, the Club quarters being full, I quartered myself upon Strickland. It was a desirable bungalow, eight-roomed and heavily thatched against any chance of leakage from rain. Under the pitch of the roof ran a ceiling-cloth which looked just as neat as a white-washed ceiling. The landlord had repainted it when Strickland took the bungalow. Unless you knew how Indian bungalows were built you would never have suspected that above the cloth lay the dark three-cornered cavern of the roof, where the beams and the underside of the thatch harboured all manner of rats, bats, ants, and foul things.

Tietjens met me in the verandah with a bay like the boom of the bell of St. Paul's, putting her paws on my shoulder to show she was glad to see me. Strickland had contrived to claw together a sort of meal which he called lunch, and immediately after it was finished went out about his business. I was left alone with Tietjens and my own affairs. The heat of the summer had broken up and turned to the warm damp of the rains. There was no motion in the heated air, but the rain fell like ramrods on the earth, and flung up a blue mist when it splashed back. The bamboos, and the custard-apples, the poinsettias, and the mango-trees in the garden stood still while the warm water lashed through them, and the frogs began to sing among the aloe hedges. A little before the light failed, and when the rain was at its worst, I sat in the back verandah and heard the water roar from the eaves, and scratched myself because I was covered with the thing called prickly-heat. Tietjens came out with me and put her head in my lap and was very sorrowful; so I gave her biscuits when tea was ready, and I took tea in the back verandah on account of the little coolness found there. The rooms of the house were dark behind me. I could smell Strickland's saddlery and the oil on his guns, and I had no desire to sit among these things. My own servant came to me in the twilight, the muslin of his clothes clinging tightly to his drenched body, and told me that a gentleman had called and wished to see some one. Very much against my will, but only because of the darkness of the rooms, I went into the naked drawing-room, telling my man to bring the lights. There might or might not have been a caller waiting – it seemed to me that I saw a figure by one of the windows – but when the lights came there was nothing save the spikes of the rain without, and the smell of the drinking earth in my nostrils. I explained to my servant that he was no wiser than he ought to be, and went back to the verandah to talk to Tietjens. She had gone out into the wet, and I could hardly coax her back to me; even with biscuits with sugar tops. Strickland came home, dripping wet, just before dinner, and the first thing he said was:

"Has any one called?"

I explained, with apologies, that my servant had summoned me into the drawing-room on a false alarm; or that some loafer had tried to call on Strickland, and thinking better of it had fled after giving his name. Strickland ordered dinner, without comment, and since it was a real dinner with a white tablecloth attached, we sat down.

At nine o'clock Strickland wanted to go to bed, and I was tired too. Tietjens, who had been lying underneath the table, rose up, and swung into the least exposed verandah as soon as her master moved to his own room, which was next to the stately chamber set apart for Tietjens. If a mere wife had wished to sleep out of doors in that pelting rain it would not have mattered; but Tietjens was a dog, and therefore the better animal. I looked at Strickland, expecting to see him flay her with a whip. He smiled queerly, as a man would smile after telling some unpleasant domestic tragedy. "She has done this ever since I moved in here," said he. "Let her go."

The dog was Strickland's dog, so I said nothing, but I felt all that Strickland felt in being thus made light of. Tietjens encamped outside my bedroom window, and storm after storm came up, thundered on the thatch, and died away. The lightning spattered the sky as a thrown egg spatters a barn-door, but the light was pale blue, not yellow; and, looking through my split bamboo blinds, I could see the great dog standing, not sleeping, in the verandah, the hackles aloft on her back and her feet anchored as tensely as the drawn wire-rope of a suspension bridge. In the very short pauses of the thunder I tried to sleep, but it seemed that some one wanted me very urgently. He, whoever he was, was trying to call me by name, but his voice was no more than a husky whisper. The thunder ceased, and Tietjens went into the garden and howled at the low moon. Somebody tried to open my door, walked about and about through the house and stood breathing heavily in the verandahs, and just when I was falling asleep I fancied that I heard a wild hammering and clamouring above my head or on the door.

I ran into Strickland's room and asked him whether he was ill, and had been calling for me. He was lying on his bed half dressed, a pipe in his mouth. "I thought you'd come," he said. "Have I been walking round the house recently?"

I explained that he had been tramping in the dining-room and the smoking-room and two or three other places, and he laughed and told me to go back to bed. I went back to bed and slept till the morning, but through all my mixed dreams I was sure I was doing some one an injustice in not attending to his wants. What those wants were

I could not tell; but a fluttering, whispering, bolt-fumbling, lurking, loitering. Someone was reproaching me for my slackness, and, half awake, I heard the howling of Tietjens in the garden and the threshing of the rain.

I lived in that house for two days. Strickland went to his office daily, leaving me alone for eight or ten hours with Tietjens for my only companion. As long as the full light lasted I was comfortable, and so was Tietjens; but in the twilight she and I moved into the back verandah and cuddled each other for company. We were alone in the house, but none the less it was much too fully occupied by a tenant with whom I did not wish to interfere. I never saw him, but I could see the curtains between the rooms quivering where he had just passed through; I could hear the chairs creaking as the bamboos sprung under a weight that had just quitted them; and I could feel when I went to get a book from the dining-room that somebody was waiting in the shadows of the front verandah till I should have gone away. Tietjens made the twilight more interesting by glaring into the darkened rooms with every hair erect, and following the motions of something that I could not see. She never entered the rooms, but her eyes moved interestedly: that was quite sufficient. Only when my servant came to trim the lamps and make all light and habitable she would come in with me and spend her time sitting on her haunches, watching an invisible extra man as he moved about behind my shoulder. Dogs are cheerful companions.

I explained to Strickland, gently as might be, that I would go over to the Club and find for myself quarters there. I admired his hospitality, was pleased with his guns and rods, but I did not much care for his house and its atmosphere. He heard me out to the end, and then smiled very wearily, but without contempt, for he is a man who understands things. "Stay on," he said, "and see what this thing means. All you have talked about I have known since I took the bungalow. Stay on and wait. Tietjens has left me. Are you going too?"

I had seen him through one little affair, connected with a heathen idol, that had brought me to the doors of a lunatic asylum, and I had no desire to help him through further experiences. He was a man to whom unpleasantnesses arrived as do dinners to ordinary people.

Therefore I explained more clearly than ever that I liked him immensely, and would be happy to see him in the daytime; but that I did not care to sleep under his roof. This was after dinner, when Tietjens had gone out to lie in the verandah.

" 'Pon my soul, I don't wonder," said Strickland, with his eyes on the ceiling-cloth. "Look at that!"

The tails of two brown snakes were hanging between the cloth and the cornice of the wall. They threw long shadows in the lamplight.

"If you are afraid of snakes of course –" said Strickland.

I hate and fear snakes, because if you look into the eyes of any snake you will see that it knows all and more of the mystery of man's fall, and that it feels all the contempt that the Devil felt when Adam was evicted from Eden. Besides which its bite is generally fatal, and it twists up trouser legs.

"You ought to get your thatch overhauled," I said.

"Give me a mahseer-rod, and we'll poke 'em down."

"They'll hide among the roof-beams," said Strickland. "I can't stand snakes overhead. I'm going up into the roof. If I shake 'em down, stand by with a cleaning-rod and break their backs."

I was not anxious to assist Strickland in his work, but I took the cleaning-rod and waited in the dining-room, while Strickland brought a gardener's ladder from the verandah, and set it against the side of the room.

The snake-tails drew themselves up and disappeared. We could hear the dry rushing scuttle of long bodies running over the baggy ceiling-cloth. Strickland took a lamp with him, while I tried to make clear to him the danger of hunting roof-snakes between a ceiling-cloth and a thatch, apart from the deterioration of property caused by ripping out ceiling-cloths.

"Nonsense!" said Strickland. "They're sure to hide near the walls by the cloth. The bricks are too cold for 'em, and the heat of the room is just what they like." He put his hand to the corner of the stuff and ripped it from the cornice. It gave with a great sound of tearing, and Strickland put his head through the opening into the dark of the angle of the roof-beams. I set my teeth and lifted the rod, for I had not the least knowledge of what might descend.

"H'm!" said Strickland, and his voice rolled and rumbled in the roof. "There's room for another set of rooms up here, and, by Jove, some one is occupying 'em!"

"Snakes?" I said from below.

"No. It's a buffalo. Hand me up the two last joints of a mahseer-rod, and I'll prod it. It's lying on the main roof-beam."

I handed up the rod.

"What a nest for owls and serpents! No wonder the snakes live here," said Strickland, climbing farther into the roof. I could see his elbow thrusting with the rod. "Come out of that, whoever you are! Heads below there! It's falling."

I saw the ceiling-cloth nearly in the centre of the room bag with a shape that was pressing it downwards and downwards towards the lighted lamp on the table. I snatched the lamp out of danger and stood back. Then the cloth ripped out from the walls, tore, split, swayed, and shot down upon the table something that I dared not look at, till Strickland had slid down the ladder and was standing by my side.

He did not say much, being a man of few words; but he picked up the loose end of the tablecloth and threw it over the remnants on the table.

"It strikes me," said he, putting down the lamp, "our friend Imray has come back. Oh! You would, would you?"

There was a movement under the cloth, and a little snake wriggled out, to be back-broken by the butt of the mahseer-rod. I was sufficiently sick to make no remarks worth recording.

Strickland meditated, and helped himself to drinks. The arrangement under the cloth made no more signs of life.

"Is it Imray?" I said.

Strickland turned back the cloth for a moment, and looked.

"It is Imray," he said; "and his throat is cut from ear to ear."

Then we spoke, both together and to ourselves: "That's why he whispered about the house."

Tietjens, in the garden, began to bay furiously. A little later her great nose heaved open the dining-room door.

She sniffed and was still. The tattered ceiling-cloth hung down almost to the level of the table, and there was hardly room to move away from the discovery.

Tietjens came in and sat down; her teeth bared under her lip and her forepaws planted. She looked at Strickland.

"It's a bad business, old lady," said he. "Men don't climb up into the roofs of their bungalows to die, and they don't fasten up the ceiling cloth behind 'em. Let's think it out."

"Let's think it out somewhere else," I said.

"Excellent idea! Turn the lamps out. We'll get into my room."

I did not turn the lamps out. I went into Strickland's room first, and allowed him to make the darkness. Then he followed me, and we lit tobacco and thought. Strickland thought. I smoked furiously, because I was afraid.

"Imray is back," said Strickland. "The question is – who killed Imray? Don't talk, I've a notion of my own. When I took this bungalow I took over most of Imray's servants. Imray was guileless and inoffensive, wasn't he?"

I agreed; though the heap under the cloth had looked neither one thing nor the other.

"If I call in all the servants they will stand fast in a crowd and lie like Aryans. What do you suggest?"

"Call 'em in one by one," I said.

"They'll run away and give the news to all their fellows," said Strickland. "We must segregate "em. Do you suppose your servant knows anything about it?"

"He may, for aught I know; but I don't think it's likely. He has only been here two or three days," I answered. "What's your notion?"

"I can't quite tell. How the dickens did the man get the wrong side of the ceiling-cloth?"

There was a heavy coughing outside Strickland's bedroom door. This showed that Bahadur Khan, his body-servant, had waked from sleep and wished to put Strickland to bed.

"Come in," said Strickland. "It's a very warm night, isn't it?"

Bahadur Khan, a great, green-turbaned, six-foot Mahomedan, said that it was a very warm night; but that there was more rain pending, which, by his Honour's favour, would bring relief to the country.

"It will be so, if God pleases," said Strickland, tugging off his boots. "It is in my mind, Bahadur Khan, that I have worked thee remorselessly for many days – ever since that time when thou first earnest into my service. What time was that?"

"Has the Heaven-born forgotten? It was when Imray Sahib went secretly to Europe without warning given; and I – even I – came into the honoured service of the protector of the poor."

"And Imray Sahib went to Europe?"

"It is so said among those who were his servants."

"And thou wilt take service with him when he returns?"

"Assuredly, Sahib. He was a good master, and cherished his dependants."

"That is true. I am very tired, but I go buck-shooting tomorrow. Give me the little sharp rifle that I use for black-buck; it is in the case yonder."

The man stooped over the case; handed barrels, stock, and fore-end to Strickland, who fitted all together, yawning dolefully. Then he reached down to the gun-case, took a solid-drawn cartridge, and slipped it into the breech of the 360 Express.

"And Imray Sahib has gone to Europe secretly! That is very strange, Bahadur Khan, is it not?"

"What do I know of the ways of the white man. Heaven-born?"

"Very little, truly. But thou shalt know more anon. It has reached me that Imray Sahib has returned from his so long journeyings, and that even now he lies in the next room, waiting his servant."

"Sahib!"

The lamplight slid along the barrels of the rifle as they levelled themselves at Bahadur Khan's broad breast.

"Go and look!" said Strickland. "Take a lamp. Thy master is tired, and he waits thee. Go!"

The man picked up a lamp, and went into the dining-room, Strickland following, and almost pushing him with the muzzle of the rifle. He looked for a moment at the black depths behind the ceiling-cloth; at the writhing snake under foot; and last, a gray glaze settling on his face, at the thing under the tablecloth.

"Hast thou seen?" said Strickland after a pause.

"I have seen. I am clay in the white man's hands. What does the Presence do?"

"Hang thee within the month. What else?"

"For killing him? Nay, Sahib, consider. Walking among us, his servants, he cast his eyes upon my child, who was four years old. Him he bewitched, and in ten days he died of the fever – my child!"

"What said Imray Sahib?"

"He said he was a handsome child, and patted him on the head; wherefore my child died. Wherefore I killed Imray Sahib in the twilight, when he had come back from office, and was sleeping. Wherefore I dragged him up into the roof-beams and made all fast behind him. The Heaven-born knows all things. I am the servant of the Heaven-born."

Strickland looked at me above the rifle, and said, in the vernacular, "Thou art witness to this saying? He has killed."

Bahadur Khan stood ashen gray in the light of the one lamp. The need for justification came upon him very swiftly. "I am trapped," he said, "but the offence was that man's. He cast an evil eye upon my child, and I killed and hid him. Only such as are served by devils," he glared at Tietjens, couched stolidly before him, "only such could know what I did."

"It was clever. But thou shouldst have lashed him to the beam with a rope. Now, thou thyself wilt hang by a rope. Orderly!"

A drowsy policeman answered Strickland's call. He was followed by another, and Tietjens sat wondrous still.

"Take him to the police-station," said Strickland. "There is a case toward."

"Do I hang, then?" said Bahadur Khan, making no attempt to escape, and keeping his eyes on the ground.

"If the sun shines or the water runs – yes!" said Strickland.

Bahadur Khan stepped back one long pace, quivered, and stood still. The two policemen waited further orders.

"Go!" said Strickland.

"Nay; but I go very swiftly," said Bahadur Khan. "Look! I am even now a dead man."

He lifted his foot, and to the little toe there clung the head of the half-killed snake, firm fixed in the agony of death.

"I come of land-holding stock," said Bahadur Khan, rocking where he stood. "It were a disgrace to me to go to the public scaffold: therefore I take this way. Be it remembered that the Sahib's shirts are correctly enumerated, and that there is an extra piece of soap in his washbasin. My child was bewitched, and I slew the wizard. Why should you seek to slay me with the rope? My honour is saved, and – and – I die."

At the end of an hour he died, as they die who are bitten by the little brown karait, and the policemen bore him and the thing under the tablecloth to their appointed places. All were needed to make clear the disappearance of Imray.

"This," said Strickland, very calmly, as he climbed into bed, "is called the nineteenth century. Did you hear what that man said?"

"I heard," I answered. "Imray made a mistake."

"Simply and solely through not knowing the nature of the Oriental, and the coincidence of a little seasonal fever. Bahadur Khan had been with him for four years."

I shuddered. My own servant had been with me for exactly that length of time. When I went over to my own room I found my man waiting, impassive as the copper head on a penny, to pull off my boots.

"What has befallen Bahadur Khan?" said I.

"He was bitten by a snake and died. The rest the Sahib knows," was the answer.

"And how much of this matter hast thou known?"

"As much as might be gathered from One coming in in the twilight to seek satisfaction. Gently, Sahib. Let me pull off those boots."

I had just settled to the sleep of exhaustion when I heard Strickland shouting from his side of the house –

"Tietjens has come back to her place!"

And so she had. The great deerhound was couched stately on her own bedstead on her own blanket, while, in the next room, the idle, empty, ceiling-cloth waggled as it trailed on the table.

Less than Katherine

Claude Lalumière

I ASK the two detectives if they want tea; when they rang the doorbell, I was about to pour myself the first cup of the day. "Herbal," I warn them. I try to avoid caffeine now – it makes my heart palpitate; my doctor says it's my imagination, but I don't believe her. I can't resist the temptation unless I keep no black tea or coffee in the house. The cops each mumble something that I take to mean *no*.

I invite them to sit on the couch while I fetch my cup. They wait for me to come back to the living room, set my cane down, and settle in my armchair before they say anything.

The older cop, a man who looks to be in his early fifties, corpulent but not fat, with powerful hands, unruly hair, and a trim beard that tries too hard to make him look trendy, launches right into it. "Mister Cray, where were you last night, from nine to midnight?"

It's been thirty-odd years since I was last interrogated by a detective. I am gripped with an intuition that this is somehow about Katherine, but it can't be. Not again. I made sure of that.

"I go to bed every night by ten. I was here. Before you ask, Detective Logan: I was alone, and I can't think of any way to corroborate my alibi." At the word *alibi*, the two detectives exchange a glance and a nod, and I chide myself for using so charged a word. "I mean, if I need an alibi. You still haven't said why you're here. You can understand that it would make anyone nervous to have two police detectives show up on their doorstep first thing in the morning."

Logan nods to his junior partner, a short-haired brunette in her mid-thirties with a stern mouth but kind eyes who was earlier introduced as Detective Mahfud. She says, "When did you last speak to your daughter?"

"Katherine?" So it is about her. I don't have to lie. At least, not yet. "Katherine and I aren't close. It's been ... I don't know, three or four months? She came over for dinner one night, unannounced. Getting over a breakup. I didn't pry. I was happy to see her. I so rarely do." Maybe that was too much. Only give answers to what they ask, I remind myself. Don't volunteer information.

Detective Mahfud raises her left index finger. "Rupert Shaw." She uncurls the next finger. "Svend Patrickson." She uncurls a third finger. "Teddy Atkins. Do any of those names mean anything to you?"

I want to lie, but then I'd have to remember that I'd lied, in case they question me again. My mind isn't nimble enough to trust with things like that anymore. "Yes, yes they do. But please answer my question. Why are you here? Has something happened to Katherine?" I ask that knowing in my gut that's not quite why they're here. Katherine is not the one *something* has happened to.

Detective Logan takes over. "Sir, these three men were found murdered last night. For formality's sake, tell us how you know their names."

"You already know the answer, clearly. They're some of Katherine's past boyfriends. The only times I see her are when she gets her heart broken. So I remember the names of the men responsible for sending her here crying. I'm always a little grateful to them. They never seem like particularly bad men, although I've never met any of them. I know my daughter's not easy to love." Again, I'm revealing too much. When did I stop being able to control what I say? Is it decrepitude or loneliness that makes me blather so much? Probably both.

I'm not so addled yet that I can't hold up at least a minimal pretense. In a frightened tone, I ask, "Do you think Katherine's in danger, too?"

"Sir," Logan answers, "we can't locate your daughter anywhere. We compared the contact lists of the victims' phones, and hers was the only name that appeared on all three. She's not at her apartment, and her workplace says she's on vacation. She's not answering her phone. Any idea where she could be?"

I suspect there's only one place she can be. I answer, "No."

Detective Mahfud asks if I remember the names of any other ex-boyfriends. My memory has become both erratic and unpredictable, yet a half-dozen names rise to the surface of my awareness. I list them for the detectives.

Logan's gaze probes me. "You know, by this time, most people would have asked us how the men were killed."

"I don't appreciate your tone, Detective Logan. I'm sorry I'm not following your script." I use the anger to hide that, yes, I already know.

He says, "They were stabbed."

Of course.

He continues, "The weird thing is, they were killed at approximately the same time, but they live in three different sectors of the city. It would take at least forty minutes to go from one location to another. They were all killed the same way. Same wounds. Looks like the same weapon. The same killer."

Detective Mahfud takes an envelope for the inside pocket of her jacket, opens it, and lays down three photographs on the table. I can't help but stare at the gory images.

"Do these stab wounds look familiar, Mister Cray?"

The detectives know they do. They did their research before coming here.

* * *

When the five of us were still a family, we used to spend as much time as we could at the cottage up north. My wife, Jaqueline; our eldest daughter, Katherine; the young twins, Danielle and Denise. Holidays. Weekends. Whenever we could manage to get away. It was only a two-hour drive from the city. Jaqueline had inherited the place from her parents. It was a small one-room cabin that afforded no privacy whatsoever, but we were a close family and the place symbolized the wonder of childhood for her. To hear her say it, she'd spent her entire childhood there, exploring caves and, as a prelude to her later career as an archeologist, dug up old stones and shards and forgotten objects and dreamt up fantastic pasts to explain her finds. She wanted to instill that same sense of wonder in our children. Jaqueline loved exploring and playing in the woods with the kids.

Starting at age eight, Katherine was allowed to go wander off by herself. It was two years later, the day after her tenth birthday, that she came back to the cottage with the stone dagger. She said she found it in the stream that runs through the property.

In some ways Katherine was very much her mother's daughter: she, too, possessed a vivid imagination, the products of which she was always eager to share. Unlike Jaqueline, though, whose childhood daydreams had been filled with adventure, Katherine's mind turned to the grotesque and the macabre. It was all too easy for her to concoct a bloody and murderous past for this rock that, Jaqueline and I assumed at first, time and erosion had shaped into the approximate form of a knife.

"Millions of years ago, a priest used this dagger to prepare sacrifices for the gods of his people," Katherine said with a grimace, stabbing downward as if an invisible victim lay before her.

Jaqueline responded, "Millions of years? That's a long, long time. Are you sure there were priests back then?" Academia had made Jaqueline a little pedantic. I could tell she regretted the question as soon as she uttered it.

"Yes! But his people weren't people the same way that we're people. They were more like fish, except they breathed air and walked on two legs."

We always encouraged Katherine's fanciful imagination.

"Every wound made by the dagger let in a different god. The priests stabbed the sacrifices thirteen times. Thirteen wounds for their thirteen gods. The sacrifices never knew they were chosen. Because the dagger stabbed them from a distance. All the priest needed was to steal something that belonged to the sacrifices, and the dagger would find its victims. The gods swarmed the wounded bodies and ate them from the inside. The priest had to sacrifice all of his people to feed his *unquenchable*," she stressed the word, awkwardly trotting it out for the first time, "gods. In the end, he had to sacrifice even himself. Then the gods died, too, because they were no fish-people left to eat. They've been dead for millions of years. The knife is still alive, though. Even after all this time. And it's hungry."

I ask her, "How do you know all this, Katherine?"

"Because the knife told me. Didn't you listen to me? I said it was alive. It wants me to be its new priest." Katherine paused for effect. She was a natural-born storyteller. "The twins will be my first sacrifices."

She pointed the artefact at her sisters, who were two years younger than she was. Danielle stuck her tongue out and shouted back, "No we won't! Sacrifice yourself!" Denise, always the crybaby, reacted in character and hid her sobbing face behind her stronger twin.

Jaqueline said, "Okay, Katherine, that's enough playing with the knife. Daddy and I love your stories, but you shouldn't scare your sisters like that. You shouldn't threaten to hurt them."

Danielle shouted, "I'm not scared of Katherine. She's weird and stupid."

Katherine shouted back, "You're the stupid ones, Deedees." That was Katherine's name for the twins.

Jaqueline held out her hand. "Give me the stone."

"No! It's mine! And it's not a stone. It's a dagger. A sacred dagger. You can't take it. Nobody else can touch it! I'm the new priest. Me! Not you! I'll sacrifice you, too." She pointed the stone dagger at her mother.

Katherine stormed out of the cabin. The sun was starting to set. I said to my wife, "Let her ride it out. She'll come back when she's calmed down. You know how she is. She'll find some other object, dream up some other story. She knows she was bad. If we make too big a deal out of it, she'll dig in her heels and make it worse."

But I was the worrier, not Jaqueline. She and the girls fell asleep quickly after sunset. I wouldn't be able to nod off until Katherine was back home safe. I extricated myself from

Jaqueline and went to sit on the porch. The moon was full and bright. Soon enough, to my relief, Katherine emerged from the woods and walked toward me.

I didn't say a word. I nodded and smiled at her. She climbed on my lap and nestled into me. I could tell she'd been crying. She whispered into my chest, "I love you, Daddy."

I stroked her back and murmured back my love for her.

I noticed that she was still clutching the stone dagger, but I didn't say anything.

She said, "I'll go to bed."

She walked inside, with the dagger still in hand. I resisted the impulse to try to take it away from her.

A minute or two later, I heard an unusual and loud thump. I rushed inside. Everyone had been woken up by the commotion. Katherine was gone. I looked out the side window, and there were signs that someone had jumped down onto the dirt.

I explained that Katherine had returned. "She told me was coming inside to sleep." I didn't say anything about the dagger. "I don't understand why she ran off again."

In the morning we noticed a few things were missing: Jacqueline's sun hat; Denise's favourite stuffed animal, a giraffe; one of Danielle's dirty T-shirts.

* * *

Detective Logan leaves his card. Asks to call him if I hear from Katherine. He doesn't say she's a suspect. He doesn't say I'm a suspect. But he doesn't say we we're not under suspicion, either.

But how can he prove anything? The evidence won't add up.

* * *

Katherine stayed away all day. We were leaving the next morning, so in the afternoon Jaqueline and I started to pack up and load the car. The sun set, and still our eldest daughter was missing.

The twins were paying attention only to each other, probably more relieved than worried. Katherine took up a lot of social space and loved to taunt them. But Jaqueline and I exchanged worried glances, clasped and unclasped each other's hands, and fidgeted. I finally broke down. "One of us should go look for her. The other should st–"

I never finished that sentence. A bloody wound opened on Jaqueline's chest. She clutched her hands to the injury, her eyes wide with pain and shock. Impossibly, another wound appeared on her belly. On her thigh. On her shoulder. Her neck. The side of the head...

In my mind, Katherine's voice echoed: *...the dagger stabbed them from a distance...*

I screamed, "Katherine! Stop! Don't! Katherine!" But it was too late. Jaqueline was dead. The twins shrieked. I turned to them.

"Katherine! No! Please, please ... stop."

Danielle ran trying to avoid the invisible blows of Katherine's stone dagger. She stumbled dead and bloodied.

Denise died clutching her twin, her wounds leaking onto her sister as they appeared on her own all-too fragile body.

* * *

Four days later, the phone rings. "Daddy, I'm at the police station." It's Katherine. "Can you come pick me up?"

When I get there, Detective Logan is waiting for me. He says, "Turns out your daughter was at the family cottage up north. There's surveillance footage from the nearby village that backs up her story. Where she had dinner. A bar. A bank machine. All on the night of the murders. Not at the precise time of the murders, but close enough to make it impossible for her to have been in the city when they occurred."

I don't say anything in response.

He waits a few beats, then asks, "How about you? Have you been there recently?"

"I would never go back there," I tell him. "I can never go back. You must know what happened."

"I don't believe the cockamamie story that's in the report. I don't think you do, either. I don't think *she* does. You're the only ones who know the truth."

"Detective, she was only ten years old."

"I'm thinking, maybe we need to reopen that case."

I don't say anything. Detective Mahfud emerges from the door behind the reception with my daughter in tow. Katherine looks cheerful – too cheerful. She grabs my arm, gives me a peck on the cheek, and says, "Let's go." She waves goodbye at the detectives with the fake smile of a celebrity saluting her fans.

* * *

I don't know how much time elapsed before Katherine came running back to the cottage, tightly gripping the stone dagger. The moon was still preternaturally bright. The woods were eerily quiet, as if all the animals were afraid of making the slightest noise, of revealing their presence.

She stopped abruptly and gaped at the carnage.

In the heavy silence, I heard my eldest daughter whisper, "But it was only a game ... It was only supposed to be a game..."

It wasn't my daughter who did this, who murdered my family. It couldn't be her fault. It couldn't. That rock, that dagger was to blame.

I rushed to her and knocked the evil thing out of her hand. She kept repeating, "It was only a game ... only a game," not reacting to me at all.

I took the dagger and ran deep into the woods. I could hear it whisper to me. Whisper images of violence and bloodshed and unholy rituals and inhuman creatures. Maybe it was my imagination, remembering the stories Katherine had told us earlier. Regardless, I didn't want to be touching that filthy thing. I tried to shatter it against a big rock, but I only succeeded in chipping away at the bigger stone. Finally I buried the dagger under that big rock, hoping no one would ever find it again.

When I returned to the cottage, Katherine was sitting on the steps of the porch. She looked straight at me and said coldly, "They'll think you did it, Daddy. They'll think you killed them."

She was right. And I thought, *I'll let them think that. This one moment can't ruin my daughter's entire life. It wasn't her. It was that rock. That dagger. That thing.*

Shaking with grief, I sat on the chair. She climbed and nestled into me. We were both crying. She whispered into my chest, "I love you, Daddy."

I noticed that she was clutching a knife. A big chef's knife from the kitchen.

She plunged the knife into my thigh and twisted it. I struggled not to scream.

"Trust me, Daddy. They mustn't think you did it."

She pulled out the knife – it hurt even more as she did that – and ran off to throw it into the small stream that ran next to the house. She came back with a heavy rock. I was writhing in pain on the ground.

"When they ask you," she said, "tell them you didn't see anything. Tell them you were looking for me. You were attacked first." She repeated: "You didn't see anything." Then, she brought the rock down on my head. Once, twice, forever.

* * *

The police visit regularly. Always the same two detectives. Logan and Mahfud. Every month, on the night following the full moon, there's always a string of murders. Same wounds. Same lack of evidence. They only have one thing in common. The victims are always acquainted with my daughter. Co-workers. Boyfriends. Old schoolmates. Teachers. Bosses. Doctors. Shop clerks. Every victim came into contact with my daughter at some point. Most times, the detectives can dig up a story of some previous argument or altercation, some motive for a grudge. For revenge. In every case, my daughter can account for being nowhere near the crime scene.

The detectives have been coming to see me for a year now. Detective Logan says, "I know she's responsible. Somehow. It doesn't make any sense. But I know it's her. And she killed your wife, too. Her sisters. Why are you covering up for her? Help us, man. Help her. You know there's something dangerously wrong with your daughter."

I've long ago stopped responding to their taunts. I sip my tea until the two of them have exhausted whatever they want to say.

They have no evidence. They have nothing.

Me. I only have one thing. I have my daughter. That's all I have. I can't bear the thought of having less than that. Less than one daughter. Less than Katherine.

* * *

I woke up in the hospital. A police officer sat in the chair next to the bed.

I gurgled some kind of noncommittal noise.

The cop stood up, opened the door, and said, "He's awake."

Suddenly, the small room was packed. The police guard. Two plainclothes detectives. A doctor. A nurse.

After a lot of fussing, one of the plainclothes detectives asked me, "What's the last thing you remember?"

I remembered too much. Including what Katherine asked me to do. I lied: "I don't know. I was shouting for my daughter. For Katherine. We hadn't seen her all day. Then a blow to the back of my head? Then – nothing. Is she… Is she okay? Is she safe?" All I could see in my mind's eye were my daughters and my wife. Dead. I teared up. I knew I shouldn't. But maybe they wouldn't make anything of it. They'd think it was about Katherine.

The police were all over me for weeks, trying to pin the murders on me, but Katherine was adamant: from her hiding spot in the woods she saw two men attack me, and then she ran to the village to get help. She'd always been a good storyteller.

I stuck to Katherine's script. They never believed us. But there was no evidence against us. No motive. Sure, they found the kitchen knife Katherine had used on my thigh. But they couldn't make it tell the story they wanted.

Finally, they closed the case. Unsolved.

I wished I'd stayed a good father to my daughter Katherine. Maybe she wouldn't have turned out the way she did. But after the dust settled I could barely ever bring myself to speak to her. I ignored all her attempts at closeness. But I gave her anything she wanted. Except a good father. I wasn't a bad father. I was barely a father at all.

When she moved out at age sixteen, I only vaguely noticed.

When I turned sixty, I began to yearn for her company. But I never reached out. Sometimes, when she was at her most desperate, she would show up. I cooked for her, and she'd tell me stories about her life. The more she revealed, the more I realized she was incapable of sustaining any kind of friendship or relationship. Regardless of how badly she herself behaved, she always painted herself as the victim. Even through the lens of her distorted, damaged, self-serving perspective, it was horribly obvious that she was toxic and dangerous.

I barely ever said anything to her. When she'd had her say, eaten her food, she'd stumble out, back into her broken life and out of my nonexistent one.

* * *

Katherine is home, with me. She never asked to move in; one day, I noticed that she had taken over the unused guest bedroom. Spray cans, feminine lotions in tubes and bottles and small jars, and sundry beauty products invaded my tiny bathroom.

With my chaotic daughter in the apartment, it has become a constant chore to keep the premises in a habitable state of order and cleanliness. Still, it gives me satisfaction and even a hint of serenity to have her here.

It was the full moon last night. The first full moon since she started staying with me.

She gazes out the window at the fading light while I put away the dinner dishes.

When it gets fully dark, she turns to me and says, "Let's play a game."

It's only then that I notice she's holding the stone dagger.

In her other hand, she's holding two business cards. They're too far for my failing eyesight to read, but I think I know what they are.

She goes to the phone and punches a number. "Hello, may I speak to Detective Logan, please? My name? Katherine Cray. Thank you." Katherine smiles at me, like a naughty little girl trapped in a forty-two-year-old body. "Hello, Detective Logan. Is Detective Mahfud there with you? She is? Good." She hangs up without another word.

"Let's give the cops at the station a good show. Let's see them try to solve those murders."

She lays down the two cards on the long table in the living room.

I say, "Katherine, don't. Please. Please stop. You have to stop this."

"You know, all these years I never ceased hearing the dagger whisper to me. Even from so far away. For decades I resisted, but finally I went back. What other friend do I have? What other family? The stone dagger needs me. It wants me. It was easy to find. It told me where you'd hidden it."

A memory of pain shoots through the old wound on my leg. The hand on my cane trembles.

"I love you, Daddy. Even if you can't love me. I understand that you can't. I'm sorry."

I swallow. There's nothing I can say.

"You don't know how hungry the stone dagger is, Daddy. How good it makes me feel to give it what it wants. What it needs. What I need."

She stabs the two cards – Detective Logan's, Detective Mahfud's – again and again.

The phone rings. We both ignore it. She continues to stab. Again and again and again.

Shared Losses

Gerri Leen

THERE IS A DARK WORLD you can only get to through love, when you realize you've given all you can, and it's still not enough to hold on to someone. There's power when you have nothing left to lose.

You think of these things as you walk briskly down the crowded aisles of the store, high heels clicking a warning to those ahead. You pass men, not looking for long enough to catch their eye. You stop a woman who seems to work there and ask her where the ties are kept.

Dark ones. Ties suitable for a funeral.

The clerk's face shines with compassion. She points, then grabs your arm as if she cannot bear the thought of you wandering the store, searching alone for a tie for such a sad occasion.

"Was it someone close?" she asks, her voice husky, but not uncertain. This is a woman who has lost someone in her life. Only those who've swum grief's waters know how to navigate them for others.

"A lover," you say and your voice catches. It is affected but effective. The woman does not question; her eyes betray no suspicion. She believes you feel pain.

She does not understand that you also cause it.

"I lost my uncle three years ago. He practically raised me. I still go to call him sometimes, then I remember he's gone." She smiles, the sad smile of one survivor to another.

You nod. There is nothing required of you in this situation, nothing to say to make the pain better for either of you. Her with her old pain, you with your new.

Pain born and pain dealt.

"Were you with him long?" she asks, deftly navigating through some tightly packed racks, pushing an errant coat back into order in a way that says she's done it a hundred times before.

"Not long enough."

I need to talk to you. About us.

"It never is, is it?" She pushes past a woman with young children. The boy won't move, and you can tell by the look on the clerk's face that she does not like children.

You weren't terribly fond of them, either. Until yours started to grow inside you.

I was with someone.

The clerk stops suddenly and slowly turns, a frown starting. "Who is the tie for?"

"Him." You look down, as if the question is just too painful to go into more detail.

"Oh. Oh... yes, of course." She looks like she regrets having asked – having caused you more pain. "You have to decide what he'll wear in the cask – I guess something new just feels right?"

"Something new generally does."

I love her.

The clerk nods. You notice her hand strays to her belly, lying on top of it as if she's protecting something inside.

She's carrying my child.

"Are you pregnant?" you ask her, nodding at the way she is cupping her stomach.

"Oh, God, no." She blushes. "Just cramps."

You nod and smile the sympathetic grimace of remembered pain. You know cramps. From your periods and from the time when you should not have bled. When the child you would have given him came out in a mass of blood and tissue, your body cramping so badly that all you could do was lie on the floor, a sodden towel under you, cry useless tears, and moan.

And him nowhere to be found.

I just can't be with you anymore.

He left you alone to bleed.

He left you alone to spew his child on that tile floor while his new woman kept his other child safe.

"I was pregnant," you tell the clerk. "I miscarried."

She turns, more pity in her eyes. "I'm so sorry."

You nod; you're sorry, too. "Nothing to remember him by."

He hadn't known to warn this woman who carried his child that you might not take it well. Hadn't done more than just keep the two of you separate. He really never understood you very well, it turned out. She didn't know what you looked like, didn't know to be afraid when you struck up a conversation on the train into the city.

She didn't think it odd when you were always in the car she was in.

Didn't question whether it was a good idea to start getting coffee – milk for her, of course – with you before work. To start having lunch with you. To become quite so fond of you, fond enough to trust you, to share secret hopes for her future. Her future with him – God, how you had to work to hide how much you hated hearing about him with her.

Even though it was clear he hadn't warned her about you, you took precautions. You used a different name. You wore a wig and heavier makeup. Sported a lot of wool and tweed, found glasses that were bookish and dark.

Even he wouldn't have recognized you. Not from far away.

She invited you to her house one night when he was out of town. She had movies for you to watch. Chick flicks, she said. The kind with "meet cutes" and improbable coincidences that led to the inevitable happy ending. The kind of movies she said her boyfriend didn't like.

Her boyfriend.

Your boyfriend.

Out of town.

Out of reach.

You made sure he would find her when he got back. Left her halfway down the stairs, popcorn spilled around her, the hand-painted blue bowl she said they'd picked out together lying unhurt at the bottom.

Her neck was at an odd angle. You didn't put it that way; she just fell so pretty, all on her own. Got dizzy, the paramedics no doubt said. Lost her balance as pregnant women sometimes do.

You were careful not to touch anything you couldn't wipe off later, when you got rid of any trace that you'd been there. You had napkins in your hand when you pushed her.

She didn't scream when she fell. That was disappointing. You wanted something, you wanted to know she felt it – the physical as well as emotional pain. Not just a little "Oh!" and then the thud.

But you'd already been taught that you wouldn't always get what you want, so you let your disappointment go and took what fate offered.

You waited a long time before you left, making sure she wasn't just hurt – that she was good and dead. You stared at her belly, wondering if she'd bleed out the brat the way your baby had leaked out. But there was no blood. Her baby died as quietly as she did.

You left through the back door, walked the three blocks to the subway stop, and rode the train home waiting to see if guilt would sink in eventually.

It didn't.

You put the wig and the glasses in a box you hid in the attic. That person was gone. That person who she thought was her friend. She never knew the real you. It's possible no one but you and the ghost of a baby bled out on a bathroom floor know the real you.

It didn't surprise you at all that he came to you after he found her the next night. He was clearly in shock with his eyes red and puffy. He came to you. Out of habit, you think.

Something's happened.

You didn't hug him. You stared hard at him, waiting, but no more words came out of him as he stood in the light from the streetlamp and ran his hands through hair that was already mussed.

You walked away from him, down the walkway, back to the door of the house the two of you shared for three years. But just when you thought he was ready to turn and go, you looked back. That kind of look you've seen described in the sort of books that make words into poetry. The backward glance. The gesture that said, "You'll always own my heart."

That you forgave him. That you would help him. That you cared no matter what he'd done to you.

I'm so sorry. I...

You could see his pain. You thought he wasn't actually sorry for what he'd done to you. He was sorry for her having died. For their baby never getting past those stairs to the basement, with that rough Berber carpeting beneath its mother's skin and popcorn all around. The butter smell oozing up.

The smell should have made you sick since that night. It didn't.

You popped some as he paced the kitchen, not talking, just moving, as if he was some kind of heartbroken shark that would die if it stopped. You pretended not to understand why he shied away from the popcorn you offered him. Had to hide the smirk at the face he'd made. And then you told him to sit as you took the opposing chair. It was like old times, only with just you eating. He was looking increasingly sick the more you ate.

You took your time before you finally pushed the half-filled bag away.

What now?

You shrugged. He hadn't told you what had happened, not really. You owed him no reaction until he did.

He got up slowly, staring at the popcorn as if it had been the thing to kill his woman. You looked up at him, waiting.

I have to go.

But he didn't go. He stood and looked helpless, his eyes finding yours the way they used to, when he needed bailing out at a cocktail party or a family holiday. He stood by the table that you used to share with him – so many meals eaten here, so many fights, so many tears – and he played with his tie since it was clear he had no idea what else to do. It was a bright tie. Wine and turquoise, with patches of yellow. Abstract. Not one you bought for him.

But you'll buy one for him now.

The clerk is handing you a dark tie. Black with a pattern you can barely see in red with tiny streaks of antique gold. It makes you think of blood and popcorn drowning in a sea of tar.

"It's perfect," you say.

She rings it up and takes extra care with wrapping it in tissue paper so it won't wrinkle or scrunch up in the bag. She's trying so hard you think she is probably a good person. Someone who rushes to hold doors for old ladies and tells people when they drop something on the sidewalk. She's a person who would never leave someone lying crumpled on the stairs with a dying baby inside them.

But you can be good. Look at you now, buying him a tie. Not a bright, loud, bought-by-somebody-else tie. But a mournful tie that you'll take to him.

"For the funeral," you will say.

And he will look touched. He will look helpless and want to hug you, because that's how he says "Thank you." He's been by several times since she died. You've been sweet to him. You've been comforting. As if you can forgive him. As if you love him enough to want to help him when he needs you.

He never knew about your baby; he wasn't there when you needed him, when you cleaned up the mess.

Bleach and scouring powder. That's what babies smell like to you. You hate those smells, now.

But babies can smell like popcorn, too, and that smell still doesn't bother you.

You don't eat popcorn around him, anymore. Not since he told you what happened. After all, you're a caring person. You wouldn't want to torture him.

You've been so understanding.

"I am sorry." The clerk hands you the bag. "To lose your lover..."

You nod and give her the saddest look you can. But as you turn and push your way through the aisles, you smile, and you know in what used to be your heart that it is not a pretty expression. "I didn't say it was my lover."

The Hound

H.P. Lovecraft

IN MY TORTURED EARS there sounds unceasingly a nightmare whirring and flapping, and a faint distant baying as of some gigantic hound. It is not dream – it is not, I fear, even madness – for too much has already happened to give me these merciful doubts.

St John is a mangled corpse; I alone know why, and such is my knowledge that I am about to blow out my brains for fear I shall be mangled in the same way. Down unlit and illimitable corridors of eldritch phantasy sweeps the black, shapeless Nemesis that drives me to self-annihilation.

May heaven forgive the folly and morbidity which led us both to so monstrous a fate! Wearied with the commonplaces of a prosaic world; where even the joys of romance and adventure soon grow stale, St John and I had followed enthusiastically every aesthetic and intellectual movement which promised respite from our devastating ennui. The enigmas of the symbolists and the ecstasies of the pre-Raphaelites all were ours in their time, but each new mood was drained too soon, of its diverting novelty and appeal.

Only the somber philosophy of the decadents could help us, and this we found potent only by increasing gradually the depth and diablism of our penetrations. Baudelaire and Huysmans were soon exhausted of thrills, till finally there remained for us only the more direct stimuli of unnatural personal experiences and adventures. It was this frightful emotional need which led us eventually to that detestable course which even in my present fear I mention with shame and timidity – that hideous extremity of human outrage, the abhorred practice of grave-robbing.

I cannot reveal the details of our shocking expedition, or catalogue even partly the worst of the trophies adorning the nameless museum we jointly dwelt, alone and servantless. Our museum was a blasphemous, unthinkable place, where with the satanic taste of neurotic virtuosi we had assembled an universe of terror and a secret room, far, far, underground; where huge winged daemons carven of basalt and onyx vomited from wide grinning mouths weird green and orange light, and hidden pneumatic pipes ruffled into kaleidoscopic dances of death the line of red charnel things hand in hand woven in voluminous black hangings. Through these pipes came at will the odors our moods most craved; sometimes the scent of pale funeral lilies; sometimes the narcotic incense of imagined Eastern shrines of the kingly dead, and sometimes – how I shudder to recall it! – the frightful, soul-upheaving stenches of the uncovered-grave.

Around the walls of this repellent chamber were cases of antique mummies alternating with comely, lifelike bodies perfectly stuffed and cured by the taxidermist's art, and with headstones snatched from the oldest churchyards of the world. Niches here and there contained skulls of all shapes, and heads preserved in various stages of dissolution. There one might find the rotting, bald pates of famous noblemen, and the flesh and radiantly golden heads of new-buried children.

Statues and painting there were, all of fiendish subjects and some executed by St John and myself. A locked portfolio, bound in tanned human skin, held certain unknown and unnameable drawings which it was rumored Goya had perpetrated but dared not acknowledge. There were nauseous musical instruments, stringed, brass, wood-wind, on which St John and I sometimes produced dissonances of exquisite morbidity and cacodaemoniacal ghastliness; whilst in a multitude of inlaid ebony cabinets reposed the most incredible and unimaginable variety of tomb-loot ever assembled by human madness and perversity. It is of this loot in particular that I must not speak. Thank God I had the courage to destroy it long before I thought of destroying myself!

The predatory excursions on which we collected our unmentionable treasures were always artistically memorable events. We were no vulgar ghouls, but worked only under certain conditions of mood, landscape, environment, weather, season, and moonlight. These pastimes were to us the most exquisite form of aesthetic expression, and we gave their details a fastidious technical care. An inappropriate hour, a jarring lighting effect, or a clumsy manipulation of the damp sod, would almost totally destroy for us that ecstatic titillation which followed the exhumation of some ominous, grinning secret of the earth. Our quest for novel scenes and piquant conditions was feverish and insatiate – St John was always the leader, and he it was who led the way at last to that mocking, accursed spot which brought us our hideous and inevitable doom.

By what malign fatality were we lured to that terrible Holland churchyard? I think it was the dark rumor and legendry, the tales of one buried for five centuries, who had himself been a ghoul in his time and had stolen a potent thing from a mighty sepulchre. I can recall the scene in these final moments – the pale autumnal moon over the graves, casting long horrible shadows; the grotesque trees, drooping sullenly to meet the neglected grass and the crumbling slabs; the vast legions of strangely colossal bats that flew against the moon; the antique ivied church pointing a huge spectral finger at the livid sky; the phosphorescent insects that danced like death-fires under the yews in a distant corner; the odors of mould, vegetation, and less explicable things that mingled feebly with the night-wind from over far swamps and seas; and, worst of all, the faint deep-toned baying of some gigantic hound which we could neither see nor definitely place. As we heard this suggestion of baying we shuddered, remembering the tales of the peasantry; for he whom we sought had centuries before been found in this selfsame spot, torn and mangled by the claws and teeth of some unspeakable beast.

I remember how we delved in the ghoul's grave with our spades, and how we thrilled at the picture of ourselves, the grave, the pale watching moon, the horrible shadows, the grotesque trees, the titanic bats, the antique church, the dancing death-fires, the sickening odors, the gently moaning night-wind, and the strange, half-heard directionless baying of whose objective existence we could scarcely be sure.

Then we struck a substance harder than the damp mould, and beheld a rotting oblong box crusted with mineral deposits from the long undisturbed ground. It was incredibly tough and thick, but so old that we finally pried it open and feasted our eyes on what it held.

Much – amazingly much – was left of the object despite the lapse of five hundred years. The skeleton, though crushed in places by the jaws of the thing that had killed it, held together with surprising firmness, and we gloated over the clean white skull and its long, firm teeth and its eyeless sockets that once had glowed with a charnel fever like our own. In the coffin lay an amulet of curious and exotic design, which had apparently been worn around the sleeper's neck. It was the oddly conventionalised figure of a crouching winged hound, or sphinx with a semi-canine face, and was exquisitely carved in antique Oriental fashion from a small piece of green jade. The expression of its features was repellent in the extreme, savoring at once of death, bestiality and malevolence. Around the base was an inscription in characters which neither St John nor I could identify; and on the bottom, like a maker's seal, was graven a grotesque and formidable skull.

Immediately upon beholding this amulet we knew that we must possess it; that this treasure alone was our logical pelf from the centuried grave. Even had its outlines been unfamiliar we would have desired it, but as we looked more closely we saw that it was not wholly unfamiliar. Alien it indeed was to all art and literature which sane and balanced readers know, but we recognized it as the thing hinted of in the forbidden Necronomicon of the mad Arab Abdul Alhazred; the ghastly soul-symbol of the corpse-eating cult of inaccessible Leng, in Central Asia. All too well did we trace the sinister lineaments described by the old Arab daemonologist; lineaments, he wrote, drawn from some obscure supernatural manifestation of the souls of those who vexed and gnawed at the dead.

Seizing the green jade object, we gave a last glance at the bleached and cavern-eyed face of its owner and closed up the grave as we found it. As we hastened from the abhorrent spot, the stolen amulet in St John's pocket, we thought we saw the bats descend in a body to the earth we had so lately rifled, as if seeking for some cursed and unholy nourishment. But the autumn moon shone weak and pale, and we could not be sure.

So, too, as we sailed the next day away from Holland to our home, we thought we heard the faint distant baying of some gigantic hound in the background. But the autumn wind moaned sad and wan, and we could not be sure.

Less than a week after our return to England, strange things began to happen. We lived as recluses; devoid of friends, alone, and without servants in a few rooms of an ancient manor-house on a bleak and unfrequented moor; so that our doors were seldom disturbed by the knock of the visitor.

Now, however, we were troubled by what seemed to be a frequent fumbling in the night, not only around the doors but around the windows also, upper as well as lower. Once we fancied that a large, opaque body darkened the library window when the moon was shining against it, and another time we thought we heard a whirring or flapping sound not far off. On each occasion investigation revealed nothing, and we began to ascribe the occurrences to imagination which still prolonged in our ears the faint far baying we thought we had heard in the Holland churchyard. The jade amulet now reposed in a niche in our museum, and sometimes we burned a strangely scented candle before it. We read much in Alhazred's Necronomicon about its properties, and about the relation of ghosts' souls to the objects it symbolized; and were disturbed by what we read.

Then terror came.

On the night of September 24, 19–, I heard a knock at my chamber door. Fancying it St John's, I bade the knocker enter, but was answered only by a shrill laugh. There was no one in the corridor. When I aroused St John from his sleep, he professed entire ignorance of the event, and became as worried as I. It was the night that the faint, distant baying over the moor became to us a certain and dreaded reality.

Four days later, whilst we were both in the hidden museum, there came a low, cautious scratching at the single door which led to the secret library staircase. Our alarm was now divided, for, besides our fear of the unknown, we had always entertained a dread that our grisly collection might be discovered. Extinguishing all lights, we proceeded to the door and threw it suddenly open; whereupon we felt an unaccountable rush of air, and heard, as if receding far away, a queer combination of rustling, tittering, and articulate chatter. Whether we were mad, dreaming, or in our senses, we did not try to determine. We only realized, with the blackest of apprehensions, that the apparently disembodied chatter was beyond a doubt in the Dutch language.

After that we lived in growing horror and fascination. Mostly we held to the theory that we were jointly going mad from our life of unnatural excitements, but sometimes it pleased us more to dramatize ourselves as the victims of some creeping and appalling doom. Bizarre manifestations were now too frequent to count. Our lonely house was seemingly alive with the presence of some malign being whose nature we could not guess, and every night that daemoniac baying rolled over the wind-swept moor, always louder and louder. On October 29 we found in the soft earth underneath the library window a series of footprints utterly impossible to describe. They were as baffling as the hordes of great bats which haunted the old manor-house in unprecedented and increasing numbers.

The horror reached a culmination on November 18, when St John, walking home after dark from the dismal railway station, was seized by some frightful carnivorous thing and torn to ribbons. His screams had reached the house, and I had hastened to the terrible scene in time to hear a whir of wings and see a vague black cloudy thing silhouetted against the rising moon.

My friend was dying when I spoke to him, and he could not answer coherently. All he could do was to whisper, "The amulet – that damned thing–"

Then he collapsed, an inert mass of mangled flesh.

I buried him the next midnight in one of our neglected gardens, and mumbled over his body one of the devilish rituals he had loved in life. And as I pronounced the last daemoniac sentence I heard afar on the moor the faint baying of some gigantic hound. The moon was up, but I dared not look at it. And when I saw on the dim-lighted moor a wide-nebulous shadow sweeping from mound to mound, I shut my eyes and threw myself face down upon the ground. When I arose, trembling, I know not how much later, I staggered into the house and made shocking obeisances before the enshrined amulet of green jade.

Being now afraid to live alone in the ancient house on the moor, I departed on the following day for London, taking with me the amulet after destroying by fire and burial the rest of the impious collection in the museum. But after three nights I heard the baying again, and before a week was over felt strange eyes upon me whenever it was dark. One evening as I strolled on Victoria Embankment for some needed air, I saw a black shape obscure one of the reflections of the lamps in the water. A wind, stronger than the night-wind, rushed by, and I knew that what had befallen St John must soon befall me.

The next day I carefully wrapped the green jade amulet and sailed for Holland. What mercy I might gain by returning the thing to its silent, sleeping owner I knew not; but I felt that I must try any step conceivably logical. What the hound was, and why it had pursued me, were questions still vague; but I had first heard the baying in that ancient churchyard, and every subsequent event including St John's dying whisper had served to connect the curse with the stealing of the amulet. Accordingly I sank into the nethermost abysses of despair when, at an inn in Rotterdam, I discovered that thieves had despoiled me of this sole means of salvation.

The baying was loud that evening, and in the morning I read of a nameless deed in the vilest quarter of the city. The rabble were in terror, for upon an evil tenement had fallen a red death beyond the foulest previous crime of the neighborhood. In a squalid thieves' den an entire family had been torn to shreds by an unknown thing which left no trace, and those around had heard all night a faint, deep, insistent note as of a gigantic hound.

So at last I stood again in the unwholesome churchyard where a pale winter moon cast hideous shadows and leafless trees drooped sullenly to meet the withered, frosty grass and cracking slabs, and the ivied church pointed a jeering finger at the unfriendly sky, and the night-wind howled maniacally from over frozen swamps and frigid seas. The baying was very faint now, and it ceased altogether as I approached the ancient grave I had once violated, and frightened away an abnormally large horde of bats which had been hovering curiously around it.

I know not why I went thither unless to pray, or gibber out insane pleas and apologies to the calm white thing that lay within; but, whatever my reason, I attacked the half frozen sod with a desperation partly mine and partly that of a dominating will outside myself. Excavation was much easier than I expected, though at one point I encountered a queer interruption; when a lean vulture darted down out of the cold sky and pecked frantically at the grave-earth until I killed him with a blow of my spade. Finally I reached the rotting oblong box and removed the damp nitrous cover. This is the last rational act I ever performed.

For crouched within that centuried coffin, embraced by a closepacked nightmare retinue of huge, sinewy, sleeping bats, was the bony thing my friend and I had robbed; not clean and placid as we had seen it then, but covered with caked blood and shreds of alien flesh and hair, and leering sentiently at me with phosphorescent sockets and sharp ensanguined fangs yawning twistedly in mockery of my inevitable doom. And when it gave from those grinning jaws a deep, sardonic bay as of some gigantic hound, and I saw that it held in its gory filthy claw the lost and fateful amulet of green jade, I merely screamed and ran away idiotically, my screams soon dissolving into peals of hysterical laughter.

Madness rides the star-wind ... claws and teeth sharpened on centuries of corpses ... dripping death astride a bacchanale of bats from nigh-black ruins of buried temples of Belial ... Now, as the baying of that dead fleshless monstrosity grows louder and louder, and the stealthy whirring and flapping of those accursed web-wings circles closer and closer, I shall seek with my revolver the oblivion which is my only refuge from the unnamed and unnameable.

From Beyond

H.P. Lovecraft

HORRIBLE beyond conception was the change which had taken place in my best friend, Crawford Tillinghast. I had not seen him since that day, two months and a half before, when he had told me toward what goal his physical and metaphysical researches were leading; when he had answered my awed and almost frightened remonstrances by driving me from his laboratory and his house in a burst of fanatical rage, I had known that he now remained mostly shut in the attic laboratory with that accursed electrical machine, eating little and excluding even the servants, but I had not thought that a brief period of ten weeks could so alter and disfigure any human creature. It is not pleasant to see a stout man suddenly grown thin, and it is even worse when the baggy skin becomes yellowed or grayed, the eyes sunken, circled, and uncannily glowing, the forehead veined and corrugated, and the hands tremulous and twitching. And if added to this there be a repellent unkemptness; a wild disorder of dress, a bushiness of dark hair white at the roots, and an unchecked growth of white beard on a face once clean-shaven, the cumulative effect is quite shocking. But such was the aspect of Crawford Tillinghast on the night his half-coherent message brought me to his door after my weeks of exile; such was the specter that trembled as it admitted me, candle in hand, and glanced furtively over its shoulder as if fearful of unseen things in the ancient, lonely house set back from Benevolent Street.

That Crawford Tillinghast should ever have studied science and philosophy was a mistake. These things should be left to the frigid and impersonal investigator, for they offer two equally tragic alternatives to the man of feeling and action; despair, if he fail in his quest, and terrors unutterable and unimaginable if he succeed. Tillinghast had once been the prey of failure, solitary and melancholy; but now I knew, with nauseating fears of my own, that he was the prey of success. I had indeed warned him ten weeks before, when he burst forth with his tale of what he felt himself about to discover. He had been flushed and excited then, talking in a high and unnatural, though always pedantic, voice.

"What do we know," he had said, "of the world and the universe about us? Our means of receiving impressions are absurdly few, and our notions of surrounding objects infinitely narrow. We see things only as we are constructed to see them, and can gain no idea of their absolute nature. With five feeble senses we pretend to comprehend the boundlessly complex cosmos; yet other beings with a wider, stronger, or different range of senses might not only see very differently the things we see, but might see and study whole worlds of matter, energy, and life which lie close at hand yet can never be detected with the senses we have. I have always believed that such strange, inaccessible worlds exist at our very elbows, and now I believe I have found a way to break down the barriers. I am not joking.

Within twenty-four hours that machine near the table will generate waves acting on unrecognized sense-organs that exist in us as atrophied or rudimentary vestiges. Those waves will open up to us many vistas unknown to man, and several unknown to anything we consider organic life. We shall see that at which dogs howl in the dark, and that at which cats prick up their ears after midnight. We shall see these things, and other things which no breathing creature has yet seen. We shall overleap time, space, and dimensions, and without bodily motion peer to the bottom of creation."

When Tillinghast said these things I remonstrated, for I knew him well enough to be frightened rather than amused; but he was a fanatic, and drove me from the house. Now he was no less a fanatic, but his desire to speak had conquered his resentment, and he had written me imperatively in a hand I could scarcely recognize. As I entered the abode of the friend so suddenly metamorphosed to a shivering gargoyle, I became infected with the terror which seemed stalking in all the shadows. The words and beliefs expressed ten weeks before seemed bodied forth in the darkness beyond the small circle of candlelight, and I sickened at the hollow, altered voice of my host. I wished the servants were about, and did not like it when he said they had all left three days previously. It seemed strange that old Gregory, at least, should desert his master without telling as tried a friend as I. It was he who had given me all the information I had of Tillinghast after I was repulsed in rage.

Yet I soon subordinated all my fears to my growing curiosity and fascination. Just what Crawford Tillinghast now wished of me I could only guess, but that he had some stupendous secret or discovery to impart, I could not doubt. Before I had protested at his unnatural pryings into the unthinkable; now that he had evidently succeeded to some degree I almost shared his spirit, terrible though the cost of victory appeared.

Up through the dark emptiness of the house I followed the bobbing candle in the hand of this shaking parody on man. The electricity seemed to be turned off, and when I asked my guide he said it was for a definite reason.

"It would be too much ... I would not dare," he continued to mutter. I especially noted his new habit of muttering, for it was not like him to talk to himself.

We entered the laboratory in the attic, and I observed that detestable electrical machine, glowing with a sickly, sinister violet luminosity. It was connected with a powerful chemical battery, but seemed to be receiving no current; for I recalled that in its experimental stage it had sputtered and purred when in action. In reply to my question Tillinghast mumbled that this permanent glow was not electrical in any sense that I could understand.

He now seated me near the machine, so that it was on my right, and turned a switch somewhere below the crowning duster of glass bulbs. The usual sputtering began, turned to a whine, and terminated in a drone so soft as to suggest a return to silence. Meanwhile the luminosity increased, waned again, then assumed a pale, outré color or blend of colors which I could neither place nor describe. Tillinghast had been watching me, and noted my puzzled expression.

"Do you know what that is?" he whispered. "That is ultra-violet " He chuckled oddly at my surprise. "You thought ultra-violet was invisible, and so it is – but you can see that and many other invisible things now.

"Listen to me! The waves from that thing are waking a thousand sleeping senses in us; senses which we inherit from eons of evolution from the state of detached electrons to the state of organic humanity. I have seen truth, and I intend to show it to you. Do you wonder how it will seem? I will tell you."

Here Tillinghast seated himself directly opposite me, blowing out his candle and staring hideously into my eyes.

"Your existing sense-organs – ears first, I think – will pick up many of the impressions, for they are closely connected with the dormant organs. Then there will be others. You have heard of the pineal gland? I laugh at the shallow endocrinologist, fellow-dupe and fellow-parvenu of the Freudian. That gland is the great sense organ of organs – I have found out. It is like sight in the end, and transmits visual pictures to the brain. If you are normal, that is the way you ought to get most of it … I mean get most of the evidence from beyond."

I looked about the immense attic room with the sloping south wall, dimly lit by rays which the everyday eye cannot see. The far corners were all shadows, and the whole place took on a hazy unreality which obscured its nature and invited the imagination to symbolism and phantasm. During the interval that Tillinghast was silent I fancied myself in some vast and incredible temple of long-dead gods; some vague edifice of innumerable black stone columns reaching up from a floor of damp slabs to a cloudy height beyond the range of my vision.

The picture was very vivid for a while, but gradually gave way to a more horrible conception; that of utter, absolute solitude in infinite, sightless, soundless space. There seemed to be a void, and nothing more, and I felt a childish fear which prompted me to draw from my hip pocket the revolver I always carried after dark since the night I was held up in East Providence. Then, from the farther-most regions of remoteness, the sound softly glided into existence. It was infinitely faint, subtly vibrant, and unmistakably musical, but held a quality of surpassing wildness which made its impact feel like a delicate torture of my whole body. I felt sensations like those one feels when accidentally scratching ground glass. Simultaneously there developed something like a cold draft, which apparently swept past me from the direction of the distant sound. As I waited breathlessly I perceived that both sound and wind were increasing; the effect being to give me an odd notion of myself as tied to a pair of rails in the path of a gigantic approaching locomotive.

I began to speak to Tillinghast, and as I did so all the unusual impressions abruptly vanished. I saw only the man, the glowing machine, and the dim apartment Tillinghast was grinning repulsively at the revolver which I had almost unconsciously drawn, but from his expression I was sure he had seen and heard as much as I, if not a great deal more. I whispered what I had experienced, and he bade me remain as quiet and receptive as possible.

"Don't move," he cautioned, "for in these rays we are able to be seen as well as to see. I told you the servants left, but I didn't tell you how. It was that thick-witted housekeeper – who turned on the lights downstairs after I had warned her not to, and the wires picked up sympathetic vibrations. It must have been frightful – I could hear the screams up here in spite of all I was seeing and hearing from another direction, and later it was rather awful to find those empty heaps of clothes around the house. Mrs. Updike's clothes were close to the front hall switch – that's how I know she did it. It got them all. But so long as we don't move we're fairly safe. Remember we're dealing with a hideous world in which we are practically helpless… Keep still!"

The combined shock of the revelation and of the abrupt command gave me a kind of paralysis, and in my terror my mind again opened to the impressions coming from what Tillinghast called 'beyond'. I was now in a vortex of sound and motion, with confused pictures before my eyes. I saw the blurred outlines of the room, but from some point in space there seemed to be pouring a seething column of unrecognizable shapes or clouds, penetrating the solid roof at a point ahead and to the right of me. Then I glimpsed the temple-like effect again, but this time the pillars readied up into an aerial ocean of light, which sent down one blinding beam along the path of the cloudy column I had seen before.

After that the scene was almost wholly kaleidoscopic, and in the jumble of sights, sounds, and unidentified sense-impressions I felt that I was about to dissolve or in some way lose the solid form. One definite flash I shall always remember. I seemed for an instant to behold a patch of strange night sky filled with shining, revolving spheres, and as it receded I saw that the glowing suns formed a constellation or galaxy of settled shape; this shape being the distorted face of Crawford Tillinghast. At another time I felt huge animate things brushing past me and occasionally walking or drifting through my supposedly solid body, and thought I saw Tillinghast look at them as though his better-trained senses could catch them visually. I recalled what he had said of the pineal gland, and wondered what he saw with this preternatural eye.

Suddenly I myself became possessed of a kind of augmented sight. Over and above the luminous and shadowy chaos arose a picture which, though vague, held the elements of consistency and permanence. It was indeed somewhat familiar, for the unusual part was superimposed upon the usual terrestrial scene much as a cinema view may be thrown upon the painted curtain of a theater. I saw the attic laboratory, the electrical machine, and the unsightly form of Tillinghast opposite me; but of all the space unoccupied by familiar objects not one particle was vacant. Indescribable shapes both alive and otherwise were mixed in disgusting disarray, and close to every known thing were whole worlds of alien, unknown entities. It likewise seemed that all the known things entered into the composition of other unknown things, and vice versa.

Foremost among the living objects were inky, jellyish monstrosities which flabbily quivered in harmony with the vibrations from the machine. They were present in loathsome profusion, and I saw to my horror that they overlapped; that they were semi-fluid and capable of passing through one another and through what we know as solids. These things were never still, but seemed ever floating about with some malignant purpose. Sometimes they appeared to devour one another, the attacker launching itself at its victim and instantaneously obliterating the latter from sight. Shudderingly I felt that I knew what had obliterated the unfortunate servants, and could not exclude the things from my mind as I strove to observe other properties of the newly visible world that lies unseen around us. But Tillinghast had been watching me, and was speaking.

"You see them? You see them? You see the things that float and flop about you and through you every moment of your life? You see the creatures that form what men call the pure air and the blue sky? Have I not succeeded in breaking down the barrier; have I not shown you worlds that no other living men have seen?"

I heard his scream through the horrible chaos, and looked at the wild face thrust so offensively close to mine. His eyes were pits of flame, and they glared at me with what I now saw was overwhelming hatred. The machine droned detestably.

"You think those floundering things wiped out the servants? Fool, they are harmless! But the servants are gone, aren't they? You tried to stop me; you discouraged me when I needed every drop of encouragement I could get; you were afraid of the cosmic truth, you damned coward, but now I've got you! What swept up the servants? What made them scream so loud? ... Don't know, eh? You'll know soon enough. Look at me – listen to what I say – do you suppose there are really any such things as time and magnitude? Do you fancy there are such things as form or matter? I tell you, I have struck depths that your little brain can't picture. I have seen beyond the bounds of infinity and drawn down demons from the stars… I have harnessed the shadows that stride from world to world to sow death and madness … space belongs to me, do you hear? Things are hunting me now – the things that devour and dissolve – but I know how to elude them. It is you they will get, as they got the servants…

"Stirring, dear sir? I told you it was dangerous to move; I have saved you so far by telling you to keep still – saved you to see more sights and to listen to me. If you had moved, they would have been at you long ago. Don't worry, they won't hurt you. They didn't hurt the servants – it was the seeing that made the poor devils scream so. My pets are not pretty, for they come out of places where aesthetic standards are – very different. Disintegration is quite painless, I assure you – but I want you to see them. I almost saw them, but I knew how to stop.

"You are not curious? I always knew you were no scientist. Trembling, eh? Trembling with anxiety to see the ultimate things I have discovered? Why don't you move, then? Tired? Well, don't worry, my friend, for they are coming … Look, look, curse you, look … it's just over your left shoulder…"

What remains to be told is very brief, and may be familiar to you from the newspaper accounts. The police heard a shot in the old Tillinghast house and found us there – Tillinghast dead and me unconscious. They arrested me because the revolver was in my hand, but released me in three hours, after they found that it was apoplexy which had finished Tillinghast and saw that my shot had been directed at the noxious machine which now lay hopelessly shattered on the laboratory floor. I did not tell very much of what I had seen, for I feared the coroner would be skeptical; but from the evasive outline I did give, the doctor told me that I had undoubtedly been hypnotized by the vindictive and homicidal madman.

I wish I could believe that doctor. It would help my shaky nerves if I could dismiss what I now have to think of the air and the sky about and above me. I never feel alone or comfortable, and a hideous sense of pursuit sometimes comes chillingly on me when I am weary. What prevents me from believing the doctor is this one simple fact – that the police never found the bodies of those servants whom they say Crawford Tillinghast murdered.

Drive Safe

K.A. Mielke

THE WOMAN SITS on the side of the road, naked and shivering, with her knees pulled up to her chin.

Beside me, Cameron looks up from her cell phone, her freckled face glowing in the light of the screen. "Oh my god, Kyle, stop the car."

We speed past her.

"What are you doing?" Cameron says, twisting around in her seat to look out the rear windshield.

I shrug. "What if it's some elaborate ploy by a serial killer? Set a pretty lady up on the side of the road, wait for some chivalrous opportunist to come save her, and WHAM! Best case scenario, we're the next mysterious naked people hoping to be rescued on the side of the road."

"You can't be serious."

I shrug again as guilt settles into my stomach. "She could be a victim of him, or she could be working with him –"

"Or there could be no serial killer and she could just be a woman in need," Cameron said, her gaze hard and kinda terrifying.

I sigh and make a U-turn.

When we see her again, still curled up in a ball, I pull over. Gravel scatters beneath my tires. The woman doesn't seem to notice us.

Cameron practically flies out of the car. I unbuckle and step out.

It's freezing, the wind cutting through my jacket and burning my cheeks. I slip in the slush on my way to her, snowflakes catching in my hair and shooting into my eyes.

"Are you okay?" I shout above the wind. The woman doesn't hear me, or maybe she's too frozen to respond. Maybe she's dying.

Cameron stands beside her and shouts something at me, but the wind steals her words. Cameron holds out her hand, urging. I guess at what she wants, taking off my coat and wrapping it around the hitchhiker's shoulders. The woman doesn't even look at me.

"We're going to help you," Cameron says. "It's going to be okay. Let's get her in the car."

My bare arms stinging in the cold, I crouch behind the woman and help lift her to her feet.

She steps with us, slowly, shaking and shaking and shaking. I duck my head and pay attention to my feet, trying not to think about how slow our pace is or how long it'll take to reach the car when every footstep is a painful, freezing eternity –and then we've reached the car. We lay the woman in the backseat, and I run back to the driver's side and slam the door.

My teeth chatter enough to chip, especially in the cold. I crank the heat and rub my hands together over the heaters.

Cameron's breathing heavy, and for a moment we all sit in the quiet, me, my girlfriend, and the dying hitchhiker girl in the back seat. Finally, Cameron says, "We should go."

I look over my shoulder, hoping she isn't dead, praying we got to her in time – and wishing we'd never stopped in the first place.

Her shivering seems less violent, her skin less blue.

The woman looks at me with the deepest, bluest eyes I've ever seen, so deep and blue they look artificial. Like dyed flowers. I've never seen eyes that beautiful.

I turn around when I realize I'm staring. "The nearest hospital can't be far," I say, shifting into drive.

"I'll Google it," Cameron says.

We've been on the road for a couple days now. I woke up Thursday morning with Cameron on top of me, hair in my face, and saying, "I've always wanted to go on a road trip." So I sat up and packed our bags, throwing her over my shoulder and setting out. Right now, driving through a blizzard, we've come to admit that doing a huge road trip during winter was not a well-thought-out plan.

At least it worked out for somebody.

Cameron sets the GPS in her phone and mantles it to the dashboard.

I signal and pull out.

A horn blares and I slam on the brakes as a transport truck swerves out of the way and barrels by us. Our car rocks in the wind.

"Jesus!" Cameron says

"Sorry. I wasn't paying attention."

Cameron doesn't say anything to that. She's not the kind of person to rub something in if you're already feeling bad. I don't think I've ever been more grateful for that.

I thoroughly check for oncoming traffic, looking in both mirrors and my blind spot until my neck hurts and my eyes ache.

I pull out.

As we drive, the only sounds are the vents pumping warm air and our own erratic breathing.

My grip on the steering wheel tightens as I struggle against nature. The wipers work overtime to clear away all the snow, but I still can barely see in front of us – except for the neon sign passing on the right that says DRIVE SAFE.

It might be kinda funny, once we get off the road and into the warmth of a motel bed.

Cameron turns on the radio and leans in to me. She cycles through stations until she finds country music. She had to put up with David Bowie's entire discography up until now, so I can't argue.

She looks back at the woman curled up in the backseat. "What do you think happened to her?" she whispers.

"I don't know," I say.

"Do you think she was... you know, hurt? Like that?"

"I don't know," I say again, snippier this time, feeling anger begin to flush my face. Then, "Sorry."

She takes my hand. She's warmer than I am, her hand practically burning mine. "It's okay. She's going to be okay. She's already looking better."

I adjust the rear-view to look at her. Colour is returning to her olive skin, and she seems more alert, looking around like she isn't sure how she got in our car.

She sits up, my coat falling off her shoulders, her body exposed. My heart thunders in my chest. When I look at her, my body feels light, as if my soul's rising out from the dead weight of my flesh. It's a feeling I've only experienced when drunk, but I've been sober for years. After how Cameron found me last time...

Embarrassed, I look away from the woman, keeping my eyes on the road and not at her bare chest betraying how cold she is. The feeling starts to fade.

"Hungry," she says.

That's when I fall completely, irreparably in love with her. It's not the perfect curves like a winding mountain road, or the way her eyes look so much deeper than anyone else's, like there are whole worlds contained in the vastness of her irises. It's not her helplessness, even though I am very literally her hero right now and that is admittedly hot. No, it's her voice, uttering a single word we can all relate to, and it shoots me so full of endorphins I'm suddenly a giddy teenager having his first kiss all over again.

You have to understand, I love my girlfriend. She's the most helpful, beautiful, kind person I've ever met. We both like Indian food and hate fancy coffees, and we've spent so much time together she feels less like she was once a stranger and more like she's always been a part of me.

But there's just something about this woman that makes none of that matter. There's a tugging that I can feel in my gut, my body yearning to be inside her.

Cameron opens the glove compartment and pulls out a chocolate bar. She holds it out to the woman.

Our hitchhiker just stares. "I'm hungry," she says again.

"It might be a little frozen, but it's better than nothing."

The woman says nothing.

"We're probably about half an hour from the nearest diner," Cameron says helpfully, putting the chocolate back. "We can stop there and get something to eat. We can get out my suitcases, too. I'm sure some of my clothes will fit you."

"No," the woman says. She turns to me. "I need to feed *now*."

"Anything," I say without thinking.

"What exactly are we going to feed her?" Cameron hisses.

"Anything," I say again. "Find anything."

"I'm not going to give her crumbs off the floor, Kyle," she says. She starts looking around the car, checking hidden pockets and cup holders. "Do we have any jerky left?"

"Your lover," the woman says. "Give me your lover."

The colour goes from Cameron's face as she looks back in horror. My own body, however, is reacting like she's just said she loves me and we're having a baby and everything is going to be all right. The pit of my stomach flares with warmth. "Excuse me?" Cameron says.

The hitchhiker leans over me, mouth wet on my ear, breasts on my arm. "I'm going to eat your lover," she says, and it's like she told me I've won an all-expenses-paid vacation to Hawaii, freeing me from the endless cold and bringing me to the oceanside.

With her. For ever with her.

"What the fuck?" Cameron screams. "Kyle, stop the car."

"Don't stop the car, Kyle," the woman says.

It's not even a struggle wondering who to listen to.

The hitchhiker turns to Cameron and straddles the centre console.

Cameron's sobbing. "Don't let her do this!"

The woman dips her face in quickly, once, like a bird pecking its food. Cameron screams and cries hard. She presses her hand to her neck, blood leaking through her fingers. "Oh my god," Cameron says through her tears. "What are you?"

She screams again, loud and curdled and more visceral than anything you could ever experience reading a book or watching a movie. A sound that explodes in my brain into fireworks of every colour.

Somehow, even with her mouth full of flesh, the woman sings. It's this country-pop Top 40 ballad that's all over the radio, something Cameron would have loved. Which means normally it's the auditory equivalent of chewing glass. But with my new love singing, it's my favourite song, my favourite sound in a world full of children's laughter and kittens mewing and love-laced moans.

Cameron bats the hitchhiker away with all the power of a baby, her struggling easing into complacency. The hitchhiker tears off Cameron's ear.

I blink and, just for a second, she changes. She has wings, broken so the bone sticks out, huge and feathered where her arms should be. She's still naked, her bare back soft and smooth in the light of the car GPS, but her eyes look darker, almost black, and her mouth is contorted in a single, hard, sharp beak.

And then I blink again and she's back to the woman who makes my heart race and my body sweat and my dick throb, and I can't control myself around her.

She swallows, and she turns to me.

"I'm still hungry," she says.

I know what she wants. I expose my neck for her.

She leans in.

I close my eyes, and I can feel her breath on my neck, warm and wet, and her soft, plush lips too.

And her teeth. Her tooth. Her sharp beak at my neck, breaking my skin so the first drop of blood trickles down and pools in my collarbone.

From behind my eyelids, there's a light, and I almost think I'm in Heaven. My heart hurts, I'm so happy to be giving myself to this woman.

Then the horn starts.

And in that second I see her for what she is, her beady eyes staring at the oncoming truck, her beak hung open over my neck, the headlights outlining every feather on her body. And I see Cameron, too, my beautiful, smart, funny Cameron, torn apart and slumped against the passenger side door.

I swerve out of the way, the truck's bumper an inch away from taking us out, my hands turning the wheel left and right and left as the back of the car fishtails and the wheels catch on a patch of black ice and suddenly the car is out of my control completely, spinning around as the trees and the road and the black form a panorama of the middle of nowhere and then –

The car flips over –

Glass shatters and cuts open my face –

Metal bends as the roof dents and caves in –

Blood squirts into my mouth, though I don't know if it's mine or Cameron's or the hitchhiker's –

And everything stops. I hang upside down, seatbelt pressed into my chest as it supports my weight, airbags deflating.

I look over at Cameron, ignoring the screaming pain in my neck. The airbag is covered in blood, and Cameron is everywhere, bits of her stuck to the ceiling and the chair.

The naked woman – her top half now entirely bird, her bottom half still impossibly woman – lies with her eyes closed in the back. Blood trickles out of her head, over her feathers.

I sit in a daze for a few moments, feeling the cold of the snow coming in through broken windows, trying to focus on something, anything – and then I remember where I am. What caused the accident.

I scramble for the seatbelt. It releases, dropping me to the ceiling. I open the door and fall into the snow.

My arms and face are on fire, the snow burning and burning until I'm numb to the pain.

The car door slams behind me. I spin around, slipping in the loose snow, limping through the trees.

She cries out to me, cries like a bird whose wings I've broken. Feathers release from her, catching in the wind of the blizzard and blowing away until there's nothing left. Like she was never here at all.

I cross my arms, climb up the ditch, and kneel on the gravel shoulder. I pray for someone kind, someone like Cameron, to stop and help a hitchhiker.

In the Dark

Edith Nesbit

IT MAY have been a form of madness. Or it may be that he really was what is called haunted. Or it may – though I don't pretend to understand how – have been the development, through intense suffering, of a sixth sense in a very nervous, highly strung nature. Something certainly led him where They were. And to him They were all one.

He told me the first part of the story, and the last part of it I saw with my own eyes.

Chapter I

HALDANE AND I were friends even in our school-days. What first brought us together was our common hatred of Visger, who came from our part of the country. His people knew our people at home, so he was put on to us when he came. He was the most intolerable person, boy and man, that I have ever known. He would not tell a lie. And that was all right. But he didn't stop at that. If he were asked whether any other chap had done anything-been out of bounds, or up to any sort of lark – he would always say, "I don't know, sir, but I believe so." He never did know – we took care of that. But what he believed was always right. I remember Haldane twisting his arm to say how he knew about that cherry-tree business, and he only said, "I don't know – I just feel sure. And I was right, you see." What can you do with a boy like that?

We grew up to be men. At least Haldane and I did. Visger grew up to be a prig. He was a vegetarian and a teetotaller, and an all-wooler and Christian Scientist, and all the things that prigs are – but he wasn't a common prig. He knew all sorts of things that he oughtn't to have known, that he couldn't have known in any ordinary decent way. It wasn't that he found things out. He just knew them. Once, when I was very unhappy, he came into my rooms – we were all in our last year at Oxford – and talked about things I hardly knew myself. That was really why I went to India that winter. It was bad enough to be unhappy, without having that beast knowing all about it.

I was away over a year. Coming back, I thought a lot about how jolly it would be to see old Haldane again. If I thought about Visger at all, I wished he was dead. But I didn't think about him much.

I did want to see Haldane. He was always such a jolly chap – gay, and kindly, and simple, honourable, upright, and full of practical sympathies. I longed to see him, to see the smile in his jolly blue eyes, looking out from the net of wrinkles that laughing had made round them, to hear his jolly laugh, and feel the good grip of his big hand. I went straight from the docks to his chambers in Gray's Inn, and I found him cold, pale, anaemic, with dull eyes and a limp hand, and pale lips that smiled without mirth, and uttered a welcome without gladness.

He was surrounded by a litter of disordered furniture and personal effects half packed. Some big boxes stood corded, and there were cases of books, filled and waiting for the enclosing boards to be nailed on.

"Yes, I'm moving," he said. "I can't stand these rooms. There's something rum about them – something devilish rum. I clear our tomorrow."

The autumn dusk was filling the corners with shadows. "You got the furs," I said, just for something to say, for I saw the big case that held them lying corded among the others.

"Furs?" he said. "Oh yes. Thanks awfully. Yes. I forgot about the furs." He laughed, out of politeness, I suppose, for there was no joke about the furs. They were many and fine – the best I could get for money, and I had seen them packed and sent off when my heart was very sore. He stood looking at me, and saying nothing.

"Come out and have a bit of dinner," I said as cheerfully as I could.

"Too busy," he answered, after the slightest possible pause, and a glance round the room – "look here – I'm awfully glad to see you – If you'd just slip over and order in dinner – I'd go myself – only – Well, you see how it is."

I went. And when I came back, he had cleared a space near the fire, and moved his big gate-table into it. We dined there by candle light. I tried to be amusing. He, I am sure, tried to be amused. We did not succeed, either of us. And his haggard eyes watched me all the time, save in those fleeting moments when, without turning his head, he glanced back over his shoulder into the shadows that crowded round the little lighted place where we sat.

When we had dined and the man had come and taken away the dishes, I looked at Haldane very steadily, so that he stopped in a pointless anecdote, and looked interrogatively at me. "Well?" I said.

"You're not listening," he said petulantly. "What's the matter?"

"That's what you'd better tell me," I said.

He was silent, gave one of those furtive glances at the shadows, and stooped to stir the fire to – I knew it – a blaze that must light every corner of the room.

"You're all to pieces," I said cheerfully. "What have you been up to? Wine? Cards? Speculation? A woman? If you won't tell me, you'll have to tell your doctor. Why, my dear chap, you're a wreck."

"You're a comfortable friend to have about the place," he said, and smiled a mechanical smile not at all pleasant to see.

"I'm the friend you want, I think," said I. "Do you suppose I'm blind? Something's gone wrong and you've taken to something. Morphia, perhaps? And you've brooded over the thing till you've lost all sense of proportion. Out with it, old chap. I bet you a dollar it's not so bad as you think it."

"If I could tell you – or tell anyone," he said slowly, "it wouldn't be so bad as it is. If I could tell anyone, I'd tell you. And even as it is, I've told you more than I've told anyone else."

I could get nothing more out of him. But he pressed me to stay – would have given me his bed and made himself a shake-down, he said. But I had engaged my room at the Victoria, and I was expecting letters. So I left him, quite late – and he stood on the stairs, holding a candle over the bannisters to light me down.

When I went back next morning, he was gone. Men were moving his furniture into a big van with somebody's Pantechnicon painted on it in big letters.

He had left no address with the porter, and had driven off in a hansom with two portmanteaux-to Waterloo, the porter thought.

Well, a man has a right to the monopoly of his own troubles, if he chooses to have it. And I had troubles of my own that kept me busy.

Chapter II

IT WAS MORE than a year later that I saw Haldane again. I had got rooms in the Albany by this time, and he turned up there one morning, very early indeed – before breakfast in fact. And if he looked ghastly before, he now looked almost ghostly. His face looked as though it had worn thin, like an oyster shell that has for years been cast up twice a day by the sea on a shore all pebbly. His hands were thin as bird's claws, and they trembled like caught butterflies.

I welcomed him with enthusiastic cordiality and pressed breakfast on him. This time, I decided, I would ask no questions. For I saw that none were needed. He would tell me. He intended to tell me. He had come here to tell me, and for nothing else.

I lit the spirit lamp – I made coffee and small talk for him, and I ate and drank, and waited for him to begin. And it was like this that he began:

"I am going," he said, "to kill myself – oh, don't be alarmed," – I suppose I had said or looked something – "I shan't do it here, or now. I shall do it when I have to – when I can't bear it any longer. And I want someone to know why. I don't want to feel that I'm the only living creature who does know. And I can trust you, can't I?"

I murmured something reassuring.

"I should like you, if you don't mind, to give me your word, that you won't tell a soul what I'm going to tell you, as long as I'm alive. Afterwards… you can tell whom you please." I gave him my word.

He sat silent looking at the fire. Then he shrugged his shoulders.

"It's extraordinary how difficult it is to say it," he said, and smiled. "The fact is – you know that beast, George Visger."

"Yes," I said. "I haven't seen him since I came back. Some one told me he'd gone to some island or other to preach vegetarianism to the cannibals. Anyhow, he's out of the way, bad luck to him."

"Yes," said Haldane, "he's out of the way. But he's not preaching anything. In point of fact, he's dead."

"Dead?" was all I could think of to say.

"Yes," said he; "it's not generally known, but he is."

"What did he die of?" I asked, not that I cared. The bare fact was good enough for me.

"You know what an interfering chap he always was. Always knew everything. Heart to heart talks – and have everything open and above board. Well, he interfered between me and some one else – told her a pack of lies."

"Lies?"

"Well, the things were true, but he made lies of them the way he told them – you know." I did. I nodded. "And she threw me over. And she died. And we weren't even friends. And I couldn't see her-before-I couldn't even… Oh, my God… But I went to the funeral. He was there. They'd asked him. And then I came back to my rooms. And I was sitting there, thinking. And he came up. He would do. It's just what he would do. The beast! I hope you kicked him out."

"No, I didn't. I listened to what he'd got to say. He came to say, no doubt it was all for the best. And he hadn't known the things he told her. He'd only guessed. He'd guessed right, damn him. What right had he to guess right? And he said it was all for the best, because, besides that, there was madness in my family. He'd found that out too –"

"And is there?"

"If there is, I didn't know it. And that was why it was all for the best. So then I said, 'There wasn't any madness in my family before, but there is now,' and I got hold of his throat. I am not sure whether I meant to kill him; I ought to have meant to kill him. Anyhow, I did kill him. What did you say?"

I had said nothing. It is not easy to think at once of the tactful and suitable thing to say, when your oldest friend tells you that he is a murderer.

"When I could get my hands out of his throat – it was as difficult as it is to drop the handles of a galvanic battery – he fell in a lump on the hearth-rug. And I saw what I'd done. How is it that murderers ever get found out?"

"They're careless, I suppose," I found myself saying, "they lose their nerve."

"I didn't," he said. "I never was calmer, I sat down in the big chair and looked at him, and thought it all out. He was just off to that island – I knew that. He'd said goodbye to everyone. He'd told me that. There was no blood to get rid of – or only a touch at the corner of his slack mouth. He wasn't going to travel in his own name because of interviewers. Mr Somebody Something's luggage would be unclaimed and his cabin empty. No one would guess that Mr Somebody Something was Sir George Visger, FRS. It was all as plain as plain. There was nothing to get rid of, but the man. No weapon, no blood – and I got rid of him all right."

"How?"

He smiled cunningly.

"No, no," he said; "that's where I draw the line. It's not that I doubt your word, but if you talked in your sleep, or had a fever or anything. No, no. As long as you don't know where the body is, don't you see, I'm all right. Even if you could prove that I've said all this – which you can't – it's only the wanderings of my poor unhinged brain. See?"

I saw. And I was sorry for him. And I did not believe that he had killed Visger. He was not the sort of man who kills people. So I said:

"Yes, old chap, I see. Now look here. Let's go away together, you and I – travel a bit and see the world, and forget all about that beastly chap."

His eyes lighted up at that.

"Why," he said, "you understand. You don't hate me and shrink from me. I wish I'd told you before – you know – when you came and I was packing all my sticks. But it's too late now."

"Too late? Not a bit of it," I said. "Come, we'll pack our traps and be off tonight – out into the unknown, don't you know."

"That's where I'm going," he said. "You wait. When you've heard what's been happening to me, you won't be so keen to go travelling about with me."

"But you've told me what's been happening to you," I said, and the more I thought about what he had told me, the less I believed it.

"No," he said, slowly, "no – I've told you what happened to him. What happened to me is quite different. Did I tell you what his last words were? Just when I was coming at him.

Before I'd got his throat, you know. He said, 'Look out. You'll never to able to get rid of the body – Besides, anger's sinful.' You know that way he had, like a tract on its hind legs. So afterwards I got thinking of that. But I didn't think of it for a year. Because I did get rid of his body all right. And then I was sitting in that comfortable chair, and I thought, 'Hullo, it must be about a year now, since that –' and I pulled out my pocket-book and went to the window to look at a little almanac I carry about – it was getting dusk – and sure enough it was a year, to the day. And then I remembered what he'd said. And I said to myself, 'Not much trouble about getting rid of your body, you brute.' And then I looked at the hearth-rug and – Ah!" he screamed suddenly and very loud – "I can't tell you – no, I can't."

My man opened the door – he wore a smooth face over his wriggling curiosity. "Did you call, sir?"

"Yes," I lied. "I want you to take a note to the bank, and wait for an answer."

When he was got rid of, Haldane said: "Where was I?"

"You were just telling me what happened after you looked at the almanac. What was it?"

"Nothing much," he said, laughing softly, "oh, nothing much – only that I glanced at the hearthrug – and there he was – the man I'd killed a year before. Don't try to explain, or I shall lose my temper. The door was shut. The windows were shut. He hadn't been there a minute before. And he was there then. That's all."

Hallucination was one of the words I stumbled among.

"Exactly what I thought," he said triumphantly, "but – I touched it. It was quite real. Heavy, you know, and harder than live people are somehow, to the touch – more like a stone thing covered with kid the hands were, and the arms like a marble statue in a blue serge suit. Don't you hate men who wear blue serge suits?" "There are halllucinations of touch too," I found myself saying…

"Exactly what I thought," said Haldane more triumphant than ever, "but there are limits, you know – limits. So then I thought someone had got him out – the real him – and stuck him there to frighten me – while my back was turned, and I went to the place where I'd hidden him, and he was there – ah! – just as I'd left him. Only… it was a year ago. There are two of him there now."

"My dear chap," I said "this is simply comic."

"Yes," he said, "It is amusing. I find it so myself. Especially in the night when I wake up and think of it. I hope I shan't die in the dark, Winston: That's one of the reasons why I think I shall have to kill myself. I could be sure then of not dying in the dark."

"Is that all?" I asked, feeling sure that it must be.

"No," said Haldane at once. "That's not all. He's come back to rue again. In a railway carriage it was. I'd been asleep. When I woke up, there he was lying on the seat opposite me. Looked just the same. I pitched him out on the line in Red Hill Tunnel. And if I see him again, I'm going out myself. I can't stand it. It's too much. I'd sooner go. Whatever the next world's like, there aren't things in it like that. We leave them here, in graves and boxes and… You think I'm mad. But I'm not. You can't help me – no one can help me. He knew, you see. He said I shouldn't be able to get rid of the body. And I can't get rid of it. I can't. I can't. He knew. He always did know things that he couldn't know. But I'll cut his game short. After all, I've got the ace of trumps, and I'll play it on his next trick. I give you my word of honour, Winston, that I'm not mad."

"My dear old man," I said, "I don't think you're mad. But I do think your nerves are very much upset. Mine are a bit, too. Do you know why I went to India? It was because of you and her. I couldn't stay and see it, though I wished for your happiness and all that; you know I did. And when I came back, she… and you… Let's see it out together," I said. "You won't keep fancying things if you've got me to talk to. And I always said you weren't half a bad old duffer."

"She liked you," he said.

"Oh, yes," I said, "she liked me."

Chapter III

THAT WAS HOW we came to go abroad together. I was full of hope for him. He'd always been such a splendid chap – so sane and strong. I couldn't believe that he was gone mad, gone for ever, I mean, so that he'd never come right again. Perhaps my own trouble made it easy for me to see things not quite straight. Anyway, I took him away to recover his mind's health, exactly as I should have taken him away to get strong after a fever. And the madness seemed to pass away, and in a month or two we were perfectly jolly, and I thought I had cured him. And I was very glad because of that old friendship of ours, and because she had loved him and liked me.

We never spoke of Visger. I thought he had forgotten all about him. I thought I understood how his mind, over-strained by sorrow and anger, had fixed on the man he hated, and woven a nightmare web of horror round that detestable personality. And I had got the whip hand of my own trouble. And we were as jolly as sandboys together all those months.

And we came to Bruges at last in our travels, and Bruges was very full, because of the Exhibition. We could only get one room and one bed. So we tossed for the bed, and the one who lost the toss was to make the best of the night in the armchair. And the bedclothes we were to share equitably.

We spent the evening at a café chantant and finished at a beer hall, and it was late and sleepy when we got back to the Grande Vigne. I took our key from its nail in the concierge's room, and we went up. We talked awhile, I remember, of the town, and the belfry, and the Venetian aspect of the canals by moonlight, and then Haldane got into bed, and I made a chrysalis of myself with my share of the blankets and fitted the tight roll into the armchair. I was not at all comfortable, but I was compensatingly tired, and I was nearly asleep when Haldane roused me up to tell me about his will.

"I've left everything to you, old man," he said. "I know I can trust you to see to everything." "Quite so," said I, "and if you don't mind, we'll talk about it in the morning."

He tried to go on about it, and about what a friend I'd been, and all that, but I shut him up and told him to go to sleep. But no. He wasn't comfortable, he said. And he'd got a thirst like a lime kiln. And he'd noticed that there was no water-bottle in the room. "And the water in the jug's like pale soup," he said.

"Oh, all right," said I. "Light your candle and go and get some water, then, in Heaven's name, and let me get to sleep."

But he said, "No – you light it. I don't want to get out of bed in the dark. I might – I might step on something, mightn't I – or walk into something that wasn't there when I got into bed."

"Rot," I said, "walk into your grandmother." But I lit the candle all the same. He sat up in bed and looked at me – very pale – with his hair all tumbled from the pillow, and his eyes blinking and shining. "That's better," he said. And then, "I say – look here. Oh – yes – I see. It's all right. Queer how they mark the sheets here. Blest if I didn't think it was blood, just for the minute." The sheet was marked, not at the corner, as sheets are marked at home, but right in the middle where it turns down, with big, red, cross-stitching.

"Yes, I see," I said, "it is a queer place to mark it."

"It's queer letters to have on it," he said. "G.V."

"Grande Vigne," I said. "What letters do you expect them to mark things with? Hurry up."

"You come too," he said. "Yes, it does stand for Grande Vigne, of course. I wish you'd come down too, Winston."

"I'll go down," I said and turned with the candle in my hand.

He was out of bed and close to me in a flash.

"No," said he, "I don't want to stay alone in the dark."

He said it just as a frightened child might have done.

"All right then, come along," I said. And we went. I tried to make some joke, I remember, about the length of his hair, and the cut of his pajamas – but I was sick with disappointment. For it was almost quite plain to me, even then, that all my time and trouble had been thrown away, and that he wasn't cured after all. We went down as quietly as we could, and got a carafe of water from the long bare dining table in the sale à manger. He got hold of my arm at first, and then he got the candle away from me, and went very slowly, shading the light with his hand, and looking very carefully all about, as though he expected to see something that he wanted very desperately not to see. And of course, I knew what that something was. I didn't like the way he was going on. I can't at all express how deeply I didn't like it. And he looked over his shoulder every now and then, just as he did that first evening after I came back from India.

The thing got on my nerves so that I could hardly find the way back to our room. And when we got there, I give you my word, I more than half expected to see what he had expected to see – that, or something like that, on the hearth-rug. But of course there was nothing.

I blew out the light and tightened my blankets round me – I'd been trailing them after me in our expedition. And I was settled in my chair when Haldane spoke.

"You've got all the blankets," he said.

"No, I haven't," said I, "only what I've always had." "I can't find mine then," he said and I could hear his teeth chattering. "And I'm cold. I'm..."

"For God's sake, light the candle. Light it. Light it. Something horrible..."

And I couldn't find the matches.

"Light the candle, light the candle," he said, and his voice broke, as a boy's does sometimes in chapel. "If you don't he'll come to me. It is so easy to come at any one in the dark. Oh Winston, light the candle, for the love of God! I can't die in the dark."

"I am lighting it," I said savagely, and I was feeling for the matches on the marble-topped chest of drawers, on the mantelpiece – everywhere but on the round centre table where I'd put them. "You're not going to die. Don't be a fool," I said. "It's all right. I'll get a light in a second."

He said, "It's cold. It's cold. It's cold," like that, three times. And then he screamed aloud, like a woman-like a child-like a hare when the dogs have got it. I had heard him scream like that once before.

"What is it?" I cried, hardly less loud. "For God's sake, hold your noise. What is it?" There was an empty silence. Then, very slowly:

"It's Visger," he said. And he spoke thickly, as through some stifling veil.

"Nonsense. Where?" I asked, and my hand closed on the matches as he spoke.

"Here," he screamed sharply, as though he had torn the veil away, "here, beside me. In the bed." I got the candle alight. I got across to him.

He was crushed in a heap at the edge of the bed. Stretched on the bed beyond him was a dead man, white and very cold.

Haldane had died in the dark.

It was all so simple.

We had come to the wrong room. The man the room belonged to was there, on the bed he had engaged and paid for before he died of heart disease, earlier in the day. A French commis-voyageur representing soap and perfumery; his name, Felix Leblanc.

Later, in England, I made cautious enquiries. The body of a man had been found in the Red Hill tunnel – a haberdasher man named Simmons, who had drunk spirits of salts, owing to the depression of trade. The bottle was clutched in his dead hand.

For reasons that I had, I took care to have a police inspector with me when I opencd the boxes that came to me by Haldane's will. One of them was the big box, metal lined, in which I had sent him the skins from India-for a wedding present, God help us all!

It was closely soldered.

Inside were the skins of beasts? No. The bodies of two men. One was identified, after some trouble, as that of a hawker of pens in city offices – subject to fits. He had died in one, it seemed. The other body was Visger's, right enough.

Explain it as you like. I offered you, if you remember, a choice of explanations before I began the story. I have not yet found the explanation that can satisfy me.

The Cask of Amontillado

Edgar Allan Poe

THE THOUSAND INJURIES of Fortunato I had borne as I best could, but when he ventured upon insult, I vowed revenge. You, who so well know the nature of my soul, will not suppose, however, that I gave utterance to a threat. *At length* I would be avenged; this was a point definitely settled – but the very definitiveness with which it was resolved, precluded the idea of risk. I must not only punish, but punish with impunity. A wrong is unredressed when retribution overtakes its redresser. It is equally unredressed when the avenger fails to make himself felt as such to him who has done the wrong.

It must be understood that neither by word nor deed had I given Fortunato cause to doubt my good will. I continued, as was my wont, to smile in his face, and he did not perceive that my smile *now* was at the thought of his immolation.

He had a weak point – this Fortunato – although in other regards he was a man to be respected and even feared. He prided himself on his connoisseurship in wine. Few Italians have the true virtuoso spirit. For the most part their enthusiasm is adopted to suit the time and opportunity – to practise imposture upon the British and Austrian *millionaires*. In painting and gemmary, Fortunato, like his countrymen, was a quack – but in the matter of old wines he was sincere. In this respect I did not differ from him materially: I was skillful in the Italian vintages myself, and bought largely whenever I could.

It was about dusk, one evening during the supreme madness of the carnival season, that I encountered my friend. He accosted me with excessive warmth, for he had been drinking much. The man wore motley. He had on a tight-fitting parti-striped dress, and his head was surmounted by the conical cap and bells. I was so pleased to see him, that I thought I should never have done wringing his hand.

I said to him – "My dear Fortunato, you are luckily met. How remarkably well you are looking today! But I have received a pipe of what passes for Amontillado, and I have my doubts."

"How?" said he. "Amontillado? A pipe? Impossible! And in the middle of the carnival!"

"I have my doubts," I replied; "and I was silly enough to pay the full Amontillado price without consulting you in the matter. You were not to be found, and I was fearful of losing a bargain."

"Amontillado!"

"I have my doubts."

"Amontillado!"

"And I must satisfy them."

"Amontillado!"

"As you are engaged, I am on my way to Luchesi. If any one has a critical turn, it is he. He will tell me –"

"Luchesi cannot tell Amontillado from Sherry."

"And yet some fools will have it that his taste is a match for your own."

"Come, let us go."

"Whither?"

"To your vaults."

"My friend, no; I will not impose upon your good nature. I perceive you have an engagement. Luchesi –"

"I have no engagement; – come."

"My friend, no. It is not the engagement, but the severe cold with which I perceive you are afflicted. The vaults are insufferably damp. They are encrusted with nitre."

"Let us go, nevertheless. The cold is merely nothing. Amontillado! You have been imposed upon. And as for Luchesi, he cannot distinguish Sherry from Amontillado."

Thus speaking, Fortunato possessed himself of my arm. Putting on a mask of black silk, and drawing a *roquelaire* closely about my person, I suffered him to hurry me to my palazzo.

There were no attendants at home; they had absconded to make merry in honour of the time. I had told them that I should not return until the morning, and had given them explicit orders not to stir from the house. These orders were sufficient, I well knew, to insure their immediate disappearance, one and all, as soon as my back was turned.

I took from their sconces two flambeaux, and giving one to Fortunato, bowed him through several suites of rooms to the archway that led into the vaults. I passed down a long and winding staircase, requesting him to be cautious as he followed. We came at length to the foot of the descent, and stood together on the damp ground of the catacombs of the Montresors.

The gait of my friend was unsteady, and the bells upon his cap jingled as he strode.

"The pipe," said he.

"It is farther on," said I; "but observe the white web-work which gleams from these cavern walls."

He turned towards me, and looked into my eyes with two filmy orbs that distilled the rheum of intoxication.

"Nitre?" he asked, at length.

"Nitre," I replied. "How long have you had that cough?"

"Ugh! ugh! ugh! – Ugh! ugh! ugh! – Ugh! ugh! ugh! – Ugh! ugh! ugh! – Ugh! ugh! ugh!"

My poor friend found it impossible to reply for many minutes.

"It is nothing," he said, at last.

"Come," I said, with decision, "we will go back; your health is precious. You are rich, respected, admired, beloved; you are happy, as once I was. You are a man to be missed. For me it is no matter. We will go back; you will be ill, and I cannot be responsible. Besides, there is Luchesi –"

"Enough," he said; "the cough is a mere nothing; it will not kill me. I shall not die of a cough."

"True – true," I replied; "and, indeed, I had no intention of alarming you unnecessarily – but you should use all proper caution. A draught of this Medoc will defend us from the damps."

Here I knocked off the neck of a bottle which I drew from a long row of its fellows that lay upon the mould.

"Drink," I said, presenting him the wine.

He raised it to his lips with a leer. He paused and nodded to me familiarly, while his bells jingled.

"I drink," he said, "to the buried that repose around us."

"And I to your long life."

He again took my arm, and we proceeded.

"These vaults," he said, "are extensive."

"The Montresors," I replied, "were a great and numerous family."

"I forget your arms."

"A huge human foot d'or, in a field azure; the foot crushes a serpent rampant whose fangs are imbedded in the heel."

"And the motto?"

"*Nemo me impune lacessit.*"

"Good!" he said.

The wine sparkled in his eyes and the bells jingled. My own fancy grew warm with the Medoc. We had passed through walls of piled bones, with casks and puncheons intermingling, into the inmost recesses of catacombs. I paused again, and this time I made bold to seize Fortunato by an arm above the elbow.

"The nitre!" I said; "See, it increases. It hangs like moss upon the vaults. We are below the river's bed. The drops of moisture trickle among the bones. Come, we will go back ere it is too late. Your cough –"

"It is nothing," he said; "let us go on. But first, another draught of the Medoc."

I broke and reached him a flagon of De Grave. He emptied it at a breath. His eyes flashed with a fierce light. He laughed and threw the bottle upwards with a gesticulation I did not understand.

I looked at him in surprise. He repeated the movement – a grotesque one.

"You do not comprehend?" he said.

"Not I," I replied.

"Then you are not of the brotherhood."

"How?"

"You are not of the masons."

"Yes, yes," I said; "yes, yes."

"You? Impossible! A mason?"

"A mason," I replied.

"A sign," he said, "a sign."

"It is this," I answered, producing a trowel from beneath the folds of my *roquelaire*.

"You jest," he exclaimed, recoiling a few paces. "But let us proceed to the Amontillado."

"Be it so," I said, replacing the tool beneath the cloak and again offering him my arm. He leaned upon it heavily. We continued our route in search of the Amontillado. We passed through a range of low arches, descended, passed on, and descending again, arrived at a deep crypt, in which the foulness of the air caused our flambeaux rather to glow than flame.

At the most remote end of the crypt there appeared another less spacious. Its walls had been lined with human remains, piled to the vault overhead, in the fashion of the great catacombs of Paris. Three sides of this interior crypt were still ornamented in this manner. From the fourth side the bones had been thrown down, and lay promiscuously upon the earth, forming at one point a mound of some size. Within the wall thus exposed by the displacing of the bones, we perceived a still interior recess, in depth about four feet in width three, in height six or seven. It seemed to have been constructed for no especial use within itself, but formed merely the interval between two of the colossal supports of the roof of the catacombs, and was backed by one of their circumscribing walls of solid granite.

It was in vain that Fortunato, uplifting his dull torch, endeavoured to pry into the depth of the recess. Its termination the feeble light did not enable us to see.

"Proceed," I said; "herein is the Amontillado. As for Luchesi –"

"He is an ignoramus," interrupted my friend, as he stepped unsteadily forward, while I followed immediately at his heels. In an instant he had reached the extremity of the niche, and finding his progress arrested by the rock, stood stupidly bewildered. A moment more and I had fettered him to the granite. In its surface were two iron staples, distant from each other about two feet, horizontally. From one of these depended a short chain, from the other a padlock. Throwing the links about his waist, it was but the work of a few seconds to secure it. He was too much astounded to resist. Withdrawing the key I stepped back from the recess.

"Pass your hand," I said, "over the wall; you cannot help feeling the nitre. Indeed, it is *very* damp. Once more let me *implore* you to return. No? Then I must positively leave you. But I must first render you all the little attentions in my power."

"The Amontillado!" ejaculated my friend, not yet recovered from his astonishment.

"True," I replied; "the Amontillado."

As I said these words I busied myself among the pile of bones of which I have before spoken. Throwing them aside, I soon uncovered a quantity of building stone and mortar. With these materials and with the aid of my trowel, I began vigorously to wall up the entrance of the niche.

I had scarcely laid the first tier of the masonry when I discovered that the intoxication of Fortunato had in a great measure worn off. The earliest indication I had of this was a low moaning cry from the depth of the recess. It was *not* the cry of a drunken man. There was then a long and obstinate silence. I laid the second tier, and the third, and the fourth; and then I heard the furious vibrations of the chain. The noise lasted for several minutes, during which, that I might hearken to it with the more satisfaction, I ceased my labours and sat down upon the bones. When at last the clanking subsided, I resumed the trowel, and finished without interruption the fifth, the sixth, and the seventh tier. The wall was now nearly upon a level with my breast. I again paused, and holding the flambeaux over the mason-work, threw a few feeble rays upon the figure within.

A succession of loud and shrill screams, bursting suddenly from the throat of the chained form, seemed to thrust me violently back. For a brief moment I hesitated – I trembled. Unsheathing my rapier, I began to grope with it about the recess; but the thought of an instant reassured me. I placed my hand upon the solid fabric of the catacombs, and felt satisfied. I reapproached the wall; I replied to the yells of him who clamoured. I re-echoed – I aided – I surpassed them in volume and in strength. I did this, and the clamourer grew still.

It was now midnight, and my task was drawing to a close. I had completed the eighth, the ninth, and the tenth tier. I had finished a portion of the last and the eleventh; there remained but a single stone to be fitted and plastered in. I struggled with its weight; I placed it partially in its destined position. But now there came from out the niche a low laugh that erected the hairs upon my head. It was succeeded by a sad voice, which I had difficulty in recognizing as that of the noble Fortunato. The voice said –

"Ha! ha! ha! – he! he! he! – a very good joke indeed – an excellent jest. We shall have many a rich laugh about it at the palazzo – He! he! he! – over our wine – He! he! he!"

"The Amontillado!" I said.

"He! he! he! – He! he! he! – yes, the Amontillado. But is it not getting late? Will not they be awaiting us at the palazzo, the Lady Fortunato and the rest? Let us be gone."

"Yes," I said, "let us be gone."

"For the love of God, Montresor!"

"Yes," I said, "for the love of God!"

But to these words I hearkened in vain for a reply. I grew impatient. I called aloud –

"Fortunato!"

No answer. I called again –

"Fortunato –"

No answer still. I thrust a torch through the remaining aperture and let it fall within. There came forth in reply only a jingling of the bells. My heart grew sick on account of the dampness of the catacombs. I hastened to make an end of my labour. I forced the last stone into its position; I plastered it up. Against the new masonry I re-erected the old rampart of bones. For the half of a century no mortal has disturbed them. *In pace requiescat!*

The Azure Ring

Arthur B. Reeve

FILES OF NEWSPAPERS and innumerable clippings from the press bureaus littered Kennedy's desk in rank profusion. Kennedy himself was so deeply absorbed that I had merely said good evening as I came in and had started to open my mail. With an impatient sweep of his hand, however, he brushed the whole mass of newspapers into the waste-basket.

"It seems to me, Walter," he exclaimed in disgust, "that this mystery is considered insoluble for the very reason which should make it easy to solve – the extraordinary character of its features."

Inasmuch as he had opened the subject, I laid down the letter I was reading. "I'll wager I can tell you just why you made that remark, Craig," I ventured. "You're reading up on that Wainwright-Templeton affair."

"You are on the road to becoming a detective yourself, Walter," he answered with a touch of sarcasm. "Your ability to add two units to two other units and obtain four units is almost worthy of Inspector O'Connor. You are right and within a quarter of an hour the district attorney of Westchester County will be here. He telephoned me this afternoon and sent an assistant with this mass of dope. I suppose he'll want it back," he added, fishing the newspapers out of the basket again. "But, with all due respect to your profession, I'll say that no one would ever get on speaking terms with the solution of this case if he had to depend solely on the newspaper writers."

"No?" I queried, rather nettled at his tone.

"No," he repeated emphatically. "Here one of the most popular girls in the fashionable suburb of Williston, and one of the leading younger members of the bar in New York, engaged to be married, are found dead in the library of the girl's home the day before the ceremony. And now, a week later, no one knows whether it was an accident due to the fumes from the antique charcoal-brazier, or whether it was a double suicide, or suicide and murder, or a double murder, or – or – why, the experts haven't even been able to agree on whether they have discovered poison or not," he continued, growing as excited as the city editor did over my first attempt as a cub reporter.

"They haven't agreed on anything except that on the eve of what was, presumably, to have been the happiest day of their lives two of the best known members of the younger set are found dead, while absolutely no one, as far as is known, can be proved to have been near them within the time necessary to murder them. No wonder the coroner says it is simply a case of asphyxiation. No wonder the district attorney is at his wits' end. You fellows have hounded them with your hypotheses until they can't see the facts straight. You suggest one solution and before –"

The door-bell sounded insistently, and without waiting for an answer a tall, spare, loose-jointed individual stalked in and laid a green bag on the table.

"Good evening, Professor Kennedy," he began brusquely. "I am District Attorney Whitney, of Westchester. I see you have been reading up on the case. Quite right."

"Quite wrong," answered Craig. "Let me introduce my friend, Mr. Jameson, of the *Star*. Sit down. Jameson knows what I think of the way the newspapers have handled this case. I was about to tell him as you came in that I intended to disregard everything that had been printed, to start out with you as if it were a fresh subject and get the facts at first hand. Let's get right down to business. First tell us just how it was that Miss. Wainwright and Mr. Templeton were discovered and by whom."

The district attorney loosened the cords of the green bag and drew out a bundle of documents. "I'll read you the affidavit of the maid who found them," he said, fingering the documents nervously. "You see, John Templeton had left his office in New York early that afternoon, telling his father that he was going to visit Miss. Wainwright. He caught the three-twenty train, reached Williston all right, walked to the Wainwright house, and, in spite of the bustle of preparation for the wedding, the next day, he spent the rest of the afternoon with Miss. Wainwright. That's where the mystery begins. They had no visitors. At least, the maid who answers the bell says they had none. She was busy with the rest of the family, and I believe the front door was not locked – we don't lock our doors in Williston, except at night."

He had found the paper and paused to impress these facts on our minds.

"Mrs. Wainwright and Miss. Marian Wainwright, the sister, were busy about the house. Mrs. Wainwright wished to consult Laura about something. She summoned the maid and asked if Mr. Templeton and Miss. Wainwright were in the house. The maid replied that she would see, and this is her affidavit. Ahem! I'll skip the legal part: 'I knocked at the library door twice, but obtaining no answer, I supposed they had gone out for a walk or perhaps a ride across country as they often did. I opened the door partly and looked in. There was a silence in the room, a strange, queer silence. I opened the door further and, looking toward the davenport in the corner, I saw Miss. Laura and Mr. Templeton in such an awkward position. They looked as if they had fallen asleep. His head was thrown back against the cushions of the davenport, and on his face was a most awful look. It was discoloured. Her head had fallen forward on his shoulder, sideways, and on her face, too, was the same terrible stare and the same discolouration. Their right hands were tightly clasped.

"'I called to them. They did not answer. Then the horrible truth flashed on me. They were dead. I felt giddy for a minute, but quickly recovered myself, and with a cry for help I rushed to Mrs. Wainwright's room, shrieking that they were dead. Mrs. Wainwright fainted. Miss. Marian called the doctor on the telephone and helped us restore her mother. She seemed perfectly cool in the tragedy, and I do not know what we servants should have done if she had not been there to direct us. The house was frantic, and Mr. Wainwright was not at home.

"'I did not detect any odour when I opened the library door. No glasses or bottles or vials or other receptacles which could have held poison were discovered or removed by me, or to the best of my knowledge and belief by anyone else.'"

"What happened next?" asked Craig eagerly.

"The family physician arrived and sent for the coroner immediately, and later for myself. You see, he thought at once of murder."

"But the coroner, I understand, thinks differently," prompted Kennedy.

"Yes, the coroner has declared the case to be accidental. He says that the weight of evidence points positively to asphyxiation. Still, how can it be asphyxiation? They could have escaped from the room at any time; the door was not locked. I tell you, in spite of the fact that the tests for poison in their mouths, stomachs, and blood have so far revealed nothing, I still believe that John Templeton and Laura Wainwright were murdered."

Kennedy looked at his watch thoughtfully. "You have told me just enough to make me want to see the coroner himself," he mused. "If we take the next train out to Williston with you, will you engage to get us a half-hour talk with him on the case, Mr. Whitney?"

"Surely. But we'll have to start right away. I've finished my other business in New York. Inspector O'Connor – ah, I see you know him – has promised to secure the attendance of anyone whom I can show to be a material witness in the case. Come on, gentlemen: I'll answer your other questions on the train."

As we settled ourselves in the smoker, Whitney remarked in a low voice, "You know, someone has said that there is only one thing more difficult to investigate and solve than a crime whose commission is surrounded by complicated circumstances and that is a crime whose perpetration is wholly devoid of circumstances."

"Are you so sure that this crime is wholly devoid of circumstances?" asked Craig.

"Professor," he replied, "I'm not sure of anything in this case. If I were I should not require your assistance. I would like the credit of solving it myself, but it is beyond me. Just think of it: so far we haven't a clue, at least none that shows the slightest promise, although we have worked night and day for a week. It's all darkness. The facts are so simple that they give us nothing to work on. It is like a blank sheet of paper."

Kennedy said nothing, and the district attorney proceeded: "I don't blame Mr. Nott, the coroner, for thinking it an accident. But to my mind, some master criminal must have arranged this very baffling simplicity of circumstances. You recall that the front door was unlocked. This person must have entered the house unobserved, not a difficult thing to do, for the Wainwright house is somewhat isolated. Perhaps this person brought along some poison in the form of a beverage, and induced the two victims to drink. And then, this person must have removed the evidences as swiftly as they were brought in and by the same door. That, I think, is the only solution."

"That is not the only solution. It is one solution," interrupted Kennedy quietly.

"Do you think someone in the house did it?" I asked quickly.

"I think," replied Craig, carefully measuring his words, "that if poison was given them it must have been by someone they both knew pretty well."

No one said a word, until at last I broke the silence. "I know from the gossip of the *Star* office that many Williston people say that Marian was very jealous of her sister Laura for capturing the catch of the season. Williston people don't hesitate to hint at it."

Whitney produced another document from that fertile green bag. It was another affidavit. He handed it to us. It was a statement signed by Mrs. Wainwright, and read:

> "Before God, my daughter Marian is innocent. If you wish to find out all, find out more about the past history of Mr. Templeton before he became engaged to Laura. She would never in the world have committed suicide. She was too bright and cheerful for that, even if Mr. Templeton had been about to break off the engagement. My daughters Laura and Marian were always treated by Mr. Wainwright and myself exactly alike. Of course they had their quarrels, just as all sisters do, but there was never, to my certain knowledge, a serious disagreement, and I was always close enough to my girls to know. No, Laura was murdered by someone outside."

Kennedy did not seem to attach much importance to this statement. "Let us see," he began reflectively. "First, we have a young woman especially attractive and charming in both person and temperament. She is just about to be married and, if the reports are to be believed, there was no cloud on her happiness. Secondly, we have a young man whom everyone agrees to have been of an ardent, energetic, optimistic temperament. He had everything to live for, presumably. So far, so good. Everyone who has investigated this case, I understand, has tried to eliminate the double-suicide and the suicide-and-murder theories. That is all right, providing the facts are as stated. We shall see, later, when we interview the coroner. Now, Mr. Whitney, suppose you tell us briefly what you have learned about the past history of the two unfortunate lovers."

"Well, the Wainwrights are an old Westchester family, not very wealthy, but of the real aristocracy of the county. There were only two children, Laura and Marian. The Templetons were much the same sort of family. The children all attended a private school at White Plains, and there also they met Schuyler Vanderdyke. These four constituted a sort of little aristocracy in the school. I mention this, because Vanderdyke later became Laura's first husband. This marriage with Templeton was a second venture."

"How long ago was she divorced?" asked Craig attentively.

"About three years ago. I'm coming to that in a moment. The sisters went to college together, Templeton to law school, and Vanderdyke studied civil engineering. Their intimacy was pretty well broken up, all except Laura's and Vanderdyke's. Soon after he graduated he was taken into the construction department of the Central Railroad by his uncle, who was a vice-president, and Laura and he were married. As far as I can learn he had been a fellow of convivial habits at college, and about two years after their marriage his wife suddenly became aware of what had long been well known in Williston, that Vanderdyke was paying marked attention to a woman named Miss. Laporte in New York."

"No sooner had Laura Vanderdyke learned of this intimacy of her husband," continued Whitney, "than she quietly hired private detectives to shadow him, and on their evidence she obtained a divorce. The papers were sealed, and she resumed her maiden name.

"As far as I can find out, Vanderdyke then disappeared from her life. He resigned his position with the railroad and joined a party of engineers exploring the upper Amazon. Later he went to Venezuela. Miss. Laporte also went to South America about the same time, and was for a time in Venezuela, and later in Peru.

"Vanderdyke seems to have dropped all his early associations completely, though at present I find he is back in New York raising capital for a company to exploit a new asphalt concession in the interior of Venezuela. Miss. Laporte has also reappeared in New York as Mrs. Ralston, with a mining claim in the mountains of Peru."

"And Templeton?" asked Craig. "Had he had any previous matrimonial ventures?"

"No, none. Of course he had had love affairs, mostly with the country-club set. He had known Miss. Laporte pretty well, too, while he was in law school in New York. But when he settled down to work he seems to have forgotten all about the girls for a couple of years or so. He was very anxious to get ahead, and let nothing stand in his way. He was admitted to the bar and taken in by his father as junior member of the firm of Templeton, Mills & Templeton. Not long ago he was appointed a special master to take testimony in the get-rich-quick-company prosecutions, and I happen to know that he was making good in the investigation."

Kennedy nodded. "What sort of fellow personally was Templeton?" he asked.

"Very popular," replied the district attorney, "both at the country club and in his profession in New York. He was a fellow of naturally commanding temperament – the Templetons were always that way. I doubt if many young men even with his chances could have gained such a reputation at thirty-five as his. Socially he was very popular, too, a great catch for all the sly mamas of the country club who had marriageable daughters. He liked automobiles and outdoor sports, and he was strong in politics, too. That was how he got ahead so fast.

"Well, to cut the story short, Templeton met the Wainwright girls again last summer at a resort on Long Island. They had just returned from a long trip abroad, spending most of the time in the Far East with their father, whose firm has business interests in China. The girls were very attractive. They rode and played tennis and golf better than most of the men, and this fall Templeton became a frequent visitor at the Wainwright home in Williston.

"People who know them best tell me that his first attentions were paid to Marian, a very dashing and ambitious young woman. Nearly every day Templeton's car stopped at the house and the girls and some friend of Templeton's in the country club went for a ride. They tell me that at this time Marian always sat with Templeton on the front seat. But after a few weeks the gossips – nothing of that sort ever escapes Williston – said that the occupant of the front seat was Laura. She often drove the car herself and was very clever at it. At any rate, not long after that the engagement was announced."

As he walked up from the pretty little Williston station Kennedy asked: "One more question, Mr. Whitney. How did Marian take the engagement?"

The district attorney hesitated. "I will be perfectly frank, Mr. Kennedy," he answered. "The country-club people tell me that the girls were very cool toward each other. That was why I got that statement from Mrs. Wainwright. I wish to be perfectly fair to everyone concerned in this case."

We found the coroner quite willing to talk, in spite of the fact that the hour was late. "My friend, Mr. Whitney, here, still holds the poison theory," began the coroner, "in spite of the fact that everything points absolutely toward asphyxiation. If I had been able to discover the slightest trace of illuminating-gas in the room I should have pronounced it asphyxia at once. All the symptoms accorded with it. But the asphyxia was not caused by escaping illuminating-gas.

"There was an antique charcoal-brazier in the room, and I have ascertained that it was lighted. Now, anything like a brazier will, unless there is proper ventilation, give rise to carbonic oxide or carbon monoxide gas, which is always present in the products of combustion, often to the extent of from five to ten per cent. A very slight quantity of this gas, insufficient even to cause an odour in a room, will give a severe headache, and a case is recorded where a whole family in Glasgow was poisoned without knowing it by the escape of this gas. A little over one per cent of it in the atmosphere is fatal, if breathed for any length of time. You know, it is a product of combustion, and is very deadly – it is the much-dreaded white damp or afterdamp of a mine explosion.

"I'm going to tell you a secret which I have not given out to the press yet. I tried an experiment in a closed room today, lighting the brazier. Some distance from it I placed a cat confined in a cage so it could not escape. In an hour and a half the cat was asphyxiated."

The coroner concluded with an air of triumph that quite squelched the district attorney.

Kennedy was all attention. "Have you preserved samples of the blood of Mr. Templeton and Miss. Wainwright?" he asked.

"Certainly. I have them in my office."

The coroner, who was also a local physician, led us back into his private office.

"And the cat?" added Craig.

Doctor Nott produced it in a covered basket.

Quickly Kennedy drew off a little of the blood of the cat and held it up to the light along with the human samples. The difference was apparent.

"You see," he explained, "carbon monoxide combines firmly with the blood, destroying the red colouring matter of the red corpuscles. No, Doctor, I'm afraid it wasn't carbonic oxide that killed the lovers, although it certainly killed the cat."

Doctor Nott was crestfallen, but still unconvinced. "If my whole medical reputation were at stake," he repeated, "I should still be compelled to swear to asphyxia. I've seen it too often, to make a mistake. Carbonic oxide or not, Templeton and Miss. Wainwright were asphyxiated."

It was now Whitney's chance to air his theory.

"I have always inclined toward the cyanide-of-potassium theory, either that it was administered in a drink or perhaps injected by a needle," he said. "One of the chemists has reported that there was a possibility of slight traces of cyanide in the mouths."

"If it had been cyanide," replied Craig, looking reflectively at the two jars before him on the table, "these blood specimens would be blue in colour and clotted. But they are not. Then, too, there is a substance in the saliva which is used in the process of digestion. It gives a reaction which might very easily be mistaken for a slight trace of cyanide. I think that explains what the chemist discovered; no more, no less. The cyanide theory does not fit."

"One chemist hinted at *nux vomica*," volunteered the coroner. "He said it wasn't *nux vomica*, but that the blood test showed something very much like it. Oh, we've looked for morphine chloroform, ether, all the ordinary poisons, besides some of the little known alkaloids. Believe me, Professor Kennedy, it was asphyxia."

I could tell by the look that crossed Kennedy's face that at last a ray of light had pierced the darkness. "Have you any spirits of turpentine in the office?" he asked.

The coroner shook his head and took a step toward the telephone as if to call the drug-store in town.

"Or ether?" interrupted Craig. "Ether will do."

"Oh, yes, plenty of ether."

Craig poured a little of one of the blood samples from the jar into a tube and added a few drops of ether. A cloudy dark precipitate formed. He smiled quietly and said, half to himself, "I thought so."

"What is it?" asked the coroner eagerly. "*Nux vomica?*"

Craig shook his head as he stared at the black precipitate. "You were perfectly right about the asphyxiation, Doctor," he remarked slowly, "but wrong as to the cause. It wasn't carbon monoxide or illuminating-gas. And you, Mr. Whitney, were right about the poison, too. Only it is a poison neither of you ever heard of."

"What is it?" we asked simultaneously.

"Let me take these samples and make some further tests. I am sure of it, but it is new to me. Wait till tomorrow night, when my chain of evidence is completed. Then you are all cordially invited to attend at my laboratory at the university. I'll ask you, Mr. Whitney, to come armed with a warrant for John or Jane Doe. Please see that the Wainwrights, particularly Marian, are present. You can tell Inspector O'Connor that Mr. Vanderdyke and Mrs. Ralston are required as material witnesses – anything so long as you are sure that these five persons are present. Good night, gentlemen."

We rode back to the city in silence, but as we neared the station, Kennedy remarked: "You see, Walter, these people are like the newspapers. They are floundering around in a sea of unrelated facts. There is more than they think back of this crime. I've been revolving in my mind how it will be possible to get some inkling about this concession of Vanderdyke's, the mining claim of Mrs. Ralston, and the exact itinerary of the Wainwright trip in the Far East. Do you think you can get that information for me? I think it will take me all day tomorrow to isolate this poison and get things in convincing shape on that score. Meanwhile if you can see Vanderdyke and Mrs. Ralston you can help me a great deal. I am sure you will find them very interesting people."

"I have been told that she is quite a female high financier," I replied, tacitly accepting Craig's commission. "Her story is that her claim is situated near the mine of a group of powerful American capitalists, who are opposed to having any competition, and on the strength of that story she has been raking in the money right and left. I don't know Vanderdyke, never heard of him before, but no doubt he has some equally interesting game."

"Don't let them think you connect them with the case, however," cautioned Craig.

Early the next morning I started out on my quest for facts, though not so early but that Kennedy had preceded me to his work in his laboratory. It was not very difficult to get Mrs. Ralston to talk about her troubles with the government. In fact, I did not even have to broach the subject of the death of Templeton. She volunteered the information that in his handling of her case he had been very unjust to her, in spite of the fact that she had known him well a long time ago. She even hinted that she believed he represented the combination of capitalists who were using the government to aid their own monopoly and prevent the development of her mine. Whether it was an obsession of her mind, or merely part of her clever scheme, I could not make out. I noted, however, that when she spoke of Templeton it was in a studied, impersonal way, and that she was at pains to lay the blame for the governmental interference rather on the rival mine-owners.

It quite surprised me when I found from the directory that Vanderdyke's office was on the floor below in the same building. Like Mrs. Ralston's, it was open, but not doing business, pending the investigation by the Post-Office Department.

Vanderdyke was a type of which I had seen many before. Well dressed to the extreme, he displayed all those evidences of prosperity which are the stock in trade of the man with securities to sell. He grasped my hand when I told him I was going to present the other side of the post-office cases and held it between both of his as if he had known me all his life. Only the fact that he had never seen me before prevented his calling me by my first name. I took mental note of his stock of jewellery, the pin in his tie that might almost have been the Hope diamond, the heavy watch chain across his chest, and a very brilliant seal ring of lapis lazuli on the hand that grasped mine. He saw me looking at it and smiled.

"My dear fellow, we have deposits of that stuff that would make a fortune if we could get the machinery to get at it. Why, sir, there is lapis lazuli enough on our claim to make enough ultramarine paint to supply all the artists to the end of the world. Actually we could afford to crush it up and sell it as paint. And that is merely incidental to the other things on the concession. The asphalt's the thing. That's where the big money is. When we get started, sir, the old asphalt trust will simply melt away, melt away."

He blew a cloud of tobacco smoke and let it dissolve significantly in the air.

When it came to talking about the suits, however, Vanderdyke was not so communicative as Mrs. Ralston, but he was also not so bitter against either the post-office or Templeton.

"Poor Templeton," he said. "I used to know him years ago when we were boys. Went to school with him and all that sort of thing, you know, but until I ran across him, or rather he ran across me, in this investigation I hadn't heard much about him. Pretty clever fellow he was, too. The state will miss him, but my lawyer tells me that we should have won the suit anyhow, even if that unfortunate tragedy hadn't occurred. Most unaccountable, wasn't it? I've read about it in the papers for old time's sake, and can make nothing out of it."

I said nothing, but wondered how he could pass so lightheartedly over the death of the woman who had once been his wife. However, I said nothing. The result was he launched forth again on the riches of his Venezuelan concession and loaded me down with 'literature,' which I crammed into my pocket for future reference.

My next step was to drop into the office of a Spanish-America paper whose editor was especially well informed on South American affairs.

"Do I know Mrs. Ralston?" he repeated, thoughtfully lighting one of those black cigarettes that look so vicious and are so mild. "I should say so. I'll tell you a little story about her. Three or four years ago she turned up in Caracas. I don't know who Mr. Ralston was – perhaps there never was any Mr. Ralston. Anyhow, she got in with the official circle of the Castro government and was very successful as an adventuress. She has considerable business ability and represented a certain group of Americans. But, if you recall, when Castro was eliminated pretty nearly everyone who had stood high with him went, too. It seems that a number of the old concessionaires played the game on both sides. This particular group had a man named Vanderdyke on the anti-Castro side. So, when Mrs. Ralston went, she just quietly sailed by way of Panama to the other side of the continent, to Peru – they paid her well – and Vanderdyke took the title role.

"Oh, yes, she and Vanderdyke were very good friends, very, indeed. I think they must have known each other here in the States. Still they played their parts well at the time. Since things have settled down in Venezuela, the concessionaires have found no further use for Vanderdyke either, and here they are, Vanderdyke and Mrs. Ralston, both in New York now, with two of the most outrageous schemes of financing ever seen on Broad Street. They have offices in the same building, they are together a great deal, and now I hear that the state attorney-general is after both of them."

With this information and a very meagre report of the Wainwright trip to the Far East, which had taken in some out-of-the-way places apparently, I hastened back to Kennedy. He was surrounded by bottles, tubes, jars, retorts, Bunsen burners, everything in the science and art of chemistry, I thought.

I didn't like the way he looked. His hand was unsteady, and his eyes looked badly, but he seemed quite put out when I suggested that he was working too hard over the case. I was worried about him, but rather than say anything to offend him I left him for the rest of the afternoon, only dropping in before dinner to make sure that he would not forget to eat something. He was then completing his preparations for the evening. They were of the simplest kind, apparently. In fact, all I could see was an apparatus which consisted of a rubber funnel, inverted and attached to a rubber tube which led in turn into a jar about a quarter full of water. Through the stopper of the jar another tube led to a tank of oxygen.

There were several jars of various liquids on the table and a number of chemicals. Among other things was a sort of gourd, encrusted with a black substance, and in a corner was a box from which sounds issued as if it contained something alive.

I did not trouble Kennedy with questions, for I was only too glad when he consented to take a brisk walk and join me in a thick porterhouse.

It was a large party that gathered in Kennedy's laboratory that night, one of the largest he had ever had. Mr. and Mrs. Wainwright and Miss. Marian came, the ladies heavily veiled.

Doctor Nott and Mr. Whitney were among the first to arrive. Later came Mr. Vanderdyke and last of all Mrs. Ralston with Inspector O'Connor. Altogether it was an unwilling party.

"I shall begin," said Kennedy, "by going over, briefly, the facts in this case."

Tersely he summarised it, to my surprise laying great stress on the proof that the couple had been asphyxiated.

"But it was no ordinary asphyxiation," he continued. "We have to deal in this case with a poison which is apparently among the most subtle known. A particle of matter so minute as to be hardly distinguishable by the naked eye, on the point of a needle or a lancet, a prick of the skin scarcely felt under any circumstances and which would pass quite unheeded if the attention were otherwise engaged, and not all the power in the world – unless one was fully prepared – could save the life of the person in whose skin the puncture had been made."

Craig paused a moment, but no one showed any evidence of being more than ordinarily impressed.

"This poison, I find, acts on the so-called endplates of the muscles and nerves. It produces complete paralysis, but not loss of consciousness, sensation, circulation, or respiration until the end approaches. It seems to be one of the most powerful sedatives I have ever heard of. When introduced in even a minute quantity it produces death finally by asphyxiation – by paralysing the muscles of respiration. This asphyxia is what so puzzled the coroner.

"I will now inject a little of the blood serum of the victims into a white mouse."

He took a mouse from the box I had seen, and with a needle injected the serum. The mouse did not even wince, so lightly did he touch it, but as we watched, its life seemed gently to ebb away, without pain and without struggle. Its breath simply seemed to stop.

Next he took the gourd I had seen on the table and with a knife scraped off just the minutest particle of the black licorice-like stuff that encrusted it. He dissolved the particle in some alcohol and with a sterilised needle repeated his experiment on a second mouse. The effect was precisely similar to that produced by the blood on the first.

It did not seem to me that anyone showed any emotion except possibly the slight exclamation that escaped Miss. Marian Wainwright. I fell to wondering whether it was prompted by a soft heart or a guilty conscience.

We were all intent on what Craig was doing, especially Doctor Nott, who now broke in with a question.

"Professor Kennedy, may I ask a question? Admitting that the first mouse died in an apparently similar manner to the second, what proof have you that the poison is the same in both cases? And if it is the same can you show that it affects human beings in the same way, and that enough of it has been discovered in the blood of the victims to have caused their death? In other words, I want the last doubt set aside. How do you know absolutely that this poison which you discovered in my office last night in that black precipitate when you added the ether – how do you know that it asphyxiated the victims?"

If ever Craig startled me it was by his quiet reply. "I've isolated it in their blood, extracted it, sterilised it, and I've tried it on myself."

In breathless amazement, with eyes riveted on Craig, we listened.

"Altogether I was able to recover from the blood samples of both of the victims of this crime six centigrams of the poison," he pursued. "Starting with two centigrams of it as a moderate dose, I injected it into my right arm subcutaneously. Then I slowly worked my way up to three and then four centigrams. They did not produce any very appreciable results other than to cause some dizziness, slight vertigo, a considerable degree of lassitude, and an extremely painful headache of rather unusual duration. But five centigrams considerably improved on this. It caused a degree of vertigo and lassitude that was most distressing, and six centigrams, the whole amount which I had recovered from the samples of blood, gave me the fright of my life right here in this laboratory this afternoon.

"Perhaps I was not wise in giving myself so large an injection on a day when I was overheated and below par otherwise because of the strain I have been under in handling this case. However that may be, the added centigram produced so much more on top of the five centigrams previously taken that for a time I had reason to fear that that additional centigram was just the amount needed to bring my experiments to a permanent close.

"Within three minutes of the time of injection the dizziness and vertigo had become so great as to make walking seem impossible. In another minute the lassitude rapidly crept over me, and the serious disturbance of my breathing made it apparent to me that walking, waving my arms, anything, was imperative. My lungs felt glued up, and the muscles of my chest refused to work. Everything swam before my eyes, and I was soon reduced to walking up and down the laboratory with halting steps, only preventing falling on the floor by holding fast to the edge of this table. It seemed to me that I spent hours gasping for breath. It reminded me of what I once experienced in the Cave of the Winds of Niagara, where water is more abundant in the atmosphere than air. My watch afterward indicated only about twenty minutes of extreme distress, but that twenty minutes is one never to be forgotten, and I advise you all, if you ever are so foolish as to try the experiment, to remain below the five-centigram limit.

"How much was administered to the victims, Doctor Nott, I cannot say, but it must have been a good deal more than I took. Six centigrams, which I recovered from these small samples, are only nine-tenths of a grain. Yet you see what effect it had. I trust that answers your question."

Doctor Nott was too overwhelmed to reply.

"And what is this deadly poison?" continued Craig, anticipating our thoughts. "I have been fortunate enough to obtain a sample of it from the Museum of Natural History. It comes in a little gourd, or often a calabash. This is in a gourd. It is blackish brittle stuff encrusting the sides of the gourd just as if it was poured in in the liquid state and left to dry. Indeed, that is just what has been done by those who manufacture this stuff after a lengthy and somewhat secret process."

He placed the gourd on the edge of the table where we could all see it. I was almost afraid even to look at it.

"The famous traveller, Sir Robert Schomburgh first brought it into Europe, and Darwin has described it. It is now an article of commerce and is to be found in the United States Pharmacopoeia as a medicine, though of course it is used in only very minute quantities, as a heart stimulant."

Craig opened a book to a place he had marked:

"At least one person in this room will appreciate the local colour of a little incident I am going to read – to illustrate what death from this poison is like. Two natives of the part of the world whence it comes were one day hunting. They were armed with blowpipes and quivers full of poisoned darts made of thin charred pieces of bamboo tipped with this stuff. One of them aimed a dart. It missed the object overhead, glanced off the tree, and fell down on the hunter himself. This is how the other native reported the result:

"'*Quacca takes the dart out of his shoulder. Never a word. Puts it in his quiver and throws it in the stream. Gives me his blowpipe for his little son. Says to me goodbye for his wife and the village. Then he lies down. His tongue talks no longer. No sight in his eyes. He folds his arms. He rolls over slowly. His mouth moves without sound. I feel his heart. It goes fast and then slow. It stops. Quacca has shot his last woorali dart.'"*

We looked at each other, and the horror of the thing sank deep into our minds. Woorali. What was it? There were many travellers in the room who had been in the Orient, home of poisons, and in South America. Which one had run across the poison?

"Woorali, or curare," said Craig slowly, "is the well-known poison with which the South American Indians of the upper Orinoco tip their arrows. Its principal ingredient is derived from the Strychnos toxifera tree, which yields also the drug *nux vomica*."

A great light dawned on me. I turned quickly to where Vanderdyke was sitting next to Mrs. Ralston, and a little behind her. His stony stare and laboured breathing told me that he had read the purport of Kennedy's actions.

"For God's sake, Craig," I gasped. "An emetic, quick – Vanderdyke."

A trace of a smile flitted over Vanderdyke's features, as much as to say that he was beyond our interference.

"Vanderdyke," said Craig, with what seemed to me a brutal calmness, "then it was you who were the visitor who last saw Laura Wainwright and John Templeton alive. Whether you shot a dart at them I do not know. But you are the murderer."

Vanderdyke raised his hand as if to assent. It fell back limp, and I noted the ring of the bluest lapis lazuli.

Mrs. Ralston threw herself toward him. "Will you not do something? Is there no antidote? Don't let him die!" she cried.

"You are the murderer," repeated Kennedy, as if demanding a final answer.

Again the hand moved in confession, and he feebly moved the finger on which shone the ring.

Our attention was centred on Vanderdyke. Mrs. Ralston, unobserved, went to the table and picked up the gourd. Before O'Connor could stop her she had rubbed her tongue on the black substance inside. It was only a little bit, for O'Connor quickly dashed it from her lips and threw the gourd through the window, smashing the glass.

"Kennedy," he shouted frantically, "Mrs. Ralston has swallowed some of it."

Kennedy seemed so intent on Vanderdyke that I had to repeat the remark.

Without looking up, he said: "Oh, one can swallow it – it's strange, but it is comparatively inert if swallowed even in a pretty good-sized quantity. I doubt if Mrs. Ralston ever heard of it before except by hearsay. If she had, she'd have scratched herself with it instead of swallowing it."

If Craig had been indifferent to the emergency of Vanderdyke before, he was all action now that the confession had been made. In an instant Vanderdyke was stretched on the floor and Craig had taken out the apparatus I had seen during the afternoon.

"I am prepared for this," he exclaimed quickly. "Here is the apparatus for artificial respiration. Nott, hold that rubber funnel over his nose, and start the oxygen from the tank. Pull his tongue forward so it won't fall down his throat and choke him. I'll work his arms. Walter, make a tourniquet of your handkerchief and put it tightly on the muscles of his left arm. That may keep some of the poison in his arm from spreading into the rest of his body. This is the only antidote known – artificial respiration."

Kennedy was working feverishly, going through the motions of first aid to a drowned man. Mrs. Ralston was on her knees beside Vanderdyke, kissing his hands and forehead whenever Kennedy stopped for a minute, and crying softly.

"Schuyler, poor boy, I wonder how you could have done it. I was with him that day. We rode up in his car, and as we passed through Williston he said he would stop a minute and wish Templeton luck. I didn't think it strange, for he said he had nothing any longer against Laura Wainwright, and Templeton only did his duty as a lawyer against us. I forgave John for prosecuting us, but Schuyler didn't, after all. Oh, my poor boy, why did you do it? We could have gone somewhere else and started all over again – it wouldn't have been the first time."

At last came the flutter of an eyelid and a voluntary breath or two. Vanderdyke seemed to realise where he was. With a last supreme effort he raised his hand and drew it slowly across his face. Then he fell back, exhausted by the effort.

But he had at last put himself beyond the reach of the law. There was no tourniquet that would confine the poison now in the scratch across his face. Back of those lack-lustre eyes he heard and knew, but could not move or speak. His voice was gone, his limbs, his face, his chest, and, last, his eyes. I wondered if it were possible to conceive a more dreadful torture than that endured by a mind which so witnessed the dying of one organ after another of its own body, shut up, as it were, in the fulness of life, within a corpse.

I looked in bewilderment at the scratch on his face. "How did he do it?" I asked.

Carefully Craig drew off the azure ring and examined it. In that part which surrounded the blue lapis lazuli, he indicated a hollow point, concealed. It worked with a spring and communicated with a little receptacle behind, in such a way that the murderer could give the fatal scratch while shaking hands with his victim.

I shuddered, for my hand had once been clasped by the one wearing that poison ring, which had sent Templeton, and his fiancee and now Vanderdyke himself, to their deaths.

Redux

Alexandra Camille Renwick

WINNIE RAISED HERSELF UP on one elbow and squinted in the direction of her bedroom doorway. The room was so dark it was like staring at a sheet of solid tar. The sound came again, a whisper of fabric followed by a nearly inaudible intake of breath. She saw a silhouette move, person-sized, person-shaped, a darker patch of darkness, and her still half-asleep brain struggled to make sense of what was happening. She fumbled with the lamp, clicked it on, saw the person standing in the doorway, and though she began to ask *Peter, is that you?,* with all the confusion, the lack of comprehension, the slow lickings of the dawning understanding of danger, her lips barely compressed into the first letter of his name before he raised the gun he held and shot her twice in the center of the chest.

* * *

Winnie raised herself up on one elbow and squinted in the direction of her bedroom doorway, dislodging the book she'd fallen asleep reading. It slid off the vintage satin coverlet to the floor with a crash.

She reached down to rescue the book, to smooth its fresh-bent pages and close it properly, when an odd sensation of extra stillness made her pause.

She glanced again at the doorway leading to the hall. Had something flickered there, in the blackness? She clicked the bedside lamp on and squinted at the pitch-dark rectangle of the open door.

"Hello?" she called out, her voice sounding feeble, wobbly. She felt instantly foolish. Stupid. Embarrassed, even alone with no one to witness her being all squirrelly and girly and scared.

Shaking her head, she got up to head for the bathroom. She stepped into her slippers – puffy ridiculous moonfaced panda slippers, a gift from her mother last Christmas – and grabbed her garish pink and purple chrysanthemum kimono off its hook by the door, shrugging into it more from habit than a need for warmth or modesty in the empty house. As soon as she stepped into the hallway a hammer smashed into her left temple.

With a soft startled cry she fell sideways, knocking a framed picture off the wall. Glass crunched and tinkled as she crawled over it. Her head felt hot, but the alarm bells going off in her brain drowned out any immediate sensation of pain. Warm sticky wetness trickled into her left ear. Her palms trailed red smears on the wall as she pulled herself upright and turned to see her neighbor Peter standing with a bloody hammer in his hand. Weak light spilled from her bedroom, casting his face half in shadow. A weirdly rounded cap perched on his short blonde hair, like a compact bike helmet with a too-thin strap running under his chin. There was not an ounce of any emotion she could understand or even recognize as he lifted his arm again to send the hammer crashing down into her skull.

* * *

Winnie raised herself up on one elbow and squinted in the direction of her bedroom doorway. Had something woken her? She'd been dreaming about her mother. Her mother turning into a goldfish the size of a city bus and swimming down the street, obeying traffic laws with other vehicles half her size.

Shit, it must be late. Winnie rolled to the far edge of the bed – a bed too big, now she and Liz had split for good – and grabbed her phone off what used to be Liz's nightstand. 2:22 a.m. A nice solid number, but way too early to wake up.

Rustling in the hallway. Not her imagination.

Silent, phone in hand, she slithered off the coverlet onto the floor. Her naked skin hardly made a whisper on the vintage satin. She pressed the cold flat glass face of the phone hard between her breasts, trying to cover any light it might emit, hoping she could keep it from making inadvertent sounds. She thought she heard breathing in the hallway just outside her bedroom door – not labored breathing, but tight, irregular, excited, as though the breather fought to keep it under control.

With some wriggling, Winnie managed to squeeze mostly under the bed. It was disgusting under there, grittily colonized with dust creatures the size of kittens – neither she nor Liz had been vacuum-under-the-bed types. Even in the dark she could see the lower legs of someone entering the room. The person attached to the legs approached the bed, not seeming particularly stealthful and certainly without the hesitancy Winnie would expect of anyone unaccustomed to navigating her bedroom at night without light. Whoever it was even sidestepped her ridiculous slippers where they lay as they'd fallen when she'd kicked them off going to bed, one humped up onto the other's back as though intending to populate her room with plush moonfaced panda babies.

She held her breath as the person stood beside the bed. Her heart beat too fast, slamming against the flat face of her phone, the sound reverberating so loudly she was sure it echoed up into the room, giving her away.

"Winnie? Where are you?"

Winnie's heart skipped its next beat as she recognized the voice. Peter, from next door. Why the hell would he be in her room in the middle of the night? Had softhearted Liz extended him an open-ended invitation to drop in that she'd neglected to mention? Or maybe Winnie herself had once made some offhand neighborly comment about him being welcome any time – something no sane person would take so literally? Maybe he was in trouble, hurt or bleeding from some freak kitchen accident, desperate for his only nearby neighbor to drive him to the hospital. A dozen implausible notions scrambled to present themselves as plausible scenarios, to explain away the intense weirdness of a neighbor she barely knew being her in her bedroom uninvited after two in the morning.

The fabric of his trousers made a whisking sound as he knelt to peer under the bed. His bland-handsome face was a pale splotch swimming in darkness. His head looked strangely over-rounded, misshapen as though he wore a fitted lumpy hat.

"There you are," he said. "That's a first."

Trapped. Winnie felt trapped, without enough room for her lungs to expand, to breathe the dust-choked air. Cold wood floorboards pressed hard against her naked spine. She felt flushed all over, simultaneous ice and heat, fear and the flight urge competing, suffocating her, adding to the confusion of *what the hell was happening*.

He reached under the bed as though to drag her out and she squirmed out the other side, not even enough room to roll, her skin scraping along the dust-gritted floor. It was a relief to stand. The relief hit her like a betrayal, a false promise of improved circumstances. Nothing was improved.

Peter straightened to regard her from across the rumpled bed. He stood between Winnie and the door. Her brain raced, sketching a hasty plan, something to do with leaping onto the bed, launching past him in the darkness, dashing down the hall, running naked out into the night toward the vague safety of *away*. She and Peter were the sole residents of this particular cul-de-sac, but the builder had never gotten around to connecting streetlights, so perhaps the cover of darkness would help her. Could she make it to the next cluster of occupied homes some distance down the main road, naked and barefoot? Buying her very own house had seemed a dream-come-true at the time, getting in at the ground floor, so to speak, with a developer desperate to sell units in an unestablished neighborhood at the ass-end of town. But then she'd gotten Liz, and a small but nice house near enough to the woods that they saw deer in the evenings, more birds than they could count... even a persistent coyote, leggy and lonesome and – she'd observed with a tinge of guilt – clearly displaced by the suburban encroachment on his natural habitat. No noisy neighbors to shatter the peace out here; only one quiet, corporate-drone sort of guy, Peter, who kept to himself, rarely spoke, never brought home friends. Mostly he seemed to hole up in his garage and fiddle with expensive tools, inscrutably tinkering on unrecognizable projects like any number of random suburban yuppie-type dudes. Winnie and Liz had tried to create a circle of friendly proximity and always waved, said hello when appropriate, were careful to respect the neat hedgerow dividing their pie-wedge yards, but privately referred to him as Khakipants.

The windowsill Winnie had backed up against dug into the flesh of her upper thigh. More half-baked plans and thoughts scrambled for attention in her brain (*open window, tear through screen? fall from second storey? survive fall?*) when Peter stepped back and flipped the overhead light switch.

Blinking against the sharp stab of sudden brightness, Winnie said, "Peter, I don't know what you're doing here but you have to leave now. I've already called 911." She hadn't. Shit, shit, she hadn't. Everything was happening so fast. She fumbled with her phone – unlock! unlock! – and wildly started thumbing for the keypad.

Her vision had adjusted quickly enough that she saw him shrug. "Doesn't matter," he said. "I'll finish up and travel back before they get here. I'd wanted to try this tonight, you know, for strangling..." Tangled in the fingers of his left hand was a loop of strong soft cord, an unmistakable garrote which he crumpled in his fist and shoved in his pocket. "...But I always bring a gun just in case."

Her lips barely compressed into the first letter of his name before he raised the gun he held and shot her twice in the center of the chest.

Flat on her back in the gap between bed and wall, Winnie watched the ceiling turning red – or was something in her eyes? Her chest felt heavy, as though her heart had turned to lead and now weighed her down, pressing her to the hard wood floor. She dimly understood the wet gurgling as herself, sucking breath through the mess of her shredded lungs. All thoughts of rescue, of Liz, of rage, of fear even, left Winnie's brain like air from a burst balloon. The sole remaining thing, the one thought burning away all the rest in the final moment, was *why?*

"Peter, why?" The words wheezed from her, bubbling and nearly unrecognizable even to her own ears. He walked around the end of the bed to stand over her, to lean down with a look of polite inquiry on his innocuous, unremarkable features.

"To test my chronofluxic resonator." He tapped the thin plastic shell of the small helmet he wore, laced with braided wires visibly embedded with dozens of old-fashioned computer chips. "I needed to do something irrevocable. Something, you know, *important*. Something the world would notice. Had to make sure everything worked before I take it public. That was why, the first time."

The ceiling was all red now. Peter's face, hovering above, was washed in pink. Her chest hurt, but not so bad as it had a few moments earlier. She tried to speak but the words ended as a ragged cough. She tried again. Again Peter leaned over to hear her, tilting his head with that same impersonal politeness one might use with an elderly stranger.

"How ... many?" Winnie burbled. Warm trails ran from the corners of her mouth. "How many times?"

Peter smiled. It was the first recognizable emotion to come into his face, reach all the way to his eyes. He nudged the end of the gun gently against her left temple.

"This is number twelve," he said, and pulled the trigger.

* * *

Winnie raised herself on one elbow and squinted in the direction of her bedroom doorway. Groggy, mind thick with sleep, she reached for her phone lying on what used to be Liz's nightstand. 2:20 a.m. A nice solid number, but way too early to wake up.

She'd been dreaming Liz was trying to tell her some urgent thing, trying to wake her, though it wasn't Liz but her mother, and then it wasn't her mother but her eighth-grade French teacher. *Rise and shine, lazybones*, her mother had chimed in that maternal singsong she'd often used to get Winnie ready for school; *Attention, mademoiselle!* Madame Giroux had snapped; *Wake up, Winnie!* Liz had shouted. *Wake the fuck up!*

Winnie rolled out of bed, shoved her feet into her slippers. She was awake, she might as well use the bathroom; it was one of her mother's dearest and most firmly held beliefs that the font of all nightmares was a sleeper's need to urinate.

With one hand she grabbed her garish pink and purple chrysanthemum kimono off its hook by the door, shrugging into it more from habit than anything else. She was about to step into the hall when something made her freeze. Not a sound, not a movement – a disturbance in the silence? Winnie pressed back against the wall behind the door and strained to listen to the inky nighttime darkness. Her heart thudded against the flat square face of the phone she still clutched, now in one fist, pressed hard against her chest as she listened to the quiet.

The unmistakable sound of someone walking up the stairs. Not Liz, who'd moved back east, leaving Winnie heartbroken and three thousand miles away. Not her mother, whose arthritis these days prevented her from driving, much less from tackling even the most forgiving staircase without a fistful of painkillers. No one else came to Winnie's mind as anyone who might have any claim to be in her home in the middle of the night. So when the intruder – taller than she was, a masculine frame – stepped into the open doorway, Winnie slammed the door into him with as much force as she could.

The door ricocheted off the collision with his solid body with more force than Winnie had anticipated, slamming her back against the wall. The intruder staggered to his feet and lunged, striking wildly in her direction with something sharp enough to slice the loose fabric off her kimono sleeve at the first pass. The second pass missed her face by an inch, notching her earlobe, and the third bit deep into the flesh of her left forearm, bared of its sleeve, before tugging free.

A bellow of rage erupted from deep in Winnie's chest as though it had amassed and been waiting, surprising her, infusing her with unexpected strength as she tackled him. They fell into the hallway, her landing heavily on top. His surprised grunt was enough for her to recognize her neighbor Peter.

"Stop!" he cried. "You'll damage my prototype!"

Hot blood rained down from her sliced ear as she raised her right fist and let it fall onto his face. Her injured arm pressed against his throat. Her thumb, sticky-slick, slid across the screen of the phone still clutched in her left hand, activating the torch function. Hard white light flooded his face, blinding them both. In the afterimage snapshot fused to her retinas she saw why he hadn't dislodged her immediately: he was trying to protect some strange hat he wore made of plastic and braided wire, twisting to keep her blows from striking it.

She ground her injured arm harder against his throat, wishing she'd paid closer attention to that stupid Wreal Wrestling reality show Liz liked – would he really pass out this way? She bellowed again, bearing down, fist tight over the illuminated phone. Red drops and smears looked like fake blood under the harsh mechanical light, like stage blood, like gory theater.

Her other fist fell again toward his baffling headwear. He managed to deflect the blow while keeping grip on his bloodstained knife, a wicked dagger-point item she imagined was designed to gut deer like those for which she and Liz used to leave buckets of water in the yard on hot summer days. The skin over Winnie's knuckles parted as she was forced to make a glancing punch at his jaw rather than in the middle of his face where she'd aimed. The strap holding his helmet snapped. The contraption skittered across the wood floor.

With renewed vigor he threw Winnie off. Her phone went flying from her hand, its blinding light spinning crazily down the hall, throwing shadows, making everything dance in the strobe effect. Peter scrambled to retrieve his helmet. Fueled by an engulfing rage beyond her surface understanding, Winnie lunged after him. Some internal scale tipped inside her, stuttered into being like a flame ignited by flint. Not even the urge to run could overpower her urge to stop him from doing it again.

Even as she swiped at him, missed, hooked her fingers in his jacket pocket instead, the query scampered across Winnie's forebrain: *again*? Stop him from doing what, *again?*

A loud ripping came as Peter's pocket tore free, spilling its contents into her hand. The gun was cold. Winnie had never held a gun, never pointed one, never wanted to.

In the faint electroluminescent wash from the phone down the hall, Winnie struggled to her feet. The metal of the gun was so cold it burned her fingers. She watched Peter retrieve his helmet, clamp it with one hand down over his short blond hair – pink hair at his temple, with her blood smeared across. There was nothing in his expression she could recognize.

"How did you know I was coming? Was it the chronometric reverb?" he said, not to her so much as to himself, musing aloud.

Winnie was shaking. She gripped the gun in both fists, pointing it at him, hoping she held it properly, wondering how to retrieve her phone and dial 911 without letting him overpower her, wondering if she could last long enough for help to arrive without passing out from the pain in her arm, her hand, the side of her head, the dozen other shallow cuts leaking her blood and turning the wood floor sticky. Her teeth chattered so hard, it was a struggle to force words out: "What have you done to me?"

He glanced up as though startled to see her standing there. He made a dismissive gesture. "There was a small possibility repeated actions would set up a kind of pre-verberation. A precursive echo, if you like." His fingers fiddled with the braided wires dangling from his headwear, trying to press them up back under the plastic, twiddling things back into place. "Don't worry. I'll tinker a little more, find a different chronometral fold to access. I'll adjust the parameters and you won't know a thing next time."

"Next time?"

She recognized something suffuse his expression then. It wasn't guilt, exactly. Closer to a rueful admission of weakness.

"Unforeseen variable – I didn't know I'd like it so much," he said. At her blank stare he added the words her mind filled in, words she'd dismissed in some last ditch effort to keep any semblance of feeling sane. "I didn't know I'd like it so much, killing someone. You. Killing you. Over and over, every way I can think of. Night after night."

The sheepish look on his face shifted to triumph as his fingers found the right wire, shoved the right chip back into its slot. The contraption on his head flickered, humming with power, coming alive. Two blue lights blinked at Winnie like two mischievous eyes, sparkling and mirthful. *Next time*, they seemed to promise. *See you next time.*

He surprised her, leaping, slamming into her chest so the gun was crushed between them. She'd forgotten the red-slick knife still in the grip of his off-hand, the hand not clamped over the crazy helmet. She felt the blade where he held it to her ribs, pushing aside the open kimono, but her attention kept riveted on the mocking blue lights blinking, turning his pinkened hair purple as they made ready to engage at his command. *Next time*, they winked at Winnie: *next time.*

As his blade parted the flesh between her ribs she twisted. Her arm sprang free of their slick and awkward embrace. The arm with the hand holding the gun.

His knife pressed deeper. Winnie's skin parted like ripe cheese. The helmet lights blinked faster. Peter began to feel less substantial in her grip. In a moment she would be dead with his knife in her heart and he, if she understood him, if she believed him, would be gone. The lights would win, would see her next time.

Reverberation from the gunshot tore through her injured arm. The knife slipped from her chest with a sickening glide, then thudded onto the bloody floor with a wet plop. Peter sagged against her, thickening, growing heavier and more substantial as he fell. Winnie staggered backward under his weight, aiming at the winking lights again, firing again. She had to silence those mocking blue lights for good, disable them and never let them return. That Peter's head happened to be underneath them was, it felt in the moment, of only distant concern.

She let his body slide to the floor. Gripping the gun in numb hands she fired another shot into the sputtering blue lights, then dropped to her knees and smashed them with the bloody butt of the pistol, again and again, until she was absolutely sure she wouldn't have to do this again next time.

The First Seven Deaths of Mildred Orly

Fred Senese

THE DETECTIVE set down the chocolate bar and the soda pop I'd asked for. She'd also brought me a box of tissues and a hand mirror. I winced at that: she was considerate.

She touched a button on the recorder. "I understand that you've waived the right to have a lawyer present today, Ms. Bissel. Is that correct?"

"I'll represent myself," I said. "If it comes to that. And it won't. Ask me anything you like."

She cleared her throat. "Testimony of Eva Bissel. 3/20/16. PI Amy Stark."

I tried to smile at her. She looked wise, crisp and confident in her tailored suit. I liked how her hair was swept up; I'd never thought of doing mine like that. Gorgeous patent leather pumps with kitten heels, and an expensive manicure – maybe this wasn't going to be so bad. Though she was older than I'd have liked.

I unwrapped the chocolate bar. I put a square on my tongue and let it melt. The detective watched me – she'd never seen a runway model eating chocolate before, I'll bet – and I offered her a square. She shook her head.

Chocolate has always made me feel better, wherever and whoever I've been. It's magic. Not real magic, not my strongest magic, but it's close. This was factory chocolate, not as rich as Marie's chocolate, but it was good enough. I felt it working on me. It took away my cold, hungry ache. It took me home. It made me feel the way I did when I was just me.

The conium I'd swallowed in the bathroom was working on me, too. It was already numbing my toes. I didn't have long now. Maybe half an hour.

I opened my eyes again and smiled at the detective. She smiled back. A kind smile.

I told her everything.

* * *

I was Mildred Orly and I was a normal human being until I turned 13.

That's when my body betrayed me. It was the year I got my period and boys started noticing me, not because I was becoming a woman, but because I was rapidly expanding into a shapeless, monstrous sack they could torment.

One morning I could barely button my blue plaid jumper. It fit just fine the day before. The boys at school said I looked like a sausage in a kilt.

And that was only the beginning. Fat piled under the straps of my training bra and between my thighs and below my navel. My arms thickened, my waist spread, my face rounded and softened and sprouted fiery red pimples that wouldn't heal after I popped them.

I went to the bathroom so often to weigh myself that Mama hid the scale. Then she took the mirror from my room. "This will pass," she said. "Perfection is a child of time. You'll see. All of us go through this. I went through it. Your grandmother went through it–"

I loved her for that before I hated her. It was crazy, what she told me, or so I thought at the time. She never changed because she was stuck being my mama. She was stuck with me, just as I was stuck with my potato body and my chewed-up nails and my bloated moon-face.

It was her job to lie to me. I was her job.

I got a job, too. I did deliveries for Marie's, a little chocolatier's shop on the corner. I was just a kid, so my pay was that I could pick out whatever chocolate I wanted, or whatever cut flowers no one wanted at the end of the day. I always went for the chocolate. My daddy hated that – he would never stop telling me about how I'd ruin my 'figure.' I didn't listen. I was already ruined.

Marie wouldn't say a word to me when I claimed my pay. She was twenty-six, the perfect age, I thought. Her mother and father had just moved to Florida and they left her the shop and their house and their car.

Marie was tall and thin and she had this creamy, poreless skin that glowed from underneath. Lush red hair with just a hint of a wave to it, full lips and a tiny button nose. She'd read *Vogue* and *Cosmo* and *Oxygen* while I was in the shop. She'd barely look up from her magazine when she was giving me a bunch of flowers or a box of chocolate to deliver. She had a fiancé, too. Robert. He was so handsome. They were going to be married that June. He was nice to me back then.

Every night in bed I'd close my eyes and whisper to myself, "*I am Marie*". Over and over again. I'd lie still until my feet fell asleep, until I couldn't tell whether my hands were palm-up or palm-down by my sides. I'd dream I was Marie. I had her beautiful hair, her sweet voice, her elegant hands. Her Robert. I'd cry when the morning light chased that dream away.

The horrible night before my fourteenth birthday, I'd been picking at my face again. I'd made a wound that I knew would never go away. I didn't bother to put tissue on it.

Daddy had left for a business trip. Mama had trouble sleeping when he was away. She left the pills that made her sleep on the bathroom counter. And just like that, I knew what I had to do.

I swallowed the whole bottle. It took a while. When I was done I whispered, "*I should have been Marie*."

* * *

The detective wrote something in her book. "Marie Kasselli," she said, and it wasn't a question.

"That's right," I told her. "That was how you figured it out, right?"

"Figured what out?" she said, carefully.

"The connection." I clasped my hands together on top of the table to keep them from shaking. The conium was moving into my chest.

"Poison," I said. "It hurts more than you would think. I got terrible cramps before I passed out. It was like being on fire from the inside."

"You survived, though," the detective said.

"No. And yes. When I woke up, I was Marie."

The detective blinked twice. "Yes," she whispered. "You were happy about that?"

"For a while, yes. I was in heaven. It's so much nicer being 26 than 14. I had... everything."

"What changed, then?"

"Robert," I said. "He learned to hate me. He told me that if I kept wolfing down chocolate, I'd get fat. Fatter, is what he said. And he was right. Marie was growing a little pooch, even before I... and this ugly scar on her tummy? They cut something out of her when she was a girl. It was creepy, thinking about whatever was missing inside of me. I couldn't stop touching it –"

"What happened to Mildred?"

"The paper said the funeral was the Sunday after I left her. I thought I'd go, but then decided that I'd better not. I didn't know how things worked, you see. Maybe someone would recognize me? I thought it was all a dream, at first." I sat back and looked at my long red nails. They were beautiful. The most flawless nails I'd ever had, though the polish on my left pinkie was a little chipped where I'd nibbled it this morning.

"Marie Kasselli shot herself in the mouth with her father's handgun on the third of June 2012," the detective said.

"Yes."

"Why?"

"I told you. Robert couldn't love me. I was getting fat. He hated my scar. And I started tearing out my hair–"

The detective put on her reading glasses and looked at her notebook. "Marie's friend Karen Crane opened her wrists in September 2013. And Karen's sister Sasha Crane-Harrel hung herself in her bedroom in July 2014."

"You missed Keely Fletcher," I said. My voice trembled. "Marie's chocolate supplier."

The detective wrote the name in her book. "Cause of death?"

"Cyanide," I said.

"Date?"

"December 2015."

She was quiet for a moment. Then she said, "After Mildred... died, did you have any contact with your mother? With Mrs. Eileen Orly?"

"Yes."

"She told you what you needed to know, then, didn't she? She told you what you were."

"Please," I said. "You understand. I know you do, Detective Stark. Amy. They'll lock me away. They'll study me, they'll dissect me–"

She sat back in her chair and studied me. "No. No one will believe what you can do. No one will believe what you are. You know that. And I know it too." She leaned forward. "All this can stop. I'll erase this interview from the recorder. All you have to do is give me what I want."

"What do you want?"

"I want you to stop."

"I want that, too! Don't you think I hate this? Don't you think I know what happens to people when I take them? But I can't– I can't live like this–"

"When I first understood your situation," the detective said, "I thought you were wearing them. Like shoes. Like new clothes. But it's not that way. You aren't like that." She picked up the hand mirror she'd brought for me and held it up. "Look at yourself. What do you see?"

"What do you mean?" I turned my head frantically from side to side. "What's wrong with my face?"

"Nothing. That's just it. You're beautiful, Eva… Mildred. You're perfect. You know you are – you're a model, people *pay* to see you wearing their clothes. People *pay* to put your face in their ads, they *pay* for the magazines those ads are in. What more proof do you need?"

She reached across the table and touched my wrist. "What your mother told you was true. Right or wrong, time has brought you here. The child is grown. It's over." She squeezed my hand. "You can stop now. You can rest."

"I can't." My throat had closed up and my tongue felt like a lump of raw meat in my mouth. It was starting.

"Why not?"

The ceiling tilted and the floor spun. I couldn't keep my eyes open for much longer. I looked at the mirror. I'd loved being Eva. Though I think my eyes were about a quarter inch too close together.

"Because you know," I said. And I made my wish. It was the last thing Eva wished.

The detective's screaming was the last thing Eva heard.

It hurts for them, too.

* * *

That night I picked up my notebook. Under the line about Keely I wrote, *Eva Bissel, 3/20/2016. Apparent heart failure*. It was strange how my handwriting looked now.

I wrote a question mark after that, because the autopsy would not be done for a few days. The detective had known that; I hadn't.

Mama warned me to be careful after Marie died. To choose a home. To choose carefully. Well, I could be even more careful now: I was a lot smarter than I'd ever been before.

I live in the most beautiful part of the City. Old Town, down along the river. Quaint shops and cobblestone streets, the kind of things tourists love to see.

There's actually a chocolatier's shop. The woman behind the counter is getting to know my new name faster than I am. As I walked out of her shop this morning I caught sight of my reflection in the glass door. It horrified me. Those crow's feet, those little grey wisps in my hair, that sagging chin.

I turned away. I couldn't bear to look.

The woman at the register said, "Did you forget something, Ms. Stark?"

Cornsilk hair that fell past her shoulders, but plaited like a crown around her head. Her lashes swept over her eyes like white feathers.

"Are you ok? Can I help you?"

"Maybe," I said.

Markheim

Robert Louis Stevenson

"YES," said the dealer, "our windfalls are of various kinds. Some customers are ignorant, and then I touch a dividend on my superior knowledge. Some are dishonest," and here he held up the candle, so that the light fell strongly on his visitor, "and in that case," he continued, "I profit by my virtue."

Markheim had but just entered from the daylight streets, and his eyes had not yet grown familiar with the mingled shine and darkness in the shop. At these pointed words, and before the near presence of the flame, he blinked painfully and looked aside.

The dealer chuckled. "You come to me on Christmas Day," he resumed, "when you know that I am alone in my house, put up my shutters, and make a point of refusing business. Well, you will have to pay for that; you will have to pay for my loss of time, when I should be balancing my books; you will have to pay, besides, for a kind of manner that I remark in you today very strongly. I am the essence of discretion, and ask no awkward questions; but when a customer cannot look me in the eye, he has to pay for it." The dealer once more chuckled; and then, changing to his usual business voice, though still with a note of irony, "You can give, as usual, a clear account of how you came into the possession of the object?" he continued. "Still your uncle's cabinet? A remarkable collector, sir!"

And the little pale, round-shouldered dealer stood almost on tip-toe, looking over the top of his gold spectacles, and nodding his head with every mark of disbelief. Markheim returned his gaze with one of infinite pity, and a touch of horror.

"This time," said he, "you are in error. I have not come to sell, but to buy. I have no curios to dispose of; my uncle's cabinet is bare to the wainscot; even were it still intact, I have done well on the Stock Exchange, and should more likely add to it than otherwise, and my errand today is simplicity itself. I seek a Christmas present for a lady," he continued, waxing more fluent as he struck into the speech he had prepared; "and certainly I owe you every excuse for thus disturbing you upon so small a matter. But the thing was neglected yesterday; I must produce my little compliment at dinner; and, as you very well know, a rich marriage is not a thing to be neglected."

There followed a pause, during which the dealer seemed to weigh this statement incredulously. The ticking of many clocks among the curious lumber of the shop, and the faint rushing of the cabs in a near thoroughfare, filled up the interval of silence.

"Well, sir," said the dealer, "be it so. You are an old customer after all; and if, as you say, you have the chance of a good marriage, far be it from me to be an obstacle. Here is a nice thing for a lady now," he went on, "this hand glass – fifteenth century, warranted; comes from a good collection, too; but I reserve the name, in the interests of my customer, who was just like yourself, my dear sir, the nephew and sole heir of a remarkable collector."

The dealer, while he thus ran on in his dry and biting voice, had stooped to take the object from its place; and, as he had done so, a shock had passed through Markheim, a start both of hand and foot, a sudden leap of many tumultuous passions to the face. It passed as swiftly as it came, and left no trace beyond a certain trembling of the hand that now received the glass.

"A glass," he said hoarsely, and then paused, and repeated it more clearly. "A glass? For Christmas? Surely not?"

"And why not?" cried the dealer. "Why not a glass?"

Markheim was looking upon him with an indefinable expression. "You ask me why not?" he said. "Why, look here – look in it – look at yourself! Do you like to see it? No! Nor I – nor any man."

The little man had jumped back when Markheim had so suddenly confronted him with the mirror; but now, perceiving there was nothing worse on hand, he chuckled. "Your future lady, sir, must be pretty hard favoured," said he.

"I ask you," said Markheim, "for a Christmas present, and you give me this – this damned reminder of years, and sins and follies – this hand-conscience! Did you mean it? Had you a thought in your mind? Tell me. It will be better for you if you do. Come, tell me about yourself. I hazard a guess now, that you are in secret a very charitable man?"

The dealer looked closely at his companion. It was very odd, Markheim did not appear to be laughing; there was something in his face like an eager sparkle of hope, but nothing of mirth.

"What are you driving at?" the dealer asked.

"Not charitable?" returned the other, gloomily. Not charitable; not pious; not scrupulous; unloving, unbeloved; a hand to get money, a safe to keep it. Is that all? Dear God, man, is that all?"

"I will tell you what it is," began the dealer, with some sharpness, and then broke off again into a chuckle. "But I see this is a love match of yours, and you have been drinking the lady's health."

"Ah!" cried Markheim, with a strange curiosity. "Ah, have you been in love? Tell me about that."

"I," cried the dealer. "I in love! I never had the time, nor have I the time today for all this nonsense. Will you take the glass?"

"Where is the hurry?" returned Markheim. "It is very pleasant to stand here talking; and life is so short and insecure that I would not hurry away from any pleasure – no, not even from so mild a one as this. We should rather cling, cling to what little we can get, like a man at a cliff's edge. Every second is a cliff, if you think upon it – a cliff a mile high – high enough, if we fall, to dash us out of every feature of humanity. Hence it is best to talk pleasantly. Let us talk of each other: why should we wear this mask? Let us be confidential. Who knows, we might become friends?"

"I have just one word to say to you," said the dealer. "Either make your purchase, or walk out of my shop!"

"True true," said Markheim. "Enough, fooling. To business. Show me something else."

The dealer stooped once more, this time to replace the glass upon the shelf, his thin blond hair falling over his eyes as he did so. Markheim moved a little nearer, with one hand in the pocket of his greatcoat; he drew himself up and filled his lungs; at the same time many different emotions were depicted together on his face – terror, horror, and resolve, fascination and a physical repulsion; and through a haggard lift of his upper lip, his teeth looked out.

"This, perhaps, may suit," observed the dealer: and then, as he began to re-arise, Markheim bounded from behind upon his victim. The long, skewerlike dagger flashed and fell. The dealer struggled like a hen, striking his temple on the shelf, and then tumbled on the floor in a heap.

Time had some score of small voices in that shop, some stately and slow as was becoming to their great age; others garrulous and hurried. All these told out the seconds in an intricate, chorus of tickings. Then the passage of a lad's feet, heavily running on the pavement, broke in upon these smaller voices and startled Markheim into the consciousness of his surroundings. He looked about him awfully. The candle stood on the counter, its flame solemnly wagging in a draught; and by that inconsiderable movement, the whole room was filled with noiseless bustle and kept heaving like a sea: the tall shadows nodding, the gross blots of darkness swelling and dwindling as with respiration, the faces of the portraits and the china gods changing and wavering like images in water. The inner door stood ajar, and peered into that leaguer of shadows with a long slit of daylight like a pointing finger.

From these fear-stricken rovings, Markheim's eyes returned to the body of his victim, where it lay both humped and sprawling, incredibly small and strangely meaner than in life. In these poor, miserly clothes, in that ungainly attitude, the dealer lay like so much sawdust. Markheim had feared to see it, and, lo! It was nothing. And yet, as he gazed, this bundle of old clothes and pool of blood began to find eloquent voices. There it must lie; there was none to work the cunning hinges or direct the miracle of locomotion – there it must lie till it was found. Found! Ay, and then? Then would this dead flesh lift up a cry that would ring over England, and fill the world with the echoes of pursuit. Ay, dead or not, this was still the enemy. "Time was that when the brains were out," he thought; and the first word struck into his mind. Time, now that the deed was accomplished – time, which had closed for the victim, had become instant and momentous for the slayer.

The thought was yet in his mind, when, first one and then another, with every variety of pace and voice – one deep as the bell from a cathedral turret, another ringing on its treble notes the prelude of a waltz – the clocks began to strike the hour of three in the afternoon.

The sudden outbreak of so many tongues in that dumb chamber staggered him. He began to bestir himself, going to and fro with the candle, beleaguered by moving shadows, and startled to the soul by chance reflections. In many rich mirrors, some of home design, some from Venice or Amsterdam, he saw his face repeated and repeated, as it were an army of spies; his own eyes met and detected him; and the sound of his own steps, lightly as they fell, vexed the surrounding quiet. And still, as he continued to fill his pockets, his mind accused him with a sickening iteration, of the thousand faults of his design. He should have chosen a more quiet hour; he should have prepared an alibi; he should not have used a knife; he should have been more cautious, and only bound and gagged the dealer, and not killed him; he should have been more bold, and killed the servant also; he should have done all things otherwise: poignant regrets, weary, incessant toiling of the mind to change what was unchangeable, to plan what was now useless, to be the architect of the irrevocable past. Meanwhile, and behind all this activity, brute terrors, like the scurrying of rats in a deserted attic, filled the more remote chambers of his brain with riot; the hand of the constable would fall heavy on his shoulder, and his nerves would jerk like a hooked fish; or he beheld, in galloping defile, the dock, the prison, the gallows, and the black coffin.

Terror of the people in the street sat down before his mind like a besieging army. It was impossible, he thought, but that some rumour of the struggle must have reached their ears and set on edge their curiosity; and now, in all the neighbouring houses, he divined them sitting motionless and with uplifted ear – solitary people, condemned to spend Christmas dwelling alone on memories of the past, and now startingly recalled from that tender exercise; happy family parties struck into silence round the table, the mother still with raised finger: every degree and age and humour, but all, by their own hearths, prying and hearkening and weaving the rope that was to hang him. Sometimes it seemed to him he could not move too softly; the clink of the tall Bohemian goblets rang out loudly like a bell; and alarmed by the bigness of the ticking, he was tempted to stop the clocks. And then, again, with a swift transition of his terrors, the very silence of the place appeared a source of peril, and a thing to strike and freeze the passer-by; and he would step more boldly, and bustle aloud among the contents of the shop, and imitate, with elaborate bravado, the movements of a busy man at ease in his own house.

But he was now so pulled about by different alarms that, while one portion of his mind was still alert and cunning, another trembled on the brink of lunacy. One hallucination in particular took a strong hold on his credulity. The neighbour hearkening with white face beside his window, the passer-by arrested by a horrible surmise on the pavement – these could at worst suspect, they could not know; through the brick walls and shuttered windows only sounds could penetrate. But here, within the house, was he alone? He knew he was; he had watched the servant set forth sweet-hearting, in her poor best, "out for the day" written in every ribbon and smile. Yes, he was alone, of course; and yet, in the bulk of empty house above him, he could surely hear a stir of delicate footing – he was surely conscious, inexplicably conscious of some presence. Ay, surely; to every room and corner of the house his imagination followed it; and now it was a faceless thing, and yet had eyes to see with; and again it was a shadow of himself; and yet again behold the image of the dead dealer, reinspired with cunning and hatred.

At times, with a strong effort, he would glance at the open door which still seemed to repel his eyes. The house was tall, the skylight small and dirty, the day blind with fog; and the light that filtered down to the ground story was exceedingly faint, and showed dimly on the threshold of the shop. And yet, in that strip of doubtful brightness, did there not hang wavering a shadow?

Suddenly, from the street outside, a very jovial gentleman began to beat with a staff on the shop-door, accompanying his blows with shouts and railleries in which the dealer was continually called upon by name. Markheim, smitten into ice, glanced at the dead man. But no! He lay quite still; he was fled away far beyond earshot of these blows and shoutings; he was sunk beneath seas of silence; and his name, which would once have caught his notice above the howling of a storm, had become an empty sound. And presently the jovial gentleman desisted from his knocking, and departed.

Here was a broad hint to hurry what remained to be done, to get forth from this accusing neighbourhood, to plunge into a bath of London multitudes, and to reach, on the other side of day, that haven of safety and apparent innocence – his bed. One visitor had come: at any moment another might follow and be more obstinate. To have done the deed, and yet not to reap the profit, would be too abhorrent a failure. The money, that was now Markheim's concern; and as a means to that, the keys.

He glanced over his shoulder at the open door, where the shadow was still lingering and shivering; and with no conscious repugnance of the mind, yet with a tremor of the belly, he drew near the body of his victim. The human character had quite departed. Like a suit half-stuffed with bran, the limbs lay scattered, the trunk doubled, on the floor; and yet the thing repelled him. Although so dingy and inconsiderable to the eye, he feared it might have more significance to the touch. He took the body by the shoulders, and turned it on its back. It was strangely light and supple, and the limbs, as if they had been broken, fell into the oddest postures. The face was robbed of all expression; but it was as pale as wax, and shockingly smeared with blood about one temple. That was, for Markheim, the one displeasing circumstance. It carried him back, upon the instant, to a certain fair-day in a fishers' village: a gray day, a piping wind, a crowd upon the street, the blare of brasses, the booming of drums, the nasal voice of a ballad singer; and a boy going to and fro, buried over head in the crowd and divided between interest and fear, until, coming out upon the chief place of concourse, he beheld a booth and a great screen with pictures, dismally designed, garishly coloured: Brown-rigg with her apprentice; the Mannings with their murdered guest; Weare in the death-grip of Thurtell; and a score besides of famous crimes. The thing was as clear as an illusion; he was once again that little boy; he was looking once again, and with the same sense of physical revolt, at these vile pictures; he was still stunned by the thumping of the drums. A bar of that day's music returned upon his memory; and at that, for the first time, a qualm came over him, a breath of nausea, a sudden weakness of the joints, which he must instantly resist and conquer.

He judged it more prudent to confront than to flee from these considerations; looking the more hardily in the dead face, bending his mind to realise the nature and greatness of his crime. So little a while ago that face had moved with every change of sentiment, that pale mouth had spoken, that body had been all on fire with governable energies; and now, and by his act, that piece of life had been arrested, as the horologist, with interjected finger, arrests the beating of the clock. So he reasoned in vain; he could rise to no more remorseful consciousness; the same heart which had shuddered before the painted effigies of crime, looked on its reality unmoved. At best, he felt a gleam of pity for one who had been endowed in vain with all those faculties that can make the world a garden of enchantment, one who had never lived and who was now dead. But of penitence, no, not a tremor.

With that, shaking himself clear of these considerations, he found the keys and advanced towards the open door of the shop. Outside, it had begun to rain smartly; and the sound of the shower upon the roof had banished silence. Like some dripping cavern, the chambers of the house were haunted by an incessant echoing, which filled the ear and mingled with the ticking of the clocks. And, as Markheim approached the door, he seemed to hear, in answer to his own cautious tread, the steps of another foot withdrawing up the stair. The shadow still palpitated loosely on the threshold. He threw a ton's weight of resolve upon his muscles, and drew back the door.

The faint, foggy daylight glimmered dimly on the bare floor and stairs; on the bright suit of armour posted, halbert in hand, upon the landing; and on the dark wood-carvings, and framed pictures that hung against the yellow panels of the wainscot. So loud was the beating of the rain through all the house that, in Markheim's ears, it began to be distinguished into many different sounds. Footsteps and sighs, the tread of regiments marching in the distance, the chink of money in the counting, and the creaking of doors held stealthily ajar, appeared to mingle with the patter of the drops upon the cupola and the gushing of the water in the pipes. The sense that he was not alone grew upon him to the verge of madness. On every side he was haunted and begirt by presences. He heard them moving in the upper chambers; from the shop, he heard the dead man getting to his legs; and as he began with a great effort to mount the stairs, feet fled quietly before him and followed stealthily behind. If he were but deaf, he thought, how tranquilly he would possess his soul! And then again, and hearkening with ever fresh attention, he blessed himself for that unresting sense which held the outposts and stood a trusty sentinel upon his life. His head turned continually on his neck; his eyes, which seemed starting from their orbits, scouted on every side, and on every side were half-rewarded as with the tail of something nameless vanishing. The four-and-twenty steps to the first floor were four-and-twenty agonies.

On that first storey, the doors stood ajar, three of them like three ambushes, shaking his nerves like the throats of cannon. He could never again, he felt, be sufficiently immured and fortified from men's observing eyes, he longed to be home, girt in by walls, buried among bedclothes, and invisible to all but God. And at that thought he wondered a little, recollecting tales of other murderers and the fear they were said to entertain of heavenly avengers. It was not so, at least, with him. He feared the laws of nature, lest, in their callous and immutable procedure, they should preserve some damning evidence of his crime. He feared tenfold more, with a slavish, superstitions terror, some scission in the continuity of man's experience, some wilful illegality of nature. He played a game of skill, depending on the rules, calculating consequence from cause; and what if nature, as the defeated tyrant overthrew the chess-board, should break the mould of their succession? The like had befallen Napoleon (so writers said) when the winter changed the time of its appearance. The like might befall Markheim: the solid walls might become transparent and reveal his doings like those of bees in a glass hive; the stout planks might yield under his foot like quicksands and detain him in their clutch; ay, and there were soberer accidents that might destroy him: if, for instance, the house should fall and imprison him beside the body of his victim; or the house next door should fly on fire, and the firemen invade him from all sides. These things he feared; and, in a sense, these things might be called the hands of God reached forth against sin. But about God himself he was at ease; his act was doubtless exceptional, but so were his excuses, which God knew; it was there, and not among men, that he felt sure of justice.

When he had got safe into the drawing-room, and shut the door behind him, he was aware of a respite from alarms. The room was quite dismantled, uncarpeted besides, and strewn with packing cases and incongruous furniture; several great pier-glasses, in which he beheld himself at various angles, like an actor on a stage; many pictures, framed and unframed, standing, with their faces to the wall; a fine Sheraton sideboard, a cabinet of marquetry, and a great old bed, with tapestry hangings. The windows opened to the floor; but by great good fortune the lower part of the shutters had been closed, and this concealed him from the neighbours. Here, then, Markheim drew in a packing case before the cabinet, and began to search among the keys. It was a long business, for there were many; and it was irksome, besides; for, after all, there might be nothing in the cabinet, and time was on the wing. But the closeness of the occupation sobered him. With the tail of his eye he saw the door – even glanced at it from time to time directly, like a besieged commander pleased to verify the good estate of his defences. But in truth he was at peace. The rain falling in the street sounded natural and pleasant. Presently, on the other side, the notes of a piano were wakened to the music of a hymn, and the voices of many children took up the air and words. How stately, how comfortable was the melody! How fresh the youthful voices! Markheim gave ear to it smilingly, as he sorted out the keys; and his mind was thronged with answerable ideas and images; church-going children and the pealing of the high organ; children afield, bathers by the brookside, ramblers on the brambly common, kite-flyers in the windy and cloud-navigated sky; and then, at another cadence of the hymn, back again to church, and the somnolence of summer Sundays, and the high genteel voice of the parson (which he smiled a little to recall) and the painted Jacobean tombs, and the dim lettering of the Ten Commandments in the chancel.

And as he sat thus, at once busy and absent, he was startled to his feet. A flash of ice, a flash of fire, a bursting gush of blood, went over him, and then he stood transfixed and thrilling. A step mounted the stair slowly and steadily, and presently a hand was laid upon the knob, and the lock clicked, and the door opened.

Fear held Markheim in a vice. What to expect he knew not, whether the dead man walking, or the official ministers of human justice, or some chance witness blindly stumbling in to consign him to the gallows. But when a face was thrust into the aperture, glanced round the room, looked at him, nodded and smiled as if in friendly recognition, and then withdrew again, and the door closed behind it, his fear broke loose from his control in a hoarse cry. At the sound of this the visitant returned.

"Did you call me?" he asked, pleasantly, and with that he entered the room and closed the door behind him.

Markheim stood and gazed at him with all his eyes. Perhaps there was a film upon his sight, but the outlines of the new comer seemed to change and waver like those of the idols in the wavering candle-light of the shop; and at times he thought he knew him; and at times he thought he bore a likeness to himself; and always, like a lump of living terror, there lay in his bosom the conviction that this thing was not of the earth and not of God.

And yet the creature had a strange air of the commonplace, as he stood looking on Markheim with a smile; and when he added: "You are looking for the money, I believe?" it was in the tones of everyday politeness.

Markheim made no answer.

"I should warn you," resumed the other, "that the maid has left her sweetheart earlier than usual and will soon be here. If Mr. Markheim be found in this house, I need not describe to him the consequences."

"You know me?" cried the murderer.

The visitor smiled. "You have long been a favourite of mine," he said; "and I have long observed and often sought to help you."

"What are you?" cried Markheim: "The devil?"

"What I may be," returned the other, "cannot affect the service I propose to render you."

"It can," cried Markheim; "it does! Be helped by you? No, never; not by you! You do not know me yet; thank God, you do not know me!"

"I know you," replied the visitant, with a sort of kind severity or rather firmness. "I know you to the soul."

"Know me!" cried Markheim. "Who can do so? My life is but a travesty and slander on myself. I have lived to belie my nature. All men do; all men are better than this disguise that grows about and stifles them. You see each dragged away by life, like one whom bravos have seized and muffled in a cloak. If they had their own control – if you could see their faces, they would be altogether different, they would shine out for heroes and saints! I am worse than most; myself is more overlaid; my excuse is known to me and God. But, had I the time, I could disclose myself."

"To me?" inquired the visitant.

"To you before all," returned the murderer. "I supposed you were intelligent. I thought – since you exist – you would prove a reader of the heart. And yet you would propose to judge me by my acts! Think of it; my acts! I was born and I have lived in a land of giants; giants have dragged me by the wrists since I was born out of my mother – the giants of circumstance. And you would judge me by my acts! But can you not look within? Can you not understand that evil is hateful to me? Can you not see within me the clear writing of conscience, never blurred by any wilful sophistry, although too often disregarded? Can you not read me for a thing that surely must be common as humanity – the unwilling sinner?"

"All this is very feelingly expressed," was the reply, "but it regards me not. These points of consistency are beyond my province, and I care not in the least by what compulsion you may have been dragged away, so as you are but carried in the right direction. But time flies; the servant delays, looking in the faces of the crowd and at the pictures on the hoardings, but still she keeps moving nearer; and remember, it is as if the gallows itself was striding towards you through the Christmas streets! Shall I help you; I, who know all? Shall I tell you where to find the money?"

"For what price?" asked Markheim.

"I offer you the service for a Christmas gift," returned the other.

Markheim could not refrain from smiling with a kind of bitter triumph. "No," said he, "I will take nothing at your hands; if I were dying of thirst, and it was your hand that put the pitcher to my lips, I should find the courage to refuse. It may be credulous, but I will do nothing to commit myself to evil."

"I have no objection to a death-bed repentance," observed the visitant.

"Because you disbelieve their efficacy!" Markheim cried.

"I do not say so," returned the other; "but I look on these things from a different side, and when the life is done my interest falls. The man has lived to serve me, to spread black looks under colour of religion, or to sow tares in the wheat-field, as you do, in a course of weak compliance with desire. Now that he draws so near to his deliverance, he can add but one act of service – to repent, to die smiling, and thus to build up in confidence and hope the more timorous of my surviving followers. I am not so hard a master. Try me. Accept my help. Please yourself in life as you have done hitherto; please yourself more amply, spread your elbows at the board; and when the night begins to fall and the curtains to be drawn, I tell you, for your greater comfort, that you will find it even easy to compound your quarrel with your conscience, and to make a truckling peace with God. I came but now from such a deathbed, and the room was full of sincere mourners, listening to the man's last words: and when I looked into that face, which had been set as a flint against mercy, I found it smiling with hope."

"And do you, then, suppose me such a creature?" asked Markheim. "Do you think I have no more generous aspirations than to sin, and sin, and sin, and, at the last, sneak into heaven? My heart rises at the thought. Is this, then, your experience of mankind? Or is it because you find me with red hands that you presume such baseness? And is this crime of murder indeed so impious as to dry up the very springs of good?"

"Murder is to me no special category," replied the other. "All sins are murder, even as all life is war. I behold your race, like starving mariners on a raft, plucking crusts out of the hands of famine and feeding on each other's lives. I follow sins beyond the moment of their acting; I find in all that the last consequence is death; and to my eyes, the pretty maid who thwarts her mother with such taking graces on a question of a ball, drips no less visibly with human gore than such a murderer as yourself. Do I say that I follow sins? I follow virtues also; they differ not by the thickness of a nail, they are both scythes for the reaping angel of Death. Evil, for which I live, consists not in action but in character. The bad man is dear to me; not the bad act, whose fruits, if we could follow them far enough down the hurtling cataract of the ages, might yet be found more blessed than those of the rarest virtues. And it is not because you have killed a dealer, but because you are Markheim, that I offer to forward your escape."

"I will lay my heart open to you," answered Markheim. "This crime on which you find me is my last. On my way to it I have learned many lessons; itself is a lesson, a momentous lesson. Hitherto I have been driven with revolt to what I would not; I was a bond-slave to poverty, driven and scourged. There are robust virtues that can stand in these temptations; mine was not so: I had a thirst of pleasure. But today, and out of this deed, I pluck both warning and riches – both the power and a fresh resolve to be myself. I become in all things a free actor in the world; I begin to see myself all changed, these hands the agents of good, this heart at peace. Something comes over me out of the past; something of what I have dreamed on Sabbath evenings to the sound of the church organ, of what I forecast when I shed tears over noble books, or talked, an innocent child, with my mother. There lies my life; I have wandered a few years, but now I see once more my city of destination."

"You are to use this money on the Stock Exchange, I think?" remarked the visitor; "And there, if I mistake not, you have already lost some thousands?"

"Ah," said Markheim, "but this time I have a sure thing."

"This time, again, you will lose," replied the visitor quietly.

"Ah, but I keep back the half!" cried Markheim.

"That also you will lose," said the other.

The sweat started upon Markheim's brow. "Well, then, what matter?" he exclaimed. "Say it be lost, say I am plunged again in poverty, shall one part of me, and that the worse, continue until the end to override the better? Evil and good run strong in me, haling me both ways. I do not love the one thing, I love all. I can conceive great deeds, renunciations, martyrdoms; and though I be fallen to such a crime as murder, pity is no stranger to my thoughts. I pity the poor; who knows their trials better than myself? I pity and help them; I prize love, I love honest laughter; there is no good thing nor true thing on earth but I love it from my heart. And are my vices only to direct my life, and my virtues to lie without effect, like some passive lumber of the mind? Not so; good, also, is a spring of acts."

But the visitant raised his finger. "For six-and-thirty years that you have been in this world," said he, "through many changes of fortune and varieties of humour, I have watched you steadily fall. Fifteen years ago you would have started at a theft. Three years back you would have blenched at the name of murder. Is there any crime, is there any cruelty or meanness, from which you still recoil? – Five years from now I shall detect you in the fact! Downward, downward, lies your way; nor can anything but death avail to stop you."

"It is true," Markheim said huskily, "I have in some degree complied with evil. But it is so with all: the very saints, in the mere exercise of living, grow less dainty, and take on the tone of their surroundings."

"I will propound to you one simple question," said the other; "and as you answer, I shall read to you your moral horoscope. You have grown in many things more lax; possibly you do right to be so – and at any account, it is the same with all men. But granting that, are you in any one particular, however trifling, more difficult to please with your own conduct, or do you go in all things with a looser rein?"

"In any one?" repeated Markheim, with an anguish of consideration. "No," he added, with despair, "in none! I have gone down in all."

"Then," said the visitor, "content yourself with what you are, for you will never change; and the words of your part on this stage are irrevocably written down."

Markheim stood for a long while silent, and indeed it was the visitor who first broke the silence. "That being so," he said, "shall I show you the money?"

"And grace?" cried Markheim.

"Have you not tried it?" returned the other. "Two or three years ago, did I not see you on the platform of revival meetings, and was not your voice the loudest in the hymn?"

"It is true," said Markheim; "and I see clearly what remains for me by way of duty. I thank you for these lessons from my soul; my eyes are opened, and I behold myself at last for what I am."

At this moment, the sharp note of the door-bell rang through the house; and the visitant, as though this were some concerted signal for which he had been waiting, changed at once in his demeanour.

"The maid!" he cried. "She has returned, as I forewarned you, and there is now before you one more difficult passage. Her master, you must say, is ill; you must let her in, with an assured but rather serious countenance – no smiles, no overacting, and I promise you success! Once the girl within, and the door closed, the same dexterity that has already rid you of the dealer will relieve you of this last danger in your path. Thenceforward you have the whole evening – the whole night, if needful – to ransack the treasures of the house and to make good your safety. This is help that comes to you with the mask of danger. Up!" he cried; "Up, friend; your life hangs trembling in the scales: up, and act!"

Markheim steadily regarded his counsellor. "If I be condemned to evil acts," he said, "there is still one door of freedom open – I can cease from action. If my life be an ill thing, I can lay it down. Though I be, as you say truly, at the beck of every small temptation, I can yet, by one decisive gesture, place myself beyond the reach of all. My love of good is damned to barrenness; it may, and let it be! But I have still my hatred of evil; and from that, to your galling disappointment, you shall see that I can draw both energy and courage."

The features of the visitor began to undergo a wonderful and lovely change: they brightened and softened with a tender triumph, and, even as they brightened, faded and dislimned. But Markheim did not pause to watch or understand the transformation. He opened the door and went downstairs very slowly, thinking to himself. His past went soberly before him; he beheld it as it was, ugly and strenuous like a dream, random as chance-medley – a scene of defeat. Life, as he thus reviewed it, tempted him no longer; but on the further side he perceived a quiet haven for his bark. He paused in the passage, and looked into the shop, where the candle still burned by the dead body. It was strangely silent. Thoughts of the dealer swarmed into his mind, as he stood gazing. And then the bell once more broke out into impatient clamour.

He confronted the maid upon the threshold with something like a smile.

"You had better go for the police," said he: "I have killed your master."

The Dualitists

Bram Stoker

Chapter I: Bis Dat Qui Non Cito Dat

THERE WAS joy in the house of Bubb.

For ten long years had Ephraim and Sophonisba Bubb mourned in vain the loneliness of their life. Unavailingly had they gazed into the emporia of baby-linen, and fixed their searching glances on the basket-makers' warehouses where the cradles hung in tempting rows. In vain had they prayed, and sighed, and groaned, and wished, and waited, and wept, but never had even a ray of hope been held out by the family physician.

* * *

But now at last the wished-for moment had arrived. Month after month had flown by on leaden wings, and the destined days had slowly measured their course. The months had become weeks; the weeks had dwindled down to days; the days had been attenuated to hours; the hours had lapsed into minutes, the minutes had slowly died away, and but seconds remained.

Ephraim Bubb sat cowering on the stairs, and tried with high-strung ears to catch the strain of blissful music from the lips of his first-born. There was silence in the house – silence as of the deadly calm before the cyclone. Ah! Ephra Bubb, little thinkest thou that another moment may for ever destroy the peaceful, happy course of thy life, and open to thy too craving eyes the portals of that wondrous land where Childhood reigns supreme, and where the tyrant infant with the wave of his tiny hand and the imperious treble of his tiny voice sentences his parent to the deadly vault beneath the castle moat. As the thought strikes thee thou becomest pale. How thou tremblest as thou findest thyself upon the brink of the abyss! Wouldst that thou could recall the past!

But hark! The die is cast for good or ill. The long years of praying and hoping have found an end at last. From the chamber within comes a sharp cry, which shortly after is repeated. Ah! Ephraim, that cry is the feeble effort of childish lips as yet unused to the rough, worldly form of speech to frame the word Father. In the glow of thy transport all doubts are forgotten; and when the doctor cometh forth as the harbinger of joy he findeth thee radiant with new found delight.

"My dear sir, allow me to congratulate you – to offer two fold felicitations. Mr. Bubb, sir, you are the father of Twins!"

Chapter II: Halcyon Days

THE TWINS were the finest children that ever were seen – so at least said the cognoscenti, and the parents were not slow to believe. The nurse's opinion was in itself a proof.

It was not, ma'am, that they was fine for twins, but they was fine for singles, and she had ought to know, for she had nussed a many in her time, both twins and singles. All they wanted was to have their dear little legs cut off and little wings on their dear little shoulders, for to be put one on each side of a white marble tombstone, cut beautiful, sacred to the relic of Ephraim Bubb, that they might, sir, if so be that missus was to survive the father of two such lovely twins – although she would make bold to say, and no offence intended, that a handsome gentleman, though a trifle or two older than his good lady, though for the matter of that she heerd that gentlemen was never too old at all, and for her own part she liked them the better for it: not like bits of boys that didn't know their own minds – that a gentleman what was the father of two such 'eavenly twins (God bless them!) couldn't be called anything but a boy; though for the matter of that she never knowed in her experience – which it was much – of a boy as had such twins, or any twins at all so much for the matter of that.

The twins were the idols of their parents, and at the same time their pleasure and their pain. Did Zerubbabel cough, Ephraim would start from his balmy slumbers with an agonised cry of consternation, for visions of innumerable twins black in the face from croup haunted his nightly pillow. Did Zacariah rail at aethereal expansion, Sophonisba with pallid hue and dishevelled locks would fly to the cradle of her offspring. Did pins torture or strings afflict, or flannel or flies tickle, or light dazzle, or darkness affright, or hunger or thirst assail the synchronous productions, the household of Bubb would be roused from quiet slumbers or the current of its manifold workings changed.

The twins grew apace; were weaned; teethed; and at length arrived at the stage of three years!

"They grew in beauty side by side. They filled one home," etc.

Chapter III: Rumours of Wars

HARRY MERFORD and Tommy Santon lived in the same range of villas as Ephraim Bubb. Harry's parents had taken up their abode in No. 25, No. 27 was happy in the perpetual sunshine of Tommy's smiles, and between these two residences Ephraim Bubb reared his blossoms, the number of his mansion being 26. Harry and Tommy had been accustomed from the earliest times to meet each other daily. Their primal method of communication had been by the housetops, till their respective sires had been obliged to pay compensation to Bubb for damages to his roof and dormer windows; and from that time they had been forbidden by the home authorities to meet, whilst their mutual neighbour had taken the precaution of having his garden walls pebble-dashed and topped with broken glass to prevent their incursions. Harry and Tommy, however, being gifted with daring souls, lofty ambitions, impetuous natures, and strong seats to their trousers, defied the rugged walls of Bubb and continued to meet in secret.

Compared with these two youths, Castor and Pollux, Damon and Pythias, Eloisa and Abelard are but tame examples of duality or constancy and friendship. All the poets from Hyginus to Schiller might sing of noble deeds done and desperate dangers held as naught for friendship's sake, but they would have been mute had they but known of the mutual affection of Harry and Tommy. Day by day, and often night by night, would these two brave the perils of nurse, and father, and mother, of whip and imprisonment, and hunger and thirst, and solitude and darkness to meet together. What they discussed in secret none other knew. What deeds of darkness were perpetrated in their symposia none could tell. Alone they met, alone they remained, and alone they departed to their several abodes. There was in the garden of Bubb a summer house overgrown with trailing plants, and surrounded by young poplars which the fond father had planted on his children's natal day, and whose rapid growth he had proudly watched. These trees quite obscured the summerhouse, and here Harry and Tommy, knowing after a careful observation that none ever entered the place, held their conclaves. Time after time they met in full security and followed their customary pursuit of pleasure. Let us raise the mysterious veil and see what was the great Unknown at whose shrine they bent the knee.

Harry and Tommy had each been given as a Christmas box a new knife; and for a long time – nearly a year – these knives, similar in size and pattern, were their chief delights. With them they cut and hacked in their respective homes all things which would not be likely to be noticed; for the young gentlemen were wary and had no wish that their moments of pleasure should be atoned for by moments of pain. The insides of drawers, and desks, and boxes, and underparts of tables and chairs, the backs of picture frames, even the floors, where corners of the carpets could surreptitiously be turned up, all bore marks of their craftsmanship; and to compare notes on these artistic triumphs was a source of joy. At length, however, a critical time came, some new field of action should be opened up, for the old appetites were sated, and the old joys had begun to pall. It was absolutely necessary that the existing schemes of destruction should be enlarged; and yet this could hardly be done without a terrible risk of discovery, for the limits of safety had long since been reached and passed. But, be the risk great or small, some new ground should be broken – some new joy found, for the old earth was barren, and the craving for pleasure was growing fiercer with each successive day.

The crisis had come: who could tell the issue?

Chapter IV: The Tucket Sounds

THEY MET in the arbour, determined to discuss this grave question. The heart of each was big with revolution, the head of each was full of scheme and strategy, and the pocket of each was full of sweet-stuff, the sweeter for being stolen. After having despatched the sweets, the conspirators proceeded to explain their respective views with regard to the enlargement of their artistic operations. Tommy unfolded with much pride a scheme which he had in contemplation of cutting a series of holes in the sounding board of the piano, so as to destroy its musical properties. Harry was in no wise behindhand in his ideas of reform. He had conceived the project of cutting the canvas at the back of his great grandfather's portrait, which his father held in high regard among his lares and penates, so that in time when the picture should be moved the skin of paint would be broken, the head fall bodily out from the frame.

At this point of the council a brilliant thought occurred to Tommy. "Why should not the enjoyment be doubled, and the musical instruments and family pictures of both establishments be sacrificed on the altar of pleasure?" This was agreed to nem. con.; and then the meeting adjourned for dinner. When they next met it was evident that there was a screw loose somewhere – that there was "something rotten in the state of Denmark." After a little fencing on both sides, it came out that all the schemes of domestic reform had been foiled by maternal vigilance, and that so sharp had been the reprimand consequent on a partial discovery of the schemes that they would have to be abandoned – till such time, at least, as increased physical strength would allow the reformers to laugh to scorn parental threats and injunctions.

Sadly the two forlorn youths took out their knives and regarded them; sadly, sadly they thought, as erst did Othello, of all the fair chances of honour and triumph and glory gone for ever. They compared knives with almost the fondness of doting parents. There they were – so equal in size and strength and beauty-dimmed by no corrosive rust, tarnished by no stain, and with unbroken edges of the keenness of Saladin's sword.

So like were the knives that but for the initials scratched in the handles neither boy could have been sure which was his own. After a little while they began mutually to brag of the superior excellence of their respective weapons. Tommy insisted that his was the sharper, Harry asserted that his was the stronger of the two. Hotter and hotter grew the war of words. The tempers of Harry and Tommy got inflamed, and their boyish bosoms glowed with manly thoughts of daring and of hate. But there was abroad in that hour a spirit of a bygone age – one that penetrated even to that dim arbour in the grove of Bubb. The world-old scheme of ordeal was whispered by the spirit in the ear of each, and suddenly the tumult was allayed. With one impulse the boys suggested that they should test the quality of their knives by the ordeal of the Hack.

No sooner said than done. Harry held out his knife edge uppermost; and Tommy, grasping his firmly by the handle, brought down the edge of the blade crosswise on Harry's. The process was then reversed, and Harry became in turn the aggressor. Then they paused and eagerly looked for the result. It was not hard to see; in each knife were two great dents of equal depth; and so it was necessary to renew the contest, and seek a further proof.

What needs it to relate seriatim the details of that direful strife? The sun had long since gone down, and the moon with fair, smiling face had long risen over the roof of Bubb, when, wearied and jaded, Harry and Tommy sought their respective homes. Alas! The splendour of the knives was gone for ever. Ichabod! – Ichabod! The glory had departed and naught remained but two useless wrecks, with keen edges destroyed, and now like unto nothing save the serried hills of Spain.

But though they mourned for their fondly cherished weapons, the hearts of the boys were glad; for the bygone day had opened to their gaze a prospect of pleasure as boundless as the limits of the world.

Chapter V: The First Crusade

FROM THAT DAY a new era dawned in the lives of Harry and Tommy. So long as the sources of the parental establishments could hold out so long would their new amusement continue. Subtly they obtained surreptitious possession of articles of family cutlery not in general use, and brought them one by one to their rendezvous. These came fair and spotless from the sanctity of the butlers' pantry. Alas! They returned not as they came.

But in course of time the stock of available cutlery became exhausted, and again the inventive faculties of the youths were called into requisition. They reasoned thus: "The knife game, it is true, is played out, but the excitement of the Hack is not to be dispensed with. Let us carry, then, this Great Idea into new worlds; let us still live in the sunshine of pleasure; let us continue to hack, but with objects other than knives."

It was done. Not knives now engaged the attention of the ambitious youths. Spoons and forks were daily flattened and beaten out of shape; pepper castor met pepper castor in combat, and both were borne dying from the field; candlesticks met in fray to part no more on this side of the grave; even epergnes were used as weapons in the crusade of Hack.

At last all the resources of the butler's pantry became exhausted, and then began a system of miscellaneous destruction that proved in a little time ruinous to the furniture of the respective homes of Harry and Tommy. Mrs. Santon and Mrs. Merford began to notice that the wear and tear in their households became excessive. Day after day some new domestic calamity seemed to have occurred. Today a valuable edition of some book whose luxurious binding made it an object for public display would appear to have suffered some dire misfortune, for the edges were frayed and broken and the back loose if not altogether displaced; tomorrow the same awful fate would seem to have followed some miniature frame; the day following the legs of some chair or spider-table would show signs of extraordinary hardship. Even in the nursery the sounds of lamentation were heard. It was a thing of daily occurrence for the little girls to state that when going to bed at night they had laid their dear dollies in their beds with tender care, but that when again seeking them in the period of recess they had found them with all their beauty gone, with legs and arms amputated and faces beaten from all semblance of human form.

Then articles of crockery began to be missed. The thief could in no case be discovered, and the wages of the servants, from constant stoppages, began to be nominal rather than real. Mrs. Merford and Mrs. Santon mourned their losses, but Harry and Tommy gloated day after day over their spoils, which lay in an ever-increasing heap in the hidden grove of Bubb. To such an extent had the fondness of the Hack now grown that with both youths it was an infatuation – a madness – a frenzy.

At length one awful day arrived. The butlers of the houses of Merford and Santon, harassed by constant losses and complaints, and finding that their breakage account was in excess of their wages, determined to seek some sphere of occupation where, if they did not meet with a suitable reward or recognition of their services, they would, at least, not lose whatever fortune and reputation they had already acquired. Accordingly, before rendering up their keys and the goods entrusted to their charge, they proceeded to take a preliminary stock of their own accounts, to make sure of their accredited accuracy. Dire indeed was their distress when they knew to the full the havoc which had been wrought; terrible their anguish of the present, bitter their thoughts of the future. Their hearts, bowed down with weight of woe, failed them quite; reeled the strong brains that had erst overcome foes of deadlier spirit than grief; and fell their stalwart forms prone on the floors of their respective sancta sanctorum.

Late in the day when their services were required they were sought for in bower and hall, and at length discovered where they lay.

But alas for justice! They were accused of being drunk and for having, whilst in that degraded condition, deliberately injured all the property on which they could lay hands. Were not the evidences of their guilt patent to all in the hecatombs of the destroyed? Then they were charged with all the evils wrought in the houses, and on their indignant denial Harry and Tommy, each in his own home, according to their concerted scheme of action, stepped forward and relieved their minds of the deadly weight that had for long in secret borne them down. The story of each ran that time after time he had seen the butler, when he thought that nobody was looking, knocking knives together in the pantry, chairs and books and pictures in the drawing-room and study, dolls in the nursery, and plates in the kitchen. Then, indeed, was the master of each household stern and uncompromising in his demands for justice. Each butler was committed to the charge of myrmidons of the law under the double charge of drunkenness and wilful destruction of property.

* * *

Softly and sweetly slept Harry and Tommy in their little beds that night. Angels seemed to whisper to them, for they smiled as though lost in pleasant dreams. The rewards given by proud and grateful parents lay in their pockets, and in their hearts the happy consciousness of having done their duty.

Truly sweet should be the slumbers of the just.

Chapter VI: "Let the Dead Past Bury its Dead."

IT MIGHT be supposed that now the operations of Harry and Tommy would be obliged to be abandoned.

Not so, however. The minds of these youths were of no common order, nor were their souls of such weak nature as to yield at the first summons of necessity. Like Nelson, they knew not fear; like Napoleon, they held "impossible" to be the adjective of fools; and they revelled in the glorious truth that in the lexicon of youth is no such word as 'fail.' Therefore on the day following the éclaircissement of the butlers' misdeeds, they met in the arbour to plan a new campaign.

In the hour when all seemed blackest to them, and when the narrowing walls of possibility hedged them in on every side, thus ran the deliberations of these dauntless youths:

"We have played out the meaner things that are inanimate and inert; why not then trench on the domains of life? The dead have lapsed into the regions of the forgotten past – let the living look to themselves."

That night they met when all households had retired to balmy sleep, and naught but the amorous wailings of nocturnal cats told of the existence of life and sentience. Each bore into the arbour in his arms a pet rabbit and a piece of sticking-plaster. Then, in the peaceful, quiet moonlight, commenced a work of mystery, blood, and gloom. The proceedings began by the fixing of a piece of sticking-plaster over the mouth of each rabbit to prevent it making a noise, if so inclined. Then Tommy held up his rabbit by its scutty tail, and it hung wriggling, a white mass in the moonlight. Slowly Harry raised his rabbit holding it in the same manner, and when level with his head brought it down on Tommy's client.

But the chances had been miscalculated. The boys held firmly to the tails, but the chief portions of the rabbits fell to earth. Ere the doomed beasts could escape, however, the operators had pounced upon them, and this time holding them by the hind legs renewed the trial.

Deep into the night the game was kept up, and the Eastern sky began to show signs of approaching day as each boy bore triumphantly the dead corse of his favourite bunny and placed it within its sometime hutch.

Next night the same game was renewed with a new rabbit on each side, and for more than a week – so long as the hutches supplied the wherewithal – the battle was sustained. True that there were sad hearts and red eyes in the juveniles of Santon and Merford as one by one the beloved pets were found dead, but Harry and Tommy, with the hearts of heroes steeled to suffering and deaf to the pitiful cries of childhood, still fought the good fight on to the bitter end.

When the supply of rabbits was exhausted, other munition was not wanting, and for some days the war was continued with white mice, dormice, hedgehogs, guinea pigs, pigeons, lambs, canaries, parroqueets, linnets, squirrels, parrots, marmots, poodles, ravens, tortoises, terriers, and cats. Of these, as might be expected, the most difficult to manipulate were the terriers and the cats, and of these two classes the proportion of the difficulties in the way of terrier-hacking was, when compared with those of cat-hacking, about that which the simple Lac of the British Pharmacopoeia bears to water in the compound which dairymen palm off upon a too confiding public as milk. More than once when engaged in the rapturous delights of cat-hacking had Harry and Tommy wished that the silent tomb could open its ponderous and massy jaws and engulf them, for the feline victims were not patient in their death agonies, and often broke the bonds in which the security of the artists rested, and turned fiercely on their executioners.

At last, however, all the animals available were sacrificed; but the passion for hacking still remained. How was it all to end?

Chapter VII: A Cloud with Golden Lining

TOMMY AND HARRY sat in the arbour dejected and disconsolate. They wept like two Alexanders because there were no more worlds to conquer. At last the conviction had been forced upon them that the resources available for hacking were exhausted. That very morning they had had a desperate battle, and their attire showed the ravages of direful war. Their hats were battered into shapeless masses, their shoes were soleless and heelless and had the uppers broken, the ends of their braces, their sleeves, and their trousers were frayed, and had they indulged in the manly luxury of coat tails these too would have gone.

Truly, hacking had become an absorbing passion with them. Long and fiercely had they been swept onward on the wings of the demon of strife, and powerless at the best of times had been the promptings of good; but now, heated with combat, maddened by the equal success of arms, and with the lust for victory still unsated, they longed more fiercely than ever for some new pleasure: like tigers that have tasted blood they thirsted for a larger and more potent libation.

As they sat, with their souls in a tumult of desire and despair, some evil genius guided into the garden the twin blossoms of the tree of Bubb. Hand in hand Zacariah and Zerubbabel advanced from the back door; they had escaped from their nurses, and with the exploring instinct of humanity, advanced boldly into the great world – the terra incognita, the Ultima Thule of the paternal domain.

In the course of time they approached the hedge of poplars, from behind which the anxious eyes of Harry and Tommy looked for their approach, for the boys knew that where the twins were the nurses were accustomed to be gathered together, and they feared discovery if their retreat should be cut off.

It was a touching sight, these lovely babes, alike in form, feature, size, expression, and dress; in fact, so like each other that one 'might not have told either from which.' When the startling similarity was recognised by Harry and Tommy, each suddenly turned, and, grasping the other by the shoulder, spoke in a keen whisper:

"Hack! They are exactly equal! This is the very apotheosis of our art!"

With excited faces and trembling hands they laid their plans to lure the unsuspecting babes within the precincts of their charnel house, and they were so successful in their efforts that in a little time the twins had toddled behind the hedge and were lost to the sight of the parental mansion.

Harry and Tommy were not famed for gentleness within the immediate precincts of their respective homes, but it would have delighted the heart of any philanthropist to see the kindly manner in which they arranged for the pleasures of the helpless babes. With smiling faces and playful words and gentle wiles they led them within the arbour, and then, under pretence of giving them some of those sudden jumps in which infants rejoice, they raised them from the ground. Tommy held Zacariah across his arm with his baby moon-face smiling up at the cobwebs on the arbour roof, and Harry, with a mighty effort, raised the cherubic Zerubbabel aloft.

Each nerved himself for a great endeavour, Harry to give, Tommy to endure a shock, and then the form of Zerubbabel was seen whirling through the air round Harry's glowing and determined face. There was a sickening crash and the arm of Tommy yielded visibly.

The pasty face of Zerubbabel had fallen fair on that of Zacariah, for Tommy and Harry were by this time artists of too great experience to miss so simple a mark. The putty-like noses collapsed, the putty-like cheeks became for a moment flattened, and when in an instant more they parted, the faces of both were dabbled in gore. Immediately the firmament was rent with a series of such yells as might have awakened the dead. Forthwith from the house of Bubb came the echoes in parental cries and footsteps. As the sounds of scurrying feet rang through the mansion, Harry cried to Tommy:

"They will be on us soon. Let us cut to the roof of the stable and draw up the ladder."

Tommy answered by a nod, and the two boys, regardless of consequences, and bearing each a twin, ascended to the roof of the stable by means of a ladder which usually stood against the wall, and which they pulled up after them.

As Ephraim Bubb issued from his house in pursuit of his lost darlings, the sight which met his gaze froze his very soul. There, on the coping of the stable roof, stood Harry and Tommy renewing their game. They seemed like two young demons forging some diabolical implement, for each in turn the twins were lifted high in air and let fall with stunning force on the supine form of its fellow. How Ephraim felt none but a tender and imaginative father can conceive. It would be enough to wring the heart of even a callous parent to see his children, the darlings of his old age – his own beloved twins – being sacrificed to the brutal pleasure of unregenerate youths, without being made unconsciously and helplessly guilty of the crime of fratricide.

Loudly did Ephraim and also Sophonisba, who, with dishevelled locks, had now appeared upon the scene, bewail their unhappy lot and shriek in vain for aid; but by rare ill chance no eyes save their own saw the work of butchery or heard the shrieks of anguish and despair. Wildly did Ephraim, mounting on the shoulders of his spouse, strive, but in vain, to scale the stable wall.

Baffled in every effort, he rushed into the house and appeared in a moment bearing in his hands a double-barrelled gun, into which he poured the contents of a shot pouch as he ran. He came anigh the stable and hailed the murderous youths:

"Drop them twins and come down here or I'll shoot you like a brace of dogs."

"Never!" exclaimed the heroic two with one impulse, and continued their awful pastime with a zest tenfold as they knew that the agonised eyes of parents wept at the cause of their joy.

"Then die!" shrieked Ephraim, as he fired both barrels, right-left, at the hackers.

But, alas! Love for his darlings shook the hand that never shook before. As the smoke cleared off and Ephraim recovered from the kick of his gun, he heard a loud twofold laugh of triumph and saw Harry and Tommy, all unhurt, waving in the air the trunks of the twins – the fond father had blown the heads completely off his own offspring.

Tommy and Harry shrieked aloud in glee, and after playing catch with the bodies for some time, seen only by the agonised eyes of the infanticide and his wife, flung them high in the air. Ephraim leaped forward to catch what had once been Zacariah, and Sophonisba grabbed wildly for the loved remains of her Zerubbabel.

But the weight of the bodies and the height from which they fell were not reckoned by either parent, and from being ignorant of a simple dynamical formula each tried to effect an object which calm, common sense, united with scientific knowledge, would have told them was impossible. The masses fell, and Ephraim and Sophonisba were stricken dead by the falling twins, who were thus posthumously guilty of the crime of parricide.

An intelligent coroner's jury found the parents guilty of the crimes of infanticide and suicide, on the evidence of Harry and Tommy, who swore, reluctantly, that the inhuman monsters, maddened by drink, had killed their offspring by shooting them into the air out of a cannon – since stolen – whence like curses they had fallen on their own heads; and that then they had slain themselves suis manibus with their own hands.

Accordingly Ephraim and Sophonisba were denied the solace of Christian burial, and were committed to the earth with 'maimed rites,' and had stakes driven through their middles to pin them down in their unhallowed graves till the Crack of Doom.

Harry and Tommy were each rewarded with National honours and were knighted, even at their tender years.

Fortune seemed to smile upon them all the long after years, and they lived to a ripe old age, hale of body, and respected and beloved of all.

Often in the golden summer eves, when all nature seemed at rest, when the oldest cask was opened and the largest lamp was lit, when the chestnuts glowed in the embers and the kid turned on the spit, when their great-grandchildren pretended to mend fictional armour and to trim an imaginary helmet's plume, when the shuttles of the good wives of their grandchildren went flashing each through its proper loom, with shouting and with laughter they were accustomed to tell the tale of *The Dualists; or, the Death-doom of the Double-born*.

The Burial of the Rats

Bram Stoker

LEAVING PARIS by the Orleans road, cross the Enceinte, and, turning to the right, you find yourself in a somewhat wild and not at all savoury district. Right and left, before and behind, on every side rise great heaps of dust and waste accumulated by the process of time.

Paris has its night as well as its day life, and the sojourner who enters his hotel in the Rue de Rivoli or the Rue St. Honore late at night or leaves it early in the morning, can guess, in coming near Montrouge – if he has not done so already – the purpose of those great waggons that look like boilers on wheels which he finds halting everywhere as he passes.

Every city has its peculiar institutions created out of its own needs; and one of the most notable institutions of Paris is its rag-picking population. In the early morning – and Parisian life commences at an early hour – may be seen in most streets standing on the pathway opposite every court and alley and between every few houses, as still in some American cities, even in parts of New York, large wooden boxes into which the domestics or tenement-holders empty the accumulated dust of the past day. Round these boxes gather and pass on, when the work is done, to fresh fields of labour and pastures new, squalid, hungry-looking men and women, the implements of whose craft consist of a coarse bag or basket slung over the shoulder and a little rake with which they turn over and probe and examine in the minutest manner the dustbins. They pick up and deposit in their baskets, by aid of their rakes, whatever they may find, with the same facility as a Chinaman uses his chopsticks.

Paris is a city of centralisation – and centralisation and classification are closely allied. In the early times, when centralisation is becoming a fact, its forerunner is classification. All things which are similar or analogous become grouped together, and from the grouping of groups rises one whole or central point. We see radiating many long arms with innumerable tentaculae, and in the centre rises a gigantic head with a comprehensive brain and keen eyes to look on every side and ears sensitive to hear – and a voracious mouth to swallow.

Other cities resemble all the birds and beasts and fishes whose appetites and digestions are normal. Paris alone is the analogical apotheosis of the octopus. Product of centralisation carried to an ad absurdum, it fairly represents the devil fish; and in no respects is the resemblance more curious than in the similarity of the digestive apparatus.

Those intelligent tourists who, having surrendered their individuality into the hands of Messrs. Cook or Gaze, 'do' Paris in three days, are often puzzled to know how it is that the dinner which in London would cost about six shillings, can be had for three francs in a cafe in the Palais Royal. They need have no more wonder if they will but consider the classification which is a theoretic speciality of Parisian life, and adopt all round the fact from which the chiffonier has his genesis.

The Paris of 1850 was not like the Paris of today, and those who see the Paris of Napoleon and Baron Haussmann can hardly realise the existence of the state of things forty-five years ago.

Amongst other things, however, which have not changed are those districts where the waste is gathered. Dust is dust all the world over, in every age, and the family likeness of dust-heaps is perfect. The traveller, therefore, who visits the environs of Montrouge can go back in fancy without difficulty to the year 1850.

In this year I was making a prolonged stay in Paris. I was very much in love with a young lady who, though she returned my passion, so far yielded to the wishes of her parents that she had promised not to see me or to correspond with me for a year. I, too, had been compelled to accede to these conditions under a vague hope of parental approval. During the term of probation I had promised to remain out of the country and not to write to my dear one until the expiration of the year.

Naturally the time went heavily with me. There was no one of my own family or circle who could tell me of Alice, and none of her own folk had, I am sorry to say, sufficient generosity to send me even an occasional word of comfort regarding her health and well-being. I spent six months wandering about Europe, but as I could find no satisfactory distraction in travel, I determined to come to Paris, where, at least, I would be within easy hail of London in case any good fortune should call me thither before the appointed time. That 'hope deferred maketh the heart sick' was never better exemplified than in my case, for in addition to the perpetual longing to see the face I loved there was always with me a harrowing anxiety lest some accident should prevent me showing Alice in due time that I had, throughout the long period of probation, been faithful to her trust and my own love. Thus, every adventure which I undertook had a fierce pleasure of its own, for it was fraught with possible consequences greater than it would have ordinarily borne.

Like all travellers I exhausted the places of most interest in the first month of my stay, and was driven in the second month to look for amusement whithersoever I might. Having made sundry journeys to the better-known suburbs, I began to see that there was a terra incognita, in so far as the guide book was concerned, in the social wilderness lying between these attractive points. Accordingly I began to systematise my researches, and each day took up the thread of my exploration at the place where I had on the previous day dropped it.

In process of time my wanderings led me near Montrouge, and I saw that hereabouts lay the Ultima Thule of social exploration-a country as little known as that round the source of the White Nile. And so I determined to investigate philosophically the chiffonier-his habitat, his life, and his means of life.

The job was an unsavoury one, difficult of accomplishment, and with little hope of adequate reward. However, despite reason, obstinacy prevailed, and I entered into my new investigation with a keener energy than I could have summoned to aid me in any investigation leading to any end, valuable or worthy.

One day, late in a fine afternoon, toward the end of September, I entered the holy of holies of the city of dust. The place was evidently the recognised abode of a number of chiffoniers, for some sort of arrangement was manifested in the formation of the dust heaps near the road. I passed amongst these heaps, which stood like orderly sentries, determined to penetrate further and trace dust to its ultimate location.

As I passed along I saw behind the dust heaps a few forms that flitted to and fro, evidently watching with interest the advent of any stranger to such a place. The district was like a small Switzerland, and as I went forward my tortuous course shut out the path behind me.

Presently I got into what seemed a small city or community of chiffoniers. There were a number of shanties or huts, such as may be met with in the remote parts of the Bog of Allan – rude places with wattled walls, plastered with mud and roofs of rude thatch made from stable refuse – such places as one would not like to enter for any consideration, and which even in water-colour could only look picturesque if judiciously treated. In the midst of these huts was one of the strangest adaptations – I cannot say habitations – I had ever seen. An immense old wardrobe, the colossal remnant of some boudoir of Charles VII or Henry II, had been converted into a dwelling-house. The double doors lay open, so that the entire menage was open to public view. In the open half of the wardrobe was a common sitting-room of some four feet by six, in which sat, smoking their pipes round a charcoal brazier, no fewer than six old soldiers of the First Republic, with their uniforms torn and worn threadbare. Evidently they were of the mauvais sujet class; their blear eyes and limp jaws told plainly of a common love of absinthe; and their eyes had that haggard, worn look which stamps the drunkard at his worst, and that look of slumbering ferocity which follows hard in the wake of drink. The other side stood as of old, with its shelves intact, save that they were cut to half their depth, and in each shelf of which there were six, was a bed made with rags and straw. The half-dozen of worthies who inhabited this structure looked at me curiously as I passed; and when I looked back after going a little way I saw their heads together in a whispered conference. I did not like the look of this at all, for the place was very lonely, and the men looked very, very villainous. However, I did not see any cause for fear, and went on my way, penetrating further and further into the Sahara. The way was tortuous to a degree, and from going round in a series of semi-circles, as one goes in skating with the Dutch roll, I got rather confused with regard to the points of the compass.

When I had penetrated a little way I saw, as I turned the corner of a half-made heap, sitting on a heap of straw an old soldier with threadbare coat.

"Hallo!" said I to myself; "the First Republic is well represented here in its soldiery."

As I passed him the old man never even looked up at me, but gazed on the ground with stolid persistency. Again I remarked to myself: "See what a life of rude warfare can do! This old man's curiosity is a thing of the past."

When I had gone a few steps, however, I looked back suddenly, and saw that curiosity was not dead, for the veteran had raised his head and was regarding me with a very queer expression. He seemed to me to look very like one of the six worthies in the press. When he saw me looking he dropped his head; and without thinking further of him I went on my way, satisfied that there was a strange likeness between these old warriors.

Presently I met another old soldier in a similar manner. He, too, did not notice me whilst I was passing.

By this time it was getting late in the afternoon, and I began to think of retracing my steps. Accordingly I turned to go back, but could see a number of tracks leading between different mounds and could not ascertain which of them I should take. In my perplexity I wanted to see someone of whom to ask the way, but could see no one. I determined to go on a few mounds further and so try to see someone – not a veteran.

I gained my object, for after going a couple of hundred yards I saw before me a single shanty such as I had seen before – with, however, the difference that this was not one for living in, but merely a roof with three walls open in front. From the evidences which the neighbourhood exhibited I took it to be a place for sorting. Within it was an old woman wrinkled and bent with age; I approached her to ask the way.

She rose as I came close and I asked her my way. She immediately commenced a conversation; and it occurred to me that here in the very centre of the Kingdom of Dust was the place to gather details of the history of Parisian rag-picking – particularly as I could do so from the lips of one who looked like the oldest inhabitant.

I began my inquiries, and the old woman gave me most interesting answers – she had been one of the ceteuces who sat daily before the guillotine and had taken an active part among the women who signalised themselves by their violence in the revolution. While we were talking she said suddenly: "But m'sieur must be tired standing," and dusted a rickety old stool for me to sit down. I hardly liked to do so for many reasons; but the poor old woman was so civil that I did not like to run the risk of hurting her by refusing, and moreover the conversation of one who had been at the taking of the Bastille was so interesting that I sat down and so our conversation went on.

While we were talking an old man-older and more bent and wrinkled even than the woman-appeared from behind the shanty. "Here is Pierre," said she. "M'sieur can hear stories now if he wishes, for Pierre was in everything, from the Bastille to Waterloo." The old man took another stool at my request and we plunged into a sea of revolutionary reminiscences. This old man, albeit clothed like a scare-crow, was like any one of the six veterans.

I was now sitting in the centre of the low hut with the woman on my left hand and the man on my right, each of them being somewhat in front of me. The place was full of all sorts of curious objects of lumber, and of many things that I wished far away. In one corner was a heap of rags which seemed to move from the number of vermin it contained, and in the other a heap of bones whose odour was something shocking. Every now and then, glancing at the heaps, I could see the gleaming eyes of some of the rats which infested the place. These loathsome objects were bad enough, but what looked even more dreadful was an old butcher's axe with an iron handle stained with clots of blood leaning up against the wall on the right hand side. Still these things did not give me much concern. The talk of the two old people was so fascinating that I stayed on and on, till the evening came and the dust heaps threw dark shadows over the vales between them.

After a time I began to grow uneasy, I could not tell how or why, but somehow I did not feel satisfied. Uneasiness is an instinct and means warning. The psychic faculties are often the sentries of the intellect; and when they sound alarm the reason begins to act, although perhaps not consciously.

This was so with me. I began to bethink me where I was and by what surrounded, and to wonder how I should fare in case I should be attacked; and then the thought suddenly burst upon me, although without any overt cause, that I was in danger.

Prudence whispered: "Be still and make no sign," and so I was still and made no sign, for I knew that four cunning eyes were on me. "Four eyes – if not more." My God, what a horrible thought! The whole shanty might be surrounded on three sides with villains! I might be in the midst of a band of such desperadoes as only half a century of periodic revolution can produce.

With a sense of danger my intellect and observation quickened, and I grew more watchful than was my wont. I noticed that the old woman's eyes were constantly wandering toward my hands. I looked at them too, and saw the cause – my rings. On my left little finger I had a large signet and on the right a good diamond.

I thought that if there was any danger my first care was to avert suspicion. Accordingly I began to work the conversation round to rag-picking – to the drains – of the things found there; and so by easy stages to jewels. Then, seizing a favourable opportunity, I asked the old woman if she knew anything of such things. She answered that she did, a little. I held out my right hand, and, showing her the diamond, asked her what she thought of that. She answered that her eyes were bad, and stooped over my hand. I said as nonchalantly as I could: "Pardon me! You will see better thus!" and taking it off handed it to her. An unholy light came into her withered old face, as she touched it. She stole one glance at me swift and keen as a flash of lightning.

She bent over the ring for a moment, her face quite concealed as though examining it. The old man looked straight out of the front of the shanty before him, at the same time fumbling in his pockets and producing a screw of tobacco in a paper and a pipe, which he proceeded to fill. I took advantage of the pause and the momentary rest from the searching eyes on my face to look carefully round the place, now dim and shadowy in the gloaming. There still lay all the heaps of varied reeking foulness; there the terrible blood-stained axe leaning against the wall in the right hand corner, and everywhere, despite the gloom, the baleful glitter of the eyes of the rats. I could see them even through some of the chinks of the boards at the back low down close to the ground. But stay! These latter eyes seemed more than usually large and bright and baleful!

For an instant my heart stood still, and I felt in that whirling condition of mind in which one feels a sort of spiritual drunkenness, and as though the body is only maintained erect in that there is no time for it to fall before recovery. Then, in another second, I was calm – coldly calm, with all my energies in full vigour, with a self-control which I felt to be perfect and with all my feeling and instincts alert.

Now I knew the full extent of my danger: I was watched and surrounded by desperate people! I could not even guess at how many of them were lying there on the ground behind the shanty, waiting for the moment to strike. I knew that I was big and strong, and they knew it, too. They knew also, as I did, that I was an Englishman and would make a fight for it; and so we waited. I had, I felt, gained an advantage in the last few seconds, for I knew my danger and understood the situation. Now, I thought, is the test of my courage-the enduring test: the fighting test may come later!

The old woman raised her head and said to me in a satisfied kind of way:

"A very fine ring, indeed – a beautiful ring! Oh, me! I once had such rings, plenty of them, and bracelets and earrings! Oh! For in those fine days I led the town a dance! But they've forgotten me now! They've forgotten me! They? Why they never heard of me! Perhaps their grandfathers remember me, some of them!" and she laughed a harsh, croaking laugh. And then I am bound to say that she astonished me, for she handed me back the ring with a certain suggestion of old-fashioned grace which was not without its pathos.

The old man eyed her with a sort of sudden ferocity, half rising from his stool, and said to me suddenly and hoarsely:

"Let me see!"

I was about to hand the ring when the old woman said:

"No! No, do not give it to Pierre! Pierre is eccentric. He loses things; and such a pretty ring!"

"Cat!" said the old man, savagely. Suddenly the old woman said, rather more loudly than was necessary:

"Wait! I shall tell you something about a ring." There was something in the sound of her voice that jarred upon me. Perhaps it was my hyper-sensitiveness, wrought up as I was to such a pitch of nervous excitement, but I seemed to think that she was not addressing me. As I stole a glance round the place I saw the eyes of the rats in the bone heaps, but missed the eyes along the back. But even as I looked I saw them again appear. The old woman's "Wait!" had given me a respite from attack, and the men had sunk back to their reclining posture.

"I once lost a ring – a beautiful diamond hoop that had belonged to a queen, and which was given to me by a farmer of the taxes, who afterwards cut his throat because I sent him away. I thought it must have been stolen, and taxed my people; but I could get no trace. The police came and suggested that it had found its way to the drain. We descended – I in my fine clothes, for I would not trust them with my beautiful ring! I know more of the drains since then, and of rats, too! But I shall never forget the horror of that place – alive with blazing eyes, a wall of them just outside the light of our torches. Well, we got beneath my house. We searched the outlet of the drain, and there in the filth found my ring, and we came out.

"But we found something else also before we came! As we were coming toward the opening a lot of sewer rats – human ones this time – came toward us. They told the police that one of their number had gone into the drain, but had not returned. He had gone in only shortly before we had, and, if lost, could hardly be far off. They asked help to seek him, so we turned back. They tried to prevent me going, but I insisted. It was a new excitement, and had I not recovered my ring? Not far did we go till we came on something. There was but little water, and the bottom of the drain was raised with brick, rubbish, and much matter of the kind. He had made a fight for it, even when his torch had gone out. But they were too many for him! They had not been long about it! The bones were still warm; but they were picked clean. They had even eaten their own dead ones and there were bones of rats as well as of the man. They took it cool enough those other – the human ones – and joked of their comrade when they found him dead, though they would have helped him living. Bah! What matters it – life or death?"

"And had you no fear?" I asked her.

"Fear!" she said with a laugh. "Me have fear? Ask Pierre! But I was younger then, and, as I came through that horrible drain with its wall of greedy eyes, always moving with the circle of the light from the torches, I did not feel easy. I kept on before the men, though! It is a way I have! I never let the men get it before me. All I want is a chance and a means! And they ate him up – took every trace away except the bones; and no one knew it, nor no sound of him was ever heard!" Here she broke into a chuckling fit of the ghastliest merriment which it was ever my lot to hear and see. A great poetess describes her heroine singing: "Oh! To see or hear her singing! Scarce I know which is the divinest."

And I can apply the same idea to the old crone – in all save the divinity, for I scarce could tell which was the most hellish – the harsh, malicious, satisfied, cruel laugh, or the leering grin, and the horrible square opening of the mouth like a tragic mask, and the yellow gleam of the few discoloured teeth in the shapeless gums. In that laugh and with that grin and the chuckling satisfaction I knew as well as if it had been spoken to me in words of thunder that my murder was settled, and the murderers only bided the proper time for its accomplishment. I could read between the lines of her gruesome story the commands to her accomplices. "Wait," she seemed to say, "bide your time. I shall strike the first blow. Find the weapon for me, and I shall make the opportunity! He shall not escape! Keep him quiet, and then no one will be wiser. There will be no outcry, and the rats will do their work!"

It was growing darker and darker; the night was coming. I stole a glance round the shanty, still all the same! The bloody axe in the corner, the heaps of filth, and the eyes on the bone heaps and in the crannies of the floor.

Pierre had been still ostensibly filling his pipe; he now struck a light and began to puff away at it. The old woman said:

"Dear heart, how dark it is! Pierre, like a good lad, light the lamp!"

Pierre got up and with the lighted match in his hand touched the wick of a lamp which hung at one side of the entrance to the shanty, and which had a reflector that threw the light all over the place. It was evidently that which was used for their sorting at night.

"Not that, stupid! Not that! The lantern!" she called out to him.

He immediately blew it out, saying: "All right, mother, I'll find it," and he hustled about the left corner of the room – the old woman saying through the darkness:

"The lantern! The lantern! Oh! That is the light that is most useful to us poor folks. The lantern was the friend of the revolution! It is the friend of the chiffonier! It helps us when all else fails."

Hardly had she said the word when there was a kind of creaking of the whole place, and something was steadily dragged over the roof.

Again I seemed to read between the lines of her words. I knew the lesson of the lantern.

"One of you get on the roof with a noose and strangle him as he passes out if we fail within."

As I looked out of the opening I saw the loop of a rope outlined black against the lurid sky. I was now, indeed, beset!

Pierre was not long in finding the lantern. I kept my eyes fixed through the darkness on the old woman. Pierre struck his light, and by its flash I saw the old woman raise from the ground beside her where it had mysteriously appeared, and then hide in the folds of her gown, a long sharp knife or dagger. It seemed to be like a butcher's sharpening iron fined to a keen point.

The lantern was lit.

"Bring it here, Pierre," she said. "Place it in the doorway where we can see it. See how nice it is! It shuts out the darkness from us; it is just right!"

Just right for her and her purposes! It threw all its light on my face, leaving in gloom the faces of both Pierre and the woman, who sat outside of me on each side.

I felt that the time of action was approaching; but I knew now that the first signal and movement would come from the woman, and so watched her.

I was all unarmed, but I had made up my mind what to do. At the first movement I would seize the butcher's axe in the right-hand corner and fight my way out. At least, I would die hard. I stole a glance round to fix its exact locality so that I could not fail to seize it at the first effort, for then, if ever, time and accuracy would be precious.

Good God! It was gone! All the horror of the situation burst upon me; but the bitterest thought of all was that if the issue of the terrible position should be against me Alice would infallibly suffer. Either she would believe me false – and any lover, or any one who has ever been one, can imagine the bitterness of the thought – or else she would go on loving long after I had been lost to her and to the world, so that her life would be broken and embittered, shattered with disappointment and despair. The very magnitude of the pain braced me up and nerved me to bear the dread scrutiny of the plotters.

I think I did not betray myself. The old woman was watching me as a cat does a mouse; she had her right hand hidden in the folds of her gown, clutching, I knew, that long, cruel-looking dagger. Had she seen any disappointment in my face she would, I felt, have known that the moment had come, and would have sprung on me like a tigress, certain of taking me unprepared.

I looked out into the night, and there I saw new cause for danger. Before and around the hut were at a little distance some shadowy forms; they were quite still, but I knew that they were all alert and on guard. Small chance for me now in that direction.

Again I stole a glance round the place. In moments of great excitement and of great danger, which is excitement, the mind works very quickly, and the keenness of the faculties which depend on the mind grows in proportion. I now felt this. In an instant I took in the whole situation. I saw that the axe had been taken through a small hole made in one of the rotten boards. How rotten they must be to allow of such a thing being done without a particle of noise.

The hut was a regular murder-trap, and was guarded all around. A garroter lay on the roof ready to entangle me with his noose if I should escape the dagger of the old hag. In front the way was guarded by I know not how many watchers. And at the back was a row of desperate men – I had seen their eyes still through the crack in the boards of the floor, when last I looked – as they lay prone waiting for the signal to start erect. If it was to be ever, now for it!

As nonchalantly as I could I turned slightly on my stool so as to get my right leg well under me. Then with a sudden jump, turning my head, and guarding it with my hands, and with the fighting instinct of the knights of old, I breathed my lady's name, and hurled myself against the back wall of the hut.

Watchful as they were, the suddenness of my movement surprised both Pierre and the old woman. As I crashed through the rotten timbers I saw the old woman rise with a leap like a tiger and heard her low gasp of baffled rage. My feet lit on something that moved, and as I jumped away I knew that I had stepped on the back of one of the row of men lying on their faces outside the hut. I was torn with nails and splinters, but otherwise unhurt. Breathless I rushed up the mound in front of me, hearing as I went the dull crash of the shanty as it collapsed into a mass.

It was a nightmare climb. The mound, though but low, was awfully steep, and with each step I took the mass of dust and cinders tore down with me and gave way under my feet. The dust rose and choked me; it was sickening, foetid, awful; but my climb was, I felt, for life or death, and I struggled on. The seconds seemed hours; but the few moments I had in starting, combined with my youth and strength, gave me a great advantage, and, though several forms struggled after me in deadly silence which was more dreadful than any sound, I easily reached the top. Since then I have climbed the cone of Vesuvius, and as I struggled up that dreary steep amid the sulphurous fumes the memory of that awful night at Montrouge came back to me so vividly that I almost grew faint.

The mound was one of the tallest in the region of dust, and as I struggled to the top, panting for breath and with my heart beating like a sledge-hammer, I saw away to my left the dull red gleam of the sky, and nearer still the flashing of lights. Thank God! I knew where I was now and where lay the road to Paris!

For two or three seconds I paused and looked back. My pursuers were still well behind me, but struggling up resolutely, and in deadly silence. Beyond, the shanty was a wreck – a mass of timber and moving forms. I could see it well, for flames were already bursting out; the rags and straw had evidently caught fire from the lantern. Still silence there! Not a sound! These old wretches could die game, anyhow.

I had no time for more than a passing glance, for as I cast an eye round the mound preparatory to making my descent I saw several dark forms rushing round on either side to cut me off on my way. It was now a race for life. They were trying to head me on my way to Paris, and with the instinct of the moment I dashed down to the right-hand side. I was just in time, for, though I came as it seemed to me down the steep in a few steps, the wary old men who were watching me turned back, and one, as I rushed by into the opening between the two mounds in front, almost struck me a blow with that terrible butcher's axe. There could surely not be two such weapons about!

Then began a really horrible chase. I easily ran ahead of the old men, and even when some younger ones and a few women joined in the hunt I easily distanced them. But I did not know the way, and I could not even guide myself by the light in the sky, for I was running away from it. I had heard that, unless of conscious purpose, hunted men turn always to the left, and so I found it now; and so, I suppose, knew also my pursuers, who were more animals than men, and with cunning or instinct had found out such secrets for themselves: for on finishing a quick spurt, after which I intended to take a moment's breathing space, I suddenly saw ahead of me two or three forms swiftly passing behind a mound to the right.

I was in the spider's web now indeed! But with the thought of this new danger came the resource of the hunted, and so I darted down the next turning to the right. I continued in this direction for some hundred yards, and then, making a turn to the left again, felt certain that I had, at any rate, avoided the danger of being surrounded.

But not of pursuit, for on came the rabble after me, steady, dogged, relentless, and still in grim silence.

In the greater darkness the mounds seemed now to be somewhat smaller than before, although – for the night was closing – they looked bigger in proportion. I was now well ahead of my pursuers, so I made a dart up the mound in front.

Oh joy of joys! I was close to the edge of this inferno of dustheaps. Away behind me the red light of Paris in the sky, and towering up behind rose the heights of Montmartre – a dim light, with here and there brilliant points like stars.

Restored to vigour in a moment, I ran over the few remaining mounds of decreasing size, and found myself on the level land beyond. Even then, however, the prospect was not inviting. All before me was dark and dismal, and I had evidently come on one of those dank, low-lying waste places which are found here and there in the neighbourhood of great cities. Places of waste and desolation, where the space is required for the ultimate agglomeration of all that is noxious, and the ground is so poor as to create no desire of occupancy even in the lowest squatter. With eyes accustomed to the gloom of the evening, and away now from the shadows of those dreadful dust-heaps, I could see much more easily than I could a little while ago. It might have been, of course, that the glare in the sky of the lights of Paris, though the city was some miles away, was reflected here. Howsoever it was, I saw well enough to take bearings for certainly some little distance around me.

In front was a bleak, flat waste that seemed almost dead level, with here and there the dark shimmering of stagnant pools. Seemingly far off on the right, amid a small cluster of scattered lights, rose a dark mass of Fort Montrouge, and away to the left in the dim distance, pointed with stray gleams from cottage windows, the lights in the sky showed the locality of Bicetre. A moment's thought decided me to take to the right and try to reach Montrouge. There at least would be some sort of safety, and I might possibly long before come on some of the cross roads which I knew. Somewhere, not far off, must lie the strategic road made to connect the outlying chain of forts circling the city.

Then I looked back. Coming over the mounds, and outlined black against the glare of the Parisian horizon, I saw several moving figures, and still a way to the right several more deploying out between me and my destination. They evidently meant to cut me off in this direction, and so my choice became constricted; it lay now between going straight ahead or turning to the left. Stooping to the ground, so as to get the advantage of the horizon as a line of sight, I looked carefully in this direction, but could detect no sign of my enemies. I argued that as they had not guarded or were not trying to guard that point, there was evidently danger to me there already. So I made up my mind to go straight on before me.

It was not an inviting prospect, and as I went on the reality grew worse. The ground became soft and oozy, and now and again gave way beneath me in a sickening kind of way. I seemed somehow to be going down, for I saw round me places seemingly more elevated than where I was, and this in a place which from a little way back seemed dead level. I looked around, but could see none of my pursuers. This was strange, for all along these birds of the night had followed me through the darkness as well as though it was broad daylight. How I blamed myself for coming out in my light-coloured tourist suit of tweed. The silence, and my not being able to see my enemies, whilst I felt that they were watching me, grew appalling, and in the hope of some one not of this ghastly crew hearing me I raised my voice and shouted several times. There was not the slightest response; not even an echo rewarded my efforts. For a while I stood stock still and kept my eyes in one direction. On one of the rising places around me I saw something dark move along, then another, and another. This was to my left, and seemingly moving to head me off.

I thought that again I might with my skill as a runner elude my enemies at this game, and so with all my speed darted forward.

Splash!

My feet had given way in a mass of slimy rubbish, and I had fallen headlong into a reeking, stagnant pool. The water and the mud in which my arms sank up to the elbows was filthy and nauseous beyond description, and in the suddenness of my fall I had actually swallowed some of the filthy stuff, which nearly choked me, and made me gasp for breath. Never shall I forget the moments during which I stood trying to recover myself almost fainting from the foetid odour of the filthy pool, whose white mist rose ghostlike around. Worst of all, with the acute despair of the hunted animal when he sees the pursuing pack closing on him, I saw before my eyes whilst I stood helpless the dark forms of my pursuers moving swiftly to surround me.

It is curious how our minds work on odd matters even when the energies of thought are seemingly concentrated on some terrible and pressing need. I was in momentary peril of my life: my safety depended on my action, and my choice of alternatives coming now with almost every step I took, and yet I could not but think of the strange dogged persistency of these old men. Their silent resolution, their steadfast, grim, persistency even in such a cause commanded, as well as fear, even a measure of respect. What must they have been in the vigour of their youth. I could understand now that whirlwind rush on the bridge of Arcola, that scornful exclamation of the Old Guard at Waterloo! Unconscious cerebration has its own pleasures, even at such moments; but fortunately it does not in any way clash with the thought from which action springs.

I realised at a glance that so far I was defeated in my object, my enemies as yet had won. They had succeeded in surrounding me on three sides, and were bent on driving me off to the left-hand, where there was already some danger for me, for they had left no guard. I accepted the alternative-it was a case of Hobson's choice and run. I had to keep the lower ground, for my pursuers were on the higher places. However, though the ooze and broken ground impeded me my youth and training made me able to hold my ground, and by keeping a diagonal line I not only kept them from gaining on me but even began to distance them. This gave me new heart and strength, and by this time habitual training was beginning to tell and my second wind had come. Before me the ground rose slightly. I rushed up the slope and found before me a waste of watery slime, with a low dyke or bank looking black and grim beyond. I felt that if I could but reach that dyke in safety I could there, with solid ground under my feet and some kind of path to guide me, find with comparative ease a way out of my troubles. After a glance right and left and seeing no one near, I kept my eyes for a few minutes to their rightful work of aiding my feet whilst I crossed the swamp. It was rough, hard work, but there was little danger, merely toil; and a short time took me to the dyke. I rushed up the slope exulting; but here again I met a new shock. On either side of me rose a number of crouching figures. From right and left they rushed at me. Each body held a rope.

The cordon was nearly complete. I could pass on neither side, and the end was near.

There was only one chance, and I took it. I hurled myself across the dyke, and escaping out of the very clutches of my foes threw myself into the stream.

At any other time I should have thought that water foul and filthy, but now it was as welcome as the most crystal stream to the parched traveller. It was a highway of safety!

My pursuers rushed after me. Had only one of them held the rope it would have been all up with me, for he could have entangled me before I had time to swim a stroke; but the many hands holding it embarrassed and delayed them, and when the rope struck the water I heard the splash well behind me. A few minutes' hard swimming took me across the stream. Refreshed with the immersion and encouraged by the escape, I climbed the dyke in comparative gaiety of spirits.

From the top I looked back. Through the darkness I saw my assailants scattering up and down along the dyke. The pursuit was evidently not ended, and again I had to choose my course. Beyond the dyke where I stood was a wild, swampy space very similar to that which I had crossed. I determined to shun such a place, and thought for a moment whether I would take up or down the dyke. I thought I heard a sound – the muffled sound of oars, so I listened, and then shouted.

No response; but the sound ceased. My enemies had evidently got a boat of some kind. As they were on the up side of me I took the down path and began to run. As I passed to the left of where I had entered the water I heard several splashes, soft and stealthy, like the sound a rat makes as he plunges into the stream, but vastly greater; and as I looked I saw the dark sheen of the water broken by the ripples of several advancing heads. Some of my enemies were swimming the stream also.

And now behind me, up the stream, the silence was broken by the quick rattle and creak of oars; my enemies were in hot pursuit. I put my best leg foremost and ran on. After a break of a couple of minutes I looked back, and by a gleam of light through the ragged clouds I saw several dark forms climbing the bank behind me. The wind had now begun to rise, and the water beside me was ruffled and beginning to break in tiny waves on the bank. I had to keep my eyes pretty well on the ground before me, lest I should stumble, for I knew that to stumble was death. After a few minutes I looked back behind me. On the dyke were only a few dark figures, but crossing the waste, swampy ground were many more. What new danger this portended I did not know – could only guess. Then as I ran it seemed to me that my track kept ever sloping away to the right. I looked up ahead and saw that the river was much wider than before, and that the dyke on which I stood fell quite away, and beyond it was another stream on whose near bank I saw some of the dark forms now across the marsh. I was on an island of some kind.

My situation was now indeed terrible, for my enemies had hemmed me in on every side. Behind came the quickening roll of the oars, as though my pursuers knew that the end was close. Around me on every side was desolation; there was not a roof or light, as far as I could see. Far off to the right rose some dark mass, but what it was I knew not. For a moment I paused to think what I should do, not for more, for my pursuers were drawing closer. Then my mind was made up. I slipped down the bank and took to the water. I struck out straight ahead, so as to gain the current by clearing the backwater of the island for such I presume it was, when I had passed into the stream. I waited till a cloud came driving across the moon and leaving all in darkness. Then I took off my hat and laid it softly on the water floating with the stream, and a second after dived to the right and struck out under water with all my might. I was, I suppose, half a minute under water, and when I rose came up as softly as I could, and turning, looked back. There went my light brown hat floating merrily away. Close behind it came a rickety old boat, driven furiously by a pair of oars. The moon was still partly obscured by the drifting clouds, but in the partial light I could see a man in the bows holding aloft ready to strike what appeared to me to be that same dreadful pole-axe which I had before escaped. As I looked the boat drew closer, closer, and the man struck savagely. The hat disappeared. The man fell forward, almost out of the boat. His comrades dragged him in but without the axe, and then as I turned with all my energies bent on reaching the further bank, I heard the fierce whirr of the muttered "Sacre!" which marked the anger of my baffled pursuers.

That was the first sound I had heard from human lips during all this dreadful chase, and full as it was of menace and danger to me it was a welcome sound for it broke that awful silence which shrouded and appalled me. It was as though an overt sign that my opponents were men and not ghosts, and that with them I had, at least, the chance of a man, though but one against many.

But now that the spell of silence was broken the sounds came thick and fast. From boat to shore and back from shore to boat came quick question and answer, all in the fiercest whispers. I looked back – a fatal thing to do-for in the instant someone caught sight of my face, which showed white on the dark water, and shouted. Hands pointed to me, and in a moment or two the boat was under weigh, and following hard after me. I had but a little way to go, but quicker and quicker came the boat after me. A few more strokes and I would be on the shore, but I felt the oncoming of the boat, and expected each second to feel the crash of an oar or other weapon on my head. Had I not seen that dreadful axe disappear in the water I do not think that I could have won the shore. I heard the muttered curses of those not rowing and the laboured breath of the rowers. With one supreme effort for life or liberty I touched the bank and sprang up it. There was not a single second to spare, for hard behind me the boat grounded and several dark forms sprang after me. I gained the top of the dyke, and keeping to the left ran on again. The boat put off and followed down the stream. Seeing this I feared danger in this direction, and quickly turning, ran down the dyke on the other side, and after passing a short stretch of marshy ground gained a wild, open flat country and sped on.

Still behind me came on my relentless pursuers. Far away, below me, I saw the same dark mass as before, but now grown closer and greater. My heart gave a great thrill of delight, for I knew that it must be the fortress of Bicetre, and with new courage I ran on. I had heard that between each and all of the protecting forts of Paris there are strategic ways, deep sunk roads, where soldiers marching should be sheltered from an enemy. I knew that if I could gain this road I would be safe, but in the darkness I could not see any sign of it, so, in blind hope of striking it, I ran on.

Presently I came to the edge of a deep cut, and found that down below me ran a road guarded on each side by a ditch of water fenced on either side by a straight, high wall.

Getting fainter and dizzier, I ran on; the ground got more broken-more and more still, till I staggered and fell, and rose again, and ran on in the blind anguish of the hunted. Again the thought of Alice nerved me. I would not be lost and wreck her life: I would fight and struggle for life to the bitter end. With a great effort I caught the top of the wall. As, scrambling like a catamount, I drew myself up, I actually felt a hand touch the sole of my foot. I was now on a sort of causeway, and before me I saw a dim light. Blind and dizzy, I ran on, staggered, and fell, rising, covered with dust and blood.

"Halt la!"

The words sounded like a voice from heaven. A blaze of light seemed to enwrap me, and I shouted with joy.

"Qui va la?" The rattle of musketry, the flash of steel before my eyes. Instinctively I stopped, though close behind me came a rush of my pursuers.

Another word or two, and out from a gateway poured, as it seemed to me, a tide of red and blue, as the guard turned out. All around seemed blazing with light, and the flash of steel, the clink and rattle of arms, and the loud, harsh voices of command. As I fell forward, utterly exhausted, a soldier caught me. I looked back in dreadful expectation, and saw the mass of dark forms disappearing into the night. Then I must have fainted. When I recovered my senses I was in the guard room. They gave me brandy, and after awhile I was able to tell them something of what had passed. Then a commissary of police appeared, apparently out of the empty air, as is the way of the Parisian police officer. He listened attentively, and then had a moment's consultation with the officer in command. Apparently they were agreed, for they asked me if I were ready now to come with them.

"Where to?" I asked, rising to go.

"Back to the dust heaps. We shall, perhaps, catch them yet!"

"I shall try!" said I.

He eyed me for a moment keenly, and said suddenly:

"Would you like to wait awhile or till tomorrow, young Englishman?" This touched me to the quick, as, perhaps, he intended, and I jumped to my feet.

"Come now!" I said; "now! Now! An Englishman is always ready for his duty!"

The commissary was a good fellow, as well as a shrewd one; he slapped my shoulder kindly. "Brave garcon!" he said. "Forgive me, but I knew what would do you most good. The guard is ready. Come!"

And so, passing right through the guard room, and through a long vaulted passage, we were out into the night. A few of the men in front had powerful lanterns. Through courtyards and down a sloping way we passed out through a low archway to a sunken road, the same that I had seen in my flight. The order was given to get at the double, and with a quick, springing stride, half run, half walk, the soldiers went swiftly along. I felt my strength renewed again – such is the difference between hunter and hunted. A very short distance took us to a low-lying pontoon bridge across the stream, and evidently very little higher up than I had struck it. Some effort had evidently been made to damage it, for the ropes had all been cut, and one of the chains had been broken. I heard the officer say to the commissary:

"We are just in time! A few more minutes, and they would have destroyed the bridge. Forward, quicker still!" And on we went. Again we reached a pontoon on the winding stream; as we came up we heard the hollow boom of the metal drums as the efforts to destroy the bridge was again renewed. A word of command was given, and several men raised their rifles.

"Fire!" A volley rang out. There was a muffled cry, and the dark forms dispersed. But the evil was done, and we saw the far end of the pontoon swing into the stream. This was a serious delay, and it was nearly an hour before we had renewed ropes and restored the bridge sufficiently to allow us to cross.

We renewed the chase. Quicker, quicker we went towards the dust heaps.

After a time we came to a place that I knew. There were the remains of a fire – a few smouldering wood ashes still cast a red glow, but the bulk of the ashes were cold. I knew the site of the hut and the hill behind it up which I had rushed, and in the flickering glow the eyes of the rats still shone with a sort of phosphorescence. The commissary spoke a word to the officer, and he cried:

"Halt!"

The soldiers were ordered to spread around and watch, and then we commenced to examine the ruins. The commissary himself began to lift away the charred boards and rubbish. These the soldiers took and piled together. Presently he started back, then bent down and rising beckoned me.

"See!" he said.

It was a gruesome sight. There lay a skeleton face downwards, a woman by the lines – an old woman by the coarse fibre of the bone. Between the ribs rose a long spike-like dagger made from a butcher's sharpening knife, its keen point buried in the spine.

"You will observe," said the commissary to the officer and to me as he took out his note book, "that the woman must have fallen on her dagger. The rats are many here – see their eyes glistening among that heap of bones – and you will also notice" – I shuddered as he placed his hand on the skeleton – "that but little time was lost by them, for the bones are scarcely cold!"

There was no other sign of any one near, living or dead; and so deploying again into line the soldiers passed on. Presently we came to the hut made of the old wardrobe. We approached. In five of the six compartments was an old man sleeping – sleeping so soundly that even the glare of the lanterns did not wake them. Old and grim and grizzled they looked, with their gaunt, wrinkled, bronzed faces and their white moustaches.

The officer called out harshly and loudly a word of command, and in an instant each one of them was on his feet before us and standing at "attention!"

"What do you here?"

"We sleep," was the answer.

"Where are the other chiffoniers?" asked the commissary.

"Gone to work."

"And you?"

"We are on guard!"

"Peste!" laughed the officer grimly, as he looked at the old men one after the other in the face and added with cool deliberate cruelty, "Asleep on duty! Is this the manner of the Old Guard? No wonder, then, a Waterloo!"

By the gleam of the lantern I saw the grim old faces grow deadly pale, and almost shuddered at the look in the eyes of the old men as the laugh of the soldiers echoed the grim pleasantry of the officer.

I felt in that moment that I was in some measure avenged.

For a moment they looked as if they would throw themselves on the taunter, but years of their life had schooled them and they remained still.

"You are but five," said the commissary; "where is the sixth?" The answer came with a grim chuckle.

"He is there!" and the speaker pointed to the bottom of the wardrobe. "He died last night. You won't find much of him. The burial of the rats is quick!"

The commissary stooped and looked in. Then he turned to the officer and said calmly:

"We may as well go back. No trace here now; nothing to prove that man was the one wounded by your soldiers' bullets! Probably they murdered him to cover up the trace. See!" Again he stooped and placed his hands on the skeleton. "The rats work quickly and they are many. These bones are warm!"

I shuddered, and so did many more of those around me.

"Form!" said the officer, and so in marching order, with the lanterns swinging in front and the manacled veterans in the midst, with steady tramp we took ourselves out of the dust-heaps and turned backward to the fortress of Bicetre.

* * *

My year of probation has long since ended, and Alice is my wife. But when I look back upon that trying twelvemonth one of the most vivid incidents that memory recalls is that associated with my visit to the City of Dust.

Mister Ted

Donald Jacob Uitvlugt

MISTER TED had done a bad thing. Again.

He didn't mean to. He loved Sophie with all of his fluffy heart. He truly did. Why didn't she understand? Why did she make him do the things he did? It wasn't fair.

He remembered the first day Sophie came into his life. He had waited in the store for so long. Each time someone picked him up, he felt his stuffing tighten in hope. Every time they set him down, he died a little inside. He wanted to cry from his plastic eyes, but of course he couldn't. By the time Christmas Eve came, he had resigned himself to being thrown into the clearance bin or given away to charity as a tax write-off.

The hands that picked him up were rough and not clean. Alcohol reeked from every wrinkle of the man's suit. A bleary-eyed teenager scanned his barcode and stuffed him into a plastic bag. He had expected Christmas to be a glossy box with shiny paper in bright colors. A bow wouldn't be too much.

Instead, he got shoved under a plastic tree shedding plastic needles on his plastic bag. The other presents moved away from him. This was not the Christmas the other toys told him about. He curled into a ball and trembled with silent sobs.

Then came Christmas morning.

"Daddy! This one's from you?"

His heart beat faster as gentle hands pulled him from the bag. Eyes the color of the morning sky studied him. A smile crowned the angelic face. The girl embraced him. He breathed deeply of her long blond hair.

He was in love.

"Oh, Daddy. He's perfect. I'm going to call him Mister Ted."

And just like that, he had a name and an owner. It was the happiest day of his life. This was why he had been stitched. Sophie had lots of other presents, but he sat on her lap as she opened them all. He was the one she constantly hugged and whispered to. He was the one her mother had to set an extra place for at Christmas dinner. He was the favorite.

He could endure all the stares and the silent treatment from the other toys. They were jealous, because Sophie was his and he was hers. And he was the one she took to bed at night. She fell asleep holding him in her arms.

Her mother and father came to the doorway to check on Sophie. Mister Ted noted how the man tried to put his arm around the woman but she shrugged out of his embrace.

"You think this makes up for anything, Dale? One lousy stuffed animal stinking of booze? Why didn't you wrap it in a whisky sack? It'd be more honest."

Mister Ted sniffed himself. He didn't smell of anything but Sophie. And he certainly didn't have lice. He was not sure he liked Sophie's mother.

"Don't pick a fight. You said you wanted me to be more in her life."

"She needs a father every day of the year. Not someone who swoops in and upstages everything I've worked so hard to give her."

The man snorted. "That's what really gets you, isn't it? In spite of what any judge or cop says she still chooses me instead of you."

The woman pushed the man away from her. "You're bad news, Dale. You were bad for me. You're bad for her. That teddy bear loves her more than you ever will. I don't want to see you break her heart again. I'm through cleaning up after your messes."

The man opened his mouth to say something, when Sophie moaned in her sleep. Her mother rushed to her side and stroked her hair until her breathing calmed. She pulled up the covers over her daughter and tucked them tight around Sophie and Mister Ted both. Perhaps the woman wasn't so bad after all.

She pulled the man from the doorway. "We'll finish this conversation downstairs."

Mister Ted snuggled right up against Sophie. He thought long and hard about everything he had heard. He would win the mother over. He knew he could. But the father seemed to be a horrible man. He understood what it was like to be left alone and unloved. He knew what it was like to have hope rise in your heart again and again, only to have it snatched away. Sophie would never suffer that pain. Not if he could help it.

The mother was right. He loved Sophie more than her father ever would. She didn't need her father any more.

He waited until he thought both adults were settled in for the night, the woman in her room, the man on the couch downstairs. He counted to a hundred, to make sure, and slipped from Sophie's arms. He stroked her silken hair and hopped down off the bed.

It was no problem getting down the stairs, though he tumbled more than climbed down them. Climbing back up would be a challenge. He made his way to the living room, quiet as cotton fluff.

The man still wore his clothes. Drool leaked from a corner of his open mouth. Mister Ted shook his head. Such a waste of a man. The best thing he ever did was give him to Sophie. Sophie had him now. He would never leave her.

He picked up the pillow the man had kicked to the floor. It wasn't easy to climb on the man's stomach, but Mister Ted did. He pressed the pillow into the man's face.

The man didn't realize what was happening at first. When he did, Mister Ted's love was stronger than his struggles. At last the man gave up on life, like he had given up on everything else.

"Dale?"

Mister Ted froze. The stairs. The woman's voice came from the top of the stairs. She hadn't seen yet. He threw the pillow to the floor and then himself. He tumbled into the shadows just as the woman reached the landing.

"Dale, are you awake?" She ran her hand over the back of the couch. "I'm sorry. Sophie needs a father, and if you're serious about being in her life – Dale?"

As she bent to check the man's pulse and ran to call an ambulance, Mister Ted hurried up the stairs. His return took him less time than he had feared. He was back in Sophie's arms by the time the ambulance arrived.

The next few weeks and months were among the happiest in Mister Ted's life. Sure, Sophie was sad. But she sought consolation in Mister Ted. She cried into his faux fur until he was wet and sticky. She couldn't fall asleep without him. He was the last thing her daddy had given to her, and she would never let him go. That suited Mister Ted fine.

Sophie held him tight all through the funeral. He rode with her in the limo. She clung to him at the graveside, her tears falling on his head. The day was bright and sunny, so was Mister Ted's spirit. His heart sang with the twittering birds. He was loved, he was loved. He was loved!

Even after the funeral, Sophie took him everywhere. Mister Ted went with her to relatives and friends of her mother, to the grocery store and the library. He spent every day with her at school. The other children whispered about Sophie when they thought she wasn't looking. Mister Ted heard what they said, but they didn't matter. They were only jealous. They didn't have someone in their lives like Mister Ted. They weren't loved.

Life settled into a happy routine for Sophie and Mister Ted. He woke up every morning in her arms. She held him as long as she could, letting him go only when her mother forced her into her clothes for the day. He sat at her side during breakfast and on her lap during the bus ride to school. Her teacher understood the grief Sophie had suffered. Mister Ted sat under Sophie's desk in her backpack. She would hold him during lunch and recess.

Then came the bus ride home and Mister Ted's favorite part of the day. Playtime. Sophie made the best tea. But she was also a brave explorer of alien worlds and had saved him many times from tentacled creatures. Or she was President of the United States and he was her Vice President. Each day held new adventures. Mister Ted always learned so much from Sophie.

Bedtime always came far too soon but brought pleasures all its own. When Sophie was safe in her pajamas, her mother would tuck her and Mister Ted into bed together, kiss both of them on the head, and turn off the light. Sophie held him close. Sometimes she talked to him, told him all about her thoughts and plans and dreams. No one listened like Mister Ted. Sometimes she rubbed her face against his fur.

Before she fell asleep, every night, Sophie whispered into his ear, "I love you, Mister Ted."

His heart soared at the words each and every time. They had a love eternal. No one would ever get in the way of their love.

Summer vacation was playtime squared. Then the new school year began. Sophie's new teacher was a dried up old thing, clearly unloved. The first day of school she drew Sophie's mother aside. Mister Ted didn't think Sophie overheard the two adults, but he did.

"Does she always bring that toy to school?"

Sophie's mother had a distant look in her eyes. "It was a gift from her late father."

"Ah. My condolences. She's welcome to have it today. But in the future, she will have to keep the bear in her backpack. It would be a distraction to the other children."

"I see."

The teacher started to leave but turned back to Sophie's mother. She rested a hand on her arm. "Does she spend a lot of time with the toy?"

"They're inseparable."

The teacher nodded. "That's what I thought. Of course it isn't my place to say, but I wonder if she might heal from her grief more quickly if they didn't spend so much time together?"

"Oh, I couldn't take Mister Ted from Sophie." But Mister Ted could see the calculating look in the eyes of Sophie's mother.

"I wouldn't suggest anything so radical, but perhaps a gradual...weaning. After all, what we both want is for the girl to grow up into a mature, self-reliant adult."

That wasn't what Mister Ted wanted at all. He loved Sophie. He needed her, and he knew she needed him. He decided to watch Sophie's mother and this teacher very carefully.

Being zipped up in the backpack wasn't so bad, even if he couldn't hear everything quite as clearly. Sophie still played with him most recesses, though she surprised him once when she left him under the desk to play with another girl instead. A flash of jealousy filled his heart when Sophie told him about her fun later in the evening. Sophie's mother came to tuck them in.

"You know, Mister Ted is looking a little ratty."

Mister Ted lifted his nose slightly. He wasn't ratty. He was well-loved.

"I guess."

"How about I give him a bath? I'll have him back to you, good as new."

Mister Ted hated bath time. Sophie's mother never let him play with her during bath time. He didn't imagine his own bath would be with Sophie either.

Sophie looked from Mister Ted to her mother and back again. "You promise?"

"Cross my heart."

Before Sophie said anything else, her mother took Mister Ted from her and tucked only the girl into the bed. Only she got the goodnight kiss. Sophie's mother turned off the light and carried him not to the bathroom, but to the laundry room where she deposited him on top of a pile of dirty clothes. Mister Ted didn't smell nearly as bad as the nasty clothes Sophie's mother wore. She hummed a little as she fiddled with the washing machine. And then she grabbed an armful of the dirty clothes, with Mister Ted on top, and dumped them in the machine.

He hated the tune the woman hummed as she heaped more clothes on top of him. But true hell came afterwards. The lid came down with a loud bang and the washing machine began to fill with water. Mister Ted felt himself grow heavy as faux fur and stuffing became saturated. The water began to spin and churn. He tried to push up the lid but the water swirled him away from it. He tumbled over and over again until he would likely have lost his mind. Only the image of Sophie's face kept him sane.

At last the torture ended. All he had to do to escape was push up the lid of the washing machine. But he couldn't get his sodden limbs to respond. He was trapped. He did not know how long he stayed in the dark of the washing machine. He tried to summon Sophie with every beat of his heart. She never came.

He dozed for a while only to awake to the sound of the school bus pulling away. Sophie had gone to school without him! Anger burned in his heart. No. That wasn't like Sophie at all. It had to be her mother. Her mother and teacher had conspired against him and his love for Sophie. They had to be stopped.

Sophie's mother ran into the laundry room and threw Mister Ted and the clothes into the dryer before heading to her job at the office. The dryer was another kind of hell, but as his limbs dried, his strength returned to him. As he tumbled, ideas formed in his head. The beginning of a plan took shape and he smiled.

The dryer finally stopped. It took all of his strength, but Mister Ted finally pushed open the door. He had discerned from the summer Sophie's mother always came home for lunch. Today, she would get a surprise. He would do something about the teacher later.

The woman was distracted as she let herself into the side door. As she grabbed the makings of a sandwich, she picked up a phone and spoke excitedly to the person on the other end.

"He asked me out! Yes, I understand what you say about office romances, but it's only a date. Besides, he loves kids, he told me so himself. If tonight goes well, I'll take Sophie to meet him. Ow –"

She set down the phone at the first slash of the knife at her ankles. This was his Sophie she was talking about. Introducing her to some strange man? He slashed out with the blade again. Sophie's mother screamed. Someone trying to take the place of her father? A slash across the throat. Blood sprayed. Trying to take his place? He drove his knife with all his strength.

Only when Sophie's mother lay still did Mister Ted realize he had done a bad thing. Blood stained his faux fur, and who would wash it with Sophie's mother gone? He climbed to the sink and tried to wash himself as best as he could. With Sophie's mother gone, who would tuck them both in at night? Who would kiss them both on the forehead? He kept washing, even long after the stains were gone.

He was going to have to be strong. He was going to have to be father and mother both to Sophie now. Mister Ted did his best to wring out his fur and climbed down, careful not to track through the blood on the floor. He climbed up the stairs and onto Sophie's bed. His heart thudded nervously as he waited her arrival.

Sophie's key opened the front door and she bounced up the stairs. She smiled wide as she glimpsed him. "Mom washed you!" Sophie threw her backpack aside and picked him up in her arms. She whirled him around and hugged him tight. If she noticed he remained damp, she didn't say anything. She held him as she went back downstairs to get a snack while she waited for her mother to get home from work. Mister Ted wondered how she couldn't feel his heart pound.

Her eyes grew wide when she spotted her mother's body. Her mouth opened but no sound came out at first. Then came a high-pitched wail. She fell to her knees in her mother's blood. She crushed Mister Ted to her chest. She still loved him. In spite of what he had done, she still loved him. She must never know what he did. He would never be bad again. He would spend the rest of his life protecting his Sophie.

Sophie was different after her mother's funeral. Oh, she still clung to him as much as before. But there was less playtime and fewer bedtime talks. She didn't cry much, and only late at night. Each tear broke Mister Ted's heart. He offered what comfort he could, but every day he was reminded he was only a stuffed bear.

Sophie went from relative to relative, tossed about like debris in a hurricane. She clung to Mister Ted as to a life preserver. He should have been happy, but he wasn't. As the cold winds and waves of indifference drove Sophie here and there, he felt almost seasick.

And through the storm, Sophie grew up. Toys had less and less of a place in her life. Now she spent her time on makeup and friends and gossip about boys. Time was an enemy Mister Ted could not fight. Instead, he struggled to maintain any hold on Sophie's heart at all. With each new home, he made sure he was always front and center, at least in her room; on the dresser, in the chair, in the middle of the bed. He was the last thing she saw when she went to school and the first thing she saw when she got home.

He tried to be good too, not that he wasn't tempted; the fifth-grade friend that wanted Sophie to trade him for two tubes of lipstick, the eighth-grade friend that counseled her to "get rid of that ratty old thing." The worst was her date to the junior prom. She brought him back to her room after the event. Mister Ted wanted to kill him, but he didn't. A few kicks and jabs with a needle from under the bed, and the boy left the room anyway.

When Sophie turned eighteen, she got a place of her own. She couldn't afford much on her tips as a waitress, but she didn't need a lot. She had Mister Ted. She told him so often, the first few months in the apartment. She held him close, so close, and cried softly. It was almost like those first golden days when he had been new. His heart soared as it had not dared soar for a long time. He realized if Sophie continued to love him and confide in him, everything would work out beautifully.

Sophie's mood improved and Mister Ted was convinced his plan had worked. All his being good had paid off. One day Sophie came home from work all smiles. She picked him up from the center of the bed and twirled him around. He knew it. He knew their love was for the ages.

"I've met somebody, Mister Ted. You're going to love him."

Mister Ted did not love Kevin, not at all. He did not like his name, did not like the way Sophie always talked about him, did not like the way he looked when he came over to the apartment. He especially did not like it when Kevin spent the night.

But Mister Ted had faith in Sophie. He understood everyone eventually left her, and in the end, she would be his and his alone. They were made for each other. He just had to wait Kevin out. A few well-placed needles wouldn't hurt either.

Then came the night when Kevin let himself in with the key Sophie had given him. He set down the bag he had been carrying, and pulled out a small blue box. He opened it and showed the ring inside to Mister Ted.

"I'm going to ask her to marry me, Mister Ted."

He didn't hear anything else Kevin had to say. He glowered at him as he lit candles and spread flower petals over the floor. His heart pounded. When Kevin turned the music on, Mister Ted had too much. He picked up one of the wine glasses Kevin brought and did a bad thing.

The candles had almost burned themselves out when Sophie opened the door to the apartment. Her purse fell to the floor. Her eyes grew wide. Mister Ted smiled up at her from Kevin's chest. His paws were red. On the floor he had written, "I love you, Sophie," in the man's blood. At last she knew. She knew completely how he felt about her.

She would be his forever. Only his.

Cheese

Ethel Lina White

THIS STORY begins with a murder. It ends with a mousetrap.

The murder can be disposed of in a paragraph. An attractive girl, carefully reared and educated for a future which held only a twisted throat. At the end of seven months, an unsolved mystery and a reward of £500.

It is a long way from a murder to a mouse-trap – and one with no finger-posts; but the police knew every inch of the way. In spite of a prestige punctured by the press and public, they had solved the identity of the killer. There remained the problem of tracking this wary and treacherous rodent from his unknown sewer in the underworld into their trap.

They failed repeatedly for lack of the right bait.

And unexpectedly, one spring evening, the bait turned up in the person of a young girl.

Cheese.

Inspector Angus Duncan was alone in his office when her message was brought up. He was a red-haired Scot, handsome in a dour fashion, with the chin of a prize-fighter and keen blue eyes.

He nodded.

"I'll see her."

It was between the lights. River, government offices and factories were all deeply dyed with the blue stain of dusk. Even in the city, the lilac bushes showed green tips and an occasional crocus cropped through the grass of the public-gardens, like strewn orange-peel. The evening star was a jewel in the pale green sky.

Duncan was impervious to the romance of the hour. He knew that twilight was but the prelude to night and that darkness was a shield for crime.

He looked up sharply when his visitor was admitted. She was young and flower-faced – her faint freckles already fading away into pallor. Her black suit was shabby, but her hat was garnished for the spring with a cheap cowslip wreath.

As she raised her blue eyes, he saw that they still carried the memory of country sweets... Thereupon he looked at her more sharply for he knew that of all poses, innocence is easiest to counterfeit.

"You say Roper sent you?" he enquired.

"Yes, Maggie Roper."

He nodded. Maggie Roper – Sergeant Roper's niece – was already shaping as a promising young Stores' detective.

"Where did you meet her?"

"At the Girls' Hostel where I'm staying."

"Your name?"

"Jenny Morgan."

"From the country?"

"Yes. But I'm up now for good."

For good? ... He wondered.

"Alone?"

"Yes."

"How's that?" He looked at her mourning. "People all dead?"

She nodded. From the lightning sweep of her lashes, he knew that she had put in some rough work with a tear. It prejudiced him in her favour. His voice grew more genial as his lips relaxed.

"Well, what's it all about?"

She drew a letter from her bag.

"I'm looking for work and I advertised in the paper. I got this answer. I'm to be companion-secretary to a lady, to travel with her and be treated as her daughter – if she likes me. I sent my photograph and my references and she's fixed an appointment."

"When and where?"

"The day after tomorrow, in the First Room in the National Gallery. But as she's elderly, she is sending her nephew to drive me to her house."

"Where's that?"

She looked troubled.

"That's what Maggie Roper is making the fuss about. First, she said I must see if Mrs. Harper – that's the lady's name – had taken up my references. And then she insisted on ringing up the Ritz where the letter was written from. The address was *printed*, so it was bound to be genuine, wasn't it?"

"Was it? What happened then?"

"They said no Mrs. Harper had stayed there. But I'm sure it must be a mistake." Her voice trembled. "One must risk something to get such a good job."

His face darkened. He was beginning to accept Jenny as the genuine article.

"Tell me," he asked, "have you had any experience of life?"

"Well, I've always lived in the country with Auntie. But I've read all sorts of novels and the newspapers."

"Murders?"

"Oh, I love those."

He could tell by the note in her childish voice that she ate up the newspaper accounts merely as exciting fiction, without the slightest realisation that the printed page was grim fact. He could see the picture: a sheltered childhood passed amid green spongy meadows. She could hardly cull sophistication from clover and cows.

"Did you read about the Bell murder?" he asked abruptly.

"Auntie wouldn't let me." She added in the same breath, "Every word."

"Why did your aunt forbid you?"

"She said it must be a specially bad one, because they'd left all the bad parts out of the paper."

"Well, didn't you notice the fact that that poor girl – Emmeline Bell – a well-bred girl of about your own age, was lured to her death through answering a newspaper advertisement?"

"I – I suppose so. But those things don't happen to oneself."

"Why? What's there to prevent your falling into a similar trap?"

"I can't explain. But if there was something wrong, I should know it."

"How? D'you expect a bell to ring or a red light to flash 'Danger?'"

"Of course not. But if you believe in right and wrong, surely there must be some warning."

He looked sceptical. That innocence bore a lily in its hand, was to him a beautiful phrase and nothing more. His own position in the sorry scheme of affairs was, to him, proof positive of the official failure of guardian angels.

"Let me see that letter, please," he said.

She studied his face anxiously as he read, but his expression remained inscrutable. Twisting her fingers in her suspense, she glanced around the room, noting vaguely the three telephones on the desk and the stacked files in the pigeonholes. A Great Dane snored before the red-caked fire. She wanted to cross the room and pat him, but lacked the courage to stir from her place.

The room was warm, for the windows were opened only a couple of inches at the top. In view of Duncan's weather-tanned colour, the fact struck her as odd.

Mercifully, the future is veiled. She had no inkling of the fateful part that Great Dane was to play in her own drama, nor was there anything to tell her that a closed window would have been a barrier between her and the yawning mouth of hell.

She started as Duncan spoke.

"I want to hold this letter for a bit. Will you call about this time tomorrow? Meantime, I must impress upon you the need of utmost caution. Don't take one step on your own. Should anything fresh crop up, 'phone me immediately. Here's my number."

When she had gone, Duncan walked to the window. The blue dusk had deepened into a darkness pricked with lights. Across the river, advertisement-signs wrote themselves intermittently in coloured beads.

He still glowed with the thrill of the hunter on the first spoor of the quarry. Although he had to await the report of the expert test, he was confident that the letter which he held had been penned by the murderer of poor ill-starred Emmeline Bell.

Then his elation vanished at a recollection of Jenny's wistful face. In this city were scores of other girls, frail as windflowers too – blossom-sweet and country-raw – forced through economic pressure into positions fraught with deadly peril.

The darkness drew down overhead like a dark shadow pregnant with crime. And out from their holes and sewers stole the rats...

At last Duncan had the trap baited for his rat.

A young and pretty girl – ignorant and unprotected. Cheese.

When Jenny, punctual to the minute, entered his office, the following evening, he instantly appraised her as his prospective decoy. His first feeling was one of disappointment. Either she had shrunk in the night or her eyes had grown bigger. She looked such a frail scrap as she stared at him, her lips bitten to a thin line, that it seemed hopeless to credit her with the necessary nerve for his project.

"Oh, please tell me it's all perfectly right about that letter."

"Anything but right."

For a moment, he thought she was about to faint. He wondered uneasily whether she had eaten that day. It was obvious from the keenness of her disappointment that she was at the end of her resources.

"Are you sure?" she insisted. "It's – very important to me. Perhaps I'd better keep the appointment. If I didn't like the look of things, I needn't go on with it."

"I tell you, it's not a genuine job," he repeated. "But I've something to put to you that is the goods. Would you like to have a shot at £500?"

Her flushed face, her eager eyes, her trembling lips, all answered him.

"Yes, please," was all she said.

He searched for reassuring terms.

"It's like this. We've tested your letter and know it is written, from a bad motive, by an undesirable character."

"You mean a criminal?" she asked quickly.

"Um. His record is not good. We want to get hold of him."

"Then why don't you?"

He suppressed a smile.

"Because he doesn't confide in us. But if you have the courage to keep your appointment tomorrow and let his messenger take you to the house of the suppositious Mrs. Harper, I'll guarantee it's the hiding-place of the man we want. We get him – you get the reward. Question is – have you the nerve?"

She was silent. Presently she spoke in a small voice.

"Will I be in great danger?"

"None. I wouldn't risk your safety for any consideration. From first to last, you'll be under the protection of the Force."

"You mean I'll be watched over by detectives in disguise?"

"From the moment you enter the National Gallery, you'll be covered doubly and trebly. You'll be followed every step of the way and directly we've located the house, the place will be raided by the police."

"All the same, for a minute or so, just before you can get into the house, I'll be alone with – *him*?"

"The briefest interval. You'll be safe at first. He'll begin with overtures. Stall him off with questions. Don't let him see you suspect – or show you're frightened."

Duncan frowned as he spoke. It was his duty to society to rid it of a dangerous pest and in order to do so, Jenny's cooperation was vital. Yet, to his own surprise, he disliked the necessity in the case of this especial girl.

"Remember we'll be at hand," he said. "But if your nerve goes, just whistle and we'll break cover immediately."

"Will *you* be there?" she asked suddenly.

"Not exactly in the foreground. But I'll be there."

"Then I'll do it." She smiled for the first time. "You laughed at me when I said there was something inside me which told me – things. But I just know I can trust *you*."

"Good." His voice was rough. "Wait a bit. You've been put to expense coming over here. This will cover your fares and so on."

He thrust a note into her hand and hustled her out, protesting. It was a satisfaction to feel that she would eat that night. As he seated himself at his desk, preparatory to work, his frozen face was no index of the emotions raised by Jenny's parting words.

Hitherto, he had thought of women merely as 'skirts.' He had regarded a saucepan with an angry woman at the business end of it, merely as a weapon. For the first time he had a domestic vision of a country girl – creamy and fragrant as meadowsweet – in a nice womanly setting of saucepans.

Jenny experienced a thrill which was almost akin to exhilaration when she entered Victoria station, the following day. At the last moment, the place for meeting had been altered in a telegram from 'Mrs. Harper.'

Immediately she had received the message, Jenny had gone to the telephone-box in the hostel and duly reported the change of plan, with a request that her message should be repeated to her, to obviate any risk of mistake.

And now – the incredible adventure was actually begun.

The station seemed filled with hurrying crowds as she walked slowly towards the clock. Her feet rather lagged on the way. She wondered if the sinister messenger had already marked the yellow wreath in her hat which she had named as her mark of identification.

Then she remembered her guards. At this moment they were here, unknown, watching over her slightest movement. It was a curious sensation to feel that she was spied upon by unseen eyes. Yet it helped to brace the muscles of her knees when she took up her station under the clock with the sensation of having exposed herself as a target for gunfire.

Nothing happened. No one spoke to her. She was encouraged to gaze around her...

A few yards away, a pleasant-faced smartly dressed young man was covertly regarding her. He carried a yellowish sample-bag which proclaimed him a drummer.

Suddenly Jenny felt positive that this was one of her guards. There was a quality about his keen clean-shaven face – a hint of the eagle in his eye – which reminded her of Duncan. She gave him the beginnings of a smile and was thrilled when, almost imperceptibly, he fluttered one eyelid. She read it as a signal for caution. Alarmed by her indiscretion, she looked fixedly in another direction.

Still – it helped her to know that even if she could not see him, he was there.

The minutes dragged slowly by. She began to grow anxious as to whether the affair were not some hoax. It would be not only a tame ending to the adventure but a positive disappointment. She would miss the chance of a sum which – to her – was a little fortune. Her need was so vital that she would have undertaken the venture for five pounds. Moreover, after her years of green country solitude, she felt a thrill at the mere thought of her temporary link with the underworld. This was life in the raw; while screening her as she aided him, she worked with Angus Duncan.

She smiled – then started as though stung.

Someone had touched her on the arm.

"Have I the honour, happiness and felicity of addressing Miss. Jenny Morgan? Yellow wreath in the lady's hat. Red Flower in the gent's buttonhole, as per arrangement."

The man who addressed her was young and bull-necked, with florid colouring which ran into blotches. He wore a red carnation in the buttonhole of his check overcoat.

"Yes, I'm Jenny Morgan."

As she spoke, she looked into his eyes. She felt a sharp revulsion – an instinctive recoil of her whole being.

"Are you Mrs. Harper's nephew?" she faltered.

"That's right. Excuse a gent keeping a lady waiting, but I just slipped into the bar for a glass of milk. I've a taxi waiting if you'll just hop outside."

Jenny's mind worked rapidly as she followed him. She was forewarned and protected. But – were it not for Maggie Roper's intervention – she would have kept this appointment in very different circumstances. She wondered whether she would have heeded that instinctive warning and refused to follow the stranger.

She shook her head. Her need was so urgent that, in her wish to believe the best, she knew that she would have summoned up her courage and flouted her fears as nerves. She would have done exactly what she was doing – accompanying an unknown man to an unknown destination.

She shivered at the realisation. It might have been herself. Poor defenceless Jenny – going to her doom.

At that moment she encountered the grave scrutiny of a stout clergyman who was standing by the book-stall. He was ruddy, wore horn-rimmed spectacles and carried the *Church Times*.

His look of understanding was almost as eloquent as a vocal message. It filled her with gratitude. Again she was certain that this was a second guard. Turning to see if the young commercial traveller were following her, she was thrilled to discover that he had preceded her into the station yard. He got into a taxi at the exact moment that her companion flung open the door of a cab which was waiting. It was only this knowledge that Duncan was thus making good his promise which induced her to enter the vehicle. Once again her nerves rebelled and she was rent with sick forebodings.

As they moved off, she had an overpowering impulse to scream aloud for help to the porters – just because all this might have happened to some poor girl who had not her own good fortune.

Her companion nudged her.

"Bit of all right, joy-riding, eh?"

She stiffened, but managed to force a smile.

"Is it a long ride?"

"Ah, now you're asking."

"Where does Mrs. Harper live?"

"Ah, that's telling."

She shrank away, seized with disgust of his blotched face so near her own.

"Please give me more room. It's stifling here."

"Now, don't you go taking no liberties with me. A married man I am, with four wives all on the dole." All the same, to her relief, he moved further away. "From the country, aren't you? Nice place. Lots of milk. Suit me a treat. Any objection to a gent smoking?"

"I wish you would. The cab reeks of whisky."

They were passing St Paul's which was the last landmark in her limited knowledge of London. Girls from offices passed on the pavement, laughing and chatting together, or hurrying by intent on business. A group was scattering crumbs to the pigeons which fluttered on the steps of the cathedral.

She watched them with a stab of envy. Safe happy girls.

Then she remembered that somewhere, in the press of traffic, a taxi was shadowing her own. She took fresh courage.

The drive passed like an interminable nightmare in which she was always on guard to stem the advances of her disagreeable companion. Something seemed always on the point of happening – something unpleasant, just out of sight and round the corner – and then, somehow she staved it off.

The taxi bore her through a congested maze of streets. Shops and offices were succeeded by regions of warehouses and factories, which in turn gave way to areas of dun squalor where gas-works rubbed shoulders with grimed laundries which bore such alluring signs as 'Dewdrop' or 'White Rose'.

From the shrilling of sirens, Jenny judged that they were in the neighbourhood of the river, when they turned into a quiet square. The tall lean houses wore an air of drab respectability. Lace curtains hung at every window. Plaster pineapples crowned the pillared porches.

"Here's our 'destitution.'"

As her guide inserted his key in the door of No. 17, Jenny glanced eagerly down the street, in time to see a taxi turn the corner.

"Hop in, dearie."

On the threshold Jenny shrank back.

Evil.

Never before had she felt its presence. But she knew. Like the fumes creeping upwards from the grating of a sewer, it poisoned the air.

Had she embarked on this enterprise in her former ignorance, she was certain that at this point, her instinct would have triumphed.

"I would never have passed through this door."

She was wrong. Volition was swept off the board. Her arm was gripped and before she could struggle, she was pulled inside.

She heard the slam of the door.

"Never loiter on the doorstep, dearie. Gives the house a bad name. This way. Up the stairs. All the nearer to heaven."

Her heart heavy with dread, Jenny followed him. She had entered on the crux of her adventure – the dangerous few minutes when she would be quite alone.

The place was horrible – with no visible reason for horror. It was no filthy East-end rookery, but a technically clean apartment-house. The stairs were covered with brown linoleum. The mottled yellow wallpaper was intact. Each landing had its marble-topped table, adorned with a forlorn aspidistra – its moulting rug at every door. The air was dead and smelt chiefly of dust.

They climbed four flights of stairs without meeting anyone. Only faint rustlings and whispers within the rooms told of other tenants. Then the blotched-faced man threw open a door.

"Young lady come to see Mrs. Harper about the situation. Too-tel-oo, dearie. Hope you strike lucky."

He pushed her inside and she heard his step upon the stairs.

In that moment, Jenny longed for anyone – even her late companion.

She was vaguely aware of the figure of a man seated in a chair. Too terrified to look at him, her eyes flickered around the room.

Like the rest of the house, it struck the note of parodied respectability. Yellowish lace curtains hung at the windows which were blocked by pots of leggy geraniums. A walnut-wood suite was upholstered in faded bottle-green rep with burst padding. A gilt-framed mirror surmounted a stained marble mantelpiece which was decorated with a clock – permanently stopped under its glass case – and a bottle of whisky. On a small table by the door rested a filthy cage, containing a grey parrot, its eyes mere slits of wicked evil between wrinkled lids.

It had to come. With an effort, she looked at the man.

He was tall and slender and wrapped in a once-gorgeous dressing-gown of frayed crimson quilted silk. At first sight, his features were not only handsome but bore some air of breeding. But the whole face was blurred – as though it were a waxen mask half-melted by the sun and over which the Fiend – in passing – had lightly drawn a hand. His eyes drew her own. Large and brilliant, they were of so light a blue as to appear almost white. The lashes were unusually long and matted into spikes.

The blood froze at Jenny's heart. The girl was no fool. Despite Duncan's cautious statements, she had drawn her own deduction which linked an unsolved murder mystery and a reward of £500.

She knew that she was alone with a homicidal maniac – the murderer of ill-starred Emmeline Bell.

In that moment, she realised the full horror of a crime which, a few months ago, had been nothing but an exciting newspaper-story. It sickened her to reflect that a girl – much like herself – whose pretty face smiled fearlessly upon the world from the printed page, had walked into this same trap, in all the blindness of her youthful confidence. No one to hear her cries. No one to guess the agony of those last terrible moments.

Jenny at least understood that first rending shock of realisation. She fought for self-control. At sight of that smiling marred face, she wanted to do what she knew instinctively that other girl had done – precipitating her doom. With a desperate effort she suppressed the impulse to rush madly round the room like a snared creature, beating her hands against the locked door and crying for help. Help which would never come.

Luckily, common sense triumphed. In a few minutes' time, she would not be alone. Even then a taxi was speeding on its mission; wires were humming; behind her was the protection of the Force.

She remembered Duncan's advice to temporise. It was true that she was not dealing with a beast of the jungle which sprang on its prey at sight.

"Oh, please." She hardly recognised the tiny pipe. "I've come to see Mrs. Harper about her situation."

"Yes." The man did not remove his eyes from her face. "So you are Jenny?"

"Yes, Jenny Morgan. Is – is Mrs. Harper in?"

"She'll be in presently. Sit down. Make yourself at home. What are you scared for?"

"I'm not scared."

Her words were true. Her strained ears had detected faintest sounds outside – dulled footsteps, the cautious fastening of a door.

The man, for his part, also noticed the stir. For a few seconds he listened intently. Then to her relief, he relaxed his attention.

She snatched again at the fiction of her future employer.

"I hope Mrs. Harper will soon come in."

"What's your hurry? Come closer. I can't see you properly."

They were face to face. It reminded her of the old nursery story of 'Little Red Riding Hood.'

"What big eyes you've got, Grandmother."

The words swam into her brain.

Terrible eyes. Like white glass cracked in distorting facets. She was looking into the depths of a blasted soul. Down, down…That poor girl. But she must not think of *her*. She must be brave – give him back look for look.

Her lids fell… She could bear it no longer.

She gave an involuntary start at the sight of his hands. They were beyond the usual size – unhuman – with long knotted fingers.

"What big hands you've got."

Before she could control her tongue, the words slipped out.

The man stopped smiling.

But Jenny was not frightened now. Her guards were near. She thought of the detective who carried the bag of samples. She thought of the stout clergyman. She thought of Duncan.

At that moment, the commercial traveller was in an upper room of a wholesale drapery house in the city, holding the fashionable blonde lady buyer with his magnetic blue eye, while he displayed his stock of crêpe-de-Chine underwear.

At that moment, the clergyman was seated in a third-class railway carriage, watching the hollows of the Downs fill with heliotrope shadows. He was not quite at ease. His thoughts persisted on dwelling on the frightened face of a little country girl as she drifted by in the wake of a human vulture.

"I did wrong. I should have risked speaking to her."

But – at that moment – Duncan was thinking of her.

Jenny's message had been received over the telephone wire, repeated and duly written down by Mr. Herbert Yates, shorthand-typist – who, during the absence of Duncan's own secretary, was filling the gap for one morning. At the sound of his chief's step in the corridor outside, he rammed on his hat, for he was already overdue for a lunch appointment with one of the numerous 'only girls in the world.'

At the door he met Duncan.

"May I go to lunch now, sir?"

Duncan nodded assent. He stopped for a minute in the passage while he gave Yates his instructions for the afternoon.

"Any message?" he enquired.

"One come this instant, sir. It's under the weight."

Duncan entered the office. But in that brief interval, the disaster had occurred.

Yates could not be held to blame for what happened. It was true that he had taken advantage of Duncan's absence to open a window wide, but he was ignorant of any breach of rules. In his hurry he had also written down Jenny's message on the nearest loose-leaf to hand, but he had taken the precaution to place it under a heavy paper-weight.

It was Duncan's Great Dane which worked the mischief. He was accustomed at this hour to be regaled with a biscuit by Duncan's secretary who was an abject dog-lover. As his dole had not been forthcoming he went in search of it. His great paws on the table, he rooted among the papers, making nothing of a trifle of a letter-weight. Over it went. Out of the window – at the next gust – went Jenny's message. Back to his rug went the dog.

The instant Duncan was aware of what had happened, a frantic search was made for Yates. But that wily and athletic youth, wise to the whims of his official superiors, had disappeared. They raked every place of refreshment within a wide radius. It was not until Duncan's men rang up to report that they had drawn a blank at the National Gallery, that Yates was discovered in an underground dive, drinking coffee and smoking cigarettes with his charmer.

Duncan arrived at Victoria forty minutes after the appointed time.

It was the bitterest hour of his life. He was haunted by the sight of Jenny's flower-face upturned to his. She had trusted him. And in his ambition to track the man he had taken advantage of her necessity to use her as a pawn in his game.

He had played her – and lost her.

The thought drove him to madness. Steeled though he was to face reality, he dared not let himself think of the end. Jenny – country-raw and blossom-sweet – even then struggling in the grip of murderous fingers.

Even then.

Jenny panted as she fought, her brain on fire. The thing had rushed upon her so swiftly that her chief feeling was of sheer incredulity. What had gone before was already burning itself up in a red mist. She had no clear memory afterwards of those tense minutes of fencing. There was only an interlude filled with a dimly comprehended menace – and then this.

And still Duncan had not intervened.

Her strength was failing. Hell cracked, revealing glimpses of unguessed horror.

With a supreme effort she wrenched herself free. It was but a momentary respite, but it sufficed for her signal – a broken tremulous whistle.

The response was immediate. Somewhere outside the door a gruff voice was heard in warning.

"Perlice."

The killer stiffened, his ears pricked, every nerve astrain. His eyes flickered to the ceiling which was broken by the outline of a trap-door.

Then his glance fell upon the parrot.

His fingers on Jenny's throat, he paused. The bird rocked on its perch, its eyes slits of malicious evil.

Time stood still. The killer stared at the parrot. Which of the gang had given the warning? Whose voice? Not Glass-eye. Not Mexican Joe. The sound had seemed to be within the room.

That parrot.

He laughed. His fingers tightened. Tightened to relax.

For a day and a half he had been in Mother Bargery's room. During that time the bird had been dumb. Did it talk?

The warning echoed in his brain. Every moment of delay was fraught with peril. At that moment his enemies were here, stealing upwards to catch him in their trap. The instinct of the human rodent, enemy of mankind – eternally hunted and harried – prevailed. With an oath, he flung Jenny aside and jumping on the table, wormed through the trap of the door.

Jenny was alone. She was too stunned to think. There was still a roaring in her ears, shooting lights before her eyes. In a vague way, she knew that some hitch had occurred in the plan. The police were here – yet they had let their prey escape.

She put on her hat, straightened her hair. Very slowly she walked down the stairs. There was no sign of Duncan or of his men.

As she reached the hall, a door opened and a white puffed face looked at her. Had she quickened her pace or shown the least sign of fear she would never have left that place alive. Her very nonchalance proved her salvation as she unbarred the door with the deliberation bred of custom.

The street was deserted, save for an empty taxi which she hailed.

"Where to, miss?" asked the driver.

Involuntarily she glanced back at the drab house, squeezed into its strait-waistcoat of grimed bricks. She had a momentary vision of a white blurred face flattened against the glass. At the sight, realisation swept over her in wave upon wave of sick terror.

There had been no guards. She had taken every step of that perilous journey – alone.

Her very terror sharpened her wits to action. If her eyesight had not deceived her, the killer had already discovered that the alarm was false. It was obvious that he would not run the risk of remaining in his present quarters. But it was possible that he might not anticipate a lightning swoop; there was nothing to connect a raw country girl with a preconcerted alliance with a Force.

"The nearest telephone-office," she panted. "Quick."

A few minutes later, Duncan was electrified by Jenny's voice gasping down the wire.

"He's at 17 Jamaica Square, SE. No time to lose. He'll go out through the roof... Quick, quick."

"Right. Jenny, where'll you be?"

"At your house. I mean, Scot – Quick."

As the taxi bore Jenny swiftly away from the dun outskirts, a shrivelled hag pattered into the upper room of that drab house. Taking no notice of its raging occupant, she approached the parrot's cage.

"Talk for mother, dearie."

She held out a bit of dirty sugar. As she whistled, the parrot opened its eyes.

"Perlice."

It was more than two hours later when Duncan entered his private room at Scotland Yard.

His eyes sought Jenny.

A little wan, but otherwise none the worse for her adventure, she presided over a teapot which had been provided by the resourceful Yates. The Great Dane – unmindful of a little incident of a letter-weight – accepted her biscuits and caresses with deep sighs of protest.

Yates sprang up eagerly.

"Did the cop come off, chief?"

Duncan nodded twice – the second time towards the door, in dismissal.

Jenny looked at him in some alarm when they were alone together. There was little trace left of the machine-made martinet of the Yard. The lines in his face appeared freshly re-tooled and there were dark pouches under his eyes.

"Jenny," he said slowly, "I've – sweated – blood."

"Oh, was he so very difficult to capture? Did he fight?"

"Who? That rat? He ran into our net just as he was about to bolt. He'll lose his footing all right. No."

"Then why are you –"

"*You.*"

Jenny threw him a swift glance. She had just been half-murdered after a short course of semi-starvation, but she commanded the situation like a lion tamer.

"Sit down," she said, "and don't say one word until you've drunk this."

He started to gulp obediently and then knocked over his cup.

"Jenny, you don't know the hell I've been through. You don't understand what you ran into. That man –"

"He was a murderer, of course. I knew that all along."

"But you were in deadliest peril –"

"I wasn't frightened, so it didn't matter. I knew I could trust you."

"Don't Jenny. Don't turn the knife. I failed you. There was a ghastly blunder."

"But it *was* all right, for it ended beautifully. You see, something told me to trust you. I always know."

During his career, Duncan had known cases of love at first sight. So, although he could not rule them out, he always argued along Jenny's lines.

Those things did not happen to him.

He realised now that it had happened to him – cautious Scot though he was.

"Jenny," he said, "it strikes me that I want someone to watch *me.*"

"I'm quite sure you do. Have I won the reward?"

His rapture was dashed.

"Yes."

"I'm so glad. I'm rich." She smiled happily. "So this can't be pity for me."

"Pity? Oh, Jenny –"

Click. The mouse-trap was set for the confirmed bachelor with the right bait.

A young and friendless girl – homely and blossom-sweet.

Cheese.

Corpses Removed,
No Questions Asked

Dean H. Wild

FROM THE TOP of the stairs their entrance hall looked cramped because Barry's body took up most of it.

"Well, what do you do now, Mrs. Jessup?" Marie asked herself and dropped the baseball bat at her feet. It was from Barry's childhood. Lil' Slugger, it was called. "Check that. It's *Widow* Jessup now, from the looks of things. Cover the mirrors and call the pall bearers. Oh, Jesus."

She lowered herself onto the next step, her heart jackhammering, her head still spinning. One minute she was telling Barry he needn't bother coming home after his latest, money-devouring trip with his fat friend Trevor. She rushed to the upstairs hall closet when she did it because she meant to toss a few of his personal items onto the floor for effect (the closet was a bottomless jumble of bric-a-brac from his past). What stopped her was his suitcase right inside the closet door – the big suitcase – with a box of condoms bearing the ridiculous name Cherry Slips sticking out of the top flap. The overflowing powder keg of rage at her core ignited. It must have telegraphed through the air because at that same moment Barry lunged at her, one of his mean lunges full of brute blindness. "You're gonna be sorry if you touch one single thing in there."

She reached into the closet, spiteful, and clamped onto the next closest item, the Lil' Slugger. She turned around and put her weight into the swing. The rest, as they say, was history. Now, in the layering silence, she moved with painstaking slowness as if his split and oozing forehead, his impossibly bent neck, and his staring eyes made this an occasion to creep.

She stepped down to the next riser.

Who would find him if she left right this minute, while the ten o'clock news wrapped up and the traffic lights downtown switched over to an endless yellow blink? Would it matter? According to the Friday night TV shows cases like this were solved with mystifying ease, the sentence practically levied the minute the deed was done. Marie Jessup, you're under arrest for the murder of your husband, Barrington Peter Jessup. Cue the slam of a jail cell. Fade to black.

An airy squeak escaped her. "I can't go like that. What am I supposed to do?"

In response, the bat pursued her, roll/clunk, roll/clunk, and bumped her heels. Great, and for our next number the kitchen napkins and paper towels will roll out to soak up the blood coming out of your husband's ears to the tune of 'Whistle While You Work.'

The doorbell rang, three quick double note chimes that filled the apartment.
Her fingers strained on the railing.

A trio of knocks on the front door followed, rapid and forceful. She thought she might need to throw up.

"Missus," the man's voice from outside was stern, but somehow sympathetic. "I think you need to open up. He's too heavy for you to move and he certainly isn't going to get up and walk out on his own. Not anymore."

She had no idea how long she stood there contemplating, had no memory of reaching a decision. But you never knew, a part of her reasoned, what waited on the other side of a door. Answering doors was how people got flowers and surprise out-of-town visitors, it was how they found out they won the jackpot from Publishers Clearing House. It was also how she met Barry. The neighbors had called a cab and Barry pulled up to the wrong address in the rain. He was kind, apologetic and somehow dashing in his Citywide Cab jacket. They hit it off right away. And it was wonderful, at least until the gambling trips with his greasy friends started.

A shudder rifled through her as she hurried down to the entrance hall. The bat picked its way down a few more steps – roll/clunk, roll/clunk – as if to get a better view. She stepped around Barry and opened the door just wide enough to see out. "Who is it?"

"Evening, Missus. Where might I find the pick up?"

The silver-haired man on her doorstep pointed to the letters embroidered on the breast of his green coveralls – NQA. Then he indicated the white van idling at the curb just behind him as if that explained it all. The words on the side panel were large and black.

CORPSES REMOVED, NO QUESTIONS ASKED

She opened the door far enough to snatch at the collar of his coveralls. "Are you crazy? You can't park that here."

"Calm down now," he said, and patted her hand. "This is all going to come out okay."

"But the neighbors will see that rolling billboard out there. They'll know –"

When he shook his head the wattles on his neck jiggled. "They won't. They can't. It's all part of the service. Now let's get down to business."

He slipped past her and produced a small computer tablet from somewhere. He tapped it with a stylus while he paced around Barry's sprawled form.

She leaned against the door to close it. "What service? What are you doing? How did you know I was... Barry was...?"

"Embrace the providential, Missus." He gathered up a handful of Barry's hair and cranked her husband's head out of the blood pool, made an agreeable grunt of assessment and let it drop again. *Thump*. "So many folks can't manage it."

"Providential," she said as she watched his battered work boots, darkly stained but dry, step through Barry's blood. Inside, she felt unanchored, jostled between reasonless possibilities, and she decided this was what the brink of insanity must feel like: a rough coach ride seated between precarious stacks of heavy, potentially crushing luggage. But – like the man said – manage it. "And what's the fee, Mr. NQA? My soul? Is that how stuff like this works? Because I have to tell you, at the moment I'm not sure I have one."

He laughed and his hand clap was like a smart gunshot in the room. Where the tablet and stylus went, she could not say. "Nothing like that. Now step away from that door. I'm going to open her up."

She complied, her mind racing. "Where will you take him? It won't do me much good if he turns up in the dumpster behind the building. Or in the river. I don't know why anyone dumps bodies in the river. The cops find them almost right away, it seems. It's in the news all the time."

"Don't you worry none," the man crouched and gave the bloody flap between Barry's eyes a two-fingered flick. "This open fracture is nice work, by the way. He was dead before he hit the bottom on the stairs, I'd say."

"Thank you," she said. It sounded like a croak.

"Thank me after everything is back to rights and it's like I was never here tonight. Like *he* was never here tonight." He rolled Barry's eyelids down. She was glad for it. One of Barry's pupils was blown and it gave his stare an accusatory albeit broken intensity. "That's part of the primo plan you're getting. Full package, introductory offer, that sort of thing."

Her mind raced faster. *Like Barry was never here tonight.* "I can go with the full package. No trouble."

"Good deal."

The door opened like a sprung trap. She craned her neck to see.

A rectangular sheet of mist hovered near the ground outside, flat, slab-like. It glided into the hall, inches from the floor, like a low riding ambulance stretcher on invisible wheels. It lowered over Barry, hid him from view.

The NQA man's gaze grew heavy. "Any goodbyes?"

"No," she said.

The sheet/slab shimmered. A soft sizzle emanated. Bitter vapors rose into the air.

"God, that's awful," she said, her hand over her mouth. "How long will this take?"

"Almost done, actually," the man in green grinned. "If you check your stairs, the residual stuff, stains and such, are already gone. All part of the service."

She tried to return the smile. "Well then, crack the champagne and hold the Pine Sol."

"You're not like most folks who find themselves in this situation. You've got control. I like you, Missus. Really." He chuckled. "And with that, we're done. Your husband is no more."

"You like me, do you? Maybe you shouldn't."

"Now, don't be so worrisome. We all make mistakes."

"I nailed mine, didn't I?"

The sheet/slab slipped out of the door with silent importance. Gone, like it never happened. The idea filled her with an unfathomable sense of relief. The floor where Barry had rested was not entirely bare however. Stray items remained – a house key, a cell phone, a packet of greenbacks which was no doubt the last of their savings earmarked as casino-and-brothel money. The arrangement struck her as some sort of grim still life, something titled *Barry Undone or Rat Bastard's Remains*.

"How do they explain it?" she asked after a moment. "People in my position. What do they say when – ?"

She was alone. It was just her and the night air rushing in the open door.

"Okay, like the man said, you're in control. Get to work, Mrs. Jessup. And make it good."

She went over to the phone.

* * *

Knock knock.

She replayed the harried call to the police over and over while she tried to sleep. Her husband left for work that morning and never returned; what was she to do? The sleepy man on the other end of the line apologized about the 48-hour missing persons protocol and assured her that every detail of her account was on record. All she needed to do was call back after another 36 hours if her husband didn't show. Thirty-five hours now, soon to be 34.

The other sound did not register until it came again.

Knock-knock.

She sat up in the ticking dark. The front door, downstairs. Police, perhaps checking in early. Groundwork, after all, had been laid and she needed to play the part. She crossed the catwalk and hurried down the stairs. "Who is it?"

The voice from the outside made her cringe. "It's Trevor. Is Barry ready? We've got an early flight."

She opened up, hating his loathsome, whiskey-dead eyes.

"I'm sorry, I haven't seen him since this morning. His work hours have been just terrible lately."

"That's weird." His warty knuckles rasped on his doughy cheek. "When I dropped him off earlier, I'm pretty sure I saw you meet him at the door. That was, what? Shit. Four hours ago?"

Her breath caught in her chest. "Dropped him?"

"You know, gave him a ride home. It's what cabbies do, right? We do for each other, watch out for each other."

"He must have stepped out and lost track of time. I'd call him but his phone is… here. Why don't you come in?" She squeezed the words through her suddenly too-tight vocal cords. "Have a drink while you wait."

* * *

The Lil' Slugger clipped the back of Trevor's head and plowed up a flap of scalp. He sprawled over the kitchen table with a loud *oouf* sound. His glass of bourbon shattered on the floor. He surprised her by standing upright a second later and staggered toward the doorway and the entrance hall beyond. She tossed the bat aside and snatched a knife from the standing block on the counter. Then she dove on him. The knife went in hard between his shoulder blades, angular and not deep enough. He pitched into the entrance hall and landed face down, his sides wobbling, the back of his neck a series of sweaty, bloated rolls. His hands fluttered at his sides.

She crashed to her knees and wrapped both hands around the jutting knife handle. One of Trevor's hands snaked around, clamped down on her wrist and then twisted. Pain exploded there. She heard small bones snap. With a cry she shoved downward until the knife crunched through bone and cartilage. Trevor gurgled, released her and went limp.

She stood up. Pain pulsed from her injured wrist in waves. Goddamn Trevor.

She eyed the front door with a lingering, tainted hope.

The knock came a moment later, restrained, a couplet of light taps. She fell on the door like a starving woman upon something edible, but then opened it only a crack. The man from NQA was there, his coveralls replaced by a gray sweatshirt, baggy and yellow at the collar, and a pair of rumpled beige pants.

"Evening, Missus," he said with a smile of familiarity as yellow as his armpits. "Nice to see you again. Twice in one night. Happens more than you'd think."

She stepped aside to give him a view of what was inside. "I didn't know what else... he knew Barry came home... I just..."

"Nothing to fret over. I'll get right to work," he said.

He toted a rectangular black box inside and set it next to Trevor's head. She noticed there was no van outside this time. A tan wood-side station wagon with glaring rectangular headlamps idled at the curb instead. A magnetic sign advertising CORPSES REMOVED was stuck to the passenger side panel. She closed the door but kept her hand on the doorknob.

"Will I need to let that misty sheet thing in?"

"Isn't one," he said and put on a pair of thick black-rimmed glasses. They made him look like a teacher from an ancient high school yearbook. "Eradication sheets are only available to punched-in employees and my shift was done at eleven. When you – well, you know, I rushed over to the plant and snatched up what I could find. All older stuff."

Her heart fluttered a little. "You came just for me?"

"I have a good feeling about you, Missus," he shrugged and opened the black case, which was tall and narrow, like a strong box. "And about where this is headed."

"Well, I'm glad to have your attention," she said and flicked her gaze toward Trevor's massive bulk.

"It's a pleasure," the man said and reached into the box.

He removed a bundle of narrow metal rods and adeptly assembled them. When he was done a freestanding arch as wide as Trevor's shoulders and just slightly taller than his bulky form stood before him. It reminded her of a wire hoop from a gigantic croquet game, provided said hoop was equipped with a tripod of wheels at the base of each leg. He positioned it near the top of Trevor's head and then took out a pair of metal clips tethered to the inside of the box by coiled wire. When he attached them to opposing points on the arch, sparks flashed.

"Looks like she's going to work just fine," he said, eyes alight.

The arch lurched forward on its wheels and began to pass over Trevor with intimate slowness. Nowhere did it touch the body, but as it passed over, flesh melted like wax. Bones slid apart and swam in the ooze. Marie reeled back from the sudden reek of gore and ozone.

NQA gave her a sideways grin. "It looks sloppy now, but the second pass will dry up all the leavings."

The arch finished at Trevor's feet and then reversed direction. As promised, the remains were reduced to fine ash studded with small, dark objects. Coins, shoe grommets and dental fillings. Her kitchen knife.

"Wouldn't you know? I forgot my broom," NQA said happily as he straightened up and hitched his pants. "I better get it out of the car. Take care of that noise, would you? It messes with the machinery when those things go off."

She scowled at the sparse remains in front of her. Trevor's cell phone, half buried in the ash, flashed and issued a tinny beep, paused, did it again. On the screen an icon in the shape of an envelope blinked. She crouched down and pulled it out, and when she glanced at the message on the screen she went cold.

Got a late fare after I dropped you. Will be back in about twenty to pick up you and Barry. Vegas, baby! – Roger

NQA slipped up next to her and stubbed the bristles of his broom between his shoes. "Trouble, Missus?"

She held out the phone and he tipped his head to read it. "Oh, that is a bugger-boo."

"Ridiculous is more like it. Jesus! Did he invite the whole damn cab company?"

She flung the phone back into the ash heap.

NQA gave his head a dismissive shake and began to sweep. At the touch of the bristles Trevor's ash vanished with the ease of shadows evaporating under a wash of light. "We're all cleaning up on behalf of somebody, Missus. Ain't it the truth?"

She turned to answer him, her heart hammering. He was gone.

* * *

"Get inside," she said to the man on her front step.

The name *Roger* was stitched on the pocket of his Citywide Cab uniform and he goggled at the 9mm in her hand with a sort of dumb terror. Barry called the gun his Ride-Along because it went to work with him most nights. It had been in his suitcase, right on top, next to a plastic bag of marijuana and a tube of Mr. Slider's coconut flavored joy jelly. This man was older than Barry or Trevor. He put up his hands as if this was some sort of bank robbery and he jumped a little when she slammed the door and locked it behind him.

"What's the deal?" he asked. His eyes darted around. "Where's Barry?"

She trained the gun on a spot just below where his Adams apple bobbed up and down. "Did you bring your cab? Alone?"

"Yeah. Look lady, I'm just picking up some friends. I don't want no trouble."

She gave the gun a shake and directed him away from the door, toward the hall table where Barry liked to dump the *Daily Mail* along with his tips. "And the dispatch office? Do they know you're here?"

"No. No, they sure as hell don't. Nobody knows I'm here."

Her smile came slow and broad. She mouthed the words *last one* around it.

Roger's hands pistoned out so fast she barely realized it. He flipped the hall table at her. She tried to jump back but the descending table edge caught her injured wrist. She fired the gun out of reflex. The sledgehammer sensation unleashed by the gun surprised her and the Ride Along tumbled out of her hand. It bounced right over to Roger as he scrabbled with the front door deadbolt. She might as well have walked over and handed it to him. He regarded the weapon at his feet with dreamlike slowness.

She leapt to the stairs because it seemed the only place left to go. When she was halfway up, the creak of the bottom riser took all the forward motion out of her.

"Hey, lady," Roger called up to her.

She turned around and the gasp she made sounded more like a laugh. Roger approached, the gun held out, a bullet hole above his left eye leaking a trail of crimson that forked perfectly over each side of his eyebrow and dribbled down his cheek. The eye on that side was turned outward like that of a broken toy.

Why, Mrs. Jessup, it seems your one and only and thoroughly accidental shot was a good one. How very providential.

"Don't go nowhere," he said, feet slogging, his tongue lolling like a wet rag. "I means it. Meanzit."

His hand tightened on the gun, his knuckles turning white. She scrambled backward, up one step, then another. There would be no real avenue of escape once she was at the top of the stairs, just the catwalk that ended at the bedroom door. She made the trip anyway and once at the top she found a relief so complete she nearly sobbed. The Lil' Slugger was propped against the bedroom doorjamb. She had put it there earlier, after – well, after Trevor – and she had forgotten about it, but now there it was like an old friend.

"I mean it, lady," Roger said from behind her. His feet clomped on the top step.

She raised the bat one-handed. "We all do."

This is where he shoots you, Mrs. Jessup. Do you realize that? You open up and he drops you like a junkyard rat before you can crack his skull –

"Missus," the voice from below seemed to blare as the door opened to the night air. "I'm back."

Roger turned toward the sounds, baffled. Marie's strength seemed to come all the way from her heels as she brought the bat down on his skull. The blow was perfectly centered, accompanied by a satisfying crunch. Roger pitched sideways over the railing. The crumpling sound as he struck the hall floor was heavy and final.

"He's the last one," she called down to NQA through a self-satisfied smile that she couldn't help. "I'm out of the woods. Of course, we'll have to drop his cab someplace."

"That's good, Missus," NQA said. He watched the tips of his shoes as he mounted the stairs. He wore a black fedora and a dark, pinstriped suit. A tie the color of dried blood was knotted at his throat. In his hand was a single red rose. "I hope it all comes out for you, then."

Her heart plunged inside of her, an elevator car whose cables just snapped. "You hope? No, you have to do this for me. Help me. Why aren't you going to help me?"

"I got the call when I got home. Those last two of yours put me over. My retirement's in," he said. He removed his hat, slow and mannerly, as he climbed toward her. "I came to thank you."

"That can't be right." Her voice trembled as she rushed to the topmost step to meet him. "I mean, you wouldn't be here if you weren't going to –"

NQA waited on the next-to-top step, nearly face to face with her. He extended the rose in a trembling hand. "I'm here to check out, Missus. Simple as that."

Her fingers tightened on the bat. "You can't leave me with this mess. I want to be done, damn you. I can't manage this alone."

He turned his back, stiff, on silent feet. "You've learned enough to manage. At least, I hope you have."

"Why the hell did I ever open the door for you?"

The bat seemed to lash out on its own, dragging her arm with it, and it cracked against the miserable hunch between his shoulder blades. His fall was heavy and noisy, a series of grunts and brittle snaps. His forehead struck the ground floor newel post; it had the same motion-halting effect a brick wall might have on a careening car. A slack frown drew his lips downward, fixed as if in lifeless clay.

Great. Punch the clock and break out the Bermudas, you old son of a bitch.

The strength ran out of her and she collapsed on the top step. The Lil' Slugger slipped out of her hand and rolled down the stairs with a harsh wooden chuckle. The air smelled of blood again, as unforgiving as rusty metal bars. The thudding of her heart became a rap of isolation, delivered again and again without mercy. She glanced at the rose, which had landed on the top step. It was black. Dry.

After a moment, the doorbell rang.

Lord Arthur Savile's Crime: A Study of Duty

Oscar Wilde

Chapter I

IT WAS Lady Windermere's last reception before Easter, and Bentinck House was even more crowded than usual. Six Cabinet Ministers had come on from the Speaker's Levée in their stars and ribands, all the pretty women wore their smartest dresses, and at the end of the picture-gallery stood the Princess Sophia of Carlsrühe, a heavy Tartar-looking lady, with tiny black eyes and wonderful emeralds, talking bad French at the top of her voice, and laughing immoderately at everything that was said to her. It was certainly a wonderful medley of people. Gorgeous peeresses chatted affably to violent Radicals, popular preachers brushed coat-tails with eminent sceptics, a perfect bevy of bishops kept following a stout prima-donna from room to room, on the staircase stood several Royal Academicians, disguised as artists, and it was said that at one time the supper-room was absolutely crammed with geniuses. In fact, it was one of Lady Windermere's best nights, and the Princess stayed till nearly half-past eleven.

As soon as she had gone, Lady Windermere returned to the picture-gallery, where a celebrated political economist was solemnly explaining the scientific theory of music to an indignant virtuoso from Hungary, and began to talk to the Duchess of Paisley. She looked wonderfully beautiful with her grand ivory throat, her large blue forget-me-not eyes, and her heavy coils of golden hair. *Or pur* they were – not that pale straw colour that nowadays usurps the gracious name of gold, but such gold as is woven into sunbeams or hidden in strange amber; and they gave to her face something of the frame of a saint, with not a little of the fascination of a sinner. She was a curious psychological study. Early in life she had discovered the important truth that nothing looks so like innocence as an indiscretion; and by a series of reckless escapades, half of them quite harmless, she had acquired all the privileges of a personality. She had more than once changed her husband; indeed, Debrett credits her with three marriages; but as she had never changed her lover, the world had long ago ceased to talk scandal about her. She was now forty years of age, childless, and with that inordinate passion for pleasure which is the secret of remaining young.

Suddenly she looked eagerly round the room, and said, in her clear contralto voice, "Where is my cheiromantist?"

"Your what, Gladys?" exclaimed the Duchess, giving an involuntary start.

"My cheiromantist, Duchess; I can't live without him at present."

"Dear Gladys! You are always so original," murmured the Duchess, trying to remember what a cheiromantist really was, and hoping it was not the same as a cheiropodist.

"He comes to see my hand twice a week regularly," continued Lady Windermere, "and is most interesting about it."

"Good heavens!" said the Duchess to herself, "he is a sort of cheiropodist after all. How very dreadful. I hope he is a foreigner at any rate. It wouldn't be quite so bad then."

"I must certainly introduce him to you."

"Introduce him!" cried the Duchess; "you don't mean to say he is here?" and she began looking about for a small tortoise-shell fan and a very tattered lace shawl, so as to be ready to go at a moment's notice.

"Of course he is here; I would not dream of giving a party without him. He tells me I have a pure psychic hand, and that if my thumb had been the least little bit shorter, I should have been a confirmed pessimist, and gone into a convent."

"Oh, I see!" said the Duchess, feeling very much relieved; "he tells fortunes, I suppose?"

"And misfortunes, too," answered Lady Windermere, "any amount of them. Next year, for instance, I am in great danger, both by land and sea, so I am going to live in a balloon, and draw up my dinner in a basket every evening. It is all written down on my little finger, or on the palm of my hand, I forget which."

"But surely that is tempting Providence, Gladys."

"My dear Duchess, surely Providence can resist temptation by this time. I think every one should have their hands told once a month, so as to know what not to do. Of course, one does it all the same, but it is so pleasant to be warned. Now if someone doesn't go and fetch Mr. Podgers at once, I shall have to go myself."

"Let me go, Lady Windermere," said a tall handsome young man, who was standing by, listening to the conversation with an amused smile.

"Thanks so much, Lord Arthur; but I am afraid you wouldn't recognise him."

"If he is as wonderful as you say, Lady Windermere, I couldn't well miss him. Tell me what he is like, and I'll bring him to you at once."

"Well, he is not a bit like a cheiromantist. I mean he is not mysterious, or esoteric, or romantic-looking. He is a little, stout man, with a funny, bald head, and great gold-rimmed spectacles; something between a family doctor and a country attorney. I'm really very sorry, but it is not my fault. People are so annoying. All my pianists look exactly like poets, and all my poets look exactly like pianists; and I remember last season asking a most dreadful conspirator to dinner, a man who had blown up ever so many people, and always wore a coat of mail, and carried a dagger up his shirt-sleeve; and do you know that when he came he looked just like a nice old clergyman, and cracked jokes all the evening? Of course, he was very amusing, and all that, but I was awfully disappointed; and when I asked him about the coat of mail, he only laughed, and said it was far too cold to wear in England. Ah, here is Mr. Podgers! Now, Mr. Podgers, I want you to tell the Duchess of Paisley's hand. Duchess, you must take your glove off. No, not the left hand, the other."

"Dear Gladys, I really don't think it is quite right," said the Duchess, feebly unbuttoning a rather soiled kid glove.

"Nothing interesting ever is," said Lady Windermere: "*on a fait le monde ainsi*. But I must introduce you. Duchess, this is Mr. Podgers, my pet cheiromantist. Mr. Podgers, this is the Duchess of Paisley, and if you say that she has a larger mountain of the moon than I have, I will never believe in you again."

"I am sure, Gladys, there is nothing of the kind in my hand," said the Duchess gravely.

"Your Grace is quite right," said Mr. Podgers, glancing at the little fat hand with its short square fingers, "the mountain of the moon is not developed. The line of life, however, is excellent. Kindly bend the wrist. Thank you. Three distinct lines on the *rascette*! You will live to a great age, Duchess, and be extremely happy. Ambition – very moderate, line of intellect not exaggerated, line of heart–"

"Now, do be indiscreet, Mr. Podgers," cried Lady Windermere.

"Nothing would give me greater pleasure," said Mr. Podgers, bowing, "if the Duchess ever had been, but I am sorry to say that I see great permanence of affection, combined with a strong sense of duty."

"Pray go on, Mr. Podgers," said the Duchess, looking quite pleased.

"Economy is not the least of your Grace's virtues," continued Mr. Podgers, and Lady Windermere went off into fits of laughter.

"Economy is a very good thing," remarked the Duchess complacently; "when I married Paisley he had eleven castles, and not a single house fit to live in."

"And now he has twelve houses, and not a single castle," cried Lady Windermere.

"Well, my dear," said the Duchess, "I like–"

"Comfort," said Mr. Podgers, "and modern improvements, and hot water laid on in every bedroom. Your Grace is quite right. Comfort is the only thing our civilisation can give us.

"You have told the Duchess's character admirably, Mr. Podgers, and now you must tell Lady Flora's"; and in answer to a nod from the smiling hostess, a tall girl, with sandy Scotch hair, and high shoulder-blades, stepped awkwardly from behind the sofa, and held out a long, bony hand with spatulate fingers.

"Ah, a pianist! I see," said Mr. Podgers, "an excellent pianist, but perhaps hardly a musician. Very reserved, very honest, and with a great love of animals."

"Quite true!" exclaimed the Duchess, turning to Lady Windermere, "absolutely true! Flora keeps two dozen collie dogs at Macloskie, and would turn our town house into a menagerie if her father would let her."

"Well, that is just what I do with my house every Thursday evening," cried Lady Windermere, laughing, "only I like lions better than collie dogs."

"Your one mistake, Lady Windermere," said Mr. Podgers, with a pompous bow.

"If a woman can't make her mistakes charming, she is only a female," was the answer. "But you must read some more hands for us. Come, Sir Thomas, show Mr. Podgers yours"; and a genial-looking old gentleman, in a white waistcoat, came forward, and held out a thick rugged hand, with a very long third finger.

"An adventurous nature; four long voyages in the past, and one to come. Been shipwrecked three times. No, only twice, but in danger of a shipwreck your next journey. A strong Conservative, very punctual, and with a passion for collecting curiosities. Had a severe illness between the ages sixteen and eighteen. Was left a fortune when about thirty. Great aversion to cats and Radicals."

"Extraordinary!" exclaimed Sir Thomas; "you must really tell my wife's hand, too."

"Your second wife's," said Mr. Podgers quietly, still keeping Sir Thomas's hand in his. "Your second wife's. I shall be charmed"; but Lady Marvel, a melancholy-looking woman, with brown hair and sentimental eyelashes, entirely declined to have her past or her future exposed; and nothing that Lady Windermere could do would induce Monsieur de Koloff, the Russian Ambassador, even to take his gloves off. In fact, many people seemed afraid to face the odd little man with his stereotyped smile, his gold spectacles, and his bright, beady eyes; and when he told poor Lady Fermor, right out before everyone, that she did not care a bit for music, but was extremely fond of musicians, it was generally felt that cheiromancy was a most dangerous science, and one that ought not to be encouraged, except in a *tête-à-tête*.

Lord Arthur Savile, however, who did not know anything about Lady Fermor's unfortunate story, and who had been watching Mr. Podgers with a great deal of interest, was filled with an immense curiosity to have his own hand read, and feeling somewhat shy about putting himself forward, crossed over the room to where Lady Windermere was sitting, and, with a charming blush, asked her if she thought Mr. Podgers would mind.

"Of course, he won't mind," said Lady Windermere, "that is what he is here for. All my lions, Lord Arthur, are performing lions, and jump through hoops whenever I ask them. But I must warn you beforehand that I shall tell Sybil everything. She is coming to lunch with me tomorrow, to talk about bonnets, and if Mr. Podgers finds out that you have a bad temper, or a tendency to gout, or a wife living in Bayswater, I shall certainly let her know all about it."

Lord Arthur smiled, and shook his head. "I am not afraid," he answered. "Sybil knows me as well as I know her."

"Ah! I am a little sorry to hear you say that. The proper basis for marriage is a mutual misunderstanding. No, I am not at all cynical, I have merely got experience, which, however, is very much the same thing. Mr. Podgers, Lord Arthur Savile is dying to have his hand read. Don't tell him that he is engaged to one of the most beautiful girls in London, because that appeared in the *Morning Post* a month ago.

"Dear Lady Windermere," cried the Marchioness of Jedburgh, "do let Mr. Podgers stay here a little longer. He has just told me I should go on the stage, and I am so interested."

"If he has told you that, Lady Jedburgh, I shall certainly take him away. Come over at once, Mr. Podgers, and read Lord Arthur's hand."

"Well," said Lady Jedburgh, making a little *moue* as she rose from the sofa, "if I am not to be allowed to go on the stage, I must be allowed to be part of the audience at any rate."

"Of course; we are all going to be part of the audience," said Lady Windermere; "and now, Mr. Podgers, be sure and tell us something nice. Lord Arthur is one of my special favourites."

But when Mr. Podgers saw Lord Arthur's hand he grew curiously pale, and said nothing. A shudder seemed to pass through him, and his great bushy eyebrows twitched convulsively, in an odd, irritating way they had when he was puzzled. Then some huge beads of perspiration broke out on his yellow forehead, like a poisonous dew, and his fat fingers grew cold and clammy.

Lord Arthur did not fail to notice these strange signs of agitation, and, for the first time in his life, he himself felt fear. His impulse was to rush from the room, but he restrained himself. It was better to know the worst, whatever it was, than to be left in this hideous uncertainty.

"I am waiting, Mr. Podgers," he said.

"We are all waiting," cried Lady Windermere, in her quick, impatient manner, but the cheiromantist made no reply.

"I believe Arthur is going on the stage," said Lady Jedburgh, "and that, after your scolding, Mr. Podgers is afraid to tell him so."

Suddenly Mr. Podgers dropped Lord Arthur's right hand, and seized hold of his left, bending down so low to examine it that the gold rims of his spectacles seemed almost to touch the palm. For a moment his face became a white mask of horror, but he soon recovered his *sang-froid*, and looking up at Lady Windermere, said with a forced smile, "It is the hand of a charming young man."

"Of course it is!" answered Lady Windermere, "but will he be a charming husband? That is what I want to know."

"All charming young men are," said Mr. Podgers.

"I don't think a husband should be too fascinating," murmured Lady Jedburgh pensively, "it is so dangerous."

"My dear child, they never are too fascinating," cried Lady Windermere. "But what I want are details. Details are the only things that interest. What is going to happen to Lord Arthur?"

"Well, within the next few months Lord Arthur will go a voyage–"

"Oh yes, his honeymoon, of course!"

"And lose a relative."

"Not his sister, I hope?" said Lady Jedburgh, in a piteous tone of voice.

"Certainly not his sister," answered Mr. Podgers, with a deprecating wave of the hand, "a distant relative merely."

"Well, I am dreadfully disappointed," said Lady Windermere. "I have absolutely nothing to tell Sybil tomorrow. No one cares about distant relatives nowadays. They went out of fashion years ago. However, I suppose she had better have a black silk by her; it always does for church, you know. And now let us go to supper. They are sure to have eaten everything up, but we may find some hot soup. François used to make excellent soup once, but he is so agitated about politics at present, that I never feel quite certain about him. I do wish General Boulanger would keep quiet. Duchess, I am sure you are tired?"

"Not at all, dear Gladys," answered the Duchess, waddling towards the door. "I have enjoyed myself immensely, and the cheiropodist, I mean the cheiromantist, is most interesting. Flora, where can my tortoise-shell fan be? Oh, thank you, Sir Thomas, so much. And my lace shawl, Flora? Oh, thank you, Sir Thomas, very kind, I'm sure"; and the worthy creature finally managed to get downstairs without dropping her scent-bottle more than twice.

All this time Lord Arthur Savile had remained standing by the fireplace, with the same feeling of dread over him, the same sickening sense of coming evil. He smiled sadly at his sister, as she swept past him on Lord Plymdale's arm, looking lovely in her pink brocade and pearls, and he hardly heard Lady Windermere when she called to him to follow her. He thought of Sybil Merton, and the idea that anything could come between them made his eyes dim with tears.

Looking at him, one would have said that Nemesis had stolen the shield of Pallas, and shown him the Gorgon's head. He seemed turned to stone, and his face was like marble in its melancholy. He had lived the delicate and luxurious life of a young man of birth and fortune, a life exquisite in its freedom from sordid care, its beautiful boyish insouciance; and now for the first time he became conscious of the terrible mystery of Destiny, of the awful meaning of Doom.

How mad and monstrous it all seemed! Could it be that written on his hand, in characters that he could not read himself, but that another could decipher, was some fearful secret of sin, some blood-red sign of crime? Was there no escape possible? Were we no better than chessmen, moved by an unseen power, vessels the potter fashions at his fancy, for honour or for shame? His reason revolted against it, and yet he felt that some tragedy was hanging over him, and that he had been suddenly called upon to bear an intolerable burden. Actors are so fortunate. They can choose whether they will appear in tragedy or in comedy, whether they will suffer or make merry, laugh or shed tears. But in real life it is different. Most men and women are forced to perform parts for which they have no qualifications. Our Guildensterns play Hamlet for us, and our Hamlets have to jest like Prince Hal. The world is a stage, but the play is badly cast.

Suddenly Mr. Podgers entered the room. When he saw Lord Arthur he started, and his coarse, fat face became a sort of greenish-yellow colour. The two men's eyes met, and for a moment there was silence.

"The Duchess has left one of her gloves here, Lord Arthur, and has asked me to bring it to her," said Mr. Podgers finally. "Ah, I see it on the sofa! Good evening."

"Mr. Podgers, I must insist on your giving me a straightforward answer to a question I am going to put to you."

"Another time, Lord Arthur, but the Duchess is anxious. I am afraid I must go."

"You shall not go. The Duchess is in no hurry."

"Ladies should not be kept waiting, Lord Arthur," said Mr. Podgers, with his sickly smile. "The fair sex is apt to be impatient."

Lord Arthur's finely-chiselled lips curled in petulant disdain. The poor Duchess seemed to him of very little importance at that moment. He walked across the room to where Mr. Podgers was standing, and held his hand out.

"Tell me what you saw there," he said. "Tell me the truth. I must know it. I am not a child."

Mr. Podgers's eyes blinked behind his gold-rimmed spectacles, and he moved uneasily from one foot to the other, while his fingers played nervously with a flash watch-chain.

"What makes you think that I saw anything in your hand, Lord Arthur, more than I told you?"

"I know you did, and I insist on your telling me what it was. I will pay you. I will give you a cheque for a hundred pounds."

The green eyes flashed for a moment, and then became dull again.

"Guineas?" said Mr. Podgers at last, in a low voice.

"Certainly. I will send you a cheque tomorrow. What is your club?"

"I have no club. That is to say, not just at present. My address is – but allow me to give you my card"; and producing a bit of gilt-edge pasteboard from his waistcoat pocket, Mr. Podgers handed it, with a low bow, to Lord Arthur, who read on it:

Mr. SEPTIMUS R. PODGERS
Professional Cheiromantist
103a West Moon Street

"My hours are from ten to four," murmured Mr. Podgers mechanically, "and I make a reduction for families."

"Be quick," cried Lord Arthur, looking very pale, and holding his hand out.

Mr. Podgers glanced nervously round, and drew the heavy *portière* across the door.

"It will take a little time, Lord Arthur, you had better sit down."

"Be quick, sir," cried Lord Arthur again, stamping his foot angrily on the polished floor.

Mr. Podgers smiled, drew from his breast-pocket a small magnifying glass, and wiped it carefully with his handkerchief.

"I am quite ready," he said.

Chapter II

TEN MINUTES LATER, with face blanched by terror, and eyes wild with grief, Lord Arthur Savile rushed from Bentinck House, crushing his way through the crowd of fur-coated footmen that stood round the large striped awning, and seeming not to see or hear anything. The night was bitter cold, and the gas-lamps round the square flared and flickered in the keen wind; but his hands were hot with fever, and his forehead burned like fire. On and on he went, almost with the gait of a drunken man. A policeman looked curiously at him as he passed, and a beggar, who slouched from an archway to ask for alms, grew frightened, seeing misery greater than his own. Once he stopped under a lamp, and looked at his hands. He thought he could detect the stain of blood already upon them, and a faint cry broke from his trembling lips.

Murder! That is what the cheiromantist had seen there. Murder! The very night seemed to know it, and the desolate wind to howl it in his ear. The dark corners of the streets were full of it. It grinned at him from the roofs of the houses.

First he came to the Park, whose sombre woodland seemed to fascinate him. He leaned wearily up against the railings, cooling his brow against the wet metal, and listening to the tremulous silence of the trees. "Murder! Murder!" he kept repeating, as though iteration could dim the horror of the word. The sound of his own voice made him shudder, yet he almost hoped that Echo might hear him, and wake the slumbering city from its dreams. He felt a mad desire to stop the casual passer-by, and tell him everything.

Then he wandered across Oxford Street into narrow, shameful alleys. Two women with painted faces mocked at him as he went by. From a dark courtyard came a sound of oaths and blows, followed by shrill screams, and, huddled upon a damp doorstep, he saw the crook-backed forms of poverty and eld. A strange pity came over him. Were these children of sin and misery predestined to their end, as he to his? Were they, like him, merely the puppets of a monstrous show?

And yet it was not the mystery, but the comedy of suffering that struck him; its absolute uselessness, its grotesque want of meaning. How incoherent everything seemed! How lacking in all harmony! He was amazed at the discord between the shallow optimism of the day, and the real facts of existence. He was still very young.

After a time he found himself in front of Marylebone Church. The silent roadway looked like a long riband of polished silver, flecked here and there by the dark arabesques of waving shadows. Far into the distance curved the line of flickering gas-lamps, and outside a little walled-in house stood a solitary hansom, the driver asleep inside. He walked hastily in the direction of Portland Place, now and then looking round, as though he feared that he was being followed. At the corner of Rich Street stood two men, reading a small bill upon a hoarding. An odd feeling of curiosity stirred him, and he crossed over. As he came near, the word 'Murder', printed in black letters, met his eye. He started, and a deep flush came into his cheek. It was an advertisement offering a reward for any information leading to the arrest of a man of medium height, between thirty and forty years of age, wearing a billy-cock hat, a black coat, and check trousers, and with a scar upon his right cheek. He read it over and over again, and wondered if the wretched man would be caught, and how he had been scarred. Perhaps, someday, his own name might be placarded on the walls of London. Someday, perhaps, a price would be set on his head also.

The thought made him sick with horror. He turned on his heel, and hurried on into the night.

Where he went he hardly knew. He had a dim memory of wandering through a labyrinth of sordid houses, of being lost in a giant web of sombre streets, and it was bright dawn when he found himself at last in Piccadilly Circus. As he strolled home towards Belgrave Square, he met the great waggons on their way to Covent Garden. The white-smocked carters, with their pleasant sunburnt faces and coarse curly hair, strode sturdily on, cracking their whips, and calling out now and then to each other; on the back of a huge grey horse, the leader of a jangling team, sat a chubby boy, with a bunch of primroses in his battered hat, keeping tight hold of the mane with his little hands, and laughing; and the great piles of vegetables looked like masses of jade against the morning sky, like masses of green jade against the pink petals of some marvellous rose. Lord Arthur felt curiously affected, he could not tell why. There was something in the dawn's delicate loveliness that seemed to him inexpressibly pathetic, and he thought of all the days that break in beauty, and that set in storm. These rustics, too, with their rough, good-humoured voices, and their nonchalant ways, what a strange London they saw! A London free from the sin of night and the smoke of day, a pallid, ghost-like city, a desolate town of tombs! He wondered what they thought of it, and whether they knew anything of its splendour and its shame, of its fierce, fiery-coloured joys, and its horrible hunger, of all it makes and mars from morn to eve. Probably it was to them merely a mart where they brought their fruits to sell, and where they tarried for a few hours at most, leaving the streets still silent, the houses still asleep. It gave him pleasure to watch them as they went by. Rude as they were, with their heavy, hob-nailed shoes, and their awkward gait, they brought a little of a ready with them. He felt that they had lived with Nature, and that she had taught them peace. He envied them all that they did not know.

By the time he had reached Belgrave Square the sky was a faint blue, and the birds were beginning to twitter in the gardens.

CHAPTER III

WHEN LORD ARTHUR woke it was twelve o'clock, and the midday sun was streaming through the ivory-silk curtains of his room. He got up and looked out of the window. A dim haze of heat was hanging over the great city, and the roofs of the houses were like dull silver. In the flickering green of the square below some children were flitting about like white butterflies, and the pavement was crowded with people on their way to the Park. Never had life seemed lovelier to him, never had the things of evil seemed more remote.

Then his valet brought him a cup of chocolate on a tray. After he had drunk it, he drew aside a heavy *portière* of peach-coloured plush, and passed into the bathroom. The light stole softly from above, through thin slabs of transparent onyx, and the water in the marble tank glimmered like a moonstone. He plunged hastily in, till the cool ripples touched throat and hair, and then dipped his head right under, as though he would have wiped away the stain of some shameful memory. When he stepped out he felt almost at peace. The exquisite physical conditions of the moment had dominated him, as indeed often happens in the case of very finely-wrought natures, for the senses, like fire, can purify as well as destroy.

After breakfast, he flung himself down on a divan, and lit a cigarette. On the mantelshelf, framed in dainty old brocade, stood a large photograph of Sybil Merton, as he had seen her first at Lady Noel's ball. The small, exquisitely-shaped head drooped slightly to one side, as though the thin, reed-like throat could hardly bear the burden of so much beauty; the lips were slightly parted, and seemed made for sweet music; and all the tender purity of girlhood looked out in wonder from the dreaming eyes. With her soft, clinging dress of *crêpe-de-chine*, and her large leaf-shaped fan, she looked like one of those delicate little figures men find in the olive-woods near Tanagra; and there was a touch of Greek grace in her pose and attitude. Yet she was not *petite*. She was simply perfectly proportioned – a rare thing in an age when so many women are either over life-size or insignificant.

Now as Lord Arthur looked at her, he was filled with the terrible pity that is born of love. He felt that to marry her, with the doom of murder hanging over his head, would be a betrayal like that of Judas, a sin worse than any the Borgia had ever dreamed of. What happiness could there be for them, when at any moment he might be called upon to carry out the awful prophecy written in his hand? What manner of life would be theirs while Fate still held this fearful fortune in the scales? The marriage must be postponed, at all costs. Of this he was quite resolved. Ardently though he loved the girl, and the mere touch of her fingers, when they sat together, made each nerve of his body thrill with exquisite joy, he recognised none the less clearly where his duty lay, and was fully conscious of the fact that he had no right to marry until he had committed the murder. This done, he could stand before the altar with Sybil Merton, and give his life into her hands without terror of wrongdoing. This done, he could take her to his arms, knowing that she would never have to blush for him, never have to hang her head in shame. But done it must be first; and the sooner the better for both.

Many men in his position would have preferred the primrose path of dalliance to the steep heights of duty; but Lord Arthur was too conscientious to set pleasure above principle. There was more than mere passion in his love; and Sybil was to him a symbol of all that is good and noble. For a moment he had a natural repugnance against what he was asked to do, but it soon passed away. His heart told him that it was not a sin, but a sacrifice; his reason reminded him that there was no other course open. He had to choose between living for himself and living for others, and terrible though the task laid upon him undoubtedly was, yet he knew that he must not suffer selfishness to triumph over love. Sooner or later we are all called upon to decide on the same issue – of us all, the same question is asked. To Lord Arthur it came early in life – before his nature had been spoiled by the calculating cynicism of middle-age, or his heart corroded by the shallow, fashionable egotism of our day, and he felt no hesitation about doing his duty. Fortunately also, for him, he was no mere dreamer, or idle dilettante. Had he been so, he would have hesitated, like Hamlet, and let irresolution mar his purpose. But he was essentially practical. Life to him meant action, rather than thought. He had that rarest of all things, common sense.

The wild, turbid feelings of the previous night had by this time completely passed away, and it was almost with a sense of shame that he looked back upon his mad wanderings from street to street, his fierce emotional agony. The very sincerity of his sufferings made them seem unreal to him now. He wondered how he could have been so foolish as to rant and rave about the inevitable. The only question that seemed to trouble him was, whom to make away with; for he was not blind to the fact that murder, like the religions of the Pagan world, requires a victim as well as a priest. Not being a genius, he had no enemies, and indeed he felt that this was not the time for the gratification of any personal pique or dislike, the mission in which he was engaged being one of great and grave solemnity. He accordingly made out a list of his friends and relatives on a sheet of notepaper, and after careful consideration, decided in favour of Lady Clementina Beauchamp, a dear old lady who lived in Curzon Street, and was his own second cousin by his mother's side. He had always been very fond of Lady Clem, as everyone called her, and as he was very wealthy himself, having come into all Lord Rugby's property when he came of age, there was no possibility of his deriving any vulgar monetary advantage by her death. In fact, the more he thought over the matter, the more she seemed to him to be just the right person, and, feeling that any delay would be unfair to Sybil, he determined to make his arrangements at once.

The first thing to be done was, of course, to settle with the cheiromantist; so he sat down at a small Sheraton writing-table that stood near the window, drew a cheque for £105, payable to the order of Mr. Septimus Podgers, and, enclosing it in an envelope, told his valet to take it to West Moon Street. He then telephoned to the stables for his hansom, and dressed to go out. As he was leaving the room he looked back at Sybil Merton's photograph, and swore that, come what may, he would never let her know what he was doing for her sake, but would keep the secret of his self-sacrifice hidden always in his heart.

On his way to the Buckingham, he stopped at a florist's, and sent Sybil a beautiful basket of narcissus, with lovely white petals and staring pheasants' eyes, and on arriving at the club, went straight to the library, rang the bell, and ordered the waiter to bring him a lemon-and-soda, and a book on Toxicology. He had fully decided that poison was the best means to adopt in this troublesome business. Anything like personal violence was extremely distasteful to him, and besides, he was very anxious not to murder Lady Clementina in any way that might attract public attention, as he hated the idea of being lionised at Lady Windermere's, or seeing his name figuring in the paragraphs of vulgar society – newspapers. He had also to think of Sybil's father and mother, who were rather old-fashioned people, and might possibly object to the marriage if there was anything like a scandal, though he felt certain that if he told them the whole facts of the case they would be the very first to appreciate the motives that had actuated him. He had every reason, then, to decide in favour of poison. It was safe, sure, and quiet, and did away with any necessity for painful scenes, to which, like most Englishmen, he had a rooted objection.

Of the science of poisons, however, he knew absolutely nothing, and as the waiter seemed quite unable to find anything in the library but *Ruff's Guide* and *Bailey's Magazine*, he examined the book-shelves himself, and finally came across a handsomely-bound edition of the *Pharmacopoeia*, and a copy of Erskine's *Toxicology*, edited by Sir Mathew Reid, the President of the Royal College of Physicians, and one of the oldest members of the Buckingham, having been elected in mistake for somebody else; a *contretemps* that so enraged the Committee, that when the real man came up they black-balled him unanimously. Lord Arthur was a good deal puzzled at the technical terms used in both books, and had begun to regret that he had not paid more attention to his classics at Oxford, when in the second volume of Erskine, he found a very interesting and complete account of the properties of aconitine, written in fairly clear English. It seemed to him to be exactly the poison he wanted. It was swift – indeed, almost immediate, in its effect – perfectly painless, and when taken in the form of a gelatine capsule, the mode recommended by Sir Mathew, not by any means unpalatable. He accordingly made a note, upon his shirt-cuff, of the amount necessary for a fatal dose, put the books back in their places, and strolled up St. James's Street, to Pestle and Humbey's, the great chemists. Mr. Pestle, who always attended personally on the aristocracy, was a good deal surprised at the order, and in a very deferential manner murmured something about a medical certificate being necessary. However, as soon as Lord Arthur explained to him that it was for a large Norwegian mastiff that he was obliged to get rid of, as it showed signs of incipient rabies, and had already bitten the coachman twice in the calf of the leg, he expressed himself as being perfectly satisfied, complimented Lord Arthur on his wonderful knowledge of Toxicology, and had the prescription made up immediately.

Lord Arthur put the capsule into a pretty little silver *bonbonnière* that he saw in a shop window in Bond Street, threw away Pestle and Hambey's ugly pill-box, and drove off at once to Lady Clementina's.

"Well, *monsieur le mauvais sujet*," cried the old lady, as he entered the room, "why haven't you been to see me all this time?"

"My dear Lady Clem, I never have a moment to myself," said Lord Arthur, smiling.

"I suppose you mean that you go about all day long with Miss. Sybil Merton, buying *chiffons* and talking nonsense? I cannot understand why people make such a fuss about being married. In my day we never dreamed of billing and cooing in public, or in private for that matter."

"I assure you I have not seen Sybil for twenty-four hours, Lady Clem. As far as I can make out, she belongs entirely to her milliners."

"Of course; that is the only reason you come to see an ugly old woman like myself. I wonder you men don't take warning. *On a fait des folies pour moi*, and here I am, a poor rheumatic creature, with a false front and a bad temper. Why, if it were not for dear Lady Jansen, who sends me all the worst French novels she can find, I don't think I could get through the day. Doctors are no use at all, except to get fees out of one. They can't even cure my heartburn."

"I have brought you a cure for that, Lady Clem," said Lord Arthur gravely. "It is a wonderful thing, invented by an American."

"I don't think I like American inventions, Arthur. I am quite sure I don't. I read some American novels lately, and they were quite nonsensical."

"Oh, but there is no nonsense at all about this, Lady Clem! I assure you it is a perfect cure. You must promise to try it"; and Lord Arthur brought the little box out of his pocket, and handed it to her.

"Well, the box is charming, Arthur. Is it really a present? That is very sweet of you. And is this the wonderful medicine? It looks like a *bonbon*. I'll take it at once."

"Good heavens! Lady Clem," cried Lord Arthur, catching hold of her hand, "you mustn't do anything of the kind. It is a homoeopathic medicine, and if you take it without having heartburn, it might do you no end of harm. Wait till you have an attack, and take it then. You will be astonished at the result."

"I should like to take it now," said Lady Clementina, holding up to the light the little transparent capsule, with its floating bubble of liquid aconitine. I am sure it is delicious. The fact is that, though I hate doctors, I love medicines. However, I'll keep it till my next attack."

"And when will that be?" asked Lord Arthur eagerly. "Will it be soon?"

"I hope not for a week. I had a very bad time yesterday morning with it. But one never knows."

"You are sure to have one before the end of the month then, Lady Clem?"

"I am afraid so. But how sympathetic you are today, Arthur! Really, Sybil has done you a great deal of good. And now you must run away, for I am dining with some very dull people, who won't talk scandal, and I know that if I don't get my sleep now I shall never be able to keep awake during dinner. Goodbye, Arthur, give my love to Sybil, and thank you so much for the American medicine."

"You won't forget to take it, Lady Clem, will you?" said Lord Arthur, rising from his seat.

"Of course I won't, you silly boy. I think it is most kind of you to think of me, and I shall write and tell you if I want any more."

Lord Arthur left the house in high spirits, and with a feeling of immense relief.

That night he had an interview with Sybil Merton. He told her how he had been suddenly placed in a position of terrible difficulty, from which neither honour nor duty would allow him to recede. He told her that the marriage must be put off for the present, as until he had got rid of his fearful entanglements, he was not a free man. He implored her to trust him, and not to have any doubts about the future. Everything would come right, but patience was necessary.

The scene took place in the conservatory of Mr. Merton's house, in Park Lane, where Lord Arthur had dined as usual. Sybil had never seemed more happy, and for a moment Lord Arthur had been tempted to play the coward's part, to write to Lady Clementina for the pill, and to let the marriage go on as if there was no such person as Mr. Podgers in the world. His better nature, however, soon asserted itself, and even when Sybil flung herself weeping into his arms, he did not falter. The beauty that stirred his senses had touched his conscience also. He felt that to wreck so fair a life for the sake of a few months' pleasure would be a wrong thing to do.

He stayed with Sybil till nearly midnight, comforting her and being comforted in turn, and early the next morning he left for Venice, after writing a manly, firm letter to Mr. Merton about the necessary postponement of the marriage.

Chapter IV

IN VENICE he met his brother, Lord Surbiton, who happened to have come over from Corfu in his yacht. The two young men spent a delightful fortnight together. In the morning they rode on the Lido, or glided up and down the green canals in their long black gondola; in the afternoon they usually entertained visitors on the yacht; and in the evening they dined at Florian's, and smoked innumerable cigarettes on the Piazza. Yet somehow Lord Arthur was not happy. Every day he studied the obituary column in the *Times*, expecting to see a notice of Lady Clementina's death, but every day he was disappointed. He began to be afraid that some accident had happened to her, and often regretted that he had prevented her taking the aconitine when she had been so anxious to try its effect. Sybil's letters, too, though full of love, and trust, and tenderness, were often very sad in their tone, and sometimes he used to think that he was parted from her for ever.

After a fortnight Lord Surbiton got bored with Venice, and determined to run down the coast to Ravenna, as he heard that there was some capital cock-shooting in the Pinetum. Lord Arthur at first refused absolutely to come, but Surbiton, of whom he was extremely fond, finally persuaded him that if he stayed at Danieli's by himself he would be moped to death, and on the morning of the 15th they started, with a strong nor'-east wind blowing, and a rather choppy sea. The sport was excellent, and the free, open-air life brought the colour back to Lord Arthur's cheek, but about the 22nd he became anxious about Lady Clementina, and, in spite of Surbiton's remonstrances, came back to Venice by train.

As he stepped out of his gondola on to the hotel steps, the proprietor came forward to meet him with a sheaf of telegrams. Lord Arthur snatched them out of his hand, and tore them open. Everything had been successful. Lady Clementina had died quite suddenly on the night of the 17th!

His first thought was for Sybil, and he sent her off a telegram announcing his immediate return to London. He then ordered his valet to pack his things for the night mail, sent his gondoliers about five times their proper fare, and ran up to his sitting-room with a light step and a buoyant heart. There he found three letters waiting for him. One was from Sybil herself, full of sympathy and condolence. The others were from his mother, and from Lady Clementina's solicitor. It seemed that the old lady had dined with the Duchess that very night, had delighted everyone by her wit and *esprit*, but had gone home somewhat early, complaining of heartburn. In the morning she was found dead in her bed, having apparently suffered no pain. Sir Mathew Reid had been sent for at once, but, of course, there was nothing to be done, and she was to be buried on the 22nd at Beauchamp Chalcote. A few days before she died she had made her will, and left Lord Arthur her little house in Curzon Street, and all her furniture, personal effects, and pictures, with the exception of her collection of miniatures, which was to go to her sister, Lady Margaret Rufford, and her amethyst necklace, which Sybil Merton was to have. The property was not of much value; but Mr. Mansfield, the solicitor, was extremely anxious for Lord Arthur to return at once, if possible, as there were a great many bills to be paid, and Lady Clementina had never kept any regular accounts.

Lord Arthur was very much touched by Lady Clementina's kind remembrance of him, and felt that Mr. Podgers had a great deal to answer for. His love of Sybil, however, dominated every other emotion, and the consciousness that he had done his duty gave him peace and comfort. When he arrived at Charing Cross, he felt perfectly happy.

The Mertons received him very kindly. Sybil made him promise that he would never again allow anything to come between them, and the marriage was fixed for the 7th June. Life seemed to him once more bright and beautiful, and all his old gladness came back to him again.

One day, however, as he was going over the house in Curzon Street, in company with Lady Clementina's solicitor and Sybil herself, burning packages of faded letters, and turning out drawers of odd rubbish, the young girl suddenly gave a little cry of delight.

"What have you found, Sybil?" said Lord Arthur, looking up from his work, and smiling.

"This lovely little silver *bonbonnière*, Arthur. Isn't it quaint and Dutch? Do give it to me! I know amethysts won't become me till I am over eighty."

It was the box that had held the aconitine.

Lord Arthur started, and a faint blush came into his cheek. He had almost entirely forgotten what he had done, and it seemed to him a curious coincidence that Sybil, for whose sake he had gone through all that terrible anxiety, should have been the first to remind him of it.

"Of course you can have it, Sybil. I gave it to poor Lady Clem myself."

"Oh! Thank you, Arthur; and may I have the *bonbon* too? I had no notion that Lady Clementina liked sweets. I thought she was far too intellectual."

Lord Arthur grew deadly pale, and a horrible idea crossed his mind.

"*Bonbon*, Sybil? What do you mean?" he said in a slow, hoarse voice.

"There is one in it, that is all. It looks quite old and dusty, and I have not the slightest intention of eating it. What is the matter, Arthur? How white you look!"

Lord Arthur rushed across the room, and seized the box. Inside it was the amber-coloured capsule, with its poison-bubble. Lady Clementina had died a natural death after all!

The shock of the discovery was almost too much for him. He flung the capsule into the fire, and sank on the sofa with a cry of despair.

Chapter V

MR. MERTON was a good deal distressed at the second postponement of the marriage, and Lady Julia, who had already ordered her dress for the wedding, did all in her power to make Sybil break off the match. Dearly, however, as Sybil loved her mother, she had given her whole life into Lord Arthur's hands, and nothing that Lady Julia could say could make her waver in her faith. As for Lord Arthur himself, it took him days to get over his terrible disappointment, and for a time his nerves were completely unstrung. His excellent common sense, however, soon asserted itself, and his sound, practical mind did not leave him long in doubt about what to do. Poison having proved a complete failure, dynamite, or some other form of explosive, was obviously the proper thing to try.

He accordingly looked again over the list of his friends and relatives, and, after careful consideration, determined to blow up his uncle, the Dean of Chichester. The Dean, who was a man of great culture and learning, was extremely fond of clocks, and had a wonderful collection of timepieces, ranging from the fifteenth century to the present day, and it seemed to Lord Arthur that this hobby of the good Dean's offered him an excellent opportunity for carrying out his scheme. Where to procure an explosive machine was, of course, quite another matter. The London Directory gave him no information on the point, and he felt that there was very little use in going to Scotland Yard about it, as they never seemed to know anything about the movements of the dynamite faction till after an explosion had taken place, and not much even then.

Suddenly he thought of his friend Rouvaloff, a young Russian of very revolutionary tendencies, whom he had met at Lady Windermere's in the winter. Count Rouvaloff was supposed to be writing a life of Peter the Great, and to have come over to England for the purpose of studying the documents relating to that Tsar's residence in this country as a ship carpenter; but it was generally suspected that he was a Nihilist agent, and there was no doubt that the Russian Embassy did not look with any favour upon his presence in London. Lord Arthur felt that he was just the man for his purpose, and drove down one morning to his lodgings in Bloomsbury, to ask his advice and assistance.

"So you are taking up politics seriously?" said Count Rouvaloff, when Lord Arthur had told him the object of his mission; but Lord Arthur, who hated swagger of any kind, felt bound to admit to him that he had not the slightest interest in social questions, and simply wanted the explosive machine for a purely family matter, in which no one was concerned but himself.

Count Rouvaloff looked at him for some moments in amazement, and then seeing that he was quite serious, wrote an address on a piece of paper, initialled it, and handed it to him across the table.

"Scotland Yard would give a good deal to know this address, my dear fellow."

"They shan't have it," cried Lord Arthur, laughing; and after shaking the young Russian warmly by the hand he ran downstairs, examined the paper, and told the coachman to drive to Soho Square.

There he dismissed him, and strolled down Greek Street, till he came to a place called Bayle's Court. He passed under the archway, and found himself in a curious *cul-de-sac*, that was apparently occupied by a French Laundry, as a perfect network of clothes-lines was stretched across from house to house, and there was a flutter of white linen in the morning air. He walked right to the end, and knocked at a little green house. After some delay, during which every window in the court became a blurred mass of peering faces, the door was opened by a rather rough-looking foreigner, who asked him in very bad English what his business was. Lord Arthur handed him the paper Count Rouvaloff had given him. When the man saw it he bowed, and invited Lord Arthur into a very shabby front parlour on the ground floor, and in a few moments Herr Winckelkopf, as he was called in England, bustled into the room, with a very wine-stained napkin round his neck, and a fork in his left hand.

"Count Rouvaloff has given me an introduction to you," said Lord Arthur, bowing, "and

I am anxious to have a short interview with you on a matter of business. My name is Smith, Mr. Robert Smith, and I want you to supply me with an explosive clock."

"Charmed to meet you, Lord Arthur," said the genial little German, laughing. "Don't look so alarmed, it is my duty to know everybody, and I remember seeing you one evening at Lady Windermere's. I hope her ladyship is quite well. Do you mind sitting with me while I finish my breakfast? There is an excellent *pâté*, and my friends are kind enough to say that my Rhine wine is better than any they get at the German Embassy," and before Lord Arthur had got over his surprise at being recognised, he found himself seated in the back-room, sipping the most delicious Marcobrünner out of a pale yellow hock-glass marked with the Imperial monogram, and chatting in the friendliest manner possible to the famous conspirator.

"Explosive clocks," said Herr Winckelkopf, "are not very good things for foreign exportation, as, even if they succeed in passing the Custom House, the train service is so irregular, that they usually go off before they have reached their proper destination. If, however, you want one for home use, I can supply you with an excellent article, and guarantee that you will he satisfied with the result. May I ask for whom it is intended? If it is for the police, or for anyone connected with Scotland Yard, I am afraid I cannot do anything for you. The English detectives are really our best friends, and I have always found that by relying on their stupidity, we can do exactly what we like. I could not spare one of them."

"I assure you," said Lord Arthur, "that it has nothing to do with the police at all. In fact, the clock is intended for the Dean of Chichester."

"Dear me! I had no idea that you felt so strongly about religion, Lord Arthur. Few young men do nowadays."

"I am afraid you overrate me, Herr Winckelkopf," said Lord Arthur, blushing. "The fact is, I really know nothing about theology."

"It is a purely private matter then?"

"Purely private."

Herr Winckelkopf shrugged his shoulders, and left the room, returning in a few minutes with a round cake of dynamite about the size of a penny, and a pretty little French clock, surmounted by an ormolu figure of Liberty trampling on the hydra of Despotism.

Lord Arthur's face brightened up when he saw it. "That is just what I want," he cried, "and now tell me how it goes off."

"Ah! There is my secret," answered Herr Winckelkopf, contemplating his invention with a justifiable look of pride; "let me know when you wish it to explode, and I will set the machine to the moment."

"Well, today is Tuesday, and if you could send it off at once–"

"That is impossible; I have a great deal of important work on hand for some friends of mine in Moscow. Still, I might send it off tomorrow."

"Oh, it will be quite time enough!" said Lord Arthur politely, "if it is delivered tomorrow night or Thursday morning. For the moment of the explosion, say Friday at noon exactly. The Dean is always at home at that hour."

"Friday, at noon," repeated Herr Winckelkopf, and he made a note to that effect in a large ledger that was lying on a bureau near the fireplace.

"And now," said Lord Arthur, rising from his seat, "pray let me know how much I am in your debt."

"It is such a small matter, Lord Arthur, that I do not care to make any charge. The dynamite comes to seven and sixpence, the clock will be three pounds ten, and the carriage about five shillings. I am only too pleased to oblige any friend of Count Rouvaloff's."

"But your trouble, Herr Winckelkopf?"

"Oh, that is nothing! It is a pleasure to me. I do not work for money; I live entirely for my art."

Lord Arthur laid down £4, 2s. 6d. on the table, thanked the little German for his kindness, and, having succeeded in declining an invitation to meet some Anarchists at a meat-tea on the following Saturday, left the house and went off to the Park.

For the next two days he was in a state of the greatest excitement, and on Friday at twelve o'clock he drove down to the Buckingham to wait for news. All the afternoon the stolid hall-porter kept posting up telegrams from various parts of the country giving the results of horse-races, the verdicts in divorce suits, the state of the weather, and the like, while the tape ticked out wearisome details about an all-night sitting in the House of Commons, and a small panic on the Stock Exchange. At four o'clock the evening papers came in, and Lord Arthur disappeared into the library with the *Pall Mall*, the *St. James's*, the *Globe*, and the *Echo*, to the immense indignation of Colonel Goodchild, who wanted to read the reports of a speech he had delivered that morning at the Mansion House, on the subject of South African Missions, and the advisability of having black Bishops in every province, and for some reason or other had a strong prejudice against the *Evening News*. None of the papers, however, contained even the slightest allusion to Chichester, and Lord Arthur felt that the attempt must have failed. It was a terrible blow to him, and for a time he was quite unnerved. Herr Winckelkopf, whom he went to see the next day was full of elaborate apologies, and offered to supply him with another clock free of charge, or with a case of nitro-glycerine bombs at cost price. But he had lost all faith in explosives, and Herr Winckelkopf himself acknowledged that everything is so adulterated nowadays, that even dynamite can hardly be got in a pure condition. The little German, however, while admitting that something must have gone wrong with the machinery, was not without hope that the clock might still go off, and instanced the case of a barometer that he had once sent to the military Governor at Odessa, which, though timed to explode in ten days, had not done so for something like three months. It was quite true that when it did go off, it merely succeeded in blowing a housemaid to atoms, the Governor having gone out of town six weeks before, but at least it showed that dynamite, as a destructive force, was, when under the control of machinery, a powerful, though a somewhat unpunctual agent. Lord Arthur was a little consoled by this reflection, but even here he was destined to disappointment, for two days afterwards, as he was going upstairs, the Duchess called him into her boudoir, and showed him a letter she had just received from the Deanery.

"Jane writes charming letters," said the Duchess; "you must really read her last. It is quite as good as the novels Mudie sends us."

Lord Arthur seized the letter from her hand. It ran as follows:

> The Deanery, Chichester,
> 27th May

My Dearest Aunt,

Thank you so much for the flannel for the Dorcas Society, and also for the gingham. I quite agree with you that it is nonsense their wanting to wear pretty things, but everybody is so Radical and irreligious nowadays, that it is difficult to make them see that they should not try and dress like the upper classes. I am sure I don't know what we are coming to. As papa has often said in his sermons, we live in an age of unbelief.

We have had great fun over a clock that an unknown admirer sent papa last Thursday. It arrived in a wooden box from London, carriage paid, and papa feels it must have been sent by someone who had read his remarkable sermon, 'Is Licence Liberty?' for on the top of the clock was a figure of a woman, with what papa said was the cap of Liberty on her head. I didn't think it very becoming myself, but papa said it was historical, so I suppose it is all right. Parker unpacked it, and papa put it on the mantelpiece in the library, and we were all sitting there on Friday morning, when just as the clock struck twelve, we heard a whirring noise, a little puff of smoke came from the pedestal of the figure, and the goddess of Liberty fell off, and broke her nose on the fender! Maria was quite alarmed, but it looked so ridiculous, that James and I went off into fits of laughter, and even papa was amused. When we examined it, we found it was a sort of alarum clock, and that, if you set it to a particular hour, and put some gunpowder and a cap under a little hammer, it went off whenever you wanted. Papa said it must not remain in the library, as it made a noise, so Reggie carried it away to the schoolroom, and does nothing but have small explosions all day long. Do you think Arthur would like one for a wedding present? I suppose they are quite fashionable in London. Papa says they should do a great deal of good, as they show that Liberty can't last, but must fall down. Papa says Liberty was invented at the time of the French Revolution. How awful it seems!

I have now to go to the Dorcas, where I will read them your most instructive letter. How true, dear aunt, your idea is, that in their rank of life they should wear what is unbecoming. I must say it is absurd, their anxiety about dress, when there are so many more important things in this world, and in the next. I am so glad your flowered poplin turned out so well, and that your lace was not torn. I am wearing my yellow satin, that you so kindly gave me, at the Bishop's on Wednesday, and think it will look all right. Would you have bows or not? Jennings says that everyone wears bows now, and that the underskirt should be frilled. Reggie has just had another explosion, and papa has ordered the clock to be sent to the stables. I don't think papa likes it so much as he did at first, though he is very flattered at being sent such a pretty and ingenious toy. It shows that people read his sermons, and profit by them.

Papa sends his love, in which James, and Reggie, and Maria all unite, and, hoping that Uncle Cecil's gout is better, believe me, dear aunt, ever your affectionate niece,

Jane Percy.

PS. – Do tell me about the bows. Jennings insists they are the fashion.

Lord Arthur looked so serious and unhappy over the letter, that the Duchess went into fits of laughter.

"My dear Arthur," she cried, "I shall never show you a young lady's letter again! But what shall I say about the clock? I think it is a capital invention, and I should like to have one myself."

"I don't think much of them," said Lord Arthur, with a sad smile, and, after kissing his mother, he left the room.

When he got upstairs, he flung himself on a sofa, and his eyes filled with tears. He had done his best to commit this murder, but on both occasions he had failed, and through no fault of his own. He had tried to do his duty, but it seemed as if Destiny herself had turned traitor. He was oppressed with the sense of the barrenness of good intentions, of the futility of trying to be fine. Perhaps, it would be better to break off the marriage altogether. Sybil would suffer, it is true, but suffering could not really mar a nature so noble as hers. As for himself, what did it matter? There is always some war in which a man can die, some cause to which a man can give his life, and as life had no pleasure for him, so death had no terror. Let Destiny work out his doom. He would not stir to help her.

At half-past seven he dressed, and went down to the club. Surbiton was there with a party of young men, and he was obliged to dine with them. Their trivial conversation and idle jests did not interest him, and as soon as coffee was brought he left them, inventing some engagement in order to get away. As he was going out of the club, the hall-porter handed him a letter. It was from Herr Winckelkopf, asking him to call down the next evening, and look at an explosive umbrella, that went off as soon as it was opened. It was the very latest invention, and had just arrived from Geneva. He tore the letter up into fragments. He had made up his mind not to try any more experiments. Then he wandered down to the Thames Embankment, and sat for hours by the river. The moon peered through a mane of tawny clouds, as if it were a lion's eye, and innumerable stars spangled the hollow vault, like gold dust powdered on a purple dome. Now and then a barge swung out into the turbid stream, and floated away with the tide, and the railway signals changed from green to scarlet as the trains ran shrieking across the bridge. After some time, twelve o'clock boomed from the tall tower at Westminster, and at each stroke of the sonorous bell the night seemed to tremble. Then the railway lights went out, one solitary lamp left gleaming like a large ruby on a giant mast, and the roar of the city became fainter.

At two o'clock he got up, and strolled towards Blackfriars. How unreal everything looked! How like a strange dream! The houses on the other side of the river seemed built out of darkness. One would have said that silver and shadow had fashioned the world anew. The huge dome of St. Paul's loomed like a bubble through the dusky air.

As he approached Cleopatra's Needle he saw a man leaning over the parapet, and as he came nearer the man looked up, the gas-light falling full upon his face.

It was Mr. Podgers, the cheiromantist! No one could mistake the fat, flabby face, the gold-rimmed spectacles, the sickly feeble smile, the sensual mouth.

Lord Arthur stopped. A brilliant idea flashed across him, and he stole softly up behind. In a moment he had seized Mr. Podgers by the legs, and flung him into the Thames. There was a coarse oath, a heavy splash, and all was still. Lord Arthur looked anxiously over, but could see nothing of the cheiromantist but a tall hat, pirouetting in an eddy of moonlit water. After a time it also sank, and no trace of Mr. Podgers was visible. Once he thought that he caught sight of the bulky misshapen figure striking out for the staircase by the bridge, and a horrible feeling of failure came over him, but it turned out to be merely a reflection, and when the moon shone out from behind a cloud it passed away. At last he seemed to have realised the decree of destiny. He heaved a deep sigh of relief, and Sybil's name came to his lips.

"Have you dropped anything, sir?" said a voice behind him suddenly.

He turned round, and saw a policeman with a bull's-eye lantern.

"Nothing of importance, sergeant," he answered, smiling, and hailing a passing hansom, he jumped in, and told the man to drive to Belgrave Square.

For the next few days he alternated between hope and fear. There were moments when he almost expected Mr. Podgers to walk into the room, and yet at other times he felt that Fate could not be so unjust to him. Twice he went to the cheiromantist's address in West Moon Street, but he could not bring himself to ring the bell. He longed for certainty, and was afraid of it.

Finally it came. He was sitting in the smoking-room of the club having tea, and listening rather wearily to Surbiton's account of the last comic song at the Gaiety, when the waiter came in with the evening papers. He took up the *St. James's*, and was listlessly turning over its pages, when this strange heading caught his eye:

Suicide of a Cheiromantist.

He turned pale with excitement, and began to read. The paragraph ran as follows:

Yesterday morning, at seven o'clock, the body of Mr. Septimus R. Podgers, the eminent cheiromantist, was washed on shore at Greenwich, just in front of the Ship Hotel. The unfortunate gentleman had been missing for some days, and considerable anxiety for his safety had been felt in cheiromantic circles. It is supposed that he committed suicide under the influence of a temporary mental derangement, caused by overwork, and a verdict to that effect was returned this afternoon by the coroner's jury. Mr. Podgers had just completed an elaborate treatise on the subject of the Human Hand, that will shortly be published, when it will no doubt attract much attention. The deceased was sixty-five years of age, and does not seem to have left any relations.

Lord Arthur rushed out of the club with the paper still in his hand, to the immense amazement of the hall-porter, who tried in vain to stop him, and drove at once to Park Lane. Sybil saw him from the window, and something told her that he was the bearer of good news. She ran down to meet him, and, when she saw his face, she knew that all was well.

"My dear Sybil," cried Lord Arthur, "let us be married tomorrow!"

"You foolish boy! Why, the cake is not even ordered!" said Sybil, laughing through her tears.

Chapter VI

When the wedding took place, some three weeks later, St. Peter's was crowded with a perfect mob of smart people. The service was read in the most impressive manner by the Dean of Chichester, and everybody agreed that they had never seen a handsomer couple than the bride and bridegroom. They were more than handsome, however – they were happy. Never for a single moment did Lord Arthur regret all that he had suffered for Sybil's sake, while she, on her side, gave him the best things a woman can give to any man – worship, tenderness, and love. For them romance was not killed by reality. They always felt young.

Some years afterwards, when two beautiful children had been born to them, Lady Windermere came down on a visit to Alton Priory, a lovely old place, that had been the Duke's wedding present to his son; and one afternoon as she was sitting with Lady Arthur under a lime-tree in the garden, watching the little boy and girl as they played up and down the rose-walk, like fitful sunbeams, she suddenly took her hostess's hand in hers, and said, "Are you happy, Sybil?"

"Dear Lady Windermere, of course I am happy. Aren't you?"

"I have no time to be happy, Sybil. I always like the last person who is introduced to me; but, as a rule, as soon as I know people I get tired of them."

"Don't your lions satisfy you, Lady Windermere?"

"Oh dear, no! Lions are only good for one season. As soon as their manes are cut, they are the dullest creatures going. Besides, they behave very badly, if you are really nice to them. Do you remember that horrid Mr. Podgers? He was a dreadful impostor. Of course, I didn't mind that at all, and even when he wanted to borrow money I forgave him, but I could not stand his making love to me. He has really made me hate cheiromancy. I go in for telepathy now. It is much more amusing."

"You mustn't say anything against cheiromancy here, Lady Windermere; it is the only subject that Arthur does not like people to chaff about. I assure you he is quite serious over it."

"You don't mean to say that he believes in it, Sybil?"

"Ask him, Lady Windermere, here he is"; and Lord Arthur came up the garden with a large bunch of yellow roses in his hand, and his two children dancing round him.

"Lord Arthur?"

"Yes, Lady Windermere."

"You don't mean to say that you believe in cheiromancy?"

"Of course I do," said the young man, smiling.

"But why?"

"Because I owe to it all the happiness of my life," he murmured, throwing himself into a wicker chair.

"My dear Lord Arthur, what do you owe to it?"

"Sybil," he answered, handing his wife the roses, and looking into her violet eyes.

"What nonsense!" cried Lady Windermere. "I never heard such nonsense in all my life."

Fragments of Me

Nemma Wollenfang

TODAY I am Rhodine Glastonbury, or so the roulette dictates. That does not mean this will not change before nightfall; the timing is incalculable and prone to spontaneity. Simply put, I am this person… for now. But tomorrow, who knows? There are seven possible versions of me.

At this moment I am Rhodine, and Rhodine wanders the halls of Fleetwood's Psychiatric Unit looking for some fun. She soon finds it, it's like she has radar.

"Well-well, Nurse Romano, someone has been working out," she says, eyeing the new orderly with appreciation. Honed, tall, swarthy – all of her favourite attributes. "Been weighing the dumb-bells again, I see."

Rhodine is the typical cliché of a high-school cheerleader – preppy, bubbly and bright. In her mind, the title naturally equates to being a shameless flirt too, and her taste for young and cute guys like the strikingly handsome Nurse Romano is notorious.

"Good morning, Rhodine," he sighs as he arranges pill pots on a tray. He spares her only a glance. "How are you today?"

"I am just *perfect*." She rolls her 'r's and gifts him with a sly little smile. Minx.

Nurse Romano rolls his eyes and internally the rest concur.

"But these pyjamas are totally horrid," she continues. "Shapeless, hospital-issue green does nothing for my complexion. And I have a great complexion, don't you think?"

Nurse Romano sighs once more as he fills another tray, deigning her with a nod and a gentle smile. "You do, Rhodine. Of course you do. Even in those awful pyjamas you are as lovely as ever."

He is a gentleman and unfailingly polite, however I know that he finds Rhodine's brazen come-ons trying rather than endearing… but he likes her better than Morgan.

Nobody likes Morgan.

* * *

By one o'clock I am Billy.

And Billy is allowed to play with his Lego set! The box says it is only for ages seven to twelve but Billy is a big boy. He builds a skyscraper, because it is big and tall and because he can. Nurse Hammond supervises him. They do not want him to eat the pieces as he did last week. Nurse Hammond is a plump lady with red cheeks who puffs a lot to keep up, but she is very nice and she smiles a lot. He likes Nurse Hammond.

* * *

When the clock strikes three I am Hector Bowes-Lyon: frustrated genius and musician extraordinaire – who frantically scribbles.

"No, not right, yes, no, *no…*"

Pen in mouth, he writes in hectic lines of darting italic. The symphony is there, *right there*, in our head. I can hear its intricate melody siphoning off his thoughts. He cannot write it down fast enough – daaar-da-da-dum-da-da – it's aggravating!

"Argh!"

Frustration has driven him to the brink!

"Hector?" a young orderly ventures. She takes a tentative step in his direction. Hector stiffens and stills. "Are you okay?" she continues. "Do you need any help?"

Hector gives the girl a long, measured look – under such vicious scrutiny she gulps and steps back – before he returns to his scattered sheet music and ignores her.

Although he can talk, Hector says nothing. He does not speak to menials. They are not worth his time.

* * *

When the setting sun colours the sky with rose and gold, I am Zuri Okoro.

Zuri is pleasant: happy and genial and friendly with everyone. Her hair sways from side to side in its neat ponytail as she jogs the length of the outdoor track.

One two, one two, one two…

She breathes steadily as she keeps an even pace, monitoring her steps closely.

"You're picking up some good speed there, Zuri!" Nurse Romano calls from an open door, and as she passes he bestows an encouraging smile.

"At the next Olympics I'm going for gold!" she calls back and he laughs good-naturedly.

Inside our head, Rhodine broils. She does not like the affinity that those two share, and although it is nothing but friendship she quietly sulks, resenting even that.

Nurse Romano is mine, she silently hisses. Zuri says nothing. Her only focus is running. *One two, one two, one two…*

* * *

The evening is quiet and during dinner I am Sister Mary – the novice nun.

The food is a little lacking in taste but it is nutritious and she prompts the other inmates in green pyjamas to give thanks for this generous bounty. "Let us pray."

Some of the patients clasp their hands and dutifully dip their heads but others ignore her completely. One rocks back and forth in her seat with glazed eyes. Another recites the alphabet on a quiet loop as he arranges his peas and carrots in concentric circles. They are all God's children and she prays for them all.

"Give us this day our daily bread, and forgive our trespasses –"

Rhodine sticks out her tongue and makes a rude noise inside our head. No one can hear it but the seven of us. Regardless, Sister Mary's lips thin with disapproval.

She and Rhodine have always shared a turbulent relationship but it is not one-sided. Sister Mary often rants about her audacious behaviour and lack of propriety. Last week she called her a 'godless hussy' – strong words from Sister Mary. Rhodine called her something stronger in return.

The prayer concludes and we settle down for dinner. Morgan does not trouble us and we have a peaceful meal. This is not her usual routine, not her *modus operandi*. It is not the way Morgan operates. Always there is some disruption. She never speaks, not like the others, and that is something that has always unnerved me. But sometimes I can sense her – as an underlying quiver, a ripple of malcontent – and there are the out-of-place actions. A random pinch here, a leg stuck out to trip an orderly there, a sinister cackle for no obvious reason. Those I attribute to her. They are typical Morgan, expected Morgan. Minor nuisances that are easy to live with. But today there is none of that. That is why the new silence concerns me.

Yet the others are not so worried: Billy hums a nonsensical tune, Rhodine quietly examines our nails, Hector stews over another section of his concerto, and Zuri plans a two mile run for tomorrow. No one anticipates an outburst, no one prepares for disaster. The tranquillity encourages them not to.

Studiously, I ponder the phrase: 'the calm before the storm'.

* * *

After dinner we watch TV in the common-room, or at least we try to. Happy-go-lucky Rhodine is in charge again and she cannot *sit still*. Eventually she spots Nurse Romano leaving the room, alone, and vacates our chair in search of dessert (as she puts it).

Sister Mary clucks in disapproval and Billy whines – he had wanted to watch Ghostbusters. As usual, I go with the flow, another passenger along for the ride.

Sometimes it is hard, being in such a crowded head, and with other much more domineering personalities like Hector and Rhodine, it is not often that I 'get out'. I seldom have my chance to shine. Tonight, again, I have been side-lined while another takes centre-stage, hogging the spotlight. *But, tomorrow*, I tell myself, *maybe tomorrow…*

My chance will come again.

And so I spin the casino wheel – let the little white ball fall where it may. Red, black, red, black… Fate is the decider, our Lady of Roulette. And in this way I gamble with every second of every day on my own uncertain lottery.

But, as Rhodine often says, *isn't that the same for everyone else?*

"Everyone else has one body to one mind," I gripe. My tongue and limbs are not my own, they are a shared commodity. That is not something I can easily forget. But at least I am never alone. That is perhaps the one positive aspect of my situation. These extra fragments can be caring and kind and in some ways they can be like family.

With the one glaring exception.

Nurse Romano is folding sheets and placing them neatly on a trolley in the main corridor. Rhodine dallies with fantasies of him, of his hands and lips running over her skin, of luring him into the utility closet where she can have her wicked way with him. He always says no but still she holds out hope – ignoring the fact that it would cost him his job. Like a lioness on the hunt, Rhodine prowls forward, releasing a giggle as she closes in on her unsuspecting orderly. His back stiffens with awareness. Busted!

"Rhodine," he sighs as he turns, his black hair shining, "shouldn't you be back in the lounge watching TV?"

"I'd much rather be out here with you, darling," she smiles, all sugary sweet.

But as she saunters closer, intent on bad behaviour, her steps falter. A spike of alarm pierces her chest.

Alert, I rise to attention. *Rhodine, what's wrong?*

Then I sense it. Darkness stirs in the recesses of our mind. A chill begins to spread through our veins; an awful, familiar feeling that crystallises our blood with dread. *Oh no.*

Hector puts aside his thoughts of music, Sister Mary crosses herself and starts to pray, Zuri backs away and Billy begins to whimper, and all the while the darkness builds.

It chills and chokes, it sends stinging tingles along our skin.

"Are you alright?" Nurse Romano asks. He must have seen the fear in our eyes.

The others scatter like mice before a hawk and for that moment we are left speechless, so I try to take the podium myself.

"I…" want to say *Call Dr. Abernathy*, "I…" want to say *help* and hear the static on his walkie-talkie buzz as he requests immediate assistance in Corridor A.

But I cannot. My throat constricts in a boa's grip. The darkness seeps into our vision, smothering the light. We fight to see, to push through the stormy fog, but our efforts are futile and one by one we fall back. We never are strong enough, even together.

"What is it?" Nurse Romano asks, his voice faint and distant but distinctly concerned. He clasps our shoulders, fingers digging in. "Speak to me Rhodine. What's wrong?"

In a final plaintive keen, we cry as one, "It's Morgan!"

But the sound never leaves our lips. Instead, another silken voice answers.

"Nothing," it says calmly. "It's nothing."

Everything goes black.

* * *

Rain clings to my cheeks as I walk along a puddle-strewn pavement, fresh from school and shouldering my gym-bag. My surroundings are blurred and grainy, with the consistency of memory. I know this place, know where I am. I'm in the terminable in-between. A place I get shoved whenever Morgan takes over. Stuck living my past, our past, *Morgan's* past.

Home-time traffic fills an intersection up ahead, horns blast and drivers holler. The tang of petrol fills the air. It tastes like yesterday. I hate these times. At least when the others are out I can hear and see and feel what they do. I *know* what is going on. But Morgan allows no such luxury; she blocks me off and cuts me out. I cannot even hear the others.

No doubt she will show me what she was up to later though, she always does. Bragging without words. For now though I can only live history… and revise her first emergence.

Ahead a group of boys laugh. Popular boys. Pretty boys. The kind who all own Audis and throw ragers at their parent's lake-houses. One of them tripped me in gym earlier, sending me sprawling across the court. I have a technicolour patchwork of developing bruises to prove it. He'd thought he was being funny and when he laughed so had his friends.

At the sight of them, at the reminder, fresh pain and humiliation bubble beneath the surface, making my eyes sting. But there is something else too, a new sensation – a darkness that ripples and uncoils, like a snake preparing to strike. It happens so quickly, it rises and engulfs me where I stand, banishing me to the recesses of my mind with barely a whimper. It's as simple as that – a shiver and a snap – a sudden and smooth coup. The tears vanish.

Outwardly nothing has changed. But it's not me anymore who scans their happy little crowd of five, it's not me who silently broils, it's not me who eyes the blonde one on the end who wears a blue parker that matches his eyes. The one who laughed the loudest.

It's another, a new presence – one I could only describe then as 'Her'.

Blue Eyes sees her watching and smiles, appearing surprised. He steps away from his friends, towards her. They don't even notice, walking on ahead. And as he gets closer she moves away. He follows where she leads, straight into the depths of a damp dark alley, where the sound of the street fades to a dull murmur. After so many crime shows with this same clichéd beginning he should have known better, but he just smiles that happy oblivious smile.

Like a deer that does not recognise danger.

"Hey," he says, as she stops behind a dumpster, "about earlier, I'm sorry I laughed at you. Nathan's an ass and I shouldn't ha –"

She strikes. In the shadows, against a brick wall, with the sour-sweet rot of garbage all around, her fingers dig deep into his windpipe cutting of air. He fights, of course, those bright blue eyes silently shriek *Why?!* as he grips and pushes. Somehow she prevails. Such a tiny form should not be so strong. But it is. Her grip tightens, constricts, crushes. Chokes the life from him until his lips turn blue and his flailing slows. Lowering him to the ground she straddles his chest as his struggles weaken, and watches as the light seeps out of his eyes.

There... gone.

He is not laughing anymore, and never will again.

The horror does not end there. From his pocket she extracts a hip flask, from another a lighter. She empties one over him and flicks the other. Smiling into the dancing flames.

Morgan's predilections have always been... vengeful.

Vicious, brutal, *hateful*.

Once, this reminiscence could reduce me to messy tears, but it does not jar as it once did. I have seen it too many times now. Become desensitised with repetition, I think. It is one of several that Morgan replays whenever she takes charge – her reel of past victories.

I heard a phrase once, perhaps in a movie, that some people do not care about anything. They just want to watch the world burn. That is Morgan.

* * *

When I wake up the next day I am me. Pure, undiluted me.

This is a rare and unusual thing and immediately I am suspicious.

The only time I am allowed to the front is when something very bad has happened and no one else wants to take the blame and...

Yes, something bad has happened.

I try to move and cannot shift an inch. I am strapped down tight, buckled to a gurney. Internally, I groan, striving to remember. Nurse Romano, Corridor A. *What did Morgan do?*

There are no voices. No one answers. For once I am alone.

Nurse Hammond arrives to release me then – not Nurse Romano, I note – but before she does she examines my face with shrewd speculation.

"Are you calm?" she asks.

"Yes."

A moment passes as she quietly assesses the truth of this.

"Come with me," she eventually says, unstrapping the restraints. She knows the danger has passed. "Dr. Abernathy would like to speak with you."

I wait in his office on a plush red couch and remember the first time I sat here with my parents, and the police, just two years before – the day I was admitted. After the conviction I could have ended up somewhere much worse, should have really, but

Daddy had connections and as long as I was locked safely away no one particularly seemed to care where.

It had been a hard time, fresh from school and another disastrous 'incident' in which half of the library had burnt down. People had been hurt that day, people had died.

I had not known what was going on then. The others had been quiet whispers, easy to ignore, and I had held control. I thought. The lapsed hours and lost sleep had been easy to overlook and the nightmares were just that – nightmares. The truth had an ugly face.

There had been CCTV cameras in the library however – undeniable proof. There had never been cameras before, or witnesses. Crafty Morgan had meticulously avoided evidence. That time, however, she'd gotten sloppy. My only wish now is that I had been caught sooner.

So many could have been saved…

Now, I survey the endless bookcases and the dark mahogany desk – an antique. There is a photo there, one among many, of a young schoolgirl with dark auburn hair. She is not stunningly beautiful, but definitely pretty, a little geeky, and wears a black and white uniform as she holds up a golden trophy. It reads '1st Place Science Award'. I know her well. She was an honours student: top of her class in all but gym… At sixteen, I had held such promise.

Outside, the nurses speak in hushed tones of the horrendous antics of Morgan the Hellcat. That's what they call her, *that* fragment. It makes her sound so quaint, like an angry kitten. They would not call her that if they truly knew her, they would not dare.

The sound of footsteps quiets them.

Dr. Abernathy walks in and sets his coffee down – *on* the placemat, very important – and proceeds to his desk and files while barely giving me a second glance.

"So, who do I have the pleasure of talking to today?" he asks.

Of course, he does not know. No one ever does.

"Mary? Hector? Zuri?" He lists the names off like items on a shopping list. I suppose I should be grateful, some people have trouble remembering just one let alone seven. "I know it's not Morgan," he continues, "she vanished quickly enough last night when caught and left us with a crying Billy. It's Rhodine, isn't it? You're usually the forerunner."

"Dr. Abernathy –"

"Whoever it is, we need to talk about what happened," he sighs, weary.

"Dr. Abernathy, it's me."

A weight of silence follows, stony silence, and this time I know he has heard.

It's me. Two words that mean little when said by a patient suffering from my particular affliction, but he understands. Those two words mean everything.

"Em?" Closing the file he holds, he steps closer and takes the opposite seat. Behind his wire-rimmed spectacles his eyes are trained on me. I have his attention now.

"How long do we have? How long can you talk for?"

"I don't know," I say, and it's true. No one ever knows how long they have and I have less time than most. Already the others are stirring. I can feel their restlessness.

"How are you? Have they been treating you well?"

"Fine, I guess." What else can I say? The voices in my head are behaving today… Then I remember the nurses' whisperings. "I hear Morgan set a fire last night when she broke out. I'm sorry about that. I would have stopped her if I could."

Morgan and her obsession with fire have gotten me into trouble many times. No matter where she is, whenever she is out, the pyromaniac somehow manages to set something alight. But fire on its own is usually the least disastrous outcome – an infrequent path she chooses just to cause a little chaos, to distract from her more insidious acts. If she had not been contained, it would have been worse. At least, in here, they know her and what to expect.

Dr. Abernathy waves my apology away. "It wasn't your fault, Em," he says. "We know that."

"Did anyone get hurt?" That's the important question; the one that will determine whether I sleep tonight.

Nurse Romano? Rhodine ventures quietly – the first to re-emerge. Her worry is plain and, for once, her attitude is not so breezy.

Dr. Abernathy hesitates, but he knows I prefer full disclosure. Morgan will show me all at some future date anyway.

"Nurse Romano sustained some bruises from trying to contain her," he gravely reports. "He understood who had emerged and called in assistance, but she gave him the slip. Later he and two other orderlies gained some minor burns from putting out the flames – she set fire to a supply closet – but they are okay," he hastens to add. Then, with a weak smile, he says, "Only our supply of toilet rolls were harmed. Other than that, Morgan only scared a few of the patients during her rampage, but nothing was damaged beyond repair."

A blessing, considering. They were lucky this time.

That was not always the case.

"Okay," I say, exhaling sharply. "Please tell Nurse Romano that I am very sorry for what Morgan did, just in case I don't… well…" *In case I don't get the chance.*

"I'll pass along the message," he assures. "But he knows that it wasn't you."

Wasn't it? In a way, all of my personalities are me.

* * *

By the time my parents arrive that afternoon I am Billy again, playing with Lego.

All three – Mommy, Daddy, the doctor-man – look down with disappointment. Billy wonders what he has done wrong. Are they upset that he put finger-paints on the wall?

When he asks as much, Mommy bursts into tears and the doctor-man has to take her away for some strong tea. Billy starts to cry too but Daddy stays with him. Daddy stays and they build a castle from his Lego bricks and defend it from space-pirates.

He watches Billy while they play, hoping for someone else but not seeing her.

But maybe… just maybe…

The roulette wheel spins again and the ball is set in play. Today I am Billy, but tomorrow who knows? It could be one of seven fragments of me.

Biographies & Sources

Sara Dobie Bauer
The Wendigo Goes Home
(Originally Published in *Flapperhouse Magazine*, Winter 2016)
Sara Dobie Bauer is an American writer, model, and mental health advocate with a creative writing degree from Ohio University. She spends most days at home in her pajamas as a book nerd and sex-pert for SheKnows.com. Her short story 'Don't Ball the Boss' was nominated for the Pushcart Prize, inspired by her shameless crush on Benedict Cumberbatch. She lives with her hottie husband and two precious pups in Northeast Ohio, although she would really like to live in a Tim Burton film. She is the author of *Bite Somebody*, a paranormal romantic comedy. Learn more at SaraDobieBauer.com.

Steen Steensen Blicher
The Rector of Veilbye
(Originally Published in *Nordlyset*, 1829)
The Danish writer Steen Steensen Blicher (1782–1848) was a pioneer of the short story form in Denmark. A clergyman like his father, Blicher showed active interest in politics, lived in relative poverty and was known to lapse into alcoholism. He published his first collection of poems in 1814, and went on to produce a number of short stories, infused with a curious mix of humour and melancholy and usually concerning Central Jutland and its people. 'The Rector of Veilbye' is regarded as the first work of Danish crime fiction. Based on a true case, the story demonstrates an early use of an unreliable narrator in Danish literature.

Ambrose Bierce
The Death of Halpin Frayser
(Originally Published in *The Wave*, 1891)
The Moonlit Road
(Originally Published in *Cosmopolitan*, 1907)
Ambrose Bierce (1824–c. 1914) was born in Ohio, America. He was a famous journalist and author known for writing *The Devil's Dictionary*. After fighting in the American Civil War, Bierce used his combat experience to write stories based on the war, such as in *An Occurrence at Owl Creek Bridge*. Following the separate deaths of his ex-wife and two of his three children he gained a sardonic view of human nature and earned the name 'Bitter Bierce'. His disappearance at the age of 71 on a trip to Mexico remains a great mystery and continues to spark speculation.

Michael Cebula
Funeral
(Originally Published in *Thuglit*, September 2014)
Michael Cebula lives with his wife and two sons in Chicago, Illinois. His fiction and nonfiction have appeared in a variety of publications, including the crime fiction journals *ThugLit* and *All Due Respect*. His favorite authors of murder and mayhem include Richard Price, Jim Thompson, Elmore Leonard, Agatha Christie, William Gay, James Carlos Blake, Daniel Woodrell, Larry Brown, Joe R. Lansdale, Tom Franklin, James Ellroy, Dennis Lehane, Hubert Selby, Jr., Bret Easton Ellis, and Donald Ray Pollock.

Carolyn Charron

Into the Blue

(First Publication)

Carolyn Charron is a Canadian writer whose short stories have appeared in *The Saturday Evening Post, Fabula Argentea*, and *Enchanted Conversations,* among others. She writes all forms of speculative fiction, reads slush for the Hugo-nominated *Apex Magazine*, and has workshopped with Richard Thomas and Paula Guran. She spends far too much time on Facebook and not enough on her blog or Twitter. She lives in Toronto with her family and is currently writing a novel blending Canadian history with clockworks and potato batteries.

G.K. Chesterton

Dr. Hyde, Detective, and the White Pillars Murder

(Originally Published in *English Life*, 1925)

Gilbert Keith Chesterton (1874–1936) is best known for his creation of the worldly priest-detective Father Brown, although he did write crime fiction with other protagonists too. The Edwardian writer's literary output was immense: around 200 short stories, nearly 100 novels and about 4000 essays, as well as weekly columns for multiple newspapers. Chesterton was a valued literary critic, and his own authoritative works included biographies of Charles Dickens and Thomas Aquinas, and the theological book *The Everlasting Man*. Chesterton debated with such notable figures as George Bernard Shaw and Bertrand Russell, and even broadcasted radio talks.

Wilkie Collins

The Traveller's Story of a Terribly Strange Bed

(Originally Published in *Household Words*, 1852)

Who Killed Zebedee?

(Originally Published in *The Seaside Library*, 1881)

Wilkie Collins (1824–89) was born in London's Marylebone and he lived there almost consistently for 65 years. Writing over 30 major books, 100 articles, short stories and essays and a dozen or more plays, he is best known for *The Moonstone*, often credited as the first detective story, and *The Woman in White*. He was good friends with Charles Dickens, with whom he collaborated, as well as took inspiration from, to help write novels like *The Lighthouse* and *The Frozen Deep*. Finally becoming internationally reputable in the 1860s, Collins truly showed himself as the master of his craft as he wrote many profitable novels in less than a decade and earned himself the title of a successful English novelist, playwright and author of short stories.

Charles Dickens

The Trial for Murder

(Originally Published as 'To Be Taken With a Grain of Salt' in *All the Year Round*, 1865)

The iconic and much-loved Charles Dickens (1812–70) was born in Portsmouth, England, though he spent much of his life in Kent and London. At the age of 12 Charles was forced into working in a factory for a couple of months to support his family. He never forgot his harrowing experience there, and his novels always reflected the plight of the working class. A prolific writer, Dickens kept up a career in journalism as well as writing short stories and novels, with much of his work being serialized before being published as books. He gave a view of contemporary England with a strong sense of realism, yet incorporated the occasional ghost and horror elements. He continued to work hard until his death in 1870, leaving *The Mystery of Edwin Drood* unfinished.

Dick Donovan

The Problem of Dead Wood Hall

(Originally Published in *Riddles Read*, Chatto & Windus, 1896)

Dick Donovan (1843–1934) was the pseudonym of J.E. Preston Muddock. Born near Southampton, England, Muddock became a journalist and travelled the globe. 'Dick Donovan' was the name of Muddock's fictional Glasgow detective – a character who so rivalled the popularity of Sherlock Holmes that Muddock later chose Donovan as his own pen name. This technique of using a fictional detective as a pseudonym was used later by Ellery Queen and Nick Carter. He was incredibly prolific in crime and horror genres in particular, and some theorize that the origin of the term 'Dick' to mean an American private detective may be linked back to him.

James Dorr

Mr. Happy Head

(Originally Published in *Wicked Mystic*, Spring 1996)

Indiana (USA) writer James Dorr's *The Tears of Isis* was a 2014 Bram Stoker Award® nominee for Superior Achievement in a Fiction Collection. Other books include *Strange Mistresses: Tales of Wonder and Romance, Darker Loves: Takes of Mystery and Regret*, and his all-poetry *Vamps (A Retrospective)*. Currently in press is a novel in stories, *Tombs: A Chronicle of Latter-day Times of Earth*. An Active Member of HWA and SFWA with nearly 400 individual appearances from *Alfred Hitchcock's Mystery Magazine* to *Xenophilia*, Dorr invites readers to visit his blog at jamesdorrwriter. wordpress.com.

Arthur Conan Doyle

The Brazilian Cat

(Originally Published in *The Strand Magazine*, 1898)

Arthur Conan Doyle (1859–1930) was born in Edinburgh, Scotland, and became a well-known writer, poet and physician. As a medical student he was so impressed by his professor's powers of deduction that he was inspired to create the illustrious and much-loved figure Sherlock Holmes. In contrast to this scientific background, however, Doyle became increasingly interested in spiritualism, leaving him keen to explore fantastical elements in his stories. Paired with his talent for storytelling he wrote great tales of terror, such as 'The Horror of Heights' and 'The Leather Funnel'. Doyle's vibrant and remarkable characters have breathed life into all of his stories, engaging readers throughout the decades.

Tim Foley

Nineteen Sixty-Five Ford Falcon

(First Publication)

Tim Foley was born in western New York, educated in Massachusetts, and lives in northern California. He has traveled extensively in Europe and South America, and studied economics at the University of Durham. His dark fiction and critical essays have appeared in various publications on both sides of the Atlantic, including *All Hallows, Dark Hollow, Wormwood, Supernatural Tales*, and *West Marin Review*. He has read every Chandler novel and his favorite is *The Long Goodbye*.

Steven Thor Gunnin
"Mama Said"
(First Publication)
Steven Thor Gunnin is a lifelong fan of all things horror who finds little more terrifying than human beings. As an author and graphic artist, he attempts to offer a different perspective on everyday horrors and unique horrors as well. His work is influenced by everyone from George Orwell and George Romero to Norman Rockwell. His short stories have previously been featured in anthologies from *Twin Trinity Media*, as well as in an Australian touring exhibit 'Tactics Against Fear'. Originally from southern California, he now lives near Philadelphia with his wife and one spoiled cat.

Kate Heartfield
Six Aspects of Cath Baduma
(Originally Published in *Postscripts to Darkness: Volume 4*, October 2013)
Kate Heartfield is a journalist and fiction writer in Ottawa, Canada. Her short stories have appeared in places such as *Strange Horizons, Escape Pod* and *Daily Science Fiction*. Her novella 'The Course of True Love' was published in 2016 by Abaddon Books, part of the collection *Monstrous Little Voices: New Tales from Shakespeare's Fantasy World*. She has a steampunk story in the 2016 anthology *Clockwork Canada* from Exile Editions, and a science fiction story in the May 2016 issue of *Lackington's*. She is represented by Jennie Goloboy of Red Sofa Literary.

William Hope Hodgson
The House Among the Laurels
(Originally Published in *The Idler*, 1910)
The Thing Invisible
(Originally Published in *The New Magazine*, 1912)
William Hope Hodgson (1877–1918) was born in Essex, England but moved several times with his family, including living for some time in County Galway, Ireland – a setting that would later inspire *The House on the Borderland*. Hodgson made several unsuccessful attempts to run away to sea, until his uncle secured him some work in the Merchant Marine. This association with the ocean would unfold later in his many sea stories. After some initial rejections of his writing, Hodgson managed to become a full-time writer of both novels and short stories, which form a fantastic legacy of adventure, mystery and horror fiction.

David M. Hoenig
Freedom is Not Free
(Originally Published in *Nebula Rift (Fiction Magazines): Volume 3, Number 7*, 2015)
David is a practicing physician for whom writing is his 'second career'. He's won 2 short fiction contests (Dark Chapter Press, Espec Books) and has multiple stories published in different anthologies with Horrified Press, Zoetic Press/NonBinary Review, Drunk Monkeys Literary, Dark Chapter Press, Elder Signs Press, and *Nebula Rift Magazine*. He lives in New York where he is working on his first novel. Slowly. He particularly loves sci fi and fantasy, and finds inspiration like the Highlander, in 'lots of different places'.

E.T.A. Hoffmann
Mademoiselle de Scudéri
(First Published in *Yearbook for 1820*, 1819)
E.T.A. Hoffmann (1776–1822) was a musician and a painter as well as a successful writer. Born in Germany and raised by his uncle, Hoffmann followed a legal career until his interests drew him to composing operas and ballets. He began to write richly imaginative stories that helped secure his reputation as an influential figure during the German Romantic movement, with many of his tales inspiring stage adaptations, such as *The Nutcracker* and *Coppélia*. 'Mademoiselle de Scudéri' is considered one of the earliest examples of crime fiction, as it carries many of the essential plot devices now associated with detective stories.

Liam Hogan
How to Build a Mass-Murderer
(Originally Published in *Liars' League*, Fame & Fortune theme, June 2008)
Liam Hogan was abandoned in a library at the tender age of 3, only to emerge blinking into the sunlight many years later, with a head full of words and an aversion to loud noises. He's the host of the award winning monthly literary event, Liars' League, and the Winner of Quantum Shorts 2015 and Sci-Fest LA's Roswell Award 2016. He's been published at DailyScienceFiction, *Sci-Phi Journal*, NoSleep Podcast, and in well over a dozen anthologies. He lives in London and dreams in Dewey Decimals. Find out more at: happyendingnotguaranteed.blogspot.co.uk.

Robert E. Howard
Pigeons from Hell
(Originally Published in *Weird Tales*, 1938)
The American writer Robert E. Howard (1906–36) was born in Peaster, Texas. An intellectual and athletic man, Howard wrote within the genres of westerns, boxing, historical and horror fiction, and is credited with having formed the subgenre within fantasy known as 'Sword and Sorcery'. His novella 'Pigeons from Hell', which Stephen King quotes as the one of the finest horror stories of the century, exemplifies his dark yet realistic style. Howard's work is strongly associated with the pulp magazine *Weird Tales*, in which he published many horror and fantasy stories, including those featuring the character Conan the Barbarian.

Patrick Hurley
The Two-Out-of-Three Rule
(First Publication)
Patrick Hurley worked for The Great Books Foundation in Chicago for ten years and now finds himself an editor at becker&mayer! books in Seattle. Patrick has had fiction and poetry published in *Abyss & Apex*, *Penumbra*, *Big Pulp*, *T. Gene Davis's Speculative Blog*, *Allegory*, *The Willows*, *Niteblade*, *Cast Macabre*, *Well Told Tales*, and *The Drabblecast*. When Patrick is not training for a marathon or exploring the pubs and coffee shops of Seattle, he is finalizing revisions on his first novel. His biggest authorial influences are Stephen King, Neil Gaiman, and Terry Pratchett.

W.W. Jacobs
The Well
(Originally Published in *The Lady of the Barge*, Thomas Nelson and Sons, 1902)
William Wymark ('W.W.') Jacobs (1863–1943) was born in Wapping, London, and he is known for his deeply humorous and horrifying works. Drawing upon his childhood experiences, Jacobs

wrote many works reflecting on his father's profession as a dockhand and wharf manager. His first volume of stories, *Many Cargoes*, was a great success and gave Jacobs the courage to publish other stories such as 'The Monkey's Paw', which was published along with 'The Well' in the collection *The Lady of the Barge*. Jacobs used realistic experiences as well as a combination of superstition, terror, exotic adventure and humour in each one of his famous tales.

Franz Kafka
In the Penal Colony
(Originally Published by Kurt Wolff Verlag, 1919)
Franz Kafka (1883–1924) has become synonymous with the surreal and the bizarre. He was born in Prague, which was then in Austria-Hungary, into a Jewish middle-class family. His stories often touch on themes of alienation, guilt and fear, and his most famous work, *The Metamorphosis*, has become lauded as a key piece of literature. Kafka died at the age of 40 from tuberculosis, never having gained much acclaim for his writing, and left his work to his friend Max Brod, with express instructions to burn it after his death. Brod, ignoring Kafka's wishes, published many of Kafka's writings, which have since seen Kafka posthumously praised as one of the great writers of the twentieth century.

Michelle Ann King
Getting Shot in the Face Still Stings
(Originally published in *Black Treacle*, 2013)
Michelle Ann King was born in East London and now lives in Essex. She writes science fiction, fantasy and horror, and her stories have appeared in over 70 different venues, including *Interzone*, *Strange Horizons* and *Black Static*. Her favourite author is Stephen King (sadly, no relation), and she also loves zombies, Las Vegas, and good Scotch whisky. She is currently working on her second short story collection — the first, *Transient Tales*, is available in ebook and paperback now from Amazon and other online retailers.

Rudyard Kipling
The Return of Imray
(Originally Published in *Life's Handicap: Being Stories of Mine Own People*, Macmillan & Co., 1891)
English writer and poet Rudyard Kipling (1865–1936) was born in Bombay, India. He was educated in England but returned to India in his youth which would inspire many of his later writings, most famously seen in *The Jungle Book*, as well as here in 'The Return of Imray'. He would later return to England and after travelling the States settled in Vermont, America. He was awarded the Nobel Prize for Literature in 1907, which made him the first English-language writer to receive the accolade. His narrative style is inventive and engaging, making it no surprise that his works of fiction and poetry have become classics.

Claude Lalumière
Less than Katherine
(Originally Published in *Playground of Lost Toys* (Exile Editions 2015), edited by Colleen Anderson & Ursula Pflug)
Claude Lalumière (claudepages.info) was born and raised in Montreal. He's the author of *Objects of Worship* (2009), *The Door to Lost Pages* (2011), and *Nocturnes and Other Nocturnes* (2013). His fourth book, *Venera Dreams*, is forthcoming in 2017. His first

fiction – 'Bestial Acts' – appeared in Interzone in 2002, and he has since published more than 100 stories; his work has been translated into French, Italian, Polish, Spanish, and Serbian and adapted for stage, screen, audio, and comics. In summer 2016, he was one of 21 international short-fiction writers showcased at Serbia's Kikinda Short 11: The New Deal.

Gerri Leen
Shared Losses
(Originally published online on the Shred of Evidence webzine, 2007)
Gerri Leen lives in Northern Virginia and originally hails from Seattle. She has stories and poems published by: Daily Science Fiction, Escape Pod, Grimdark, Enchanted Conversation, and others. She is seeking representation for *Bluegrass Dreams Aren't for Free*, a collection of interconnected shorts about genetically modified racehorses that manage their own careers, and is finalizing *Handle with Care*, an urban fantasy novel. Her first solo editing gig, the *A Quiet Shelter There* anthology published by Hadley Rille Books, was released in Fall 2015 and benefits homeless animals, a cause she passionately supports. See more at www.gerrileen.com.

H.P. Lovecraft
The Hound
(Originally Published in *Weird Tales*, 1924)
From Beyond
(Originally Published in *The Fantasy Fan*, 1934)
Howard Philips Lovecraft (1890–1937) was born in Providence, Rhode Island. Although now Lovecraft is one of the most significant American authors in the genre of horror fiction, he did not receive much of his highly deserved recognition until after his death. His inspiration came predominantly from various astronomers and the writings of Edgar Allan Poe. Having nightmares repeatedly throughout his adulthood, he was inspired to write his dark and strange fantasy tales. Lovecraft's most famous story 'The Call of Cthulhu' went on to inspire many authors, as well as movies, art and games.

K.A. Mielke
Drive Safe
(First Publication)
K.A. Mielke is a freelance writer from Guelph, Ontario, a fearsome city overrun with rabid environmentalists. His short fiction has appeared in *Every Day Fiction*, *Niteblade Magazine*, and *The Running Bunny*, among other publications. He enjoys panicking about his writing career, watching entirely too much television, and reading *Coraline* to his children whether they like it or not. His three main literary influences (and impulse buys) are Neil Gaiman, Chuck Palahniuk, and Patrick Ness, and yes, he does think that is a rather disparate jumble of artists.

Edith Nesbit
In the Dark
(Originally Published in *Fear*, Stanley Paul & Co., 1910)
Edith Nesbit (1858–1924) was born in Surrey, England. Although she is best remembered for her children's stories, such as *The Railway Children* and *Five Children and It*, she

wrote several tales for adults, including some horror short story collections. Nesbit was also a strong political activist, who helped to found the socialist organization the Fabian Society. When she first married, her writing was essential for helping to bring in money, and her success later allowed them to buy Well Hall in Eltham, where they hosted such literary members of society as H.G. Wells and George Bernard Shaw.

Edgar Allan Poe
The Cask of Amontillado
(Originally Published in *Godey's Lady's Book*, 1846)
Versatile writer Edgar Allan Poe (1809–49) was born in Boston, Massachusetts. Poe is well known for being an author, poet, editor and literary critic during the American Romantic Movement. He is generally considered the inventor of the detective fiction genre, and his works are famously filled with terror, mystery, death and haunting. His better known works include *The Tell Tale Heart, The Raven* and *The Fall of the House of Usher.* The dark, mystifying characters from his tales have captured the public's imagination and reflect the struggling, poverty-stricken lifestyle he lived his whole life.

Arthur B. Reeve
The Azure Ring
(Originally Published in *The Silent Bullet*, Harper & Brothers, 1910)
Arthur B. Reeve (1880–1936) was born in New York, graduating from Princeton and going on to study law. However he ended up working as an editor and journalist, writing about several famous crime cases, before gaining wide popularity for his stories about fictional detective Professor Craig Kennedy, the first of which were published in *Cosmopolitan* magazine. Kennedy shares many similarities with both Conan Doyle's Holmes and Freeman's Dr. Thorndyke, as he solves crimes with science, logic and a knowledge of technology, as well as having a companion in several stories who chronicles his work, very similarly to Watson.

Alexandra Camille Renwick
Redux
(First Publication)
Alexandra Camille Renwick is a dual Canadian/American author raised in sunny Austin, Texas who recently moved into a crumbling snowbound mansion in Ottawa, Ontario. Her stories appear in *Ellery Queen's* and *Alfred Hitchcock's Mystery Magazines, The Exile Book of New Canadian Noir*, and the special Monsters Issue of *Mslexia Magazine*. Her short-fiction collection *Push of the Sky* (written as Camille Alexa) earned a starred review in Publishers Weekly and was shortlisted for the Endeavour Award, a prize given annually for an outstanding book of speculative fiction.

Christopher P. Semtner
Foreword: Murder Mayhem Short Stories
The Curator of the Edgar Allan Poe Museum in Richmond, Christopher Semtner has written a number of books and articles about Poe, visual art, and history. He has appeared on BBC4, PBS, Military History Channel, and many other stations to speak about the author. Semtner is also an internationally exhibited visual artist whose paintings have entered several public and private collections.

Fred Senese

The First Seven Deaths of Mildred Orly

(First Publication)

Fred Senese is a former NASA scientist who teaches chemistry at a small university in rural Appalachia. He is the author of three books and an award-winning science website that has been recognized by *Scientific American, The San Francisco Chronicle*, and others. His stories have appeared or are forthcoming in *Spark: A Creative Anthology, Bartleby Snopes, Triptych Tales, Firewords Quarterly, Zetetic Record, The Molotov Cocktail*, and others. He is currently working on two books on symbolic mathematics and dozens of strange short stories. Find him at fredsenese.com, @fsenese on Twitter, and at facebook.com/fredsenesewrites.

Robert Louis Stevenson

Markheim

(Originally Published in *The Broken Shaft: Tales of Mid-Ocean* as part of *Unwin's Christmas Annual*, 1885)

Robert Louis Stevenson (1850–1894) was born in Edinburgh, Scotland. He became a well-known novelist, poet and travel writer, publishing the famous works *Treasure Island, Kidnapped* and *The Strange Case of Dr Jekyll and Mr Hyde*. All of his works were highly admired by many other artists, as he was a literary celebrity during his lifetime. Travelling a lot for health reasons and because of his family's business, Stevenson ended up writing many of his journeys into his stories and wrote works mainly related to children's literature and the horror genre.

Bram Stoker

The Dualitists

(Originally Published in *The Theatre Annual: Containing Stories, Reminiscences and Verses*, Carson & Comerford, 1886–87)

The Burial of the Rats

(Originally Published in *Lloyd's Weekly Newspaper*, London, 1896 and *The Boston Herald*, Boston, 1896)

Abraham 'Bram' Stoker (1847-1912) was born in Dublin, Ireland. Often ill during his childhood, he spent a lot of time in bed listening to his mother's grim stories, sparking his imagination. Striking up a friendship as an adult with the actor Henry Irving, Stoker eventually came to work and live in London, meeting notable authors such as Arthur Conan Doyle and Oscar Wilde. Stoker wrote several stories based on supernatural horror, such as the gothic masterpiece *Dracula* which has left an enduring and powerful impact on the genre, as well as chilling mysteries like *The Lair of the White Worm*.

Donald Jacob Uitvlugt

Mister Ted

(Originally Published in Satan's Toybox: Terrifying Teddies by Angelic Knight Press, 2012)

Donald Jacob Uitvlugt lives on neither coast of the United States, but mostly in a haunted memory palace of his own design. His short fiction has appeared in numerous print and online venues, including *Cirsova* magazine and the Chaosium anthology *Mark of the Beast*. He also regularly serves as a judge at the weekly one-on-one writing competition at TheWritersArena.com. Donald strives to write what he calls 'haiku fiction': stories that are small in scale but big in impact. If you enjoyed 'Mister Ted', let him know at his webpage: haikufiction.blogspot.com or via Twitter: @haikufictiondju.

Ethel Lina White
Cheese
(Originally Published in 1941)
Ethel Lina White (1876–1944) was a British crime writer born in Monmouthshire, Wales. White's most famous work is the novel *The Wheel Spins*, which Alfred Hitchcock based his successful film *The Lady Vanishes* on. Her passion for writing started early in her life and she contributed articles and poetry to children's papers, before writing short stories and eventually full length novels by the time she reached adulthood. Although her name is lesser known these days, in her heyday of the 1930s and 1940s she was a renowned writer of crime fiction.

Dean H. Wild
Corpses Removed, No Questions Asked
(First Publication)
Dean H. Wild grew up in east central Wisconsin and has lived in the area, primarily in small towns surrounding the city of Fond du Lac, all his life. He wrote his first short horror story at the tender age of seven and continued to write dark fiction while he pursued careers in retail, the newspaper industry and real estate. His short stories have seen publication in various magazines and anthologies including *Bell, Book & Beyond*, *A Feast of Frights*, *Night Lights* and *Night Terrors II*. He and his wife, Julie, currently reside in the village of Brownsville.

Oscar Wilde
Lord Arthur Savile's Crime
(Originally Published in *Court and Society Review*, 1887)
Oscar Wilde (1854–1900) was born in Dublin, Ireland, and was a successful author, poet, philosopher and playwright with an impressive gift for language. With several acclaimed works including his novel *The Picture of Dorian Gray* and the play *The Importance of Being Earnest*, Wilde was known for his biting wit and flamboyant personality in the Victorian era. He was famously imprisoned on homosexual charges, which proved disastrous to his health. He continued to write while in prison, and following his release he left for France and spent his remaining days in exile, essentially in poverty.

Nemma Wollenfang
Fragments of Me
(First Publication)
Nemma is an MSc Postgraduate and prize-winning steampunk short story writer who lives in Northern England. Generally she adheres to Science Fiction – perhaps as a result of years in the laboratory cackling like a mad scientist – but she has been known to branch out. Her stories have appeared in several anthologies, including: *A Bleak New World* (RIP), *Come Into the House* (Corazon Books), and *Masked Hearts* (Roane Publishing) as well as magazines. Her story 'Clockwork Evangeline' is also in Flame Tree's *Science Fiction Short Stories* and two of her unpublished novels have now been shortlisted in, or won, awards.

FLAME TREE PUBLISHING
Short Story Series
New & Classic Writing

**Flame Tree's Gothic Fantasy books offer a carefully curated series of
new titles, each with combinations of original and classic writing:**

Chilling Horror Short Stories
Chilling Ghost Short Stories
Science Fiction Short Stories
Murder Mayhem Short Stories
Crime & Mystery Short Stories
Swords & Steam Short Stories
Dystopia Utopia Short Stories
Supernatural Horror Short Stories
Lost Worlds Short Stories
Time Travel Short Stories
Heroic Fantasy Short Stories
Pirates & Ghosts Short Stories
Agents & Spies Short Stories
Endless Apocalypse Short Stories
Alien Invasion Short Stories

**as well as new companion titles which offer rich collections of
classic fiction and legendary tales:**

H.G. Wells Short Stories • *Lovecraft Short Stories*
Sherlock Holmes Collection • *Edgar Allan Poe Collection*
Bram Stoker Horror Stories • *Celtic Myths & Tales*
Norse Myths & Tales • *Greek Myths & Tales*
King Arthur & The Knights of the Round Table

Available from all good bookstores, worldwide, and online at
flametreepublishing.com

...and coming soon:

FLAME TREE PRESS | FICTION WITHOUT FRONTIERS
New and original writing in Horror, Crime, SF and Fantasy